NICHOLAS EVERARD

MARINER OF ENGLAND: 1

by Alexander Fullerton

THE BLOODING OF THE GUNS
SIXTY MINUTES FOR ST GEORGE
PATROL TO THE GOLDEN HORN

WARNER BOOKS

A *Warner* Book

This omnibus edition published in Great Britain in 2001
simultaneously by Warner Books and Little, Brown and Company
Copyright © Alexander Fullerton 2001

The Blooding of the Guns first published in Great Britain in 1976
by Michael Joseph Ltd
Published in 1993 by Little, Brown and Company
Published in 1998 by Warner Books
Copyright © Alexander Fullerton 1976

Sixty Minutes for St George first published in Great Britain in 1977
by Michael Joseph Ltd
Published in 1994 by Little, Brown and Company
Published in 1998 by Warner Books
Copyright © Alexander Fullerton 1977

Patrol to the Golden Horn first published in Great Britain in 1978
by Michael Joseph Ltd
Published in 1994 by Little, Brown and Company
Published in 2001 by Warner Books
Copyright © Alexander Fullerton 1978

The moral right of the author has been asserted.

A CIP catalogue record for this book
is available from the British Library.

ISBN 0 7515 3200 2

Printed and bound in Great Britain by Clays Ltd, St Ives plc

Warner Books
A Division of
Little, Brown and Company (UK)
Brettenham House
Lancaster Place
London WC2E 7EN

www.littlebrown.co.uk

Alexander Fullerton, born in Suffolk and brought up in France, s~ ᵇᵉ ᵥears 1938–41 at the RN College, Dartmouth, and the ╷ ⌐¹ Surface!, based on his experiences as gunnery and torpedo ᴏₙₙₑr of HM Submarine *Seadog* in the Far East, 1944–5, in which capacity he was mentioned in despatches for distinguished service – was published in 1953. It became an immediate bestseller, with five reprints in six weeks, and he likes to recall that, working for a Swedish shipping company at the time, he wrote it in office hours, on the backs of old cargo manifests. He has lived solely on his writing since 1967, and is one of the most borrowed authors from British libraries.

Alexander Fullerton's nine-volume Everard series – of which *The Blooding of the Guns, Sixty Minutes for St George* and *Patrol to the Golden Horn* are the first three titles – has secured his reputation as the finest of modern writers about naval warfare.

THE BLOODING
OF THE GUNS

Iron Duke
18th June 1916

The Secretary
of the **ADMIRALTY**,

SIR,

Be pleased to inform the Lords Commissioners of the Admiralty that the German High Sea Fleet was brought to action on 31st May 1916, to the westward of the Jutland Bank, off the coast of Denmark.

(Opening paragraph of Sir John Jellicoe's despatch)

AUTHOR'S NOTE

To provide homes for fictional characters, three fictional ships – HMS *Nile* (battleship), *Bantry* (cruiser) and *Lanyard* (destroyer) have been added to those which actually fought at Jutland.

All other ships and their movements are as recorded in despatches, narratives, personal reminiscences et cetera, and are described as the fictional characters would have seen them from their own areas of the battle.

For readers who may find it useful or of interest, 'cast' of the Grand Fleet's ships, squadrons and flotillas may be found overleaf.

Finally, two technical assurances to readers whose own more recent naval experience may suggest that – as the instructors used to say – 'error has crep' in'. (1) It is a fact that at the time of the 1914–18 war a port helm order was needed to produce a turn to starboard; (2) it is also a fact that at this time four-inch and even smaller calibre ammunition was separate, not 'fixed'.

THE GRAND FLEET
Squadrons and flotillas as on 30th May 1916

(A) AT SCAPA AND CROMARTY

BATTLE FLEET (Fleet flagship *Iron Duke*)
2ND BATTLE SQUADRON (at Cromarty)
1st Div: *King George V – Ajax – Centurion – Erin*
2nd Div: *Orion – Monarch – Conqueror – Thunderer*

4TH BATTLE SQUADRON
3rd Div: *Iron Duke – Royal Oak – Superb – Canada*
4th Div: *Benbow – Bellerophon – Temeraire – Vanguard*

1ST BATTLE SQUADRON
5th Div: *Colossus – Collingwood – Neptune – St Vincent*
6th Div: *Marlborough – Revenge – Hercules – Agincourt*

BATTLE CRUISERS (Temporarily attached, ex Rosyth force)
Invincible – Inflexible – Indomitable

CRUISERS
1ST CRUISER SQUADRON (at Cromarty)
Defence – Warrior – Duke of Edinburgh – Black Prince

2ND CRUISER SQUADRON
*Minotaur – Hampshire – Cochrane – Shannon – Bantry**

LIGHT CRUISERS
4TH LIGHT CRUISER SQUADRON: 5 ships, plus 6
temporarily attached

DESTROYERS
4TH FLOTILLA: 19 ships   11TH FLOTILLA: 16 ships
12TH FLOTILLA: 16 ships

(B) AT ROSYTH

BATTLE CRUISER FLEET (Fleet flagship *Lion*)
1ST BATTLE CRUISER SQUADRON
Lion – Princess Royal – Queen Mary – Tiger

2ND BATTLE CRUISER SQUADRON
New Zealand – Indefatigable

5TH BATTLE SQUADRON (*Queen Elizabeth* class battleships)
*Barham – Valiant – Warspite – Malaya – Nile**

LIGHT CRUISERS
1ST LIGHT CRUISER SQUADRON: *Galatea* plus 3

2ND LIGHT CRUISER SQUADRON: *Southampton* plus 3

3RD LIGHT CRUISER SQUADRON: *Falmouth* plus 3

DESTROYERS
1ST FLOTILLA: 10 ships

9TH FLOTILLA: 8 ships

13TH FLOTILLA: 12 ships including *Lanyard**

*fictional ships

CHAPTER 1

'Sub!'

Nick took his eyes off the wilderness of black, grey-flecked sea. It was still dark, but greyer eastward as dawn approached. The glow from the binnacle lit the bony sharpness of his captain's face.

'Sir?'

'What's the date?'

'May thirtieth, 1916, sir.'

All destroyer captains were mad. One knew that; everyone did.

'Sure it's not the thirty-first?'

'Certain, sir.'

'What's the displacement of this ship?'

'Eight hundred and seven tons, sir.'

'How d'ye know that?'

'Looked it up, sir.'

'Devil you did . . . Where were we built?'

'Yarrow, sir.'

'What's our horsepower, d'ye look that up?'

Sub-Lieutenant Nick Everard, Royal Navy, with salt water streaming down his face, neck and inside his shirt, nodded as he grabbed at a stanchion for support. 'Twenty-four thousand, sir.' *Lanyard* lurched, staggered, her stubby bow seeming to catch in a trough of sea like a boot-toe in a furrow; spray rattled against splinter-mattresses lashed to the bridge rail. Nick had forgotten, until now, that the bridge of an eight-hundred-ton torpedo-boat destroyer, when she was steaming head-on into even as moderate a sea as a Force Four wind kicked up, was like the back of a frisky horse only wetter. Mortimer, her captain, spat a lungful of salt water down-wind; he'd appeared on the bridge a few minutes ago, wearing a long striped nightgown and a red woollen hat with a bobble on it; he'd looked like something out of a slapstick comedy

1

even before the nightgown had been soaked through, plastered against his tall, angular frame like a long wet bathing-suit. He spat again, and laughed.

'You're wrong, Sub! Twenty-four thousand five hundred!'

The inaccuracy seemed to have elated him. Nick stared back, not yet sure of him, wary that what looked like a friendly grin might turn out to be a grimace of fury. One couldn't be sure of any of these people yet. Nick had joined *Lanyard* only forty-eight hours ago – he'd been ordered to her suddenly, without any sort of warning, transferred at a moment's notice from the dreadnought battleship that had housed him for the last two years. It had seemed so unbelievable that there'd had to be some snag in it. In spite of the sensation of relief and escape, he was still ready to find the snag, and meanwhile all his experience of officers senior to himself warned him to be cautious, to look every gift horse in the mouth.

'Everard.'

'Sir?'

'My first lieutenant informs me that you have the reputation of being lazy, ignorant and insubordinate. Would you dispute that?'

Nick stared straight ahead at the empty, foam-washed sea. Johnson, *Lanyard*'s first lieutenant, was a contemporary and friend of Nick's elder brother David. He was standing behind, and holding on to the binnacle, beside Mortimer and within about three feet of Nick's own position. You couldn't be very much farther from each other than that, on a bridge about as large and which seemed just about as solid as a chicken-house roof. Johnson was officer of the watch, and Nick, who lacked as yet a watchkeeping certificate, was acting as his dogsbody. In the last few minutes the first lieutenant had been listening to Nick's exchanges with Mortimer while pretending either not to hear or to have no interest in them.

Nick said stiffly, 'No, sir.'

'You don't dispute it?'

'I'd rather not contradict the first lieutenant, sir.'

'Hear that, Number One?' Johnson nodded, poker-faced. He had a thin, pale face, dark-jowled, needing two shaves a day by the looks of it. Rather a David-type face, Nick thought gloomily. *Lanyard* had her bow up, scooting along like a duck landing on a pond; Mortimer asked Nick, 'What's cordite, when it's at home?'

'Blend of nitro-glycerine and nitrocellulose gelatinised with five per cent vaseline, sir.'

'Vaseline?'

2

'Petroleum jelly, sir, to lubricate the bore of the gun.'

'What's the average speed of a twenty-one-inch White-head torpedo when it's set for seven thousand yards?'

'Forty-five knots, sir.'

He was wondering when the difficult questions were going to start. But Mortimer was apparently satisfied, for the time being.

'Number One!'

Johnson turned to him. 'Sir.'

'I suspect you may have been partially misinformed. This officer is neither wholly ignorant nor pathologically insubordinate. Only time will tell us whether or not he's lazy. Give him plenty to do, and if he shirks it kick his arse.'

'Aye aye, sir . . .' Johnson pointed out over the starboard bow. 'Everard. Fishing vessel there, steering east, bearing steady. What action if any would you take?'

'Alter course to starboard, sir, until past and clear.'

'Right. Come here.'

Nick stepped closer.

'Our course is south fifteen west, two hundred and sixty revolutions. Take over the ship.'

'Aye aye, sir.'

'I'll be in the chartroom.' He tapped the starboard voice-pipe's copper rim. '*This* pipe. Let me know the minute we raise May Island.'

Nick watched Johnson and Mortimer leave the bridge together. Things really did seem, so far, to have changed quite strikingly for the better!

Not that one could count on it. Johnson, until he proved otherwise, was an enemy. He'd obey Mortimer's orders to the letter, but whether or not a man was 'lazy' was a matter for individual interpretation, and 'kicks' came in different shapes and sizes. Most disconcerting of all was the fact that this Johnson was a friend of brother David's who was up in Scapa as navigating officer of the cruiser *Bantry*. Bright, successful, correct brother David, whom one tried not to let into one's thoughts too often. Johnson's decision to leave one up here alone in charge of the watch wasn't any sign of trust or encouragement. An officer in a destroyer who couldn't keep a watch was a semi-passenger, leaving a lesser number of watchkeepers on the roster, and since the only way to get a watchkeeping certificate was to acquire experience it was in Johnson's interests to make sure he got some.

3

It was in Nick's too, though – for present convenience, not career reasons. He'd decided long ago that he'd quit the Service when he could. There'd been no point in mentioning it to anyone, not even to Sarah, his stepmother, to whom he confided most things. As long as the war lasted, one was stuck; one could only think of it as something that mercifully wouldn't last for ever. Like a prisoner sitting out a gaol sentence. And in those terms, the events of the past two days had left him feeling like a long-term convict unexpectedly offered parole.

He'd been in his battleship's gunroom, writing a letter to Sarah, at Mullbergh. She was the only person he ever did write to. He wrote about once a month, and never mentioned the Navy or the war. What would there have been to say about it? There was no action – only pomposity and boredom. Somewhere distant, other men were fighting and being killed.

He wrote a lot about the Magnussons – he'd never told another soul about these Orcadian friends of his – and fishing, and the landscape of the Orkneys, that kind of thing. The Magnusson family and fishing provided the escape which as a midshipman and then junior sub-lieutenant in a battleship in the Grand Fleet he'd so badly needed; escape from boredom drills, bugle-calls, and from such horrors, too, as 'gunroom evolutions'.

Being well able to look after himself physically, he hadn't suffered much from the bullying rituals which were justified by the word 'tradition'; but he'd had to witness them, and pretend to take part in them. And they'd be in full swing again now, in the gunroom he'd just left. When he'd been promoted sub-lieutenant and become mess president, he'd stopped it all; but he knew the man who'd taken his place, and there was no doubt the 'evolutions' would have been re-established; evolutions such as 'Angostura Trail'. A midshipman would be blindfolded, forced to his hands and knees and made to follow with his nose a winding trail of Angostura bitters; if he lost the scent, all the others would lay into him. Or 'Running Torpedoes', which involved a boy being launched off the gunroom table as hard and fast as his messmates could manage it; if he tried to shield his head or break his fall, he'd be thrashed.

Nick thrashed a sub-lieutenant, once. The evolution had been 'scuttle drill'. The victim had to haul himself out of one scuttle and swing along the outside of the ship to the next, and pull himself back into the gunroom through it, and only a well-grown midship-

4

man had the length of body or arm-reach for it. The reigning sub-lieutenant was insisting on a particularly small lad – barely fifteen, and undersized – attempting to perform the impossible. The boy was shaking with fright, close to tears, and what broke Nick's self-control was that in the faces of the other midshipmen, this small one's friends, he could see the same sadistic excitement as in the sub-lieutenant's. He grabbed the sub-lieutenant by an arm, swung him round and hit him; within a minute the mess president had been knocked down three times and lost several front teeth.

Midshipman Everard was awarded twelve cuts with a cane, and a dozen more unofficially with a rope's end, and three months' stoppage of shore leave. He was also given extra duties which meant that during those three months he had only short periods of sleep and never time to finish a meal. And with that, it was pointed out, he'd been let off lightly; for an attack on a superior officer he could have been courtmartialled and dismissed the Service.

There'd been two possible reasons for the leniency. One was that Nick's uncle, Hugh Everard, had just returned from the Falklands battle, the destruction of Admiral Graf von Spee's squadron. Only a week before he hit the sub-lieutenant Midshipman Everard had been summoned to pace the quarterdeck beside his godlike captain, and to listen to a summary of the battle and its results. What it had boiled down to had been that the name of Everard was in favour at that higher level; Nick, the captain told him, had 'a great deal to live up to'. The other point was that the investigation into what had provoked the assault had established that the little midshipman could not have reached from one scuttle to the other, would therefore have fallen into the Flow, and quite likely might have drowned.

Killed on active service, would his family have been told? So many shams, right from one's earliest memories. Mullbergh: being woken in that freezing mausoleum of a house with his father's bellows of anger echoing through its corridors . . . Sir John Everard was a man of power and influence; Master of his own hounds, magistrate, Deputy Lieutenant of the county. He was a brigadier now, and doubtless he'd come back from France a major-general, covered in medals, even more of a respected figure. With his young wife – Sarah was twenty-eight, closer to his sons' ages than to his own – at his side. So beautiful and so loved!

Poor, lovely, Sarah . . .

To whom he'd been starting a letter, two days ago. He'd sat

down at the gunroom table which was no longer used as a launching ramp for human torpedoes and he'd got as far as putting the date, *28 May 1916*, at the head of the first sheet of paper, when a messenger had arrived to summon him to the ship's commander. He'd hurried up two decks, to the senior officers' cabin flat, and knocked on the wood surround of the commander's doorway.

'Sir!'

The commander was three parts bald; his face was dark red and he had ginger hair curling on his cheekbones.

'You're leaving us, Everard. Or did you know it already?'

'Sir?'

The commander growled, 'The destroyer *Lanyard* sails for Rosyth tomorrow. You will join her this afternoon. *Now.*'

Nick failed to understand.

'Sir, d'you mean I'm taking passage to—'

'Who the blazes said anything about taking passage?'

'I'm sorry, sir, I—'

'You are joining *Lanyard*. You are to report aboard her forthwith. Pack your gear, then present my compliments to the officer of the watch and ask him kindly to provide a boat.'

'Aye aye, sir!'

This was actually happening . . .

When those three months of stopped shore leave were over, he didn't give the Magnussons any reason for his not having seen them recently. It would have been difficult to explain, something so foreign to them that it wouldn't have made sense.

They'd probably thought he'd been away at sea and couldn't speak of it. Ships came, ships went; there were so many of them, and why should the crofters know their names, or care?

Greta almost referred to his long absence. She'd told him, 'The spring run were grand, Nick. Ye'd no've believed the fish we took!'

'Very glad to hear it.' He'd hesitated. 'I wish I'd—'

'Och, ye'll get your chance.' Her father had put an end to the need to talk about it. Nick could read the thought in the old man's eyes; if you had something to say, you'd say it, and if on the other hand you preferred to hold your tongue . . .

'I've missed you all.'

Greta had laughed; 'So I should hope!'

'Come intae the hoose, lad.' The old man stooped, leading the way into his gloomy little cottage. Greta stood back, smiling, making Nick go next.

He'd met the old man fishing. Over a period of months they'd encountered each other from time to time, at first with no more than a wave, a grunt. Then they'd begun to exchange a word or two – the weather, or the fish, or how the sheep were doing. Finally one afternoon Magnusson had invited him to the croft for 'a dram tae keep the cold oot', and he'd met Greta and her mother.

Escape and a lack of any kind of sham. The Magnussons had made Scapa bearable. They'd be wondering in a day or two where he'd got to; there'd been no way to send a message.

Peering into the binnacle, he saw suddenly that *Lanyard* had swung nearly ten degrees off course.

'Watch your steering, quartermaster!'

'Aye aye, sir!'

Searching the horizon again, he checked suddenly: on the beam, that dark smear was the low protuberance of Fife. 'Sub-Lieutenant, sir!' The signalman was pointing ahead. 'May Island, sir!'

Everything came in sight at once, as if a curtain had been rung up suddenly on the day. May Island's lighthouse was a white pimple poking out of a grey corrugated horizon. Nick put his face down to the other voicepipe.

'Chartroom!'

Johnson's voice floated out of the copper funnel: 'Chartroom.'

'Fife Ness is in sight to starboard, sir, and May Island's fine on the port bow.'

There was silence, for about three seconds. Then Johnson told him, 'I'm coming up.'

He was chewing, when he reached the bridge, and his lips were wet. He crossed to the starboard side of the bridge and studied the land; glanced ahead, frowning, at the clearing shape of May Island.

'How long have you had land in sight?'

'I suppose a minute, or—'

'Look.' Johnson pointed. 'The Ness is well abaft the beam. It was no further from us ten minutes ago than the nearer land is now.'

Nick agreed. 'Visibility's improved a lot in the last few minutes.'

'Hardly that much.' Pale eyes flickered at him, and away again. Judged – condemned. Nick, smarting, held his tongue.

The destroyer's motion eased rapidly as she closed May Island;

7

there was shelter from the gradually engulfing land and at the same time the wind was dying. Johnson turned to him again.

'Go down and get some breakfast. Back up here in thirty minutes.'

'Aye aye, sir.'

And the hell with you, too!

But he was still a damn sight better off, he told himself, than he'd been two days ago. He moved to the back of the bridge, over the lower level that served as signal-bridge and was dominated by the searchlight above it and, a few feet abaft the searchlight mounting, the slanting tube of the foremast. He nodded to the port-side lookout – a man of about his own age, with a freckled face, a missing tooth, a gingerish tinge of beard. The sailor asked him, 'You'd be the Forth we're enterin', would it, sir?'

'It would, yes. What's your name?'

'MacIver, sir.'

MacIver. Ginger, freckles, tooth missing. There were a lot of names to learn; he'd start a list, add a dozen a day until he knew the whole ship's company. He let himself down the ladder from the destroyer's salt-wet, black-painted bridge, down to the upper deck. Turning aft, he passed the ship's boats lashed and gripped in their turned-in davits, with the galley between them. Now the foremost of the pair of funnels: *Lanyard* was one of a small number of her class that had only two instead of three. Walking aft, he scanned the deck layout as he went, passing the midship four-inch gun and then the second funnel, and aft of that the first pair of twenty-one-inch torpedo tubes, now the after searchlight platform, and the other pair of tubes. Mainmast: and an inch-wide brass strip marked the start of the quarterdeck. There was superstructure amidships here, a sort of deckhouse with a door in it, and inside the door a ladder led down to the wardroom and the officers' cabin flat. Abaft it was the stern four-inch.

Nick paused and leant beside the door. The land was easy to see now, even from this lower level. *Lanyard* was only about five miles offshore, and the sun rising in the east was floodlighting that coast for her at the same time as it would be blinding anyone ashore: the light-gauge, Uncle Hugh had called it, explaining how an admiral would try to deploy his ships so as to have the advantage of it. It was strange how thinking back to Uncle Hugh's talk about the Navy still gave one a whiff of excitement and enthusiasm; it was as if Hugh Everard's own attitudes were infectious, strong enough to break through one's own more recent disillusionment and renew the longing for things which one now suspected to be myths. Daydreams; rose-coloured, like this sunrise flush that was turning the sea milky while a pink glow seeped through slats of cloud low on the diffuse horizon. But how could one explain Uncle Hugh's attitude to a Service that had treated him so shabbily?

In any case, thanks to the boost which the Falklands success had given to his resumed career, he was back now almost to where he would have been if they hadn't forced him out. Hugh Everard was captain of the brand-new battleship *Nile*, one of the crack Queen Elizabeth class super-dreadnoughts. *Nile*, with the others of the fifth Battle Squadron, had left Scapa for Rosyth only a day ahead of *Lanyard*; and might Uncle Hugh, Nick wondered, have had something to do with this move of his? Might he have pulled a string with the admirals before he sailed?

There was no reason why he should have. Nick hadn't asked for anything, or complained; he hadn't said a single word to anyone, not even to Sarah – from whom, if he had told her anything about his feelings of dead-end hopelessness, it might have got back to his uncle.

He shrugged. It had happened, that was all. All he had to do was take advantage of it, make a go of things here in *Lanyard* – if they'd let him. And meanwhile – breakfast. Nick shot down the ladder, almost colliding with the surgeon lieutenant, Samuels, who'd been starting up it.

'Sorry—'

'If you break your neck, don't ask me to mend it.'

They seemed a friendly bunch. Reynolds, whose quiet voice and high forehead made him seem more like an academic than a naval officer, was eating breakfast. Hastings, a Reserve sub-lieutenant who was *Lanyard*'s navigator, had just finished. Tall, fair, with the skin of his cheeks pitted, presumably by smallpox; he'd pushed his chair back and he was stuffing a pipe with tobacco.

Nick sat down. 'Good morning.' He nodded to the steward: 'Morning, Blewitt.'

'Morning, sir. Bacon and egg, sir?'

'Please.' Nick told Hastings, 'We're almost up to May Island.'

'I know. I looked.'

'You'd imagine—' Reynolds addressed Nick – 'that a pilot worth his salt would be up there looking after this vessel's safety. Eh?' Nick didn't commit himself. Reynolds shook his head. 'Not

9

this one. He sits here eating hearty meals while we officers of the watch do his job for him. What truly aggravates him is to have to use his sextant – should stars happen to become visible at night, or a sun at noon, or—'

'Don't worry.' Hastings raised a hand in greeting as the gunner, Mr Pilkington, joined them. Wizened, wiry, like a jockey. 'I'll con the old hooker in for you, by and by.'

'My dear fellow, how kind you are!'

Nick told them, 'I'll be up there too.'

'Haven't you just come down?'

'I gather I'm on permanent watch until I'm considered safe to do it on my own.'

'Well, that's reasonable.'

Hastings asked him, 'Haven't you done any destroyer time before this?'

'A few months, earlier on. Most of that in the Flow and Lough Swilly.'

'Ah.' The navigator winked at Reynolds. 'Reckon he'll be getting some destroyer *sea-time* soon enough.'

Reynolds frowned. 'Even if there was anything to it, Hastings—'

'To what?'

Hastings answered Nick, 'I had to go with the CO to a briefing before we sailed. Carry the chart for him, you know? Anyway, it seems there's the makings of a flap. Or there may not be, but—'

'Flap?'

'It's no more than the weekly buzz, Sub.' Reynolds was testy. 'Meaningless, like all the others.'

'The Hun sailed sixteen U-boats on May seventeenth. Thirteen days ago. And none of 'em's showed up anywhere. Not so much as the tip of a periscope. Well, a fortnight at sea's about their limit; so if it's some fleet operation they're out to cover, it must be about due. Right?'

'Unless—' Reynolds sighed – 'they've sailed right back again, and our clever cipher boys only *think* they're still out. Or they're out and looking for targets and haven't found any yet. Or—'

'The other titbit, Everard—' Hastings raised his voice, to drown out Reynolds's attempts to cut him off 'the other meaningless item of intelligence is that there's been the devil of a lot of wireless signalling going on over there. As one knows, our wireless interception's quite hot stuff these days.'

'Your breakfast, sir.' Blewitt put a plate in front of Nick. 'Take my advice, sir, eat it while it's 'ot. Cold, it's 'orrible.'

'I'm sure you're right.' Hastings, with the steward present, had stopped talking. Reynolds muttered, getting to his feet, 'I'll see you lads up there, by and by.' He looked at Nick. 'Here's advice for you, Sub. Before you come up topsides, treat yourself to a shave.' He lowered his voice. 'Our captain may adopt a somewhat bizarre appearance when at sea, but informality is not encouraged in his officers.'

'Right. Thank you.'

'Good day.' Worsfold, the commissioned engineer, slid into a chair at the end of the table. Dark, small-boned, with deepset eyes. The others nodded to him: 'Morning, Chief.' Reynolds had gone. Nick, chewing bacon, stared at Hastings, thinking *U-boats, wireless activity: we do hear it once a week.*

CHAPTER 2

The Firth of Forth was misty, shiny-grey; the snake-humps of the bridge two miles seaward looked from here as if it was mist they floated on, banks of haze they linked. The mist would rise soon, as the day warmed up; there might even be blue skies later, and one of those days when grey old Edinburgh perked up, grass and granite sparkling . . . It was good, Hugh Everard thought, to see Edinburgh again.

He turned at the stern end of his battleship's quarterdeck and paced briskly for'ard again, with his hands clasped behind his back. It was going to be good – more than good, thrilling, to see Sarah again, too; after – what, a year? He gazed out over *Nile*'s starboard side, to Queensferry and beyond – way beyond, where the Pentland Hills' blueish shapes rose dimly above land-haze. Edinburgh itself lay between him and those distant ridges, while here, close to his own ship, were moored the others of the Fifth Battle Squadron: *Malaya, Warspite, Valiant*, and at the head of the line Admiral Evan-Thomas's flagship *Barham*. Each of them displacing about thirty thousand tons, with fifteen-inch guns and an armour belt thirteen inches thick, they were the most powerful ships in Jellicoe's Grand Fleet, all as yet untested in battle. One wondered, sometimes, whether they'd ever be more than the crack squadron of a 'fleet in being'.

The name-ship of the squadron, *Queen Elizabeth*, was in dock for a refit, here at Rosyth. She, at least, had fired her guns in anger: she'd done a stint in the Dardanelles, as a bombardment ship in support of the Gallipoli landings – until Jackie Fisher had insisted on withdrawing her, and had a blazing row with Lord Kitchener in consequence.

Seaward, close to the bridge, Hugh could see Beatty's six battle cruisers: the flagship *Lion*, with *Princess Royal, Queen Mary, Tiger,*

New Zealand and *Indefatigable*. The battle cruisers were faster, sacrificing armour and fire-power for a few extra-knots. The 'strategic cavalry of the fleet', Churchill had called them; and it had been Churchill, not Jellicoe or Fisher, who'd put Sir David Beatty in command of them.

One had such faith in Jellicoe; as a seaman, a leader, a professional. One was less sure of Beatty's suitability for high command. You couldn't help thinking, for instance, of the Dogger Bank action, last year, when Beatty with his 'cavalry' had managed to sink one German armoured cruiser, the *Bluecher*, while the more powerful units of the German raiding squadron steamed away to safety. It was all very well to blame Rear-Admiral Moore for it; the simple truth was that Beatty's ambiguous and unnecessary flag-hoists had muddled his subordinate commanders. The public, ignorant as ever, had applauded a great victory; but the frightening thing, to Hugh Everard's mind, was that Beatty had seemed to regard it in the same light. His flagship *Lion* had been badly mauled; he'd claimed innumerable hits on the German ships, whereas Intelligence reports had now indicated that the British shooting had been extremely poor. Beatty remained arrogant, confident, the public's sailor-hero, with his cap at a slant and his uniform cut to his own design. Hugh Everard frowned, questioning his own feelings – whether there might be envy, jealousy sharpening them. Beatty, after all, was exactly his own age . . . *Cavalry of the fleet?* Confidence was fine – so long as there was some basis, some reason for it. But mere dash, panache, an assumption of Nelsonian superiority: that, in terms of what was needed in a modern fleet commander, was more dangerous than beneficial. No, one's view was not distorted by personal feelings. Sir David Beatty's ambitions and his view of himself were his own business, but the effectiveness of a vitally important section of the fleet was a matter in which others were entitled to be concerned.

Commander Tom Crick came stooping under 'Y' turret's massive barrels. Straightening his long, ungainly frame, he saluted.

'Boat's alongside, sir.'

Crick was tall – several inches taller than his captain, who was himself only a hair's breadth under six foot and pink-faced, with ears that stuck out like wings, seeming to support his cap. He'd served with Hugh Everard in the Falklands expedition, and when Hugh had been offered command of *Nile* Crick had come with him as second-in-command.

He fell in beside his captain, pacing aft, picking up the step. Hugh asked him, 'Any problems?'

'None worth bothering you with, sir.'

'Defaulters?'

Crick pulled at one of his outsize ears. 'We seem to have made some inroads into the crime rate, sir.'

Hugh's glance rested on Lady Beatty's yacht *Sheelah* which, fitted out now as a hospital tender, was anchored half a mile off Hawes Pier.

'I'll be out at Aberdour. Until about the middle of the afternoon, probably. If you need to, you can reach me by telephone at this number.'

The deep-water moorings had shore telephone connections at their buoys. Crick's long fingers pushed the folded sheet of signal-pad into a pocket of his reefer jacket. He asked diffidently, 'Are you visiting the Admiral, sir?'

The Beattys had a house at Aberdour.

'No. It's a – a personal – er—' he hesitated: then he finished gruffly, annoyed with himself for being self-conscious about it, 'A private visit, Tom.'

His own words echoed in his head as he tested them, wondering how they'd sounded, and at the same time aware of a distinctly pleasant feeling of excitement and expectation. He'd written from Scapa, when he'd been told of the squadron's forthcoming move south, to suggest to Sarah that she might find it a good time to visit her father, who was living in retirement near Aberdour. It might do her good, he'd suggested, to get away for a while from that great, gloomy house down in Yorkshire.

It was more than a year since he'd seen her. Writing that letter, he'd rejected the thought that his motives for proposing what amounted to a clandestine meeting might be open to misunderstanding. What was wrong with seeing his brother's wife in her own father's house, her father's presence, probably? He'd hinted, rather than put the proposal bluntly; but she'd replied by telegram. He'd thought, reading her wire and immediately crumpling it in his fist, *She feels it too, then . . .* And then at once, angry with himself, he'd questioned, *feels what?* He liked her, cared for her, his feelings for her might be avuncular or paternal or big-brotherly, there could be no question of any sort of – well, there *was* no such question. Neither he nor Sarah felt anything except friendship, affection, empathy.

14

He was concerned for her. With John away in France she must be feeling very much alone now.

Although – to be truthful about it – with John at home, he'd have had even more sympathy for her.

He told Crick, 'It's my brother's wife's family. I'm sure you'd be more than welcome, Tom, if you'd care to test your land-legs one day?'

'Most kind, sir.' Crick beamed. Genial, lobster-pink Crick was a torpedo specialist, and a great deal cleverer than he looked. They'd halted now: Hugh Everard had, and then his commander had followed suit: they stood side by side, looking towards the light cruiser squadrons' anchorage. Three squadrons, twelve cruisers; those were the scouts, the eyes of the fleet. Hugh looked to his right, at the new destroyer pens and inshore moorings crowded with the low, black hulls of the first, ninth, tenth, and thirteenth flotillas. There were about thirty destroyers altogether, with two more light cruisers as their leaders.

'Well, I'll be on my way.' As he turned towards the gangway he was aware of Crick's signal to the officer of the watch, Lieutenant Mowbray. Mowbray snapped, 'Man the side!' There was a swift surge of movement round the gangway's head: the side-boys mustering, the Marine corporal of the watch hurrying to join them, the bosun's mate wetting his lips and thumbing the mouthpiece of his silver call as he took his place there. Hugh murmured to Crick, 'Telephone me if you should need to. Otherwise grant shore leave as usual. I'll let you know when I want the gig inshore again.'

'Aye aye, sir.'

The commander nodded, understanding perfectly what had *not* been said. His captain had carefully not mentioned the talk of a 'flap', the rumours that were circulating about activity on the German side. There'd been so many alarms and so much disappointment; one didn't want to add credence to fleet gossip. Mowbray, a big, slow-moving man who looked too old for his lieutenant's stripes, ordered quietly, 'Pipe!' His hand jerked up to the salute as the bosun's call shrilled; a low note that swelled higher, hovered, fell away again. Crick was saluting too. Hugh put a hand to his cap as he stepped on to the platform at the head of the ladder and saw his gig waiting at its foot, bowman and stroke oar holding her there with boathooks whose brass fittings gleamed like pale gold. The other four crewmen had their oars turned fore-and-

15

aft and sat to attention as Able Seaman Bates, Hugh's coxswain, saluted him.

He stepped into the boat and sat down, picking up the yokelines of the tiller. He nodded to Bates, who sat down in the sternsheets a few feet further for'ard.

The role of captain's coxswain made George Bates much more than just the man who looked after this gig and steered it when Hugh wasn't actually in it. He was also butler, valet, messenger and general factotum. Domestically, he organised Hugh's life for him. He was a short, wiry man, with grizzled curly hair and a monkeyish face. His eyes seemed particularly like a monkey's, brown, watchful, crafty. Toughness made up for lack of bulk. It was said that during a bar-room brawl in Durban before the war Bates had driven his fist clean through a solid oak door – an opponent having had the sense to duck.

He'd done more than his share of bar brawling – which was why he'd never made petty officer or even leading seaman. But at least he had all three good conduct badges back now, and since he'd had the job with Hugh he'd stayed out of trouble. He'd been with him at the Falklands battle, too.

Hugh ordered, 'Shove off for'ard and aft!'

Sunlight glittered on the boathooks as they were shipped.

'Oars forward! Give way together!'

They rowed with the slow, sweeping, ceremonial stroke exclusive to a captain's personal crew. They were a privileged bunch of men, and proud of their jobs. If Hugh had had a house of his own ashore he could have used them to mow grass, fell trees, groom horses, drive motors. The gig was his private conveyance, and its crew his personal staff. But apart from manning the boat and looking after it, either at the boom or inboard, and cleaning Hugh's cabins under Bates's supervision, he hadn't much work to offer them. At sea, of course, they kept watches and had their various action stations, like any other members of the ship's company.

Hugh took a quick glance astern, to check the straightness of the course that he was steering; his eyes rested for a few seconds on *Nile*'s warlike bulk. He was proud of her, of his command of her. But it struck him suddenly that while aboard that ship he was God, here and now in this small boat heading for North Queensferry he felt more like a schoolboy playing truant. And with a rather schoolboyish sense of defiance. He could quite easily have had himself put ashore in, say, the steam pinnace. This gig, even without his pendant flying in its bows – as it would be on a more formal occasion – was patently his, Hugh Everard's boat. Or at least, *Nile*'s captain's boat. He was clearly in view here at its tiller; and this was the forenoon, when nobody went ashore except on duty, and when Vice-Admiral Sir David Beatty might quite likely be on *Lion*'s quarterdeck with a telescope at his eye.

Beatty could put it to his eye, Hugh thought coarsely, or wherever else he pleased. And if he wanted to see how a ship should be run efficiently and happily, he could take some time off himself and pay *Nile* a visit . . .

He must have grunted, or made some sound. Bates's eyes were on him, questioningly. Hugh shook his head.

He liked Bates. Tom Crick didn't. Crick, who'd read Bates's Service documents, the record of his past crimes, regarded him with wary suspicion. But Hugh was satisfied that a new leaf had been turned in that interesting – if not immaculate – career. He'd noticed the trouble Bates was taking to keep it turned – by, for instance, the simple though somewhat drastic expedient of hardly ever going ashore, unless Hugh actually sent him on some errand. Bates obviously knew his limitations, one of which was that in shoreside bars he tended to become provoked.

All up and down the Firth, warships lay as still as rocks in the glassy, shimmering tide. The mist was lifting rapidly, except down near the bridge where it still hung about in patches. A collier was casting-off from a destroyer depotship; picket-boats traced lines across the polished surface. A tug puffed up-stream with barges placid as ducks astern of her, but leaving a great roll of wash to rock ammunition-lighters moored in trots in St Margaret's Bay. A string of multi-coloured bunting broke at a cruiser's yardarm, hung limply in the windless air; within seconds a red-and-white answering pendant slid up above another ship in the same squadron. A shore signal-station sprang to life, sputtering a message to seaward in blinding flashes. Out of habit, Hugh watched it, piecing words together: *Berth on oiler at number . . .* Turning, he saw the narrow, almost bow-on shape of a destroyer coming up from the direction of the bridge at about five or six knots, with her signal letters flying and her searchlight above the stubby bridge acknowledging in quick stabs of brilliance each word as it reached her from the shore.

Hugh called, 'Oars!'

His men took one more slow stroke, then sat stiff, motionless, holding their oars horizontal, blades flat to the river's surface. But

17

the destroyer had appeared suddenly out of the seaward mists and the gig still had way on which would take her too quickly into the wash.

'Hold water!'

As upright in the stern as the crew were on their thwarts, he used rudder to compensate for the boat's tendency to slew, until the way came off her.

'Oars!' He sat still and waited for the destroyer to pass ahead.

Lieutenant-Commander Mortimer, immaculate now in what was probably his best uniform – a destroyer captain, who with various special allowances was paid more than three hundred pounds a year, could afford to pay his Gieves bills – glared at *Lanyard*'s navigator, Sub-Lieutenant Hastings.

'Well? Which *is* number eleven buoy?'

Hastings had been comparing the marked chart in his hands with the actual scene into which *Lanyard* had been steaming at what had felt, in the last couple of minutes, like breakneck speed. But he'd sorted it out now; he pointed, trying to look as if the matter had never really been in doubt.

'There sir. That's our oiler.'

Mortimer raised his glasses. He muttered, 'And that's a destroyer alongside her. If they'd meant us to double up, they'd have said so.' Lowering the glasses, he looked round at Hastings. 'Are you certain that's the oiler?'

Hastings nodded. 'Perhaps we're supposed to berth on her other side?'

'Who took that signal?'

'I did, sir.'

Mortimer looked round, and asked the man who'd spoken, 'Garret, are you certain the number was eleven, not twelve?'

'Number eleven they said, sir.' Garret was bony, haggard-looking, with pale blue eyes burning in a narrow, sea-tanned face and dark hair greying at the temples. A leading signalman, he was the senior signal rating in the ship.

'We'll take a chance on her inshore side, then. Pilot, come round a point to starboard. Number One, we'll be berthing port side to the oiler.'

'Aye aye, sir . . . Everard!'

'Sir?' Hastings was calling down to the quartermaster for a change of course; now Mortimer was pushing him aside and taking over. It all seemed haphazard – a pleasant contrast to the battleship rituals one was used to.

'Yes, sir?'

'Go aft, tell Lieutenant Reynolds port side to, and stay there and assist him.'

'Aye aye, sir.' Heading for the ladder, he heard Mortimer call for slow speed, then the clang of telegraphs from the steering-position, the lower bridge. Nick dropped down to the upper deck and hurried aft . . . A gig lay on its oars, bow-on; he'd only glimpsed it out of the corner of his eye, and by the time he'd stopped and turned to look at her more closely she'd been left astern. But a six-oared gig, with a tallish senior officer at her tiller – Nick had been left with a snapshot-like impression of a broad-shouldered man and a gold-peaked cap.

Might it have been his uncle? It could be: that was the Fifth Battle Squadron over there. But he'd been thinking about Hugh Everard, and he might have imagined it: the boat had appeared and then dropped astern so fast. He could see her again now, a long way back, see the slow sweep of her oars as she pitched across *Lanyard*'s wake.

He saluted Reynolds, whose berthing party of a dozen sailors was lined up 'at ease' on the quarterdeck. 'First lieutenant says port side to, sir, and I'm to stay and help you.'

'You're entirely welcome.' Reynolds glanced to his left. 'Hear that, Petty Officer Shaw?'

'Yessir.' Shaw took a pace forward and turned about. 'Port side to, then. Thomson, 'Arris, Wills – jump to it!'

Reynolds asked Nick, 'What's Morty doing? Singing hymns, this morning?' Nick looked surprised. Reynolds added, 'He does quite often, entering harbour. He's quite cracked, you know.'

Cracked or not, Mortimer handled *Lanyard* as if she were a skiff. Within minutes, she was secured alongside the oiler, and if there'd been a crate of eggs floating at the waterline they'd all have remained intact. One had heard often enough that destroyer captains tended to be both marvellous ship-handlers and person-ally insane. He was coming aft now, followed by his first lieutenant, to whom Nick was waiting to report.

The oil pipes were already being dragged over and screwed to *Lanyard*'s fuel intakes up for'ard, under Mr Worsfold's sharp-eyed supervision. Mortimer glanced at Nick.

'What are you giving Everard to do this forenoon, Number One?'

19

'I'll be instructing him in his duties as assistant GCO, sir. After that he can lend a hand with storing ship.'

'Good. Now look here – I need someone to go into Edinburgh for me. God knows whether we'll be granting shore leave, but at least we're safe until we've fuelled and stored and I have to go and pay my respects to Captain (D.) Who can you spare?'

'Garret, sir?'

'Why him?'

'Well, sir, as you know, he got spliced, two days before we left here. I understand he's – well, anxious to – er—'

Mortimer shook his head. 'The possibility that Leading Signalman Garret may be in a state of – er – suspended animation, shall we say, is hardly relevant. I'm not offering someone a run ashore, I simply want a package delivered to my bank.'

'Garret would still be a suitable messenger, sir.' Johnson glanced over his shoulder. 'Wouldn't you say so, Cox'n?'

Chief Petty Officer Cuthbertson nodded. He was a heavy man; thick-necked, bulky round the middle. If he let himself get out of condition, he'd be fat.

' 'Ighly suitable, sir. Very responsible 'and, is Garret.'

Mortimer gave in. 'All right. Send him along, right away.'

'Aye aye, sir.' The captain went below. Johnson cocked an eye at Cuthbertson: 'All right, Cox'n?'

'Garret's messmates 'll bless you, sir. They say it's bin like livin' with a mad stallion on 'ot bricks.'

'Tell him to report to the Captain. And warn him not to let us down. If he spends half an hour with his wife, we shan't know about it; but if he stays there an hour or more . . .'

The coxswain's eyebrows twitched. 'What I'm told, sir, five an' a 'alf minutes is about what 'e'll need.'

On the bridge, Johnson showed Nick how to operate the Bar and Stroud fire-control transmitter.

'Three dials, which are manually set according to my orders. The guns are laid and trained individually by their crews, and the gunlayers apply ranges and deflection as they read them off their receivers – which of course show the same as I put on here. D'you follow that?'

Nick was relieved that the system was so simple.

'Third dial here shows the orders: load, fire, rapid independent, cease fire . . . Clear enough?'

'Yes sir.'

'I order settings and corrections and our wardroom steward, Blewitt, puts them on the transmitter. It's easy for me to control the for'ard gun, since it's just down there, I can actually look down on it and talk to the layer by voicepipe. But you'll take charge as officer of the quarters aft – of both the other guns. If I'm knocked out, you take my place here. Same if the captain's hit – I take his job, you take mine.' He stared at Nick as if he was trying to see inside his skull. 'Is that all clear, Everard?'

Nick asked a few questions and Johnson answered them without impatience or criticism. Talking directly to the point like this, he seemed far less of a David-type character; his professional interest in the subject under discussion seemed to clear away the personal prejudices or reservations. It was possible, Nick began to think, that things might not turn out too badly.

'We'll go aft now, and take a look at the guns themselves. And one other vitally important aspect, namely—' He checked, and asked Nick, 'Namely *what*?'

'Ammunition supply.'

'Good.' The man actually looked pleased. 'I've made some changes in the after supply parties. They seem to know what they're doing, but you'll need to keep an eye on 'em while they settle down. And you must see to it they learn each others' jobs, so they can switch around and no hangups in the routine if we get casualties.'

Casualties . . . Walking aft, half listening to Johnson, glancing round at the quiet although busy harbour scene, the idea of deaths or woundings seemed remote. Obviously it was not, and one had to realise it and be prepared; this was a warship, designed and built for battle. But to imagine damage, shell-bursts, here where a group of bluejackets were chipping away old paint, others polishing brass, another neatly flemishing a boat's fall; Nick closed his eyes, trying to imagine what it would feel like to be under fire.

'What the *blazes* are you doing, Everard?'

Opening his eyes, he found Johnson staring at him; with that Davidish expression . . .

'Sarah – I couldn't begin to tell you how much I've been looking forward—'

'Ah, Everard!'

He turned, with his sister-in-law's hands still clasped in his, as her father came slowly through the door of the morning room. 'Well, sir! Splendid to see you again!'

21

'A great pleasure to see *you*, sir.' White-haired, lame from gout, Sir Robert Buchanan extended a limp hand towards his guest. Then he gestured towards the bell-cord: 'Pull that, will ye, gel?' Hugh glanced round the stuffy, high-ceilinged room; a long-dead salmon topped a book-case, and stags' heads stared down glassily, resentfully even, from the brownish-papered walls. He told Buchanan, 'You're looking well, sir.' Like an old, tired sheep, he thought. 'But Sarah's rather pale, would you agree?'

'Which is more than anyone could say of *you*, Hugh dear.' She smiled as she returned to them. 'You're as brown as a sailor ought to be. Is it all sunshine in the Orkneys?'

'How long shall we have you with us, Everard?'

'Ah.' Glancing back at her father. 'It's hard to tell. Not very long, I fancy. But more to the point, how long is Sarah to be here with you?'

'I think I should *like*—' Sarah paused, as a servant appeared and her father sent him to fetch biscuits and madeira – 'I think I should like to come and live here permanently – I mean, while John's at the front. You can't imagine how dreary Mullbergh's become, Hugh, and since Father's on his own here—'

'First-class idea. Wouldn't you say so, sir?' Looking back at Sarah, he said, 'You'd leave a few people to keep Mullbergh warm, I suppose?'

'Warm? *Mullbergh?*'

'I needn't tell you, my dear, you'd be more than welcome here.' The white head nodded. 'Sit down, Everard . . . Entirely welcome, whenever you like and for as long as you like. Longer the better, in fact. But don't you think your husband might rather you kept his home fires burning?'

Hugh coughed. 'My brother's first thought would surely be for Sarah's comfort.' But he thought, *last thought, more likely*. He was studying Sarah, her hazel eyes and soft brown hair and that tender, vulnerable mouth. She was paler than she should have been; but even if she'd turned bright blue, he thought, she'd still have been beautiful.

'Since Mullbergh's lonely for you, and it was always a damp, cold place why not tell John you propose to come up here?'

Buchanan, Sarah's father, was a widower, and rich. He'd been a shipowner twenty years ago. Now they'd found coal under land which he owned here in Scotland, and he was piling up yet another fortune from the royalties.

'I'd like to – I'd *adore* to. But it's quite impossible.' Sarah was telling Hugh, more than her father. 'Mullbergh has to be looked after. It's my—' she made a face – 'war-work, I'm afraid.'

They talked about Hugh's brother, and what he'd said in recent letters. He'd spent a leave at Mullbergh several months ago; Sarah had no idea when she'd see him next. The fighting was still fierce around Verdun, where French losses were hideous in the face of a German onslaught which hadn't slackened since it began three months ago, and there was talk of a new British offensive being mounted to make the Hun relax that pressure. It would be on the Somme, people said.

War-talk with madeira and the old man crunching biscuits. Small, rapid jaw movements; like a rat's, Hugh thought.

'A pity you don't expect to be here long, Everard. It must be grand to come under the orders of Sir David Beatty, after your stuffed-shirt Jellicoe up there!'

'Jellicoe's the best we could have, sir!' Hugh spoke sharply. 'Certainly no stuffed shirt. He's brilliant – and the whole fleet loves him. Believe me, he is the one man we trust.'

'But Beatty, surely—'

'Beatty holds his command *under* Admiral Jellicoe, our Commander-in-Chief.'

'Would you not say that Beatty was – was an exceptionally able and inspiring leader?'

Hugh hesitated. One could hardly express one's views on such a matter to an outsider like Buchanan, or to anyone, in fact, except close friends in the Navy. Beatty was – well, as a young lieutenant he'd commanded a gunboat on the Nile during Kitchener's campaign against the Mahdi, and out of that he'd won a DSO and promotion to commander years ahead of his contemporaries. Then he was on the China station when the Boxer Rebellion started, and he was landed with a party of sailors and marines to break through to the relief of the Peking legations. Another display of dash and courage – he was wounded, decorated and promoted to post captain at the age of twenty-nine.

Hugh said carefully, 'His early achievements were certainly spectacular.'

'And isn't he the sort of leader our Navy needs? Not just the Navy – the *country*?'

'Well . . .' Hugh rubbed his jaw. 'There's always room for leadership, certainly.'

But did a young, hot-blooded, self-opinionated Irishman who was useful with a cutlass in a rough-house necessarily grow into a modern fleet commander?

Buchanan said stuffily, 'Sir David and Lady Beatty reside now, as you're perhaps aware, at Aberdour House here. Lady Beatty is the most charming, delightful person. A major asset, I may say, to our small community.'

'I'm sure she must be.'

She was American. Back from China with wounds newly healed, the glamorous young Captain Beatty had married the daughter of a Chicago millionaire, Marshall Field. London's society lay open to him. In 1910 he'd become the youngest admiral since – Nelson and Nelson had only completed the course in one year less. But that comparison, in Hugh Everard's view, was ludicrous.

Buchanan was like a dog with a bone . . .

'Was it not Winston Churchill who appointed him to command the battle cruisers?'

Churchill had made Beatty his naval secretary in 1911. Despite that meteoric rise, Beatty had seemed to have reached his ceiling; he was on half-pay and close to being compulsorily retired. He'd refused an appointment in the Atlantic Fleet, considering it beneath him, and Their Lordships were not thinking of offering him alternatives. They'd warned Churchill that the young admiral had already been over-promoted; but Churchill took to him, liked the vigour of his personality, which he'd felt matched his own.

Beatty, Hugh Everard felt, had had a run of stupendous luck. For the Navy's sake one had to hope that it had not run out.

Leading Signalman Garret of HMS *Lanyard* was so sick of jokes and innuendo about his marital condition that he'd considered, just for a moment, asking to be excused the privilege of carrying the captain's package to the bank.

He'd hesitated, seeing in the corners of his imagination the winks and nudges, hearing his messmates' guffaws . . . But the hell with them! He wasn't passing-up a chance to see Margaret.

'Aye aye, Cox'n.'

'Don't look so sad about it, lad. It's a favour we're doin' you!'

The destroyer berthed on the oiler's other side had had a boat actually alongside and about to cross to Hawes Pier; Sub-Lieutenant Hastings, acting as officer of the day, had arranged for Garret to steal a ride in it. From Hawes Pier it was only a stone's throw to Dalmeny Station, and from there a short train journey to the Caledonian Station.

From Princes Street he turned into Hanover Street and found the bank, where an elderly assistant manager in striped trousers took the package and gave him a signature for it on the captain's chit.

Duty done. Now to surprise Margaret. He'd get a tram and then cut through the back streets. He hoped to God he'd find her at home. She'd been about to start finding out what jobs might be going; until now she'd helped her mother in the shop, but they were determined to start saving, so she wanted to earn money now, not just pocket-money. There was no certainty he'd find her, only hope. Fearing disappointment, he warned himself as he hurried up Hanover Street and turned right into Queen Street, crossing it diagonally then towards the tram stop, don't count your chickens, lad!

They'd known before the wedding that *Lanyard* and the rest of her flotilla would be sailing in a day or two for Scapa. What they had not known was that having arrived there she'd develop trouble with an A-bracket and have to dock to fix it; worse still, have to wait more than a week until the one and only floating dock was able to receive her.

He was burning to see Margaret, see she was all right; see her, speak with her; to establish contact, that was the urgent need. At first he'd put up easily with the shipboard humour; then he'd begun to hate it, and his increasingly short temper with his messmates' teasing had only made things worse. They were decent lads, but in the last few days he'd come close to loathing them.

He was smiling at his own thoughts . . . They were all right. He'd let it get him down, but from now on everything would be back to normal. He was rattling north-eastwards . . . This wasn't his town, it was Margaret's – and she called it a 'toon'! He smiled again as he dropped off the tram at a corner which he recognised by its horse-trough with angels over it.

He broke into a trot. The thought that he might just miss her by minutes or even seconds tormented him. He was in a bit of a jumpy state, he knew that; but he knew also that taking Margaret's hands in his, looking into her eyes and talking to her, hearing her voice, was the only medicine likely to do him good. Rounding a corner, he had to slam on starboard rudder to avoid collision with a hawker's cart, a load of vegetables; his cap went skidding, he stumbled, scooped it up, ran on, an old man's cracked laughter floating after him. At the end of this cobbled part he'd come into the wider, newer street, and just a short way up it was the shop.

The skipper had been as fair as he could have been. 'Back aboard by noon, Garret. That'll allow you – oh, an hour or more, for your own purposes.'

Say half an hour. There'd be other days, and shore leave granted. Sundays would be the best, if he could swap watches with unmarried men – which wouldn't be difficult, since three-quarters of *Lanyard*'s ship's company were bachelors – because whatever job she found herself, on Sundays Margaret wouldn't have to work. And since all shore leave expired at sunset . . . Well, they'd known, both of them, they'd faced quite clearly what sort of half-life they'd be leading in terms of marriage; it was the war, the way things had to be in wartime. What they were investing their lives in was a long-term future, the time when there'd be no war.

The bell on the shop door clanged dully as Garret burst in, breathless.

'Mrs McKie, it's me! Where's—'

'Wha's that? Wha's that ye—'

Margaret's mother had swung round, as cumbersome as a turret in a battleship. Now she was goggling at him across the counter. There was practically nothing in the shop; Lord only knew how they made a living.

'Och, *you* back wi' us, Geoffrey!'

He nodded, anxious, and already edging towards the back, the stairs door. 'Is Margaret in? Upstairs, is she?'

'Aye, but – I'd thought tae let her sleep, she's been sae—'

'She's not ill?'

'I'd not say ill, no, I couldn't say *ill*, Geoffrey; but she's no' been hersel', she's—'

He realised that she'd shifted her broad-based bulk so that it was now blanking-off the doorway. And was Margaret ill, or wasn't she? He thought he saw confusion – hesitance, a sort of fear, even – in the woman's face. He stared at her. She was uneasy, caught off-guard, it was as evident as the black hairs curling on her chin.

Pushing past her, Garret hurled himself up the stairs; narrow, curving, hollow-sounding under his heavy boots. Before he was halfway up he heard Margaret's voice call sharply 'Who's there? Who's that?' He wrenched the door open.

'Geoff! *Geoff!* Och, I canna *believe* it!'

He could hardly believe his eyes, either. She wasn't dressed nor quite undressed either. Just enough on for decoration, to make her look like something wicked – something that stunned him, winded him. He kicked the door shut with his heel.

It was necessary, he realised, to speak.

'What's she on about, you being ill?'

Margaret laughed, put a finger to her lips. She was kneeling on the bed. He'd forgotten how she thrilled him: or *had* she, had she ever, quite like this? He could hardly get his breath in or out.

'She doesn'ae want me lookin' for work, that's a'!' Laughing: he laughed with her. He'd forgotten what suspicions had been in his mind when he'd come rushing up the stairs. She asked him softly, 'Lock the door?'

He'd only come to see her, talk to her.

They'd lunched late and very slowly, and then Buchanan had wanted to smoke a cigar with his guest before he'd hauled his old bones away to rest them. It was nearly five before Hugh had Sarah to himself, and by that time he was uncomfortably divided in his impulses. He'd had no real chance to talk to her, but he felt he should soon be starting back; on the other hand it had been his idea that she should come up from Yorkshire. He could hardly spend so short a time and just rush away.

The chance of the fleet being ordered to sea was nothing new. The ships were always at short notice, and there were always 'buzzes'. Besides, there'd be no time wasted in getting back, since the old man had placed his motor and chauffeur at his disposal.

Still, the feeling of being an absentee persisted. There was a tension in him which refused to be dispelled.

Sarah had asked him a question about Nick.

'Hasn't he written to you lately?'

She nodded. 'He writes quite often. But about everything except the Navy.' She touched her brown hair; a filtered ray of sun from the window gave golden tints to it. 'I worry for him. He's so – so *wholehearted*, and responsive to friendship. One might almost imagine he'd never had any! He admires *you*, enormously, but you're—' she gestured upwards – 'out of his reach. The Navy seems to – isolate people, somehow?'

Hugh cleared his throat.

'What Nick had to learn is that one has to fit into one's surroundings as one finds them. We – the Navy – have our faults,

27

there's no body or organisation that doesn't. But we know the faults, and we work to remove them. It's no good just—' he turned back from the window – 'Nick's too ready to stand at bay, so to speak, and tell everyone to go to the devil. Perhaps that's how he's learnt to cope with – oh—'

'With his father?'

'In the Navy, it won't do.' Hugh frowned. 'One thing that might help him, probably, would be some action. That's my fault, I dare say – when he was younger I rather fed him the glamour of the Service; battles, victories, the great days . . . And as you say, he's – a forthright lad, at heart. All he's seen has been Scapa Flow and a lot of drills and no fighting – and this in time of war, too. I suppose that is a lot of his trouble.' He raised his eyebrows and spread his hands. 'But for heaven's sake, it's the same for all the rest of us – and nobody can whistle up the German fleet just to please one discontented little sub-lieutenant!'

Sarah smiled. He went on, 'Strictly between us, though – I've done what I can towards getting him a second chance.'

'Has he lost some first chance?'

'He's in danger of going "under report", as it's called. It'd mean he'd be kept more or less for ever in a capital ship and have reports on his conduct submitted to the Admiralty. It's a system I'd like to see abolished, frankly – it does no good, and often makes matters much worse. Very few sublieutenants who get to that stage ever get promoted to lieutenant, I can tell you.' He sat down. 'As you can imagine, I'd like to avoid it happening to Nick.'

'And you think it's just that he's bored – disappointed at not to have been in any fighting?'

'I don't know . . . except he's got to pull himself together. Did you know that when he was still a midshipman he physically assaulted a sub-lieutenant?'

She shook her head.

'I'm sure he must have had good reason.'

'During an evening of what's called "gunroom evolutions". It's a sort of traditional horseplay they indulge in. I think Nick was largely in the right, but you can't have people striking their superior officers, you see. These "evolutions" are harmless enough if they aren't overdone; but up at Scapa, cooped up in gunrooms with no real outlets for their adolescent energies . . .' He shook his head. 'It can get, well – it can degenerate into plain bullying. I've put a stop to it in my own ship – had the doors

28

taken off the gunroom, so the young savages have less privacy than they'd like.'

Beatty, he'd been told, encouraged 'evolutions', even insisted on them for his own after-dinner entertainment.

Sarah asked him, 'What sort of second chance?'

'I don't know if anything's been done. I sent a note – a letter – to Doveton Sturdee.'

'The Admiral?' Hugh nodded. She asked him, 'Now, how is it I know of him?'

'You'll have heard of him because he commanded the Falklands operation. It was through him that I went out there. He's an extremely capable and forthright man, and a good friend. He also happens to be flag officer of the Fourth Division of the battle fleet, and the Fourth Division includes Nick's ship. I asked him whether he'd forestall the inevitable by having Nick moved to a destroyer or a light cruiser. If it's at all possible, I think he'll do it for me.'

'I'll pray for it.'

'Then between us we'll have a double-barrelled prayer.'

Sarah laughed. 'You are simply *not* the ironclad you're supposed to be!'

'Me? Ironclad?'

'Oh, what's said, here and there. Perhaps you don't hear it. The brilliant Captain Everard, who should never have been allowed to leave the Navy and who's bound now to become an admiral?'

'More power to their sooth-saying!'

'It truly does matter to you, doesn't it? More than – anything?'

'Perhaps.' The window, with the bright colours of the garden, drew his eyes. 'Yes, I suppose so.'

'What are you really after, Hugh? To square accounts?'

'Good Lord, who with? Fisher's gone. In any case, he had his reasons. No.'

'You want to prove you can do it.' He nodded. She asked him, 'Prove it to whom?'

'Perhaps to men of my own vintage who saw me forced out. Or younger ones who've shot up the ladder since. Look here, it's said I've done well since I've been back – and perhaps I have – but there's a man named Dreyer who's captain of *Iron Duke*, Jellicoe's flagship. I'm forty-five, and he's only thirty-eight and he's where I would've been, d'you see?'

'And this is *your* second chance. It's vitally important to you, isn't it? Before any other consideration.'

Her hands moved expressively. She was inviting comment, and he'd none to make. She said more quietly, 'I'm sorry. It's none of my business. I've no right to pry or criticise.'

'It would be the most glorious thing imaginable if you did have such a right.'

He'd heard himself say it. He could still hear the words. And see Sarah's eyes on him, wide and startled.

Was this how lives were changed, re-directed? By words that spoke themselves? There'd been no forethought, he'd not had the least intention . . .

They were staring at each other as if each was trying to test the solidity, the safety of new ground. And there was no safety in it whatsoever, he realised. It would be as reckless as it would be – marvellous. As damaging as the idea of it was thrilling. How long had it been in his mind – without his knowing it?

It must have been there. I've just put it into words . . .

To act on it would be suicide. His brother's wife: the war, and his brother at the front. How much more of a destructive scandal could one invite?

'You mustn't—' Sarah looked away – 'we mustn't allow ourselves even to think of—'

'I know.'

Two words, as final as 'full stop.' As if a door had been open a crack and suddenly slammed shut. If he'd answered in some quite different way . . .

Well, he hadn't. He'd made the opening: or it had made itself: and he'd looked through it into a new world, a whole new future. And then – shut the door. For the sake of – safety? But what did one want most?

Looking at her, he thought he knew the answer.

'Sarah, Sarah, listen . . .'

Her eyes rested on his face. He'd paused: he was lost, he needed time to test the words before he uttered them. She shook her head just slightly, almost imperceptibly, as if it was some idea of her own she was rejecting. She asked him, rather stiffly, 'If they let Nick move as you've asked, would it make so much difference to him?'

'It could.'

His mind was still on her, not Nick.

'What if he's just not interested? I know how you feel about the Navy, but does that mean *he* has to?'

The change of subject was a tide one went with, unwillingly. He said, 'There've been Everards in the Navy List for two hundred years.'

'But the Navy List has you in it, and it has David. Isn't that good enough reading for you?'

It wouldn't have been easy to explain, even if his mind had been fully on it. He thought Nick was right for the Navy, but he was less sure about David. Some lack of stamina or leadership, that one sensed? Hard to say why, in the light of Nick's performance so far, one should have such feelings: and a feeling was all it was, an *instinct*. He explained, 'Nick's *in* the Navy. It's what he always wanted to do. It's up to him to make a go of it.' He set himself to play devil's advocate. 'As David has. David's won first-class passes in all subjects, he's well thought of in his present appointment, he's—'

'He's the most selfish—'

She'd glanced round, at the door. Hugh heard it too: the telephone bell. He thought immediately of *Nile*, and that it might well be Tom Crick calling him back aboard. There was a clink out there in the hall as the old butler, McEwan, lifted the receiver. Hugh checked the time and saw that it was five forty-five, later than he'd thought . . .

'Indeed he is, sir. If ye'd hold the line a wee moment?'

'Sarah, excuse me?'

He was out of the room, dodging the heavyweight McEwan as he crossed the hall. The receiver was hanging on its cord; he scooped it up, put it to his ear, stooped to reach the mouthpiece. Buchanan was a small man and he'd had the thing mounted too low on the wall for comfort. 'Everard here.'

'Crick here, sir. We've orders to raise steam. May I send your boat in?'

'Yes. At once please, Tom.'

Hanging up, turning, he saw the butler hovering and Sarah in the doorway of the drawing-room.

'I'm sorry, Sarah. I've no time even to thank your father for his hospitality.'

Sarah spoke to McEwan. 'Would you tell Alec to bring the motor to the front, please?'

'Certainly, m'lady.'

The old man lumbered away. Hugh took Sarah's hand.

'We've had so little time to talk. And – what I began to say earlier—'

'You should not have.' She smiled. It was kind and friendly, nothing else. She laughed. 'And now your country needs you!'

'Sarah—'

'Are you off to sea again – off to fight the foe?'

McEwan came shuffling ponderously back into the hall. Hugh shook his head. 'No such luck.'

'Shall I be seeing you again soon, then?'

'I can't tell.' He saw her frown and added, 'But stay a while? I'll telephone when I can.' He heard the car arriving, and as he let go of her hand his thoughts left her too, settled five, six miles away where a fleet was raising steam, recalling libertymen, would soon be hoisting-in boats, shortening-in anchor cables or passing slip-wires at the buoys. There'd be bunting fluttering from the yardarms, searchlights winking out their messages, boat traffic heavy for a while and then decreasing, dwindling until the capstans turned and bugle-calls floated across a darkening Firth which, when daylight came tomorrow, the citizens of Edinburgh would find empty.

Just this Rosyth force, he wondered? Or the whole Grand Fleet, the squadrons and flotillas from Scapa and Invergordon too?

CHAPTER 3

'By May 28th it became clear that some considerable movement was on foot, and at noon on 30th May a message was
sent to the Commander-in-Chief, Grand Fleet, that there
were indications of the German fleet coming out. The position still remained obscure . . . At 5.16 pm a message went off
to the Commander-in-Chief, and Senior Officer, Battle Cruiser Force, to raise steam, followed by a further wire at 5.40
pm ordering the fleet to concentrate to eastward of Long
Forties ready for eventualities. The operations had begun.'
Narrative of the Battle of Jutland
(H.M. Stationery Officer, 1924)

Another North Sea sweep; one was used to them by now. David
Everard peered into the dimly lit binnacle as *Bantry*, port screw
going slow astern and the other slow ahead, swung her stern to
starboard so that her bow would point south-east towards Hoxa
Sound. She and the other cruisers and after them Hood's battle
cruisers and then the dreadnought squadrons, would be parading
southwards through that two-mile gap during the next ninety
minutes. It was nine forty pm. Ten minutes ago the destroyer
flotillas had left their moorings and, invisible in the gathering
night, streamed southwards through the destroyer exit, Switha
Sound, while at the same time the light cruiser squadrons had
weighed and started south. Boom vessels would at this moment be
dragging back the great steel-mesh nets which guarded the fleet's
base against torpedo and submarine attack; beyond them, mine-
sweepers had been busy for the last two hours, ensuring clear water
as far down as Swona Island.
'Light cruisers passing ahead, sir.'
Commander Clark, hunched in a wing of the bridge with

binoculars at his eyes, made the quiet report. Wilmott, *Bantry*'s captain, raised his own glasses to watch the low, grey ships slide past. He was close on David's right; his light-brown, neatly trimmed beard shone like gold in the binnacle's soft radiance.

'Pilot, how's her head?'

David called down the voicepipe to the helmsman, 'Stop port.' He told Wilmott, 'A point to go, sir.' He'd been watching the slowly circling lubber's line as it crept round the compass card. He called down again now, after a fifteen-second pause, 'Stop starboard.' None of the ships showed any lights. The routine for leaving the Flow in darkness, established in great detail in the commander-in-chief's standing orders, could be initiated and conducted with few signals and no wasted time. Jellicoe had made his first signal at five forty pm, 'All ships prepare for sea'. At that point, a thousand different preparations had automatically been put in hand. At eight seven the second signal had come, 'Fleet will leave harbour at nine thirty pm by the DT3 method'. No further instruction had been necessary; with nine thirty established as zero-hour, all ships and squadrons knew the order of departure, the intervals at which they'd point ship, weigh anchor and move out. There'd be a gap of four thousand yards between the rear ship of each squadron of big ships and the leading ship of the next squadron following, and successive squadrons would pass alternately north or south of the Pentland Skerries, the last small, jagged bits of rock they'd see as they steamed east.

There'd been no wireless signals to alert the enemy to Grand Fleet movements. Even the Admiralty's orders to Jellicoe and Beatty had been sent by land-line.

'Cable's up-and-down, sir!'

'Vast heaving.' Wilmott stooped, looking intently through his glasses. *Bantry* would follow astern of the ships of the Second Cruiser Squadron and act as one of them; they had to weigh and pass her first and she'd tag on behind. Tomorrow – Admiral Heath had passed the information by light some while ago to Wilmott – the Scapa force would be joined at sea by the ships from Cromarty, and when the rendezvous had been made *Bantry* would transfer to the first Cruiser Squadron, to which she now belonged.

'*Minotaur*'s under way, sir.' Nobby Clark spoke quietly. The whole movement, the whole Flow, was quiet. A watcher ashore, even if he should be on a shore as close as Flotta's, might not

34

become aware before tomorrow's dawn that a single ship had sailed. Clark added gruffly, 'And *Hampshire*, sir – and *Cochrane*—'

'I see them, thank you . . . Tell the foc'sl stand by to weigh anchor.'

The sailor manning the navyphone to the cable-party said sharply into his mouthpiece, 'Stand by to weigh!' David called less urgently into his voicepipe, 'Slow astern starboard.' *Bantry* had over-swung a little. 'Slow ahead port.' His own orders floated back to him as the quartermaster re-intoned them, and he heard the clash of engine-room telegraphs down there in the steering position, felt the vibration through the soles of his half-boots as the ship's engines were put to work. But not much was needed: he called down, 'Stop both engines.' One could imagine the engineers glancing at each other: *what the 'ell they playin' at, up there?* He heard the commander's voice from the bridge's wing: '*Shannon* is about to pass ahead, sir.'

'Weigh anchor.'

A muffled shout from for'ard; clanking resumed, as the last shackles were hove in. *Shannon* loomed ahead, her four tall funnels duplicates of *Bantry*'s – visible against the night sky as she passed.

'Anchor's aweigh, sir!'

They were waiting for the next report, and it came soon enough.

'Clear anchor!' Meaning that the anchor was out of water, in sight from the foc'sl and not fouled by anything such as another ship's wires or cables. *Bantry* was in fact clear of the seabed, a free agent.

Wilmott muttered, 'Carry on, Everard.'

'Slow ahead together.'

'Slow ahead together, sir! Both telegraphs slow ahead, sir!'

Straightening from the voicepipe, David raised his binoculars to watch *Bantry*'s bow and *Shannon*'s track ahead of her. He felt the churning of the screws, a vibration right through the ship as she gathered way; fifteen thousand tons of her, and twenty-seven thousand horsepower inside a six-inch armour belt to overcome the vast inertia and then drive her – when speed might be called for, later – at her designed rate of twenty-three knots. At a pinch, she might manage a shade more than that.

Wilmott was impassive, immobile, watching *Shannon* through his glasses but leaving the handling of the ship to his navigator. David called down, 'Port fifteen.'

Bantry's bow swung to starboard just inside the wake left by

Shannon; her forward momentum as she turned would carry her right into it, so that she'd finish precisely astern of that next-ahead. He stooped again: 'Half ahead together.'

'Half ahead together, sir!' He ordered revolutions for twelve knots.

Astern of the cruisers would come Admiral Hood's *Invincible, Inflexible* and *Indomitable* – they were up here from Rosyth, for gunnery practice, and *Nile* with her squadron of Queen Elizabeths had been sent south to take their place temporarily in Beatty's force – and then the battle fleet led by Jellicoe in *Iron Duke*. While at this same moment Vice-Admiral Sir Martyn Jerram would be leading the Second Battle Squadron and Arbuthnot's cruisers out of the Cromarty Firth, Invergordon. Beatty, presumably, would be putting out from Rosyth with his battle cruisers and the Fifth Battle Squadron, including *Nile*: and young Nick's destroyer with them.

Nick's pierhead jump into *Lanyard* still infuriated David. Obviously Uncle Hugh had arranged it somehow. Otherwise that bloody-minded little tyke who'd been about to go under report – which effectively would have put a stopper on his naval career – could never have been even considered for a destroyer job!

They ganged up – Hugh, Nick, Sarah . . .

Would Captain Hugh Everard, Royal Navy, have lifted as much as one finger to help his older nephew, David Everard? Would he, hell!

David bent to the voicepipe and called down, 'Steer three degrees to port!'

Uncle Hugh, and Sarah. His own brother's wife, for God's sake. It had been skirt-chasing that had wrecked Hugh Everard's career and marriage, years ago. Whatever he *said*, everyone knew that was the truth of it . . . Wilmott spoke suddenly out of the darkness, 'Which side of the Skerries do we go?'

'South of them, sir.'

They were passing through Hoxa Sound now, beacons flashing dimly on each side; no stars visible; wind south-east, force three. *Bantry* trembled under her engines' gentle thrust; she'd begun to pitch a little, as if sensing the open sea ahead and lengthening her stride for it. Below, in stifling-hot boiler-rooms, stokers would already be glistening with sweat as they swung their shovels with piston-like rhythm into the banks of coal and slung it into roaring furnaces . . . The boom-vessels, trawlers which operated the net defences by hauling them to and fro to allow ships to pass through them, loomed up suddenly out of the dark. For a moment or two they seemed so close that one might have reached out and touched them before they fell away astern and disappeared. As *Bantry* passed the second pair, the outer gate, David called, 'Porter – note the time, in the log.'

'Aye aye, sir.'

A useful lad, David's 'tanky'.

Wilmott ordered, 'Secure the foc's'l.'

They'd be shivering with cold down there by now, but until a ship was clear of harbour an anchor had to be kept ready for letting go, in case of some emergency. Now it would be cranked home into its hawse-pipe, the screw-slip hammered on and tightened, Blake slip secured and lashed, lashings and securing tackles would be rigged between the two cables, port and starboard, hove taut and secured. *Bantry* was out now, her pitching to the long, smooth swell more pronounced as she steamed in *Shannon*'s wake towards Swona Island five miles ahead. It was in the vicinity of Swona that one felt the impact of the Pentland tide-rip, a current of as much as ten knots which, if the bridge and quartermaster weren't alert and ready for it, could take a ship's bow as she steamed into it and swing her clear around through sixteen points.

A new arrival on the bridge approached Wilmott. David saw that it was Harrington, *Bantry*'s first lieutenant, up from his duties as cable officer.

'Foc's'l secured for sea, sir.'

'Thank you. Pilot, are we falling astern?'

David bent to the voicepipe and ordered an increase in revolutions. He hadn't noticed the slight widening of the gap between *Bantry* and the ship ahead of her. He told himself, *Come on, wake up.* It was an illusion that Wilmott had left it to him to take the ship out of harbour; the man was at his elbow, watching each move, every detail. Discovering – as a new CO had to, of course – whom he could rely on, who might need watching. He'd only taken over just over a week ago, and he'd not had his fourth stripe much longer than a month; he was a man bent on further swift strides up the promotion ladder, and David was aware that the coat-tails of a young, ambitious post captain weren't bad things to snatch a tow from. So far, touch wood, Wilmott seemed to approve of his young navigating lieutenant. David told himself, *I don't need my damned uncle's help, I don't even want it! I detest the lot of them!*

They'd see, one day – Hugh, Nick, Sarah – who had the whip hand. It might not be all that long before they saw it, either. As elder son and therefore heir to a baronet – father currently occupied in – or at least not far behind – the Flanders trenches, one was fully aware of the possibilities. The French were saying *Ils ne passeront pas*: but a Hun breakthrough at Verdun, where the bloodiest fighting of the war had been going on for months now, wouldn't surprise anyone. Wilmott broke into his thoughts.

'How many miles to Swona, Pilot?'

'Roughly ten, sir, but I'll—'

'That's near enough. What's course and speed after we pass the Skerries?'

'South seventy-three east, sir, seventeen knots.'

'And our disposition?'

'Number one, sir, with ourselves added on the starboard wing. But we're to remain in close order ten miles ahead of the battle fleet until daylight, and then spread out.'

'Ah.'

Wilmott had known the answers before he'd asked the questions; the orders for the cruisers' disposition had been passed by light from *Minotaur* while the fleet had still been raising steam. David bent his tall, thin body again, to put his mouth to the voicepipe. 'Quartermaster.'

'Sir!'

'In a few minutes we'll feel the Firth tide. Watch your steering very closely.'

'Aye aye, sir.'

'Pilot—' Wilmott again 'what revolutions will give us seventeen knots?'

'One hundred, sir, near enough.'

'Damned odd!'

'Yes sir.' The ratio of revolutions to speed was unusual, in this class of ship. Wilmott paced over to stand beside Clark, his second-in-command, and David heard him mutter, 'I'd like to be past Swona before we fall out special sea-dutymen.' He was coming back now. 'Whose watch will it be?'

Aubrey Steel, who'd been loitering somewhere at the back of the bridge, answered the question.

'Mine, sir.'

'Who's that?'

'Lieutenant Steel, sir.'

'Oh, Steel . . .'

When Swona was astern, and *Bantry* pounding along at seventeen knots on the new south-easterly course, David handed the ship over to Steel and went down to the wardroom. He'd have a cup of coffee, he thought, before turning in. As navigator one had no watch to keep, but one did have to put in a fair amount of time on the bridge – particularly with Wilmott watching like a bearded hawk . . . It was warm here in the wardroom. Overhead lights shone on white-enamelled bulkheads and on the high polish of the mahogany mess table; *Bantry* quivered as she rose and fell; driving rhythmically into a low swell and light headwind. Her padre, the Reverend Pickering, was dozing on the sofa, Maudsley and Laidlaw – both watchkeeping lieutenants – were playing a game of *Attaque*, and Rutherford the surgeon lieutenant was fiddling half-heartedly with a jigsaw. Other officers dropped in and drifted out again while the ship relaxed into her cruising routine. There was an air of boredom; this was just another sweep, and the Grand Fleet would draw another blank, and then it would be Scapa again and next week another sweep . . . For the Grand Fleet this war seemed to be a matter of fighting not Germans so much as boredom. The Hun didn't care to face the fire-power of the British dreadnoughts; he'd make his occasional sneak raid on the English coast, lob shells into Hartlepool or Scarborough and kill or maim a few civilians, but he'd always nip back quickly to his bases in the Elbe or Jade before anyone could make him pay for it. Time and again Jellicoe had led his fleet in sweeps across the North Sea, hoping to catch Germans in his net; or on coat-trailing exercises on the Hun doorstep, tempting him to come out and fight. The Hun was wary; his strategy was to lure the Royal Navy over mines or submarines, or trick some detached squadron into facing the full weight of the High Seas Fleet. The Germans wanted odds clearly in their favour, in order to whittle down the superior British strength without risking losses of their own: and Jellicoe, who knew that the continued existence of British naval power was as vital to Britain and her Empire as a heart was vital to a living body, wasn't being had. It was difficult to see much prospect of real action for the Grand Fleet's big ships.

'Hello, David.'

Johnny West, *Bantry*'s gunnery lieutenant. Plump, balding, cheerful. In a few months he'd be putting up the extra half-stripe that would make him a lieutenant-commander. It was still a bit of a novelty, a rank introduced in 1914 for lieutenants of eight and more years' seniority. He'd flopped into an armchair next to David's, and reached back to the table to grab yesterday morning's *Daily Mail*. The wardroom door banged open again and Commander Clark came in, pushing the door shut behind him with his heel. A stocky, aggressive-looking man, he walked with a kind of strut. Blue-eyed, and red-faced from the cold night air, he stared round at each officer in turn. His glance swept over David, barely pausing; he nodded to Johnny West.

'Anyone done anything about coffee?'

'Not yet, sir.'

West had answered. David shook his head; he was reading a report about the forthcoming trial of Sir Roger Casement. Clark banged his fist on the sliding hatch to the wardroom pantry. It opened, and a young steward's pale face was framed in the square of it.

'Coffee in here, steward!'

One forty am, 31 May: *Minotaur*'s searchlight split the pre-dawn light as it winked out an order to the cruisers to spread into screening formation. Sunrise wouldn't be until after three o'clock, but even now one could see two or more miles through the misty, salt-laden air.

Sub-Lieutenant Denham was officer of the watch. David had just arrived on the bridge; Denham had sent his midshipman to shake the captain and at the same time had warned the engine-room that more power would be called for presently.

Wilmott appeared from his sea-cabin alert and immaculately dressed. His short, jutting beard gave him a cocky, terrier look. 'No executive signal yet?'

'No, sir,' Denham said. 'I've warned the engine-room.'

Wilmott trained his glasses on the flagship. 'Do we have a course to open on?'

'Yes, sir.' David had worked it out on the Battenberg, Prince Louis' invention that solved so instantly all kinds of station-keeping problems, the triangles of relative velocities. He'd given the course to Denham.

Wilmott muttered, 'You seem to have matters reasonably well in hand, Everard.'

That was a compliment, presumably.

'Executive signal, sir!'

'Carry on, Denham.'

The sub-lieutenant called down, 'Port fifteen! One hundred and ten revolutions!'

'Port fifteen, sir. Fifteen o' port helm on, sir. One hundred an' ten—'

Bantry was sheering too sharply away to starboard.

'Midships!'

'Helm's amidships, sir. One-one-oh revolutions on, sir.'

Denham gave the quartermaster the new course to steer. The cruisers were dividing, fanning out to their new stations. They'd end up in line abreast with a gap of five miles between each pair of ships and the centre – *Minotaur* – ten miles ahead of the battle fleet. Another ten miles in front of *Minotaur*, Admiral Hood with his three battle cruisers screened by two light cruisers, *Canterbury* and *Chester*, spearheaded the advance.

David, crouching at the binnacle, watched the line of bearing as the squadron spread. Wilmott stood a yard away, feet apart, hands pushed flatly into reefer pockets, chin belligerently thrust forward. Might it have been conscious, David wondered, the adoption of that Beatty-type stance?

Wilmott spoke suddenly, gruffly.

'We'll meet no Huns this time, Pilot.'

'Shan't we, sir?'

'Hipper's scouting force may be out. But the Admiralty's just wirelessed the C-in-C – Scheer's flagship's still in the Jade River. Flagship'd hardly be in port if the battle fleet were at sea, now would it?'

Hugh Everard stood with his back against the port for'ard corner of *Nile*'s fore bridge and listened to reports arriving by navyphone and voicepipe as the ship's company closed up at their action stations and went through the routines of testing gear and communications.

It was two forty-two am, and in thirty minutes the sun would rise – technically speaking – on this last day of May. Technically only, because it would not itself be visible through the mist and low cloud which obscured horizon and sky alike; but its growing brightness during the next half-hour would still produce the confusing, varying visibility which made it essential for ships to stand-to, on the alert against surprise attack.

Nile's fifteen-inch turrets had been trained out on the beams: A

41

and X to starboard, B and Y to port. Brook, the gunnery lieutenant, was at his station in the control top, fifty feet above this platform, and he'd just reported that all quarters were closed up and circuits tested. Knox-Wilson, the torpedo lieutenant, had reported similarly from the torpedo control tower aft. Tom Crick, the commander, had been receiving reports on the closing of watertight doors and hatches and the readiness of his damage control parties, below decks. Lieutenant-Commander Rathbone, the battleship's navigating officer, was all this time at the binnacle, where he'd taken over ten minutes ago from Mowbray, conning the ship as she kept up her anti-submarine zigzag astern of the others of her squadron on a mean course of south eighty-one degrees east.

Almost due east, in fact. Beatty's force had cleared the Forth Estuary by eleven last night, and had held this course at eighteen knots since then. Jellicoe had given Beatty a position some eighty miles off the Skaggerak which he was to reach by approximately two pm this afternoon, and then, failing a sight of the enemy, turn north to rendezvous with the main body of the Grand Fleet.

Hugh stared down over his ship's port side. The secondary armament, the six-inch batteries, had been trained outboard too; their barrels pointed menacingly towards the black-hulled torpedo craft which, in line ahead, steamed on the same course two thousand yards away. On this side were five destroyers of the first flotilla; to starboard four others were trailing their flotilla leader, the light cruiser *Fearless*. The destroyers were lifting and plunging heavily to the swell which *Nile*'s immensity merely thrust aside.

'*Lion* signalling, sir!'

Hugh turned and raised his binoculars, focusing on the distant, winking light. Beatty's *Lion* and the five other battle cruisers were about five miles south-east; Beatty had the ninth, tenth and thirteenth destroyer flotillas with him, and three squadrons of light cruisers disposed in screening formation another eight miles ahead. The seaplane-carrier *Engadine* was up there with the cruisers, too; with them, or ahead of them.

It wasn't for *Nile* to acknowledge Beatty's signal. *Barham* was this battle squadron's flagship, and Admiral Evan-Thomas would take care of it. Hugh lowered his binoculars.

'What's it about, Chief Yeoman?'

'Speed alteration, sir.' Chief Petty Officer Peppard, the chief yeoman of signals, had his telescope at his eye. 'Speed of the fleet nineteen and a half knots, sir!'

'What revolutions will that call for, Rathbone?'

The navigator's round, yellowish face turned to him. 'Two-three-oh, sir.'

Hugh told Crick, 'Warn the Engineer Commander, will you?' He raised his glasses again. One could make out – just – grey smudges against an unclearly defined horizon: Beatty's battle cruisers. Two groups of them, slightly separated, and the speed signal had been flashed from the right-hand group.

'Executive signal for nineteen and a half knots, sir.'

Sallis, that had been.

'Carry on, Rathbone.'

If you were slow on it, you'd drop astern of station, and then you'd need even more revs in order to close up again. Rathbone had passed the order to the quartermaster; he was watching *Malaya*, the next ahead, through narrowed eyes; to get inside the distance would be as bad as to fall astern of it. Hugh turned away, rested his eyes on the grey specks that were Beatty's battle cruisers. He was remembering how after the Falklands battle he'd met Jellicoe – who'd been persuaded to leave his Grand Fleet in other hands while he attended some conference or other, at the Admiralty. The small, quiet-mannered commander-in-chief had asked him some questions about the Falklands action then he'd put another: 'What views, if any, Everard, have you formed on the subject of our enemy's capabilities?'

Hugh had mentally taken a deep breath. There were quarters in which it was not thought seemly to respect the Hun.

'I think we should forget all we've been brought up to believe, sir, about our unquestionable superiority at sea. The Germans' shooting is first class, and they're as brave as lions.'

Scharnhorst had sunk with her starboard batteries still firing. *Gneisenau* had fought on until all her guns were wrecked and she'd no steam in her boilers; then she'd blown herself up. Nearly all *Leipzig*'s crew had died with her, fighting.

'I'm inclined to agree with you, Everard,' Jellicoe had nodded. 'We must never for a moment underestimate them; and we must make our own shooting *better* than first class.'

He and his battle squadrons had been working at that, ever since; doggedly, persistently; practice after practice, in all weathers, week in and week out.

Had Beatty? Or did Beatty trust more to his 'cavalry's natural élan and dash'?

Never underestimate them. He could still hear Jellicoe's dry, emphatic tones. And the recollection triggered something else which had been lurking abrasively in the back of his mind . . .

'Captain, sir.'

Tom Crick loomed beside him, bat-ears stark against a lightening sky. 'Secure from action stations, sir?'

'Yes, please. Secure.'

But still thinking . . . The bugle-call was sounding as he moved aft, down the three port-side steps from monkeys' island to the lower fore bridge. He pulled back the sliding door of the chartroom, and went in. The chart, spread over the long table which took up exactly half the space, had been marked by Rathbone with positions, courses and times which he'd obtained from Admiral Evan-Thomas's staff before they'd sailed. There was the position off the south-western tip of Norway where Jellicoe intended to be at two thirty this afternoon; and here was the spot, a hundred miles south-east of that, which Beatty had been told to reach at roughly the same time – and then, failing a sight of an enemy, to turn northwards and link up with Jellicoe.

The Grand Fleet was operating, as usual, right in the Germans' back yard. Which corresponded with Jackie Fisher's dictum, that Britain's frontiers were the enemy's coastlines. Hugh Everard frowned as he stared down at the chart and allowed the last few hours' orders and signals to filter through his brain.

It came to him, suddenly. That Admiralty signal telling Jellicoe that Scheer was still at Wilhelmshaven; it had stuck in his mind like a piece of grit, mentally indigestible, and now with time to think about it he knew why. Hadn't there been an item in an Intelligence summary, at that time when he'd been kicking his heels in the Admiralty in London, about a German trick of transferring their C-in-C's call-sign to the shore signal-station when he took his fleet to sea? So that a wireless bearing on the transmitter which was continuing to use that call-sign would seem to indicate that the flagship hadn't moved?

If the Admiralty had blundered – Scheer might be at sea now with the whole of the High Seas Fleet, while Jellicoe was being assured that he was still in port!

Hugh leant on his elbows on the chart table, with his chin resting in his hands, and put his mind to it. If that was the situation, what difference might it make?

44

The chartroom door slid back. Able Seaman Bates's wide shoulders filled the gap. Hugh didn't move, or look at him.

'Captain, sir?'

If Jellicoe realised Scheer *might* be at sea – and if the Germans had pulled that trick it would suggest some kind of trap was being laid – if Jellicoe knew it, wouldn't he want to be closer to Beatty, close enough to move quickly to his support?

'All right, sir?'

'Eh?' Hugh glanced round. 'Oh. What is it, Bates?'

'I've put some tongue sandwiches and a pot o' coffee in your sea-cabin, sir. Case you was feelin' peckish.'

'Thank you, Bates.'

There was a gleam in the monkeyish eyes.

'Reckon we'll get a bit of a scrap this time, sir?' It was the fact that they were out with Beatty, of course, that was making every-one imagine this sweep might be different from all the others that had drawn blank. Beatty was supposed to be the fighter, the man who got to grips with Germans.

Hugh shook his head, 'Damned if I know.' He stared down at the chart, and said again, more to himself than to his coxswain, 'Damned if I know.'

45

CHAPTER 4

Bantry was starboard wing ship in an extended cruiser screen sixteen miles ahead of the battle fleet. She was steering south fifty degrees east at fifteen knots, which allowing for the anti-submarine zigzag was giving a speed-of-advance of fourteen. The smear on her port beam was the cruiser *Black Prince*.

David had been working in his chartroom since lunch-time; he'd come up on the bridge for a look-around and a breath of air. Aubrey Steel had the watch; it was just after two pm, with a flat, grey sea and low cloud and a light south-east wind; there was nothing in sight except one attendant destroyer zigzagging astern like a dog on a lead, and that smudge in the north-east.

She – *Bantry* – belonged to the First Cruiser Squadron now, and her consorts were *Black Prince, Duke of Edinburgh, Defence* – who was Sir Robert Arbuthnot's flagship – and *Warrior. Defence* was in the centre of the fifty-mile spread of cruisers. *Warrior*, three miles astern of her, and *Hampshire* six miles astern of *Minotaur*, were link-ships for visual signalling purposes with the battle fleet. And the battle fleet was now a huge concentration of power: six divisions of battleships, the divisions disposed abeam of each other and each consisting of four dreadnoughts in line ahead; a great square of armour and big guns: *King George V* leading *Ajax, Centurion* and *Erin, Orion* leading *Monarch, Conqueror* and *Thunderer*, Jellicoe's flagship *Iron Duke* leading *Royal Oak, Superb* and *Canada*. On Jellicoe's starboard beam *Benbow* was followed by *Bellerophon, Temeraire* and *Vanguard*; then the Fifth Division with *Colossus* leading *Collingwood, Neptune* and *St Vincent*, and the Sixth comprising *Marlborough, Revenge, Hercules* and *Agincourt*. There had been sixteen battleships when he'd sailed from Scapa, and Admiral Jerram had joined him with the other eight this morning.

Light cruisers formed an inner screen. And twenty miles ahead,

46

Rear-Admiral the Honourable Horace Hood's three battle cruisers were still the vanguard of the fleet.

It was more than a fleet: it was an armada. To David Everard it all seemed rather pointless – so much effort, such vast expenditure of fuel and other energies, all in the vain hope of encountering an enemy who hadn't left his anchorage. When it was *known* he hadn't!

David mooted this thought to Captain Wilmott, who'd just come back to the bridge after a snack lunch in his sea-cabin. Wilmott had seemed to be in a jolly mood; he'd cracked a joke with Steel, and now he'd commented to David in his brusque, clipped manner that the fleet was an hour astern of schedule.

'Of course, having to stop to search those trawlers hasn't helped.'

Neutrals, who might turn out to be disguised enemy scouts, had to be examined whenever they were met, and Jellicoe had slowed the whole fleet several times for this purpose. If he hadn't, the destroyers conducting the searches would have needed to have raced at full power to catch up again, depleting fuel reserves which were never more than barely adequate.

David suggested, 'We could as well go home, sir. Since Scheer's not coming out?'

Wilmott's head turned slowly. One eyebrow rose. Then he looked away again, as if he wasn't going to answer. Finally he growled, 'Hipper may be at sea, mayn't he? Scheer's not the only Hun there is, is he?'

'Of course not, sir.'

David tried to make himself sound agreeable; afterwards, he wished he'd kept his mouth shut. 'But aren't Sir David Beatty's battle cruisers a match for Hipper's?'

Wilmott sighed. He made a thumb-print on the compass glass.

'Here's Beatty, Everard, close to the Hun bases. And here, let us say, might be Hipper, out ahead of him. D'you see?'

David nodded. Wilmott's fingernails, he noticed, were jagged, as if he bit them.

'We'd have him caught between our—'

'God's sake, man, d'you propose the Commander-in-Chief should leave the route northwards open to him? D'you think a Hun battle cruiser force should be let out into the Atlantic? What d'you imagine our blockade of the German ports is all about, for God's sake? Why d'you think we sit in *Scapa*, of all places, month after month? To count sheep?'

David's face burned and it embarrassed him acutely to know

that he was blushing. In front of Steel and the snotty of the watch – Ackroyd – and the bridge messenger, duty signalman, captain's coxswain . . .

Wilmott had swung away from him.

'Keep the lookouts on their toes, Steel.' His arm scythed, a gesture covering miles of grey, empty sea; grey-green, with a dull shine on it from the steely, cloud-filtered light. David was taut, sweating with resentment of his captain's unnecessary rudeness. He told himself as he moved out into the unoccupied port wing of the bridge, with his back to Wilmott, that henceforth he'd remain correct in manner and as efficient as any navigator could be, but socially, Wilmott would not exist. His nerves were racked tight; he felt as he did when he thought about his family. He told himself to forget it – think about something else . . . the next leave, for instance: Ellaline Teriss in *Broadway Jones* – he'd see that – and *The Bing Boys* at the Alhambra, with George Robey in it. Pat Johnson, who was now Nick's first lieutenant, had told him the other day that *The Bing Boys* had made him laugh his head off.

'W/T signal, sir, urgent!'

The yeoman, Petty Officer Sturgis, was taking it to Wilmott. Sturgis had come pounding up the ladder from the signal bridge like an elephant run amok. He looked dishevelled, as if he'd buttoned his jacket and stuck his cap on his small, round head on his way up. It was warm in the signals office, of course; they did sit around in shirt-sleeves, because they had the heat of the foremost funnel within a few feet of them. Wilmott had taken the clipboard from his yeoman's hands. Perusing the top signal, he'd glanced up at him, then down again; a hand rose slowly to stroke his beard while he read the message for a second time. Flipping back, now, over signals that he must have been shown earlier . . . David, aware of the act that was being put on and of his own disdain for it, could hear Midshipman Ackroyd squeaking away, lecturing the wretched lookouts.

Wilmott glanced his way and beckoned. The zigzag bell rang; Steel told the quartermaster, 'Port ten, steer south forty east!'

The quartermaster was repeating the order as David read the signal. It was from *Galatea*, flagship of the First Light Cruiser Squadron, which was part of Beatty's scouting force, and it was addressed to Beatty – Flag Officer, Battle Cruiser Fleet – and to C-in-C. Time of Origin two twenty pm. It read: *Two cruisers, probably hostile, in sight bearing E.S.E. course unknown. My position Lat 56 degs 48'N Long 5 degs 21'E.*

Wilmott called, 'Midshipman Ackroyd. My compliments to the commander, and would he kindly join me on the compass platform.'

'Aye aye, sir!'

Ackroyd scuttled away. Wilmott cocked a bushy eyebrow: 'Still think we should "go home", Everard?'

At nineteen knots, *Lanyard* felt to Nick as if she were doing forty. It was like a bumpy, windy, exhilarating canter; noisy too, with the wind thundering on jolting steel and the crashing of the destroyer's bow as she met and smashed through the ridges of the low swell. And there was the throbbing clatter of the ship herself driving forward, ploughing a broad white streak across leaden-tinted sea, stumbling, shaking herself like a dog and plunging on, an answering pendant cracking like a whip in the wind as it raced to her yardarm, acknowledging the preparatory order to turn north. *Lanyard* and the rest of the thirteenth flotilla, led by the light cruiser *Champion*, were grouped closely around *Lion* and the other three ships of the First Battle Cruiser Squadron. They were clustered so closely that, looking to his left as he clung to the port-side rail – this was the side of the destroyer's bridge, all there was to it, just a single rail supported on corner stanchions and with a painted canvas screen lashed to it – Nick could see the cluster of gold-peaked caps on *Lion*'s high compass-platform. Sir David Beatty, and his staff . . . Astern of *Lion* pounded *Princess Royal, Queen Mary* and *Tiger*, the four great ships hemmed in by the two lines of destroyers, while the close, solid phalanx of grey steel hid from *Lanyard*, for the moment, the other battle cruiser squadron which, surrounded by destroyers of the ninth and tenth flotillas, thrashed eastward on the same course six thousand yards north-eastward.

Lieutenant Reynolds had the watch, and Mortimer, *Lanyard*'s captain, was also on the bridge. Nick stared up at the wildly fluttering answering pendant; looking down again, he found Mortimer watching him, half-smiling. Nick, still holding tight to the port-side rail, returned the stare, and Mortimer shouted, his voice high and with a cutting edge to it to beat the bedlam of sound around them, 'Think you'll make a destroyer man, do you, Everard?'

As it happened, that *was* what he'd been thinking. If being a destroyer man involved this kind of thrill, this heady feeling of swift movement, exuberance – in a way, a kind of freedom – well, yes, why not? Mortimer was yelling down a voicepipe now. Nick took another look at *Lion*'s bridge; he knew how it would be up there. Ritual, deference, pomposity. Middle-rank officers murmuring, junior officers whispering; cold eyes staring down noses under gilded peaks . . .

When that signal at *Lion*'s yard came fluttering down, the battle cruisers would swing north and steer for the rendezvous with Jellicoe and the battle fleet. Beatty had already re-disposed his cruiser screen. The centre of it lay south-east from here, and it extended on a line north-east, south-west; so he'd have the screen astern of him, spread across twenty or thirty miles of sea between him and the German bases. And he'd put the Fifth Battle Squadron five miles on his port quarter, in other words north-west; when he swung his whole force to a course of north-by-east it would find itself in a V-formation with the battleships in the port wing, Beatty and his First Squadron behind in the V's apex, and the Second Squadron on the starboard wing.

Mortimer had explained it to Nick ten minutes ago, down in the chartroom. He'd said, 'Damn shame, no Huns this time. This is the limit of the sweep, you see . . . Never mind, young Everard – we'll find ourselves a skirmish for you, one day!'

Nick wondered what he'd done to deserve such decent treatment. Did destroyer men become human beings at sea? Or might Mortimer be a friend of his uncle's? He hadn't mentioned him. Nor had Johnson. And most startling of all was what Johnson – supposedly brother David's friend – had said earlier this morning, when they'd been on watch together. It was still difficult to believe . . . Nick's eyes were on that flag-hoist above Beatty's battle cruiser; suddenly he saw it jerk and begin its downward rush. He shouted, 'Executive!' He realised that Leading Signalman Garret had yelled it almost simultaneously. The answering pendant was falling like a shot bird. Nick grinned at Garret and the signalman wagged his head, a sort of wink. Reynolds was shouting down to the quartermaster, 'Four hundred revolutions!' Not full power, but not much short of it; the starboard-side destroyers had to race now to maintain their station on the outside of the turn. Noise rising, the rush of the wind increasing, *Lion* swinging, foreshortening as she went round, Reynolds yelling down the voicepipe, 'Steer five degrees to port!' Cutting the corner, *Lanyard* was thrashing forward like a racehorse, trembling with the effort or with eagerness. That was it, she did feel eager, and here on her bridge in the rush of air and spray Nick shared her keenness. A surprise, a revelation, almost!

'What?'

He looked to his right. The Captain had his ear to the voicepipe from the chartroom. He looked, Nick thought, astounded. He'd turned his head to shout into the pipe again, 'Bring it up here, Number One!'

The destroyer ahead of *Lanyard* – it was *Nomad* – suddenly looked too close. Reynolds saw it too; he'd called down for a cut in speed. Nick craned out, looking astern; *Narborough* seemed to be in perfect station. Mortimer shouted to Reynolds, '*Galatea*'s made an enemy report. Two Hun cruisers!'

'*Galatea*?'

Mortimer pointed a bit north of east. He told Reynolds, 'About fifteen miles away. Wing of the screen.' Reynolds bent to the voicepipe, 'Three-six-oh revolutions.' *Lanyard* had just about regained her station. Mortimer snapped, 'Too close. Come out a bit.' He snatched the sheet of signal-pad from Johnson's hand; when he'd read it, he looked round for Nick, and shouted above the noise of the wind and the ship's motion, 'May get that skirmish after all, Sub!'

Hun cruisers, fifteen miles away? There must be, Nick thought, six or even eight – yes, two squadrons – of our own light cruisers out there in the screen with *Galatea*. Widely spaced, but a lot closer to the enemy than this battle cruiser force was. If the German presence was as little as two cruisers, it would be dealt with long before *Lanyard* got a whiff of cordite . . .

A voicepipe squawked, 'Bridge!' It was tinny and remote. Johnson, who'd been on the point of leaving the bridge and was nearest to the pipe, answered it. 'Bridge?' He was listening to the rapid gabble, and Nick, staggering as the destroyer rolled – the swell was abeam, and it didn't take much of a crosswise sea to roll a ship whose beam measurement was eight feet nine inches – shifting his feet and grabbing at the rail again, saw it was the voicepipe from the wireless office, which was immediately below the bridge on the starboard side.

Johnson straightened. Mortimer, with an elbow crooked round one of the binnacle's correcting-spheres, was watching him, waiting for the news.

'Well?'

'*Galatea*, sir.' Johnson looked puzzled, as if he could hardly believe whatever it was they'd told him. 'Two more signals to *Lion* and C-in-C. First one saying *Engaging the enemy*, and the other reports—'

'Speak up, man!'

'Other one says *Large amount of smoke as though from a fleet bearing east-nor'-east*, sir!'

'*Lion* signalling, sir!'

Leading Signalman Garret's shout had a cutting, penetrating quality. Bunting was rushing upwards to the flagship's yardarm. Nick heard Johnson say, 'Addressed to destroyers!' At the same moment he recognised for himself that the top flag of the hoist was horizontally striped yellow-blue-yellow, the destroyer flag. Garret already had *Lanyard*'s red-and-white answering pendant at the dip, meaning 'Signal seen but not yet understood', and he was using a pair of binoculars one-handed to read that string of flags half a mile away. He was in profile, one hand on the halyards half-hitched on their cleat, and his lips were moving as if he was trying to read print, not flags. He muttered, to himself, '*Destroyers take up position – as anti-submarine screen—*'

Nick moved over to help him, flicked quickly through the pages of the signal manual. Garret should have had one of his three signalmen up here to help him, but there'd hardly have been room.

He'd got it, '*– when course is altered to sou'-sou'-east!*'

Garret sent the answering pendant whipping up to the yard: *Signal understood*. He turned, stared into Nick's face, hissed, 'We're goin' after 'em, sir! *Fleet*, that said!' Nick stared back at those craggy features illuminated by a glow of joy. He felt it too. He was suddenly delirious with happiness. Every face in the destroyer's bridge was either grinning broadly or tense with expectation, and Mortimer, her captain, suddenly waved his cap above his head and screamed like a banshee at the grey overlay of cloud – 'Tally ho – o!'

Hugh Everard left young Lieutenant Lovelace at the binnacle and walked out to the starboard wing of *Nile*'s bridge to look back over her quarter at the battle cruisers, or rather, at the smoke that hid them.

'Make anything of it, Chief Yeoman?'

Peppard had a telescope at his eye. He was about six feet away, on the lower level of the bridge and with his back against the handrail of the ladder that led down to it. The support helped him to keep steady while he concentrated on the difficult business of making out *Lion*'s signal.

Beatty's last flag-hoist, forewarning the destroyers of a change of course to south-south-east, had been readable from *Nile*'s bridge, but a minute or two earlier Beatty had ordered all ships to raise steam for full speed; as the battle cruisers' engineers drew their coal fires forward the funnel-smoke had thickened, blackened, so much so that from this five-mile range now one had only brief and partial glimpses of them.

'Can't read it at all, sir.' The chief yeoman hadn't given up, though. 'If they'd use a light—'

'Keep your eye on it. It might clear.' Hugh told Greenlaws, the midshipman of the watch, 'Keep in touch with the wireless office. I want to know if anything even *starts* coming through.'

'Aye aye, sir.' Greenlaws' rather burly figure moved aft; the W/T room reported by telephone to the signals office, which was next to the chartroom at the back of the bridge. Hugh leant on the binnacle as *Nile* ploughed northwards astern of *Malaya, Warspite, Valiant* and the flagship *Barham*. Admiral Evan-Thomas in *Barham* would, he knew, be staring astern just as he had been, trying to guess Beatty's intentions. If that signal had been an order to alter course to south-south-east, it might be addressed to the whole force or it could be intended only for the battle cruisers. One would hardly have expected that; but one was not supposed to guess an admiral's intentions – he was supposed to control his squadrons, not confuse them!

Surely he'd realise his flags couldn't be seen through smoke at this range? And therefore, if he wanted his signal to apply to this squadron, would have passed it by searchlight?

Nile, all thirty thousand tons of her, was as steady as a rock: as she forged on in *Malaya*'s broad, white wake. The battleships of this Queen Elizabeth class being entirely oil-fired, they weren't fouling the sky as Beatty's coal-burners were.

'Signal's hauled down, sir!'

Whatever it had been . . .

Lovelace, the officer of the watch, was calling down a helm order, maintaining the ordered zigzag which had not as yet been cancelled. Commander Crick was on the bridge; and the navigator, Rathbone, was in the chartroom, trying to make some sense or lucid pattern out of the welter of enemy-report signals which had been intercepted by *Nile*'s telegraphists. Hugh had alerted his officers to the possibility of an action developing, but there'd been no point in sending the ship's company to their battle stations – not yet. And if Beatty allowed the squadron to continue steaming *away* from the enemy, most likely not at all.

'Battle cruisers are hauling round to starboard, sir!'

He nodded, watching them. You could see, in gaps in the drifting smoke, the long, grey ships shortening as they turned; destroyers racing past them. You could see their smoke too, and the white of their bow-waves, but the general picture, from this distance and obscured as much of it was, was of a jumble of ships all going different ways. If one hadn't known what was happening, it would have been impossible to make it out.

Did Beatty intend to leave his most powerful ships steaming northwards? Perhaps he did. His alteration of course to east-south-east, when the enemy had been reported to be somewhere roughly north-east, would be aimed at putting himself between that enemy and his escape-route southwards, south-eastwards. It wasn't in-conceivable that he wanted to leave the battleships out here, so that the Germans would find themselves between the two forces, hemmed in while Jellicoe bore down from the north? But it would have been a very strange, even dangerous – in fact *highly* dangerous decision. And remembering the Dogger Bank action, the confusion of misunderstood signals – might history be repeating itself here? Hugh wondered whether, if he'd been in Evan Thomas's place in *Barham*, he wouldn't have assumed an error on Beatty's part and led the battle squadron round after him without waiting for any orders.

'Wireless signal, sir, *Tiger* to *Lion. Tiger*'s asking whether the alter-course signal should have been passed to *Barham*.'

Someone had woken up, at last.

Perhaps *Tiger* was supposed to have passed it on anyway? But the fact she hadn't, and that she'd had to ask, suggested an element of confusion in the vice-admiral's grasp of communications prob-lems. Already the gap between the battle cruisers and the QEs was more like nine miles than five. And Beatty would be cracking on at his 'cavalry's' best gallop – twenty-eight knots, when these more heavily armoured battleships could only make twenty-five at most. So if there should be a significant enemy force over there, he'd be charging at it without the support he should have had and might badly need.

'*Lion* has replied, *affirmative*, sir!'

And there it was. Dogger-Bank type manoeuvres!

'*Tiger* is signalling by searchlight, sir.'

54

Hugh stared out at the flashing light. Closer, destroyers of the first flottila thrashed white paths through the grey-green sea. Hugh saw Tom Crick watching them with a kind of hunger in his face. Crick's heart was in destroyers, where he'd spent his younger days.

Barham – Evan-Thomas – would be answering that signal. It was completed now. Hugh had caught the signing-off letters 'AR'. The chief yeoman called, 'Flags from *Barham*, sir: *alter course in succession sou'-sou'-east*, sir!'

'I'll take over, Lovelace.'

'Aye aye, sir.' The young officer of the watch stepped aside. Peppard reported, 'From *Barham*, sir: *speed twenty-five knots*.'

Admiral Evan-Thomas wasn't wasting any more time, but he had to re-dispose his destroyers ready for what would be almost a sixteen-point turn. The swift black hulls were curving out to port and starboard, heeling almost on to their beam-ends as their helms were flung over and they wheeled like a cavalry squadron scattering and then re-forming; or like wasps disturbed and now settling again, settling in screening formation on the battleships' starboard quarter where, when the big ships turned, they'd be in the right place to screen them on the new course. Astern, the two battle cruiser squadrons, grey dots recently in two separate groups, had merged into one.

'Executive signal, sir!'

'Very good.' *Barham* was sheering off to starboard. Her squat grey profile loomed, lengthening as she swung outwards, shortening as her swing continued and *Valiant* followed in the same white crescent of churned sea. Now *Warspite*'s move: *Barham* passing, steadying on the south-easterly course, destroyers falling into their positions round her . . . 'Port fifteen.'

'Port fifteen, sir . . . Fifteen of port helm on, sir!'

Nile began to turn: six hundred and fifty feet of battleship leaning to the swing of it, her stem carving, slicing round inside *Malaya*'s track. 'Ease to ten.'

'Ease to ten, sir . . . Ten of—'

'Midships!'

'Midships, sir. Helm's amidships—'

'Steady!' Now the quartermaster would keep her in the wake of the next-ahead. Hugh saw the speed signal drop from *Barham*'s yard, and he anticipated Peppard's report of it.

'Two hundred and eighty revolutions.'

Now at least they were pointing the right way; perhaps it might be possible to get some idea of what had been happening elsewhere. Hugh looked over towards Crick: 'Tom. Take over for a minute, would you?'

In the chartroom, Rathbone had translated a whole wad of cryptic signals from the scouting forces into positions and courses on a plotting-diagram.

'*Galatea*'s been hit, sir. Must be somewhere about here. She's in action against a cruiser believed to be the *Elbing*. She got one hit below the bridge, but the shell didn't explode.'

'Be nice if all the Hun shells were that kind.' Hugh pointed at the plot. 'Explain the rest of it?'

'Reports of enemy cruisers and destroyers here, here, and here, sir. *Galatea* had turned north-west, with *Phaeton* in close company and *Inconstant* and *Cordelia* not far off. She reported a few minutes ago that the enemy's following her north-westward.'

Trying to draw the Hun towards Beatty – which was not a scouting cruiser's job. A hatch slid open, and a signalman passed a message through to Rathbone.

'*Galatea* to *Lion*, sir.'

Hugh read the signal. *Galatea* was reporting that the enemy had turned north, and that more smoke indicated the approach of heavier ships . . . Now another signal: Beatty was ordering *Engadine*, a seaplane carrier with the cruiser screen, to send up an observer 'plane.

One couldn't envy any admiral having to dispose his fleet in the light of this haphazard scattering of information. Those light cruisers should have been pressing through to discover what lay behind the enemy light forces, not playing some decoy game. And a screening force wouldn't be there to screen nothing.

'Well.' He pulled the door open. Then he paused and looked back at Rathbone. He was a shy, quiet man, this navigator, with his round face and alert, quick eyes. 'Pilot, come out and take over.'

He went outside, and up the three steps to the compass platform. Evan-Thomas was grabbing a chance to close up slightly on the battle cruisers by cutting a corner instead of following astern of them. Wouldn't make all that much difference, but every yard was one in the right direction. If it should turn out to be the High Seas Fleet that Beatty was charging at on his own, the sooner this squadron could bring its fifteen-inch guns and heavier armour up, the better.

Jellicoe would have had all those signals – for what they were worth. One could imagine his impassive, steady manner covering a desperate longing for useful, detailed information. He'd be working his battle fleet up to full speed, hurrying down to Beatty's aid, still convinced that Scheer was in harbour and unaware that Beatty had managed to put twenty thousand yards, ten miles, between himself and his supporting battleships!

Rathbone had taken over the handling of the ship. Crick stepped down from the central island. He nodded in the direction of the battle cruiser squadrons.

'Unfortunate we're so far astern, sir.'

Hugh nodded. The situation, and what had caused it, was plain to both of them, but one did not, in conversation with a more junior officer, criticise one's admiral. Crick murmured phlegmatically, pulling at one of his large, pink ears, 'Want it all to themselves, perhaps.'

A signalman saluted: 'W/T signal, sir.'

It was to Beatty and commander-in-chief, from the cruiser *Nottingham*, who reported *Have sighted smoke bearing east-north-east. Five columns.*

Hugh showed it to Crick. *Nottingham* was only a few miles from Beatty, and 'five columns' sounded like Admiral Hipper's scouting-group of battle cruisers.

'Getting warmer, Tom.'

Crick looked up from reading it; he pursed his lips as he gazed out towards Beatty's smoke. 'Shall I get the hands up, sir?'

'Not yet.' As he said it, a light began to flash from that hazy, far-off line of ships. This time he'd been looking that way as it started, and he read the message for himself. Crick did too, muttering the words one by one as each burst of dots and dashes was followed by a second's pause for the acknowledging flash from *Barham*. Beatty was telling Evan-Thomas: *Speed twenty-five knots. Assume complete readiness for action. Alter course, leading ships together, the rest in succession, to east. Enemy in sight.*

Hugh told Crick, 'Belay my last order. Get the hands up.'

'Aye aye, sir.' The commander faced aft; tall, bat-eared, as benign and calm as an umpire at a cricket match: 'Bugler, sound action stations!'

Below, in the battleship's messdecks and compartments, the bugle call produced an effect similar to that of a stick pushed into an ant's nest. Men were streaming from their messes to battle stations above and below decks; some only half-dressed, pulling jumpers on as they ran; expressions were tense, excited, joyful. This ship's company had been called to action stations a thousand times, for exercises, target practices and so on, but in the last half-hour a buzz had flown round the ship that German units were at sea and perhaps not far away . . . Bit of luck, to be with David Beatty, who had a nose for Huns . . . Damage-control and fire parties stood back out of the rush as they assembled at key points, and were sworn at when they didn't; they waited for the last of the rush, so that watertight doors could be shut and clipped and the quarters reported closed-up and ready.

Petty Officer Alfred Cartwright, gunner's mate and captain of 'X' turret, heard the bugle in his sleep and was out of the POs' mess before he'd really woken; up a ladderway between S3 and S4 casemates to the foc'sl deck, emerging near the screen door into the bridge superstructure. A destroyer racing past seemed almost alongside. He noticed a sailor on her after searchlight platform who was doing some sort of jig with his arms up above his head and his mouth opening and shutting – singing, or shouting for joy. Cartwright thought, *daft bugger* . . . He raced aft – past the funnels, the lashed-down cutters, whalers, pinnaces, and the captain's gig with the sixteen-foot dinghy nestled against it like a baby just below the torpedo control tower and near the ladder – which he shot down, using his hands on the rails more than his feet on its steps – to the upper deck and the rear of his own 'X' turret. He swung himself up into it and pulled the hatch shut.

He saw at a glance that his crew was complete; Dewar, number two of the right gun, grinned at him cockily, and Cartwright scowled at the Scotsman's impudence. They'd less distance to come than he had: and he had them trained, he'd have booted a man from here to Flamborough Head if he'd not come running like a greyhound to *that* call.

'Turret's crew, number!'

Cartwright's sharp Yorkshire eyes checked each man as he sprang into position. Gunlayers, trainers and sightsetters in their places; number ones at the loading-cage levers, facing the breeches, number twos in line with their breeches and facing the muzzles; number threes in front of number twos and number fours at the sides, facing inwards to the breeches. The second captain-of-turret and numbers five and six were below, in the working-chamber. Civilians, Cartwright knew, outsiders, thought a turret was a round

58

thing with a pair of guns stuck in it; they had no idea until you told them that below the gun-house – which was what they thought was the whole thing – was a lower part, a working-chamber below decks which was about as big as the gun-house; or that a great armoured tube called a barbette extended right down into the bowels of the ship – five decks down – and contained the revolving hoist, cages in which projectiles and charges were fed up to the gun-house, plus a magazine, a handling-room and shellroom. There were eighteen men under another petty officer in the magazine, and one more petty officer plus eighteen in the shellroom.

The numbering was complete, and Cartwright nodded, satisfied. It was a happy thought that perhaps he'd be blooding his guns, by and by. He turned about, went to the cabinet at the rear of the turret. Its sound-proof door was open. It had to be sound-proof, so that the turret officer could hear and speak over his navyphones to the control top and transmitting station.

Captain Edwin Blackaby, Royal Marines, nodded affably.

'Well, Cartwright? Got your shooting boots on?'

Peculiar fellow, Mr Blackaby. Looked like a younger version of old Kitchener, and spent more time cracking his own idea of jokes than he did making sense. The men liked him, though. Behind Blackaby was Midshipman Mellors, his assistant.

'Turret's crew numbered and correct, sir.' *Nile* heeled, and he realised she must be altering course. Blackaby put his eyes to the lenses of his periscope; he murmured from that position, 'Right you are, GM. You'd best test loading gear, hadn't you? And be quick – but for heaven's sake don't let 'em go mad, eh?'

'Aye aye, sir.'

Over Blackaby's shoulder, young Mellors grinned at him. Mellors liked Cartwright. When he'd joined *Nile* – green as grass, and fresh out of Dartmouth – and been detailed as an assistant turret officer, he'd come to this gunner's mate for advice and information, and Cartwright, showing him round the turret's workings and then the cabinet's fire-control equipment, navyphones and so on, had summed up what his function would be by telling him, 'Captain Blackaby is turret officer, sir; if we're ordered to independent control 'stead o' director-firing, it's him as controls us. Tha' sits up there wi' him, and tha' works the rate-clock, and tha' takes charge if he should be killed; but 'appen if Captain Blackaby's killed sir, so'll tha' be theself . . .'

He was back behind his guns now, bellowing, 'Test main loading gear!' Number one of the right-hand gun yelled it down to the crew of the working-chamber, and like a hollow echo the voice of number six below there took it up and passed it down to the magazine and shellroom. The number twos meanwhile had grabbed the breech levers and swung the breeches open; number threes roared in unison, competing with each other for sheer noise, exuberance, 'Gun run out, breech open!' Tripping the air-blast levers, since of course nothing had run out, while number ones were trying rather perfunctorily to raise the gun-loading cages while the telegraphs showed 'not ready' and the pedals were pressed down. It couldn't be done; if it had been possible it would have proved some failure in the mechanism. Now they'd put the telegraphs to 'ready' and they were trying again with the pedal not pressed. It was as it should be; they were reporting this to Cartwright; and the number fours, who'd checked meanwhile that the chain-rammers wouldn't work when the cages weren't up, were confirming this point just as loudly. They were enjoying themselves, bawling out their reports and slamming the gear about. Cartwright warned them, shouting the whole lot down, 'Steady, lads, now *steady*!' Nobody wanted a jam-up, not at a moment such as this.

'Out rammers, free the cage!'

You couldn't do that, either. So many things you couldn't do. Safety precautions, all of them. With fifteen-inch guns you weren't dealing in weights of pounds or hundredweights, you were handling moving steel parts that weighed *tons*.

'Withdraw rammers!'

Not halfway through, yet. But routine they knew by heart, orders which they'd die – as old men if they were lucky – still knowing. After main loading gear, there was secondary gear to be tested. Then the firing circuits to be checked, and training- and elevation-receivers to be lined-up with the director-trainer's transmitter in the director tower.

'What're we fightin', GM, d'ye know?'

Number two of the right gun, Able Seaman Dewar, was glancing round over his shoulder. Cartwright ignored the question. He pointed: 'Interceptor there, ye gormless clown!' Dewar snatched at the interceptor switch, broke it, and the right gun-ready lamp went out. He looked round again, rather furtively; Cartwright told him, glaring, 'Tha'd best stay awake and lively, Dewar!' He went back to the cabinet, where Midshipman Mellors had synchronised the turret officer's receivers with those of the director and the guns; Blackaby told his turret captain, 'Load the cages with common shell, GM, and then stand by, and *don't* let 'em play that gramophone!'

'Aye aye, sir.'

Blackaby hated Dewar's gramophone. His main complaint of it had been that Dewar always put on the same record, a well-worn hit called *Everybody's Doing It*. But when Dewar had borrowed a couple of other ragtime records from some pal of his, Blackaby had been just as discouraging. *He* should worry, Cartwright thought; all *he* needed to do was shut his cabinet's sound-proof door!

'Stand to!'

Laughter and banter died away. He faced them at attention; a tallish man, deep-chested, black-browed, with a strong-boned, open face. Glancing round the turret, he met each pair of eyes in turn, asserting an essentially personal control.

'Wi' common shell, load the cages!'

Dewar jumped to the voicepipe to the working-chamber, and number three grabbed the handle of the magazine telegraph and whirled it round to rest at the word LOAD.

Three thirty-five pm: the enemy battle cruisers were in sight from *Lanyard*'s bridge. There was a mass of smoke in the north-east, and under it five grey, ship-shaped objects. They were about fifteen miles away, and steering roughly east-south-east.

Lanyard's turbines normally whined but now, at full power, they were screaming. Her bridge was juddering, jolting, wind-whipped as her funnels belched black smoke to mingle with her flotilla's and the battle cruisers'. She felt like some creature that was alive and suffering, panting, dragging each last ounce of effort out.

This fleet and the distant, silent procession of Hun warships might have been two fleets passing, without contact!

In fact they were converging on each other rapidly. Looking to his right as *Lanyard* clawed painfully up the port side of the British battle cruisers Nick saw that their turrets had been trained round to point at the far-off enemy, the great gun barrels cocked up to maximum elevation, ready to send their projectiles whirring skyward and away. Everything was silent, now; the silence of waiting, the silence of eyes at range-finders and periscopes, of guns loaded and waiting only for the fire-gongs' clang. It was a tense, not a peaceful silence; but what struck one as incongruous was the sense of detachment between the two converging fleets, the feeling that neither had anything to do with the other. It was difficult to convince oneself that in that remote grey battle line on the north-eastern horizon there were eyes watching instruments, indicator-dials clicking the ranges down, down . . .

The sky had cleared a little, or was clearing. Clouds still drifted in the light south-easterly breeze, but there were gaps now through which the sun was greening and glossing the sea's flat surface. But the sun was westering already, and the Germans would have their targets silhouetted against its brightness.

Lanyard felt and sounded as if she'd tear herself apart if she kept this pace up much longer, straining her steel guts to keep up with her flotilla and get into station ahead of the battle cruisers. Nick – Johnson had told him to stay on the bridge for the time being, although his action station was at the after four-inch guns – could almost feel the strain in his own muscles as the destroyer struggled on, overhauling the big ships easily enough but slipping back in comparison with her sisters. They were not sisters, that was the trouble; *Lanyard* was an L-class destroyer, the only one of that earlier type in a flotilla consisting otherwise of more modern, faster craft, Ns, Os and Ps. She was supposed to be the fastest of the Ls, and that was the reason for her having been included in such scintillating company. Theoretically, according to the results of fairly recent speed-trials, *Lanyard* could work up to almost her designed speed of thirty-five knots.

The theory wasn't exactly being proved today. If she was making thirty-five, then *Nestor, Nicator* and *Nomad* must have been making thirty-seven, which nobody could have claimed for them.

The ensign whipped overhead in the wind, mast and rigging hummed, the deck trembled and jolted and the canvas lashed to the bridge rail thrashed and boomed. Every loose fitting rattled and they were all, apparently, quite loose. But *Lanyard* had passed Beatty's flagship now and she was thrusting on to take up her station in the flotilla's port division astern of *Champion*, their leader, who was waiting for them now two miles ahead of *Lion*. The ninth and tenth flotillas had been ordered to get up there too, but that group's four L-class weren't making it at all; they were well astern, fouling the battle cruisers' range with their smoke. At any minute now Beatty would tell them to drop astern and clear the range, and Nick could see in the grim anxiety in his captain's face the recognition of that frightful hazard; that if *Lanyard* failed to keep up, she might be relegated, forced to join those others. It might seem logical, to some minds, to lump all the L's together. But *Lanyard* was making it, or seemed to be. So long as she didn't bust a gut.

There was one plain purpose in sending the destroyers up ahead, and that was to dispose them in a situation from which, when the vice-admiral considered the time was ripe, they could fulfil their destiny, perform the function for which they'd been designed and built and for which their officers and crews had been trained – to attack the enemy battle line with torpedoes.

Nick checked the time: three forty-five. And almost there. Mortimer had just shouted down, 'Four hundred revolutions!' He was easing her speed almost to twenty-five knots, the speed of the fleet, as *Lanyard* closed up astern of *Nicator* in the port column. Ahead of *Nicator* were *Nomad* and *Nestor*, who was the leader of this division. In the centre, *Champion* led *Obdurate, Nerissa* and *Termagant*; to starboard *Narborough* led *Pelican, Petard*, and – closing up now – *Turbulent*.

Off on *Lanyard*'s beam as she settled into station in the port column Nick saw two boats from the ninth or tenth flotillas; two M's who'd left the slower L's and pushed on to join this faster group.

Two flag-hoists had broken simultaneously at *Lion*'s yards. Mortimer straightened from the voicepipe – he'd reduced the revs again, to three hundred and eighty – and pointed: 'Garret?'

'Aye, sir, I'm—'

Having problems, by the look of it. Nick snatched up the signal manual and moved over, ready to help. Garret had binoculars pointed at the bright clusters of flags; his legs were braced apart against the ship's jolting, pounding motion . . . But he wasn't, after all, going to need the manual.

'Line-of-bearing signal to the battle cruisers, sir. Can't make him out, not—'

'What's the other?'

The glasses moved fractionally. 'Alter course east-sou'-east, sir!'

'Very good. Doesn't matter about the first one.' Nick realised that a course of east-south-east would be parallel to the enemy's; Beatty was squaring-off for the fight. That signal was fluttering down, and up ahead *Champion*'s wake grew an elbow in it as she put her helm over. Glancing back at the battle cruisers, expecting the thunder of the first salvoes to come at any moment, he saw the line-of-bearing forming as the great ships swung to their firing course; the line-of-bearing 'staggered' them, so that instead of following directly in each other's wakes, their tracks were spread. It meant that no ship would be steaming entirely in her next-ahead's funnel-smoke, and this should make it easier for the gunners. Nick stared out to port, at the distant line of Germans. He was watching them in that second as they opened fire.

A ripple of sharp, red flashes blossomed and travelled from right to left down the line of ships.

'Enemy's opened fire, sir!' Johnson had reported it.

Nick was aware of an extraordinary feeling of detachment. One heard nothing, yet. One had seen those red gun-flashes, and now . . . nothing. All silent, and those enemy ships so far away. One knew what it was about, what it meant, what would be happening here in a matter of twenty or thirty seconds, yet it seemed to be utterly remote from what was happening and visible here now.

But there was also a sense of enormous satisfaction – *relief*, it might be. This, finally, was battle.

More flags were showing from *Lion*, and Garret shouted to Mortimer, 'Distribution of fire signal, sir!' Beatty had six ships to the Germans' five; he had to tell his captains which targets each of them should aim at. Johnson had come to the after end of the bridge, where Blewitt crouched beside the Barr and Stroud transmitter; Nick had opened his mouth to ask whether he should go down now, when the sound of that distant gunfire reached them. A booming roll of far-off thunder, but it was lost immediately in a tearing, ripping noise as if the atmosphere was being forced apart, torn open, and the sea began to spout great mast-high columns of white water with dark tops; a forest of yellowish foam. All short, but already the red flashes of a second salvo were ripping down the German line, red spurts out of what looked now like a lumpy layer of smoke. Simultaneously the air astern erupted, split and split again as first *Lion* and then the ships astern of her opened fire.

You could actually see the shells, like scratch-marks against the pale-grey sky, as the battle cruisers' guns lobbed them away towards the Germans. Nick got his question through to Johnson when the volume of noise lessened. Johnson shouted, 'No, I'll tell you when to go down.' He'd explained earlier that it was preferable for Nick to stay on the bridge until the last moments before action, so that when he went down to his guns he'd know as much as possible about the tactical situation and the CO's intentions. Nick had thought perhaps that the time had come, but of course it hadn't, there was no enemy anywhere within range of the destroyers' little four-inch guns. This was a duel between giants, and it was continuous now. That reply of Johnson's had been squeezed into the last oasis of comparative silence there'd been – perhaps the last there'd *ever* be? Gunfire was no longer a matter of separate percussions or even separate salvoes, the noise of guns firing and shells falling was continuous, both fleets shooting steadily and rapidly and the fall-of-shot thick, closing-in, the German salvoes creeping closer as their gunners adjusted range, and – *Lion* had been hit! And hit *again* . . . That second hit had struck her centre turret, 'Q' turret: not just the shell-burst but a larger explosion and a shaft of flame and smoke that leapt to the height of her funnel-tops. Nick watched, fascinated, horrified: it was a blaze now, orange flames and thick, black smoke pouring back across the flagship's upperworks as she thrust on at twenty-five knots, her other three turrets all still firing. One had to remind oneself that shells would be raining down also on the enemy: in fact *that* had been a hit! He'd glanced over at the German line as the thought had come to him, and he'd seen the red-and-black explosion on their leading ship: and the third ship too, that third one might even be on fire . . . But in Beatty's squadron *Lion* wasn't the only one getting knocked about: her next astern, *Princess Royal*, had been hit on her foc'sl and the flash of the explosion had erupted from *inside* the ship. Extraordinary – horrible – to stand and watch: men must have died in there at that second, there'd be others wounded, mutilated, and the two fleets steaming on, side by side and ten miles apart and – as it seemed – indifferent . . .

Tiger was being hit now – so was *Indefatigable*. Nick whispered inside his skull, *Please God, may the Hun be getting as much as he's handing out! Indefatigable* had been hit again. The sea was a mass of leaping shell-splashes, the churned foam yellow, even the air yellowish with the explosive reek; the line of battle cruisers astern was almost entirely hidden now under the absolute smothering of German shells and – even more obscuring – their own funnel-smoke. But it was blowing clear again: suddenly he could see the whole line, and it looked as if *Indefatigable* was badly hurt. Smoke pouring from her after superstructure but no sign of any flames . . .

Lion was altering course to port – to close the range? The next ship to her, *Princess Royal*, going round too; and *Queen Mary*, and *Tiger*, and *New Zealand* and – Garret, the leading signalman, had turned to draw Nick's attention to the fact that *Indefatigable* didn't seem to have put her helm over. She was ploughing straight on across the other battle cruisers' tracks – already she was two cables or thereabouts out on *New Zealand*'s starboard quarter, and she was still steaming straight ahead. Her steering might have jammed, Nick thought; perhaps steering engine smashed; smoke billowed from her afterpart. As he watched her – with Johnson close beside him in the starboard after corner of the bridge – two more shells hit her. Nick felt himself cry out: or he thought he had. He'd felt his gut convulse and all the muscles of his body clench. But *she was all right*! The first shell had landed on her foc's'l and the other one on 'A' turret, and both had seemed to burst on impact. Had *seemed* to . . .

Indefatigable blew up.

There were those two hits, which hadn't seemed to penetrate her armour. Then perhaps half a minute in which nothing seemed to happen; he'd only continued to watch her because she held her course and still hadn't altered round with the other ships. He kept his eyes on her, aware of bedlam all around, of the continuing roar of gunfire and the fall of German shot, the sound of it screeching through the sky and then its impact mostly, but not all, in the sea, foul black water from near-misses sheeting across ships' decks. And then suddenly great flares of orange flame were leaping from *Indefatigable*'s forepart, spreading aft in a blazing mass with black smoke as well as flame, the smoke spreading until everything else had been blotted out, until that ugly, sickening pall hid the ship entirely. Above the smoke, in clear air, a fifty-foot picket boat soared, spinning like a toy. Other debris too. As it fell, the smoke was already dissipating and blowing clear, and *Indefatigable*, nineteen thousand tons of battle cruiser and more than a thousand men, had gone.

Leading Seaman Garret's mouth was open, his eyes wide and glazed with shock. His hands, up at chest-level, opened and shut convulsively, as if they were trying to find substance in thin air.

Hugh Everard told his gunnery lieutenant, speaking into the navy-phone to the control top, 'Open fire when you're ready, Brook.'

'Aye aye, sir.'

Replacing the telephone, Hugh joined Rathbone at the binnacle.

Nile heeled slightly under rudder as she followed the others of her squadron in a sharp turn to starboard, on to a firing course.

It was five minutes past four. The Fifth Battle Squadron had been straining eastward to close the gap between themselves and Beatty's battle cruisers, and even more essentially to get into hitting-distance of the enemy. Now the German battle cruisers were in sight, at a range of something like eleven miles, and Admiral Evan-Thomas was opening his squadron's broadsides to that distant target.

A minute ago, Hugh had seen *Indefatigable* blow up. He'd been watching the battle cruisers through his binoculars at the time; there'd seemed to be some alteration of course in progress, but it was a confused, smoky picture and he'd been trying to sort it out while he chatted briefly to Tom Crick. During the short exchange of conversation Crick had been standing with his back towards Beatty's ships, and consequently hadn't seen the sudden and total destruction of the battle cruiser. Probably very few men had. Indeed, hopefully . . .

Hugh had continued with the conversation. He'd kept the glasses at his eyes, hiding the shock he'd felt.

Now Rathbone was steadying *Nile* on the new course. The turrets were all trained out to about forty degrees on the port bow, which was where the Hun was. That far-off smoke, that cloudy suggestion of a line of ships was the enemy. From the top, where Brook was, the view would be much clearer, of course. But the Germans had the light on their side, and there was nothing Beatty could have done about it.

How would the Germans enjoy their first taste of fifteen-inch shells? The long barrels jutted menacingly, upward-pointing; silent, but ready to erupt. One could envisage very easily the interiors of the turrets; the warm, slightly oily atmosphere, the gleam of polished brass and steel, the quiet, and the tension in the guns' crews as they waited. The range was long, certainly, but that was no great drawback. These ships, like all those in Jellicoe's Scapa squadrons, had been trained to standards of excellence which one knew would be difficult to improve upon.

The Germans could shoot, there was no doubt of that; in the last few minutes the evidence of it had been incontrovertible. But in the next few minutes, they'd be getting experience of Jellicoe-type gunnery.

Hugh lowered his binoculars, stared up at his ship's masthead and then back at her after struts . . . It was all right. He might have known Crick would have seen to it. No less than three white ensigns and one union flag were fluttering up there. One or more might be shot away and *Nile* would still display her colours.

Barham opened fire. The thunder of that first salvo rolled back like thunder and brown cordite-smoke clung for a few seconds round her turrets. Now *Valiant* had begun: and that was *Warspite* joining in. Hugh left Rathbone, and moved out again to the port side – which shortly would be the engaged side – of the bridge, and levelled his glasses at the far-off enemy. The rearmost pair of them, the two grey shapes to the left, flickering with the red sparks of their own gunfire, had been identified as *Von der Tann* and *Moltke*, and on them – once the nearer cruisers had been dealt with – this squadron's fire would be concentrated.

Malaya had opened fire. Hugh swallowed to clear his ears from the percussion-effect of it. He put his glasses up again, and watched for the fall of *Barham*'s shells.

Five minutes ago the guns had been loaded; since then, range and deflection had been passed electrically from the TS to the director-sight in the top; and in the turrets, pointers followed the director settings.

The TS, or transmitting station, was a small compartment deep in the belly of the ship. In it, Royal Marine bandsmen fed numerous items of information into a computer called a Dreyer fire control table, which then churned out the settings that were to be applied to the guns.

In 'X' turret, Blackaby had ordered 'Salvoes! Right gun commencing!'

For the moment, that was his job done. Now it was up to the captain of the turret, PO Cartwright, out there behind the gleaming oiled steel of the great breech mechanisms, with the crew he'd trained and over whose every movement he now watched eagle-eyed. Number three, for instance; if number three had shut the interceptor switch before he'd seen the gunlayer raise his hand to confirm the pointers were in line – All right. The layer had put his hand up and three had slammed the switch shut and bellowed 'Right gun ready!'

In the TS, and in the control top where the lieutenant (G) hunched tensely at a binocular sight, and in the director tower where the director layer had his eye at the cross-wired telescope and a hand hovering close to the firing key, four out of eight 'gun ready' lights glowed brightly as in each of the four fifteen-inch turrets the crews stood by one loaded and cocked gun.

Brook, the gunnery lieutenant, who'd already had the order

from Captain Everard to commence firing, spoke clearly and unexcitedly into the mouthpiece of his telephone-set.

'Fire.'

The director layer waited a split second, until his sights rolled on. Then he pressed the key.

Moorsom, one of the tenth flotilla destroyers, had closed up astern of *Lanyard* so that the port column of the thirteenth flotilla now consisted of *Nestor, Nomad, Nicator, Lanyard, Moorsom*. It was twelve minutes past four. Almost unbelievably, that meant it was less than two hours since the first enemy report had been made by *Galatea*.

A long way astern, perhaps almost ten miles, the Fifth Battle Squadron was in action. One could hear nothing, of course, at such a distance and when the noise here was so great and so constant, but one could see the Queen Elizabeths back there in a grey clump hazed by smoke that was pierced intermittently by the spurting scarlet flashes of their guns. With binoculars you could also see their fall of shot. The fifteen-inch shells made such enormous splashes that there was no question of confusing them with the battle cruisers' smaller-calibre projectiles, and it looked as if they were straddling and hitting with impressive frequency. Their first salvoes had fallen short, but now they'd found the range and the Germans must have been feeling the effects unpleasantly; in fact the enemy rate and accuracy of fire had fallen off, or seemed to have, and the third ship in their line was clearly burning. The British battle cruisers had suffered badly enough, meanwhile; *Lion* had had the roof of one of her turrets blown clean off, and all the ships had been punished, hit time and time again. But no one would have guessed it from a quick inspection now – no one who hadn't seen the shells hitting, or didn't know that where five ships steamed now there'd been six ten minutes ago.

'Signal from *Champion*, sir!'

Garret had his glasses up, but hardly needed them. That signal whipping from the light cruiser's yard was one familiar to all destroyer men. It was the order they longed for, dreamt about.

'*Flotilla will attack the enemy with torpedoes, sir!*'

'Number One! Tell Chief I'll be calling for full power!'

'Aye aye, sir!'

Johnson started yelling into the engine-room voicepipe, and at the same time he was beckoning to Nick to come for'ard . . .

69

'Chief? Full power any second now. We'll be carrying out a torpedo attack on enemy battle cruisers. You'll—'

Interruption. Something about fuel? Johnson cut in again: 'Just everything we've got, Chief. *Everything*.' He straightened, nodding to Mortimer. Then he looked at Nick. 'Sub, listen. When we—'

Garret called, '*Champion* to thirteenth flotilla, sir: *Speed thirty knots – three-oh knots*, sir!'

'Very good.'

'Sub,' Johnson turned sideways, blocking one ear with his palm; Reynolds was bawling into a voicepipe to Pilkington, the torpedo gunner. Johnson told Nick, 'What'll happen is this. We'll push on ahead a mile or two first, and then—'

'Executive signal for thirty knots, sir!'

Mortimer was shouting now, on Nick's other side, for increased revolutions. It would be a relief to Worsfold, the engineer; *Lanyard* could manage thirty easily enough. Johnson yelled, 'When we're far enough ahead we'll haul away to port and aim for a spot out there somewhere.' He was pointing ahead and into the no-man's-land between the British and German squadrons. 'Up there on the Hun's bow, you see, for the attack. But when he sees what's happening, the Hun'll almost certainly send a flotilla or two out to meet us halfway. Perhaps light cruisers too. Understand?'

Nick nodded. *Lanyard* had the shakes again; thirty knots, and the whole flotilla in its three line-ahead divisions was racing forward on *Champion*'s heels. The first lieutenant told him, pitching his voice high above the din of increasing speed and of battle from astern, 'There'll be some high-speed gunnery before we can launch our torpedoes. Impossible to say which side the action'll develop on. Most likely both sides at once. You'll just have to watch out and shift from side to side; it'll be too fast for me to control from here.' He stared at him questioningly. 'All right?'

It was as 'all right', Nick thought, as it ever would be. The tight feeling in his stomach wasn't anything to take notice of; nor had the appalling dryness in his mouth anything to do with what was going on. Such fear as one was conscious of was – well, ninety per cent of it – was fear of not measuring-up, not doing the thing right.

Suddenly that mattered more than anything had ever mattered in his life.

70

CHAPTER 5

'Destroyers of the 13th Flotilla . . . having been ordered to attack the enemy when opportunity offered, moved out at 4.15 pm simultaneously with a similar movement on the part of the enemy. The attack was carried out in the most gallant manner and with great determination . . .'

From Vice-Admiral Sir David Beatty's report to Commander-in-Chief

Champion was flying the signal for the port column, this division, to attack, and over Nick's head at the after end of the bridge *Lanyard*'s answering pendant thrashed enthusiastically at the yard-arm. Ahead, *Nicator, Nomad* and the divisional leader *Nestor* also had their pendants close-up; astern, *Moorsom*'s ran up now.

Mortimer was hugging the binnacle in an ape-like stance with his arms spread and hooked around the spheres. Reynolds was making an adjustment to the port torpedo sight. Johnson, close to Nick on the port side farther aft, was looking through his binoculars at the head of the German line.

Behind them, Garret's yell was like a seagull's screech: 'Executive, sir!'

That signal had dropped from *Champion*'s yard; a new one climbing off the other side would be the order for the next division, the centre column, to follow this one. Mortimer, in that hunched-up position, had his face right down on the voicepipe, and he'd called down to the quartermaster for full power before Garret had had time to haul in the answering pendant. *Nestor* had put her helm over and she was careering away to port, leaning to the turn and digging her bow deep, flinging back a bow-wave like a great white scarf streaming from a runner's throat, the wave lengthening and curling aft down her sleek black side and her wash sluicing away in

71

a heaped-up curve of foam with *Nomad*'s stem sheering into it, and then *Nicator*'s into hers; and now it was *Lanyard*'s turn, Mortimer shouting 'Starboard twenty!' into increasing noise as the stoke-hold fans roared and her speed built up. Nick grasped for hand-holds on the base of the searchlight platform to steady himself against the force of the turn and the suddenly slanting deck, the sharp heel to starboard as she swung fast to port; Garret, coiling halyards with the pendant bundled temporarily under one arm, lurched round and crashed against him, muttered terse apologies as he struggled back up the sloping deck. But she was levelling again now, straightening into the straight lines of the other destroyers' wakes. Reynolds shouted into a voicepipe close to the torpedo sight, 'Stand by all tubes!' His voice, snatched away by the wind, was sharp and thin. Nobody had said anything about the guns yet; Nick was watching Johnson, who had his glasses up again to stare out over miles of grey-green sea to the dark shapes and heavy smoke-trails of Hipper's battle cruisers.

'Ah!' – Johnson from . . . *Lanyard*'s funnels were pouring smoke; it curled down to brush the welter of sea astern, stream over *Moorsom* and spread wider, drifting in the slow-moving haze of all five destroyers' smoke; it might just help to hide the next division until they burst through it, perhaps confuse the picture to German eyes. The distance between *Lanyard* and *Nicator* seemed constant so far, although down below there Worsfold and his engine-room staff must have been squeezing every ounce of pres-sure out of her. The sounds of battle were only a distant thunder now; the noise that ruled here was all ship-noise, sea-noise, wind-rush, the turbines' scream and the fans' roar and the thrum of vibration in the destroyer's plates, mast, rigging: not separate sounds, but one great orchestra of movement urgency.

'Take a look. But be *quick*!'

Johnson was holding the binoculars out towards Nick. He took them, leant back against the searchlight mounting to steady himself on the jolting bridge. It didn't work: the mounting, solid as it appeared to be, was shaking like everything else. The only way was to balance on feet spread well apart and avoid contact with bridge fittings. He saw what Johnson had wanted him to see, had prophesied; a flotilla of destroyers was moving out from the head of the enemy battle cruiser line. The counter-move. Judging by the smoke pluming astern of them, they were moving, like this flotilla, at high speed.

72

Nick nodded as he handed the glasses back. The first lieutenant stooped slightly to shout into his ear. 'Set the gunsights at ten thousand yards and I'll tell you when to open fire.' He pointed at the Barr and Stroud transmitter dials; 'I'll give you the early ranges too, on the leading ships. After that you'll have to select your own targets and carry on in "rapid independent". Understand?'

'Aye aye, sir.'

He was anxious to get on with it, do it instead of talk about it. Johnson pointed: 'Looks like we'll have 'em approaching on the starboard bow, unless they cross over. Their object'll be to force us to turn away – which of course we shan't do.' He grinned. 'Down you go, Sub.'

Nick wondered, as he climbed down the ladder, its metal runners singing like guitar-strings, whether that had been the first real smile he'd ever seen on Johnson's face. He couldn't remember seeing one before. Was this – action – what *everybody* lived for? Down here on the destroyer's upper deck the ship's motion, the sensation of her battering herself to destruction against sea, wind, and her own reluctance to move at such a speed, was even more pronounced than it had been up on the bridge. The sea's surface was so much closer, the steel of the deck less remote from the actual motion than the bridge was, stuck up there on top of it. The highest curve of the bow-wave was higher than the actual deck, so that one felt less 'on' the sea than 'in' it: and the sound of the sea matched that of the ship, like the sound of a mill-race magnified a dozen times . . . Nick moved aft, past the slung whaler and the foremost funnel, and up on to the raised platform of the midships four-inch gun.

'Layer! Leading Seaman Hooper?'

'Sir!' Hooper was a tall, thin sailor, stooped and narrow-shouldered, with a strangely triangular, narrow-eyed face. On his left arm he wore the killick-emblem of a leading hand above two good-conduct badges; on his right, the crossed gun-barrels and star of a gunlayer. He'd been peering over the top of the gunshield while the rest of the gun's crew stood waiting in its shelter . . . From the bridge, Johnson timed it perfectly: as Hooper and his men turned towards Nick, the buzzer sounded. Hooper ducked to his receivers, and a second later shouted the order 'Load!'

Nick stood back and watched. He saw that the shot-ready racks and cartridge racks had already been uncovered; shells lay nose-down, their brass bases gleaming. The number three snatched out the first one and slid it into the open breech; number four – a stout,

73

one-badge seaman with tattoos on the backs of his hands loaded a cartridge in behind it; number two – young, fresh-faced, no badges – slammed the breech shut.

'Ready!'

They all looked cheerful, eager. Nick checked the readings on the receivers against those on the sights: range ten thousand – on the dial that looked like a hundred – and deflection fifty right. It might become more, firing at a destroyer going flat-out in the opposite direction; at the full rate of crossing it could be at least sixty knots. But they'd most likely be approaching at an angle.

'Layer. Here a minute.' Out beside the gunshield, standing in the platform's saucer-shaped rim, Nick found he could just see the oncoming German boats. They were pointing straight at the thirteenth flotilla now, while in the distance way behind them, several miles farther away and indistinct in the smoke-haze left by the speeding enemy destroyers, Hipper's battle cruisers still pressed southwards.

'See 'em there?'

'Aye, sir!' Hooper grinned. 'I got me eye on 'em!'

'You'll get your open-fire order from the bridge. Follow receivers to start with, but when they're really close you'll have to shift from target to target and make your own corrections. Right?'

'Aye aye, sir!'

He dropped down to the upper deck and headed aft, to see that the quarterdeck gun's crew knew what was happening. Passing the ventilators, the roar of fans was almost deafening. It wasn't much short of a miracle that *Lanyard* was keeping up with the more modern N-class boats ahead of her; under his feet – in the engine-room and in the two boiler-rooms which he'd just passed over – was where that miracle was being worked.

He looked astern, and saw *Moorsom*, well back from her station. She'd lost a cable's length since he'd left the bridge. Beyond her – but not far beyond – the second division of the flotilla was coming flat-out on this division's heels. If *Moorsom* didn't watch out, they'd soon be overhauling her. Between him and those ships astern and in the same line of sight *Lanyard's* wake was piled like a great heap of snow, higher than her counter; it managed the trick of staying that high while at the same time it melted constantly away.

'Hey, Sub!'

Mr Pilkington, the gunner (T), was peering down at Nick from the searchlight platform between the two sets of tubes, the for'ard pair of which had been trained out to starboard and the after pair to port. Pilkington looked weird: at the best of times he had a gnome-like appearance – small, short-legged, with a large head and fiercely bristling eyebrows – and now he'd jammed his cap so hard down that its peak was almost covering his eyes. Nick nodded to him, 'About a dozen Hun destroyers, Mr Pilkington.'

'So we bin told, Sub,' the gunner nodded. 'An' so I seen. What I want you to tell me, 'owever, is would there be a light cruiser wi' em, leader sort o' thing?'

Had there been one larger shape, to the right of the flotilla, in support of it?

'There might be. I—'

'Might be!' Pilkington stared skywards, muttering his dissatisfaction. Now he was looking down – for sympathy perhaps – at his torpedo gunner's mate, an outsize petty officer squatting toad-like between the tubes of the for'ard mounting. The same position on the after tubes was occupied by a leading torpedo-man, while the number twos, lacking fixed seats, leant beside their training handwheels. Nick moved on aft, and found that the stern gun was loaded and had the right settings on its sights. He explained the general situation and intentions to Stapleton, the grey-haired gunlayer, a three-badge able seaman. Stapleton told Nick, pointing along the barrel of his gun – it was trained round as far for'ard as it would go – 'First customer's pretty near in range now, sir.'

It was a fact. But *Nestor, Nomad* and *Nicator* would be the first to open fire; there'd be that much forewarning. Looking for'ard there, *Nomad* was in sight out to starboard, on what was going to be the engaged side; and she was closer, as if she'd fallen back, perhaps changing places with *Nicator*? Or she might have swung over to try a long torpedo shot at the battle cruiser line before the German flotillas got in the way . . . Nick looked around him, checking that the ammunition-supply party was ready with the trap open. It was a circular hatch in the deck behind the gun, and it led down into the wardroom, which was the compartment immediately underneath. There was a similar trap in the deck of the wardroom, and below that were the after four-inch magazine and shell-room; the ammunition was passed up through the first hatch and through the wardroom, where a sailor on a steel ladder pushed it through to the supply ratings here on the upper deck. There were half a dozen of them, since the cartridges and projectiles had to be delivered to the midships gun as well as to this one.

And they ought to get some up there now, not wait for the midships gun to empty its shot-ready racks . . . He told the leading seaman who was in charge of the party, 'Get a dozen rounds up amidships, before the shooting starts.' He saw the movement start; a shout down through the hatch, and shells coming up, it was like pressing a switch and starting an automatic process . . . 'Sub-Lieutenant, sir!'

A bridge messenger. 'First Lieutenant says, when we engage the enemy would you start the upper deck fire-main, sir.'

'Right.'

'Shall I stand by it, sir?'

Why not? And then report back to the bridge. As Stapleton had observed, the fight would be starting at any moment now. He told the messenger, 'Yes, please.' But there was no sign of the enemy destroyers now: he started looking out on the port bow, thinking they might be crossing ahead; or perhaps this division had altered. course just slightly, putting the Germans dead ahead? The purpose of opening the fire-main would be to have a continuous flood of water over the upper deck, thus making it less easy for fires to start. Nick wondered whether Johnson had had the boats' tarpaulin covers filled with water too. Strangely, it seemed quite natural, now, to be going into action. As if one had done it before, and knew all about it. Maybe because one had imagined it so often, in one's daydreams, since the age of ten or so?

Crashes were coming suddenly from ahead. *Nestor*, he guessed, had opened fire. More gunfire now, quite rapid, and the wind into which *Lanyard* was thrusting had a stench of cordite in it. Ammunition, he noticed, was flowing for'ard smoothly. But that tightness had returned to the pit of his stomach: it was infuriating, he'd thought he'd got rid of it: he told himself, *Ignore it. Probably just physical, it's not –* A waterspout leapt, shattering the introspection; a second one; no, *three* – forty or fifty yards abeam to starboard, and *still* no enemy in sight; the gun was trained to its foremost stop and there was nothing for it yet to bear on. It sounded like the two leading destroyers firing now, the crashes were too frequent to come from just one ship. The ammunition party had come to a halt again, having built up supplies at the other gun. Nick went inside the cover of the gunshield and stood behind Stapleton to see what, if anything, might be coming through on the receivers from the bridge. To his surprise, the range was showing as 060 – six thousand yards – well inside effective range. He went out again. He was out there just in time to see the stern gun of the next ship ahead fire on a for'ard bearing, and a second later he saw the leading German destroyer sweep into sight. The Hun must have been right ahead, or almost right ahead, and now swung a point or two to port to pass on a more or less parallel but reciprocal course to the British flotilla, which meant, if he held that course and the ships astern of him did too, they'd be shooting at each other as they passed at something like point-blank range. *Lanyard*'s bow gun fired, Nick opened his mouth to shout to Stapleton, and thunder cracked right beside him as the gunlayer let rip without waiting for an order. The midships gun had opened up too.

There were three enemy in sight now; Nick could see the flashes of their guns, hear the almost continuous shooting from the thirteenth flotilla ships ahead, see waterspouts all round the Germans and the glow of hits too; the orange flare of bursting shells and black smoke streaming aft. The leading destroyer had been hit two or three times and she was swinging away, her bow down and her bridge – no, her waist, between the funnels – pouring black smoke. The range was about four thousand yards now and water was sluicing over *Lanyard*'s iron deck, her guns firing as fast as they could load and fire again, the deflection increasing as the distance lessened and the bow-on angle opened. You got used to noise; it became simply what you had around you. Shell-splashes surrounded the next-ahead. This was *Nomad*, not *Nicator*, for some reason they'd swapped places and *Lanyard* was swinging out to starboard suddenly, closing-up on *Nomad* as if Mortimer intended passing her. Well, *she'd* gone out to port, or *Lanyard* had swung to starboard, before this – otherwise she wouldn't have been in sight from aft here. And she'd been hit: amidships, where her boilers were. *Lanyard* raced past her as she slowed; the action was all to starboard and the leading German destroyer – no, the second, the first was out of it, she'd turned away and stopped, she was still being hit and she looked as if she was sinking: the nearest German was less than fifteen hundred yards away, all her guns blazing. The ammunition party's leading seaman was bawling down into the hatch: Nick saw that the flow of shells had stopped, this gun's crew snatching what they needed from the ready-use racks. Nick stooped, yelled in the man's ear, 'What is it?' His face turned, mouthing something frantically, his words lost in gun

77

crashes and the screech and explosions of enemy projectiles. Nick repeated his question, and this time he got an answer that he could hear, 'Tryin' to find out, sir, they don't seem—'

Enemy destroyers abeam now, point-blank, waterspouts all round, the gaff with the ensign on it shot away and hanging, but *Lanyard* had been lucky, *Nomad* was stopped back there astern and someone was using her for target-practice. Nick had an idea that *Lanyard* had been hit for'ard; meanwhile her own guns had sent number four in the German destroyer line reeling out to port and listing. The guns' crews were cheering as he flung himself into the deckhouse over the wardroom hatchway; he took the ladder in a single leap and crashed in through the latched-back wardroom door. He saw the trouble at a glance. The ladder to the ammo exit had come adrift, so they hadn't been able to reach that deck-head hatch, and the two men who comprised the supply-link in here – stokers, he saw, by their insignia, and both very young – were struggling frantically to fix it. The bar which ran through its top and through two eye-bolts in the deckhead by the trap hadn't been pushed through properly, so one end had come out and it had buckled. What they were trying to do was hopeless. Nick told them, 'Leave it. Get the table under, and that chair on the table, quick now!' They'd jumped to obey him. Remembering Johnson's remark about new hands in the supply party he wondered whether they'd been trained at all. He helped them slide the table into place; then the chair was on it, and one of them up there while the other handed up ammunition from the lower hatch. Nick saw the stream re-started, then he ran for the ladder to the upper deck.

Halfway up it, the blast hit him. There was a moment before he realised that he'd been knocked backwards off the ladder. Dazed, bruised, scrambling back to it and starting up again. Torpedo? The explosion had been big enough. It was already, within seconds, indistinct in his memory, but it seemed to have taken time, to have had a certain duration to it. Behind him a voice asked, 'What's happened? What was that?' Nick looked back and downwards, and saw the surgeon, Samuels. The dressing-station and emergency operating theatre was Mortimer's cabin, a dozen steps from the ladder's foot; but ten minutes ago Samuels had been up near the midships four-inch; Nick had seen him there, just before the action started, when he'd been talking to Hooper.

'I don't know yet.'

At the top of the ladder he found that the steel hutch, the

superstructure over it, had changed shape, its vertical walls con-
cave, pushed in by the blast. He could hear guns firing, but the
stern four-inch wasn't – wasn't *there*! The deck was ripped where
gun and mounting had been torn off it. Jagged, upturned edges of
the deck itself, and littered wreckage of steel that might have been
twisted around in giant hands and then flung down and stamped
on. And there'd been men in it when that had happened, there were
bodies and parts of bodies held in it, like animals caught in traps.
The rush of water from the fire-main entered this strewn, smashed
area as clear water and flowed out bright red.

Samules stood beside him, clutching his dark, curly head between both hands . . . 'My God, what *did* this?'

'Sir, I—'

A torpedoman – the number two of the after tubes. Bent sideways as he staggered aft, holding his left side: all blood, ripped
cloth and flesh. 'I been 'it, sir, I—'

Samuels caught him as he fell. Nick felt as if he woke up at that
moment; to the fact that the action was at its hottest and no
ammunition could be getting to the midships gun. Also that those
jagged holes in the deck, which were above the store compartments
immediately aft of the wardroom, had water from the fire-main
pouring into them; the fire-main had to be shut off. Ammunition
for that gun was what mattered most. He crouched down beside
the trap; the deck around it had been scoured, grooved, its bare
steel shone like silver. One of the young stokers peered at him
through the hole and began, 'Sir, is—'

'Ready, sir, they're wantin' it!'

Whipping round, Nick found two of the ammunition supply
party; they must have just returned from delivering shot to the
midships gun. He'd thought of them all as being dead. Nick told
the stoker down below, 'Come on then, get it moving!' He stood
up, and one of the two sailors said, 'It all begun to come up fast,
sudden like, faster 'n we could take it from 'em. I reckon a shell hit
a lot of 'em as was stood there, sir.' The other man looked winded,
sick. Nick grasped his arm, and told them both, 'Only two of you
now. You'll just have to damn well run with it.' The surgeon's
helpers, one sick berth attendant and one cook, had come up to
help; they were carrying the wounded torpedoman down through
the hatch, all three of them soaked already in his blood. As Nick
started for'ard a shell dropped alongside, exploding as it hit the
water. He heard the rattle of splinters on the ship's side and the

whirr of others whizzing past and overhead, but all that hit him was a douche of black, foul-smelling water. He located the fire-main, and shut it off. He headed for Pilkington now, who had the use of the searchlight crew's voicepipe to the bridge. The noise had slackened, there was still a lot of gunfire but it seemed to be all astern. 'Mr Pilkington!'

'What, you still alive?' Crouching on the platform, the torpedo gunner had only glanced down briefly. He had his torpedo-firing disc in his hand. Nick asked him, 'Would you tell the first lieutenant – stern four-inch blown overboard, crew all killed and—'

'Bloody 'ell I will!' Mr Pilkington's small eyes gleamed with anger under the jammed-down peak of his cap. 'Fill up the voicepipe wi' bloody chatter?' He stood up, pointing out on the port bow and yelling down to his beefy TGM, 'Port side only, one an' two tubes only, get 'em round!' Looking round just as the midships four-inch fired, Nick saw a shell-splash leap up astern of what must have been the last of the German flotilla. Farther back and broader on the quarter he could see two others stopped and sinking; the after part of one of them was on fire. How long had the whole action taken, from start to finish? Four, five minutes? *Lanyard* was still steaming flat out, the roar of her fans unchanged, funnel-smoke pouring astern thick and black. He could see three, four – no, *five* more destroyers following astern there, their guns still engaging the German boats: and the Germans seemed to be fanning out, disengaging. They'd still have the thirteenth flotilla's starboard division ahead of them, of course, and it was possible they'd had enough. He climbed up behind the midships gun; there was nothing for it to shoot at now, and as the supply party came panting to and fro with charges and projectiles they were refilling the ready-racks. Nick told Hooper, 'Train round to the other side. We'll be turning to starboard in a minute to fire torpedoes.' The Barr and Stroud, he saw, was showing a range of 080. He told the gunlayer as the four-inch pivoted round through the stern bearing and up the other side, 'Set range oh-eight-oh—' Shells screeched overhead. He finished, 'And deflection zero.' Shell-splashes went up astern. Shellfire was thickening now, the noise of it rising and the sea spouting like a pond from heavy rain, the air alive with the scrunch and screech of overs. He felt *Lanyard* begin her turn, deck tilting, screws pounding, wake curving crescent-like to starboard. A range of 080 meant eight thousand yards, four sea miles; good torpedo range but hardly a comfortable distance at which to loiter round five German battle cruisers whose secondary armament of six-inch guns was reserved exclusively for just such moments. Each of those ships had six six-inch on each side, which meant that now *Nestor* and *Nicator* had made their runs there'd be no less than thirty six-inch banging away at *Lanyard*.

A clanging crash came from the foc'sl and a smoke-cloud that flew aft and left a stink of high-explosive as it passed told of a hit for'ard. Now water rained down from some near miss or misses, and Nick saw the Germans suddenly as the destroyer's bow swung and they came into view while her turn continued until she was broadside-on to all of them – a sitting duck, and the deck's slant lessening as Mortimer eased her helm, levelling her for the convenience of Mr Pilkington and his torpedoes. The enemy was five vast silver-grey juggernauts with what looked like a hundred guns spitting fire and fury under a long, unbroken shroud of funnel-smoke; Hooper was firing steadily as *Lanyard* still swung and his gunsight travelled from the third in the line, past the second, to the leader – Hipper's flagship. Nick shouted in the gunlayer's ear, 'Bridge! Aim at her bridge!' A hit on the person of Vice-Admiral Hipper with a four-inch QF Mark IV might be worth scoring. But it was hard to see now through the density of shell-spouts and falling spray. A piece of the for'ard funnel suddenly flared, smoked, flew away in the wind and fell astern, and the gun was training slowly aft now – faster – Hooper keeping the flagship's bridge as his point of aim. There'd been no sign of any torpedo hit, but Nick realised that while ten seconds ago the big ships' firing had been rising to a hideous, merciless crescendo – he'd thought, as they hit that funnel, *Now this can't last* – it had just as suddenly slackened off. And the German ships were turning! Swinging away together to port, to avoid *Lanyard*'s torpedo. *Lanyard*, eight hundred tons, making a whole squadron of twenty-five-thousand-ton battle cruisers turn away! Then he saw the error in that boast, for it wasn't only *Lanyard*, but here were three – no, four others racing in, perhaps more, at this moment out of his view. The situation wasn't orderly, there were ships here, there and everywhere . . . and *Petard* seemed about to cross astern as she swung over to make her attack; Nick shouted to Hooper to hold his fire.

*   *   *

Nile's broadsides roared again: and since the Fifth Battle Squadron had opened fire fifteen minutes ago there was little doubt that the enemy were suffering. To start with, the screening cruisers had been sent scurrying; now *Moltke* and *Von der Tann* had both been hard hit and their rates of fire reduced, and it looked as if the leading ships of the squadron were reaching *Seydlitz* now as well. Hugh Everard swung his glasses to the left, to what had been the battlefield and was now once again just a grey acreage of North Sea. There, well abaft the battle squadron's port beam now, a sailing barque – tall, square-rigged – lay becalmed with all sails set. A lovely craft; a peaceful, restful and utterly incongruous sight, a total contrast to the destructive violence which during the last half-hour had thundered past on either side of her, shells hurtling in their low trajectory over her white, idle sails. With his glasses resting on her for a moment, Hugh found himself thinking of Sarah. No, not thinking of her, but forming a picture of her in his mind; her smile and her calm, friendly manner; a combination of vulnerability and quiet self-confidence. The vulnerability was something one saw oneself, of course, because when one thought of her one tended to have *him* in mind. How she'd accepted him in the first place was – well, there was no answer to it! John could turn on his charm, of course, and hide his more natural attributes. And he was a baronet, which would have delighted Buchanan, who would have used his influence . . .

Nile's guns crashed out again, just as a close pattern of German shells thumped into the sea sixty yards short. Nothing had touched *Nile* yet, and there'd been no hits so far on any of the ships ahead of her. All the shells fired at this squadron had fallen short, while their own fifteen-inch guns had had the range to hit the two rearmost Germans time and time again. The range was closing now, though, as the lines converged, and before long one might expect a taste of one's own medicine, a share of the hammering which Beatty's ships had been enduring for about forty minutes – a hammering which Beatty had positively invited by rushing in without waiting for this squadron. But meanwhile, with Rathbone piloting *Nile* in *Malaya*'s wake, and Brook up in the control top sending salvo after salvo thundering from her guns, there wasn't a great deal for her captain to be doing.

He thought he might tell Sarah, one day, how the sight of that becalmed sailing-ship had turned his thoughts to her in the middle of a battle . . .

Extraordinary, that one could reach years of discretion and still behave like an adolescent. Blurting that out to her, as he had yesterday . . .

Damn it, I meant it! I feel it now!

As she must too. Otherwise, would she have telegraphed an answer to his letter, to arrange a meeting? Well, *would* she?

He bit his lip. He'd got cold feet, that was all. He'd begun to express a fraction of what he felt for her, and then baulked at it, backed off. Career? And the idea of stealing his brother's wife? *Morality?* Where was the morality in leaving her in John's hands, for God's sake?

Tom Crick touched his arm.

'Sir.'

Drawing his attention, privately, to something on the starboard bow . . . To Beatty's ships – fine on the bow, almost right ahead. Hugh raised his glasses and focused them on the battle cruisers – still some five miles distant, still pressing southward, their guns flinging out a brownish cordite haze that mingled with clouds of heavier funnel-smoke.

He saw what Crick was showing him. Twenty minutes ago, *Indefatigable* had blown up. Now he was watching the same thing happen to *Queen Mary*. A dull, red glow faded almost before he'd seen it: another glow spread for'ard: her hull was opening, expanding outwards, and as he watched – hardly letting himself believe he was seeing it – her masts and funnels toppled inward, as if a great pit had been opened for them to fall into. Then the eruption: he saw the roofs of all four turrets blow up like corks from bottles: smoke spread, built up, a column piling, rising in great circling folds to a height of about a thousand feet. The ship astern of her had vanished into that vast cloud's base: they'd be in darkness, pieces of their sister-ship would be raining down around them as they steamed through the stench of her destruction.

Like *Indefatigable, Queen Mary* would have taken about a thousand men with her to the bottom. Some would have been trapped, and at this moment still alive, not even knowing yet what had happened . . .

Jellicoe, Hugh thought, must be getting close now. *Please God, lend him speed: Beatty has already lost his battle.*

'Signal, sir!'

Hugh took the clip-board from his chief yeoman's hand.

Jellicoe had given Beatty this Fifth Battle Squadron to support him, and Beatty had stupidly or arrogantly (or *both* adverbs might apply) left it astern and taken Hipper on alone. All right, so there must obviously be some structural defect that allowed the battle cruisers to fall such easy victims to a few hits, but they *were* lightly armoured, as Beatty well knew, and if the Queen Elizabeths had been with them the German fire would have been spread over more targets, and the German gunners would have had a much less easy time of it, because there'd have been fifteen-inch salvoes pouring down on them.

Over there in the German line, they'd be cheering themselves hoarse now.

Sick at heart, he gave his attention to the signal. It was from senior officer Second Light Cruiser Squadron – which meant Commodore Goodenough in *Southampton* and addressed to C-in-C and FO, BCF. The message, prefixed URGENT, read: *Have sighted enemy battle fleet bearing approximately south-east. Course of enemy north. My position lat 56 degs 34' N long 6 degs 20' E. Time 4.38 pm.*

Hugh looked up at Crick. He told him, 'Scheer's coming north with the High Seas Fleet. He's already almost on top of Beatty.'

'Flag signal flying from *Lion*, sir!'

Midshipman Ross-Hallet had reported it. The chief yeoman whipped his telescope to his eye as he hurried out to the bridge's starboard wing. It wasn't an easy string of flags to read, at a distance of five miles and with the flags blowing this way, end-on, and in smoke.

'What's he saying, Peppard?'

More shells were falling just short of them.

'Can't quite make—' The chief yeoman's face was screwed up in concentration. Yeoman Brannon, one of his four assistants, was beside him with another telescope. 'Looks like an alter-in-succession signal, sir, but—'

'It's coming down.' Hugh was behind the binnacle, where Rathbone had made room for him, and he had his binoculars trained on Beatty's ships. 'Doesn't matter, Peppard. He *is* turning.'

The battle cruisers were going-about, reversing course, by the looks of it. And in the circumstances, Hugh thought, that was wise enough. In fact there was nothing else Beatty could have done – short of committing suicide with all his ships and men. But there was more to it than just survival. Just as Jellicoe, misled by the Admiralty, hadn't known Scheer was at sea, so the probability was that Admiral Scheer had not the slightest idea that Jellicoe was either. Certainly not that the Grand Fleet was only fifty miles away, and coming closer at every minute. He couldn't know, because if he did he'd be steaming south, not north!

Jellicoe steaming south at, say, twenty knots – of which his slowest battleships were capable – and the ships here going north at twenty-five; in an hour, there'd be no gap! But Scheer and Hipper must be thinking they had Beatty trapped and running for his life; they could hardly guess he'd be leading them into a *British* trap.

The four surviving battle cruisers had completed their northwards turn; they were returning this way, now, towards the Fifth Battle Squadron, which Evan-Thomas was still leading south. Beatty had had quite a mauling; no doubt he wanted the more powerful battleships astern of him, where the brunt of the fighting would now be. That was reasonable and fair. Unlike the battle cruisers, these super-dreadnoughts were armoured to take punishment as well as gunned to hand it out.

'Rathbone.' Hugh passed his navigator the clip of signals. 'Put the last one on the plot, will you?'

'Sir.'

'You know, Tom—' he kept his eyes on *Malaya*, the next ahead – 'this is an odd situation. Scheer thinks he's got Beatty's goose cooked. Whereas with any sort of luck, he's practically in the oven himself!'

Crick pulled thoughtfully at an ear. 'Let's hope so, sir.'

Geoff Garret held on to the rail in the starboard after corner of *Lanyard*'s bridge and wondered how long he'd live.

It was necessary, vitally necessary now, that he should survive; but could Fate or the Almighty be counted on to recognise the necessity?

Blood – not just stains, but pools of it – in certain parts of the bridge suggested that no particular element of Divine protection was being extended over this destroyer. Against that, one might take comfort from the theory that lightning never struck twice in the same place. He told himself, *Best not to think about it. Me going soft won't help her.*

Ahead of *Lanyard, Nestor* and *Nicator* zigzagged to and fro, dodging like snipe; *Lanyard* followed in the water they'd slashed and churned, whipping to and fro just as wildly, under almost constant helm one way or the other, salvo-dodging, flinging herself from tack to tack so savagely that she was permanently on her beam ends, her deck bucking as she flung herself from side to side while the pair ahead were often hidden from sight in foam, spray, the height of their own wakes and the spouts of German shells – and battleships' shells now. The Hun dreadnoughts had only hove into sight ten minutes ago, when *Lanyard* and her two N-class consorts had been heading westward to rejoin Beatty's force, and Geoff Garret had read in other faces that he wasn't the only one who felt distinctly relieved, at that point, to be getting out from under. But relief hadn't lasted long. *Nestor* had suddenly veered out to port and begun flashing to the two boats astern of her. Garret, as he concentrated on reading the first words of *Nestor*'s morse, had heard Sub-Lieutenant Hastings exclaim: 'It's the Fifth Battle Squadron, sir. They're off on our port bow now!' After the attack, the turning and twisting to and fro, he'd been confused, as most were; whichever way you looked the sea was grey, planted here and there with groups of ships or single ships at varying distances, with patches and streaks of smoke. Those three German destroyers, for instance, two of them sinking, and *Nomad*, whom they'd had to leave, shrouded in steam escaping from her shattered boiler-rooms . . . Hastings had thought that line of big ships which had just shown themselves out of the mistier section of the horizon were the Queen Elizabeths, but the misconception was quickly dispelled. *Nestor*'s signal said *Enemy battle fleet bearing S.S.E. Intend attacking with remaining torpedoes.*

Garret had read it, calling the words out one by one as he clashed the shutter of the searchlight to acknowledge them; and during the recital of the last few words, he'd begun to wonder whether the intention which was being expressed could possibly be in his own best interests.

He'd never thought in such terms before. He'd been in action three or four times, in another boat down in the Harwich flotilla, and he'd always rather enjoyed it, same as most of the lads did. You couldn't swing round an anchor or prop up a jetty and hope to win the war; fighting was what the fleet was *for*. But he'd changed. He felt entirely different. Part of his unease was that he recognised the change and disliked it; he was uncomfortable, and the fact he was uncomfortable made him more uncomfortable.

Returning a wink from Blewitt, Garret hoped his fear didn't show. He wished he could recover the sense of excitement and anticipation he'd felt when they'd had the signal about altering course to go after the enemy. He wasn't the same man now that he'd been then.

There was a six-foot hole in the port fore corner of the bridge. There'd been steps there and a door; now it was just a pit. And three men were dead. Two of the for'ard gun's crew had been wounded, and soon after that there'd been an enormous explosion aft. It had felt and sounded like a torpedo hit. Number One had tried to find out what had happened but the voicepipes didn't work, and then he'd been busy with the for'ard gun and Blewitt's machine. It had been during the run-in to fire torpedoes that a German light cruiser's shell had smashed into that corner where the bridge connected, with three steps down and a wooden door and a short ladder inside, with the steering position. The blast went both ways: it killed the coxswain, CPO Cuthbertson, at the wheel, and Lieutenant Johnson and Lieutenant Reynolds in the bridge, and a splinter from it had cut the throat of the bridge messenger, aft on the other side.

Entrance to the lower bridge – the steering position – was through that hole now. The second coxswain had brought up a rope ladder and rigged it there.

'Hard a-starboard!'

'Hard a-starboard, sir!'

Geordie Alan was on the wheel now. He'd pulled the coxswain off it, and taken over. *Lanyard* stood on her ear as she skidded round to port, with her captain clinging to the binnacle and watching for the fall of shot; he'd order the wheel over as soon as he saw shell-spouts rise; he seemed to head *towards* each salvo.

'Midships! Meet her!'

'Meet her, sir!'

Pandemonium: the ship was jolting, crashing, swinging from side to side: you braced yourself – then you had to shift, brace differently as she flung over the other way. Mortimer had somehow jammed his body at the binnacle, and looked nowhere except ahead, at the grey shapes of the enemy with their white bow-waves looking big now as the distance lessened, and at the destroyers ahead, and the splashes of shells scrunching down right, left and – Mortimer never saw the overs, because he never looked astern.

'Hard a-port!'

'Hard a-port, sir!' The for'ard gun fired; it couldn't shoot much, with the other two destroyers in the line of fire half the time and *Lanyard* doing acrobatics when they weren't. No gunlayer on earth could have kept his sights on, the way she was throwing herself about. Near-misses shot up close to port as she sheered away to starboard; they'd gone in the drink but you felt the blow of them, and water cascaded black across the bridge. Filthy reek lingering . . .

'Midships! Starboard twenty!'

Nestor was performing a long swing to starboard. Shell-spouts hid her, then she was in sight again, pouring black smoke from her funnels, her starboard side visible almost as far down as her bilges as she heeled to the turn, but the heel lessened as she eased her wheel, and Geoff Garret realised she must be about to fire, steadying the turn so that her torpedo gunner'd be able to hold his aim on the enemy long enough to send a fish away. *Nicator* swung over, lancing through white water, dashing after her leader now to add her torpedoes to the attack.

'Hard a-port!'

Lanyard swivelled, flinging over as starboard rudder bit into the sea: 'Midships! Meet her!'

Nestor would be firing about now, and *Nicator* with her, both firing to port as they swung to starboard. Mortimer had moved, grabbed a hold on the bridge rail by the torpedo voicepipe where canvas screening flew in tatters behind splinter-mattresses which were also ripped: 'Mr Pilkington! I'm turning to port now so you'll fire to starboard. Train round to *starboard*!'

Garret heartily approved. He'd expected Mortimer to turn *Lanyard* with the others, fire on the same curve in sequence, same as it was done in practice firings; he'd been thinking that if that happened, the Germans would only have to keep dropping shells in one spot.

'Hard a-starboard!' Mortimer yelled at Hastings, pointing at the torpedo voicepipe, 'Tell Pilkington to fire when his sight comes on!'

'Aye aye, sir!'

Sub-Lieutenant Hastings looked as cool as anything. Garret hoped he looked like that. He was trying to. *Lanyard* was lifting to the turn, riding across the wall from the other two. She was going to almost scrape *Nicator*'s stern as she peeled-off to the left and *Nicator* to the right; they'd be almost on the same spot together for a moment, then they'd be dividing and you could hope the German gunners might think they were seeing things – like one ship splitting into two, and wonder which half to shoot at . . . But *Nicator* had suddenly reversed her wheel!

She'd checked her starboard swing, and begun to turn back – across *Lanyard*'s bow. Garret held his breath and thought, *Oh God, we're going to hit her* . . .

He heard Mortimer almost scream, 'Hard a-port!' Garret thought it was too late, he wouldn't make it. And he could see the reason for *Nicator*'s suicidal change of course: *Nestor* had been hit, so *Nicator* had had to reverse her wheel or run into her. *Nestor* had swung broadside-on, with her after-part pouring smoke; she'd lost all her way, and she was down by the stern. *Lanyard*'s only hope of avoiding collision had been to reverse her helm – which Mortimer had done – and try to turn inside her, the other way.

Shell-splashes spurted everywhere and within seconds *Lanyard*'s stem was going to embed itself in *Nicator*'s stern. What was more, Pilkington's tubes would be trained out on the wrong side, now. Garret whispered in his mind, *Please God, please* . . .

Nicator's stern shaved past with about a foot to spare.

Mortimer yelled down, 'Ease to ten!' Garret's breath rushed out like air from a balloon. *Nicator*'s turn had flattened; she was going over to starboard again, towards the enemy, and Mortimer had steadied *Lanyard* on a course to pass close to *Nestor*. *Nestor* was done for, the German gunners were concentrating on her, she was stopped and helpless and taking the whole weight of their fury. The small mercy of it was that for the moment there was very little coming *Lanyard*'s way.

About as much as an hour ago, one might have felt she was in the thick of it. After the last eight or nine minutes everyone knew better: this was nothing.

Mortimer called down, 'Port twenty!'

'Port twenty, sir! Twenty of port helm on, sir!'

Turning away: leaving *Nestor* to her fate – which could only be that of a target for gunnery practice by Admiral Scheer's High Seas Fleet, which within the next twenty minutes or so would be steaming past her in its stately progress, battleship after battleship, keen to draw British blood.

'Midships! Steady!'

The midships four-inch fired.

'Steady, sir! Course west by south sir!'

'Steer west.'

That midships gun fired again, and at the same time spouts from enemy shells went up fifty yards on the bow.

'Starboard ten!'

Salvo-dodging again; Mortimer began to alter towards each lot of splashes as they leapt. There was another salvo scrunching over now, and the gun aft fired again. Garret edged out as far as he could, and leant over, peering aft; the south-east wind was carrying *Lanyard*'s smoke to starboard, and on the port quarter – almost right astern – he could see a grey line of battleships, their two leaders spitting fire. *Nestor* was out there entirely alone now, surrounded by shell-spouts and smoke; *Nicator* was speeding after *Lanyard*.

Mortimer turned his head, yelled at Hastings, 'Tell 'em aft to cease fire. And get Everard up here.' He ducked to the voicepipe: 'Midships . . . Steady!'

Garret heard him mutter then, glancing aft, 'Waste of ammunition. We may well need it, later.' Garret thought, *Oh God, please don't make us need it . . .* He had to jump aside then as the engineer officer, Mr Worsfold, climbed into the bridge. Mortimer, stooped at the binnacle, didn't know Worsfold was there until he spoke.

'Captain, sir.'

'What?'

Mortimer's head jerked round . . . 'Oh. Hello, Chief. What're you doing up here?'

'I needed a word with you, sir.' Worsfold's narrow, small-boned face was set hard, and his deepset eyes were anxious. Mortimer stared at him for a second or two, then he turned to Hastings. 'Pilot, take over for a minute. Mean course west, and for God's sake keep her zigging.'

'Aye aye, sir.'

'What's up, Chief?'

'We can't keep up this speed, sir. If we try to, we'll—'

'Chief. Wait.' Mortimer held up one hand. 'There's no can't about it.' He cocked a thumb over his shoulder. 'That's the leading division of the High Seas Fleet coming up astern of us. We need every knot we've—'

'It wouldn't help us to break down, then, sir. And that's what's going to happen unless—'

'Chief.' Mortimer licked his lips. It seemed to Garret that he was making an effort to control himself. 'Listen to me. We have no option, you have no option, none whatever, but to continue at our maximum—'

'Sir. With respect, I—'

'*Damn* your respect!'

Control had been forgotten. A finger pointed, shaking, in the engineer's face. Mortimer's face seemed swollen with his rage. He shouted, 'I'll keep going at full power, Worsfold, because I bloody well have to! D'you understand? Eh? Well, understand something else, if in the next half-hour we either ease off or break down, I'll have you *shot*! I'll shoot you myself, by God!'

Hastings called down to the quartermaster, his face low on the rim of the voicepipe so that his voice seemed quiet, 'Port twenty.' The engineer's dark eyes were fixed on Mortimer's. He might have been wondering whether this was some kind of joke. Mortimer said in a more even tone than he'd just used, 'I mean it, Worsfold, I mean exactly what I say. Don't doubt it for a moment. Get back to your engines, and keep 'em going!'

Garret, not wanting to meet Mortimer's stare if he happened to glance this way, directed a professional stare at the ensign, flapping furiously at the masthead. He felt Mr Worsfold's shoulder brush against his own as the engineer came back aft without another word and climbed over on to the ladder. Garret thought, *Skipper's gone off his chump*. Glancing down again, he saw that *Nicator* was moving up to take the lead, steering a straight course to overhaul *Lanyard* on her starboard beam. Astern, the sound of gunfire hadn't slackened, while ahead, where they were going, it was like continuous, rolling thunder.

Poor old *Nestor*. She was the second of *Lanyard*'s flotilla mates they'd had to leave behind: two static, helpless targets for the Huns to knock to smithereens. Geoff Garret closed his eyes. A few minutes ago he'd foreseen, almost as if it was happening, a similar fate for *Lanyard*: he'd seen her and *Nicator* interlocked after they'd collided, lying stopped with *Lanyard*'s bow locked in the other's quarter; and the shells locating their helpless target, raining down. And Margaret, back there in Edinburgh, Margaret, for whom he needed now to live.

He shook his head, to clear away the imagery. It hadn't happened, had it? He remembered a thing he'd had to memorise at school: *The coward dies a thousand deaths, the brave man dies but one*. He knew what it meant, now.

Nick climbed off the ladder into the bridge; Hastings had sent Blewitt to him with the captain's message. Nick nodded to Garret, as the leading signalman made way for him; 'All right, are we?' Garret, he thought, looked out of sorts. Mortimer half-turned his head: 'Everard. Come here.' Hastings reported, with binoculars at his eyes, 'I believe the battle cruisers have gone round sixteen points, sir.' Mortimer, forgetting Nick, used his own glasses to check this statement. He agreed. 'But the Queen Elizabeths haven't gone about.'

'No, not yet, sir.' Hastings pointed, '*Nicator*'s mean course seems to be a point or two to starboard, though, sir.'

'Well, keep astern of her, of course!'

Lowering his glasses, Mortimer turned to Nick.

That blown-out corner of the bridge: Nick stared at it, seeing the canvas screen and the splinter-mattress ripped and charred black at the edges, and the paintwork blackened; but in the distortions of the steel deck there was a dark, glistening spillage. Like oil – but he knew it wasn't oil. He could smell it, and see its reddish tinge. A sweet, sickly smell, mixed with the stench of burning and explosive. Nick felt dazed; there was no sign of Johnson, or . . . He shook his head, and he was staring at that mess again when Mortimer told him evenly, 'Lieutenants Johnson and Reynolds have been killed, Everard.'

Nick had heard it, but there was a sense of unreality.

'Sub.' He met Mortimer's eyes. Mortimer asked him, quite pleasantly, 'Be a good fellow. Try to listen to what I'm telling you?'

'I'm sorry, sir.'

It was bewildering. Johnson, dead . . .

Johnson who'd astonished him this morning, in the darkness of the four to eight am watch on the bridge; first by becoming chatty and friendly, and then by launching what had amounted to a thunderbolt when the subject had turned to David. Nick's mind went over it all now. He'd said that David had done as well as he had in the Service – and at Osborne and Dartmouth – because he had some sort of terror of not doing well, so he'd always swotted, 'pushed himself' . . .

'Don't get on with him, do you?'

'No. But—'

'I guessed not. Nobody does, really.'

Nick had stared at him through the pre-dawn gloom. He'd never spoken on any sort of personal level to any of David's friends or term-mates. One had learnt in one's first weeks at Osborne that one did not consort with one's seniors, except on formal terms.

Johnson murmured, 'Sort of – edgy, isn't he? You say something quite harmless to him, and as often as not he thinks you're getting at him or criticising. I've always felt a bit sorry for him, really.'

92

Nick shook his head. 'And I've always thought it was just me that didn't get on with him!'

'I'll tell you what I expected you to be like. Like your brother – in other words difficult – and on top of that ignorant and useless.' Johnson smiled. 'Frankly, it's quite a relief that you're fairly normal.'

Meaning, Nick had wondered, that he thought David was abnormal?

Well, he was. But not in any way that Johnson knew.

He came back to the present with a jolt. Mortimer, staring at him, was looking considerably less than patient. Nick shook his head, as if to clear it; it was Johnson who was dead, not David.

'I'm sorry, sir.'

Mortimer told him, 'Sub-Lieutenant Hastings becomes my second-in-command. You'll assume the duties of gunnery control officer. Understood?'

'Yes, sir.'

'Now tell me what's been happening aft.'

'Excuse me, sir,' Hastings interrupted. '*Nicator*'s ceased zigzagging.'

'Then do the same, for God's sake!' Mortimer's voice had been sharp, surprised. He closed his eyes for a second, opened them, and repeated more quietly, almost apologetically, 'Do what she does, Hastings.'

'Aye aye, sir.'

'Now then, Everard.'

Nick told him: the stern gun and mounting blown overboard, that gun's crew were wiped out, three of the ammunition-supply party killed with them – probably by a shell hitting projectiles standing loose behind the gun. He added that one torpedoman had been very badly wounded at the same time.

'Why didn't you report this earlier?'

'Wasn't possible, sir. The voicepipes to the guns have been shot away, and Mr Pilkington wanted to keep his voicepipe clear for torpedo-control purposes, and I couldn't leave the other gun when we were still in action.' Mortimer turned, stared towards the smoke and grey shapes which could only be the Fifth Battle Squadron. He looked back at Nick. 'Where were you when it happened?'

'In the wardroom, sir.'

Mortimer started as violently as if he'd been kicked. Hastings glanced round and Nick caught a look of astonishment before the pock-marked face turned away again. Garret and Blewitt exchanged glances which were extraordinarily devoid of expression. Mortimer said grimly, 'Will you explain that?'

'Ammunition had stopped coming up, sir. Both guns were in action and something had to be done. I went down, put things right, and—'

'What had been wrong?'

'The ladder had carried away, sir, and the two hands in there are young stokers, new to the job, I think. They were – well, confused. I had them push the table under the hatch and forget the ladder. So it only took – well, a second or two, and I was on my way back up when—'

'I see.' Mortimer turned away. Nick resented, still, the implication which had lain behind the question, behind the way they'd all looked so shocked. Then he thought of David, and Johnson's saying, 'He thinks everyone's against him.' Their surprise had been perfectly normal; there was nothing whatsoever to resent. Mortimer added, with his eyes on the smoky mass of Beatty's battle cruisers and the Fifth Battle Squadron as they passed each other on opposite courses, 'Two men of the for'ard four-inch's crew were hit. The first lieutenant replaced them and sent them aft to the surgeon, but you'd better check the replacements know their jobs. Also, I want to know how much ammunition we've used and how much is left. Have gunlayers clean guns and refill racks. Get flexible hose from engine-room stores and rig it in place of the damaged voicepipes. And tell Surgeon Lieutenant Samuels I'd like a report from him as soon as possible.'

'Aye aye, sir.'

'Tell Mr Pilkington I'm waiting for a report from him too. D'you know how many torpedoes we have left?'

'One, sir.'

'Only one?'

'Two were fired at the battle cruisers, sir, and Mr Pilkington managed to get one away at the head of the battleship line during our final turn away.'

'Firing to port? Weren't the tubes trained starboard?'

'We got them round in time, sir.'

'We?'

Nick hadn't meant to say that. He corrected it, 'Mr Pilkington did, sir.'

Mortimer looked pleased. 'One more thing, Sub. The ensign

seems to've been shot away, aft there. Have the staff struck, and re-hoist it.'

'Aye aye, sir.'

'And see those – stokers, did you say? See they don't gum up the works next time we're in action.'

'They won't, sir.'

As he turned away, Nick found Garret and the steward watching him; they looked away. He wondered what they were thinking. Perhaps his own thought, which was when would that 'next time' be?

As it happened, he, Nick Everard, had got the tubes round. He'd seen what was happening and roused the crabby little gunner to it, and they'd been in time to get one fish on its way. Some time later Pilkington, who'd never taken his beady eyes off the enemy battle line, had seen what he'd thought might be a hit.

Pilkington could tell Mortimer, if he wanted to. The tubes were his affair. Nick began to check over in his mind, as he pushed past Garret to the ladder, the various things he had to see to. What had been done with the bodies, anyway?

'Enemy battleships have opened fire with their main armament, sir!'

Hastings had seen it, as he'd swept round to the quarter with his binoculars and seen the flashes of gunfire from the leading German ships; the head of Scheer's battle line had now crossed *Lanyard*'s stern from her port quarter to starboard. Mortimer swung round, raising his glasses to take a look, and at the same moment they all heard the whistling roar of high-calibre shells passing overhead towards the German fleet.

Hastings observed, 'Fifth Battle Squadron's engaging 'em.'

Garret thought, *Right over our bloody heads!*

CHAPTER 6

'At 4.19 a new squadron consisting of four or five ships of the
Q.E. class . . . appeared from a north-westerly direction, and
took part in the action with opening range of about 21,000
yards . . . The new opponent fired with remarkable rapidity
and accuracy.'

Admiral Scheer's official Despatch

The guns of the Fifth Battle Squadron fell silent as the battle
cruisers rushed towards them. In half a minute Beatty's ships
would be passing between these battleships and the enemy. Hugh
Everard moved out to the port wing of his bridge as the gap
between the squadrons closed at roughly fifty sea miles per hour.
Lion, with foam streaming from her enormous bow and black
smoke pouring from all three funnels rushed by *now* . . . too fast
for any detailed assessment of what Hipper's guns had done to her;
but certainly her 'X' turret was out of action – it was trained to the
disengaged side with the guns tilted up to maximum elevation –
and the smoke of an internal fire was pouring from her after
superstructure, while great black splashes of charred paintwork
showed here and there on her port side.

Now a string of flags broke at her port yardarm, close enough to
read easily with the naked eye: *Fifth Battle Squadron alter course in
succession sixteen points to starboard.*

Rathbone's yellowish face showed concern as Hugh came back
to him at the binnacle.

'A *red* turn, sir?'

Hugh had been considering exactly that point. A turn in succession, each ship following her next ahead and turning on virtually
the same spot, and the German gunnery officers knowing, once
Barham had led round, that each of her squadron would be

96

paddling round after her like tame ducks . . . well, *sitting* ducks!

The Huns would make a meal of it. Hugh didn't answer Rathbone, or look at him. What could he have said – *Our Admiral's an idiot?*

A 'blue' turn, all ships turning at once and ending on a reversed course in reverse order, would have been far better in these circumstances; and that signal should in any case have been hauled down by this time. It couldn't be acted on while it was still flying, and even if the turn was started now, this second, the interval needed for reversing the course of a squadron of battleships would mean there'd be a gap of several miles between this squadron and Beatty's. It wasn't just the time it took to turn, but the loss of speed involved in it: every second's delay now was increasing that ultimate distance apart. German shells were falling into the sea ahead and short, and those were salvoes from Scheer's battleships, from guns that had never before been fired in anger. Hugh had his glasses trained on the enemy as *Nile*, rearmost of the squadron, drew clear of the last of Beatty's smoke. Just as he was wondering why Brook hadn't yet opened fire, *Nile* shuddered from the concussion of her first salvo at the High Seas Fleet.

'Executive signal, red sixteen points, sir!'

About time . . . Hugh stepped up on to the central platform, and took over again from Rathbone.

'Shift down to the conning-tower, Pilot. Then you can take over when I call down.'

'Aye aye, sir.'

The conning-tower, lower down, was the action control position. You could only see out through a periscope and through slits in the protective armour, but it would be senseless to stay up here, exposed, when things warmed up. Hugh told his second-in-command, 'You'd as well go down too, Tom. It's likely to get fairly brisk, presently.'

Crick eyed Scheer's distant battleships – mile upon mile of them, pouring northwards. He enquired, 'And you, sir?' As calm, Hugh noticed, as a parson at evensong. He nodded. 'I shan't be long.'

Ahead, shells pock-marked the sea round *Barham* as she swung away to starboard. One hit her, when she was halfway through her turn; starboard side for'ard, that sickeningly *pretty* orange glow, black smoke rising to enfold it like foliage around a flower; then the flame was disappearing, smothered, and the smoke dissipating astern. If only Beatty had signalled, 'Follow me' or 'Alter course to

97

north', Evan-Thomas could have exercised his own judgement on the method and the timing. His flag – white, with the red St George's cross and the two red balls in the cantons next to the halyard – stood out as stiffly as a weather-vane as *Barham* – hit again – steadied on the new course. *Valiant* was going round now, through a barrage of falling shell; it was going to be worse for each ship in turn, worst of all for *Nile*, the last. *Warspite*'s helm had gone over and she was turning into a forest of shell-spouts, a curtain of high-explosive shrieking down, raising the sea in fountains. She'd been hit for'ard, two hits together and both on her foc'sl; the Hun salvoes came closely spaced, so if you got hit at all the chance was you'd get hit hard. Their gunners were firing fast, seeing this opportunity and loth to let it go, but *Malaya* was showing good sense, turning half a cable's length before she should have. If she'd held on, she'd have run into a real plastering. You could see now exactly what she'd managed to avoid, the sea leaping, alive with falling shell just off her bow as she hauled round. As it was, she'd suffered; as he bent to the voicepipe he'd seen the sudden gush of smoke. He called down, 'Starboard ten!'

'Starboard ten, sir! Ten of starboard helm on, sir!'

A diversion to port. An impromptu zigzag to throw their range out before *Nile* became the next Aunt Sally.

'Midships!'

'Midships Helm's amidships, sir.'

He watched *Malaya*'s turn. You had to do it right, when it was a 30,000-ton battleship you were handling, mistakes couldn't be corrected easily or quickly. He told himself, judging it by eye while fresh salvoes lacerated the sea on *Malaya*'s starboard quarter, *now* . . .

'Port fifteen!'

'Port fifteen, sir!'

Round she goes . . . The gunners over there in Scheer's battle-ships, with their sharp eyes on *Malaya* until about this moment, might not have noticed *Nile*'s small excursion out to port. If they hadn't, their shots as she went round now would – hopefully – be 'overs' . . .

Hearing them tearing the air like ripping calico as they passed overhead, a degree of satisfaction helped him resist the urge to duck.

'Ease to five!'

'Ease to five, sir!'

By prolonging the turn, he'd slide his ship back into line astern of *Malaya* . . . Smoke drifting in streaks and patches at masthead height might be confusing, he hoped, to Scheer's spotting officers. Another salvo crackled over, and spouts rose like the fingers of a dirty hand poked up through the surface forty yards to port.

'Midships!'

'Midships, sir. Wheel's—'

'Meet her!'

Beatty's ships were seven or eight thousand yards ahead, sparking with gun flashes as they continued to engage the German battle cruisers. Hipper had altered course, reversing it to accompany Beatty northwards and at the same time placing himself ahead of Scheer's battle squadrons. There was a gap of six miles between the two German forces: and neither could have any idea yet that Jellicoe was coming south like Nemesis.

A flag-hoist was climbing to *Barham*'s yard, curving on an arc of halyard in the wind's force and straightening as it was hauled taut. Peppard, the chief yeoman, reported that it was a distribution of fire signal. He used the manual to get its meaning: that *Barham* and *Valiant* were to engage Hipper's battle cruisers while the others took on Scheer's battleships.

Hugh called down to the conning-tower, 'Pilot?'

Rathbone answered. Hugh told him, 'Take over. I'll be with you shortly.'

'Aye aye, sir.'

'Quartermaster, obey your voicepipe from the conning-tower, now.'

'Aye aye, sir!'

He used the telephone to talk to his gunnery lieutenant in the control top.

'Brook, concentrate all your fire on the quarter, second battleship in the line. If you have to shift from him take the third.'

'Aye aye, sir.'

'Your shooting's looked good, so far. Keep it up, Brook.'

'I do believe we've scored a few, sir.'

'Score some more, a lot more.' He hung up the navy-phone. Now Beatty's four surviving battle cruisers, plus the two leading ships of this squadron, would be engaging Hipper's five ships – leaving *Nile, Warspite* and *Malaya* with Scheer's leading division of nine or ten dreadnoughts to hold off . . .

He ought, he knew, to go down to the protection of the conning-tower; and he would, in a moment. He wanted to see first what sort of practice Brook might make against those looming, pursuing battleships. He went out into the starboard wing of the bridge – it seemed particularly spacious, with only himself and the chief yeoman sharing it – and trained his binoculars on the leading ships just as *Nile*'s four turrets roared and smoked; he began to count, reckoning on a time-of-flight of something like twenty-five or thirty seconds. To his left, *Malaya* sent off a salvo, and the concussion of it with her guns firing as it were past one's ear was indescribably powerful. It wasn't only noise that split your head; it was like being hit on that ear with a sandbag at the same time. He put his hand to it, and found the plug of cotton-wool still in place; he'd thought it might have been blown into the eardrum. Focusing on the German battleships, it seemed to him that the range had closed somewhat. If it had, either Scheer's ships had more speed than was officially credited to them, or their course and this squadron's were converging . . . Twenty-six, twenty-seven – *there*! Brook's salvo spouted between the first and second ships. So there was no clue to range, you had to get the line right before you could usefully correct up or down. The guns fired again, *Warspite*'s did too, while at the same moment *Malaya*'s salvo fell, short and in line with the leading ship. Hugh decided to stay where he was for just one more salvo; he wanted to see *Nile* straddle her target, and from the tower his view would be so restricted, the tower itself so crowded. Still watching the line of Scheer's battleships, he was thinking of that shortening range: if he was right and it *was* shortening. And looking harder, taking advantage of an improving light as the mist in that quarter thinned, he saw that Scheer was indeed converging; this squadron was following Beatty on a course of about north, while those inimical grey shapes with white flecks at their stems and gun-flashes rippling constantly up and down the steadily oncoming line, must have been steering something more like north-west-by-north.

It would make sense from Scheer's point of view. His ships didn't have the guns to shoot effectively at the long ranges with which these QEs could cope. Just as it would have been making the best use of the British advantage in long-range gunnery to have kept the enemy at arm's length.

Well, you couldn't sheer off westward when the object was to lead the Germans north, into Jellicoe's embrace.

Scheer's dreadnoughts were getting the range. In the last minute two salvoes had fallen close but short, and one had gone over. Hugh watched *Nile*'s – he thought it must be hers – straddle the second ship in Scheer's line; two spouts went up short, one only showed its top beyond her quarterdeck, and the fourth struck a spark and then a flare on her stern turret. *Nile*'s guns roared again – that *must* have been her effort – and again within half a minute; Brook was firing double salvoes now he had the range. *Warspite* and *Malaya* were also keeping up the pressure, each getting a salvo into the air at about one-minute intervals. Now two or three German salvoes had gone over, and out of the corner of his eye Hugh saw a burst and blossom of flame on *Malaya*'s stern and another between her funnels. Lowering his glasses he swivelled round to look at her and saw that her after superstructure had been hit. Smoke was pouring out of both sides – from the entry-hole, probably, and another the shell had made when it exploded.

He was feeling sorry for *Malaya* when a lone shell came whirring like a bluebottle and burst on *Nile*'s foc's'l.

It didn't penetrate. It had landed close to the port cable-holder and burst against the armoured deck. All ships were firing fast now and there were practically no intervals between the falls of German salvoes; by the time one lot of spouts had collapsed back into the torn sea, another lot were leaping in their places. And hits were being scored; with any luck the Germans were being walloped too, but at this end one couldn't have denied it was becoming reasonably uncomfortable. Hugh decided that the time for loitering in such an exposed position was past: he'd go down now.

'Peppard – carry on down on the conning-tower.'

Chief Petty Officer Peppard looked surprised. 'All the same to you, sir, I'd as soon—'

'That was not an invitation, Chief Yeoman.'

'Aye aye, sir.'

With an entire division of battleships letting rip at one squadron – and probably concentrating, at that, on *Nile* and *Malaya* who were their nearest targets – one could hardly expect to emerge unscathed. He picked up a different navyphone and at the same time, glancing round, saw Peppard hesitating at the top of the port ladder, looking back at him. Then the chief yeoman started down. At the same moment a sailor's cap rose into view on the other side. Hugh stared at it exasperatedly: Bates . . .

His coxswain was carrying a tray.

'Torpedo control tower!'

'Torpedo Lieutenant, please.' That had been the midshipman who worked the plotter for Knox-Wilson.

'Lieutenant (T) here, sir.'

'Knox-Wilson, are you ranging on the quarter?'

'Yes, sir. Down to sixteen thousand, closing quite fast.'

'We're in a good position on their bow to try a long shot. This visibility's none too reliable, so don't wait for ever.'

'No, sir. But—'

'But?'

'Starboard for'ard tube's stuck, sir. They can't shift the bar.'

'Use the starboard after tube, then. And keep 'em working to clear the other.'

'Aye aye, sir.'

Knox-Wilson would have wanted to clear his for'ard tube for action before he took a long-range chance, so as to make sure of having one of the two starboard tubes functioning in case a much surer chance cropped up. But the enemy was there; you couldn't always play safe, you had to take your chances. Hugh told Knox-Wilson, 'Send Mr Askell to see what they're up to down there.' He hung up the navyphone. The action was getting hotter all the time: six to eight salvoes a minute were dropping round them. He'd felt a hit aft and seen another for'ard, and *Malaya* had been hit three times in succession, all amidships. But all guns still fired, which was not the case with the enemy. The fire from the battle cruisers had been considerably reduced – as a result, one imagined, of *Barham*'s and *Valiant*'s influence. Looking that way, he couldn't see Hipper's ships now: they'd vanished, swallowed in the mist. It freed the two leading Queen Elizabeths to join the three astern of them in this rather uneven fight with Scheer. But mist – falling visibility – Hugh murmured in his mind, *Please, God, don't let it get worse!* Just when Jellicoe should be on the point of joining in, if Scheer at just that moment should be presented with a mist to run away and hide in . . . Whose side would the Almighty seem to be on, if *that* happened?

Bates said, behind him, 'Cup o' coffee, sir. Thought you was likely gettin' a bit—'

Hugh whipped round. 'For God's sake, man, get below.'

'Aye aye, sir.' Unruffled, cheerful. 'Leave your coffee 'ere, sir, shall I?'

Nile trembled to a double explosion aft.

'I could leave it 'ere, sir, or—'

'Yes.' Hugh made himself speak levelly: his ship's guns crashed out another salvo, and Bates's hands, he noticed, holding the tray with the coffee on it, were completely steady. 'Yes, thank you, Bates. Leave it here.'

He remembered – perhaps inconsequentially – as he turned for'ard again, that Bates couldn't swim. A salvo screeched over-head. He didn't see it fall, because he'd glanced round to make sure his coxswain had left the bridge, almost dreading, as he turned his head, that he'd find those brown monkey-eyes still watching him.

The coffee was there, steaming on the ledge below the starboard Battenberg. Bates had gone below.

This patchy mist: Jellicoe wouldn't pursue an enemy at night or in bad visibility. He'd put this to the Admiralty, and their Lord-ships had approved the principle that the Grand Fleet must not be put at risk in circumstances where pure chance might play too great a part. The Germans had equipped their cruisers for mine-laying, they could lay a field of mines, unseen, ahead of a pursuing fleet, actually during the course of battle. And the newer destroyers with their new long-range, high-speed torpedoes were an unknown quantity. Britain's survival depended on the continued existence of her fleet; the way to handle it was not to handle it the way the Germans would like it handled, in conditions which gave advan-tages to the techniques of sneak-attack.

Barham was altering course to port, as Beatty had at that same point. She seemed to have a fire amidships, but it could be just her boats that were being incinerated. *Valiant*, following her in the two-point turn, had blocked off his quick view of her. *Warspite* had taken a lot of hits, and *Malaya* was suffering again as she put her helm over. *Nile* was surrounded with shell-splashes. Hugh felt her shudder, heard the explosion and the deep clang of metal striking aft: looking back there he saw a seepage of smoke drifting down-wind from her quarter but no evidence of damage. A navyphone buzzed harshly, and he crossed over to it, waiting for the guns to fire before he answered.

'Bridge. Captain.'

'Crick here, sir. Shouldn't you be coming down, sir?'

'I'm on my way. Tom, we had a shell hit us aft, just then. It might have been below the waterline.'

'I'll find out, sir.'

Against twice their own number of ships, the Queen Elizabeths were hitting at least as often as they were being hit themselves.

Beatty had been out of the action for the last twenty or thirty minutes; with Hipper's ships hidden in the mist, there'd been nothing for his guns to shoot at. No doubt he'd have been using the respite well, getting fires under control and repairing damage. Hugh focused his glasses on the battle cruisers and saw they'd just altered to starboard again, steering north, by the looks of it. To head off Hipper, or perhaps just to get back in sight of him. A salvo plunged just short, its tall spouts lashing a black salt rain across *Nile*'s forepart; then came two explosions in quick succession down near S1 and S2 casemates. He realised he'd forgotten that intention of going down to the tower.

'Captain, sir!'

Crick, at the top of the ladder, had a look of disquiet on his normally unruffled features.

'It must have been a near-miss aft, sir, the one you mentioned. It seems it—' He had to shout, as a salvo crashed overhead and raised spouts thirty yards from *Nile*'s side – 'didn't hurt us, sir!' That close, on the disengaged side and with the flat trajectory of ships' guns, those shells must have passed between her masts. Hugh hadn't looked out to port much in the last ten minutes, but he did so now, and paused to watch destroyers streaming up on the squadron's beam and bow. This must be the flotilla which had been across and made a torpedo attack on the enemy battle cruisers, an hour or so ago. And the nearest boat seemed to have lost her stern gun, so that her oddly levelled afterpart gave her the look of an attenuated tug. Training his glasses on her, he saw the rips and scars in her quarterdeck. She was one of the half-dozen L-class boats that had only two funnels instead of three; and it looked, from the lump which had been shot out of her for'ard funnel, as though she'd done her best to get down to one.

Crick, judging his moment for it between shell-bursts and gun-fire, cleared his throat loudly. Hugh glanced round at him, and nodded.

'Yes, Tom. You're right.' He turned aft and went down the steps to the lower end of the bridge. Five forty-five now. On his way down to the next level of the superstructure, he thought that it would be as well for Jellicoe to get here soon. Otherwise he wouldn't have enough hours of daylight left in which to do the job for which his Grand Fleet had been built and trained . . . He was two levels down with one more to go when he heard the crash, felt the shock and the reverberation of an explosion somewhere

104

close below the bridge; then a sound like hail lashing a tin roof –
splinters from that shell-burst, raking the compass platform. He
didn't bother to look round at Crick, who'd be wearing his told-
you-so expression.

Bantry pitched rhythmically to the low swell as she followed astern
of *Warrior* and the First Cruiser Squadron's flagship, *Defence*. A
grey, faintly lumpy sea, and greyish, rather hazy light with clearer
patches here and there. The cruiser screen had fallen back closer to
the battle fleet on account of the deteriorating visibility. *Bantry* was
less than five miles ahead of the fleet's starboard column, and
looking back over her port quarter David could see quite clearly
that concentrated mass of armoured and destructive power, as
Jellicoe held on grimly south-eastward at the speed of his slowest
dreadnought.

His ships were still in their cruising disposition of six columns.
Soon – if they were to come into contact with the enemy, which
David was convinced they would not – that solid phalanx of ships
would have to be re-formed into a single line ahead, which was the
only way a fleet could bring all its guns to bear. But in order to
deploy in the way which would give him the most advantage when
he met the enemy, Jellicoe needed the one thing he wasn't getting:
information.

There'd been a smattering of it, which *Bantry*'s W/T operators
had picked up. It amounted to only the facts that Scheer's as well as
Hipper's ships were coming north, and that the battle cruisers and
the Fifth Battle Squadron and the light forces with them had been
heavily engaged.

Bantry ploughed on south-eastward behind the other two. Four
miles on the starboard beam was *Duke of Edinburgh*, and four or
five beyond her, *Black Prince*. If anyone was going to sight the
enemy or establish contact with Beatty's cruiser screen as he came
northwards, it would be *Black Prince*. But for half an hour now,
there'd been no reports at all. Nothing. All the earlier information,
sketchy and even conflicting as it had been, had been put on the
chart – by David – and he'd set Midshipman Porter, his 'tanky', to
work producing a large-scale plot of it. It still made very little
sense.

Not, David thought, that it mattered. There'd be no action, for
the Grand Fleet. It was too late now; he felt sure of it.

Wilmott came forward and stopped beside Nobby Clark. He

said irritably, 'C-in-C must be beside himself. Why don't they tell him what they can see, for heaven's sake?'

Clark shrugged agreement. David was at the binnacle, conning the ship while Wilmott drifted about the bridge like a cat on hot bricks and paid visits to the chartroom and signals office. *Bantry* had been at action stations for nearly four hours now, and the only intelligible enemy reports had come from Commodore Good-enough in the light cruiser *Southampton*. Goodenough must have been almost alongside Scheer's battleships, at one point, to have sent back as much information as he had!

But in the jumble of reports from this source and that, positions and bearings and reported courses conflicted – confused, more than informed. Beatty, for instance, had told Jellicoe nothing that could be of any real use to him . . . But then, Beatty would be in the thick of it – as he always was, which made one wonder about Nick; might he have been in the thick of it too?

A few minutes ago Jellicoe had betrayed his impatience by signalling his own position to Beatty; and long ago he'd sent Hood away with his three battle cruisers to join Beatty and support him. There'd been no word of Hood since then – he might as well have vanished into thin air. Or – David thought, taking a look round the horizon – thickening air. The light was getting very patchy indeed. Drifting mist kept changing things: one minute it was clear in one direction and hazy in another, and next time you looked the conditions might be reversed. Visibility might drop to four or five miles, or open out to twelve. It wouldn't be the first time the North Sea's unpredictability had helped Germans out of the way of British guns. He looked astern again. As well as this squadron of armoured cruisers, and Rear-Admiral Heath's Second Squadron, with which *Bantry* had sailed from Scapa, there were ten light cruisers and thirty-nine destroyers in Jellicoe's inner screen. One could imagine him, in the centre of that mass of steel, the fleet he'd created, trained, prepared, pacing his bridge, cloaking anxiety behind a mask of imperturbability, silence and *sangfroid*, and knowing that with an armada of this size whichever of the methods of deployment he chose, it would from the moment that he ordered it become irreversible, unstoppable. It had to be not a gambler's throw, but a tactician's masterstroke.

Or if he acted on incomplete or wrong information, a tactician's blunder.

At four fifty-one – getting on for an hour ago – he'd wirelessed four words to the Admiralty: *Fleet action is imminent*. That pre-arranged message would have resulted by now in an alert being flashed to dockyards, tugs, hospitals, all the emergency services which large-scale damage and casualties would call for.

Action imminent. They'd be saying it excitedly even in London now, let alone on this cruiser's bridge; but David couldn't believe in it; his instincts denied it, he couldn't feel it as something that could ever happen.

Not to himself. If anything happened to David Everard – it wouldn't, but just imagining it, supposing – and with one's father in France, with the big push intended to relieve the pressure on Verdun expected any day now . . . Even a brigadier couldn't last for ever, you'd only to glance at the daily Roll of Honour in *The Times*. Just thinking about what could, but wouldn't, happen – well, young Nick would inherit the title, Mullbergh, everything!

The idea of that was simply – grotesque . . . One could only dismiss it, put it out of mind and replace it with an entirely contrary thought – that Nick, having through Hugh Everard's influence got himself to a destroyer, might well get his come-uppance. The torpedo craft did tend to get knocked about, and it was a fact that Nick was behind steel plating one-eighth of an inch thick, instead of the twelve-inch armour belt worn by the battleship he'd left. Nick's destroyer might well be in action at this moment. It was a tantalising thought!

'*Duke of Edinburgh* flashing, sir!'

From four miles to the south a rapid series of dots and dashes cut through the haze. In fact the visibility down there looked better, at the moment.

'W/T signal, sir.' It was a leading signalman who'd come pelting up from the office. 'To C-in-C from *Black Prince*, sir.' Commander Clark took the clip-board and passed it straight to Wilmott – who scanned it, raised his thick eyebrows and told Clark, '*Black Prince* is in contact with *Falmouth*, in Beatty's screen.' He let the signalman take the board out of his hand. Narrow-eyed, beard jutting very much like a wire-haired terrier's, he was watching that distant, flashing light. He murmured, 'We'll be at 'em soon.'

A snapshot of Nick flashed suddenly in David's memory of Nick staring at him; an accusing, condemning stare, not only judgement but dislike, contempt even, in his steady scrutiny. Insufferable little – pig! what did he know about—

'Pilot!'

107

Snapping out of nightmare: 'Sir?'

'What's the—'

Wilmott had checked, with his question unasked. Every head in the bridge had jerked round, faces turning to the sound that had come rumbling on the south-east wind. The sound of heavy guns.

It was so loud that it was surprising it hadn't been audible before. A voice squawked distantly, metallically, 'Bridge!' It was the voicepipe from the fore top, and Commander Clark was nearest to it. He bent his thickset body jerkily, like a tubby marionette, and barked, 'Bridge!'

'Ships in action on the starboard bow, sir! Looks like battle cruisers and cruisers!'

Another voicepipe call: from the wireless office, this time, and Porter took it.

'Commander-in-Chief to Admiral Beatty, sir: *Where is the enemy battle fleet?*'

Wilmott muttered something angrily into his beard. *Defence* was flashing a signal to *Iron Duke*, reporting ships in action south-south-west, course north-east. Wilmott began a conversation over the navyphone to Johnny West, the gunnery lieutenant, in the control top, asking him what he could see, and where, and what it was doing; and that whole southern sector of the horizon was suddenly full of ships and the flashes of their guns. Petty Officer Sturgis, the yeoman, reported to Wilmott, 'C-in-C to SO, BCF by W/T sir – *Where is the enemy battle fleet?*'

'We've already had that one, Yeoman.'

'No, sir.' Sturgis looked hurt. 'He's asked it again, sir. Repetition, sir.'

Bedlam increasing, as reports flowed in . . .

Wilmott had moved up close to the binnacle; he was staring ahead at *Warrior* and *Defence*. He extended his left arm with the hand open, and said to David without looking at him, 'Hand me my glasses, Pilot.' David unslung them from the brass cylinder that enclosed the flinder's bar, and placed them in the outstretched hand. Midshipman Porter, straightening from the fore top's voicepipe reported, 'Fore top can see shells falling close to the light cruisers, sir, but they can't see where they're coming from.' They were referring, presumably, to light cruisers in Beatty's screen.

David felt quite calm – not so much disinterested as detached, waiting for the visibility to clamp down. He was still sure it would.

108

Wilmott snapped suddenly, with the binoculars still at his eyes, 'Revolutions for twenty-three knots, Pilot!'

'Searchlight signalling starboard, sir!'

It was on the bow; a distant, winking light . . . David called down for maximum revs, full speed. And now he saw why Wilmott had ordered it. *Defence* and *Warrior* had surged forward, pushing out ahead, and from out to starboard *Duke of Edinburgh* and *Black Prince* were converging to join up with them. Sir Robert Arbuthnot was gathering his squadron together and speeding to close the enemy, leaving the battle fleet astern. South-eastward at full speed, towards the sound and flashes of the guns. There was an impression suddenly of things speeding up, a sense of urgency and impending action developing; David resisted it, feeling that it was only a kind of hysteria in which one should not allow oneself to become involved. The yeoman was reporting to Wilmott with a touch of excitement in his voice that the searchlight flashing from the south was Beatty's, *Lion*'s, and that the message was one answering that repeated question about the enemy battle fleet. Beatty was telling his commander-in-chief, *Have sighted enemy battle fleet bearing south-south-west*.

So now Jellicoe knew the direction of his enemy, even though he'd no information at all about distance, course or speed. And *Bantry* was picking up speed now, her steel trembling as she pressed forward, her bow rising and falling as it cut through the combined wakes of the other cruisers.

Arbuthnot, David guessed, must be watching the falling visibility and trying to hurry his squadron into action. One had not foreseen this, but had thought rather in terms of the cruisers remaining in company with the battle fleet.

'All right, Pilot,' Wilmott nodded, 'I'll take her.'

'Sir.'

Turning away and looking astern towards the broad front of the battle fleet as they began to draw away from it, he saw specks of colour sliding up to the flagship's yardarm. The yeoman had seen it too, and he whipped up his telescope. David, using binoculars, identified the blue-and-white stripes of the equal-speed pendant above the quartered black, red, blue and yellow of flag C and the red St Andrew's cross of flag L. The yeoman confirmed his accuracy.

'Equal-speed, Charlie, London, sir . . . Battle fleet deploying on—' he hesitated, staring astern still – 'on the port column, sir!'

Twenty-four dreadnought battleships were about to form into a single fighting line. Deploying on the port column meant that the leading ships of the six columns would all turn simultaneously ninety degrees to port; each division would follow its leader round, until the six divisions had thus fallen into line-ahead. Finally, the battleships would file round to starboard, a follow-my-leader turn which would bring the whole line back on to their course towards the enemy. It meant that Scheer, coming north-eastward, would find several miles of dreadnoughts across his intended line of advance: Jellicoe would have 'crossed Scheer's T', and the Grand Fleet's massed broadsides would be able to hammer Scheer's leading division into scrap-iron before more than a few German guns could be brought to bear. And Jellicoe would have the light-gauge; the westering sun would throw the German line into sharp relief while the British battleships remained invisible in the mist!

The light had not failed, after all. It was patchy, but Jellicoe had seen how he could take advantage of it. David was beginning to realise that his instincts had tricked him. Meanwhile, he had nothing to do except stand ready in case Wilmott wanted him to take over at the binnacle again.

A navyphone buzzed and flashed; he snatched it up, forestalling the commander, who'd started towards it.

'Bridge.'

It was Johnny West, calling from the control top again. David turned his eyes up towards that swaying, box-like construction on the foremast as he listened to West telling him, 'Our own light cruisers bearing south, course north-east, and the battle cruisers are in sight astern of them, same course, and in action. They're under fire from an enemy I can't see. Look as if they're going to pass ahead of us.'

David passed the message verbatim to Wilmott. Wilmott glanced at his second-in-command.

'It's going to be like a bloody circus ring, in a minute.'

David thought about it; Beatty, storming up from the south, steering north-east now to head-off Hipper's battle cruisers and force him round ahead of the deploying battle fleet. It was rather spectacular, really; Beatty was doing his job perfectly, he'd not only led the Germans up to Jellicoe but now he'd be screening the sight of Jellicoe from them until the very last moment, and Wilmott's meaning was clear: in a few minutes there'd be something like a hundred ships all rushing in different directions as

Beatty with his screening cruisers and destroyers ahead and around him raced across the front of the battle fleet.

With binoculars, you could even see it all developing from the bridge now. The light cruisers, and behind them the dark mass of the bigger ships. Shells falling among them, and more than anywhere round the battle cruisers. No sign of where they came from; just that great spread of ships all racing north-eastward, bow-waves flaring, guns flashing. They must have an enemy in sight. And *Defence* was under helm, swinging to port, with flags rushing to her yardarm.

'*Defence* to squadron, sir: *Engage enemy starboard!*'

'Tell West to open fire when he has a target.'

'Aye aye, sir.' David passed the order. *Warrior* was going round astern of the flagship. Wilmott, stooped awkwardly at the binnacle, watching *Warrior*'s piled wake gleaming as it flowed curving away behind her, kept his face low beside the voicepipe's copper rim, waiting for the exact moment to put the helm over; crouched like that, he looked to David as if he was about to defecate.

There'd hardly been time to think about how wrong he'd been. It was only about six o'clock, there were several hours of daylight left, and *Bantry* would shortly be in action.

'Starboard fifteen!'

Swinging over . . .

'Ease to five!'

'Ease to five, sir . . . Five o' starboard helm on, sir!'

The two ships ahead opened fire. Smoke burgeoned out of them to starboard, then the sharp percussions cracked astern with the stink of cordite. David put his glasses to his eyes – German cruisers. He saw three, and one other which seemed to be stopped. Everything was greyish, wrapped-up in mist. It came clear for a moment, then hazed-up again. He found himself wishing that the visibility would hold up, give Jellicoe time to get to grips with Scheer. He heard a fire-gong ring, and before the clang had lost its echo *Bantry*'s nine-inch guns flung out their first salvo.

'Midships!'

'Midships, sir—'

'Meet her, and follow the next-ahead!'

'Aye aye, sir!'

It was the nearest of the enemy ships that was lying stopped. She must have been damaged – by a destroyer's torpedo, perhaps – but her ensign was still flying. Another salvo roared away; the splashes from *Defence*'s and *Warrior*'s salvoes went up a long way short. *Defence* was hauling round to starboard; one could guess that Arbuthnot had decided to close the range and try again. She was steaming directly towards the still motionless German cruiser; *Warrior* was following her, and in *Bantry*'s bridge Wilmott was once again lowering himself into that undignified knees-bend position.

Light cruisers of Beatty's screen were on the quarter and astern, and closing rapidly at high speed. On the beam the battle fleet was extending north-eastward as Jellicoe made his deployment. The Second Cruiser Squadron – *Minotaur, Shannon* and company – was in sight in that direction too. Wherever one looked there were ships and smoke, and the smoke was mingling with the mist to create banks of impenetrable fog.

'Port fifteen!'

Wilmott turned his cruiser's bow into the swirl of *Warrior*'s wake. With the change of course, David saw that the light cruisers would now pass astern. In every direction there were ships racing at high speed, crossing each other's bows, swinging under each other's sterns, destroyers passing through cruiser squadrons and cruisers combing down between the lines of the deploying battle fleet. There was purpose in it all, and it was a display of high-speed ship-handling such as had never been seen before, but it looked like a free-for-all, a mass of ships in the hands of madmen, while shell-spouts leapt in clumps here and there between them and funnel-smoke hung and drifted everywhere.

Astern of the other two, Wilmott was turning *Bantry* to star-board in order to open fire again. But David was counting ships and there seemed to be only four battle cruisers in Beatty's force, instead of six. He decided he must be mistaken, two of them might be with that group astern? It was difficult to count them. The four battle cruisers were making an enormous amount of smoke, and it was all piling astern in that direction, and the ships were – from this angle – overlapping. His eyes ached, the glasses kept getting steamed-up from his rising breath and he couldn't hold the damn things steady.

'Midships!'

'Midships, sir . . . Wheel's amidships—'

Bantry's guns fired; the four nine-inch, and this time the broad-side of seven-point-fives joined in too. David lowered his glasses as the dirty-brown cordite fumes flew back in the wind. *Defence* and

Warrior were firing steadily, synchronising their salvoes; as a newcomer to the squadron, *Bantry* was the outsider. Looking over at the German cruiser, which was now about forty degrees on the bow and still stopped, he saw shells hitting all down her length. The shots were landing rather like match-heads hitting and striking on emery-paper, one after another and in twos and threes as *Bantry* too found the range and began to strike home. Now white smoke – no, steam, they'd hit her in a boiler-room – gushed skyward. He took his eyes off her, looked back to see a squadron of light cruisers racing past astern. Those were part of Beatty's screen, and within seconds, he realised, this squadron, *Bantry* and the other two, would have crossed the battle cruisers' bows, which meant – the position suddenly clarified in his mind – they'd be out in no-man's-land, between the battle cruisers and the German fleet!

Did Wilmott realise it? David turned back to look at him. He was standing with his eyes on that German cruiser; his fingers were caressing that beard of his, and there was something admiring in his expression, David thought. The main armament weren't firing now; it had evidently been decided to finish the Hun off with the seven-fives, but it was amazing that she hadn't already sunk.

Did Wilmott understand the position they'd put themselves in? Destroyers flashed past astern, and just abaft the beam now came Beatty's battle cruisers, bow-waves high and creamy under bleak steel bows, jutting guns flaming intermittently to starboard, black funnel-smoke pluming up and rolling astern like coils of tight black wool. *Lion*, their leader, with Beatty's flag and half a dozen ensigns whipping in the wind, had smoke belching from an enormous hole in her for'ard superstructure – but she looked magnificent: proud, angry, indestructible. David was staring at her when he heard a tearing, howling noise and shell-spouts shot up just short of *Warrior*'s quarterdeck, and half a second later another salvo crashed into the water sixty yards over, abreast *Bantry*'s second funnel. A navyphone buzzed; Commander Clark had snatched it up, but his voice sounded calm, less brusque than it did normally.

'Bridge here, West. What is it?'

Listening, his expression was bland, unworried as he glanced at Wilmott. A salvo fell short and foul water fell solidly across the for'ard nine-inch turret. They'd bracketed her now; David thought, *This isn't happening – is it?* He realised suddenly, for the first time ever, what his most compelling fear was. It wasn't just the thought of being killed, but of being killed and Nick left alive to inherit Mullbergh, the title, everything, with Uncle Hugh there as an honoured guest – and he and Sarah – No! David told himself, *It couldn't happen. It simply could not happen* . . . Himself, David, gone, and never mentioned, while they all—

'Enemy battle cruisers on the bow and stern, sir.' Clark was reporting to Wilmott what West had just told him. 'He says he only gets glimpses of them, but their course seems to be north-east.' The Commander pointed, 'You can see their gun-flashes now, sir.' Nobby Clark's tone had never been so mild.

More shells ripped over. A salvo raised the sea just short of *Warrior*'s stern; the gap between her stern and *Bantry*'s stem was two cables, four hundred yards. All guns were firing now. *Defence* had been hit; there was a spurt of bright orange flame and a puff-ball of black, oily smoke. She'd swung away to starboard, but *Warrior* seemed to be holding her course so Wilmott, who'd started his curtsey to the voicepipe, straightened again. Wilmott's clownish movements had ceased to be amusing. Minutes ago, David re-collected, everything had been calm and easy, they'd been coming up to take some pot shots at a disabled cruiser and there'd seemed to be no danger in it at all. Now in some extraordinary way they'd found themselves acting as targets for German battle cruisers. The heavens had opened, and the stuff raining out of them was explosive, steel, destruction, death. The sea was a forest of shell-spouts, and the stinking splashes of near-misses carried with them steel splinters, shell-fragments which screamed whirring across the decks, tore holes in funnels, cut halyards, brought rigging and wireless gear crashing down. A shell hit aft, and then two in quick succession for'ard. *Warrior* was all smoke and *Defence* was ploughing out to starboard, burning, smoke pouring from shell-holes below her bridge.

The navyphone called again. The commander had left the bridge, to take charge of damage-control below decks after those three hits. Had there been three – or more? David wasn't sure. Porter was answering that 'phone; he'd glanced enquiringly at David, and David hadn't moved; he was close to Wilmott, a couple of feet from the binnacle, and he hadn't felt like moving. So the midshipman had nipped over and taken the navyphone off its hook. *Warrior* had turned away about two points to starboard, and Wilmott was conning *Bantry* round astern of her. Midshipman Porter reported, 'Control top says we're being fired at by enemy battleships bearing due south, sir.'

114

'Thank you, Snotty.' Wilmott glanced sideways at David. 'Can't say I'd noticed the difference. Had you?' He bobbed down, 'Meet her.'

'Meet her, sir!'

'Steady!' He'd looked up, pointing, 'Oh, no . . .' A second ago he'd been smiling; now it was shock that David glimpsed before he looked where he was pointing, staring . . . *Defence* was reeling from a full salvo which had burst on her. Smoke was everywhere: her fore top swayed, and crashed down into the sea. A second salvo hit at that moment, as they watched: she seemed to check, like a shot animal before it drops, and then she blew up. A sheet of flame ran horizontally along her length, and then opened, swelling upwards into smoke as the ship disintegrated into blackness. Wilmott, knees bent, called down, 'Port twenty!' *Warrior* had sheered away to port – towards the enemy battle fleet. She was still being hit, and shells were plastering the sea all round her, and it wouldn't have done her the slightest good if *Bantry* had gone that way and shared what she was getting. Wilmott was taking his ship to starboard . . . 'Midships!'

'Midships, sir!'

She'd be heading roughly north now; David wasn't close enough to the binnacle to see. At least it was a course away from the High Seas Fleet . . . Porter came to Wilmott from a voicepipe he'd been answering: 'Commander says there are heavy casualties between decks, sir, and several fires which he hopes he'll shortly have under control.'

'Thank you, Snotty . . . Steady!'

'Steady, sir! Course north by west, sir!'

'Steer that, quartermaster.'

'Aye aye, sir!'

Wilmott straightened, and looked round. *Warrior* was some way off on the port beam, and she seemed to be on fire; but there were no shell-splashes there now, and it looked as if she was coming round to starboard, perhaps to follow *Bantry*. David heard Wilmott mutter to himself as he turned to watch the Fifth Battle Squadron coming up from the south-west, 'Find the other pair . . .' David guessed he was expressing an intention of joining *Duke of Edinburgh* and *Black Prince*, who'd sheered off somewhere on their own. Beyond the Queen Elizabeths, who were still heavily engaged, David saw destroyers, a pack of them tearing along on the disengaged side. Ahead, where that squadron was going, the air

115

was like soup, layers of haze drifting and mingling with banks of funnel-smoke from the dozens of ships which in the last twenty minutes of skilfully-managed chaos had dashed across this acreage of sea. The water still bore the tracks they'd made; it seethed where wakes met and clashed, swirled in whirlpools where ships, squadrons and flotillas had turned or ploughed through each other's washes . . . But in fact, David saw as the picture changed even while he was watching it, in the space of just a few minutes, the haze was splitting up. It was dividing, like curtains opening on a stage; and suddenly its drab, milky greyness was punctured by red stabs of gunfire, massed gunfire, where a minute ago one would have sworn there'd been nothing but a North Sea fog.

Wilmott announced, 'Jellicoe's at 'em, at last. Now we'll see a thing or two.'

Still in the process of deployment, the Grand Fleet's battleships had opened fire. You could see the ships behind the gun-flashes, now; this was the Sixth Division, the end of the line, opening fire as it swung in to form the tail. Wilmott raised a hand, pointing at the clouds, his eyebrows rose too, and his beard cocked. David listened to the hoarse rush of shells hurtling overhead. The main action, the trial of strength which would decide which fleet won or lost the battle, was just about beginning.

'Starboard ten!'

They were getting *Bantry* out of it, turning to pass up ahead of the Queen Elizabeths who, with their fifteen-inch guns still firing steadily, were swinging away to port – a 'blue' turn that would get them into position to form astern, presently, of Jellicoe's long battle line.

But one of the QE squadron – the third in the line – had gone on turning, on her own. Instead of steadying on the squadron's new course she was circling on, all by herself and getting closer at every second to the German battleships, whose shells were already straddling her.

The third in line; that would be – *Warspite*? Wilmott had seen it too; he had his glasses up, watching her as she swung into the enemy's welcoming arms. The German gunnery officers were grabbing their chance of an easy target: alone, close, and out of control. It was a reasonable supposition that her steering-gear had jammed: and anyone's bet whether her engineers would clear it before the Germans finished her.

Wilmott had shouted something at David, he was pointing. He

116

shouted again as David turned to look at him; he got one word '– *Nile*!'

But *Nile*, Hugh Everard's ship, was the last in that QE line, not the third. This one in the trap was *Warspite*: if Wilmott thought it was *Nile*, he was wrong. David turned his glasses, just to make sure, on to his uncle's ship.

Nile had put her helm over. She was steering out to join – or cover – *Warspite*. All her guns were blazing; she was a fantastic, splendid sight. All *Warspite*'s guns were firing too, in spite of the smothering she was getting, in which *Nile* any minute now would be sharing. David's glasses were jammed against his eyes, and his teeth were clenched. He was watching something marvellous, stupendous, and he felt he was part of it and yet wasn't; it was an extraordinary feeling. The sea all round *Nile* was spouting with shell-bursts and splashes, columns of water and black blossomings of smoke: at times you could only see the scarlet flashes of *Nile*'s guns, not the ship herself at all. She'd drawn two-thirds of the enemy's hate from *Warspite*, and she still had a long way to go: she was getting everything they had to offer now, she'd snatched a victim from their claws and they were making her pay for it with her own blood. David stood spellbound, fascinated; he heard Porter answer a navyphone and then tell Wilmott, 'Commander reports fires not yet under control, sir, and Lieutenant-Commander Harrington's among those killed.' David thought, *Harri dead?* That meant Johnny West was third in command now. Wilmott had taken no notice of what Porter had told him; he'd just shouted down to *Bantry*'s quartermaster, 'Starboard twenty!'

It was confusing. Another turn to port made no sense. Wilmott was crouched over the voicepipe in that silly squat of his; he told David, 'We'll get him out of it, now.' He pointed at the cluster of navyphones on the for'ard bulkhead: 'Tell the engine-room I want smoke!'

Bantry's head was falling off fast to port. As David jumped to the 'phone, Wilmott called down, 'Midships!'

Suddenly it was obvious what he was about to do. He was taking this cruiser and her smoke between *Nile* and the half-dozen dreadnought battleships that were shooting at her.

CHAPTER 7

'Midships!'

Rathbone repeated Hugh's order into the voicepipe. Hugh was watching through the conning-tower's periscope, and passing helm orders to his navigator. He heard the quartermaster's dirge-like repetition of that last one; immediately, instead of giving him a 'Steady' for a course to settle on, he ordered the helm the other way: 'Port fifteen!'

Rathbone's quick snap, the quartermaster's hollow bleat . . . Constant helm. And erratic too. He was planning to weave *Nile* like a picket-boat, take a leaf out of the destroyer men's book and dodge between the Germans' salvoes, even if a thirty-thousand-ton battleship *was* a somewhat ponderous dodger. Hugh wondered whether his decision to turn out of the line and cover *Warspite* might have been the one truly appalling decision of his career; whether it could even be thought of as a 'decision' at all; whether it hadn't been pure reflex.

Destroyer captains, a high proportion of whom were generally acknowledged to be raving lunatics, could be allowed such aberrations. A battleship's captain was another animal altogether – or should be.

'Midships! Starboard ten!'

He'd started it, and he and *Nile* – which meant not just an expensive heap of steel but about a thousand men – were out on the limb he'd opted for. You couldn't turn back, you had to see it through. And if of course you had the luck – tempered by a bit of judgement and timing – to pull it off, bring *Nile* back into the line intact and operative as a fighting unit with *Warspite* at least afloat, then the taking of the risk would have been justified. It was a biggish 'if'.

'Midships . . . Ask the control top what's up with "X" turret.'

'Midships—'

'Control top!' Ross-Hallet's voice was shouting.

'Wheel's amidships, sir!'

'Port fifteen!'

The enemy were out of sight sometimes, from this level, the view of them obscured by the rain of their own shell-splashes and bursts. From the control top, of course, Brook shouldn't be getting any such interference; all he had to do was keep his guns bearing, and cope with the wild zigzag. The noise was tremendous, and almost uninterrupted by any periods of quiet. It was like trying to keep one's brain working normally while trapped inside a steel drum that was being beaten continuously with sledge-hammers.

Midshipman Ross-Hallet reported, 'Lieutenant Brook says "X" is back in action, sir.'

'Good. Ease to five!'

'Ease to five, sir!'

'*Warspite* seems to be getting out of trouble, sir.' That had been Rathbone's voice imparting good news. Hell of a long way to go yet, though. Hugh told him, 'Midships the helm, then put on twenty of starboard.' The tower seemed to lurch, in a huge, close explosion, and there was an immediate tattoo of splinters or debris clanging against its armour; through the slits, there'd been an impression of a white-orange flash, more *surrounding* than localised. Among those who'd been knocked off their feet was the Secretary, Paymaster Lieutenant the Honourable James Colne-Wilshaw, whose action job was to keep the written 'narrative'. His notes of times, movements, orders and observed events were strewn about the iron deck under everyone else's feet.

'Twenty of starboard wheel on, sir.' The ship heeled under so much rudder . . .

Crick was down below; he'd be reporting, when he had a chance, on the state of things. Damage-control was a second-in-command's main responsibility. Hugh said, 'Midships, Pilot.'

'Midships!'

Rathbone, Hugh had noticed, was very cool and steady. He'd rather thought he might be, when it came to it.

'Ross-Hallet!'

'Sir?'

'Use the navyphone, tell Lieutenant Brook that within a few minutes I'll be turning away so he'll only have his after turrets bearing.'

Run for cover. If the next few minutes saw a continuance of good fortune . . .

'Captain, sir, message from the Commander, sir—'

'Wait.' It was a seaman boy, one of Tom Crick's party. Hugh said, 'Port ten, Pilot.' He looked back and down at the young messenger. 'Yes?'

'Shell burst in the W/T room, sir—'

Hugh interrupted him: 'Chief Yeoman?'

'Aye aye, sir.' Chief Petty Officer Peppard was already on his way. Hugh told him, 'Bring me a report as soon as possible.' The W/T cabinet was inside the bridge superstructure but on about its lowest level, the shelter deck. Hugh looked back at the messenger, who rattled on, 'It blew up into your sea-cabin, sir, and that's all wrecked—' Hugh thought, *Oh, God* . . . He wasn't thinking of the loss of his sea-cabin, but of the fact he'd told Bates to wait in it until he sent for him. The seaman boy concluded his report: 'Superstructure's on fire, sir, but commander says 'e'll soon 'ave it in 'and, sir.'

'Very good.' He looked round at Rathbone. 'Starboard fifteen.' By making the turns to port tighter, sharper than the ones to starboard, he was gradually easing her round; he wanted to get *Nile* round to a north-west course without making the intention so obvious that the German gunners might anticipate her movements. He also wanted news of Bates. 'Midships.'

'Captain, sir.' He looked round quickly at CPO Peppard, who told him, 'It's like the lad said, sir. W/T room's all smashed, and your cabin's gone too, sir. The fire's spread a bit but they're gettin' on top of it now.'

'Casualties?'

'One telegraphist killed, sir, three men 'urt. They've been took below, sir. Lieutenant Sallis was 'urt too, sir, an' the PO Tel, they've been took down to—'

'Ross-Hallet. Able Seaman Bates was supposed to be waiting in my sea-cabin. Go and—' he paused, while the guns fired and fresh spouts of German shells went up on the bow: he was about to finish what he'd been saying to the midshipman when something big clanged into *Nile*'s starboard side. He met Rathbone's calm, round eyes, and commented, 'That one was a dud'n.' Behind him, several men laughed. Amusement wasn't difficult to trigger. Hugh said, 'Port ten.'

Rathbone passed the helm order into the copper tube.

120

'See what you can find out, Mid.'

'Aye aye, sir.'

The chief yeoman finished his report: 'I was to tell you the commander's gone aft now, sir. Spot o' trouble – one in through the quarterdeck I believe, sir.'

'All right, Peppard.'

Crick would tell him, when he could, what was happening below. In the meantime, nobody could handle 'spots of trouble' more ably than Tom Crick . . . A shell exploded on the roof of 'B' turret, which was only a few feet from this conning-tower's hood and periscope. The smoke cleared: with his eardrums hurting, Hugh saw paintwork charred black but no other visible damage. Rathbone shouted, fiddling with his earplugs, 'Still have ten of port helm on, sir.'

'Midships!'

'B' turret had just fired, with the others, and it was comforting to think that some of *Nile*'s fifteen-inch shells would be smashing down into German ships . . .

'Starboard fifteen!'

He glanced, round at the hatch. But it was too soon for that midshipman to have got back yet.

Lanyard rang dully, sporadically, with the percussions of the Grand Fleet's salvoes. It was a distant sound, and intermittent. With the easier motion of the destroyer at this greatly reduced speed there was a sense, at least down here in the chartroom, of a lull in the storm of battle; a false lull, perhaps, which might be shattered at any moment. Meanwhile, this job was hardly a pleasant one. Nick dumped the contents of Johnson's pockets in a heap on the chart-table. There wasn't much; a wallet with some letters in it, a notebook, some stubs of pencil, a pocket-watch and a ring of keys. Reynolds' small possessions were similar, but included a silver cigarette-case and a metal match-container.

Nick weighed it for a moment in his hand. He'd seen Reynolds using this, in the wardroom, earlier this very day. Now it was an object to be packaged for transmission to the lieutenant's next of kin, so that the body could before long be 'committed' to the sea. For the time being it was outside on the foc'sl, together with the body of Pat Johnson – who'd seemed at first to be something of an ogre but who'd astounded Nick, this morning, with totally new aspects of his brother.

He'd never thought deeply about David; it had never occurred to him to try to understand him. Unpleasantness was all one had been conscious of. Coldness, hostility; resentment of his – Nick's – existence. And since in any dispute David had always had their father's backing, Nick had learnt to walk alone and avoid them both. Birds of a feather . . . Well, they were! And since that time in London, when he looked at his elder brother, what he saw in his mind's eye was a girl's face – bruised, swollen, pulpy . . .

He put Johnson's and Reynolds' keys aside. They'd be ship's keys – safes, pistol and rifle racks, the spirit store, and so on. Nick told Garret, who was helping him, 'Grab a couple of those old charts and make parcels, would you? Put their names on 'em. This pile's Lieutenant Johnson's.'

Garret complied wordlessly. Mortimer had told Nick to see to this, and as an afterthought he'd sent Garret down to help him. *Lanyard* was on the disengaged side of the battle fleet, and it was a good time for patching up, clearing away, making good. And for such tasks as this.

There'd be five men for burial, when the time for that came. Two men aft, as well as these; the torpedoman had died, and one of the for'ard gun's crew, and the coxswain, CPO Cuthbertson.

The guns had been sponged-out and greased, ready-racks re-filled, ammunition stocks counted. Jury voicepipes, halyards and wireless aerials had been rigged. A collision-mat had been spread on the quarterdeck and lashed down with a steel-wire hawser laced to and fro over battens across the damaged area. Spare splinter-mattresses had been secured around the bridge. Finally, Nick had organised the cooks and some of the ammunition-supply ratings into a canteen service to provide tea and bully-beef sandwiches to all hands at their stations.

Lanyard was lazing along now at no more than fifteen knots, keeping station on the port side of the battle fleet. The fleet had slowed, in the course of its deployment, to avoid 'bunching' as the squadrons slid into place in the great, unwieldy line. Six miles of battleships . . . And coming now was the crucial phase, the duel between the dreadnoughts. Destroyer and cruiser actions had drawn blood, cost lives and ships, and there'd surely be more of the same – more dead, and more destroyed – before darkness fell; but the heavyweights were in the ring now and the big fight, the contest for the world championship, was about to follow that earlier sparring and jockeying for position.

He'd seen his uncle's ship, when *Lanyard* had overhauled her some while ago. *Nile* had suffered some hits, but looked none the worse for it; and the Fifth Battle Squadron would be out of harm's way by this time, because the way Jellicoe had deployed his other squadrons had left the Queen Elizabeths no alternative but to tag on at the rear. But Nick could understand his uncle now, understand the strength of his feeling for the Navy; a few hours of action, some moments of fear followed by longer periods of extraordinary exhilaration; the sight of the flotilla attacking, that wild charge against the line of blazing guns; the entire experience of these last hours had convinced him that the Service was – or could be, at times – what he'd been told it was, believed it to be: and he had the key now to the riddle of Hugh Everard's having retained enthusiasm for the naval service in spite of its having kicked him in the teeth.

'My own fault . . .'

Hugh had said that to his brother, Nick's father, at luncheon at Mullbergh, one day about four years ago. Nick, David and Sarah had been there too; Sarah had become the second Lady Everard only a few months earlier. She'd asked Hugh how he'd been forced to give up his career, and he'd answered briefly, quite dispassionately. She'd been indignant, cross with him, even, for 'taking it lying down'. He'd smiled at her angry face, and Nick had seen the effect of that smile and the quick glance she'd immediately thrown at her husband. Hugh had murmured, 'My own stupidity, perhaps I should say. Jackie Fisher being the man he is, I should have – oh, been less ingenuous. Genius and rationality shouldn't be expected in one individual, you know.'

'Are you saying Lord Fisher's irrational?'

It was Sir John who was indignant now, glaring down the table at his brother. 'Surely Fisher, of all men, is the most practical, down-to-earth—'

'In directly professional matters, yes. But where personalities are concerned – why, Jackie'd smell treachery from a brick wall at a hundred paces with a clothes-peg on his nose!'

'One of the greatest men of this century, in my view.'

'I agree, John. Entirely.'

'But you feel free to blame him for your own failure?'

At the time of this conversation Nick had been seventeen, and a midshipman, not long at sea. Nineteen-twelve . . . He remembered the impression he'd had at that luncheon table that his father was trying to belittle Uncle Hugh in order to reduce him in Sarah's eyes; as if he didn't want his new, young wife to think anything of her brother-in-law. In fact they'd become the best of friends – not more than that, as David had been spiteful enough to suggest, but – well, friends. Which hadn't been enough, and still wasn't, for brother David . . . But anyway, it had been some trifling indiscretion, a social thing and quite meaningless, that had aroused Lord Fisher's displeasure. Displeasure and distrust: and Fisher was proud of his own ruthlessness. In 1904 Hugh Everard had been a member of the 'Fish Pond', a group of outstandingly promising young officers whom Fisher had inducted to the Admiralty and given influence and authority out of all proportion to their ranks or years; high-flyers all: and he promoted them over the heads of older, more experienced men, making enemies for himself and them in the process. 'Favouritism', declared Fisher, 'is the secret of efficiency!' With favouritism went despotism; at thirty-three, in 1904, Hugh had been a commander; in 1906, the year of his marriage, he was promoted to post captain, eight years ahead of the most favourable normal expectation. In 1907, Fisher broke him.

The damage hadn't been permanent, as things had turned out now. For some years Hugh had worked for a shipbuilding company, but the war had brought him back to active service and the Falklands victory had re-established him as an up-and-comer and led to his being offered the command of *Nile*. Fisher, of course, had gone. He'd built this fleet, bulldozed it into being. But a year ago his quarrels with the First Lord, Winston Churchill, had reached a climax, primarily over the Dardanelles issue. Fisher had been opposed to the Gallipoli adventure right from the beginning. A year ago, goaded beyond an old man's endurance by the young politician, he'd stalked out of the Admiralty for the last time, not so much defeated as bemused, an old dog snarling through broken teeth at enemies real and unreal.

Garret scrawled *1st Lieut* on one package, and *Lt Reynolds* on the other. He asked Nick, 'Reckon we'll come off best, sir?'

'Good God, yes! Of course!'

Garret nodded. Somewhere ahead and to starboard a battle-ship's guns fired one broadside, and fell silent. One could visualise the shifting mist-banks, the eyes pressed against periscopes and range-finders, searching constantly for targets. The signalman hardly seemed convinced; Nick explained to him that Jellicoe's course was now roughly south-east, and that Hipper's battle cruisers in the van of the German fleet had been bent off-course, eastward, first by Beatty and more recently by the deploying battle fleet. It was doubtful whether Admiral Scheer yet appreciated how powerful an enemy lay across his line of advance. The poor visibility was maddening to the Grand Fleet, but it might also be a blessing in disguise, hiding Jellicoe from Scheer. Meanwhile the German line, as Scheer's leading division followed Hipper round, was an arc, a curve that started northwards and sheered away east as it flinched from the wall of advancing British dreadnoughts.

Garret reached for his enamelled mug of dark-brown tea. Nick asked him, 'Rough up there, was it, when we—' he glanced down at the parcels on the table – 'when we got that hit?'

Garret nodded as he put his mug down. 'It's the standin', wi' no work to do. Just waitin' – you get time to think – like about if – if you're a married man, say . . .'

'Yes.' The tea tasted like liquid boot-polish. 'I'm lucky, that way, with no ties. But you only just got married, didn't you?'

Garret bit into a thick sandwich. The packages in front of them kept their voices low, reminded them of the bodies outside on the foc's'l between the for'ard four-inch ready-racks and the rattling steel bulkhead of this chartroom. Garret chewed thoughtfully, glancing at Nick and away again while his thoughts made a quick trip to Edinburgh, took a look at Margaret, and came back.

'Don't you have any—' he hesitated, as if having embarked on the question embarrassed him – 'Any young lady, as it might be, sir?'

Nick thought about it. Chewing the last of his door-stop sandwich while Garret swirled dregs of tea around the bottom of his mug. Young lady . . . Did Greta Magnusson, the Orcadian crofter's daughter, rate as a 'young lady'?

It wasn't the social aspect he was questioning. It was just that he didn't think of her in such terms, any more than he'd think of Sarah, his stepmother, as a 'young lady'. They were both, well, different . . . 'Young ladies', as he'd understood the words, were the giggly creatures one met, danced with, played tennis with, and so on, in other large Yorkshire houses. He'd never yet met one he'd found at all interesting or more than passingly attractive, and in any case they'd always directed all their interest at his brother David. He was the heir, of course, and the good-looking, taller one; the one who danced better, played better tennis, and who didn't keep falling off the horses which he was more or less forced to ride.

125

But Greta Magnusson belonged in the setting of the Orkneys. It struck him as he thought of her that if he was back there, next week, say, and told her all about this battle, how it had seemed and felt, and how he was suddenly feeling that he belonged, that this was the Navy he'd wanted, dreamt about and had begun to think didn't exist at all – well, Greta would have said something like, *Och, is that so?* and changed the subject at once, to fish, or sheep, or what her father had said yesterday.

Finishing the crust, he swallowed hard, making an effort of it to justify the length of time it had taken him to produce an answer. He shook his head.

'Not really.'

In *Nile*'s 'X' turret, everything had been running as smoothly as it ever had, until the loading rammers jammed.

Cartwright had been feeling proud of his men: and not unproud of himself, for the way he'd trained them. However hard you worked at it, and however good a performance looked when it was a wood-and-canvas target you were shooting at, you always wondered how it would pan out when it was a live target that shot back at you. And this had gone off, so far, like the best of the practice shoots; except that there was excitement, elation and a terrific sense of satisfaction in them all. Not just because this at last was action, justification for all the weary months of training and waiting; but also that they were measuring-up, matching-up to the high standards of their Service, fleet, ship. Those standards had seemed intimidatingly high, sometimes, but nobody was falling down on the job now. Nobody would, either; you could see it in their faces, in the swift, confident, skilful way they worked, keeping the guns firing – firing fast and hitting.

Information came now and then from Lieutenant Brook in the control top to his turret officers, and here in 'X' turret Captain Blackaby passed it on to the men who worked the guns.

They'd been told during the last half-hour that the German battleships *Grosser Kurfürst* and *Markgraf* had each been hit several times. Those were the two at which *Nile, Malaya* and *Warspite* had been shooting mostly, during the run northwards. Also the battle cruisers *Seydlitz, Lutzow* and *Derfflinger* were in poor shape now; *Seydlitz* particularly: she was on fire, four of her turret guns had been silenced, her secondary armament had been completely smashed, and shell-damage to her foc's'l had left her

126

down by the head and losing speed. *Von der Tann* had no turrets left that she could shoot with; she was still in the line with the other battle cruisers, but she was toothless . . . And now *Lutzow, Derfflinger* and *Markgraf* had all been hit again, during the last few minutes. 'X' turret's crew cheered as the right-hand gun fired, flung back; the cage came up – left gun fired – number two of the right gun swung the breech open and Cartwright roared 'Right gun STILL!'

He'd seen number two – Dewar, of course – open the breech too soon, before the gun had finished its run-out; the carrier arm of the breech had struck the rammer head, and metal-bound it. So the rammer had stuck and now the port rammer had too. Cartwright swore loudly and articulately as he flung himself off his seat. Until this moment, everything had gone so smoothly, easily; there'd been none of the silly over-eagerness which could be counted on to lead to this sort of jam-up and consequent delay. Up in the control top, Lieutenant Brook would be cursing when 'X' turret's gunready lamps failed to light; *Nile*, for the moment, would be firing three-gun salvoes, and Captain Blackaby, normally quite a patient man, would very shortly be exploding with Royal Marine-type fury. Cartwright shoved Dewar out of his way, taking some satisfaction in using a considerable degree of force; he snatched up a steel pinch-bar, and shoved its end in behind the rammer head. Then he jerked the lever over to the 'Run Out' position; and the rammer slid out, sweet and quick and no more bother. Cartwright brought it back again and out two more times, and there it was, gay as a lark again, right gun back in action.

'Load!'

He passed the steel bar over to the captain of the left gun, and went quickly back to his seat to lay the gun by pointer, following the director's. The gun was ready just in time, and the second the interceptor switch was shut, it fired. They were loading again: cage up, rammer thudding over, projectile up the spout and then the charge hard up behind it. Cartwright thought he'd take a look, see what was happening out there; he got up, and put his eyes to the periscope.

Nothing. They'd heard a few German shells hit, from time to time, and one of them had blown muck of some sort over the outer glass. He could see some sort of wreckage; could be anything, just black. He felt *Nile* turning. He was back on his seat quickly, eyes quick too, checking round; gun ready – fired – recoiling – running out . . . loading again, and no problems now. He spoke to Captain Blackaby on the telephone.

'Cartwright here, sir. Don't matter so bad, since we're in director-firing but this periscope's fouled up outside, sir. 'Appen we'd go in local control, wouldn't be too easy, sir. Dunno we might send a hand out?'

Blackaby peered through the cabinet's periscope. *Nile* had turned to port, and so had the ships ahead of her. It was a 'blue' turn, which had left the squadron in quarter-line, but the turrets had trained round on to the starboard quarter and still bore on the enemy.

'If we get a chance, I'll see to it.' He hung the navyphone back on its hook. Midshipman Mellors suggested, 'Say the word, sir, and I'll nip out. Shouldn't take a second.' Blackaby was using the periscope again, and for a moment or two he didn't answer. *Warspite*, for some reason that was difficult to fathom, had suddenly gone off on her own. She'd hauled out between the squadron and the enemy; and *Nile*, for the moment, couldn't shoot at all. If there was ever going to be a moment to clear that periscope, this was it. He buzzed the gunner's mate.

'Cartwright, I'm sending Midshipman Mellors out. Break both interceptors.'

'Aye aye, sir!'

With interceptor switches broken, the guns couldn't be fired. And if 'Y' turret did – which was unlikely, in the next half-minute – it would be on that after bearing, pointing the other way. It might frighten the snotty, but it wouldn't hurt him.

'Both guns at half-cock, sir!'

'Right . . . Go on, Mellors. Be damn quick, eh?'

The boy scuttled out, and the hatch clanged shut behind him. Blackaby watched through his periscope, wondering what *Warspite* was up to. She certainly couldn't be doing it for fun: she was being hit hard and often. It occurred to him that she might be out of control, with steering jammed, or – *Christ*, but the Huns were going for her! He felt *Nile*'s lurch as she began a sharp turn to starboard; checking on *Malaya*, the next ahead, he realised that this was yet another solo effort. The turret trained exactly as fast as the ship swung, since the director kept its sights trained on the enemy and the turrets followed the director. *Nile* was still under helm; still swinging, anyway: and Blackaby guessed that she was going out of the line to cover *Warspite*, who was quite obviously in bad trouble. There wasn't any other explanation.

Where the blazes was that snotty? Blackaby bit his lip; time was a peculiar thing, in action. Fifteen seconds could seem to take five minutes. But surely—

'A', 'B' and 'Y' turrets all fired.

He heard salvoes hitting, as German gunners switched to the new target which was being presented to them. Shut in an armoured turret it was difficult to know where the hits had been; there'd been savage, penetrating clangs and the deep thuds of detonations below decks. Three – four – and the other turrets had all fired again . . . Brook was calling on the navyphone from the Control Top.

'What's wrong, Blackaby?'

Blackaby told him he'd sent a man out to clear an obstructed periscope.

'Well, for God's sake get him back inside!'

'Right.'

How? Panic stations up there, by the sound of it. The moment had not, after all, been such a good one to clear that damn thing. How long had Mellors been outside – a minute? Less? Two salvoes, that would account for a minute and a third one now . . . *Nile* had steadied, but she'd begun a new turn, the other way; there was a thunderous explosion which seemed – felt – to have been astern, and Blackaby had nothing in front of his periscope but smoke.

Cartwright, waiting for his glass to be cleared, was just as anxious. He was thinking they ought to shut the interceptors and get back into action. Things were much too brisk up top for a turret to be standing idle, and it seemed obvious that the midshipman must have come to grief. Even if he hadn't, the guns would at least have burst his eardrums.

The periscope was clear, suddenly. There was smoke, where before there'd been something solid; smoke, swirling thickly. *Nile* was being battered and that smoke was from shell-bursts; if you were out there, it'd be enough to gas you if you weren't already dead. He put a hand on the navyphone and saw Midshipman Mellors' face in the smoke. The boy's eyes were staring at him – into the glass of the periscope – wide, dead eyes. Mellors was crouched on the roof of the turret, kneeling, bent over, staring at the periscope and his arms clamped across his belly. He seemed to be clasping a mass of blood and as he toppled sideways Cartwright saw it all just fall away . . . He – Cartwright – had the navyphone in his fist: he raised it, and reported, 'Midshipman Mellors is dead, ir. Periscope's clear.' Mellors' remains slid, vanished over the turret's edge. Blackaby snapped, 'Salvoes – director firing – right gun commencing – recock!'

Back to four-gun salvoes . . .

In the torpedo control tower, just above 'X' turret and for'ard of it, Midshipman Greenlaws had been watching the movements of his friend Mellors and he'd seen everything that had happened to him. Greenlaws was leaning with his face against the starboard sighting hole; he felt sick and weak. He was leaning there when the first detonation of 'X' turret's guns for two minutes flung him backwards against the corner of the range-finder, and knocked thoughts of sickness out of his head. Knox-Wilson, the torpedo lieutenant, said sharply, 'And that was your own damn fault, Mid!'

He'd spoken roughly – out of impatience and also because Greenlaws was a bright lad, by no means wet or soft, and he needed reminding of it. There was also the question of setting an example to the other members of this control tower's crew. Knox-Wilson told Pugh, the communications rating, 'Ask Mr Askell what progress he's making.' Pugh was putting his hand out to the navyphone when its light began to flash; Knox-Wilson muttered, his words lost in the screech of a salvo tearing overhead, 'Speak of the devil . . .' His eyes were on the smoke pouring out of *Nile*'s bridge superstructure, streaming away over her port quarter; sparks flew in it . . . But he was right, it was the torpedo gunner on the navyphone, and he was telling Ordinary Seaman Pugh, 'The bugger's clear now. You can use it when you want.'

'Wait, sir, please.' Pugh passed the message to Knox-Wilson, who nodded. 'Good. Tell him—' he paused, as the guns crashed out, lobbing another fifteen-inch salvo at the enemy – 'tell him—' Deep thuds and the crack of hits came from somewhere for'ard; shell-spouts leapt in a close group flinging black water at the funnels. Knox-Wilson roared, 'Tell him I'm firing soon, he'd better stay there!'

Askell was in the for'ard torpedo flat, which was way down below the waterline – six, seven decks below the air and daylight and just for'ard of 'A' turret's revolving hoist. The torpedo flat occupied the full width of the ship, with one tube aimed out on each side. The starboard one had run into trouble some while ago; they'd fired from the after torpedo flat at longish range, and as they were now a lot closer to the enemy it seemed a good time to take another shot.

'Range?'

A salvo ripped over and burst just off the quarter. *Nile* had taken a fair number of hits; there'd have been far more if it hadn't been for the way she'd been handled, the erratic dodging. Knox-Wilson wondered how many shells had penetrated, what things might be like below decks . . . 'What's the range, Kilfeather, damn it!'

He was trying to line-up his torpedo-firing disc, and being under constant helm wasn't making it any easier . . . Leading Torpedo-man Kilfeather, the range-taker, reported finally, 'One-double-oh, sir.'

'So if we take their course as north-east by east, the distance off track will be . . .' he was muttering to himself, fiddling with the disc, and now peering over Greenlaws' shoulder at the plotter. 'H'm.' He nodded, and yelled at Pugh, 'Stand by!'

Greenlaws had worked out the deflection. Kilfeather, with his eyes at the lenses of the range-finder, called suddenly, 'Range about to be hobscured, sir!' Knox-Wilson leant to the sighting hole, and stared out; he saw a cruiser laying smoke, coming southwards at high speed; she was about to pass and hang the curtain of her smoke between *Nile* and the tail end of the German line. Within seconds they'd be cut off from each other's sight; and with the cruiser where she was there was no chance of getting a torpedo away quickly, before that happened. Arriving on an opposite course as she had, she'd less approached than suddenly appeared.

The enemy's salvoes were already thinning out. But the cruiser was about to pay for interfering in the Germans' sport. Ahead of her the sea was alive with shell-fire. They were smaller splashes, probably from the battleships' secondary armament, but it amounted to a rain of fire, an explosive hailstorm she was steaming into. From the shape of her forepart, which except for the brown cordite haze flung out by her own guns was clear of smoke, he guessed she was one of the *Minotaur* class. She'd almost passed now; watching her, Knox-Wilson found himself willing her to turn, praying she'd put her helm over *now*, retire behind her own smoke-cover. She'd done the job: he whispered in his mind, *Now go on, get out of it, for God's sake!*

At last . . . He realised he'd been holding his breath. He let it out, and sat back a bit.

Nile was getting out of it, too; turning away. There'd have been

131

no chance now of firing that torpedo. She was swinging her stern towards the Germans, who would probably still have her masts and upperworks in sight above the smoke; but they wouldn't have for much longer. In any case it was the cruiser they were bombarding now. He saw a salvo hit her as she altered round; two hits amidships, twin orange bursts of flame that seemed to split the swirling smoke, and then a streak of fire that shot up the side of her bridge superstructure. Seeing it, imagining what it might be like to be on that bridge, he winced; and in the same instant a new salvo came whistling down on *Nile*.

Lieutenant-Commander Mortimer was staring aft, with his binoculars levelled at an area of smoke way out over his destroyer's starboard quarter. He was trying to catch some glimpse of *Nile* or *Warspite* or of the cruiser *Warrior*.

There was still a vast quantity of smoke down there, and he couldn't see any of them; it was only that in these changeable conditions of visibility one did from time to time get a clearance, an unexpected view through haze which as suddenly clamped down again. He'd seen *Defence* blow up; in fact her destruction must have been witnessed from as many as fifty different ships, when the battle fleet had been starting its deployment and every Tom, Dick and Harry had been rushing across its van. He'd also seen *Warrior* reeling from salvo after salvo, burning, slowing to a crawl, trying to creep away somewhere like a wounded animal to lick her wounds. That German cruiser – he'd thought she might be the *Wiesbaden* – which *Defence*'s squadron had rushed out to attack, had been still afloat though burning from end to end, and a destroyer – *Onslow*, from *Lanyard*'s own flotilla – had had a crack at her with torpedoes, and scored a hit, but got badly smashed-up herself in the process; she'd lain stopped, licking her wounds, then incredibly got going again for a solo attack on the Hun battleships. He'd lost track of her about then, because it had been at this stage that he'd seen *Warspite*'s helm jam.

Lanyard had been on the Fifth Battle Squadron's port bow, then, shaping course to get round astern of the battle fleet. There'd been no shells falling near them – which had made a pleasant change, a breathing-space – and there'd been no visible prospect of action in the immediate future; so when Everard came up to the bridge to report he'd completed various jobs, it had been a good moment to send him down to do another. Consequently Everard hadn't seen *Nile* come out and charge the enemy: and that might be just as well.

Considering all things, *Lanyard* herself had been lucky, so far. When one thought of *Nestor* and *Nomad*, left behind . . . *Nestor*'s captain, Bingham, had waved a 'leave-us-to-it' signal to *Nicator*. It wouldn't have made sense to have hung around and there would have been no time to take her in tow. Even to have attempted it would have been a matter of throwing away another ship; it would have cost lives, not saved them. But it still hadn't been easy, to steam away and leave one's friends in the lurch.

'Sir. You sent for me.'

Mortimer glanced round, and saw Worsfold, his commissioned engineer.

'So I did.' Worsfold's face was set, inscrutable. The man had that kind of face anyway, but there was also the circumstance – which was in both their minds – that the last time he'd appeared on the bridge Mortimer had threatened him with death.

It was when he'd just left *Nestor* sinking, and lost two officers and *Lanyard*'s coxswain. Worsfold had picked a bad time to come up with his bleat about how the destroyer's engines should or should not be used.

'All right now, Chief?'

'I'd say we eased up just in time, sir.' Worsfold hesitated. 'Used a lot of fuel, of course. But so long as there's no more prolonged high-speed—'

'You know damn well I can't guarantee anything of the sort!'

They stared at each other. Worsfold added, 'Slight leak on one feed-tank, sir. We can cope with it if it gets no worse.'

'What caused it?'

'A hit aft, sir. I think when the gun went overboard.'

'Yes.' Mortimer nodded. He cleared his throat. 'Chief, I'm afraid I lost my temper, earlier on. I apologise, and I congratulate you on the job you've been doing. You and your staff.'

The engineer's thin lips twitched. Mortimer had turned to stare at the destroyer ahead of *Lanyard*; she'd done a sudden jink to port, but it had probably been only a helmsman's momentary aberration. In any case, Hastings had his eyes on her. Worsfold murmured, 'No firing squad this time, sir?'

'Chief.'

'Sir.'

133

'I can't stand having my bridge cluttered-up with bloody plumbers. Get to hell off it, would you?'

Hastings winked at Worsfold as he turned away. At the same moment, the battle fleet's hitherto sporadic gunfire seemed to thicken, solidify and rise to a crescendo, as if every ship in the vast line of dreadnoughts had suddenly found a target.

Mortimer had whipped up his glasses.

'My God, look at that!'

Emerging from thick haze in the south was the head of Scheer's battle line. And the leading German battleship, as she came thrusting out of the murk into clearer air, was being hit simultaneously by *Agincourt, Bellerophon, Conqueror, Thunderer, Hercules, Colossus, Benbow, Iron Duke, Orion, Monarch, Royal Oak,* and *Revenge.*

The leading German ship had burst into flames. Her whole forepart was ablaze, and the rest was smoke.

'She's turning away!'

Mortimer added, murmuring it to himself, 'Can't say I blame her . . .'

The battle cruisers up ahead, who had also felt the rough edge of Jellicoe's welcome, had swung off to starboard, and the front division of Scheer's dreadnoughts was now following them. The entire High Seas Fleet was tightening its curve away to starboard as its leaders flinched from the concentrated fire-power of the British squadrons.

Nick, with Garret close behind him, climbed into the bridge. Blewitt muttered, pointing, 'They're blowin' the 'uns to kingdom come, sir!'

The mist was lifting. Three, four, six German battleships were in sight now, and all of them were being hit repeatedly. Scheer, the layer of traps, must know now – *now*, in what must have been his most terrible moment ever – that what he'd steamed into was the mother and father of all traps. Jellicoe's deployment, the decision he'd taken on no more than scraps of information, had put his squadrons into the perfect position for the destruction of the High Seas Fleet.

The noise of the cannonade was tremendous; and in between the crashes of gunfire and the echoes of bursting shells there was a new sound – cheering. Guns' crews, bridge and signals staffs, every man on any upper deck – their cheers rose, swelled, rolled across the grey-green sea from ship to ship and were drowned only in the

134

renewed thunder of the guns. The smoke and flames of detonating shells smothered the German line. They were shooting back, but compared to the punishment being dealt out to them-it was no more than a token resistance as their line bent, sheered away. And as the leaders turned, others were pressing up astern to get *their* rations.

Mortimer, holding his glasses in his left hand and pointing with the other, shouted, 'They're running away, by God!'

Whenever there was a view of German ships, through gaps in the British line and where the mist was thinnest, Scheer's battleships were swinging away to starboard in a simultaneous about-turn. They were reversing their course, retreating into the cover of the mist.

One had heard quite a lot of this emergency-turn manoeuvre. The Germans had one of their long words for it, which when translated, meant, 'Battle-Turn-Away' – a splendidly Teutonic euphemism for 'cut and run'!

Captain Blackaby, struggling out of his cabinet into 'X' turret's gunhouse, was blinded and half suffocated by smoke and the acrid reek of high explosive. A shell had come in through the turret roof. He'd heard and felt it and seen a great flattish disc of orange flame before his periscope had shattered. The range-finder was smashed too. In here men were choking, reeling about; some, dead or wounded, were still or writhing on the deck. He could hear questions being asked, men calling their friends' names.

'Cartwright! GM!'

He pushed someone out of his way, stumbled over a man crawling on hands and knees. Light seeped down from above, where the hole was. He found Cartwright; the petty officer was face-down, sprawled in a heap of blue serge and blood; Blackaby noticed how his boots still gleamed, and that there was no back to his head. It wasn't necessary to turn him or look more closely to know that he was dead.

'Captain Blackaby, sir?'

It was Dewar, the right gun's number two. Blackaby told him, 'Get the hatch open, Dewar, let some air through.'

'Aye aye, sir!'

It was already clearing, in fact, through the ordinary ventilation and assisted by the hole which the shell had made in the roof, in the centre plate of the sighting hood. It had burst there, detonating as it penetrated the steel armour; you could see that by the size of the hole and the way the edges of the steel were bent upwards. It occurred to Blackaby that if the shell had come right inside before its fuse fired it, things would have been a great deal worse. Men were picking themselves up – those that could – and moving back towards their places at the guns; others were trying to help the wounded. Dewar had the hatch open, and the clearing air was helping stunned men to recover. Blackaby had been slightly dazed, but he was clearer now. He shouted, 'Turret's crew, *number*!'

That way, he got them sorted out. Five men, including the gunner's mate, couldn't answer. Of those, three were still alive. There were seven others wounded, two of whom said they could carry on. Blackaby got the spare crew up from below, and the men he didn't need he detailed to get the wounded to the surgeons and the dead out on the quarter-deck. The second captain-of-turret was a young petty officer by the name of Davies.

'Test loading gear, Davies.'

'Aye aye, sir!'

Both cages were jammed. They freed the right one: the left was immovable. Luckily it had stuck in the 'down' position, where it wouldn't interfere with hand-loading, and Davies sang out, 'Left gun hand-loading in gunhouse!'

Cartwright had drilled them well. Number five had repeated the order to the magazine and shellroom; numbers six and eight of the shellroom came up into the working-chamber to become numbers nine and ten. Meanwhile five had got the main cage door off, and Petty Officer Davies had shut off pressure to the cage mechanism and slammed the door shut in the auxiliary trunk. Blackaby stood back, fingering his moustache, as the wounded were helped and carried out.

'Surgeon'll soon fix you up, you fellows. You'll see, you'll be as right as rain!'

'Aye, sir!' A sightsetter, who looked as if he'd been scalped, grinned at him; he was holding a scarlet, sodden wad of cotton-waste against his forehead. He said, 'Don't you worry about us, sir. We'll be gettin' a whack o' leave, we will!' They all cheered; Blackaby told them, 'By God, I could make Marines of you lot!' His eyes shifted, to watch the men at work around the gun; except for the dead and wounded and that hole in the roof through which steely light probed into a swirl of still faintly yellowish vapour, this might have been a practice.

'I want that right gun back in action, Davies!'

'Aye aye, sir!'

Davies was a pale, fair-haired man with a Welsh lilt and a squinting eye; now he left the left gun's hand-loading preparation to the spare left gun-captain, and shouted, 'Right gun, load!' The cage hissed up and the rammer slid across; projectile in, charge in, rammer clanking back. Dewar slammed the breech shut. The layer put his right arm up, and number three banged the interceptor shut.

'Y' turret fired, but the loaded and cocked right gun of 'X' turret remained inert.

Davies shouted, as was laid-down in the drill book, 'Still! Misfire!'

Blackaby thought it was probably the director firing circuits that had failed; most likely they'd been cut. If so, protracted misfire procedures now would be a waste of time. And since in a moment the left gun would be ready, one would very soon know for certain. The left gun's projectile had come up on the grab, the chain-hoist, and they'd eased it into its loading-tray; now the rammer did the rest, and the charge went in, and Blackaby saw number three on that side shut his interceptor.

'Left gun ready!'

It didn't fire, though, with the next salvo. Two of the spare hands were carrying Petty Officer Cartwright out. The back of the gunner's mate's head was a pulp of bone, brain and blood. The layer of the left gun shouted 'Still! Misfire!'

Both interceptors were now broken; both guns loaded. Blackaby ordered, 'Gunlayer firing, salvoes, right gun commencing!'

The fact the turret had no periscope or sights of any kind now didn't matter. The layers would keep their pointers lined-up with director's pointers, so the guns would remain on target, and they'd press their own triggers when they heard 'Y' turret fire.

The right gun fired, recoiled, ran out. Its crew were reloading as number three of the left gun shut its interceptor and reported 'Left gun ready!'

'X' turret was back in business.

Blackaby went back into his cabinet, to report to the control top. Brook said, 'Well done, Blacko. But we've nothing to shoot at, for the moment. All we can see is smoke . . . Damn sorry about Cartwright.'

'Yes.' The cabinet door opened – from the outside – and

Blackaby saw the commander stooping, peering in at him. He hung up the navyphone.

'Got yourselves to rights, eh, Soldier?'

'Yessir. Chaps've done splendidly.'

'Quite,' Crick's pink face beamed. 'Bit of a lull now, too. I should stand 'em down, one gun's crew at a time, if I were you. Give 'em a stand-easy while we're quiet?'

'Good idea, sir.'

Crick, his long frame bent double, withdrew. Blackaby got on the navyphone to Davies.

'Petty Officer Davies. Five minutes' stand-down for each gun's crew alternately. And let Dewar play his blasted gramophone if he wants to.'

'Aye aye, sir!'

Crick climbed out of the turret, and shut the hatch behind him. He moved aft around 'Y' turret, and banged with his heel on the lid of the hatch beside the capstan; the man inside it, at the top of the ladderway, knocked a retaining clip off and pushed the hatch up, and Crick eased himself down inside. The sailor had to lean out sideways on the ladder's edge to give him room.

'Thank you. Shut and clip it now. I'll go back through the ship.' He'd only come up from here a few minutes ago, when he'd had a message about Blackaby's turret. At the bottom of the ladderway he turned aft, crossed the lobby which was lined each side with cabins – including his own – and passed through the bulkhead doorway to the captain's lobby.

It was all fumes and stink. Charred paintwork, and the reek of burnt corticene; the resin under it ran like viscous, stinking glue. The captain's day-cabin and sleeping-cabin had both been wrecked; there seemed to have been two hits by large-calibre shells, something like twelve-inch, and one of these had burst in the deck of the dining-cabin, opening a ten-foot diameter hole to the secretary's clerks' office immediately below, on the middle deck. The captain's dining-table was charred, wet matchwood, but that cabin hadn't suffered as badly as the others, since the blast had all gone downwards, apparently. The day- and sleeping-cabins had been transformed into one large room in which a herd of elephants might have run amok before someone set fire to it; and a third shell had burst outside the hull at the level of the main deck and carved away most of the catwalk which ran around the ship's stern. The fire brigade had got their hoses in this way, using what was left of the captain's private balcony to stand on while they jetted water in from outside. It hadn't been possible to get in, at first, the way Crick had just come.

But it was all in hand now. Steam rose from fire-heated steel and paintwork, smoking rubbish and the gluey mess of corticene. Water from the hoses, a great deal of it, had flooded down through the holed deck into the offices below, and 'Pay' was down there cursing loudly and continuously while he and some of his writers tried to rescue ledgers and other saturated documents. But the emergency situation here was over now, and Crick had only returned to make sure of one thing: he asked the petty officer in charge of this number eight fire brigade, 'Has Able Seaman Bates gone for'ard?'

He'd found Bates here, trying to rescue the captain's personal possessions, and getting himself more or less cooked in the process. He'd ordered him for'ard; but the captain's coxswain wasn't a man who could be relied upon to obey orders with anything like alacrity – not unless the orders were issued personally by Hugh Everard.

Petty Officer Ainslie grinned, his teeth white as a nigger minstrel's in his blackened face. 'Yessir. Picked up all 'e could lay 'is 'ands on, an' 'opped it.'

'Good.' Crick glanced round the wreck of the captain's quarters. Bates, he thought, was like a one-man dog. He corrected that; a one-man ape . . . 'Nothing much more you can do here, Ainslie.'

'Just makin' sure, sir. Some of the wood's still smoulderin' inside.'

Crick told him, 'I'll send the chief carpenter along to get those holes plugged.' He meant the ones in the deckhead, the quarter-deck. But none of this was serious damage; the ship's fighting efficiency had been hardly scratched, and so far as he'd been able to discover – touch wood – there was no damage at all below the waterline.

He walked for'ard, alternating between the main, middle and upper decks, as ladderways permitted. He'd seen to the damage on the starboard side, on his way aft; there'd been two fire brigades at work there, and he'd left the chief carpenter, Mr Wise, in charge. The after starboard six-inch gun casemate had been penetrated by a shell that burst inside and killed the entire gun's crew; another shell from the same salvo had burst in the casemate lobby and wiped out almost all the starboard ammunition-supply numbers. That gun's crew had been Marines. When he'd been there on his way aft they'd already got the wounded down to the after emergency operating room, and they'd been plugging cut fire-mains, trying to stop water pouring into the ventilation trunks; the trunks had to be kept open or men down below would suffocate. Apart from the broken fire-mains, tons of water had burst in from near-miss 'shorts' deluging into the shattered casemate.

On the port side, everything was intact and happy. Marines of the six-inch ammunition-supply parties were playing cards; a noisy game, which involved flinging the cards down and shouting at each other. A corporal asked him what was happening up top; he told them that everything was fine, that *Nile* had hit the enemy a couple of dozen times and the Huns had barely bruised her paintwork; that she'd come out of it fighting-fit, and now things were so quiet up there it was like being in church. The men cheered, and the cheer was taken up right through the casemates and the lobbies. Crick went on for'ard. There really were no problems; it was astonishing how lightly *Nile* had suffered. This had been the first test, she'd stood a real, hard hammering and sailed out smiling. Casualties were fairly heavy, but nothing like they might have been; and if *Warspite* had been saved, that would put a thousand plus-marks against these minuses.

There was still one area of damage he hadn't checked. There'd been a hit up for'ard, on the starboard side, in the master-at-arms' mess. But he went over to the port side first, and told Mr Wise to transfer his expertise to the damage aft as soon as he felt he could leave this lot to his henchmen. Wise seemed to be well on top of things now, and Crick moved on for'ard, taking the bo'sun, PO Harkmore, and Ordinary Seaman Thompson, his own messenger, along with him. He'd lent them to Mr Wise when he'd had his hands full there; now he led them past the ladderway which ran up to the bridge superstructure. There'd been some hits here too, around S3 and S4 casemates, but no real harm done, just smashed lights and so on – round 'B' barbette and through the foc'slmen's mess on the starboard side. Ahead of him, he could see the damage. The inboard bulkhead of the jaunty's mess had been blown out, ripped. Jagged flanges of sheet-steel jutted towards the centre-line. The mess itself was a ruin, although the fire had been put out before it had taken a real hold. The bulkhead between this section and the ERAs' mess for'ard of it was bulged and charred. But it was all in hand; number two fire brigade were clearing up, collecting debris, sweeping up broken glass, and a party of torpedomen under Mr Askell the warrant officer, were repairing cables on the deckhead. Amidships, the skylight over the sickbay had been shattered. Crick peered in, getting a bird's-eye view of sickberth ratings attending to a queue of lightly wounded men. Some of them looked up and saw him, and there were the usual questions to which he gave the same answers – and again the men cheered.

The glass on the skylight for'ard of this one was intact. It was over the centre of the operating room. There was a man on the table and two on stretchers awaiting their turns; the one on the table was having a leg removed.

Over on the port side, the chief stokers' mess and its pantry hadn't suffered from the blast. And all the men here were exceptionally cheerful, probably because they'd been through an unusually brisk action and come out alive, fit to tell the tale . . . He turned to PO Harkmore.

'Nothing to worry us here, Bo'sun. We'd better go and see how they've managed up top.'

'Aye, sir.' Harkmore was a big man; he'd reached the semi-finals in the Fleet heavyweight boxing competition up in Scapa, and Crick had thought he should have won it. If he, Tom Crick, had been the referee, Harkmore would have.

The bridge superstructure, when he'd last seen it, had been well ablaze from the shell which had burst in the captain's sea-cabin. He went quickly up the ladder to the foc'sl deck, and then the next one to the shelter deck; one more climb brought him and his party to the level of the conning-tower.

The captain wasn't in it. Rathbone was, and a midshipman and some signalmen, and the spare director's crew, but everyone else had gone back up to monkey's island, Rathbone said. Crick walked back the thirty-odd feet to the ladder, and climbed again. The fire had spread, before they'd got it contained and stifled. The superstructure around him as he climbed the ladderways was black, distorted and stinking, but the two upper levels were undamaged. As he stepped on to the fore bridge, he saw Hugh Everard raise a cup to his lips as if he felt he needed it.

'Bates, this stuff's cold!'

Crick saw Hugh's coxswain hurry forward.

'Beg pardon, sir, that's what I give you a 'alf-hour or more ago.'

'Oh, is it?' Hugh pushed the cup into his coxswain's hand. 'Get me some fresh, will you?' He saw Crick. 'How is it, Tom?'

'Not at all bad, sir, considering – except you personally seem to have no home left.'

'So I hear.' Hugh told him, 'I'm taking Rathbone's sea-cabin. He'll doss in the chartroom.'

'On the whole, sir, we've got off lightly.'

'Good.' The wild, zigzagging course had been *intended* to let *Nile* off lightly. Hugh trained his glasses on the other ships of *Nile*'s squadron. They were six or seven miles ahead, but they'd be reducing speed as they formed astern of the battle fleet, and it wouldn't take long to close up on them.

Hugh had a feeling that he'd done a worthwhile job. *Warspite* was on her own, north-westward from here, steaming west at slow speed. Badly hurt, obviously, but at least she was still afloat.

Hugh lowered his glasses, and turned to his second-in-command. A thought struck him; he shouted, 'Bates!'

'Sir?'

The coxswain's voice had come from one deck down.

'Bring a cup for the commander as well!'

'Aye aye, sir!'

Hugh nodded to Tom Crick. 'All right, Tom. Tell me how lightly.'

CHAPTER 8

Bantry was alone. The Germans who'd been battering her, and from whom perhaps she'd saved *Nile*, had gone – eastwards. It was all mist there; grey, impenetrable.

Nile had gone, too. *Bantry* had been zigzagging haphazardly in the spreading drift of her own smoke-screen, and now that it had dissipated *Nile* was only one of several grey smudges in the hazy northern and north-eastern distance.

'Hand me my glasses, Pilot.'

Wilmott was on his left, at the binnacle. He and David were alive, but the men in the bridge's afterpart had been killed by blast or flash or both. Incredible; it seemed like a nightmare from which sooner or later one would wake up.

'*Damn* you, Pilot! Give me my glasses!'

He snatched them up and passed them over.

'Not that side, you fool!'

David turned and stared at him. Wilmott's eyes glared back above a deathly pale, strained face, a jutting beard with flecks of spit on it.

Looking downwards, David saw the reason for the *not that side*. Wilmott's arm had been wrenched off at the shoulder. There were streamers of blood-soaked superfine cloth, and sort of – *strings*, and . . .

David shut his eyes. He felt sick, and above all, out of touch, unreal. It felt as if there was madness in the air . . . Like a robot, he moved round behind his captain and placed the glasses in his left hand. Wilmott said without looking at him again, doubled sideways with his elbow hooked over the binnacle and bent to reach the glasses with his eyes, 'Find out where Commander Clark is, and tell him I want to know what the state of things below is . . . Watch your steering, quartermaster!'

143

'Aye aye, sir . . .' The voice out of the copper tube sounded normal, steady. 'She's not answering too well, sir.'

The telegraphs weren't working either. Weren't being responded to, anyway. None of the navyphones seemed to be alive. Since the final salvo had smashed down into her, there'd been two reports, both by word of messenger; one from Pike, the engineer, to the effect that the port engine-room was out of action, and then one from the commander to the effect that he'd ordered the evacuation of the maintopmen's messdeck and that there were too many fires for all of them to be coped with adequately.

All magazines had been flooded. The hands in the after steering compartment reported water rising steadily. They were trapped in there, and rescuers couldn't get to it to help from outside.

A voice bleated from a voicepipe: 'Bridge!' David located it: it was the one from the spotting top.

'Bridge.'

'Everard.' It was Johnny West. 'Tell the Captain that all electrical circuits seem to have failed. I can't even contact the TS. And before communications went dead they told me the turrets' hydraulic power's failed. I want—'

Wilmott had sharp ears, still. He snapped, 'Tell him turrets can go into hand-training.' West was saying, '– permission to abandon this spotting top and the director. I want to get the guns into local control and hand-training, and without communications I can't do a bloody thing.'

'Tell him yes!'

'Johnny? Captain says yes. Come down.'

'Pilot!'

'Sir?'

At this slow speed and on one engine, listing and down by the stern, *Bantry* was all shakes and rattles, metal groans. It felt to David as if he was standing on something that was about to fall apart. Wilmott was leaning sideways now against the binnacle, as if without its support he'd have had no balance. His whole right side was a sheet of blood, and he was standing in a pool of it. David wondered if it was possible to be in such a state and not feel pain. Might there be some brain-defeating mechanism in the nervous system, some switch that threw off? Wilmott was paler still now, absolutely white, and there was a weird light in his eyes, but he didn't seem to be aware of the drastic nature of his injury. It added to the sense of unreality, the feeling that one would suddenly be released from all this, that it didn't have to be taken seriously. David asked him, 'Yes, sir?'

'Didn't I tell you to find the Commander?'

'I'll go now, sir.' He glanced round the bridge. He'd no idea where to start – or even, really, where he was. Even the light was peculiar; milky, streaked with duller grey and a sort of khaki haze, while aft there, of course, there was only smoke . . . He heard his voice informing Wilmott, 'I'll get the surgeon up, sir. You can't—'

'Don't tell me what I can or cannot do, Pilot. Just *you* do what I've ordered you to do.' It sounded like some sort of game, or a children's argument. 'D'you understand me, Everard?' David nodded. Presumably the man was numb, and couldn't feel it. It made one ill just to look at him even at his face. *He's dead, and he doesn't realise it . . .*

Then: *Signal bridge: there'll be men down there, and I'll send them to find Clark* . . . It was a voice speaking in his head, something he listened to from outside himself. He felt grateful to it; there didn't seem to be any other kind of help around.

'*Everard!*'

'Yes, sir.' He was moving towards the after end of the bridge, to the ladder that would take him down to the signal bridge. He managed not to look at Wilmott again before he'd got past him. But he had to pass the yeoman here, and Midshipman Porter and the Marine bugler, and a signalman named Rouse; they'd all been standing here in the after part of the compass platform when that flash had shot up and enveloped it. He half-closed his eyes, so that he could see his way but not those *things*. Clothes all charred: if you brushed against them by accident they scattered like dust or dead leaves; and the bodies weren't burnt – simply discoloured, horrible.

He started down the starboard ladderway.

'Where the devil are *you* going?'

He looked up. The question seemed to cut through the surroundings, which were too appalling to be believed. There was enough beastliness here to fill a lifetime of nightmares. Commander Clark's blue eyes blazed up at him.

'I was coming to find you, sir. Captain wants a report on how things are below decks.'

'He's about to get one.' Clark came up the ladder fast, pushing past David, hauling himself up with quick, powerful tugs of his short, thick arms. Stocky, balding, belligerent, he looked as if he'd been fighting Uhlans single-handed and unarmed and then been dunked in

145

oily water. He stopped at the top of the ladder: feet apart, hands on hips, glaring at the corpses as if they were so many defaulters.

'What the devil!'

'They're dead, sir.'

'I didn't think they were dancing a bloody hornpipe.'

Clark swung to his right, took a few paces for'ard; his usual aggressive, strutting paces. When David took his eyes off the baked effigy which had been PO Sturgis, he became aware that the commander was standing with his fists on his hips again, facing a deserted bridge.

'Well? Where *is* the Captain?'

David moved up beside him. Wilmott was down beside the binnacle, on his back. His head dangled backwards over the low central step; his mouth was an open pink slit above the beard. His eyes were open too, staring upwards at the sky.

Clark bent down, put a finger to an eyeball. Then he straightened.

'Right.' He took a deep breath, and let it out again. The word and the breath signified his assumption of command. 'Get Lieutenant West down from the spotting top.'

David glanced aloft, and pointed. With his two-man crew following him, West was climbing down the rungs on the foremast. The third man – boy, rather, it was little Ackroyd – was just emerging from the lubber's hole in the base-plate of the top. David told Commander Clark, 'None of the navyphones work, sir, and the engine-room don't answer telegraphs. The quartermaster says steering's difficult.'

'That, Everard, is hardly surprising.' Clark watched as the gunnery lieutenant – who'd just become the executive officer – climbed on the foremast into the after end of the bridge, and came for'ard.

'Sir.' West glanced down at Wilmott, and caught his breath. He looked at David, then back at Clark. He seemed to square his shoulders.

'Listen, West. We're going slow ahead on one screw, but the engine-room's inaccessible, cut off by a fire which we don't seem able to make much impression on. We're badly holed, but we can't get at the holes either, and even if we could we wouldn't be able to stop them up because they're too damn big. I estimate we've about a hundred dead and about as many wounded. And as you can see—' he pointed aft – 'there is no chance whatsoever of this ship remaining afloat.'

West nodded. Clark went on, 'I want all the wounded fetched up on deck, and then I want all fit men employed making rafts. All the boats are smashed, of course – or burnt. Now listen – we should get some warning, because the main flooding's through the starboard engine-room, and that's the one that's still going. When the water gets to a certain height it'll stop it. Then we'll know time's nearly up. Understand?'

'Might we not have a chance of getting her home, sir?'

'No. Three hundred miles, in this state?' Clark's head jerked sideways in brusque dismissal of the hope. 'If there was a chance in a thousand, I'd have a shot at it. But there isn't, and the best hope of finding assistance is to stay in this area.'

'With respect, sir – might she not float longer if we drew fires in the boiler-rooms, and shut off steam?'

'I doubt if it'd make much odds, West. And if we were completely stopped it'd make us more vulnerable to any Hun that sneaks along. A submarine, for instance.' West nodded. Clark looked at David, 'Everard.'

David was thinking that Clark was right; there must have been as many as two or three hundred ships in this approximate vicinity – say within fifty miles – and that was quite a concentration. As long as one had something fairly solid to hang on to, something that floated well – surely if one could simply stay afloat, alive, sooner or later even a German would stop and—

'Are you asleep, Everard?'

'Sir?'

Clark peered at him curiously. Johnny West was giving him the same look. The commander sighed, shook his head. 'Go on down, West. Wounded up on deck, then rafts. And send young Scrimgeour up here.'

'Aye aye, sir.' West turned away, towards the ladder. 'You come and help me, Ackroyd.'

'Sir!' Piping treble . . . Clark frowned, shook his head, thinking something like *Ought to be at home, with his mother* . . . 'Now, Everard. I want you to see to the destruction of confidential books and charts.' He pointed to the back end of the compass platform. 'You can organise a bonfire right there.'

It was black and charred, skeletally gaunt where all the wood trimmings had been scorched away; there was only bare steel, blistered paintwork, and those hideous, red-indian-coloured corpses.

'Wait a minute.'

Not that he'd moved yet. Perhaps this fellow thought he had. He

147

stared into the commander's blue eyes, wondering who he was, where he'd met him. The top half of Signalman Rowse's face was white, unburnt, where he'd shielded his eyes by throwing up his hands. David could see Rowse's face as if the image of it was over-printed on his vision as he stared at Clark. Clark said, 'Before you start on the books, go down to the signal bridge and find a flag six and hoist it somewhere.'

He looked up. He could see one or two halyards still up there, flapping loose. Perhaps one of them might be serviceable.

'Flag six, sir?'

'For God's sake, man, snap out of it!' Clark clapped his hands, for some reason, in front of David's face. 'What does flag six mean when it's hoisted on its own?'

He concentrated. Six . . . He could visualise it, all right. Half blue and half yellow . . . He nodded, as the answer came to him.

'*Am in danger of sinking from damage received in action, sir.*'

Clark nodded, angrily. 'What d'you want – congratulations?'

David stared at him, wondering what he'd meant.

'Go on, man, *move!*'

Mr Pilkington, the torpedo gunner, stared up at Nick.

'Spare a minute, can ye?'

Nick had been chatting to Leading Seaman Hooper, the layer of the midships four-inch. Now that he was gunnery control officer, he had a lot to learn, and it was likely he'd pick up more useful information from an experienced gunlayer than he would from any drill book.

He climbed down from the platform, to join Pilkington. *Lanyard* was doing about five knots, using only her starboard shaft, while Worsfold did something in one of the two boiler-rooms. Nick hadn't heard all of it, when the commissioned engineer had come up to the bridge and explained to Mortimer what it was he wanted. Roughly, it was to drain one feed-tank so that his ERAs could mend or patch a leak in it; then he'd refill it from one of the reserve tanks. Mortimer had agreed reluctantly, under Worsfold's threat that a stitch in time, now, might keep *Lanyard* in the battle, whereas otherwise she might well have to drop out with bigger trouble later.

Down in the south-east, Jellicoe's battle fleet was a grey haze topped by smoke. The fleet had altered course to south now, presumably – so Mortimer had surmised, discussing it with Nick and Hastings – to impose its guns between the Germans and their escape-route south-eastwards.

'The 'uns 've turned back agin, Sub.'

Pilkington's eyes were small and bright under the beetling brows. Since he had exceptionally short legs, he was several inches shorter than Nick.

'Are you sure?'

Pilkington jerked his head towards the bridge. One of the gun's crew, prone and dozing on the platform, rolled over and raised his head to listen; up there, the man's head was on a level with their own as they stood on the upper deck below the gun.

'We just picked up a signal from *Southampton*. Wireless signal. *Enemy battle fleet steering east-sou'-bloody-east*, it said.' He pointed, 'Bring 'em up agin Jelly agin, won't it?'

'Perhaps you're right.'

'There's no *per'aps*, Sub.' The gunner demonstrated with his hands. 'Look. Scheer goin' this way, Jelly strung out 'ere. Can't 'elp fetchin' up agin each other, eh?'

'I'm glad our W/T's all right now. That leading tel's pretty good. What's his name – Williams?'

'Garn!' Pilkington screwed up his nose. 'Don't take much to rig a jury aerial. Like stringin' a bloody washin' line! You don't want to go roun' lettin' these fellers think they're bloody geniuses, you know, Sub!'

'No. I won't.' Nick thought Pilkington was all right in small doses. 'And thanks for the buzz. Let's hope the chief has us fixed up in time.' He turned away, to go back up on the platform. Pilkington's hand clamped on his forearm.

'Wasn't that I want to talk to you about, Sub.' The gunner scowled. 'No 'urry, are yer?'

'Well—'

'Come aft 'ere a minute . . .'

'All right.' They walked aft together, past both sets of tubes and the distorted superstructure over the quarterdeck ladderway. The gunner halted facing the stern, staring critically at the lashed-down collision-mat covering the gashes in the deck. Beyond it, *Lanyard*'s wake seethed gently, like soapy water seeping from a drain. Quite a difference, Nick thought, from the boiling white cauldron which, an hour or so ago, had been piled higher than the stern itself.

It felt strange that she should be alone now, and quiet. It also felt wrong; down there to the south, the outcome of a major battle was

149

being decided. Or at least, if this little man was right about *Southampton*'s signal, *about to be* decided.

'Well?'

'Listen. Am I right, you didn't let on to the Old Man about it bein' you as got the tubes roun', an' all?'

Nick thought about it.

No, he hadn't said anything about that. He remembered now. He'd felt it wasn't necessary. And Mortimer had been firing questions at him, one after another, hadn't he? Also – it was coming back, now – Mortimer had been critical, or near-critical, of Nick's account of his movements aft here during that action and the explosion; and one's natural tendency in such circumstances had always been to clam up, say as little as possible and then remove oneself from the presence of the criticiser as swiftly as possible.

'That's so – although I did have to tell him you'd fired, and that there was only one fish left, because he asked me the direct question. Don't imagine I was making your report for you, because I wasn't.'

'I know you wasn't, ol' mate.' The warrant officer nodded his rather large head. It might not have seemed as big as it did if the rest of him hadn't been so small. But then again, he was not – as Nick had thought, on first being introduced to him – anything like a jockey, because if you'd sat him on a horse he'd have seemed quite tall. It was only his legs that the midwife must have taken reefs in.

'Right.' He nodded again. 'But I mean you did it. You could 'a took the credit. An' we scored, old chum, we bloody 'it the bugger!'

'Let's hope so. I suppose it'll all come out, some day. Who fired which way at what time, and who got hit, and all that.'

'Sub, listen.' Mr Pilkington grasped his arm. 'I'm tellin' you. That fish bloody 'it. I *seen* it 'it.'

'Well.' Nick didn't know what he was supposed to say or do. At the time, Pilkington had said he'd *thought* he'd seen a torpedo hit one of the enemy ships. Now he was swearing to it. But at least he'd let go of that arm now. 'Well, good for you. Did you tell the Captain you scored?'

'Course I did!'

'Was he pleased?'

'Christ Almighty, what d'you think?'

'Well, that's fine, then. Splendid.'

The gunner was staring at him.

'You're a rum 'un, you are, Sub.'

'Why?'

150

'Thought you was a toffee-nosed young sod, when you first come aboard.'

Nick laughed. It would be a bit of a lark, back at Mullbergh, going out to one of those awful parties, if one said to one's giggly little tennis partner, 'I know that at first I give the impression of being a toffee-nosed sod, but *act*ually . . .' He smiled at Pilkington. 'I'm sorry about that. Probably shyness, first day on board, that sort of thing?'

'You're all right, Sub.' Pilkington raised a hand and began to pick a back tooth with its forefinger. Whatever he'd been after, he'd got hold of; he was examining it, now.

He'd flicked it away.

'You want a bit of 'elp, or advice, or what, any time, Sub – well, I bin in this Navy close on thirty bloody years, I oughter know a thing or two.' He slapped Nick's shoulder, suddenly. 'You get problems, you come to me. I'll see you right, old son.'

'Thanks. I'll bear it in mind.' Evidently Pilkington felt he'd done him some sort of favour. He certainly hadn't intended to.

He left the torpedo gunner beside the after searchlight platform, and went to finish his chat with the gunlayer, Hooper. The men of the four-inch's crew were all mad keen to get back into the action; none of them had any doubts of it ending in a resounding British victory, and they wanted to be in at the kill. They'd seen that cannonade, when Jellicoe's battle squadrons had hit Scheer so hard that the High Seas Fleet had had to turn about and escape into the mist, and it had convinced them all that if the Germans could be forced to stand and fight, they'd be annihilated. Nick agreed, of course.

'But it's a very difficult move to counter, isn't it? What can a boxer do if his opponent just ducks under the ropes and legs it for home?'

Hooper pursed his lips, and pushed his cap to the back of his head. 'If you 'ad a few squadrons the other side of 'im, sir?'

Hugh Everard, when he'd told Nick and David about the turn-away tactic which Scheer had been practising in the Baltic had been thinking in terms of a fast destroyer flotilla which, when such a move seemed likely, could somehow slip out to the enemy's disengaged side, so that the turning line would be enfiladed with torpedoes. But that sounded a lot easier than it would be to achieve in practice – or rather, in action. And Jellicoe's view was that the only answer to it was time, and to keep between the enemy and his bases so that sooner or later he'd have to fight.

151

Probably that was Jellicoe's intention now. But he hadn't much daylight left.

Nick went back up to the bridge. Hastings was alone in charge of it, with a bridge staff consisting of two lookouts and one signalman. Mortimer, Hastings told him, had gone down to see what was happening in the boiler-room.

'He's getting slightly frantic again.' Hastings spoke quietly to Nick, in the forefront of the bridge. *Lanyard*'s stubby bow, below them, was pushing like a snow-plough through dull-grey sea; at this speed there wasn't much movement on the ship, only rattles . . . 'I can't say I blame him. We picked up a signal from senior officer Second Light Cruiser Squadron to the effect that the Huns 've gone about again – so it could all start up again pretty well any time now, and here we are lolling around like something on a spring cruise . . . By the way, you're doing all right. Mortimer likes you . . . You know you replaced a snotty, do you?'

'I replaced a—'

'Keep your wool on.' Hastings bent to the voicepipe to give a helm order. They were altering now and then, not in a regular zigzag pattern but just an occasional change of course to make things slightly less simple for any lurking submarine. 'Steady!'

'Steady, sir . . . Course sou'-sou'-east by south, sir!'

'Steer that.'

'Steer sou'-sou'-east by south, sir.'

Hastings straightened, turned his pock-marked face to Nick. 'Poor old Mike Reynolds was due to move to another boat as first lieutenant. Mortimer had recommended him, and we'd just been deprived of our snotty. So the plan was, since you were suddenly available for some reason, that you'd take over the dogsbody jobs for a month or two, and then when it was considered you could pull your weight, Reynolds would leave us and we'd get a new midshipman. You don't have to feel insulted or—'

'Who said I—'

'All right, then.'

David would have felt insulted, according to Johnson. Nick thought, *I may be like him, in that respect. It's something I must watch out for.* He wondered where David was now, whether *Bantry* had seen any action. 'Hey!' Hastings was using his binoculars, looking ahead, southward. 'Hey, it's warming up again!'

Nick grabbed a spare pair – he thought they'd belonged to Johnson – which had been hanging from a voicepipe. As he raised them, he heard the gunfire; now he saw flashes, that now familiar red flickering. Hastings was shouting into the engine-room voice-pipe, telling them to ask the captain to come up to the bridge. Nick checked the compass while Hastings was away from it; at least *Lanyard* was pointing in the right direction, at more or less the centre of the arc of flashes. The firing was still only intermittent, but its frequency and spread seemed to be increasing.

Mortimer flung himself into the bridge, and snatched up his own glasses. Hastings told him, pointing, 'Action's resumed, sir. Can we use our engines yet?'

'If we could, we *would* be, damn you!'

Mortimer had snarled it. His hands holding the binoculars shook; Nick could almost feel the voltage of his frustration crackling out of him . . .

'Damn-fool questions . . .' He dropped his glasses on their lanyard, raised his fists and shook them at the clouds. 'It's worse than that fool Worsfold thought. We'll be an hour, at least . . .'

Derfflinger had been hit again; Hugh saw the flames shoot out of her. *Lutzow* had dropped out of the action; Hipper had abandoned her, and it wasn't likely she'd float.

The guns of the Fifth Battle Squadron were all firing; their targets were Scheer's battleships as they loomed out of the mist, vanished, reappeared. This damnable mist. But there was always some target in sight, to shift to, and everything that appeared was being shot at and hit, not only by the Queen Elizabeths; *Revenge, Colossus, Neptune, Benbow, Superb, Hercules, Agincourt, Collingwood, Bellerophon, Royal Oak, Orion, Monarch, Centurion,* Jellicoe's own *Iron Duke, Temeraire* and *Marlborough* were all in it. *Marlborough,* who'd been hit a few minutes ago by a torpedo, was maintaining her station at the head of the Sixth Division and had just scored two hits on a König-class battleship which had since disappeared. And once again, the High Seas Fleet was being hit too hard and too often to do much in reply. Hugh was on *Nile*'s open compass platform, because there was virtually no shellfire to take shelter from. Because, also, he disliked the blinkered feeling that one got in the enclosed conning-tower; visibility was bad enough without having to peer into it through a slit in a steel wall.

Tom Crick stood on his right, Rathbone close to the binnacle on his left. The chief yeoman, Peppard, was in the port after corner of the bridge, and Bates was hanging around there somewhere. Hugh was uncomfortably aware of a certain irrational quality in his current anger with Bates; he'd been enormously relieved to discover that his coxswain had not been in the sea-cabin when it was hit, and at the same time annoyed that he'd left it and gone aft without orders. Also at the back of the bridge now was the secretary; Colne-Wilshaw was taking photographs as well as keeping his diary notes up to date.

It wasn't only mist that was hiding the German dreadnoughts, it was the smoke of exploding British shells.

A navyphone flashed and buzzed. Midshipman Ross-Hallet answered it. There'd been no need, in the last ten or fifteen minutes, for communications or conversation; the Germans had appeared, and the fleet had known what to do about it. In *Nile*, Brook in the control top had set his gunnery organisation going without a second's delay or a wasted word; and Jellicoe wasn't a man to waste time with unnecessary signalling. Ross-Hallet called out the message from the control top: 'Enemy destroyers seem about to launch torpedo attack on the bow, sir!'

'Very good.' Hugh got them in his glasses. A flotilla was emerging from the head of the German line, the gap between the four battle cruisers and the battleships; and it looked as if those surviving battle cruisers were turning towards Jellicoe's line now: there were *two* flotillas of destroyers moving out to the attack. Scheer must have ordered offensive action up there in the hope of making Jellicoe turn away.

As he would. If torpedoes were fired, he'd allow an appropriate time for their run and then order turns-away of two or perhaps four points, to allow the torpedoes to run harmlessly between ships and squadrons. When they'd run through, he'd turn back.

Perhaps Scheer was planning another retreat, and using an attack by battle cruisers and destroyers as cover for it?

Nile's salvoes had a different sound to them, now that 'X' turret came later, by a split second, than the other three. And now the noise-level increased sharply as her secondary armament of six-inch guns opened up, to add to the hail of steel that was greeting the German torpedo craft as they moved out. Brook would be keeping up his fifteen-inch salvoes at the battleships; the six-inch guns had their own director towers, one each side abaft the foremast.

Crick lowered his glasses, pointed towards the head of the enemy line, those four already badly mauled battle cruisers. They were

154

steaming directly towards the British squadrons, actually charging them, and not all their for'ard turrets were still functional.

'They're trying to commit suicide!'

'I believe Scheer's about to run for it, Tom.'

The guns of the whole British line were blazing continuously now, and making better practice than they ever did against towed targets. Scheer would be mad if he did not order another 'battle-turn-away'. And those suicidal battle cruisers: *Von de Tann* had just been hit again, aft; Hugh had his glasses on her as she erupted in smoke and flame. *Derringer*, almost finished but maddeningly refusing to admit it, was being blasted from end to end. *Seydlitz* seemed to be about to sink; she was so low for'ard that her foc'sl had hardly any freeboard at all. He'd seen two – now three – of the attacking destroyers hit, and certainly one of them was foundering. And suddenly Hugh saw that his guess had been right. Scheer's battleships were turning – and not all to starboard! *This* retreat was haphazard, a desperate scramble of huge ships to escape that pulverising cannonade.

'They're beaten, Tom.' Hugh lowered his binoculars. He told Tom Crick, 'We've *broken* 'em – they can't stand up to us!'

The torpedo craft were laying smoke. It would cover Scheer's retreat; it would also cover their own – when they'd fired their torpedoes, they could slip back into it. And a third flotilla was launching itself now from the German line; as they were spotted, gunfire rose to a crescendo, until one heard no individual shots or salvoes but only a continuous roar of exploding cordite and bursting shells. Two more destroyers had been hit, and a third and one of the first to be hit had sunk. Astern, Hugh saw four British destroyers racing out to finish a Hun flotilla leader who'd been stopped, disabled, between the lines. He looked southwards again to see that the four battle cruisers had finally turned away, and were limping into the cover of the destroyers' smoke. '*Barham*'s flying the preparative, sir!'

Chief Petty Officer Peppard had kept one eye continually on the squadron flagship, and he'd just seen the blue-and-white striped flag shoot up to Evan-Thomas's port lower yard. It was the emergency-turn signal, to avoid torpedoes. Hugh watched *Malaya*, his next ahead, as *Nile*'s answering pendant ran close-up. *Malaya*'s was up, and *Valiant*'s too now. To starboard there was no German in sight, except for a few destroyers mostly hidden in shell-spouts and smoke, but from the control top Brook must still have had targets in his sights, and all turrets were still firing.

155

Another destroyer emerged from the belt of smoke; she was dodging to and fro, her bow-wave high and brilliant-white against surrounding grey-black drabness. Hugh saw a jet of flame as the popgun on her foc's'l fired. Then the sea ahead of her gushed up, and the rest of the same salvo smashed down into her vitals. She split open, disgorging smoke and a great pillar of escaping steam. When the smoke cleared, there was no trace left of her.

'Executive, sir!'

'Starboard ten.'

'Starboard ten, sir . . . Ten o' starboard wheel on, sir!'

Nile and the ships ahead of her were swinging away to port.

'Midships!'

'Midships, sir . . .'

Midshipman Ross-Hallet answered a navyphone, and shouted, 'Director tower reports torpedo passing astern, sir!'

'Very good.' Evan-Thomas had timed his avoiding-action well. 'Steady as you go.'

'Steady, sir. Course sou'-west by south, sir.'

Hugh watched the ships ahead, and waited for the signal to resume previous course. Jellicoe would obviously continue southwards now; or perhaps west of south, to keep closer to the enemy – who had once again been turned, driven back, leaving the Grand Fleet massive and remorseless between them and their homeland.

'Keep the men busy', Clark had ordered. And he'd sent David down with the same instruction, after he'd destroyed the secret charts and books. The commander had then gone down himself, to take charge of the fire-fighting, leaving Lieutenant Scrimgeour on the bridge with young Ackroyd.

Bantry's upper deck was a scrap-heap of twisted steel; it hadn't been easy to find spaces for all the wounded. Going aft for the first time since the action, David had been astonished at the amount of wreckage – the funnels full of holes, mainmast holed too, the after searchlight blown right into the third funnel; he'd thought at first it was smoking, but that was steam leaking where one of the two steam-pipes on the funnel had been cut through. He saw that someone had lashed a Union Flag to the top of the mainmast stump. The topmast and topgallant – which had carried the W/T gear – had been shot away, and the whole lot of it, with shrouds, stays, aerials and lifts, had been dumped on the after shelter-deck and across the stern turret, buckling that screen door. The ship's boats had of course all been smashed, and the ones for'ard had been burnt; the superstructure was full of holes and great black stains where exploding shells had scorched away the paint.

West had set up his raft-factory right aft on the quarter-deck. Half a dozen Carley floats were intact, but that was all, and for a hundred wounded men the able-bodied ones were lashing together any buoyant materials they could find. Timber, boxes, mattresses, oil and paint drums were being assembled into catamaran-like shapes with sections of collision-mats, boats' sails from the bosun's store below, sections of plank – stretched, nailed, lashed across as decking.

West murmured, as they picked their way for'ard, 'A lot of those contraptions may not float too well with the weight of men on 'em.' David glanced at him, wondering why he didn't tell them so, warn them. West answered the unspoken question: 'Keeps 'em occupied. That's the main thing we must do. Anyway, you never know, until you try it out.'

He'd thought of a new way to keep the hands busy now: ranging the cable on the foc's'l. To make room for it, they were going to have to shift a lot of the wounded from there up to the battery deck.

Petty Officer Toomey looked doubtful. 'Won't get many up there, sir. Dickens of a job hoistin' the badly hurt ones up them ladders, wouldn't you say?'

'I'm afraid it has to be done, Toomey.' West thought about it. Bland, plump, considering nothing but how to make the best of the situation. 'The ones we can't lift, you see, can stay on the foc's'l; just shift 'em aft as far as possible. Here, say, each side of the turret and in behind it. Eh?'

Ranging the cable, which would be the first step to take in any preparation to be taken in tow, meant heaving the great, heavy chain up out of the cable-locker and 'flaking' it to and fro – fore and aft – on the foc's'l. There was very little chance of any ship arriving to take *Bantry* in tow, and there'd be no point anyway in one doing so; but it would cheer the men to see such preparations being made.

West asked Toomey, 'Blacksmith?'

'Aft, sir, below, helping the chief carpenter.'

'We can do without him if you get his tools. But pipe for the cable party, will you?'

'Aye aye, sir.'

157

West had a light of enthusiasm in his eyes as he turned to David.

'No hope of getting steam to the capstan, so we'll have to ship its bars and do the job by man-power. Well, that's not such a bad thing, is it? If only someone had a fiddle.'

The old custom was to have a fiddler up on the capstan, a lively shanty to bring the cable up by.

David suggested, with his eyes on the smoky-grey horizon and a rumble of distant gunfire in his ears, 'Why not the Marine band, instead?'

'That's a splendid idea!'

If enough bandsmen could be mustered . . . West pointed: 'I'll put 'em up on the turret there.' He looked round. 'Braithwaite!' Like everyone else, Able Seaman Braithwaite was listening to that gunfire. Someone for'ard shouted, 'The 'un's gettin' it in the neck now, lads!' A cheer went up. West shouted again, 'Hey, Braithwaite!'

'Sir?'

'Go after Petty Officer Toomey for me, ask him to come back here.'

'Aye aye, sir!'

'Sing-song, sir?'

A smoke-blackened face was looking up at him. The man was wrapped in a blanket which was patched dark-brown where his blood had soaked through it.

'If you like, Edwards.' West crouched down beside him. 'But we're going to get the cable up and range it. Then if some decent spark comes along to offer us a tow, we'll be all ready for him.'

They cheered again. A stoker with a bandage round his neck and shoulders called out hoarsely, ' 'ome by Christmas, lads!'

Toomey came up the ladder at the foc's'l break. 'New orders, sir?'

'Yes, Toomey.' West got up. 'This is the bright-ideas department. I want you to muster all of the Marine band that you can get hold of, and tell 'em to get their instruments up on the roof of 'A' turret here.'

'Reckon that is a good idea, sir.' Toomey rubbed his hands together. From somewhere aft came the shrill note of a bosun's call, and the summons, 'Cable Party muster on the foc's'l!' West nodded. 'Capital.' With his left hand he raised his cap, and used the right one to scratch the bald area which through nine-tenths of his waking hours it hid. 'Things are looking up, Toomey!'

'Aye aye, sir!'

David remembered that down below the engineers were still

trying to get through to men trapped in compartments which were steadily filling with salt water.

'Off you go, then.' West stared round at the prostrate or reclining forms of the wounded. 'Surgeon'll get back to you chaps soon, now. He's bound to deal with the bad cases first, of course. He'll get round to you all soon enough, though.'

'Good ol' guns!'

There was more cheering. West knew that in fact the surgeons – the PMO and his assistant surgeon-lieutenant – were working in the for'ard messdeck beside the seamen's washplaces. They'd had to evacuate the main dressing-station aft, and they were labouring in cramped, over-crowded quarters lit by oil-lamps, struggling to ease the sufferings of hideously mutilated sailors and Marines, and knowing that at any minute the ship might founder. It was more than medical skill that doctors needed at such a time, it was – West frowned, baulking at words like *heroism*. They were good people, that was all, and they were measuring-up well to the situation. He heard a sailor ask, 'Anyone got a smoke?'

West didn't smoke anything but cigars, and he didn't carry those on him. He asked David, 'Have you?'

David pulled out his case. It was silver, with the Everard otter's head crest on it. He flipped it open.

'Not many. Half a dozen.'

'Pass 'em out, there's a good fellow.'

Bantry seemed suddenly to lurch; a sudden plunge. For about five seconds there was a total silence on her decks, as if everyone alive or half alive was holding his breath; that thump could have been a bulkhead going, the beginning of the end. David was bent forward with the open cigarette-case out in his left hand. He froze in that position, and the rattling and groaning of the cruiser's fabric and the rush of the sea along her sides were the only sounds anyone could hear. Then a sailor called boisterously, 'Who 'ad beans for 'is breakfast, then?'

A roar of laughter cracked the silence, and an oily hand took David's last cigarette. He snapped the case shut, and felt in another pocket: 'Here. Match . . .'

'Ah, you're a toff, sir . . . Mind lightin' it? Can't see, not too clear . . .'

Not too clear. You could see, under the edges of the strip of bandage, the cordite-burns that had blinded him.

'Look, David.' West was groping in his pockets. 'We've got

cigarettes in the wardroom store—' he cocked an eyebrow – 'and I don't think fishes smoke . . . Here. This key, the small one. And this one's the pusser's stores – there's tins of pipe and chewing tobacco, you could get them too. All you can carry. Mind you lock the wardroom store behind you; we don't want liquor circulating.'

David stared at the grey sea sliding past: it was so impersonal that it was terrifying. It swallowed whatever it was given, and afterwards it looked the same: like *that* – secretive, malevolent . . . His hand tightened on the ring of keys, and he felt their edges bite into his palm. It was knowing what was happening down there, what *had* happened. Men trapped, others working to beat the fires and cut through to them: a sweet stench of blood which on its own was enough to make you vomit, and in it the reek of burnt corticene and paint and rubber cables. Pockets of cordite gas. Worst of all, the bodies and parts of bodies. There'd been one in the armoured grating above the for'ard boiler-room; it had been blown half *through* the grating. The surgeons were dealing with the wounded, not the dead, and the engineers were trying to reach the living. The dead stayed where they'd been thrown or dropped or—

David opened his hand, stared at the keys as if he was wondering what they were, or whose . . . West was frowning, looking at him in that odd way again: 'David? Will you do that?'

'I'm – working out what's the best route.' He pointed at the base of the bridge superstructure. 'In that way, I suppose, and down to the middle deck and aft along the port side, through the messes. If the fires are still mostly on the starboard side—'

West slapped him on the back. 'That's it! Go on, they'll bless you for it!'

The blinded stoker had eased himself down on to one elbow. He waved the hand that held the cigarette: 'All together now, lads! One – two – four – *It's a long way*—'

He had a voice like a rusty hinge, but all his mates were joining in. David was on his way down the buckled ladder. He was reminding himself to walk carefully down there: the torn steel had sharp edges, razor-sharp, and it was easy enough to pick a safe path where the oil-lamps had been lit, but with a wrong step or a slip and blood in areas where the carnage had been worst did make it slippery – where the compartments weren't fully lit—

Behind him the song rose, swelling: . . . *to Tipperary, to the sweetest girl I know*—

CHAPTER 9

'At 9 pm the enemy was entirely out of sight, and the threat of torpedo boat destroyer attacks during the rapidly approaching darkness made it necessary for me to dispose the fleet for the night with a view to its safety from such attacks whilst providing for a renewal of the action at daylight. I accordingly manoeuvred to remain between the enemy and his bases . . .

'There were many gallant deeds performed by the destroyer flotillas: they surpassed the very highest expectations that I had formed of them.'

From paragraphs 20 and 24 of
Sir John Jellicoe's Despatch

Nile forged southwards into fading light, astern of the other Queen Elizabeths. In less than half an hour, it would be dark.

Hugh glanced at Mowbray, who was waiting in his usual stolid manner to take over as officer of the watch. The fleet had fallen-out from action stations; they'd stand-to again at two o'clock, just before first light.

'All right, Mowbray. Course south, two hundred revolutions. She's all yours.'

'Sir.'

Hugh wondered what thoughts – if any – passed through the head behind Lieutenant Mowbray's deadpan countenance. He'd never managed to draw the man out at all. His thoughts changed and he forgot him now, wondered what sort of night lay ahead. Jellicoe wouldn't want a night action. But if Scheer tried to break through again, he'd have one anyway.

The sea looked like oiled silk. Shiny, opalescent, with a haze like polish floating on it. Here and there, according to patches of thicker or thinner mist, the shine disappeared, and where that happened you could see that the surface was dimpled, slightly fleck-marked by the wind.

'How's the barometer, Pilot?'

'Down a little, sir.'

A wind would be an ally for Jellicoe. Wind dispersed mist, kept fog away, allowed the dog to see the bone. It was to be hoped – expected – that with the morning light of the first day of June the bone would be there to be grasped and crushed.

There'd been some kind of action about an hour ago, down in the south-west, when the battle fleet had been steaming west to get closer to the enemy. Almost certainly it had been Beatty's battle cruisers brushing against some outlying German squadron. Perhaps a cruiser action: but it had sounded like big guns. It was all quiet again now.

Without wireless – and *Nile*'s equipment was smashed beyond any kind of emergency repair – one knew very little of what was going on. Only what could be seen, and signals passed by light or flags. The destroyer flotillas, for instance, had just been ordered to take up screening stations five miles astern of the battle fleet.

The battleship divisions were each in line ahead and one mile on each other's beams. Jellicoe in *Iron Duke* was leading the Fourth Division, which came roughly in the centre of the fleet, with three files of battleships on his starboard hand and the fifth to port, between him and these Queen Elizabeths. Outside this squadron – actually on *Nile*'s port quarter, since they'd dropped back by two or three miles now were the Sixth Division, led by *Marlborough*. *Marlborough*, as a result of that torpedo hit on her earlier in the evening, was finding it difficult to maintain the ordered speed of seventeen knots.

'Mowbray – has the commander had his supper, d'you know?'

Mowbray nodded. 'He was in the wardroom for about five minutes, sir. I think he had some sandwiches. He's doing rounds of the messdecks now, sir.'

Hugh turned aft. 'Bates?'

'Sir.' A figure detached itself from the mounting of the twenty-four-inch searchlight. Bates had been chatting to the yeoman of the watch. 'Supper, sir? Ready when you like, sir.'

'Hot?'

'' 'otter 'n that, sir!'

'Right. In my – the navigating officer's sea-cabin, please.'

162

'Aye aye, sir!'

Hugh paused, looking out to starboard. There, against a dulling sky and a fading sea, was Admiral Gaunt's Fifth Division: *Colossus, Neptune, St Vincent, Collingwood.* The King's son, Sub-Lieutenant Prince Albert, was an assistant turret officer in *Collingwood.* Beyond Gaunt's division was Sturdee's – with Jellicoe leading it in *Iron Duke* – and that was where young Nick must be. There could hardly have been time for anything to have been done about his transfer to a cruiser or destroyer; one could only hope he hadn't yet actually gone under report. And at least he'd been in action, had a taste of fighting, and that might help.

David would know what action felt like too, if the smokelaying cruiser had been *Bantry.* She'd certainly been one of the Minotaurs, and Rathbone had thought it was *Bantry.* Whoever she was, a natural appreciation of her captain's intention to assist was tempered by a conviction that his judgement had been at fault. By the time he'd made his move, *Nile* had been through the worst of it; the Germans had been about to lose one target, and he'd presented them with a new one.

Nile's gauntlet-running in aid of *Warspite* had been a very different matter. For one thing, the timing had been right, and *Nile* was armoured to withstand punishment, which a cruiser of that class was not. But thinking about judgement, good or bad – in the first minute after he'd put the helm over, hadn't he been wondering whether he might have made a terrible mistake? Judgement – or snatching at a chance?

He told himself, *Judgement by instinct.* One had seen what needed doing, and that it could be done. That cruiser captain had followed suit without recognising the differences in their situations.

It was getting really dark now. He looked ahead, at *Malaya.* The gleam of white under her counter was as easy to follow as any stern-light. It would seem strange, when the war ended, to have ships festooned with lights again.

'Pilot – are we on the top line with recognition signals?'

'Yes, sir. They're listed in the chartroom.'

The yeoman of the watch, PO Brannan, said, 'Signalmen've got it all weighted-off too, sir.'

Hugh went down the ladder, to his purloined cabin. Bates was standing by a tray of food. He'd stiffened to attention; he had a tendency, in that position, to rise and fall slightly on his toes.

Hands cramped against his thighs, thumbs pointing downwards among the inverted creases of bell-bottoms.

'What's the menu, Cox'n?'

'Beef stew, dumplings, boiled spuds and carrots, sir!'

'In the middle of a battle?' Hugh sat down. 'A few hours ago I was thinking you'd have been wise if you'd gone on with your swimming lessons.'

Bates's brown eyes blinked at him. 'I got 'eavy bones, sir, that's my trouble. Waste o' time, all that . . . But beggin' your pardon, sir, you done a treat. Reckon we'll be 'oistin' an admiral's flag 'fore long, sir.'

Hugh smiled. 'Looking forward to flag rank, are you?'

'Better 'n a crack on the snout, sir, wouldn't it?' Bates looked down at the tray. 'That's the last o' the good Stilton, sir . . . Coffee after, sir?'

'No. A mug of cocoa, please. Any casualties in the gig's crew?'

'Robertson, sir. Shell-splinter in 'is arse. Must 'a bin facin' the wrong way, I tol' 'im.'

Robertson was a Glasgow man; he was a marksman, and he'd done well in the Scapa rifle-shooting competitions.

'You'll have to replace him, temporarily. Pity.'

Bates looked surprised. ''E's not 'urt bad, sir!'

'You think he can sit on a thwart and pull an oar, with a splinter in his backside?'

'Useful 'and, is Robertson.' Bates wasn't a man to change his mind once he'd made it up. ''E'll soon 'arden, sir.'

Petty Officer Toomey stood aside as they reached the ladder to the foc's'l. David stopped too, looking at him enquiringly. It was more than halfway to being dark now.

'After you, sir!' The petty officer's voice was cheerful, encouraging. David climbed the steel stairway to the higher level.

On the turret roof, Marine bandsmen were churning out their repertoire. It wasn't doing much for anyone; there was a sort of incongruity about it, and West was wishing he'd left the men to their own sing-song. The cable party had finished ranging the cable ten minutes ago, with two shackles – twenty-five fathoms – up on the foc's'l. There'd been no point getting more up, and the light was going. West had had a bar put through one link of cable above the navel-pipe; they'd hove-in until the bar had the cable's weight, then disconnected the capstan and unrigged its bars and swifter. At least the operation had made the men feel something positive was happening: the worst thing for morale was inaction. He'd told them, 'That's the best we can do, until tomorrow. Be easier in daylight.'

He saw Toomey coming with David Everard, and went aft to meet them.

'Hey, no smokes?'

'What?'

David Everard was gazing up at the bandsmen. They were at about half strength, as a band, and they were playing *Billy Boy*. Toomey told West quietly, drawing him aside, 'Found 'im just wand'rin' about, sir. Talkin' to 'imself and not makin' much sense, sir. I thought I oughter bring 'im along like – well – '

Toomey was embarrassed. West swore, under his breath. He put a hand on David's shoulder.

'Did you go to the stores, David?'

'Stores?'

Concentrating . . . Stores?

He'd been on his way aft, through the messdecks on the port side, trying not to see more than he had to on his way through. This had been the worst, here; shells had penetrated and then burst when the compartment had been full of ammunition-supply parties, damage-control parties, a standby fire brigade. None of the dead had been moved – well, who'd have done it? There were parts, bits of bodies, things your foot struck and moved . . . Had to be careful, avoid the sharp edges of lacerating steel, because a leather shoe-sole wasn't proof against them; you trod in a puddle that was dark, looked like oil, and the surface broke and it was red, bright red . . .

'Everard! Everard, my dear fellow!'

Stench . . .

'Everard, old chap?'

Pickering, the padre. Looking more like a fugitive from a chain-gang than a man of God; blackened, blood-stained, hair on end, clothes torn, eyes that seemed to be all whites in a dirty, bruised-looking face. He looked as if he'd been fighting for his life: and there was an excitement – no, desperation – in his manner as he grabbed David's arms and peered into his face.

'You're just the man I need to help me, Everard!'

'I was on my way to get some stuff for—'

'I shan't detain you long, old chap!' The chaplain's action duty was with the first-aid parties, the part-of-ship back-up to the medical organisation. David wondered what he might be doing down here on his own. In the yellowish gleam of oil lamps, there were only horrors here.

'Listen, Everard – there's someone still *alive* in this compartment! I *know* it for a fact! We were bringing the last of the stretchers through – we were using the wardroom and officers' cabins as an emergency hospital, you know, but with the water coming in aft naturally we had to move the chaps, you see – well, the last time we passed through this messdeck, just about this very spot, I heard some poor fellow cry out "Help, help me".'

Pickering had waved an arm, indicating the whole length of the compartment. David stared at that hand as it fell back to the padre's side; it was wet, gleaming red, with blood. He looked down at his own sleeves, where the man's hands had grasped him: the dark stains looked like mourning bands.

If one had to pick through bodies, heaps of dead, pieces—

'I must try to find him, Everard, d'you see? Or at least be *certain* . . . The thought that some poor creature might be lying here alive, under—' the hand waved again, and the padre smiled, a fierce, determined, almost threatening smile: 'You *will* help? My dear chap, thank you, thank you!' He'd pointed: 'I've got as far as – there . . . From the after bulkhead. If you were to start on that side, perhaps at the other end?' He seized David's arm again. 'It's not – not a pleasant task, Everard.' His voice had a shake in it. 'One needs all – all one's strength. Or it may be – God's strength?' That fanatic's smile again and then it faded. 'Well – I cannot begin to express my gratitude . . .'

Corpse by corpse. The foul, sweet stench, and everywhere the – the detritus . . .

West leant forward, peered into David's face.

'You were going to bring up some cigarettes and things.'

Everard looked surprised.

'Was I?'

'Did you not go to the store?'

'Store?' David shook his head. 'Look here.' He showed West his hands. 'It's *everywhere*.' He began to laugh.

'Oh, Christ . . .' West turned away, and spoke to the petty officer. 'All right, Toomey, thank you. I'll look after him.'

'Right, sir. But – sir—'

'Yes?'

166

'Commander Clark's down there, sir, where they're tryin' to get through to the engine-room, an' he's just about done in, sir.'

'I'll go down, in a minute.' Johnny West looked up at the bridge, at the black ridge of its forefront silhouetted against the comparative lightness of the sky. There was more wind than there'd been all day; he could feel it on his face. He wondered if he could get Everard up there, out of the crowd, where he might be able to pull himself together. This ship's company was marvellous; disciplined, brave, cheerful, more impressive than he thought he'd ever be able to express. The last thing one wanted was to have an officer wandering among them in this condition. Shock or madness – the label you put on it made no difference. Everard had seemed peculiar earlier on: then he'd seemed to get better . . . West took his arm and drew him towards the ladder.

'Let's go up on the bridge, David. Up where it's—'

The starboard engine stopped.

Sound, vibration, had abruptly ceased. There was a thin hissing sound from a steam-pipe on one of the funnels and you could see the whiteness pluming out. Like ectoplasm: *Bantry* giving up her ghost. As she lost way, she seemed to slump lower in the sea. The bandsmen stopped playing; they stopped one by one, so that the music died disjointedly, and now the silence was emphasised by the swish of sea alongside and that leaking steam.

West looked round, at the pale faces of men patiently awaiting orders, guidance.

'Lieutenant West!'

Clark, the commander, was using his short arms to haul himself jerkily up the foc'sl ladder. 'Lieutenant West here?'

'Here, sir.' West met him, and saluted. Toomey had been right, Clark did look just about all-in. He could hardly stand. He panted, clinging to the handrail of the ladder for support, 'Put lines on the rafts you've made, and get 'em over the side. Hold 'em there. Drop a scrambling-net over – then get the wounded into the rafts.'

'Aye aye, sir. Petty Officer Toomey!'

'Here, sir!'

'Bosun's Mate?'

Toomey bellowed aft, 'Bosun's Mate, report for'ard!' He edged past Clark and rattled down the ladder. 'I'll send him to you, sir.' West called after him, 'I want him to pipe all hands on deck. And send some men to the dressing-station, bring up the last of the wounded. Tell the Surgeon-Commander we're about to abandon ship.'

'Aye aye, sir.'

'Listen to me, all of you.' Clark, still clutching the handrail, struggled for breath as he turned to and fro, addressing the men on the foc'sl and those below him in the waist as well.

'Listen . . . There's no rush. We've time to do this in an orderly manner. All wounded men will be helped into the rafts. *Un*-wounded men will stay *out* of 'em, and help tow 'em clear of the ship as soon as they're filled. There are plenty of ships about – or will be, by daylight – so you can reckon on being picked up quite soon. Right then – good luck to you all.'

Nick leant in a rear corner of *Lanyard*'s bridge listening to her thrumming, thumping clatter as she tore southwards through the dark. Not at full power; Worsfold had finished his repairs at about half-past eight, and he'd implored Mortimer not to use maximum revolutions unless action situations demanded it. Mortimer, who'd been getting more and more bad-tempered during the long delay, had been so relieved at getting his ship moving again that he'd accepted the recommendation.

Worsfold had muttered as he passed Nick, behind the binnacle, 'Wonders'll never cease!'

Mortimer had half-heard him.

'What's that, Chief?'

'I said, "Now for a bit of peace", sir.'

'Meaning?'

'We've been at it pretty hard down there, sir.'

'Oh, yes.' Mortimer's suspicion faded. 'I dare say you have. Well done, Chief.'

Worsfold had then winked at Nick and left the bridge. They'd been pushing south ever since at about three-quarters speed – twenty-six knots – which should bring them up astern of the Grand Fleet's flotillas in an hour or not much more. The jury-rigged wireless aerial could receive, after a fashion, but not transmit; the telegraphists had picked up Jellicoe's course-and-speed orders, and his order to the destroyers to take station five miles astern of the battle fleet, and that was all Mortimer had had to base his calculations on. Hastings had demurred, suggesting that they didn't know which way the fleet had steered between the time they last saw it and the time – nine twenty, roughly – Jellicoe had ordered the course to be changed to south. Mortimer had told him that it didn't make much difference, a point or two this way or that;

168

you couldn't *not* come up astern of a fleet that size, with no less than four destroyer flotillas spread out astern of it.

Nick had taken over on the bridge for about an hour before the boiler-room repair had been completed. Hastings had needed a break. And during that time, the dead had been buried. Each had been given a few prayers from the 'Form for the Burial of the Dead at Sea', the shrill pipe of a bosun's call, and a volley from half a dozen rifles. The simplicity of the ceremony had emphasised its sadness. And the destroyer alone here in gathering dusk, with the sea's reflective quality fading under a slowly darkening sky: there had been an acute sense of solitude, and loss . . .

Alone on the bridge except for Garret and the helmsman and telegraphman down there below them, Nick had listened to Mortimer's voice intoning the simple prayers, and to the high, thin wails of the pipe, the rattles of rifle-fire, the splashes. He'd felt a tightness in his throat, a depth of personal sorrow which astonished him.

He'd attended only one funeral in his life. His mother's. Mary Everard had died in 1906 of pneumonia, which had grown out of a chill caught when she'd got soaking wet out hunting. Nick had been eleven, and he'd felt he was attending the funeral of a stranger. It had been so cold, so impersonal; he'd thought, *that's how she was* . . . He remembered his father's tall, black-clad figure and set, stern face; there'd been the same clothes, the same faces, everywhere Nick had looked. He'd hardly known his mother; she'd seen to her sons' wellbeing in an efficient, supervisory manner, and he'd thought of her in that way – as a kind of supervisor, or 'higher authority'. The woman who'd mothered him had been 'Old Nanny'; he knew what her real name had been, now, but he hadn't then, and she'd died recently at Harrogate, where she'd gone to live in her retirement.

David had been fourteen, and a cadet at Osborne, at the time of their mother's funeral, and he'd attended it – on orders from their father – in his uniform. Nick had been surprised, and their father had been embarrassed, when David had started weeping. It had never occurred to Nick that either of them might be so affected. When they got back to the house, their father had sent for David, and he must have given him a ticking-off; David had been sniffling again when he'd come back upstairs to the schoolroom. He'd stopped in the doorway, and glared at his smaller brother out of reddened eyes: 'You don't *care*, do you!'

'Care what?'

'That she's dead! You never loved her, like I—'

'No, I—'

'There! You admit it! You little beast, you—'

'I was trying to say I didn't *not* like – love her.' He remembered being totally confused. He didn't *know* how he'd felt about her, or even how he felt about her being dead.

Uncle Hugh had come up from London for the funeral. He'd got married only a few months before, and he'd brought his wife up with him. Nick remembered being sent down to the big drawing-room at Mullbergh, and introduced to her. She'd drawled some comment which he didn't understand, and she'd shrugged, laughing at his embarrassment. He'd always hated that room.

'Starboard ten.'

'Starboard ten, sir!'

'Steady on sou'-west by south.' He turned, met Garret's eyes as they heard yet another rattle of shots and yet another splash. Garret muttered, 'Must be the last. Poor devils.'

'They may not be feeling poor, perhaps?'

He'd just said it without thinking and immediately wished he hadn't. Garret put the thing back in an easier perspective; he said, '*I* would be.'

An hour later: twenty-five sea-miles farther south. It was pitch dark now, and an empty sea. There'd been some signals which *Lanyard* had intercepted from light cruisers reporting sightings of the enemy; it seemed fairly plain that the Germans were to the westward or south-westward of Jellicoe's southbound battle fleet.

Mortimer had said, 'He's got 'em where he wants 'em. Given any sort of luck, he'll have Scheer over a barrel in the morning!'

It was a satisfying thought that one was taking part in a major battle that was likely to end up as a major victory. Nick wondered where David was, whether his cruiser had been in action – and if so, how he'd reacted to the experience. David would come out of it all right; not that anyone could 'arrange' what happened in a battle, but simply that David would take care he personally did not come to grief. If his ship sank, he'd survive, in any situation . . . Like getting over tall hedges, out hunting – David invariably picked his spot, and usually one that a few other riders had been over first, whereas he, Nick, tended to charge the obstacle at its nearest point – and come off, yet again . . . He enjoyed it, but he usually managed to make an idiot of himself; he wasn't the right shape for a horseman, as David was, with his length of leg, balance and slimness. David's great disadvantage was his nervousness. He'd always been scared, even as a small boy. But according to their father, David was the horseman, the one who was mad keen on riding to hounds, who looked right on a horse. Nick had never heard his brother argue the point – but he'd seen his hands shaking, seen the tremble of his lips. And David, the heir, had to do it well. Sir John Everard expected nothing less, from his elder son. Was that part of David's trouble? It matched what Johnson had said about him, the idea of his being scared of not succeeding – didn't it?

Nick frowned as he thought about it. The possibility of getting some insight that might help one to like – or *cease to dislike* – one's own brother had obvious appeal, and this was why what Johnson had said had interested him so much. Then when one thought about it – about, for instance, David's concern for his own person, and in contrast, what he'd done to that wretched tart – he had *done* it, and he'd tried to pretend he hadn't, tried to suggest some other man might have been with her after he, David, had left her: he'd been desperate, almost grovelling in his attempts to persuade Nick to accept his denials, evasions. But Nick had just returned from the girl's lodging, he'd seen her, heard her: now he saw his brother's white face and frightened eyes, and it had been an effort to keep his fists at his sides.

David had begged him to go to her address. The morning after: Nick had a bad hangover from the party – a mutual friend's bachelor night, the eve of his wedding – and David had something more than a hangover. Nick hadn't realised that; on his way to see the girl he'd construed that all that was wrong with his brother was an excess of alcohol the night before and a degree of shame at having spent what had been left of the night with a prostitute he'd picked up in the street. It had been in character, that David shouldn't want to face her sober and in daylight, and Nick, on his way there in a cab, had felt no more than a familiar, mild contempt for him. It had been no more than that – until the girl opened her door to his knock and he saw her bruised, smashed-up face.

David had left his wallet, cigarette case and silver-topped cane in her room. Whatever had happened between them, he'd panicked and run away. The girl, with one eye completely closed and the other a slit in bruised flesh, stared at him through the partly opened door. She shook her head: he saw her wince.

'Not up to it, dear. See that, carn'ya?'

He'd explained. He'd wanted to fetch a doctor.

'Get one to *'im!*'

'Why, what d'you—'

'*Brain* doctor . . . Is'n 'e ravin' bloody mad?'

There was quite a lot of money in David's wallet. Nick emptied it on the chest-of-drawers. The girl almost didn't take it. When he asked her why or how it had happened, she shrugged and turned away.

'I laughed at him. Drunk, were'n 'e – I mean, 'e could'n – you know . . .'

Nick handed David back an empty wallet. He told him, 'You'll find it's empty. I gave her all you had.'

'*What?*'

Nick stared at him, seeing not only his brother but his father too. And he could have hit him, even then, before the excuses and denials had even started. David was thumbing angrily through the wallet; he muttered, 'Damn near a whole month's pay! For God's sake, Nick—'

'Leave God out of it!' David seemed to be in shock. Nick said, 'You're lucky the police aren't looking for you. I suppose she thought they wouldn't take her word for it . . .'

Like father, like son. Nick thought, on *Lanyard*'s bridge as she thrust southwards through the night, *Perhaps they can't help it. Perhaps it's in the blood. In mine too, then?*

'Everard?'

Mortimer had his binoculars at his eyes. His back was resting against the binnacle. Nick moved up beside him.

'Sir?'

Hastings was over on the port side; looking past the captain, Nick could see him and his glasses silhouetted against the night sky. Heading into such wind as there was, and into the low, choppy sea which during the last hour it had begun to push up, *Lanyard* was thumping a bit now, smashing the small waves down but making quite a fuss about it. The damage she'd suffered had of course added to her rattles. He looked down and for'ard, saw her bow-wave gleaming white, fading into a vaguer lightness and finally merging, abaft the beam, into the surrounding blackness of the sea.

Mortimer finally condescended to lower his binoculars and turn towards him.

172

'Yes, now then. Not because we're short-handed, Sub, but because I'm satisfied you're reasonably sensible – which to some extent compensates for the fact that you're still wet behind the ears and haven't been with us much more than half a dogwatch – I'm declaring you competent to take charge of a watch at sea. When time permits you may type out a watchkeeping certificate, and I'll sign it. Copy the wording from the screed I gave Hastings last year.'

'Thank you very much, sir!'

'Don't let me down, that's all.'

Nick felt wonderful. It was like being let out of the nursery, or given the key of the door!

He blinked: something had flashed, out there, a long way off.

Mortimer had whipped up his binoculars: 'What the—'

Gunfire. There'd been that single flash, and then a lot of it, flickering to and fro out there on the horizon; now its sound reached them too. Nick heard movement behind him as someone else arrived in the bridge. Mortimer was conning *Lanyard* around two points to starboard, to steer straight for the action. Behind Nick, the torpedo gunner demanded in a stage whisper, 'What's that lot, then?' Nobody was in a position to enlighten him. The gunfire was increasing, and the stabs of flame were yellowish, not red as they'd been in daylight. A searchlight beam – no, several, a whole battery of them sprang out blinding white, held for a few seconds and then went out as suddenly as they'd come on.

That flickering, ruddy-coloured point of light might be a ship on fire. The gunfire died away, and ceased altogether.

Mortimer asked without lowering his glasses, 'What is the state of the guns, Sub?'

'Midships four-inch closed-up and ready, sir. The crew of the for'ard gun are resting under the midships gun-platform. The two crews are working watch-and-watch, and ammunition parties are at their stations but standing easy, sir.'

'Have 'em all stand-to, please.'

'Aye aye, sir.'

'Mr Pilkington, is that you?'

'Yessir. After tube is closed-up, sir.'

'Our last torpedo must not be wasted, Mr Pilkington.'

'I'm countin' it won't be, sir.'

Nick had alerted the guns' crews, by voicepipe. He moved past Garret, to see what settings Blewitt had on the Barr and Stroud transmitter. 'Put zero deflection, Blewitt. And range – well, say two thousand yards.' He thought any action in the dark would most likely be fought at fairly close quarters.

'Oh-two-oh set, sir.'

'Check that the guns have the same readings.'

'Aye aye, sir.'

'Everard.' Mortimer told him, 'If we meet any Huns, my first consideration will be to use that torpedo effectively. So I don't want any guns blazing away without orders. The object will be to get in close and make as sure as possible of a torpedo hit. Make sure the gunlayers understand this.'

'Aye aye, sir.'

It was all quiet, up ahead where that brief action had taken place. The fire, if that was what it had been, had gone out too, and it felt as if *Lanyard* was entirely alone in a great emptiness of night and sea. Mortimer said to Hastings, 'Might have been ten miles away, could've been six or seven. Anyone's guess.'

'I'd have thought at least ten, sir.'

And by the time *Lanyard* got down there, Nick thought, who-ever it had been might well be another ten miles away in any direction at all . . . He went down to instruct the gunlayers. On his way back a few minutes later, abreast the whaler on the port side, he met Pilkington coming aft.

'We'll be stuck in again soon, Sub. Got yer rubber weskit on?'

But *Lanyard* was well astern of the fleet, and the Germans were down somewhere in the south-west; there seemed no reason for either fleet to turn north. The farther south Scheer went, the closer he'd be getting to his bases. With luck, *Lanyard* might come up astern of her flotilla and rejoin it, or tag on to one of the other flotillas and locate the thirteenth at daylight. One felt that Jellicoe knew there'd be no night fighting; he'd so to speak appealed against the light and drawn stumps.

Apart from which, things felt quiet . . .

A few seconds later, as he climbed up to the bridge, he heard Hastings shout, 'Port bow, sir, more—'

'I'm not blind, Pilot!'

Nick, joining them quickly, saw the new outbreak of gunfire on the port bow. Mortimer said angrily, 'It's damnable, not knowing what's going on . . .'

Whatever it was, it was happening a long way off again, much too far for it to concern *Lanyard* in any immediate sense. There was more of it than last time, though. Searchlight beams and the flashes of explosions lit lightning glimpses of ships, miniaturised silver shapes behind blazing guns. Mortimer announced, 'Light cruisers. God knows which is what.' Keeping his glasses at his eyes, he performed a long knees-bend to the voicepipe.

'Starboard ten!'

'Starboard ten, sir!'

Again he was aiming *Lanyard* towards the action; towards toy ships firing tiny guns, making sparks and pops instead of blinding flashes and the thunder of destruction. That was what one knew it was, but its remoteness and the impossibility of reaching it in time to play any part in it gave one a sense of detachment; men were being killed down there, but one couldn't *feel* it . . .

Mortimer repeated, 'Light cruisers, wouldn't you say?' Hastings mumbled something. This action was taking place much farther east than the last one had. German scouting forces – cruisers – shadowing the Grand Fleet, perhaps, probing for information to pass on to Scheer, and running up against our own cruisers or destroyers?

'Midships!'

It was a much larger-scale action than the first. Gunfire was continuous; brilliant white and softer, yellowish flashes lit the clouds. Now to the left – eastward – there was a blaze of search-lights and more rapid shooting. Smoke, illuminated by sudden flashes from inside it, vanished as the flashes ceased, then reappeared as it rolled across the searchlights, dimming them. A ripple of gunfire came from farther to the right; the spread of the action was wider, as well as its pace being hotter, than the other one.

'Steady as you go.' Mortimer slowly straightened. 'Good God, look at that!'

A ship's tall grey funnels had been lit suddenly in an enormous gout of white flame: a second column, also white, shot up close by it. Her foremast showed black against it for a moment: and then it vanished, all of it extinguished as neatly as doused candles, and there was only a peculiar glow left, pinkish and showing through smoke like a picture-postcard sunset by a rotten artist. A moment ago searchlights had been blazing: now they'd gone out with a suddenness that left sea and sky black, empty. And the guns had all ceased fire.

Hastings said to Mortimer, 'Someone met a sudden end *there*, sir.'

'You could be right. Are we on the top line with our recognitions signals? Because with all this lot barging around the North Sea we'd damn well better be!'

'I have the current signal letters, sir, and Garret has too, I think.'

'Yessir.' Garret spoke from the far side of the searchlight mounting, 'Got 'em in mind and wrote down too, sir.'

'What about you, Everard?'

'Well, sir, if Garret—'

'Look here – suppose we were to get blown up. You're left in charge. Garret's knocked out too. Now you're challenged by – *Southampton*, say. She'd have a broadside of five six-inch guns trained on you before she made the challenge, ready to blow you out of the water if you don't give the right answer *immediately*. Well, what are you going to do about it?'

There really wasn't any answer.

'Everard, you're *dead*, by now! So's every man of your ship's company!'

'I – I'll make sure I do know the signals that are in force in future, sir.'

'How?'

'I'll—' He didn't want to say 'I'll ask someone' . . . 'I'll look it up, sir.'

'D'you know how to? Sure you can do it accurately? It's not a thing you can allow yourself a mistake in, you know!'

The book was in the chartroom. But nobody had ever shown him how to check a recognition signal. In the ships he'd served in before they'd always been chalked up on a board; he'd never given much thought to how they got there. And that book might not be simple to work from without instruction.

'I know where the book is, sir. I imagine it's fairly easy to look up the—'

'Now we approach the truth . . .' Mortimer looked round, a quick check that *Lanyard*'s surroundings were still all peaceful. He turned back, and pointed.

'Leading Signalman Garret – do *you* know how to extract the recognition signal of the watch from the appropriate CB?'

'I do that, sir.'

'Then go down to the chartroom with Sub-Lieutenant Everard, and show him how to.'

'Aye aye, sir.'

To have him instructed by a leading signalman was intended, no doubt, as a small humiliation, to serve him right for not knowing

176

such a simple procedure. He should have made it his business to find out, long ago. There were quite a number of things which he should have done, in the past eighteen months, and hadn't done; such as putting in some study and practice of the taking and working-out of sun- and star-sights. He was cack-handed with a sextant, and invariably got muddled with the figures. But he could, with a bit of effort, teach himself to do it properly. And he would, now.

He swung himself on to the ladder, and climbed down, using the ladder's sides, not its rungs, as handholds, for fear of Garret's knuckle-crushing boots coming down close above him.

Hastings, sweeping the sea and horizon with his binoculars, was working to a system. From right ahead he'd sweep down the port side to right astern; then at about twice the speed he'd sweep back up to the bow. He'd do the same thing then on the starboard side, but in between he'd give extra attention right for'ard, about two points to port and two to starboard. That was the way the ship was travelling, where an enemy would appear most suddenly, be most likely to appear.

He heard Nick and Garret leave the bridge behind him, just as he paused with his glasses trained right ahead. He murmured to the Captain, 'With respect, sir, it was always Lieutenant Reynolds's job. None of the rest of us ever looked it up.'

'I know.' Mortimer was wiping sea-dew from the lenses of his binoculars. 'Matter of keeping Everard on his toes. If we push him a bit, I believe we could make a useful—'

Hastings choked; his body jerked as if he'd had an electric shock: 'Ships, starboard bow, sir! They're – *not British*!'

Mortimer whipped up his glasses . . .

A light cruiser; two of them. The twin searchlights on their foremasts above the spotting tops was a distinctive German feature and it was plain to see against the sky.

'Port ten!'

'Port ten, sir!'

'Tell Pilkington stand by to fire to starboard, target the leading cruiser!'

'Ten o' port wheel on, sir!'

Lanyard had begun a swing to starboard. Mortimer's intention was to slip in towards the enemy, close the range enough to ensure a hit, and then come round to port, firing on that turn-away.

177

'Midships!'

Hastings had alerted Pilkington.

If *Lanyard* could get in there undetected, and get the fish away before they woke up and blasted her into scrap, she'd have a good chance of a kill. She was well up on the Germans' bow – a perfect situation, and no need even to increase speed. Not until after she'd fired: *then* there'd be the little matter of getting away from two angry cruisers' guns . . . For the moment, all one had to think about was getting in there and firing.

There was every chance she'd make it. Low speed, very little bow-wave, no risk of the glow which at full power showed at funnel-tops. They certainly hadn't seen her yet: and she was low, and black-painted to match the night, and at this moment almost bow-on to them, presenting very little silhouette.

Mortimer said quietly, tensely, 'Tell Pilkington I'm about to turn to the firing course.'

Hastings passed the stand-by message. Raising his head from the voicepipe, he happened to glance out on the starboard bow.

For a split second, while he confirmed that he wasn't imagining what he was staring at, he froze . . .

'Starboard bow – battleship – about to *ram*!'

Mortimer had sprung round, and seen it. Too late. A third ship – a dreadnought battleship following astern of those cruisers: she'd swung out to port, her vast bulk was rushing at them out of the dark, and she'd take *Lanyard* on her ram with as little trouble as it might take a rhinoceros to horn a dog.

'Hard a-port! Full ahead together!'

If he'd attempted to evade by turning to port – which would have allowed him to fire his torpedo on the way round – the German would only have needed to adjust his course by a few degrees and he'd still have got her. But a turn to starboard – turning *inside* the dreadnought's own swing to port, and probably scraping paint off her as they scraped by – that was just – *might* be – possible . . .

Fifty-fifty chance? No. Two to one against.

'Helm's hard a-port, sir, both telegraphs full ahead!'

The turbines' whine rose to a scream; the vast shape of the oncoming ship loomed bigger, closer, towering, overwhelming . . . And *Lanyard*'s bow seemed to be coming round so *slowly*!

'Stop starboard!'

He'd needed speed; now he needed swing. The sea might have been treacle, she was turning so sluggishly . . . They were finished.

In seconds they'd be smashed, ridden under, ploughed into the sea. But she was getting round: with the starboard screw stopped she was fairly whistling round! Her stem pointed at the German's foc's'l – at his bridge superstructure – amidships – round, round . . . You could have touched the bastard with a boathook!

The night split. The world exploded in their faces.

Hugh Everard lowered his binoculars. Mowbray had sent the midshipman of the watch to him, and he'd come out to see the latest of several flare-ups which had lit the blackness astern of the battle squadrons. This one had ended almost before it had started.

'Short and sweet.' He thought about that: he added, 'Though perhaps not for everyone.'

Destroyer actions, probably. Something bigger, possibly.

Having no wireless, one could only guess. Reports might well be flooding in to Jellicoe in *Iron Duke*; it might be quite plain to the commander-in-chief, and to subordinate admirals and captains whose ships still had wireless equipment in working order, what was happening astern.

The 'something bigger' possibility wasn't a comfortable thought to entertain. If the Germans were not where they were believed to be; if Scheer was attempting to break through astern of the Grand Fleet and run for the minefield gap at Horns Reef . . .

One could only dismiss the thought. Jellicoe must know where Scheer was, and where he'd find him in the morning. And Jellicoe would be able to see that fighting astern just as easily as he, Hugh Everard, could.

'I'm going to get a few hours' sleep now, Mowbray. Shake me if you need to, otherwise at one forty-five.'

'Aye aye, sir.'

He found Bates waiting in the sea-cabin.

'Afraid your kye'd get cold, sir.'

'Doesn't look like it.' The mug of cocoa was steaming; he reached for it. 'Hot, all right.' He put it down again, and asked Bates, 'Where's the stuff you salvaged?'

'In 'ere, sir.' Bates dragged a suitcase up on to the bunk. 'Not much, sir. Just odds an' ends, this is. But there's some shirts as'll want dhobyin' – an' your best suit o' number fives, an' our other pair of 'alf-boots – that's in the commander's day-cabin, sir.' He saw Hugh's quick glance, and added, 'I did ask 'im, sir.'

'Good.' Hugh opened the case. He found a litter of

correspondence, bank-books, ornaments, a silver cigarette-box, the case he kept his cufflinks and studs in; and one leather folding photograph frame.

Hugh looked at his coxswain, 'Your own personal selection, Bates . . .'

'Yessir. Lot o' stuff was spoiled, sir. An' I only 'ad the one case 'andy, for these bits.'

When Bates wanted to look blank, he knew how to. Hugh surrendered. 'I'm – much obliged to you.'

'No need, sir.' With his hands on the case, to put it back on the deck, he looked at the frame in Hugh's hand. 'Keepin' that out, sir?'

Hugh nodded. He watched Bates stow the suitcase away. 'Tell me. What made you go aft when you did? When I'd told you to wait in the sea-cabin?'

Bates straightened.

'Sorry about that, sir. Didn't 'ave time to think, not really. I felt them 'its aft, an' I looks out and there's smoke comin' out where our quarters is, so I says to meself, that's us, that is, best takee look-see, sort o' thing.'

'As well you did, in view of what happened to the sea-cabin in your absence.'

Bates nodded phlegmatically. 'One way o' lookin' at it, sir . . . Be gettin' your 'ead down now, sir, will you?'

'Yes.' He'd finished the cocoa. Bates stooped, pulled out one of the bunk drawers. 'I borrowed some gear for you to be goin' on with, sir. Sweater, scarf, pair o' gloves – well, this 'ere, sir, spare socks 'n—'

'You've done well, Bates. Thank you.' Someone knocked on the door. 'Come in!'

Tom Crick peered in. Bates said quickly, tapping that drawer with the toe of his boot, 'Commander's gear, sir.'

'Oh, *is* it.' He saw enquiry in Crick's face. 'All right, Bates, I shan't need you for a couple of hours. Get some sleep.'

'Aye aye, sir.' Bates slid out. Hugh nodded to Crick. 'Kind of you to lend me your things, Tom. I hear there's some junk of mine in your day-cabin too?'

Crick pulled the door shut. 'That's so, sir. Your coxswain has what one might call a persuasive manner.'

'You don't like him, do you, Tom?'

'Only hoping he won't let you down one day, sir.'

180

'If you'd care to bet on it, I'll take your money.'

Crick smiled and shook his head. Then he cleared his throat. 'I've come to report we're in reasonably good shape below decks now, sir. We'll need a couple of weeks in the dockyard, of course, but there's nothing need concern us for the moment. The PMO asked me to tell you he'll have a detailed casualty list ready in the morning; looks like four officers and thirty-one men killed, and two plus twenty-eight wounded.' His eyebrows rose. 'Might 've been a lot worse, sir.'

'Considering the chance I took.'

'You saved hundreds in *Warspite*, sir.'

When Crick had gone, Hugh took his reefer and half-boots off, loosened his tie and collar and stretched out on the bunk. He pulled a blanket up over himself. Then he opened the leather frame that Bates had had the remarkable percipience to rescue.

Sarah smiled at him from her photograph. A gentle, rather wistful, lonely smile. Hugh had picked this one – stolen it – from a bunch of prints which a photographer had sent to brother John so he could choose one for mounting.

The puzzling thing was, there'd been quite a number of framed portraits displayed openly in the day-cabin; but this one he'd kept more discreetly in a drawer. Had Bates reasoned that it made Sarah's portrait more important than the others or did he have second sight, in those monkey eyes of his?

Hugh closed the frame and pushed it under the pillow. He thought, with his hand out to the light switch, that he had two stories now for Sarah. This indication of his coxswain's intelligence would make one, and the other was the incident of the sailing barque which, caught between the embattled fleets, had made him think of her.

If he told her of those two things, wouldn't he be telling her everything there was to tell?

He hoped he'd have the nerve to. To let her know how he felt. Not to funk it as he had the other day.

CHAPTER 10

He was alive. Mortimer and Hastings were dead.

Lanyard was still afloat, and for the time being, so far as one could tell, out of any immediate danger.

So far as one could tell: the qualification was a real one. Uncertainty, a sense of detachment and confusion, was the residue of shock, upheaval. It had to be fought against. It was as if one's mind had been switched off for several seconds, or minutes – a period of indeterminate length during which one had seemed to be struggling to retain awareness of one's surroundings, and making no headway. Now the struggle was for renewed power of thought, judgement, decision.

He was in command!

'Four hundred revolutions.'

'Four hundred—' MacIver gulped – 'revolutions, sir.' MacIver's mouth was open, and his breath whistled through the gap of a missing tooth. He looked dazed still.

'Port ten.'

'Port ten, sir.' CPO Glennie, the chief bosun's mate, spun the wheel. After Cuthbertson's death earlier in the day Glennie had become the destroyer's senior rating. Steady as a rock: he was built like one, too. Nick told him, 'Ease to five, and steady on south.'

Lanyard's sudden lurch to starboard had sent Nick and Garret flying across the chartroom. Nick had hauled himself up the slanting deck to the starboard-side door, got out through it and started climbing the ladder to the bridge. He'd been some of the way up when the German dreadnought's port batteries – her secondary armament of six-inch guns – had crashed out a broadside at point-blank range and maximum depression. For him and Garret the blast had been an incredible volume of sound and a great sheet of flame which swept across above their heads as the

182

ship lurched back against the natural heel of her swing. For about two seconds a scorching heat radiated downwards. Then she'd heeled back again, and she'd still been turning; he'd climbed a few more rungs, and stopped again when he'd discovered that *Lanyard* no longer had an upper bridge. The top part of it – with binnacle, railings, flag-lockers, everything – had been shorn off.

The steering position – lower bridge – was roofless but otherwise intact and operable as a wheelhouse. The searchlight had gone – simply wiped off. So had the for'ard gun, both boats, and several feet of the already damaged top of the for'ard funnel. The roof of the galley, the superstructure between the boats, had been stove in. Mr Pilkington, who'd arrived in the steering-position a minute ago, had told him about the funnels and the boats, and apparently that was as far aft as the area of damage extended.

Nick and Garret owed their lives first to Mortimer having sent them down to the chartroom, and second to their having been below the reach of the guns' blast, and sheltered from it by the superstructure. Otherwise they would have been dead, blown away in that blast of flame – like Mortimer, Hastings, Blewitt and the entire crew of the for'ard four-inch.

The only shell to have hit *Lanyard* had sheered through her foremast without exploding, and passed on. The foremast had toppled, snapped, and crashed overboard. All the other projectiles had passed overhead too; the battleship's six-inch guns hadn't been able to depress far enough to reach her. According to Pilkington, the two ships had been almost alongside each other at that moment.

There'd been only that one broadside. The Germans must have thought they'd finished her; she'd reeled away, and they'd steamed on into the night.

Nick's first question to Chief Petty Officer Glennie, when he'd reached the steering-position – climbing into it, through the now completely open corner where *Lanyard* had been hit during the torpedo attack in the afternoon – had been, 'Does she answer her helm?'

'Aye, sir, she does.' Glennie had shown considerable initiative in the seconds after the cataclysm. He and MacIver, the telegraph-man, had been lifted off their feet and thrown at the starboard bulkhead. Recovering, with his head ringing from the explosions and from being bounced off a steel wall, the chief buffer had put the starboard telegraph to full ahead and then grabbed the wheel to steady the ship on a north-easterly course. Finding himself on his own, with nobody up there to direct him, it had seemed sensible to steer her away from the source of trouble.

It was a stump of a bridge, now, like a broken tooth. The after part of its deck – which was also the roof of some of the chartroom and all the signals office – was still there, but all the for'ard part had been peeled off. Apart from jagged edges, it had been done quite neatly, with no bits or pieces left behind. Nick was standing now in the steering-position between Glennie and MacIver; his head was in fresh air, cold wind, and he looked straight ahead over an edge of ripped steel at the destroyer's bow thrusting through a low, black sea.

'Does the engine-room voicepipe still work, MacIver?'

'I'll test it, sir.'

'Well, get Mr Worsfold on it, if you can.'

'Aye aye, sir.' The voicepipe was on the starboard bulkhead. MacIver put his mouth to it and shouted, 'Engine-room!'

Nick asked Pilkington, 'Is that last torpedo still in its tube?'

'Course it is!' The torpedo gunner squeezed up beside him. Space was tight in here; Nick thought perhaps MacIver could be dispensed with. He had a half-inclination to keep Pilkington here with him; but he had the other half, too, which was to keep him at a distance.

Pilkington asked him, 'What d'you reckon on doin' now, Sub?'

'I'll tell you when I've had a word to Chief . . . What about the midships four-inch – is it still there?'

'I *told* yer – nothin' touched us, aft!'

'Engineer Officer's on the voicepipe, sir.'

'Thank you.' Nick thought, as he squeezed over behind Glennie, *No, I do not want Mr Pilkington with me* . . . 'Chief?'

'Yes. What have you been *doing* up there?'

'The Captain and Hastings have been killed, the top of the bridge has been shot off and we've lost the for'ard gun. Can you tell me if there's any damage to machinery or hull?'

'I've no reason to think there is, Sub.'

That was good news, indeed, and Worsfold sounded pretty cool, down there.

'What d'you intend to do now?'

'Carry on as before. Find our flotilla.'

He couldn't see he had much choice. *Lanyard* had steam, and a gun and a torpedo. If there was action in the offing, that was where she ought to be. All he had to do was find it.

He turned to Pilkington.

'You're second-in-command, and I want you aft, where you can look after the gun as well as your own department. We'll have to do something about communications—'

'Action on the starboard bow, sir!' CPO Glennie's eyes were slits in his squarish face. He'd seen the start of another firework display. A flash, white like a magnesium flare, and the familiar flickering of guns. It was a long way off.

'Come round a point to starboard.'

'Aye aye, sir.' Glennie's hands moved on the wheel. Nick called out through the open corner of the wheelhouse, 'Garret?'

'Sir?'

'There are some binoculars in the chartroom. If there are two pairs, bring them both, please.'

'Aye aye, sir.'

Nick turned back to Pilkington. 'Perhaps you could get some flexible hose and join it to the bridge voicepipe – the one from the bridge to the after searchlight platform. It'll have been cut through of course, you'll have to find the end. Join up a length of hose and bring its other end down here.'

Pilkington nodded his large head. 'I'll 'ave a shot.'

'The other thing, Mr Pilkington, is to let the ship's company know what's going on. Would you see to that?'

He wondered if he was being too polite; whether he should be telling, instead of asking. But he was, really; and at the moment he needed the gunner's help, more than his obedience. He'd already gone; and Garret arrived now with the binoculars – Johnson's, and Reynolds's.

There was no time to mourn the dead. You could only try to fill their places. As Mortimer had filled Johnson's place with Hastings, so Nick was now replacing all three of them. Johnson had been killed about six hours ago, but he was already a name and a character from the past, his death eclipsed by the more recent ones.

'Chief Petty Officer Glennie.'

'Sir!'

Nick had cleaned and focused the binoculars, and he was sweeping the sea and horizon ahead. There was no clear-cut horizon: only a fuzz, a layer that could have been either sea or sky and might have been two miles deep or five. The unobstructed arc of lookout from here was roughly beam to beam.

'I need Garret in here for signalling. We might be challenged, or need to challenge someone else.' He thought, immediately he'd said

185

it, *I shan't do that. Not with one gun. We'll mind our P's and Q's* . . .
'But there's not much room, is there? Could you manage the telegraphs as well as the wheel?'

'Easy, sir.'

'Fine. MacIver – from here we can't see abaft the beam. And there's nothing left to stand on higher up. So take that pair of glasses and go aft to the searchlight platform and keep your eyes skinned. You'll have a voicepipe to us as soon as Mr Pilkington's got it rigged.'

'Aye aye, sir.'

'Off you go, then.'

Garret coughed. 'No searchlight for'ard here, sir. For signalling. You said you want me here?'

'Oh, damn . . .'

He did need him here, under his immediate control. Answering challenges at night was a split-second business.

Glennie suggested, 'Use an 'and-lamp, sir?'

'Garret?'

'One in the signals office, sir. Well, there *was*—'

'Get it, or get something else.' He called after him, 'Those recognition signals—'

'I've got 'em, sir.'

He'd gone. Nick said, with binoculars at his eyes, 'You did extremely well, Glennie. You probably saved the ship.'

'Oh, I dunno, sir.'

'That's how it'll read in my report.'

'Let's 'ope you get to write one then, sir.'

He'd half-smiled, with his eyes on the compass-card, on the lubber's line shifting a degree or two each side of south-by-west. The wheel's brass-capped spokes passed this way and that through his large, practised hands as he corrected, more by feel and instinct than by design, the ship's tendency to roam.

Garret came back with a brass-cased hand lamp.

'Is that going to be bright enough?'

'Be all right while it's dark, sir.' The leading signalman moved round to Glennie's other side, where MacIver had been. The space was about adequate, for three men. He added, 'When it's light we can use the after searchlight, sir.'

The priority now, Nick told himself, was to be prepared, to decide now, in advance of an emergency situation suddenly confronting him, what to do in this, that or the other circumstance. An

186

unidentified ship there, coming straight for them; or a German there, broadside-on; or an enemy challenge on the beam. One knew nothing about the positions now of either one's own or enemy forces; whatever turned up, it could be either friendly or hostile, and one or two seconds in making a correct identification could spell the difference between survival and extinction. It seemed, too, that the situation might be more complicated than Mortimer had thought it was. His view had been that the Grand Fleet was near enough due south, and the Germans in the south-west. But *Lanyard* had very recently passed the time of day – in a manner of speaking – with an enemy battleship and two cruisers, and they'd been steering south-east, across the rear of the south-bound Grand Fleet . . .

Well, it had been only one battleship; and as one swallow didn't make a summer . . . But she might have been damaged, or suffered some machinery breakdown; she could have been detached to make her own way homewards with a cruiser escort.

It didn't seem likely, on reflection. Would a fleet commander in Scheer's position spare two cruisers to take a lame duck home?

It made no difference. *Lanyard* had no wireless; she couldn't send reports, any more than she could receive them. There was only one plan of action, Nick told himself: to get her back to her flotilla, add her one gun and one torpedo to its strength. En route, to attack any enemy that showed up, and to avoid either being taken by surprise by an enemy or attacked in error by one's own side.

'Garret, those recognition signals. Have you—'

'All in my head, sir. I've a note of 'em, too.'

The sea ahead was blackish-grey, patched with mist and touched here and there with whitish flecks. It wasn't a broken sea; there was just enough breeze to knock the edge off the little waves, and to whip a few drops of spray now and then from *Lanyard*'s stem to spray this rattling, foreshortened bulkhead. She was pitching just a little, but there was no roll on her at all. The slight wind, plus her progress through it, had the wreckage of the superstructure round them groaning as if it was in pain; the rattles had settled into a rhythm which one might have missed if it had stopped.

Something clanged suddenly, overhead, behind them.

'Voicepipe 'ose, sir. Someone catch it an' 'aul it in, can they?'

Garret grabbed its end and hauled in about a fathom of it; it dangled behind CPO Glennie's head.

'Shall I lash it to the bulkhead, sir?'

'Yes. Leave a couple of feet loose at the end.'

With a voicepipe rigged to the gun and that tube, *Lanyard* would be fighting fit again. Nick thought, *Now it's up to me.*

Hanbury Pike, the engineer, spat out a mouthful of North Sea, and pointed.

'She's going.'

'What? Who's—'

'*Bantry*, you damn fool!'

Everard seemed simple, child-like, and he didn't appear to realise what was happening. He was like someone having a bathe for the fun of it. They'd been in the water half an hour; Pike was cold right through to his bones and he was wishing to God he'd refused Johnny West's request that he should keep an eye on him.

Bantry was on her way to the bottom.

Black against dark-grey sea and a lighter shade of sky, the cruiser's forepart was rising, tilting up as her stern went under, deeper into the sea.

Cold . . . Pike groaned, 'Oh, God in heaven . . .'

'What's the matter, Hanbury?'

The engineer began to swim away. Towards *Bantry*, as it happened, because he'd been watching her and therefore facing that way; his only purpose, apart from needing to use his muscles before they froze solid, was to get away from Everard. He wished he hadn't said he'd stay with him; he was too tired, mentally and physically, to put up with him, let alone look after him.

They'd managed, half an hour or so ago, to cram all the badly wounded men into rafts and floats, and less serious cases had had to go in the water and hold on to the rafts' sides. When they were all down there, West had told the fit men who'd been waiting on the upper deck, 'I want two dozen strong swimmers to tow them clear and stay with them. Volunteers?'

There'd been too many. He'd picked men who had friends among the wounded. The padre and the surgeon-commander had gone with them. They climbed down the net into the sea, and pushed and towed the rafts away into the darkness. West called after them, 'Keep close together – you'll be easier to spot and pick up if you stay in a bunch. Good luck!'

Cheers had floated back to him. Someone shouted, 'Lovely

boatin' wevver!' Laughter mingled with fresh cheers. They began to sing:

> *'Oh, a life on the ocean wave*
> *Ain't fit for a bloomin' slave . . .'*

They weren't only keeping their spirits up. There'd been a mood almost of carnival since Hanbury Pike and his party of artificers and stokers, helped by the fire brigade who'd worked with them, had brought seven men alive out of the starboard engine-room. The breakthrough had come within minutes of the pipe 'All hands on deck'; they'd ignored it, because by that time they'd fought their way to one of the armoured hatches and got a tackle rigged to lift it. They'd dragged it up, and the men – seven out of the nine who'd been trapped down there – had been hauled out.

Pike had told West it was the first time in his life he'd seen a stoker petty officer cry. Not the one they'd rescued: the PO who'd been working with him.

Apparently the shell had burst in the port engine-room, wrecking it completely and killing everyone in there; and it had burst low down, close to the base of the centre-line bulkhead. The door between the two engine-rooms had been buckled, and couldn't be shifted, and in the starboard engine-room the water began to rise quite fast. After a bit it was held down to some extent by pressure in the top of the compartment, but it was over the floor-plates, which were dislodged so that the ladders weren't accessible. Two men were drowned; the other seven, before their rescue, had found themselves trapped with the gratings above their heads and the water still rising below.

West asked the men still waiting, 'Any non-swimmers?' A voice answered at once, 'Sparks 'erbert 'ere can't swim a stroke, sir!'

Telegraphist Herbert's friends began pushing him about. Another man owned up – a stoker . . . 'I never made much of an 'and at it, sir.'

'Petty Officer Toomey – make sure they've got swimming collars on. Oh, damn it, here . . .' West took off the inflatable waistcoat which he'd bought from Messrs Gieves in Bond Street. 'One of 'em can wear this. I'll use a swimming collar.'

'No, sir, you don't go givin' me your—'

'I don't need it, Herbert, I'm like a fish in that stuff. And you should bloody well've learnt to swim, anyway, d'you hear?

Toomey, the lifebuoys are abaft the second funnel. One each for these two men, and hand out the rest to weak swimmers.'

'Aye aye, sir.'

'Scrimgeour?'

The torpedo lieutenant came forward. 'Yes?'

'Is Commander Clark still on the bridge?'

'Intends to remain there.' Scrimgeour added, 'For the time being, he says.'

Toomey was distributing lifebuoys. West heard David Everard refuse the offer of one. 'My dear Toomey, I swim like a blooming otter!' He had his inflatable waistcoat on, anyway. West sent Scrimgeour to sort out a group of snotties who seemed to have neither waistcoats nor collars. Everard told Hanbury Pike, 'My brother Nick didn't cry when our mother died. Can you believe that?'

Pike stared at him open-mouthed: West put in quickly, 'David, *there* you are, old man. Now look—'

'Not even at the funeral. Not one tear! If that doesn't prove he's—'

West patted his shoulder. 'Hang on a minute, David . . . Hanbury, a word with you?' He beckoned the engineer, and they moved away from the group of waiting men. He told him, 'Everard's round the bend. Cracked. Would you keep an eye on him – I mean in the 'oggin?'

'If you think it's necessary.' Pike shrugged, without much enthusiasm. 'Are we all set now?'

'I want the rafts well clear first. Not that one expects there'd be competition for them, but—'

'Of course there wouldn't be!'

'No,' West agreed. 'Just playing safe. But I'll go and see Nobby, before we leave her.'

Ten minutes later, he'd come down from the bridge alone. Pike had been chatting to Clarence Chance, the paymaster. West told them, 'Can't budge him. He says he wants to see everyone away first. I think he means to go down with her.'

Chance removed the monocle from his left eye. 'What would that achieve?'

West couldn't tell him. Nobody had known Clark well; but he'd never seemed a happy man.

'Come on. Time we went.'

*   *   *

190

Hanbury Pike watched *Bantry* hang for a moment with her stem pointing at the sky and her stern buried in the sea.

He hoped the four men in her after steering compartment, which it had not been possible to reach, had died before this. He tried not to think of the black water rushing through her. There was not only a dreadful sadness in the last throes of a great ship; there was also a terrible malignancy in the sea that swallowed her. And he felt so damn tired . . .

She'd begun to slide. There was a roar of displaced air, like an enormous sigh.

'Sub.' It was Worsfold on the engine-room voicepipe. 'We've been burning a deuce of a lot of oil. D'you think we might ease off a bit now and then?'

Nick thought about it. There was an argument for keeping *Lanyard* plugging along at thirty knots, and two at least against it.

'All right, Chief. Make it three-six-oh revs.'

Twenty-five knots would still be eight knots faster than the speed Jellicoe had ordered for the night. So *Lanyard* ought still to be catching up. But one might have expected to have been up with the fleet by now, and if it hadn't been for the repeated outbreaks of gunfire ahead and on the bows as they'd been steaming southwards he'd have been worried that he might somehow have passed by, diverged from the Grand Fleet's course and missed that not inconsiderable target. The fleet could have altered course – might easily have done – and without wireless *Lanyard* wouldn't know of it. The desire to link up as soon as possible with other destroyers astern of the battle fleet, which was an argument in favour of maintaining a good speed, was not entirely impersonal. Nick was conscious of feeling lonely; he had a strong inclination to be in company and have other ships to follow. But at the same time that nervousness made him glad, in another way, to reduce speed. He'd had a feeling of rushing into darkness and unseen dangers at a breathless, headlong pace; he wasn't frightened, but he was unsure, aware of his inexperience and the responsibility which had dropped on him so suddenly. A few hours ago he'd felt a glow of satisfaction in being told he could have a watch-keeping certificate, for God's sake: and here he was in command; not only in command in a detached situation and in action!

Inactivity made it worse. One had time to think. He wished he could feel more confident. And the one thing which was absolutely imperative was that nobody should be allowed to see or guess how *un*confident he did feel.

He chuckled as he came back to his position on the port side of the wheelhouse. 'Odd how engineers hate their engines being used.'

The chief buffer nodded. His eyes rose from the compasscard to glance for'ard at *Lanyard*'s short, punching bow.

'Think of 'em like mothers with babies, don't they, sir?'

The course was due south again. Nick had given up the business of altering this way and that whenever some distant exchange of gunfire illuminated the horizon. The battle fleet's ordered course, or at any rate the last one they'd heard of, had been south, so that was the heading one should stick to. Those sporadic actions, almost surely clashes between scouting and screening forces, were sometimes in one direction and sometimes in another; there was no point zig-zagging about like a donkey constantly switching carrots.

Another aspect of Nick's current feeling of having lost his bearings was that the sensation was entirely new to him. The start of his naval career hadn't been exactly brilliant, but he'd never had any sense of fright or personal inadequacy in any given situation. He'd often dug his heels in, or slacked, when he'd found surroundings or subjects irksome, but he'd never thought to himself *I doubt if I can see this through* . . . To be unsure, off-balance, was foreign to him and extremely uncomfortable, and it was making him think again now, from time to time and in the back of his mind while he tried to concentrate it on the immediate situation, of David and what Johnson had said about him. Because if Johnson had been right, this might be how David had felt pretty well all his life. And what it felt like – this situation, now – was being on a horse which you knew you wouldn't be able to stop if it decided it didn't want you to.

'Starboard—'

Nick had jerked his glasses up; since he'd seen it, CPO Glennie saved his breath.

'Hell . . .'

To start with there'd been some stabs of gunfire; just three or four. But within seconds the sea and sky out there to starboard were ablaze with action; with a barrage of noise and flame, the sea spouting geysers of white water and the black shapes of destroyers darting, thrashing through them and between them, racing like greyhounds through a deluge of shellfire towards a solid line of flaming guns. The impressions – the picture which had sprung up

192

out of nothing, out of a dark void of night and sea and mist – registered and resolved themselves into the fact that a flotilla or part-flotilla of destroyers was making an attack on a line of five, or six, much larger ships . . . Which were in line ahead on a south-easterly course. Seven or eight thousand yards on *Lanyard*'s bow, and the head of the enemy line about right ahead: the gunfire was continuous, spouting and rippling the whole length of the line as the destroyers raced in towards it; one saw them in flashes and as they appeared for no more than seconds between the leaping columns of white water. They were British destroyers, obviously . . . Well, check . . . Focusing on one of the enemy he made out a battleship; she was too big to be anything else. It was misty, though, down there, one felt one should be wiping the lenses of the binoculars twice a minute, but it was sea-mist, not the glasses fogging-up. That could only be a squadron of Scheer's High Seas Fleet beating off a determined destroyer attack.

'Four hundred revolutions!'

'Four hundred revolutions, sir.'

'Garret, tell the gun and tubes to stand by. Then get ready with that lamp.'

'Aye aye, sir.'

It looked like the fiercest engagement of the night. The Germans were using every sort of gun they had – turret guns and beam armament and quick-firing weapons flickering higher up. The destroyers were turning, Nick saw, to starboard, to a course opposite to the enemy's; when they'd fired they'd be heading west or north-west. Consequently if he altered *Lanyard*'s course to starboard there might be a danger of collision when the shooting stopped and the night went dark again, with lookouts and captains half-blinded temporarily by the flashes of their own guns and the enemy's.

'Starboard ten.'

'Starboard ten, sir.'

He was taking her round to port; to steer south-east, in order to converge on to the enemy battle squadron. They'd hardly be expecting a new attack from one solitary, shaved-off destroyer. Come to think of it, there wasn't much of *Lanyard* to see now, with no foremast and no top to her bridge.

'Midships. Steer south-east by south.'

'Sou'east by south, aye aye, sir.' Glennie sounded as calm as ever, not in the least excited.

'Garret. Tell Mr Pilkington we may be firing his torpedo at a battleship in five or ten minutes' time. I can't say which side.'

'Aye aye, sir!'

Garret *did* sound excited.

'And tell him the gun is not to open fire without my order.'

He caught his breath . . .

In the middle of that display of fireworks, he'd seen a sudden splash of dark-red flame on one of the battleships; the third in the German squadron's line. The flame gushed upwards; now it had shot back the whole length of her, and in its savagely bright light he saw that she had three funnels and a large crane-derrick between the centre one and the third. She was German, certainly, and he thought Deutschland-class. The red blaze leapt higher, a soaring mass of incredibly bright fire, and sparks were flying out of it like rockets; sparks, and burning debris tracing arcs into the darker sky. Smoke grew at the fire's base and billowed upwards, folding itself outwards and around the ship, engulfing the brilliant flames, darkening the night by stages until it was all smoke and the shooting from the other ships had stopped dead, totally, as if at one signal – *finis*.

Nick still had his glasses at his eyes, but all he could see now was the thick, grey blanket of the mist. CPO Glennie allowed himself a comment.

'They done 'er, all right, sir.'

'Let's see if we can't get another.'

Glennie nodded, with his eyes on the steering-compass. 'Never know till you try, sir.'

On this slightly converging course, Nick reckoned, he ought to pick up the Germans at about thirty or forty degrees on the bow and at reasonably close range in perhaps five minutes. He'd first seen them at about three-and-a-half miles; the next meeting should be at a distance of perhaps one mile. Allowing for a further slight closing of the range, he might be able to fire the torpedo at something like fifteen hundred yards. This, of course, depended on the battleships having held their course, not turned away to avoid the other torpedoes which must have been fired at about the same time as the one which had hit.

What would Mortimer have done, or be doing now, if he was in command?

Nick put his mind to it. The only alternative to going after the enemy as he was doing now would, he thought, have been to try to join that flotilla after they'd fired and broken off the action. But they'd vanished – to start with in a north-westerly direction, but they could afterwards have gone round astern of the enemy, or northwards, or any other way. But the Germans had been on what had looked like a straight, determined course.

Why did one have that impression? Because their course had been south-east – the same course as that of the battleship which had blown *Lanyard*'s bridge off. And south-eastward was the course for Germany via Horns Reef.

Nick wiped his glasses' lenses and put them back up to his eyes. At any second, those battleships might reappear. He decided he'd fire to starboard; close in, turn away to port, firing on the turn. But if he'd miscalculated and they should turn out to be abaft the beam, he'd turn towards, close in to a good killing range, and then put her round to starboard, firing to port as those others had done.

He was pleased to find that he could think coolly and logically. It would surely make it a lot easier, when one saw the enemy, to have the alternatives clearly in one's mind.

Still nothing in sight. He was beginning to think that the squadron must have altered course, after the torpedo hit.

Well, which way?

South, most likely. But he decided he'd hold on, steer this course for another five minutes. If by that time he hadn't—

There they were!

On the starboard bow, and in line ahead, steering just east of south. So *Lanyard* was coming up astern of them, but with about one point of difference between their course and hers, so that if she held on without any alternation she'd cross their wakes.

Peculiar. How they'd got into this position, and on that course . . .

'I'll be damned!'

He'd seen it, suddenly. He'd assumed these were the ships he'd been expecting to find, and he hadn't until this moment looked at them at all closely. These weren't battleships at all, they were destroyers. This was the bunch who'd carried out that attack!

Whatever the Germans had done – and it was still puzzling – these five ships must have swung around to port, right round, and then steered due east, and had now altered to something like south by east. They must have been searching for the Germans, too; most likely had torpedoes left, and aimed to make a second attack – encouraged, no doubt, by having knocked out one battleship half an hour ago.

'Steer five degrees to starboard. Three-six-oh revolutions.'

Glennie was repeating the orders. Nick's slight adjustments of course and speed were designed to add *Lanyard* to the tail-end of that flotilla.

'Garret, tell Mr Pilkington we're approaching friendly ships. Train the tube fore-and-aft.'

'Aye aye, sir.'

'Then stand by with your lamp.'

In a minute, they'd have to identify themselves. *Lanyard* was closing-up and edging-in, still a bit out on the other destroyers' starboard quarter. About half a mile between her and the boat she was going to tag on to.

Garret had passed that message aft. He told Nick, 'Ready with the lamp, sir.'

'They're bound to challenge, soon.' He was surprised they hadn't before this. He kept his glasses on them. 'Three-four-oh revs.'

'Three-four-oh, sir.'

A light flashed: from the *head* of the destroyer line. *Lanyard* wasn't tucked-in astern of them yet; in another minute she would have been, and that challenge wouldn't have been visible.

'Give 'em the answer, Garret.'

'Sir, that *can't* be one of our—'

From about sixty degrees on the starboard bow, an answering light flashed. Garret was right: all Nick had seen was the letter 'K'. He hadn't thought about it . . . But they hadn't been challenging *Lanyard*; they'd been talking to that other ship – whatever ship it might be – almost on the beam now. Nick swung his glasses on to her.

Not 'her'. *Them*. There were three ships, closing-in at right-angles, more or less. Meanwhile *Lanyard* had fallen into station astern of the main bunch.

'Three-two-oh revolutions.'

'Three-two-oh, sir.'

Nick's mind seemed suddenly to jump, to come alive . . . Inside his skull, a voice screamed protest.

Holding his breath – his hands had begun to shake and his breathing had become rapid, short – he focused on the new arrivals as they came slanting in under helm to add themselves one by one to the line astern of *Lanyard*.

He'd seen the possibility when he'd realised that the challenge was that single letter 'K', the long-short-long; then Garret's cut-off

196

cry had put substance to the wild suspicion. It had still been a long moment of resistance before he'd surrendered to the truth of it.

Now he saw each of the three ships clearly, in profile as they turned to slip in astern. The first was a destroyer with two funnels rather far apart, the for'ard one seeming to be almost a structural part of the stunted bridge. The second funnel was set much farther aft – almost as far as the mainmast, which was just about amidships and had a boom-derrick mounted on it. He looked at her bridge again; there was hardly any foremast.

It made her a 'G' class destroyer. One of the Krupp-built boats. And the second – turning now behind the leader – was another of the same class.

The third ship was a three-funnelled light cruiser. Rather a pretty ship, with delicate, yacht-like lines. Twin searchlights on her foremast, at funnel-top height above the bridge, and another pair on the mainmast, a bit lower.

A Stettin-class cruiser.

All three of them had formed astern now. And the destroyer ahead of *Lanyard* seemed to have accepted her without question. Nick realised – guessed – that they wouldn't have been examining her closely because they'd known they were being joined by other ships anyway; and to the newcomers *Lanyard* would have been just one of that flotilla who'd fallen slightly astern of station. Also, with her shorn-off foremast, low bridge superstructure, cut-down funnel and clean-swept stern she might well, to a careless eye, pass for one of the German 'G's.

His heart was beating so hard that he thought Glennie, beside him, might be hearing it.

'Three-one-oh revolutions.'

Might as well keep good station. The last thing one wanted was to attract the attention of the other ships.

This was a nightmare. The worst he'd ever had . . .

'Three-one-oh revs on, sir.'

Chief Petty Officer Glennie's voice was low and even. Nick looked at him, wondering if he'd caught on to the situation. Glennie must have seen his head turn; he glanced at Nick fleetingly, expressionlessly, before his eyes went back to watching the stern of the German destroyer ahead. He murmured, 'Bound for Wilhelmshaven, are we, sir?'

CHAPTER 11

Pilkington's wizened face was pale.

'D'ye know what you bloody *done?*'

Nick said quietly, 'Three-one-five revolutions.'

'Three-one-five. Aye aye, sir.'

'Sub—'

'If you're thinking of swearing at me again, Mr Pilkington, you can get back aft, and quick.'

'Sub.' The gunner pointed. 'Those are 'uns. Those are bl—' He checked himself. The next bit came in a hoarse whisper: 'Germans, Sub. We're poncin' along with a whole pack—' His control broke; he ended in a shout – 'of bloody *Germans!*'

Nick lowered his binoculars.

'If we'd done anything but take station here quietly as we did, Mr Pilkington, they would have *looked* at us. And if they had, they'd have seen who we are and blown us out of the water. That happened to be the situation we were in.'

Pilkington nodded. 'So now we're up the creek. What 'appens when they start signalling at us? Which way're we bloody goin', anyway?'

Glennie glanced sideways at Nick, as if he too had some interest in the questions. Or perhaps he was wondering how much criticism Nick would take from the warrant officer before he shut him up.

'If you'd remained at your action station, Mr Pilkington, you'd have had orders from me by now. Don't come for'ard again without my permission, please. But since you are here, just stop belly-aching and *bloody well listen, will you?*'

He'd shouted that last bit. Now he leant over, checked the compass-card. Their course was south by east; so the reciprocal would be north by west. He told Garret, 'Warn the engineer officer that in a few minutes I'll be calling for full power, and when I do I want him to give us everything he's got.'

'Aye aye, sir.'

By the way Garret glanced at Pilkington, you could see he didn't think much of him.

'Listen. You too, Glennie. Remember that if I get knocked out, Mr Pilkington here would take command, and you're next in line. So you'd better have a grasp of what's happening.'

CPO Glennie nodded. His eyes didn't leave that German destroyer's wake.

'When you go aft, Mr Pilkington, train your tube out to starboard and stand by, and report to me when you're ready. When I hear that from you I'll crack on full power and put the wheel hard a-port. We should take 'em by surprise – they'd hardly be expecting an attack from one of their own ships, would they?'

Pilkington just stared at him.

'We'll circle out to starboard and you, Glennie, will steady the ship on north by east. That's the reverse of this present course. When your tube sight comes on, Mr Pilkington, you're to fire at the last ship in the line, which is the light cruiser. I want a report down the voicepipe as soon as you've fired, so I can alter course again as necessary. We'll be close enough for you to make sure of a hit, I imagine?'

Pilkington nodded. 'Should be.'

'*Very* close . . . So what about the safety range?'

'Oh . . .' Pilkington scratched his head. 'That's a problem, ain't it?'

The pistol in the warhead of a torpedo wasn't armed until the fish had travelled far enough for a small vane, propellor-shaped, to wind down, bringing the firing-pin to within one sixteenth of an inch from the detonator.

'Only one answer. You'll have to wind it halfway down before you train the tube out. Dangerous, but—'

'*Christ!*' A yelp . . . '*I'll* say it's bloody—'

'How long will it take you?'

'Couple o' minutes. But—'

'Once we start to turn out, you'll have to be damn quick. We'll be in the firing position in no time at all. And once we've passed it, that's the chance gone, finished. Right?'

'Aye aye.'

The stroppy little bastard wasn't going to say 'sir', Nick noticed. But that was the last and least thing he'd time to worry about now.

'Go back aft, then, and report when you're ready. And tell Hooper he's not to fire unless someone shoots at us first.'

Pilkington left. Nick asked the chief bosun's mate, 'Make sense to you, does it?'

'Clear enough, sir.'

'Garret, did you warn Mr Worsfold?'

'Yessir. Says he'll be ready, sir.'

'Good.'

It wouldn't do any harm to move ahead a little, and gain fifty yards or so before the turn. No more than that, because he'd want to put some speed on too, when the time came.

'Three-two-five revolutions.'

'Three-two-five, sir.'

The farther ahead she started, the longer there'd be – in terms of seconds – before the torpedo sight came on. Nick wondered what the rest of the German ships would do. Turn and give chase? One reason he'd decided to take this action immediately was that in a couple of hours it would be dawn; in an hour, even, the sky might begin to lighten. After *Lanyard* had made her move, she'd be needing all the dark there was to hide in.

But if she sank that cruiser, or crippled her, she'd have earned her keep, and he, Nick, would have made up for his idiocy. He'd passed it off rather well, he thought, in his explanation to the gunner – and it was true that if he'd turned away they most likely *would* have sunk her. A point might be made, however, by a more agile brain than Pilkington's, that she shouldn't have been in that position in the first place.

The jury voicepipe squawked. Nick answered it. 'Wheelhouse.'

'Tube's trained out an' ready, Sub.'

'With its pistol near armed?'

'I said, *ready*.'

Nick thought he could spare one minute, just to get a simple matter straight.

'Mr Pilkington. In your Drill Book, does the report "Ready" indicate anything whatsoever about that safety-vane being wound down?'

'Well, no, but—'

'Don't be so bloody stupid or so bloody insubordinate, then! Now stand by!'

Mortimer, he thought, would be proud of me . . . He told Glennie, 'Full ahead together!'

'Full ahead together, sir!' The chief buffer, Nick noticed, had a smile on his usually immobile features. He felt the surge of power as the destroyer's screws bit into the sea and thrust her forward. He waited; the more speed she could pick up before he gave the helm order, the more sharply she'd answer her rudder when it banged over.

But it would be a mistake to wait too long. For one thing, *Lanyard* would get too close to the ship ahead, and for another the piling foam under her counter would catch the eye of her next-astern.

'Hard a-port!'

'Hard a-port, sir!'

The wheel spun through Glennie's fingers; *Lanyard* leaned hard as she sliced her bow into the sea to starboard.

Already, at least the next astern and probably some of the others too would have seen her swing out of line.

One had to hope they'd be tired, and not too quick-witted.

Lanyard trembled, rattling like an old tin can as her engines thrust her forward and her rudder dragged at her stern. Nick, using his binoculars, saw that the five leading destroyers were holding on exactly as before; then, as *Lanyard*'s turn continued, he could see only four – three – two – now only the leader . . . And then *she* was blanked-off from his sight. Ahead of *Lanyard* was dark, empty sea with the woolly greyness of drifting mist. He could feel the taut thrumming of her steel under his feet, the shake in her as she battered round. He checked the compass-card: her head was coming up now to due west – past it now, and swinging on: west-north-west . . . He gave no orders, left it to Glennie, who knew his business and what was wanted. North-west by west; Glennie spun the wheel to bring the rudder amidships as the ship still skidded round, and as the lubber's line touched north-west by north he wrenched on the opposite rudder to meet and check the swing. Now he was centring the wheel again. Nick put up his glasses, and out to starboard the last of the destroyers was just passing: Pilkington should be firing about *now* . . .

'Course north by west, sir.'

'Very good.'

A shout in the voicepipe: 'Wheel'us!'

Nick grabbed it. 'Wheelhouse!'

'Torpedo's gone!'

'Right.' He told Glennie, 'Starboard ten.'

'Starboard ten, sir . . . Ten o' starboard—'

'Steer west-nor'-west.'

'West-nor'-west, sir.'

He held the cruiser's dim shape in the circle of his glasses while *Lanyard* slewed round to port. His object was to point her stern at the enemy flotilla, so that she'd be more difficult to see. As she swung, and the Germans ploughed on southwards, he realised that the cruiser would almost certainly be out of his arc of visibility before the torpedo reached her. Or passed her . . .

Please God, guide it!

'Course west-nor'-west, sir.'

The cruiser was out of his sight now. Could the Germans have guessed that a torpedo would be on its way across that strip of sea? In that situation, he asked himself, would one think of such a possibility? He thought probably not. They'd have first to cotton-on to the fact that *Lanyard* wasn't one of their own side; and that idea would take a bit of getting used to, to start with.

A white flash, like a glimpse of sheet-lightning, lit sea and sky for a brief instant before the thudding, reverberating thump of the explosion reached them. The flash lingered, brightened, died away . . .

'Nice work that, sir.'

Nick glanced at Chief Petty Officer Glennie's rock-like silhouette. He thought, *The point now is do we get away with it . . .*

A crash of gunfire astern added weight to that question.

'Starboard twenty!'

'Starboard twenty, sir . . .'

Glennie flung the spokes round. The voicepipe gurgled with a call and Nick snapped, 'Garret, answer that.' He heard the flight of a shell or shells overhead, and as the destroyer swung to port a fountain leapt within a few yards of her bow. She swung on into it as it collapsed, and stinking black water drenched down across her foc's'l; half a ton of it dropped into the roofless wheelhouse, soaking them – and worse than that blinding, suffocating with its acrid reek: it was like a heavily concentrated stench of spent fireworks.

All three of them were coughing, and streaming at the eyes; Nick breathed out to empty his lungs, and then held his breath, hoping the gas would clear by the time he had to breathe in again: but he was out of luck.

The shell burst below them – aft, but it felt as if it was close below their feet: one looked for the deck to bulge, split . . . A deep, ripping crash. It was almost like something tearing one's own gut,

202

the way you *felt* it. Its echoes rang through the ship, boomed away into the surrounding darkness. *Lanyard* had checked as if she'd steamed into a brick wall and through it and been slowed by it: it felt to Nick as if she was slumping, wallowing.

'Midships.'

'Midships, sir.' Behind Nick, Garret shouted into the voicepipe, 'Yes, I *am* still here . . . sir.' *Lanyard*'s engines were slowing, and that roar from aft was the sound of escaping steam. Boiler-room, then. Nick thought, *Finished . . .* He told himself, *Hang on. May not be all that bad.*

He wanted to scream out to somebody to tell him what was happening, what had happened. But he knew he'd hear from Worsfold as soon as the engineer could manage it. Coping with damage had priority over talking about it.

One waited, meanwhile, for the next salvo . . .

'Garret, what the hell's he—'

'Sir.' Garret let the free end of the flexible hose clang back against the bulkhead. 'Mr Pilkington says we hit the cruiser under her bridge and she looked like sinking. But that was her stern guns that fired at us, and we've been hit in the after boiler-room, sir.'

The racket of escaping steam was dying away. So was *Lanyard*'s speed. She wasn't just slowing: both engines had stopped completely.

Stopped, Nick thought. *With one gun left.*

Might as well get her round, while she still had a bit of steerage-way.

'Starboard fifteen. Steer due west.'

'Steer west, sir.'

Nick heard a call on the engine-room voicepipe; but Garret was there, and he held himself in check while the leading signalman moved over with what seemed like maddening slowness and answered it. He told Nick, 'Engineer officer wants a word, sir.'

Now that the engines were silent, one noticed other sounds. The wind humming in the broken structure of the bridge, a rhythmic creaking as *Lanyard* rose and fell, and the slapping of the sea against her bow.

If the Germans knew they'd disabled her, they'd be along, in a minute.

Johnny West had been swimming slowly, without hurrying or using up much energy, from group to group, trying to jolly them all up a bit, have a chat and a joke and then paddle away to some other lot. He went by sound; if he heard voices, he swam towards them, or he'd call 'Hello!' and then head in the direction of any faint reply.

In the last half-hour the incidence of men giving up and allowing themselves to drown had increased alarmingly. Men seemed suddenly to lose their grip, the will to live.

'Why, if it isn't the mechanical genius himself!'

Hanbury Pike revolved slowly in the water, and peered at him through the dark.

'Johnny?'

'Well done, Hanbury! And how're you keeping?'

'I'm damn tired, if you want to know.'

'And that's because you drink too much gin, you know, old lad.' West told him, 'It weakens the muscles of the brain. I'd give it up, if I were you.'

'Since when did—' Pike spat – 'brains have muscles?' He groaned. '*Christ*, but this stuff's cold!'

'I'm lucky, there. I've a few pounds of extra insulation.'

'A *few*!'

Pike had closed his eyes. West peered closely: 'Hey!'

'What?'

'Don't let yourself drop off. If you do, you won't wake up. I've seen it happen – just now, several—'

'I have not the least intention of—'

'Good. Is David Everard somewhere near us?'

'Frankly, I hope not.'

'I thought you were going to keep – hey, what's this, searchlights?'

He tried to raise himself in the water to see better. It was like a moon rising; some huge source of approaching light . . .

No moon: that was the leap of flames. A great concentration of – of fire, lighting that part of the horizon, and growing fast, or—

'What the devil?'

He saw suddenly that it was a ship, in flames. Enveloped totally in fire. You could hear her now, roaring, crackling, pounding through the sea at twenty knots or more, and she'd pass close . . . Flames sprouted the whole length of her, from foretop to waterline. The roar of them, fanned by her speed, was like the noise from an open furnace door. The edges of the blaze were jet-black with smoke darker than the night, and streaked with trails of burning, flying debris, while the sea – the waves on either side and the spreading wake astern – was lit by the yellow flames so that she steamed in the centre of a brilliant circle of her own weird light. She was passing now – a cable's length away: West felt the heat of her, heard the flames eating her as she thundered by: she'd passed, and her wash was spreading, coming to them, a great round-topped swell with curling, breaking waves behind it. Close-to he saw the black blobs of men's heads as the piling sea lifted them, rocked them and set them down again for the follow-up waves to play with. Within a few moments of her first appearing, the doomed ship was a rosette of fire dwindling northwards.

Pike gaped after her. 'Battle cruiser – German?'

'No. *Black Prince*—'

'Oh, stuff and—'

'– with her two middle funnels shot away.'

And there could not, he thought, have been a soul left alive in her. For their sakes, he hoped to God there couldn't be.

A hundred yards away, David Everard had watched her pass. She'd come closer to him than she had to West and Pike; he'd had to shield his eyes from her heat, and lumps of burning wreckage had splashed into the sea all round him, hissing as they struck the water. Now from the direction in which she'd disappeared, he heard the thunderclap of an explosion.

He was tired. Really exhausted. And so cold . . .

He'd seen several men go off to sleep, and he'd envied them. What they'd done was simply to stop swimming or treading water, and lie back in the sea.

They'd looked so *restful*. The thought that he might follow their example had infinite appeal.

He pushed his long legs out in front of him. The Gieves waistcoat was an excellent support. He let his head fall back into the softest pillow he'd ever known.

'Bloody daylight!'

He'd whispered it. Dawn, silvery-grey, was leaking from a quickly brightening sky to grey the black waste of sea in which *Lanyard* lay helpless. Mist drifted in shifting patterns and layers, like some kind of insulation adding to the surrounding quiet in which this ship, with men hammering and clattering down in her steel belly, was the only source of noise.

Garret nodded, sharing Nick's distaste for the approach of day.

205

Another hour of darkness might have seen them through. *Lanyard*, disabled and almost defenceless, badly needed the cover which yesterday had twice saved the German battle fleet from destruction.

She wasn't entirely helpless; she did have the one four-inch left, and plenty of ammunition for it. Its crew were sitting and lying around it, muffled in coats and scarves and wool helmets. Some of them lay flat out, dozing. Hooper, the gunlayer, was on his feet, leaning against the shield and using the binoculars which Nick had given him so he could help with the looking-out. Nick and Garret were farther aft. There was a good all-round view from this position, and for extra height of eye one could get up on the torpedo tubes. Also, Garret was handy to the twenty-inch searchlight in case some friendly ship might appear and challenge.

Nick had armed as many of the ship's company as possible with small-arms and cutlasses. He was wearing a revolver himself, and Garret had a rifle beside him. Pilkington and Chief Petty Officer Glennie and a few hands with them up for'ard were similarly equipped; below decks, a couple of dozen sailors lay around or snoozed with cutlasses strapped to them. If any Germans should imagine *Lanyard* was done for and try to board, they'd get a warm reception.

In fact, since she'd been crippled nothing had approached her. The destroyers must have gone on south-eastward. Either they'd been under orders not to deviate from their course – and if that was the case it would suggest the High Seas Fleet was running for home – or they hadn't realised that *Lanyard* had been hit, and had thought it would be unprofitable to chase after her.

The noise the engineers were making down there was getting on his nerves. He knew it couldn't be helped – and that unless a submarine picked it up on her hydrophones there was no enemy near enough to hear – but it still seemed to aggravate the tension. One tended, oneself, to be ultra-quiet, speaking in whispers – while that clattering and scraping got louder all the time. Nerves were jagged with the tension of inaction, the waiting.

The cruiser's shell had smashed in through the starboard side of the after boiler-room and exploded about amidships, further for'ard. The entry-hole was nothing to worry about, being small and well above the waterline, but the shell had wrecked the boiler-room, smashing both boilers and blowing a large piece of one of them out through the hull on the port side. The hole it had made

206

was large, and extended almost to the waterline: it had to be plugged, patched and shored. The other job was longer and more complicated: the steampipes and other connections between the undamaged for'ard boiler-room and the engine-room passed through the wrecked after boiler-room, and a lot of them had been cut or damaged. Worsfold had forecast that the work would take him a good two hours – *if* he ran into no unexpected snags; and that thereafter, all things being equal, and given continuing calm weather, *Lanyard* should be able to make eight or ten knots on her two for'ard boilers.

They'd been working for an hour and a half already.

'If we do get fixed up an' away home, sir—' Garret spoke quietly as he wiped his binoculars – 'if we go westward like you said—'

Pilkington had asked Nick, when the issuing of arms had been in progress, 'Sub – you better tell me, 'case we get in some bust-up and you get 'it, what course we'd steer for 'ome. North-west, is it?'

Nick had shrugged.

'Can't tell you, really.'

'Fine navigator you are!'

'I've never pretended to be a navigator.' His inclination had been to add, *you silly little shyster* . . . He was sick of the torpedo gunner and his chip-on-the-shoulder manner. He added, 'But even if I was a very good one, I couldn't tell you where we are now. We've been all over the shop, haven't we? With no plot kept and nothing to take a sight of . . .' He'd glanced up at the overcast, starless sky, and thought, *Thank God for small mercies* . . .

'Tell you what you do, though. What I'll do if Worsfold succeeds in getting us wound up again. Just steer west, until we hit something. When we hear a crunch, that'll be dear old England.' He'd thought, *Or Scotland.*

But with any luck, he might fall in with some other ship or ships which he'd be able to follow or take directions from. The first thing to think about was getting out of this hole, getting under way again. After that, one could start worrying about a course to steer.

But Garret's mind, as he reverted to the same subject, was more directional.

'Any chance we'll finish up in the Forth, sir?'

'Not much, really. I think we're probably too far south.'

'Couldn't we sort of point up a bit, sir?'

'I think I'm bound to take the shortest route home, you know, now we've got that hole in our side. Could get tricky if a gale blew up, for instance. I should think the Tyne's about our best bet, on that score. And you see, if I'm wrong and we're farther north now than I think we are, and we – as you say "point up a bit" well, that way we might miss Scotland, even!' *Hopeless navigators*, he thought, *have to play safe.*

Garret had sighed, and mumbled something in a gloomy tone. 'What?'

'Not much good to me, sir. The Tyne, I mean.'

Nick caught on to the reason for the anxiety. He told him, 'There's a perfectly good train service to Edinburgh, you know!'

Garret's head shook in the gloom. His gloom, too. 'They'd likely keep us there, sir. An' s'pose they don't, s'pose we pay off. I'm a Devonport rating, sir, they might send me down there.'

He stopped talking about it: it was too much for him. He muttered, 'I'd – skin off, sir, I would.'

'Don't be bloody daft, Garret. Talking to me about deserting?'

'Well, I'm sorry, sir, but—'

'After we dock, I'll send you on leave. How's that?'

Beside him the signalman took a deep, hard breath.

'Can you do that, sir?'

'I'm in command, aren't I?'

'I've no leave due, sir, that's the trouble. Before I got married I took it all.'

'If your commanding officer says you have leave due, you have leave due. You'll be issued with a railway warrant – and the base paymaster'll come up with an advance of pay.'

'D'you mean this, sir?'

'No skin off my nose, Garret.'

And where, he wondered, would *he* go?

First – when they let him – to Mullbergh. See Sarah. Try first to see Uncle Hugh, and ask him to help with wangling a permanent appointment to some destroyer, anything rather than getting shanghai'd back into some battle-wagon . . . Have to put it a bit tactfully; the old boy was proud of that vast thing *he* drove around.

Nick wondered how the day and night had gone with Hugh Everard and *Nile*, and how things had been for David, too. There'd been a new line of thought, hadn't there, about David. Coupling what Johnson had said about him with the undoubted fact that their father had always looked to David, as his eldest son and the future baronet, to do brilliantly – or at least do well – at everything he was supposed to do . . . Well, hence the horsemanship. Scared half to death – still an accomplished horseman, much better in the saddle than he, Nick, was – but nervous, which Nick had never been. Had David ever really *enjoyed* a day's hunting?

Nick wondered whether he could persuade David to listen to some advice – if he suggested to him, for instance, that instead of forcing himself to continue riding to hounds, he should tell their father, 'I don't enjoy it. I don't intend to hunt in future.'

He couldn't be disinherited. He was the first-born, and the estate was entailed, and the principle of primogeniture protected him completely. Their father wouldn't like a non-hunting eldest son – he'd raise hell – but did that matter? If David could be encouraged to face up to him – or in a way, face up to himself – mightn't he find himself a lot happier and perhaps in the process become easier to get on with?

The biggest 'if' of all was if David could screw up enough guts to face his father. He'd never done so yet. The old man had him cowed. Whereas he'd realised years ago he'd never scare his younger son into subservience, and as a result got into a habit of ignoring him.

The last time he and his father had faced each other in mutual anger had been a couple of years ago, at Mullbergh. Two o'clock in the morning: Nick had been woken by a succession of loud crashes: they'd been part of some dream, but as he'd woken he'd heard another and realised they'd been real: and as the realisation had taken root, he'd heard Sarah scream. He'd sprung out of bed and raced down the long, ice-cold corridor, stone-flagged and about as cheerful as a crypt: then into the central part of the house where his father and Sarah slept. He'd rushed down the half-flight of stairs to their floor.

'What the blazes are you doing here?'

His father was still in evening clothes; he was also half-drunk, and crazy-looking. Behind him, the top half of a bedroom door had been smashed in. A heavy case – it was the dumpy leather one in which the shoe and boot cleaning things were kept – lay on the floor there. Obviously his father had just used it to break down the door.

'Oh, *Nick* . . .'

He saw Sarah, as she came out into the passage. The shoulder of her dark-green evening dress had been ripped, and she was holding it up on that side.

'Is there—' he ignored his father, who was in a rage and shouting at him to go back to his room – 'anything I can do?'

'No, I – no, Nick, there isn't, thank you.' She'd smiled at him. Brown hair, all loose, fell across her face and had to be brushed back. 'I promise you, I'll be all right now. You go back to bed before you catch cold.'

Nick remembered – relived this incident every time his thoughts turned to Sarah and his father: the torn dress and her hair flopping loose and the half-frightened, half-defiant expression . . . It had marked a turning-point in his relationship with his father. From then on, his father had stopped bullying him and taken to ignoring him: as if he'd realised suddenly that Nick wasn't going to change or, in anything that really mattered, give way to him.

But whether he'd stopped bullying Sarah was another matter.

Watching the sea, the coming of the dawn, he sighed . . . The light wasn't grey now, it was silver. Overhead there was a vaguely pearly colour which became brighter, sharper in its reflection in the sea; this was probably what was producing the silvery effect. There were no waves now, only ripples, which in the middle-distance had a streaky look – over side silver, the other black. Mackerel-colour. Mist hung over everything; compared to the radiance of the sea's surface it looked dirty, colourless like sheep's wool in a thorn hedge.

Cold . . . Nick checked that the collar of his reefer was still turned up. It was, but it hadn't felt like it. And he had a sweater on, but he wished he'd put on two, now.

Worsfold had exceeded his ration of two hours, but the hammering was still going on. Nick pulled out his watch; it was light enough now to see the positions of the hands. He told Garret, 'Two thirty-five.' And at that precise moment, the noise stopped. Nick stood still with the watch in the palm of his hand, thinking, *Any second, they'll start again.*

Garret murmured, 'Got it done, sir, by the sound of it.'

Garret had grown a lot of beard, for one night. Nick touched his own jaw: it felt about as bad. He remembered Reynolds warning him, referring to Mortimer's idiosyncracies, 'informality is not encouraged in his officers . . .'

Forty-eight hours ago, Reynolds had said that! It felt as if half a lifetime had passed. For Reynolds and Mortimer, *a whole one* had.

'I think I'll go below and see what's what.' Nick stretched, yawned, and moved out towards the ship's side. There still wasn't any noise emanating from the boiler-room. He warned himself, *Don't count your chickens!*

Chief might have run into one of those snags he'd mentioned. He might be squatting there staring at it, wondering what to do about it. Nick stared out over the quarter, at the beginnings of a purpleish glow, low down where the horizon must have been – if one could have seen it – and blanketed in the mist. That glow would harden, redden, flush upwards and resolve itself eventually into the brilliance of a sunrise, and probably that would be all they'd see of the sun all day.

But it was none too soon, he thought, for *Lanyard* to be getting under way.

He told Garret, 'I'll be back in a few—'

His mouth stayed open.

Out of that tinted mist astern, a ship was looming up towards them.

German.

At a glance, and beyond a doubt. German light cruiser.

Well, that's that . . .

She was bigger than the cruiser they'd torpedoed. She had the typically low bridge and the pair of searchlights on her foremast; the searchlights looked like a crab's eyes stuck up on stalks above its head. She might be one of the Karlsrühe class – Germany's latest in light cruisers.

Not a damn thing, he thought, that one could do. The ball would be in that Hun's court, entirely. He edged back into the shadow of the searchlight platform and told Garret, 'Hun cruiser, coming up astern.' He'd whispered it. Silly, really: she was still a mile and a half or two miles away. Coming up from the quarter, steering to pass close on *Lanyard*'s starboard side.

He put his glasses on her again. She was closing at a slow, steady speed; unhurried, purposeful. She'd have a broadside – he delved into his memory – of five or six four-point-ones.

'Leading Seaman Hooper!'

'Sir?'

'Enemy light cruiser approaching on the starboard quarter. Keep your gun's crew out of sight. Everyone, keep down!'

'Aye aye, sir!' There was a quick scurry of movement across the destroyer's deck up near the gun.

'Hooper: load, set deflection six knots left and range . . .' He thought, *She'll pass within spitting distance . . .* 'Set range five

211

hundred yards.' He told Garret, 'Go for'ard and tell Mr Pilkington what's happening. Then below, and tell Mr Worsfold I don't want a pin dropped anywhere. I'll be at the gun.'

Garret shot away. Nick called after him, 'No movement on deck either, tell 'em.' He joined Hooper on the gun platform, and crouched down beside him. 'If they think we're a wreck it's just possible they may decide to leave us alone.' The gunlayer raised an eyebrow, as if to say *fat chance of that*. Nick added, 'Or they might send a boat, a boarding party.'

He thought of the men he had waiting below with cutlasses. He *hoped* the cruiser might send a boarding party.

In a greenish, cold-looking sea, bodies in lifebelts rose and fell amongst other flotsam. The areas of dead came infrequently but there'd be as much as an acre or two of them at a time; sometimes the black and sodden uniforms were British, sometimes German. When you saw them through binoculars at a distance, the humped shapes had the look of drifting mines. One saw them always on the bow, because by the time *Nile* was close to them they'd been caught in the bow-waves of *Barham, Valiant* and *Malaya* and lifted, pushed aside to form an avenue of clear sea through which the Grand Fleet's battle squadrons in line ahead and led by these Queen Elizabeths steamed north in search of the enemy.

An hour ago Jellicoe had wheeled his dreadnoughts round and disposed them in line of battle; since two am the fleet had been closed up at action stations.

Rathbone was conning the ship. Hugh left him, and joined his second-in-command in the port wing of the bridge.

'I'm sorry to say it, Tom, but I think Scheer's got away.' He pointed out towards a scattering of black dots, the last colony of drowned men they'd passed, still visible on the quarter. 'Those are the only Huns we're likely to see today.'

Crick nodded.

'It's a – a disappointment, sir.'

Understatement was a habit, with Tom Crick.

Nile still had no wireless, so one couldn't know what reports had reached Jellicoe during the night, or on what knowledge or lack of it he'd based his decision to hold on southwards. Hugh knew only that throughout the dark hours there'd been flare-ups of action astern, and that there was no sign of any enemy in the area now. The two observations weren't difficult to link.

All right – the Grand Fleet held the ring, kept the sea. Here they were, close to the German coast, ready and more than willing to resume the battle, while Scheer had run home to safety. Wisely, even cleverly; but running was still running. The victors were those left in the field. But by escaping homewards, Scheer had denied to Jellicoe the kind of victory which the Grand Fleet had sought and which it had been expected to achieve.

'Best keep the hands closed-up, Tom, for the time being. You could send 'em to breakfast by watches?'

'Aye aye, sir.'

Hugh was hungry, too. Bates, no doubt, would have something ready for him.

There'd be post-mortems, he thought, till the cows came home. The loss of ships wouldn't be well received; and there had to be some structural defect that had led to the battle cruisers blowing up. Flash to their magazines, almost certainly. By comparison, it was extraordinary how much punishment the German capital ships had been able to absorb without blowing up or sinking. And it could be that there was some deficiency in the British shells, or in their fuses. One had seen so many explode on impact instead of penetrating.

It might be asked why Beatty had rushed into action without the support of this battle squadron; whether it had resulted from the same lack of control of his ships which had made the Dogger Bank action such a fiasco, or whether Sir David's over-confidence and pursuit of fame had urged him to hog the glory for himself and his battle cruisers. But when it came to post-mortem time, the biggest question that would be asked would be how had the Germans been permitted to escape, why it hadn't ended as a twentieth-century Trafalgar.

The public wouldn't understand that at Trafalgar Nelson had drifted into action at about two knots, that once the fleets had grappled the battle had had to be fought out to its conclusion; they might not want to understand that it was a different matter to annihilate an enemy who couldn't move from the mouths of your cannon than it was to smash one who could turn and run away into fog at twenty knots.

The Navy would know what had been proved, and so would the Germans. Twice Scheer had thrown his squadrons against Jellicoe's, and twice they'd had to turn and run. What had been proved was that the High Seas Fleet was no match for the Grand Fleet.

But still – Hugh thought – if he, Everard, had been in Jellicoe's shoes, and seen the night-fighting in the north, wouldn't he have steered for Horns Reef and shut off that escape route?

Hugh remembered the post-mortems inside the Admiralty after the Falklands victory. The arguments had all been of Jackie Fisher's making. Fisher, giving Admiral Sturdee command of the operation, had had his own personal, Fisher-type aim in mind; his hope had been that Sturdee, whom he regarded as an enemy, should fail. Doveton Sturdee had been Lord Charles Beresford's Chief-of-Staff in the Mediterranean and in the Channel, and had naturally shared his chief's anti-Fisher attitude. So Fisher still wanted Sturdee broken; and to have Hugh Everard go along on the same operation made it even better – two birds with one stone!

But Sturdee had had luck – which at one stage he'd surely needed – and he'd destroyed Von Spee's squadron. So Fisher had tried to prove he should have done it better, or more quickly, than he had. Hours, days, weeks had been wasted on an exercise of malice.

Of course, Hugh thought, for years I've loathed Fisher! Who wouldn't – unless he was some kind of saint – who'd been a victim of that brand of hate?

Fisher had broken him, in 1907, because he'd suspected him of having a foot in the Beresford camp. The Navy had been split into factions by the mutual loathing between Fisher and Beresford who'd virtually provoked mutiny in other senior officers against the thrusting, forceful First Sea Lord who'd come up from nothing and rode rough-shod over anyone who opposed him. Fisher was the son of a planter in Ceylon and he looked as if he had more than a dash of Singhalese blood; 'the gentleman from Ceylon' had been Admiral Beresford's way of referring to his First Sea Lord. It hadn't been unnatural for a man of Beresford's stamp to have loathed Fisher's methods and manners; he'd done his best to thwart him, destroy him. So when the Beresfords appeared as guests at the wedding of Commander Hugh Everard, Royal Navy, and Lady Alice Cookson-Kerr, Fisher discovered that he'd been harbouring in his 'fish pond' an officer who consorted with his enemies and had therefore to be eliminated.

The Beresfords had been invited, of course, by the parents of the bride. Hugh, hearing at the last moment of their inclusion in the guest-list, had seen the danger; but it would have been impossible to have done anything about it. Even then he hadn't – or so it seemed now, looking back on it – appreciated the depth of Fisher's

214

paranoia. But he should have known what to expect; Fisher had boasted openly of his readiness to break rivals or opponents; he'd make widows of their wives, he'd promised, and dung-heaps of their houses. The Bible had always been a source of his verbal inspiration. And he'd decided within a week of Hugh's wedding that Commander Everard had 'run out of steam'. Hugh found himself shunted off, and offered appointments which the most dead-beat officers would have regarded as insulting. Within a year he'd resigned his commission. Within a further year, Alice had made it plain that being his wife was no longer to her taste. She'd married a rising star, a future Nelson, and now she found herself with a husband who worked for a firm of shipbuilders. Her friends' husbands, if they did anything except hunt foxes, were in politics or the Services.

Hugh gave her the divorce she wanted. But the story went about – and it still held water in the minds of some of his contemporaries – that his fall from grace in the Service as well as the reason for his wife divorcing him had been 'woman trouble'. Technically, a woman had provided the grounds for the divorce; and before his marriage he'd made no pretence of being a plaster saint. After the divorce – well, he'd been his own man, and there'd been *some* advantages in that unlooked-for 'freedom'.

Fisher had done him more harm than it should have been possible for one man to do another. For nearly ten years, one had been constantly aware of it.

He'd kept his feelings to himself, though, knowing that protests and recriminations couldn't improve his situation in any way, certainly wouldn't add to his chances of recovery, and could only be counted on to make him look ridiculous and sound a bore. And now that Fisher had gone, and was himself ridiculous in his senility, he could actually feel sorry for the old man, feel the sadness of former greatness lapsed into impotence, and remember the great achievements. The reforms of sailors' pay and conditions of service were probably the most important; and this – Hugh looked astern at the line of dreadnoughts extending southwards into the morning mists – this was Jackie's creation. One could recall too that Fisher, whose own nomination to naval service when he'd joined in 1854 had been signed by the last of Nelson's admirals, had been personally responsible for the grooming and appointment of Sir John Jellicoe as C-in-C of the Grand Fleet.

The torch came from hand to hand. Ships, weapons, tactics

changed. Nothing else did. Oh, conditions, certainly. One could remember Fisher's own account of joining his first ship, at the age of thirteen, in that year 1854. On the day he joined, he saw eight men flogged, and he fainted. Hugh could still hear the gruff, disjointed reminiscences emerging from that ugly, even brutish face: *Midshipman of four-foot nothing – keeping night watches, and always hungry. No baths – belly always empty* . . . He'd remembered a quartermaster of the watch once giving him a maggoty biscuit, and a lieutenant of the watch who'd sometimes let him have a sardine, or an onion, or a glass of rum . . .

'Spot o' breakfast, sir?'

Hugh nodded to his coxswain.

'Thank you, Bates. I'm ready for it.'

Lanyard drifted; silent, inert, misshapen, wreck-like.

The gun's crew, and others with weapons in their hands, lay motionless, almost held their breaths as they watched the German cruiser approaching steadily across the dawnlit sea.

She'd closed to about a thousand yards, half a sea mile, off *Lanyard*'s quarter. She still slid closer at the same slow speed; she'd pass about two cables' lengths to starboard.

Pass – or stop.

If she saw no sign of life, and sent a boat across, *Lanyard* might have a hope? If one let the boarding party come aboard, and then captured them, would a German captain fire on his own men?

No. He'd probably send more men.

It was the tension of this waiting, and the fact of being so utterly at that ship's mercy, that made one clutch at straws.

Nick put his glasses on her again. She might have been a ghost-ship creeping up, slipping closer through a silvery-greenish sea with a feather of white at her stem and only ripples spreading where she'd passed. There was no sound at all from her; all that could be heard here was the slap of water against *Lanyard*'s sides and the creak of loose gear shifting as she moved to the sea's own movement. But nothing shifted or even seemed to live on that cruiser's bridge or about her decks; she only came on steadily with her air of purpose and those twin crab's-eyes up above her bridge as if she herself was some kind of monster watching them. He shook the fantasy out of his mind. He wondered whether there might in fact be men in that bridge who were invisible from here but who'd have binoculars trained on *Lanyard* – German optical instruments being

216

far better than British ones – revealing these men lying doggo around the gun. If so, this would be their point of aim when they opened fire; and since Hooper had built up a large reserve of cartridges and projectiles handy to the gun, it wouldn't be a healthy place to be.

In about a minute the cruiser would be abeam. About then, one might expect the ordeal to begin.

'Layer – you there, 'Oops?'

Hooper looked to his left without moving his head.

'What's up, Pratt?'

'I been thinkin'.' Pratt sounded like a Londoner. 'I never did learn to play the 'arp. Teach you when you reports aboard, do they?'

'They'll give you a shovel, mate, where you're goin'. Now be a good boy'n shurrup, eh?'

Nick glanced aft, at the ensign drooping from the mainmast. Wet from the night's mist, in the almost windless air it hung straight down, limp as a dead bird hanging in a tree. The game-keepers at Mullbergh hung vermin like that . . . But it would be visible and identifiable, he thought, from the cruiser, and it would be all the justification they'd need to open fire.

Hooper hissed suddenly, 'Sir – she listin', would you say?'

Nick raised his glasses and focused on her again. He couldn't see any list.

But she was very nearly abeam now. The range was about six or seven hundred yards – farther than he'd expected. And she was moving more slowly than he'd reckoned earlier. He told Hooper, 'Deflection *three* left.'

'Three left – aye aye, sir . . . Look there!'

'What?'

'She – just sort o' leaned over, sir—'

'Hey!'

She'd lurched to port: a definite movement, which he'd seen quite clearly. He strained his eyesight now: the lenses of his binoculars were slightly fogged and he couldn't spare the time to clean them . . . 'Layer – am I dreaming, or is she down by the bow?'

Hooper laughed shortly. 'Don't reckon you're the dreamin' sort, sir.'

The cruiser's stern was rising as her bow dug lower in the sea, and she was listing so far to port now that one could see right into

217

her bridge. It was empty. He thought, *They've abandoned her . . .* But – left her engines going?

Perhaps they left a few hands aboard, and they'd left her bridge now because they'd realised she was about to sink? It was all theory – and not counting chickens: he thought suddenly, *There could still be a torpedo coming . . .*

They could have struggled this far with that intention; in such a condition wasn't it exactly what one would do?

She was going, though. Her screws were out of the water, reflecting the light of sunrise as their blades turned slowly, lazily in the air.

Nick stood up. He told the gun's crew, 'All right. She's done for. Pratt give 'em a shout below, tell 'em all to come up and see this.'

The cruiser was standing on her nose, with nearly half her length – including bridge and foremast and the first of her four funnels – buried in the sea. A German ensign hung vertically downwards, banner-like, from her mainmast which was now parallel to the sea's surface. Nick heard cheering and whoops of joy as *Lanyard*'s ship's company came pouring up on deck. He put one hand out, leant against the gun, and at that moment the enemy cruiser seemed to lift a little in the water and then slip down into it.

She'd gone. Quietly, with no fuss at all. And *Lanyard* was alone again.

Through the pandemonium of sailors cheering, dancing, going mad, one had to take this in, take stock of an entirely new situation, the abrupt removal of what had seemed like certain doom.

He realised that since he'd stood up he'd been feeling wind on his face. He looked at the sea, and saw a flurry spreading across its surface, a sort of graining with white flecks in it. He looked at the ensign, and saw that stirring too.

Coming up so suddenly out of the dawn calm, one could expect a blow. With three hundred miles of sea to cross, and *Lanyard* with only two boilers and a hole in her side.

One enemy removed itself, and another took its place.

'Sub!'

He looked down at the upper deck. He saw Worsfold, the engineer, peering up at him. Worsfold looked as if he'd spent the night working at a coal-face.

'You can take us all home now, Sub. But listen – no more 'n five knots, d'you hear?'

218

CHAPTER 12

The gig's oars swept to and fro in the lazy-looking ceremonial stroke in which Bates had trained his crew, and the waters of the Firth of Forth hissed and gurgled under the boat's stern as she gathered way towards the northern shore. It was a bright, sparkling summer day; a month had passed since the battle which people in Britain were calling 'Jutland' but which the Germans in natural perversity were referring to as the *Skagerrakschlacht*.

Hugh Everard, in his gig's sternsheets, looked back at *Nile*. She was showing no signs of rough treatment now. He'd brought her into Rosyth on the day after the battle, and since then taken her down to Portsmouth for dockyard repairs. Now this return to Rosyth was just a twenty-four-hour call to replenish ammunition, stores and fuel on the way north to Scapa.

Jellicoe was being blamed for the escape of the High Seas Fleet. Beatty was being lauded as the intrepid young seadog who'd have scuppered Hipper, Scheer – done for Kaiser Willy himself, if *he'd* been in charge! Jellicoe, being the man he was, was declining to defend himself in public, while Beatty's stock soared without his having to say a word. He uttered no word on Jellicoe's behalf either; while Jellicoe had nothing but praise for all his subordinates, including Beatty.

In a minor capacity, Hugh was coming in for a share of the limelight; his action in turning out of the line to save *Warspite* had found glowing approval in all quarters. So one's star was rising once again . . . But for the next hour or two he intended to forget the Navy; he was on his way to see Sarah, at her father's house at Aberdour. He'd spoken to Buchanan this morning on the telephone, and the old man had told him that Sarah had returned from Mullbergh a few days ago.

She'd been at Aberdour when *Nile* had docked on the morning of 2 June, but he'd had no chance of attending to any private business or pleasure with such a maelstrom of work on hand. A few days later when he did try to contact her, he was told she'd left for Mullbergh.

He glanced astern again, across the Firth to the blueish haze over Edinburgh. Like many others in the Grand Fleet, he had mixed feelings now about that town. In the early days of June, there might even have been some satisfaction in turning the fleet's guns on it!

The Rosyth ships – including Beatty's *Lion*, badly damaged and full of wounded – had been boo'd by dockyard workers as they'd limped into their berths. Then – incredibly – wounded sailors on their way to hospital had been jeered at by civilians in the streets.

Bates had turned *his* guns on Edinburgh . . .

Hugh had sent him ashore to buy a few essentials – having almost no personal possessions left he'd hardly known where to start – but Able Seaman Bates got no further than the Caledonian Street station. Some lounging porters hooted at him; one of them shouted, 'Thank the Lord we've an army tae defend us!' A few minutes later, by which time Bates had laid him and his mate out cold and thrown a railway official through the window of the ticket office, considerably enlarging the window in the process, he was arrested. A magistrate fined him for assault and damage to property, and he'd then been handed over to the naval patrol and returned aboard *Nile*, where finally he'd been hauled up in front of Crick as a defaulter. There were several charges against him under the Naval Discipline Act, and the police sergeant who'd arrested him was brought on board as a witness.

Hugh heard all about it afterwards; it was still a pleasure to visualise the scene that morning on his ship's quarterdeck. Bates at attention with his cap off, brown monkey-eyes fixed on the commander while the charges were read out. Crick, taller than anyone else present, ramrod stiff behind a small table that had been placed beside 'X' turret, listening to Lieutenant Knox-Wilson's formal report of earlier proceedings. Knox-Wilson had been officer-of-the-day when Bates had been brought back by the patrol; he'd heard the charges read out there and then, and had no choice but to pass the case on to 'commander's report'. The regulating petty officer who'd been on duty then was here now at Crick's defaulters session; so was the master-at-arms, *Nile*'s chief of police.

The police sergeant described what had taken place at the Caledonian Street station. When he'd finished and snapped his notebook shut, Crick stared down his nose at Bates.

Bates's eyes didn't waver. He was ready for more punishment, well aware that the commander was not one of his admirers.

'What's your story, Bates?'

Bates told it, not wasting words, but not missing anything out either.

'Nothing else to say?'

'No, sir.'

Crick turned to the policeman.

'D'you wish to contradict anything this man has told me?'

'I couldn'ae, sir. I wasn'ae present, not when he started bashing 'em aboot.'

Crick's eyes returned to the defaulter. 'How much did they fine you, did you say?'

'Thirteen poun' twelve an' six, sir. They gimme time to pay though, sir.'

Crick asked the policeman, 'That's a great deal of money?'

'It were a great deal o' damage, sir.'

The commander nodded slowly, staring at him.

'Would you happen to know, sergeant, how many men we lost in the recent battle?'

'No, sir, I would not.'

'More than six thousand, sergeant.'

Crick's tone had hardened. The policeman looked down at his boots, and shook his head. Crick had turned back to Bates.

'I shall pay your fine myself.' He cleared his throat. 'No. On second thoughts, I believe the wardroom officers may wish to take a share in it. If you'd permit that, Bates?'

Bates blinked, twice. He nodded. Crick snapped, 'Case dismissed!'

Hugh returned his coxswain's salute as he stepped from the gig to the pier steps.

'Carry on, Cox'n. Be here at five, please. And you know I'll be needing you later, as well.'

'Aye aye, sir.'

Bates knew what for, too. He'd have his crew working on the gig now, back at the boom; for this evening's trip she'd be as 'tiddly' as any boat that ever crossed the Firth of Forth.

221

Hugh climbed the steps, and walked up the wooden pier. Sarah was in his thoughts now.

She was – hardly the same person.

'So you're the conquering hero now, Hugh!'

'Oh, that's all rubbish . . .'

He felt as if he was talking to her through glass, a defensive barrier. He'd had things to tell her: and he knew – he'd assembled his thoughts, for about the thousandth time, during the short train journey out to Aberdour – precisely what he wanted to establish. He wanted an understanding: an indication would have been enough. More than that, in present circumstances, would have been too much to ask for. He wanted her to understand his own feelings for her, and accept them. Beyond that, time could be left to look after everything.

All right, so he'd be asking to have his cake and eat it too. But as much for her sake as for his own. And it made sense. One couldn't ignore this morning's front-page news – of the great offensive on the Somme, the long-heralded attack aimed at prising the Huns' strangle-hold off Verdun. Brother John had told Sarah months ago that when the balloon went up he'd be there; all this time his division had been training for it.

One couldn't ignore facts or discount probabilities. The war had been going on too long and the casualty lists had stretched too far for anyone to stay blind, or pretend blindness, about such things.

Sarah had greeted him effusively; that had been the first wrong sign. She'd been like a hostess receiving a visitor whom she might not have wanted to entertain. Buchanan had told him on the telephone that regrettably he wouldn't be at home himself as he was off to London that afternoon but Sarah would be, and he, Buchanan, had been worried about leaving her alone. She'd be delighted to see him.

Less delighted, Hugh realised, than on edge. Twice she'd glanced anxiously at the clock.

'So sad about David.' He told her, 'I wrote to John, of course.'

He'd been called on down in Portsmouth by *Bantry*'s padre, a man called Pickering. Pickering and a number of wounded survivors in his care had been picked up soon after dawn on 1 June by a destroyer; they'd been on make-shift rafts, apparently. He'd spoken warmly of David's courage and steadiness below decks during the ship's last hours. Conditions must have been appalling . . . So much, Hugh had thought, for one's doubts of David.

Sarah preferred to talk about young Nick.

'Isn't it wonderful, what he did?' She added, 'And that was your doing, Hugh. If you hadn't arranged for him to be moved to that destroyer—'

'Yes, well . . .'

She rattled on about Nick. Hugh found himself surrendering; it was impossible to switch the conversation to the personal level that he'd wanted. In any case, she was so different in her manner that it was like chatting to someone one hardly knew.

She said, 'I hope it won't change him too much.'

'Would you expect it to?'

There was a sort of gloss on her. Her natural prettiness had become what he'd have called a *London* prettiness.

'Well, it's highly dramatic for him, isn't it? Recommended for – "accelerated promotion", is it?'

Hugh nodded. 'He's in for a DSC as well.'

She smiled, brightly. 'What are you in for?'

He shook his head. 'You needn't fear too great a change in him. He's now back up to his neck in hot water.'

'Oh, no!'

'He sent a man on leave. He'd no business to and he knew it, he did it surreptitiously, even got him a travel warrant and an advance of pay. The fellow wasn't entitled to leave or pay, and he and his wife left their home address and couldn't be traced so he has either to be allowed to stay on leave until he chooses to come back, or it's a matter of alerting police-stations all over the country to pick him up. Nick's not in great favour, I can tell you.'

Sarah had giggled. 'I remember. He was a bit worried, when he came to Mullbergh.'

'Indeed.'

'But compared to what he *did*—'

'He can thank his stars he has something on the credit side. But if he's going to let a bit of success go to his head—'

'Oh, Nick's not like that!'

He felt better suddenly; she'd looked and sounded like her old self, then. That vehemence; her love for Nick: this was Sarah!

He tried to take advantage of the moment . . .

'Are you – you yourself, Sarah – all right?'

'I hardly know what you mean.'

Her guard was up again. And she'd allowed herself another glance at the clock.

223

'I meant, are you happy? Because – Sarah, my dear, I've had a lot of time for thinking, lately. About you, and how I—'

'Hugh.'

He waited. She forced a smile. 'I do, to be truthful, have rather a dreadful headache. I think I'll go and lie down, when you've—'

'Oh, I'm so sorry!' He got up, quickly. 'If you'd said so before, I'd—'

'It's nothing in the least serious, just—'

'Time I moved, in any case.'

Whatever she said now, it was obvious she wanted him to leave. He opened the door for her, and followed her into the hall. Perhaps when he had time to think, he'd understand this . . .

'McEwan will send the motor round.' She spoke without looking at him. 'If you don't mind, Hugh, I think I *will* go straight up and lie down.'

'Of *course*.'

She'd rung for the butler; now Hugh watched her climb the curving staircase. McEwan came shuffling from the back regions, and she stopped on the first landing to give him instructions about the motor. Hugh waited, looking up at her; she raised a hand.

'All the very best of good luck, Hugh. I'm so sorry about my silly head. You *will* forgive me?'

That had been totally artificial . . . The front door bell clanged. Sarah looked as if she'd been shot at: alarmed, flustered. McEwan, who'd begun to move towards the door of the servants' quarters, halted and turned about. Sarah was coming down the stairs: her cheeks were flushed, and she looked beautiful as well as upset.

McEwan opened the double doors to the storm porch and went through it to the outer door. As it swung back, Hugh saw an officer in the uniform of the Camerons. Sarah called out quickly – too quickly – 'Why, it's Alastair! Hugh, this is an old, old friend of my family's—'

'My *dear* Sarah.'

The Highlander advanced into the hall. Sarah told Hugh, 'Major Kinloch-Stuart. A *very* old – oh, you're a sort of cousin really, aren't you, Alastair?'

Kinloch-Stuart, Hugh thought, looked a bit surprised at that. Sarah added, 'My brother-in-law, Captain Everard.'

The two men shook hands. Kinloch-Stuart said, 'Captain of the celebrated HMS *Nile*, of course. May I say, sir, it's an honour.'

'McEwan, show Major Kinloch-Stuart into the drawing-room . . . Alastair, would you excuse us, for a few moments?'

'Of course.'

'I'll come with you to the motor, Hugh.' Hugh and Cousin Alastair exchanged courteous goodbyes. Then he was walking out into the driveway with Sarah, knowing finally what all the clock-watching had been about, and the tension and the headache . . . He felt surprise, and jealousy, and disappointment. He'd feel worse, he knew, presently, when it had sunk right in. But he'd no right to feel *anything*, he told himself. He'd assumed far too much, taken far too many things for granted.

Sarah murmured, 'I'm – sorry, Hugh, I'm so—'

'Why? Why should you?'

'It isn't – well, as it may seem, to be—'

'I've no idea why you should be upset. Or why an old friend shouldn't call on you.' Looking down at her, he met her worried, hazel eyes. He might have been looking into that photograph, the one Bates had rescued. He thought, *My God, but I've been an idiot!*

'Hugh – please understand – it is *not* as it might appear!'

He nodded, and smiled easily, seeing how desperate she was that he should believe her. He felt as if he'd been kicked in the stomach by a horse.

'It doesn't appear like anything at all. I promise you.' He could hear the motor chugging round from the stable-yard. He asked her, 'May I write to you, from up north?'

She nodded, seriously. 'Please. Soon. And – Hugh, don't stay up there too long?'

As it happened – no, he didn't expect he'd be up in Scapa very long.

Sarah had said – last time he was here, when they'd discussed Nick's future in the Navy – she said something like 'the Navy's your god, does it have to be his too?' And she'd been right, up to a point. In a way, the Navy was his god; and he was caught up in it all the more strongly, perhaps, for having been so to speak excommunicated, a decade ago. Perhaps one might profit from that now? Not only in the determination to make up for lost time, but from having been left with few illusions, no blind faith or blinkers.

Recent developments – Beatty's popularity and the criticism of Jellicoe, who was ten times the man Beatty could ever dream of becoming – was a perfect example of the need for such awareness.

Jellicoe had given his whole life and his very considerable, exceptional talents to the Navy, and it was allowing him to be treated as a whipping-boy. Kicking him upstairs. Beatty was to take over as Commander-in-Chief, and Jellicoe was to go to the Admiralty as First Sea Lord.

Hugh knew it privately, from old friends now at the Admiralty. He'd also heard a whisper – which it would probably never be safe or politic to allow past his own lips – that during the night of 31 May/1 June the Admiralty had intercepted and deciphered no fewer than seven German signals all of which had made it clear that Scheer was steering for Horns Reef, and they'd passed none of them to Jellicoe. They'd wirelessed two earlier intercepted messages to him, but these had conflicted with reports coming in at the same time from Jellicoe's own scouting cruisers. If the Admiralty had confided to their Commander-in-Chief the information they'd possessed themselves, the Grand Fleet would have been at Horns Reef at daylight and Scheer would have faced annihilation.

The car had stopped. Hugh Everard emerged with a start from his thoughts, realising he hadn't consciously seen a yard of the miles they'd covered. In the process, he'd managed not to think of Sarah.

He climbed out. 'Thank you, Hart. A very comfortable journey.'

Actually the man could have run over a cow, and Hugh wouldn't have noticed it. Half-a-crown changed hands.

'Thank ye, sir.' Hart touched his cap. 'An' guid luck tae ye all!'

Hugh wondered, *If you'd been on this shore a month ago, would you have wished us luck – or catcalled?*

The great chance had come, and it had been missed. The best one could say, perhaps, was that the High Seas Fleet would almost certainly not put out to sea again. An American commentator had summed it up neatly by observing that the Kaiser's fleet had assaulted its gaolers but was now back behind bars.

He watched the car drive away in its cloud of exhaust smoke and dust. Then he turned, strolled out along the railway pier. It wasn't much after four-thirty, but that looked like his gig leaving the boom already. Gathering way: but end-on, hard to see . . . He stopped, narrowing his eyes against the brightness on the water. And it was the gig, sure enough: he could see the slow rhythm of its oars.

Plenty of time . . .

The gig would be taking him this evening to dine aboard a

flagship with an admiral who'd intimated that he'd like to celebrate Captain Everard's imminent promotion to rear-admiral. There'd been no confirmation yet about his new appointment, but there'd been a strong hint, privately, of a cruiser squadron. This, and other flag changes which would have to be announced first, was known at present by only a few men in the Admiralty, and Jellicoe, and Evan-Thomas, and the admiral with whom Hugh would be dining tonight. Before long, though, Jackie Fisher would read of it in *The Times*; and the old man could choke, if he cared to, on his eggs and bacon!

Halfway out along the pier; and the boat was halfway from ship to shore. This evening – he wasn't looking forward to it, but it was the sort of thing he'd have to learn to handle now – this evening the gig would display his pendant in her bows. The crew's drill would be immaculate, and the admiral, glaring down from his quarter-deck, would see nothing that could fail to please a seaman's eye.

If he doesn't have one, I'll lend him mine!

He suppressed both the thought and the smile that came with it. The order of the evening must be tact, diplomacy. There'd been too many rifts, cliques, factions; the whole Service had suffered from them in past years. The thing now was to forget personal views, likes and dislikes, and get on with the job in hand.

The gig's wake was a slim streak stretching back ruler-straight to *Nile*'s impressive silhouette. And she was an impressively happy ship these days. Experience of battle had given officers and men an appreciation of each other's qualities and a sense of inter-dependence that had perhaps been lacking earlier. At the cost of lives and ships, the Navy had a new edge to it, a sense of unity it hadn't had in years.

One had now to preserve that unity, and *use* it.

He waited at the top of the steps, and watched his boat curve in towards them.

227

SIXTY MINUTES
FOR ST GEORGE

CONTENTS

Part One, chapters 1–11
Christmas to New Year: the Straits   235

Part Two, chapter 12
St George's Day: Zeebrugge   395

AUTHOR'S NOTE

Sixty Minutes for St George is a novel about the Dover Patrol in 1917–18.

The story is built around fictional ships and characters. But the general background – Dover itself, the ships, commanders and operations of the Patrol, and the assault on Zeebrugge – is as close a reflection of historical and technical fact as research has been able to make it.

PART ONE

Christmas to New Year: the Straits

CHAPTER 1

Out of the confusion of ice-cold wind and broken sea Nick Everard caught the yelled report, high and weather-cutting as a seagull's shriek: 'Clear anchor!' He glanced round towards the port fore corner of the bridge where until a moment ago his commanding officer, Lieutenant-Commander Wyatt, had been standing hunched, heavy-shouldered, muttering with impatience while the cable's rhythmic clanking had seemed to be going on and on with no end to it, the destroyer still tethered by her nose to the sand of Dunkirk Roads. The visual memory of an outbreak of gunfire to seaward, westward, six or eight minutes ago tugged at all of them – felt as if it pulled even at *Mackerel* herself – like the most powerful of magnets. Behind Nick now, Wyatt's voice was an explosion of relief: 'Half ahead together! Starboard ten!'

'Starboard ten, sir.' The coxswain, Bellamy, was at the wheel, a shorter, slimmer figure with Wyatt's bulk looming close to it. Bellamy was leaning slightly forward across the wheel's spokes and peering into the dimly lit binnacle, waiting to be given a course to steer. The engine-room telegraphs double-clinked and the ship began to tremble as her turbines drove her forward, rudder swinging her to port across wind and sea. From the dark triangle of foc's'l at which Nick was looking down across a gull's-eye view of the for'ard four-inch gun he heard the thud of the anchor slamming home into its hawsepipe and Cockcroft's simultaneous shout telling the stoker at the capstan to 'vast heaving. Then a clatter of heavy metal, the cable party working fast to get the slips on the cable and lash them down. They had to finish and clear the foc's'l before the ship gathered much way seaward, because in a matter of minutes there could be green seas bursting on that steel deck and sweeping aft; to be still on it wouldn't be just uncomfortable, it would be almost suicidal, and Wyatt wasn't waiting on anyone's convenience, not with a Hun destroyer raid in progress. There'd be precisely one aim, Nick knew, in his commanding officer's mind, and it matched the urge in his own: to get *Mackerel* out there on the raider's line of retreat, cut them off from their Belgian bases.

Proceed vicinity No. 9 buoy, the signal had ordered. *Rendezvous with Moloch and Musician*. No. 9 buoy was about halfway out along the net barrage that zigzagged between the Goodwins and Gravelines. Admiral Sir Reginald Bacon's pride and joy, that net-line with its electrically detonated mines; and he was hanging on to it, still patrolling over it with drifters, in spite of the Admiralty committee's view that it wasn't stopping any U-boats.

'What course, pilot?'

Pym, *Mackerel*'s navigator, told the captain, 'West-nor'-west to clear Snow Bank, sir, then north eighty west when Middle Dyck's abeam.'

'Midships.'

'Midships, sir.' The rate of turning slowed; wind came like a whip now, cracking across the bridge. In the Dover straits in December, warmth was hardly a commodity one could look for. You set your teeth, tried not to think about it. Wyatt had told the coxswain, 'Meet her. Steer west-nor'-west.' Compass variation in this year 1917 was slightly more than thirteen degrees west, so their next course of north eighty degrees west would be a true one of just *south* of west. The wheel spun through Chief Petty Officer Bellamy's practised hands, and Wyatt snapped – perhaps deciding that if the foc's'l hadn't been cleared by now a wetting might teach the cable party a lesson – 'Six-fifty revolutions!'

He'd make it seven hundred in a minute, when he'd allowed them some time to work her up. At her trials in 1915 *Mackerel* had clocked up thirty-six knots at seven-fifty revolutions per minute of her twin screws; but now, after two years of hard steaming, she'd be straining every nut and bolt to squeeze out thirty-three. Less, even, seeing that she was overdue for a bottom-scrape; and that wouldn't be enough to catch the modern thirty-four-knot German destroyers, whose object in their sneak raids was to create some havoc and get home fast, intact, avoiding action with anything like equal forces. To bring them to action you had to trap them, take them by surprise and then slam into them with everything you had – just as *Broke* and *Swift* had done so sensationally earlier in the year.

'Number One!'

'Sir?'

Nick reached for a handhold as he turned aft. She'd begun to pitch as well as roll, a jolting, corkscrew motion as she gathered speed with wind and sea buffeting her port bow. Wyatt shouted, 'Might be that swine Heinecke out there, eh?'

Chat – from Edward Wyatt?

There were a couple of dozen destroyer COs in the Dover Patrol under whom it would have been a pleasure to serve. Nick had had the rotten luck to fall in with this one. And his future – present, for that matter – lay in Wyatt's hands.

'Let's hope it is, sir.'

Captain Heinecke led a flotilla of outsize destroyers which Germany had been building for Argentina and taken over when the war had begun. Intelligence had reported that he was bringing them down from the Bight to base them on Zeebrugge. Not long ago he'd destroyed a Norwegian convoy; he'd also sunk a number of neutral merchantmen and allowed their crews very small chances of escape. On top of which he had the un-endearing habit of crowing about his successes in wireless broadcasts, shouting his own name in tones of Teutonic glee.

Wyatt thumped his gloved hands together. 'God, give me Herr Heinecke!'

Bellamy muttered, 'Amen to that, sir'; and Pym, the navigating lieutenant, chimed in with 'Make a nice Christmas present, I must say!'

Five days to Christmas. In Dover the shops had sprigs of holly in their windows. And *Mackerel*, due for a boiler-clean; might have the luck to be enjoying her three-day stand-off period on the 25th. On the other hand she might have finished it, and be back at sea.

But thinking of Hun raiders: although there'd been no surface attack since *Broke* and *Swift* had carved up that raiding flotilla back in April, an attack hadn't been unexpected in this present dark period. The new floodlit minefields barring the straits from Folkestone through the Varne to Gris Nez had begun to catch and kill U-boats literally within hours of lighting up, and it was only logical to anticipate a reaction from the enemy. They needed to get their submarines through, rather than send them round the top of Scotland wasting time that could otherwise be spent sinking ships in the Atlantic; it would make sense to them now to send a surface force to break up the mob of drifters, trawlers, P-boats and 'oily wads' – old, pre-war destroyers, known also as 'thirty-knotters' – that was providing the illuminations.

Wyatt hadn't increased *Mackerel*'s revolutions beyond six-fifty. Most likely he'd be keeping her a knot or two below her best speed so as not to show flames at the funnel-tops and thus advertise her arrival on the scene. And on a night like this, black as a cow's insides, thirty knots felt fast enough – through the shoals, mine-fields, unlit and often explosive waters which it was the Dover Patrol's job to hold, use, deny to the enemy.

The Army in France and Belgium was manned, supplied and fed across this neck of water. Every single day transports, hospital ships, leave ships, supply convoys had to be escorted to and fro and the sea swept clear of mines ahead of them. The Front, the trench-line, met the sea at Nieuwpoort, a dozen miles east of Dunkirk, and looking shoreward now, eastward, you could see the sporadic outbursts of artillery fire, the intermittent burst and lingering glow of starshell. Closer still, on the bit of coast *Mackerel* was leaving, an air-raid was developing over Dunkirk.

Nick heard Cockcroft, the sub-lieutenant, arrive on the bridge and report to Wyatt.

'Foc's'l secured for sea, sir!' *Mackerel* plunged, a long slither before she lifted to the swell and began her roll to starboard. There was more of it, as she left the slight shelter provided by the bulge of the Pas de Calais. But this was nothing: only a little icy spray lashed the bridge from time to time, just enough to remind them that tonight the straits were letting them off lightly. Wyatt had his glasses up; he was sweeping the black horizon on the starboard bow. Nick waited, wanting to speak to Cockcroft but making sure the skipper had nothing to say to him first.

Wyatt spoke, but his bark wasn't addressed to Cockcroft.

'Porter!'

'Sir?'

From the after end of the bridge Leading Signalman Porter pitched his voice above the turbines' high whine and the roar of wind. Wyatt bellowed, 'What's the challenge?'

'JE, sir!'

'Reply?'

'HK, sir!'

'Sure, are you?'

'Certain, sir!'

'How far to the Middle Dyck, pilot?'

Pym cleared his throat. 'Mile and a half – bit less, sir.'

'Why can't I see it, then?'

240

Charlie Pym had his glasses up too, and he'd been searching for the lightship for several minutes. It wasn't lit, of course; but at less than three thousand yards, with high-powered binoculars – and they'd all developed cats' eyes, by this stage . . .

Nick called Cockcroft. 'Sub – here a minute.'

Cockcroft came groping like some great insect along the bridge's starboard side, keeping both hands on the rail to steady his long, awkward – uncoordinated might be the better word for it – frame as he negotiated the eight or nine feet of heaving, jolting platform. Still gripping the rail above the splinter-mattresses that were lashed to the outside of it, he craned like a bent flagpole over his first lieutenant.

'Yes?'

Wyatt interrupted: 'Number One!'

'Sir?'

'Have small-arms been issued?'

'About to have it done, sir.'

'*There!*' Pym had picked up the lightship's meagre silhouette. Nick told Cockcroft, 'Go down and have pistols, cutlasses and rifles passed out. You know the drill.'

It was an idea Wyatt had borrowed from Teddy Evans, late captain of the *Broke* and now Admiral Bacon's chief-of-staff. The object was to have weapons handy for repelling boarders if one's own ship were disabled, or – more hopefully – for boarding a maimed enemy. Loaded rifles with fixed bayonets at each gun, each pair of torpedo tubes and at the after searchlight; revolvers to all petty officers, and two spares – loaded – up here on the bridge. Cutlasses at various points around the upper deck where they could be snatched up quickly. Nick pushed his bunch of keys into the sub-lieutenant's fist. 'Here. And get a move on, eh?'

'Can I borrow Hatcher?'

Hatcher, invisible at the moment at the back of the bridge, was the wardroom steward. His action duty was to operate the Barr and Stroud transmitter by which Nick as gunnery control officer passed settings and orders to the guns.

'No. Take one of your after supply party. Then inspect all quarters and tell 'em what's going on. D'you *know* what's going on?'

'Well, not quite encyclopaedically, to tell you the absolute truth, but—'

'There are Hun destroyers in the straits and we're steaming to

241

join *Moloch* and *Musician* and head 'em off. Most likely they're having a crack at the lit minefield – but they'll have to come back again . . . Clear?'

'Topping!' Cockcroft had let go of the rail as he pocketed the keys. *Mackerel* leaned hard to port: he swayed, staggered, grabbed for a handhold and just made it. Nick added, 'Tell Mr Gladwish too, will you?'

'Aye aye!' Gladwish was the torpedo gunner. As Cockcroft began to grope towards the ladder – he was a useful and a pleasant fellow, despite his verbosity and a tendency to fall about – the coxswain was bringing *Mackerel* round to her new course. If the lightship was abeam already, Nick thought, it must have been a lot closer than two miles off when Pym spotted it. Well, this was about as dark a night as one could get . . . An odd thing about Cockcroft was that despite his instability, top-heaviness or whatever it was, he could run like a hare. As a midshipman up at Rosyth he'd won the squadron athletics championships over practically every distance. One could imagine him tumbling in a welter of his own tangled limbs each time he breasted the tape . . . Nick heard Wyatt calling down the voicepipe to the chartroom, which was immediately below this bridge.

'Chartroom!'

'Chartroom, sir!' That was Midshipman William Grant's voice. Wyatt rather bullied young Grant, and he'd accused Nick recently of being too soft with him.

'He gets seasick, sir. Half the time we think he's being stupid he's just ill.'

Wyatt's eyebrows knitting as he scowled. 'What are you – his nanny?'

'Sir, I only—'

'He needs toughening-up, not babying! Good God, man, Nelson used to get seasick – and so do I and so do you!'

Nick had refrained from reminding Wyatt that Nelson, in his early days, had been undersized, a bit of a weakling, certainly not regarded as promising material. As to any toughening-up process, the sea would attend to that, and the rigorous day-and-night routines of the Patrol. Nineteen consecutive nights at sea, sometimes: in tin cockleshells and weather which in peacetime would have halted all cross-Channel traffic. They were all tough, hard as seaboots: they had to be, and if Midshipman Grant stayed with them long enough he'd soon become unrecognisable to the mother who *had*, probably, babied him.

'Grant – have there been no signals at all since we weighed?'

The wireless office was immediately abaft the chartroom, with a connecting hatch. It was the midshipman's job to receive whatever messages the telegraphists passed through to him, decode them or otherwise make sense of them in relation to the chart, and pass the results up the voicepipe to the bridge.

'Nothing at all, sir.'

'Are they *awake*, in there?'

'Oh, *yes*—'

Wyatt had straightened from the tube. Grant's voice – scratchy, still in the breaking process – died away, and Wyatt swore as he raised his binoculars again. It *was* peculiar. If there were German surface forces in the straits, surely by now there'd have been a shout from someone? A sighting report, or a call for help? That gunfire half an hour ago – *someone* had been in action or under attack, but nobody had said a word . . . Until someone did it was all guesswork, blind man's buff, and all the advantage of the blindness was with the enemy. The Germans knew that any ship they met would be hostile to them: *they* wouldn't waste time challenging . . . Nick, swaying to remain upright while *Mackerel* flung herself about, thought how much easier it must be for the intruder, the fox in the hen-run; and therefore how much more vital it was to see him first. He lifted his own glasses, adding his eyes to others already at work. Above the cloud-cap the last splinter of the old moon would be hanging; down here there was only the gleam of bow-wave spreading, curling away into a black shine streaked and laced with veins of duller white. Farther out the shine faded, the black became smudged, confused; only when a breaking wave gleamed, spread and faded again into the dark background could one tell roughly where the division came between sea and empty, salt-damp night. Empty – or *not* empty suddenly, as the glasses swung their overlapping circles over it; imagination stretched the nerves, and it was a mistake to look at any one spot too hard. The thing was to keep the glasses moving, let the eye drift on. *Mackerel* shuddered, quivering as she smashed her bow through the lifting seas, and mixed with the turbines' whine was the thrumming of her hull, the sound the sea drew from her like fingers on a string, and the rush of wind and throaty intake of the ventilators, the roar of the stokehold fans. Rattlings: sounds that had always been there and could never be identified, and other sounds that could be – like the creaking of the whaler

243

against the griping-spar in that port-side davit. Someone touched Nick's arm: 'Number One?'

Cockcroft . . .

'All done. They seem to be on their toes all right, and I've put the small-arms round.'

'Up here too?'

'Porter's stowed two pistols on the searchlight platform.'

'Good.' Nick put his glasses up again. 'You'd better go down, then.' From the Dyck lightship to No. 9 buoy was only about five miles. At thirty knots – ten minutes. Cockcroft's action station was aft, with the midships and stern guns. 'Yes, go on down.' He heard Charlie Pym call out, 'Float – Carley float with men on it – forty on the bow, sir, about two cables!'

'*Float?*' Wyatt whipping round. 'Where, for—'

'Ships starboard quarter, sir!' Porter was shouting from the searchlight platform. 'Near bow-on, sir – destroyers – *two* destroyers, sir!'

Wyatt shouted, 'Make the challenge!'

Nick reached Hatcher at the Barr and Stroud. 'All guns load, train starboard quarter and stand by.'

Wyatt rapped at the coxswain, as the shutter on the light began to clatter, 'Starboard fifteen!' He raised his voice: 'If we engage, Number One, it'll be to port.'

'Aye aye, sir.' Nick told Hatcher to follow the bearing of the enemy on his transmitter and set range two thousand yards. He went back to the port fore corner of the bridge, the torpedo sight there, and got Gladwish on the navyphone.

'Tubes stand by to port!'

Porter yelled, 'Ships are friendly, sir!'

'Very good.' Wyatt sounded disappointed. 'Ease to ten. Four hundred revolutions.' *Mackerel* rolled harder, with the sea on her beam now. Still turning . . . Wyatt had been taking her round in an almost full circle, starting from near west and turning through south and up to north-east in order finally to pass the strangers on a reciprocal course with guns and tubes all bearing. Nick said to the torpedo gunner, 'Better luck next time, Guns.' He hung up the navyphone. A lamp was flashing from the leader of the two destroyers; you could see their low black silhouette now without any need of glasses, and the froth of white around them. The lamp was saying, *Take station astern, course south-west, speed fifteen.* The leading signalman called it out word by word as it came in bright stabs of light and *Mackerel* still pivoted in a whitened pool of sea. Wyatt told the engine-room, 'Three-sixty revolutions.' Still keeping her under starboard helm, port rudder. 'Pilot, where'll that raft be now?'

'Port quarter, sir, probably about a thousand yards. I can't see it now, but—'

'Signalman. Make to *Moloch, Believe survivors on Carley float half mile south of me. Propose investigating before joining you.*'

Clatter of the lamp . . .

'Midships!'

Nick called down to the midshipman in the chartroom. 'Grant, we may be picking up some survivors in a minute. Go aft, warn the doctor, and make yourself useful.'

The 'doctor' was a young RNVR surgeon-probationer, a Scot named McAllister. If it hadn't been for the war he'd still have been a medical student in Edinburgh. Nick cranked the telephone to the after steering position.

'CPO Swan?'

'Sir?'

Swan, Chief Boatswain's Mate or more colloquially Chief Buffer, came after Bellamy, the coxswain, as the destroyer's second most senior rating.

'We may be picking up some chaps from a Carley float, Swan. Get your gear ready and stand by.'

'Aye aye, sir!'

'Better call away whaler's crew too. But have 'em just stand by the boat, don't turn it out yet.'

Moloch had replied, *Carry on. I will stay with you.*

Wyatt grunted. He said, 'Meet her, cox'n, and steer south.'

'Steer south, sir . . .' Bellamy dragged the wheel over, putting on opposite rudder to 'meet her', check her swing. Back again now, letting the spokes fly against the palms of his hands: 'Course south, sir!'

Nick asked his captain, 'D'you intend to use the whaler, sir?'

'Not unless I have to.' Wyatt, like Pym, was searching for the float. An object so low in the water would be hidden in the troughs except in the brief moments when a wave-top lifted it; it must have been sheer luck that Pym had spotted it in the first place. Wyatt said, 'We'll give 'em a lee and haul 'em up . . . *If* we find 'em.'

'Aye aye, sir.' It would be a quicker job, if it could be done without lowering a boat, and speed was a priority consideration. A

245

lot of ships had been lost already in this way – in these straits – because they'd stopped to save lives and become sitting ducks for U-boats . . . Swan knew the score: down there on the iron deck abreast the funnels he'd be preparing scrambling nets, one each side; his men would be lashing the top-ropes of the nets to ship's-side cleats and leaving them rolled, ready to shove over.

'Sir – gunfire!'

Everyone on the bridge had seen it. Lighting the horizon and the underside of the cloudcap ten or twelve miles southward, where *Mackerel*'s short black bow was pointing. Well, south-westward. Yellow-red: more of it now, in the same place exactly, and to the right a glow rising, tinting the horizon yellowish-orange: steady, hanging there quite motionless. A crackling sound – like the vibrations of a thin sheet of tin – and more sparks: all of it so distant, impersonal, but that crackling was gunfire.

Wyatt muttered, 'Ship burning . . . Pilot, come on, where's your Carley float?'

'May we use the searchlight, sir?'

'No!'

'*Moloch* signalling, sir!'

The other two destroyers were on *Mackerel*'s starboard quarter, nosing after her, watching, keeping station there, white bow-waves easily visible to the naked eye even at this low speed. But they'd be feeling less patient now; Carley floats didn't rate highly when there were German destroyers making hay down there . . . Porter called out the signal: 'From *Moloch*, sir – *You have five minutes to complete your search and rescue.*'

More gun-flashes in the south-western distance. Remote, mysterious. Now to the left of them – nearer Cap Gris Nez than the Varne – a twin pair of sparks, one red and one white, showed tiny like small gems glimpsed then lost.

'U-boat signal, sir!'

'*Where?*'

Red and white Very lights meant *U-boat in sight.* Destroyers attacking the patrolling drifters and P-boats, Nick surmised, and submarines breaking through simultaneously on the surface. The floodlighting brigade down there on the deep minefield had orders that if they were attacked by surface forces one green Very light would be the order to extinguish all illuminations; there'd been firing, so by now one could reckon the lights would have been put out, and while the attention of the patrol vessels was still occupied by the raiders, U-boats would be pushing through. Nick could only see one answer: that the Hun destroyers ought to have been stopped before they got that far west . . . Something dark lingered in the circle of his vision: he swung the glasses back, and there was the Carley float, tilting on a wave-crest.

'Float, sir, and men in it, fine on the starboard bow!'

He lowered his glasses, checked with the naked eye, narrowing his eyes against the stinging wind. He could see it easily.

'There, sir. Cable and a half off.'

'Slow together!'

'Slow together, sir!'

'Go down and get 'em up like lightning, Number One.'

'Aye aye, sir.' Nick was already at the top of the ladder. He went down it like a sack down a chute, his weight on his hands on the rails – just – and feet skimming the rungs; he hit the foc'sl deck almost as hard as if he'd jumped, and turning aft he rattled down the short flight of steel steps to the iron deck. Here, abreast the twenty-foot motorboat, two sailors crouched beside the long sausage of rolled scrambling-net.

'Chief Bosun's Mate?'

'Here, sir!'

Swan appeared ducking round the for'ard davit. A big man, bulkier still in his oilskin, very little except his eyes showing above the 'full set' of his black beard. An impressive, piratical figure of a man. Nick told him, 'Stand by this side. We're almost up to them. Five men, I think.'

'Aye aye, sir! Morgan – 'Oneycutt – starboard side 'ere!' *Mackerel* was losing way, and as she slowed her pitch and roll increased. The drone of her turbines fell away to nothing: you heard the sea now, and the wind, and the creaks and rattles.

'Get the net over.'

He was assuming as a matter of common sense that Wyatt would pick the men up over this starboard side. The raft had been on this bow when he'd spotted it, and since *Mackerel* had been pointing south with wind and sea from the south-west, this was the obvious way to do it. Nick watched the four sailors roll the bulky net over until gravity took charge and it thumped away over the side. Then he saw the Carley float.

'There they are!'

Twenty yards away: and four men, not five, he thought. One was up on his knees, waving both arms above his head, two others were

247

visible in silhouette against the sea and the fourth was a lumpy extension of the float itself. It could even be a *dead* man; surely at the moment of rescue anyone who could move would be upright and taking notice? The float swung upwards on a rising sea, tilted over; the men's hands were grasping the rope beckets that ran round its circumference. Sinking in a trough now, as *Mackerel* soared upwards; with no way on, a lot of the movement was vertical, up and down, a motion to make itself felt in even the most hardened stomach. Nick asked Swan, pitching his voice up above the ship-noises and the weather, 'Heaving line – near enough now?'

'Might be, sir . . . 'Oneycutt, get it over 'em!' Nick saw Grant, the midshipman, coming for'ard with the doctor, and two men behind them carrying folded stretchers. *Mackerel* had stopped completely now. From the dark overhead loom of the bridge superstructure Wyatt shouted, 'What are you *waiting* for, down there?' Honeycutt had about a third of the heaving-line coiled in his right hand and the rest of it in his left: he swayed back, paused while the ship began to rise to another sea: then he swung upright, body straightening and right arm swinging over and the line flying out behind its weighted turk's-head knot; forty or fifty feet away it fell neatly across the Carley float and it was the man who was up on his knees who caught it. Everybody cheered. Swan growled out of his beard at Honeycutt, 'Pull 'em in steady now, don't go an' lose 'em.' Behind Nick, Midshipman Grant asked nervously, 'Shall I climb down the net and help them?' Wyatt bawled again, 'Get a *move* on, Number One!' Nick told the snotty, 'No.' He watched the float come rocking in towards the destroyer's side; if it hadn't been for the froth of white around it, one might not have seen it even at twenty feet. But there was less movement on it as it came under *Mackerel*'s lee. *Five* men. The one sprawled on his back wasn't a corpse, but he looked as if he might be wounded; two of the others were supporting him.

Swan said, 'You – you, Nye – get down there an' grab a hold of 'em.' What Grant had offered to do: but it was work for a strong man, not a kid who, conscious of his captain's disapproval, contempt even, wanted to justify his existence. Nick remembered only too clearly his own midshipman days, that dreary gunroom up in Scapa, the dog's life snotties had been forced to lead; he had sympathy for Grant, and a corresponding distaste for Wyatt's intolerance of him; but if that wounded man had to be dragged up the vertical and highly mobile ship's side it would take two power-

248

ful men on the net and probably two more up top here to do it; the
rescue had to be completed and *Mackerel* got under way again
quickly, immediately; there wasn't time for boosting the morale of
a little midshipman who'd only get in the way. The first of the
rescued men came up over the side, with Swan lugging at his arms;
Nick asked him, 'Is one of you down there hurt?'

'Ah.' A pale, narrow face turned to nod at him. 'Skipper – got a
leg chewed up.'

'What ship, and what happened?'

'Drifter *Lovely Mornin'*. Some murderin' bloody 'Un's what
'appened, mate.' Swan had gone down on to the net to help Nye
with the wounded skipper: another man came up over the side, and
the top of a wave came with him, shooting straight up and then
collapsing on the destroyer's deck like a suddenly up-turned bath-
ful of ice. Honeycutt swore, as he helped a third man over; behind
him the first two were assuring McAllister, the doctor, that they
were right as rain. Honeycutt grumbled, 'That last 'un filled me
seaboots!' Below him, out of sight and half in the actual sea, Swan
gasped, 'Up with ye, lad. Us two'll see to this cove.' Nick shouted
down to Swan, 'Don't bother with the float. Let it go.'

'Aye aye, sir . . .' Water surging up, frothing, leaping; Swan
roaring 'Grab 'old that arm, Nye! *Grab* it, ye clumsy—' Another
sea swept up, engulfing them, swirling to their shoulders before it
drained away. A hoarse voice panted, 'Easy, mates, easy does it
. . .' That was the wounded skipper as they hauled him up the side.
Behind Nick, McAllister was telling Grant, 'Take these four down
to the wardroom, Mid. They can strip and dry off in blankets. I'll
be along presently.'

'Right.'

'Off ye go then, gentlemen.' The doctor clapped the nearest of
them on his shoulder. 'Find a tot of rum for ye, by and by.' Nick
saw Swan and Nye come over the side, manoeuvring the wounded
man between them. Grey hair and a surprised-looking, square-
shaped face. Nick cupped his hands to his mouth and shouted up
towards the bridge, 'All inboard, sir!' Wyatt didn't acknowledge it,
but the telegraph bell clanged and in a moment the hum of the
turbines and the suck of the ventilators began to rise through the
weather sounds. Nick crouched beside the prostrate skipper while
McAllister's assistants opened a stretcher on the deck and eased
him on to it.

'Can you tell me anything about the ship that sank you?'

'Aye. Bloody 'Un. An' sod 'em all, I say!'

They had him on the stretcher. A stocky, solid man. Nick asked him, 'How many destroyers were there? And heading which way after they'd sunk you?'

'West. Varne, likely. Took a swipe at us wi'out 'ardly so much as slowin' up. Four o' the devils – you say destroyers now, but—' he coughed, and spat out salt water – 'more like cruisers. *Big* . . .'

McAllister murmured, 'Fragment, was it . . . In one side an' out the other?' He was nosing at the injured leg. Nick said, straightening, 'Put him in my cabin. Tell Grant to clear my stuff out of the way.' He thought of a question he hadn't asked: 'Skipper, d'you know if they attacked any of the other drifters on the net patrol?'

'Wouldn't 'a seen no other. We're that spread out now, d'ye see.'

The net barrage was only thinly patrolled, now that so many craft were needed on the lit minefield. The Germans had happened on this one drifter, and used it for target-practice on their way by. Quite inconsequentially: the minefield patrol had almost certainly been their real target. And that was where they'd be now: where the shooting was.

'Well done, Swan. You and Nye 'd better shift into dry clothes.'

'We'll stow the gear first, sir.'

On the bridge, Nick told Wyatt as much as he knew. *Mackerel* was following astern of *Musician* now, at something like fifteen knots. Wyatt dictated a signal down the voicepipe to the wireless office, addressing it to *Moloch* – whose captain was the senior officer in this division – and repeating it to Dover. It was plain enough that the destruction of the *Lovely Morning* had been shooting which had been seen from *Mackerel*'s bridge while she'd been weighing anchor; and it seemed probable that the four big German boats were Captain Heinecke's.

It looked as if it was indeed a concerted plan: south-westward, another pair of red and white Very lights had just floated up, hovered, vanished. A concerted plan that seemed at the moment to be working well – from the German's point of view. Smash up the minefield patrol: first to put the lights out, for immediate purposes, and in the longer term in the hope of discouraging its continuance. Meanwhile, have the U-boats waiting, ready to slip through – quite likely in both directions, some on their way out to patrol in the Atlantic and some returning to Ostend and/or Zeebrugge and thence up the canals to their inland base at Bruges.

There'd been a plan to capture those ports, and Bruges. Admiral

Bacon's 'Great Landing', which was to tie in with the Army's advance towards the Belgian coast. But the Army had bogged down, at Passchendaele, and by the middle of October the scheme had been abandoned, much to Bacon's disappointment.

Wyatt muttered, watching a new outbreak of firing – more like due west, that lot, which would mean from the section of patrolled minefield between the Varne and Folkestone – 'If he comes back *this* way—'

He'd broken off: the hope, the longing to get to grips with the 'Argentinian' flotilla was too intense to be put in words. Every destroyer captain in the Patrol prayed for a meeting with 'Herr Heinecke' . . . It was a fact, Nick realised, visualising the chart – which by this time he could just about have drawn free-hand from memory, with all its buoys and shoals and known minefields, with reasonable accuracy – it was a fact that if the Germans were west of the Varne now and took the direct route homeward to the Belgian coast, this was the way they'd come. *Mackerel*, following in line astern of the other two destroyers, had crossed the net between No. 9 buoy and the Dyck – West Dyck – lightship; there was comparatively deep water under them now. Ahead, *Musician*'s wake was a greyish track ending in a small bank of white under her stern; and *Moloch* was visible to the right of her – a smaller, less clearly defined but otherwise identical shape that changed quickly, lengthening as she altered course, hauling round to starboard. *Musician* began to follow; Wyatt was silent as he watched her through his binoculars and waited for the right moment to put *Mackerel*'s helm over.

'Port ten.' He turned her with her stem cutting into the inside edge of the curve of wake, in order to end up – as she would do, carried by her own momentum – in the centre of it. The new course seemed to be just about due west.

'Midships.'

'Midships, sir.' Bellamy let the wheel centre itself.

'Steady in his wake.'

No firing now. The straits were black, silent, empty of everything except these three destroyers. And at the same time one knew they were *not* empty, not by any means: there were literally dozens of ships down there, and four of them were Germans who'd have to retire eastward while the night was still thick enough to cover them. The German squadron, Nick told himself, could appear *there* – now – or *now*—

Cold . . . Under a duffel-coat and a reefer jacket he had a towel round his neck with its ends tucked inside a flannel shirt. But the wet had got in there, as it always did. The upper half of his body might have had a film of ice on it; a single trickle was extending down his left leg. When there was work to do, you could forget about the cold; but it never forgot *you*, it waited patiently until you had time to acknowledge it again. Wyatt's voice sounded hollow in the engine-room voicepipe: 'Three-forty revolutions.' Nick heard the reduction in speed repeated back. *Mackerel* had been getting too close up on her next ahead; it was possible that the corner of that turn had been cut.

'Bridge!'

Charlie Pym answered the voicepipe from the chartroom.

'Bridge.'

'Signal, sir.' Grant's voice. 'Flag Officer Dover to SO minefield patrol: *Have you anything to report?*'

Wyatt had heard it. He muttered, 'Might well ask.' Pym cleared his throat; 'Does seem to be rather a dearth of information, sir . . . I suppose SO patrol will be the duty monitor.'

The heavyweights of the Dover force were the monitors. They were also the tortoises: five knots, and less than that into any kind of tide. Admiral Bacon used them for bombarding the enemy-held coast, as cover to inshore operations such as mine-net laying, and now apparently as searchlight platforms. Although a monitor with her twelve-inch guns should have been some deterrent to surface raiders, too. Chief Petty Officer Bellamy reported, 'Next ahead's altering to port, sir.'

Wyatt turned to look at her. He'd been staring out over the port beam, southwards where a moment ago yet another pair of red and white Very lights had soared, hung, disappeared. Bellamy was right: they were about to file round to port again. It was a toss-up for *Moloch*'s captain; he could only cover as much sea as possible, trust to luck. The enemy might be creeping up inshore of them: or he might already have got by: or be over on the Dover side.

'Follow him round, cox'n.'

'Aye aye, sir.'

'Bridge?'

Pym answered it. 'Yes, Mid?'

'SO patrol to Flag Officer, sir: *Drifter at No. 30 buoy reports trawler fired green Very light. Have had no reports about recent firing south-eastward and on bearing of Folkestone.*'

'That's all?'

'Yes, sir.'

Pym turned from the voicepipe. 'Did you hear, sir?'

Wyatt grunted. Then he struck the binnacle with his fist, and shouted, 'What the blazes is the *matter* with 'em? God help us, what's wireless *for*?'

'Red and white Very lights, sir, starboard bow!'

Porter, the Leading Signalman, had reported it. The lights dimmed, and vanished; and that was *another* U-boat through. In October – November figures hadn't appeared yet – about 290,000 tons of shipping had been sunk in the Atlantic and another 60,000 in the Channel: those soaring Very lights were like markers to German success in the form of Britain's slow strangulation. Pym was answering Wyatt: 'Some of the patrol vessels don't *have* wireless, do they, sir?'

Pym's smarmy manner with Wyatt could get on Nick's nerves, sometimes . . . Wyatt, in any case, seemed to have been irritated by the observation. He snapped, 'All the thirty-knotters have it, so 've the P-boats. Some of the drifters – *most* of the trawlers—'

'Red and white Very's, sir!'

CPO Bellamy reported, 'Steady, sir, on south-west.'

Down-straits, in fact, parallel to the coastline, with Calais about three or four miles on the beam. Nick's suspicion that the night's work was amounting to a fairly thoroughgoing mess was hardening into certainty; and he guessed, from Wyatt's tone to Charlie Pym, that his captain was feeling the same way. He tried to reassure himself: he thought, *We* could *still run into them: they can't just vanish . . .*

Couldn't they?

On a night as dark as this – stealing away cautiously, at half speed to show no tell-tale bow-waves, dead silent and alert and keeping a stringent lookout: making in fact a burglar's exit?

Herr Heinecke could be halfway home by now. Laughing himself sick.

CHAPTER 2

Dawn was silvering the sky to starboard and putting a polish on the sea as *Mackerel* followed *Musician* and *Moloch* north-eastward at ten knots between the Outer Ratel and East Dyck banks. Against that growing light Nick – leaning on the bridge rail while behind him at the binnacle Midshipman Grant performed the routine duties of an officer of the watch – could see quite clearly the low, black silhouette of the Belgian coast. From La Panne a searchlight poked at the sea like a nervous, probing finger; there'd be a monitor anchored inshore there, a nightly guardship with an attendant destroyer, watching and protecting with her guns the few miles of flat coast that lay immediately behind the Front – in case of a German landing or an attempt at one, a quick strike to turn the British Army's flank. The Huns guarded *their* backyard similarly, but with an armed trawler known to the destroyer men as 'Weary Willie'. Willie came out of Zeebrugge each evening at dusk and pottered the ten miles down-coast to drop his hook three miles off Middelkerke, on the eastern edge of the Nieuwpoort Bank; and just about now, as daylight arrived, he bumbled back again. Ostend would have been a more convenient base for him, but the Germans had abandoned Ostend as a port now, used it only as an entrance and exit for Bruges, the inland base to which like Zeebrugge it was linked by waterways and locks. Ostend had been too hard hit too often, for the Germans' liking, by Admiral Bacon's monitors.

That searchlight had been switched off. Dawn pressed up, streaked the sky; the line of the land was darkening, its edges hardening under a pinkish glow. Starshell still broke intermittently over Nieuwpoort's eastern perimeter. Nieuwpoort itself was only ruins now. Artillery fire was a steady mutter with occasional pauses and crescendos: like, Nick thought, a malfunctioning wireless receiver with erratic volume-control. Directly east, German ack-ack guns were providing a firework display over Ostend, engaging aircraft from naval squadrons which must either be attacking Ostend itself or returning over it from raids elsewhere. St Pol, the main RNAS airfield at Dunkirk, had been badly strafed a month or two ago by Hun bombers and there'd been some dispersal to other airfields and to RFC squadrons; in any case the naval fliers worked a great deal with the RFC. But they were still part of the Dover Patrol. Eight squadrons of fighters – Sopwith Camels had replaced Pups now – and four of Handley Pages and two of daylight bombers; plus odds and ends, including one huge American flying-boat that spent its time on anti-submarine patrols. That ack-ack fire might have been at RNAS fighters on their early-morning Zeppelin hunt: pilots got up there early after pre-dawn take-offs to intercept Zeppelins returning from attacks on London. Nick, watching the little sparks of fire puncturing a still half-dark sky over Belgium, wondered whether Johnny Vereker, who a few months back had bagged a Zeppelin of his own, was with his squadron or on leave again. When Vereker was in Flanders, Nick and another of Johnny's friends, Tim Rogerson, had the use of his motor-car in Dover, and if *Mackerel* was going to be allowed her boiler-clean and three-day rest period now it might come in handy.

If on the other hand Johnny was on leave, he and his motor – a 1909 Swift, with a two-cylinder water-cooled engine – would be in London. He was going great guns with a girl who called herself Lucy L'Ecstase; she was a dancer in the musical show 'Bric-à-Brac', which was still showing to packed houses at the Palace Theatre.

If Johnny was *not* on leave – might one motor up to Town oneself, take the lovely Lucy out to supper?

Intrigued by the idea – it was already almost a decision – Nick turned from the rail to glance ahead and check that Grant was keeping *Mackerel* in her proper station; at the same moment, Wyatt stepped into the bridge from the port-side ladder.

Wyatt had been down in the chartroom, eating breakfast. But an intake of food and hot coffee hadn't helped his mood. Grant jumped back smartly from the binnacle: just in time, since if he hadn't Wyatt would have walked through him or over him, as if the boy was non-existent or at least invisible.

A quick, testy glance ahead . . .

255

'You're astern of station, Number One!'

Nick didn't agree, but there was no point disputing it. Wyatt glanced round, small eyes and bull-head swivelling like a rhino suspecting the presence of some enemy on its flank, towards Grant.

'Who has the ship? You or Grant?'

'I have, sir.' Nick said it quickly before the midshipman could answer. He reached the voicepipe: 'Engine-room!'

'Engine-room . . .'

'Two-seven-five revolutions.' He looked at *Musician's* stern again. The revs would have to be reduced again pretty quickly, he realised, or they'd be running up on her quarterdeck. Wyatt said bitterly, 'More signals have been coming through. Looks as if we lost seven drifters and a trawler sunk, with two drifters and a P-boat damaged. Hardly a shot fired from our side, and not a single report that could've been any use to anyone.'

Nick frowned. Quite a few U-boats must have got through, too, while all that was going on. It was difficult to understand how such a shambles could have come about.

He called the engine-room: 'Two-six-oh revs.'

Wyatt muttered, turning his shoulder to the helmsman, 'And yet I come up here and find you practically laughing your head off.' His voice was low, but his eyes were vicious. 'Something to be *pleased* about?'

'It was – a personal thought, sir. Nothing connected with the Service.'

'Indeed.'

Wyatt's breath smelt of kippers. Mick glanced at *Musician's* stern and at the compass-card, then back at the small, censorious eyes. Wyatt told him, 'Last night was a damned disgrace. A shame on every man-jack of us. The *Patrol's* in disgrace – and the Patrol includes this ship. There's no making light of it and no time for *personal thoughts*, Everard. Understood?'

'Yes, sir.'

'I want this ship smartened up. In every way. You've been allowing things to slack off – and I shan't stand for it, d'you hear?'

If one hadn't been at Dartmouth and then in a battleship for a few years, one wouldn't have believed a man could talk such hot air and rubbish. He nodded politely. 'I'm sorry, sir.'

He thought he knew what part of the trouble was. Wyatt had made himself a reputation in the Dardanelles campaign; first as a destroyer captain, and then, after his ship had been sunk under him, commanding a naval landing-party. He'd won himself a DSC leading a bayonet attack on some vital Turkish gun battery. It had left him – Nick thought – with the impression that he was Francis Drake reborn in the hour of his country's need.

He'd brought *Mackerel* down from Harwich about six months ago, at a time when M-class boats were taking over at Dover from the older L-class. This had been partly as a result of America coming into the war in April and, by accepting her share of Atlantic convoy escort work, releasing dozens of British destroyers for other duties. Wyatt's own first lieutenant had been invalided; he'd been going deaf, with flattened eardrums from the effects of gun-blast, and it had reached a stage where he couldn't hide it any longer. Nick, appointed in his place, had moved over from one of the departing L's, where for the previous twelve months he'd been navigator. He'd been delighted to get a No. 1's job so soon – particularly as he'd blotted his copybook somewhat, just after the rather startling success – for him personally – at Jutland.

Jutland had won him promotion to lieutenant. 'Noted for early promotion' had been the official phrase; and promotion had come within weeks. They'd also given him a Mention-in-Despatches, and its oak-leaf emblem was on his shoulder now. If he hadn't fouled things up just afterwards – a piffling business, no more than sending a man on leave when he'd no leave due to him, but it had raised the roof – they'd have awarded him a DSC. So someone at the Admiralty had confided to Nick's uncle, Hugh Everard, who'd also distinguished himself at Jutland and now had his own cruiser squadron in the Grand Fleet . . . But a week *before* Jutland Nick had been in the gunroom of a battleship: bored to distraction, and marked down as a failure, a useless sub-lieutenant who'd almost certainly never be promoted. Loathing just about everything about the Service: sure, by that time, that the Navy he'd dreamt of all through his childhood and adolescence – the Navy which Uncle Hugh had told him about with such pride – didn't exist, even if conceivably it had many years ago.

And then he found it, at Jutland.

But there was another navy too. He could see it in Wyatt's eyes, hear it in his tone of voice. It reminded him of that Scapa gunroom, and of Dartmouth. Pomposity; more than a hint of sadism; and so much *sham* . . .

But one could not afford to fall foul of Wyatt. To be here, second in command of a modern, quite powerful destroyer in what was the most active and hard-worked sector of naval operations – one had, finally, a sense of one's own worth and competence and of a job worth doing. And Wyatt, if he felt so inclined, could destroy all that with one 'adverse report'. He had, naturally, all his officers' Service documents; he knew that Nicholas Everard had been a flop at Dartmouth, a misery as a midshipman and – until Jutland – a dead loss as a sub-lieutenant. One really bad report could make Nick's performance at Jutland look like a flash in the pan, a circumstance where luck had shown him up in an entirely false light. He'd be back to where he'd started, then. A failure. Wyatt knew it, knew *he* knew it. He also knew that nothing was 'slack' in *Mackerel*, that she was run about as smartly as a destroyer in Dover Patrol conditions could be run.

He stumped heavily across the bridge. The wind was astern on this course and the funnel-smoke was acrid in one's eyes and nostrils. He muttered, 'You'd better go down to breakfast, Number One.'

McAllister had wrapped Skipper Barrie's leg like a limb of an Egyptian mummy. He'd also given him Nick's old woollen dressing-gown to wear. Well, someone had.

Barrie was a thickset man of about fifty, with grey hair, grey eyes and a square-shaped, weather-darkened face.

Nick leant against the doorway, inside the hanging curtain. Admiralty-issue, blue . . . He nodded at the trussed-up leg. 'How's it feel? Doc done you any good?'

Barrie said, without smiling, 'I'd as soon have a vet to it.'

'What?'

'Pullin' *your* leg, lad . . . This your cabin, eh?'

'Not really. According to the builders' plans it's spare, for cases of serious illness. I use it, but I'm supposed to bunk with the others in the wardroom.'

'First lieutenant, eh?'

'Right.' The skipper's thick eyebrows were black, not grey, and hooped; they gave him a permanently enquiring look. The other thing Nick had noticed was that when he spoke his lips hardly opened, hardly seemed to move at all.

'Where you from? Your home, I mean?'

'Yorkshire. West Riding . . . Are your men being looked after all right, skipper?'

'Look after 'emselves, my crew can . . . Yorkshire, eh?'

'Yes.' He didn't want to have to talk about Mullbergh, that great mausoleum of a house with its seven thousand acres of keepered shooting and stables for thirty or forty horses, and more gaunt, freezing-cold rooms than anyone had ever bothered to count. Sarah, Nick's young stepmother, had turned part of it into a hospital; Nick thought it might have been kinder to wounded soldiers to leave them in their Flanders trenches.

He was heir to Mullbergh, now that his elder brother David was dead. David had drowned at Jutland.

He asked Barrie, 'Where are *you* from?'

'Tynemouth. Know it?'

'Afraid not.'

'You'd be afraid, all right. We *eat* Yorkshiremen, up there.'

Nick stared at the deadpan, grey-stubbled face. He nodded. 'That explains why you have vets instead of doctors.'

Barrie chuckled. Nick pushed himself off the bulkhead. 'They given you any breakfast yet?' The grey head shook, briefly. He said, 'I'll see you get some.' He was hungry, suddenly, in need of his own. He added, 'I expect the captain'll be down to see you presently.'

'Oh, aye?' He hesitated: as if he'd been about to add something, and then changed his mind. He asked Nick, 'Know Teddy Evans, do you?'

'*Captain* Evans?'

'Aye, if ye like . . . He's a right 'un, is Teddy.'

Evans of the *Broke*, he was talking about. He added, 'No damn side to him. You could do with more like that one!'

'Yes.' Another Evans, perhaps, and one less Wyatt. But the drifter crews and trawlermen all liked Captain Evans. He always had a word for them, or a joke over the loud-hailer, and his cheery, forthright manner appealed to them. That and his alarming way of bringing a destroyer alongside a jetty at twenty-five knots while he himself made a show of lighting a cigarette before murmuring 'Full astern together . . .' Seamanship: and style . . . The skipper patted the dressing-gown: 'This your'n?'

'What?' Trying to look as if he hadn't noticed. 'You're welcome. Keep it to use in the hospital ship, if you like.'

'Hospital ship, be buggered!'

'Eh?'

'They'll not keep George Barrie laid up, lad!' Nick glanced at the wrapped-up leg: the skipper shook his head. 'I'll hop about, all right . . . Listen – you brought a ship back from Jutland, did you? Everard, is it?'

He nodded. Everyone in Dover knew everything about everyone else, of course. One tended to forget it.

'Yes. Destroyer – *Lanyard*. I had a lot of luck.'

'Know Snargate Street?'

The conversation seemed to leap about, somewhat. But of course he knew Snargate Street; you could hardly be in Dover for half an hour *without* knowing it, and he'd been based there for some eighteen months. He nodded, wondering what might come next.

'Know the Fishermen's Arms?'

'I know where it is.'

The only pub Nick and his friends used much was called The First and Last. It was handy to the naval pier.

Barrie said, 'Back o' the Fishermen's, lad, there's a bit on its own – a bar hid away, you wouldn't see it if you didn't know to look. It's – well, you might say it's us drifter skippers' club.'

'Ah.'

The skipper stared at him. Then he nodded. 'Welcome, any time.'

'Very kind of you. Thanks.'

Barrie rubbed his jaw. 'What's breakfast, then?'

Odd cove . . . Nick went past the foot of the ladder and the door of Wyatt's cabin, and into the wardroom. Charlie Pym glanced up from his kippers, and nodded affably; Mr Watson, the commissioned engineer, raised a butter-knife in salute and muttered a 'good morning'; Percy Gladwish, the torpedo gunner, winked over a tilted coffee-cup.

Cockcroft was on the bridge. The system of bridge watch-keeping in the straits was that Wyatt and Pym took turns at sharing the navigational responsibility, while Nick and Cockcroft did the same for gunnery control. That was the general principle, when *Mackerel* wasn't closed-up for action.

Pym murmured smoothly, with a slight lift of the eyebrows, 'Hardly the most successful night in living memory, h'm?' He touched his lips delicately, fastidiously with his napkin. Nick called the steward as he sat down; then he glanced across the wardroom at the prone figure of McAllister, who was dozing in an upper bunk. The oval table was set centrally; there were bunks like shelves – with curtains that could be drawn across them – against the ship's sides.

'Doc!'

An eye opened, shut again. A hand came out of the blankets to ward off the light.

'God's teeth. What time is it?'

'Time you were up . . . Are the drifter's crew all fit, bar their skipper?'

'Fit as horses. Swan found 'em hammocks or somesuch.' The surgeon-probationer rolled over the other way, and yawned. 'The old man's wound's clean as a whistle too. Marvellous stuff, salt water.'

Gladwish was pouring himself more coffee. He asked Nick, 'Huns havin' it all their own way, weren't they?' A dark, quick-eyed man. He added, 'Made us look silly, I reckon.'

Nick told Hatcher, 'Kippers, please, and I'm in a hurry. Then take breakfast on a tray to Skipper Barrie in my cabin. No short rations, or he might bite you.'

He didn't want to spend too long down here, with Wyatt in his present mood. And he'd have to shave before he went up again. Gladwish seemed to read his mind: 'Skipper suckin' his teeth a bit, is he?'

Nick shrugged. 'He's not *happy*.' He looked at Watson, the engineer. 'All well in your department, Chief?'

Watson was three-quarters bald, and his skin had an engine-room pallor that would have taken years of sunshine to dispel. He mumbled with his mouth full, 'Couple o' weeks in dockyard 'ands, *then* we'd be all right.'

'We'll get our three days, if we're lucky.'

'But not right away, let's hope.' Pym wiped his lips again. 'I want to be on *terra firma*, this Christmas.'

Plump, always clean-looking, with carefully manicured finger-nails and hair always smoothed down, Pym was more like some shore-based admiral's flag-lieutenant than a Dover destroyer officer. Nick had no idea how he found time to groom himself so well – or why he bothered, for that matter. The fact that Wyatt always seemed well-disposed towards his navigator and surly with him, Nick Everard, who was his second in command, didn't exactly encourage friendship. He tried to ignore it and treat him equably, but the simple fact was that Pym was not Nick's sort of man. He didn't think much of him as a destroyer officer, either.

261

Wyatt . . . Nick remembered an interview in the captain's cabin a few days after he'd taken over as first lieutenant. Wyatt had told him, glowering, 'I'll be watching you, Everard. You won't let me down twice, I promise you!'

Incredible . . . He'd been asked down for a chat and a glass of gin!

'I'll do my best not to let you down at all, sir.'

Wyatt had pursed his lips, set down his empty glass and stared at the faintly pink liquor still in Nick's as if suggesting it was time he drank up and left. He hadn't said another word. That was the whole interview: one drink, one threat.

Had he felt insulted, perhaps, at having so young an officer appointed as his first lieutenant? Possibly tried to have the appointment cancelled, and been obliged to take him?

Nick pushed his kipper plate aside, and buttered a triangle of toast. He'd been down here too long already.

If *Mackerel* was to have her stand-off and boiler-clean now, she'd be ordered to a buoy or to a jetty. Otherwise, she'd be sent alongside the duty oiler to replenish with fuel, and as likely as not straight out again as soon as her tanks were full.

Nick stood by the bridge rail to starboard and watched Dover's cliffs and castle loom up ahead. It was a grey, cold morning, but there was very little wind now. What there was of it was still in the south-west, raking the crests of low, close-ranked waves.

From here, the grass slopes around the castle looked like deep green velvet.

'What's the set, pilot?'

'Very little, sir. Eastward about one knot or less.'

At some stages of the tide, the tidal streams could make for problems. In a real wind it wasn't much of a harbour anyway; a night's 'rest' at a buoy in the destroyer anchorage, for instance, could mean a night of rolling twenty degrees each way. About as restful as being out on patrol. And in a south-westerly gale – well, the distance from the outer edge of the Admiralty breakwater to where the hospital ships berthed inside it was a hundred and fifty feet, but the ships still found solid sea, green sea, crashing down on their decks.

A light was flashing from the end of the naval pier in the main harbour. *Mackerel*'s pendants, her identification signal, already fluttered from the starboard yardarm; now her searchlight's louvred shutter clashed in acknowledgement of each word as it was received. Nick read it for himself: *Berth on west jetty, tidal harbour.*

Wyatt glanced at Pym. 'Boilers, then.' Pym said sourly, 'And back at sea for Christmas, no doubt.' Mick asked Wyatt, 'Close up sea-dutymen, sir?'

'Yes, please.'

Nick glanced over his shoulder. 'Pipe it, bosun's mate!'

Wyatt bent to the voicepipe: 'Three hundred revolutions.' As *Mackerel* got inside she'd have to spin round hard to port, under the stern of the western blockship, to enter the commercial harbour between the Admiralty and Prince of Wales' piers. At the top end, half a mile up from the harbour mouth, was the narrow entrance to the small – twelve-acre – tidal harbour. It was a basin for drifters and trawlers mostly, but destroyers in their stand-off periods also used it sometimes, and there was an old steel lighter there fitted as a workshop and with a dynamo that could provide power to ships whose fires were out.

Gladwish called up the voicepipe, 'Permission to withdraw charges?'

'Yes, please.' They were almost in harbour; no need to ask Wyatt's agreement to removing the firing-charges from the torpedo tubes. Nick saw Cockcroft waiting for orders, and Wyatt studiously ignoring him; he beckoned him to come over to his side.

'Probably port side to, Sub. But have springs ready both sides, just in case. And an anchor ready, of course.'

Cockcroft nodded, and went down. Chief Petty Officer Bellamy had the wheel now. Wyatt muttered to him, squinting across the compass-bowl, 'Steer two degrees to port.'

'Two degrees to port, aye aye, sir!'

Wind was over the port quarter on this course; *Mackerel* was hammering the small waves with the starboard side of her short, black stem, flinging up intermittent bursts of spray to infuriate Cockcroft's cable party as they veered the anchor to its slip, a-cockbill from the hawse. If Wyatt got himself into any sort of trouble when he was manoeuvring inside there, one slam of the blacksmith's hammer could knock the slip off and send the cable roaring out. Nick watched the entrance seeming to widen as the destroyer ploughed up into it; then, as she thrust in between the sunken blockships, it seemed to close in on her again. The blockships, at right-angles to the gap in the harbour wall, were two old

263

Atlantic liners, both stripped, cut down to their main decks and fitted with iron supports for the torpedo netting to hang from. The one to starboard as *Mackerel* entered harbour was the former SS *Montrose*; aboard her a passenger by the name of Crippen had been arrested on a charge of murder. Wyatt straightened. 'Two hundred revolutions!'

'Two hundred—'

'Starboard fifteen!'

'Starboard fifteen, sir.' The coxswain spun his wheel. 'Fifteen o' starboard wheel on, sir!'

'Stop port.'

'Stop port, sir!' Biddulph, bosun's mate acting as telegraphman, jerked the brass handle forward and back again. *Mackerel* began to fairly spin around, and Wyatt said, 'Slow starboard, one hundred revolutions. Slow ahead port. Midships the wheel.'

Cockcroft had his men fallen-in on the foc's'l, properly at ease. At the back of the bridge the searchlight began to clash again, as a new message came stuttering from the naval pier. Signalman Hughes scrawled it on a pad, at Porter's word-by-word dictation. Then he bawled it out:

'Signal from Captain (D), sir! *You may grant shore-leave this afternoon. Boiler-cleaning party will board you noon tomorrow.*'

A cheer floated up from the waist, the iron deck, where Swan's berthing party must either have picked up the dots and dashes for themselves or heard the signalman yell it. Shore-leave: it was a rare thing, and to be prized. Destroyers got three days like this between twenty-four days of sea duty, and ten days for docking and bottom-scraping once in four months. Between those periods there was no shore-leave at all.

'Port ten.'

'Port ten, sir . . .'

Rounding the end of the Prince of Wales pier. Transports lay on the other side of it. To port, coal hulks rocked at their buoys. Tomorrow would be the 22nd, and a boiler-clean took three whole days; so with luck, they *would* have Christmas Day in harbour.

CHAPTER 3

He heard Petty Officer Clover, the gunner's mate, reporting to Cockcroft that libertymen were ready for inspection, and Cockcroft's breezy 'Ah, right-oh then, GM!'

Cockcroft *should* have said 'Very good' – in a clipped, impersonal tone. Nick had told him a dozen times about this sort of thing – for his own sake, because Wyatt and others of that stamp had deep reverence for the customs and habits of the Service; Wyatt would have just about thrown him over the side if he'd heard that chirpy 'Right-oh'.

The sailors liked Cockcroft. They called him – amongst themselves – 'Cocky-Ollie'.

Wyatt was in London. He'd gone up on the evening of the day they'd docked, two days ago, and he wasn't due back until tomorrow afternoon, the 24th. In his absence, life had been quite enjoyable. Nick had had to forego the pleasure of going up himself, the idea of an evening's dalliance with Lucy L'Ecstase; with Wyatt away, this was where he had to be. And in any case, the luscious Lucy didn't lack admirers, and might not have been available at such short notice.

He'd passed the time pleasantly enough. That first night alongside he'd appointed himself duty officer, and invited his friends over from the submarine basin. Tim Rogerson, who was first lieutenant of an E-class submarine; Harry Underhill, a CMB – coastal motor-boat – man; and Wally Bell, who commanded an ML, a motor launch. They'd come over to *Mackerel* for dinner, driving themselves round in Johnny Vereker's constantly back-firing little Swift; and on the second night – last night – Nick had dined with them aboard their depot-ship, the old *Arrogant*.

Meanwhile, *Mackerel*'s boilers were being cleaned – by dockyard stokers, to allow the ship's engine-room staff to enjoy their own rest-period – and Nick had been getting her smartened up and cleaned internally. The sailors had caught the Christmas spirit – which was an easier thing to do in Wyatt's absence – and the work had progressed rapidly and cheerfully. The only defaulters had been minor cases of drunken behaviour ashore, which Nick had dealt with swiftly and as leniently as regulations allowed, getting them disposed-of before Wyatt should return to make mountains out of molehills.

When they'd docked on the 21st, Wyatt had gone ashore at once to see Captain (D), who commanded this Sixth Flotilla. But he'd come back without having seen him. There'd been meetings going on, strange persons down from London. Bacon himself had been up at the Admiralty, and nobody would see anyone or tell anyone anything. There was an impression that far-reaching decisions were being taken behind locked doors.

Wyatt had told Nick, 'I'm not hanging about down here. I'll be at my club in Town. You can hold the fort, I suppose, while the ship's alongside?'

Nick strolled aft – wondering now, two days later, what was going on. Dover was alive with rumours. Rogerson and the others over in *Arrogant* thought Admiral Bacon was about to get the order of the boot. The destruction of several U-boats, followed by so positive an enemy reaction against the lit minefield that was catching them, proved how right it had been to light it up. Bacon had fought against it, stone-walled the Admiralty committee's recommendations as long as he could – until, one story went, Sir John Jellicoe (Jellicoe was First Sea Lord now) had finally ordered him to implement the proposals. Bacon had argued that his nets were already barring the straits to U-boats, that none at all were getting through. Now it was plain he'd been wrong: on an issue so vital that the war could be won or lost on it.

Rogerson – long, lean, red-headed – had raised his glass. 'Here's to him, anyway. He's done a thundering good job here, *and* with only half enough ships to do it.' Nodding at Nick. '*Your* sort of ships, I mean.'

Wally Bell agreed. Burly, bearded, brown-eyed: until 1914 he'd been a law student at Cambridge. He put down his glass, leant back, stared up at the white-enamelled deckhead. *Arrogant* had been launched in 1896 as a third-class cruiser, and converted to a depot ship two years before the war. In 1914 they'd brought her round from Portsmouth under tow. Since there were now only two E-class submarines in Dover, she'd become mother-ship to the

MLs and CMBs as well. Bell said, 'I doubt if people realise what a complex job the old fellow's got. What – four hundred ships? If you can *call* 'em ships . . . And airfields, dirigibles, shore guns—'

'Isn't it what admirals are for?'

Harry Underhill, the coastal motor-boat man, was a former merchant navy mate with a master's ticket; no respecter of persons, he had a direct, incisive way of summing-up either individuals or problems. A craggy, rather savage-looking individual. He added, 'In any case – the higher they fly, eh?'

He was right, Nick thought. But one could still say 'Poor old devil . . .' Rogerson added, 'Even if he *doesn't* know how to use submarines. Frankly, I wonder why they bother to keep us here.'

The CMB people had the same complaint: that they weren't used enough. Whereas the destroyers were, beyond doubt, worked to the very limit. The lightly built, high-speed motorboats were limited to fine-weather operations, that was the main restriction; they needed moonless nights, too, for their kind of work.

Nick, strolling aft, saw Cockcroft, followed by Petty Officer Clover, completing his inspection of the libertymen.

'Carry on please, Gunner's Mate.'

He'd got *that* right, anyway. He might as easily, if he'd been in true 'Cocky-Ollie' form, have said, 'Well, have a spiffing time, you chaps . . .' No – not *quite* . . . Nick smiled to himself; he liked Cockcroft. Clover had saluted, a rigidly correct, Whale Island gunnery-school salute that practically broke his wrist; and now his heels crashed together as he whipped round to face the lines of smartly turned-out, wooden-faced sailors who were about to be turned loose on Dover.

'Libertymen – right – *turn*! Rear rank, quick – *march*!'

The *Mackerels* began to file down the gangway to the jetty. Nick stopped beside the guardrail, and Cockcroft joined him. Cockcroft said, stumbling slightly as he stopped, 'Fine body of men, what?'

He was grinning after them as the front rank tailed on behind the others. Nick said, 'See 'em in three or four hours' time, and *then* say that.'

'Well, dash it, I *would*!'

'Yes. As a matter of fact, so'd I.'

He might not have, though, when he'd been Cockcroft's age. Since then he'd seen, at Jutland, how sailors who were paid next to nothing, cooped up in miserably uncomfortable and overcrowded mess-decks, subjected to a continuous, often petty and sometimes ruthless discipline and looked down on as riff-raff by quite a large section of the general public, how men like this could fight like lions, face quite terrifying danger and privation, remain disciplined, cheer themselves hoarse to keep their own spirits up, and die like heroes. He'd seen them doing all those things, at Jutland; and the knowledge, the recognition of the sort of men one led, was one of the things that made the Navy bearable.

He stood with his hands resting on the guardrail, and watched the crowd of destroyer men moving off towards the town. He murmured, 'If anyone ever had a right to get drunk now and then – well, there they go.' Cockcroft was delighted: 'I say! D'you know that's *exactly* what I was thinking when I was inspecting them just now?'

Nick glanced at him sideways. He advised him drily, 'Just remember to keep it to yourself.'

He didn't know what to do, this evening. Except for himself and Cockcroft, all the officers were ashore; and the *Arrogant* lot, his personal friends, were all otherwise engaged.

Rogerson had gone up to London, driving himself there in Vereker's motor; he'd 'found' some petrol for it. He'd wanted Nick to go with him, to dine at his parents' house in Mayfair, but it had been out of the question to leave the precincts of the port with Wyatt absent. He'd have liked to: Rogerson, who was probably his closest friend these days and perhaps the first real friend of his own age he'd ever had in the Navy, had an extremely pretty sister, Eleanor, who was a VAD at St Thomas' Hospital; she would have been there, this evening.

Wally Bell was at sea, on patrol in the Downs, and Underhill had taken his CMB over to Dunkirk.

It had been a good evening, last night in *Arrogant*. There'd been a fifth member of the party later on, an amusing RNVR friend of Rogerson's named Elkington, who was first lieutenant of *Bravo*, one of the old 'thirty-knotters'. She was so decrepit, Elkington had told him, that they all yelled 'Bravo!' whenever she covered a sea-mile without something falling off . . . Nick remembered snatches of the conversation round that after-dinner table: about Evans of the *Broke*, for instance – how, when in some emergency last year no boat had come inshore to take him off to his ship, he'd sprung into the harbour and swum back – fully uniformed, and in a stiff December blow. Wally Bell had laughed . . . 'A man of action, surely. But not – well, with all respect to him, not exactly brimming with the old grey-matter?'

Underhill had wagged a forefinger: 'Ah. *Certain* to reach the top, then.'

Nobody had argued: it was more of a truism than a joke. Rogerson cast a friendly glance at Nick: 'How does that place *you*, Nick? Are you going to the – er – top?'

Nick had taken the question seriously. 'Doubt if I'll stay on at all, when the war ends.' This had been the opening of a discussion about what any of them might do when the Navy no longer needed them, or they the Navy, and eventually it was agreed they'd team up and start a shipping line. Between them, they had the talents: Underhill from the Merchant Navy, Rogerson's rich family to provide the capital, Wally Bell with his knowledge of the Law, Elkington's father some kind of city merchant. Nick, they decided, could be chairman . . . 'After all, you'll be a blooming baronet by that time, won't you?' They laughed: 'Just what we need, a baronet!'

He'd told them he thought his father might live for ever. Sir John Everard had survived so many battles – from *somewhere* in France. He was still a brigadier, though – which was odd, when one thought of majors who'd become generals by this time. Nick never heard from him. He wondered sometimes what would happen when the fighting stopped; whether Sarah, having enjoyed several years of freedom from that cruel, overbearing bastard, would find it possible to submit to living with him again. In most ways, and for her sake, one hoped she wouldn't. And one saw, day after day, the hospital ships arriving, stretcher-cases flooding into the Marine Station here. One read the casualty lists and the 'Roll of Honour' in *The Times*. In the latter part of this year of 1917 nearly half a million men had died in the 'push' that had been swamped out at Passchendaele. And yet: he frowned, tried to clear the subject from his mind. There were enough things here to fill it with, and it was healthier not to allow that kind of speculation. The matter of inheritance had nothing to do with the way one's thoughts ran: but one was left all the same with a sense of guilt – as if it *did* have.

He found some paperwork to clear up, and listed the jobs that had to be seen to tomorrow. Then he and Cockcroft had a rather early supper – served in Hatcher's absence by Leading Steward Warburton, the captain's steward – and after it he decided to go ashore for a walk. He had a vague idea of strolling along the Marine Parade and having a nightcap in the First and Last, the tiny windowless pub quite near the admiral's house and offices. It had no windows because a hundred or two hundred years ago it had been a Revenue Officers' depot for seized contraband, and windows would have added to their security problems.

There was quite a swell running in the harbour; even in this inner basin its effects were noticeable. *Mackerel* was sawing up and down against the timber catamarans which held her off the wall; the gangway lurched with the ship's movements, its foot scraping to and fro across the stones. He stood on the jetty for a minute, watching it; Dover really was a rotten harbour, in anything like rough weather. And he wanted no accidents for Wyatt to come back to. He warned the sentry, 'I think it's likely to get worse, if anything. Make sure you keep the breasts and springs adjusted. If you've any worries on that score, let Sub-lieutenant Cockcroft know at once.'

'Aye aye, sir.'

He set off northwards, to cross the bridged gate of the Granville dock. This was drifter territory: the stubby little craft lay everywhere, singly and in pairs, or in trots of three and four. There'd be another sixty or seventy of them at sea, on barrage duty. From these in harbour, nets and other gear were spread on the jetties for repair and overhaul. And there was a smell of fish: which there should not be, because it was U-boats they were paid to look for nowadays, not plaice! He decided he wouldn't, after all, go along the Marine Parade; he'd turn inland here, to Snargate Street, see if he could find the backroom bar that Skipper Barrie of the *Lovely Morning* had called his club. He was unlikely to be there, unfortunately; McAllister had predicted at least a week in hospital for him.

In hospital *yacht*, actually. There were three of them for naval casualties: Lord Tredegar's *Liberty*, Lord Dunraven's *Grainaigh* – with his lordship still in command of her – and Mr White's *Paulina*. To one of the three Skipper Barrie had been carted off when *Mackerel* had docked two days ago.

Rounding Granville dock, Nick turned left, with the larger Wellington basin now on his right. Following his nose out through Union Street brought him into Snargate Street; and a short way down to the right, where Fishmongers' Lane led off, stood the gaunt pile of the Fishermen's Arms. Sailors were loafing round it and leaning against its dirty walls. Some were already more than cheerful, while others looked as if they'd no money left and were plainly less so. There were no women on the outside, but Nick saw a few inside as he pushed his way into the crowd. A *Mackerel* stoker spotted him, and bawled something to shipmates at the back

of the room; a leading seaman came shoving through the throng –
grinning, swaying, spilling beer.

It was McKechnie, a Glaswegian who was coxswain of the
whaler. Black-haired, ruddy-faced, blue-eyed.

'Will ye tak' a glass wi' me an' my mates, sir?'

'It's a kind suggestion. But I've come here to meet a friend.'

'Och, she'll not fret if ye tak' just *one* first, sir!'

The killick's friends were gathering round. Nick gave in. 'A half-
pint, then. Thank you very much.' McKechnie, fighting his way
towards the bar, told a disapproving-looking Petty Officer, 'Yon's
m' first lieutenant. Best officer i' the whole Patrol. I'll flatten the
face o' any man as says he's not.' Nick, divided between gratifica-
tion, surprise and embarrassment, heard a hoarse voice shout
somewhere behind him, 'Good ol' Lanyard!'

For a moment, he didn't get it. Then it sank in. *Lanyard* had
been the destroyer he'd served in at Jutland. Was that what they
called him?

'Thanks. Thanks very much indeed.' The beer slopped over his
hand as McKechnie thrust it at him. 'Here's a happy Christmas to
you all.'

Cheers, applause. Men were trying to jostle their way through,
but the *Mackerels* shouldered them away. Nick told them after a
minute, 'Look, I do have to go and find this friend of mine . . . No,
Carr, as it happens it's a he, not a she – that drifter skipper we
picked up . . . Look, d'you mind if I buy – pay for a round of
drinks? If I leave this with you?'

He was offering McKechnie a ten-bob note. The Leading Seaman pushed it back into his fist.

'No, sir. God bless you, but—'

'Oh, come on! Carr, *you* take it.'

'Well, sir—'

He fought his way through the throng and round the side of the bar.
There was a low doorway: he went through it, and found himself in a
stone-floored passage. A choice of doors confronted him, and a smell
of cooking: fish . . . The driftermen's stock-in-trade: did they swap
fish, perhaps, for their beer? Nick tried the nearest door, and he'd
guessed right: the dozen or eighteen men inside could only be either
trawlermen or drifter crew. Among them, one girl: he was staring at
her through the floating layers of pipe-smoke when a stocky figure
reclining at her side turned and stared at *him*.

'So ye found me, lad!'

271

Skipper Barrie was in an armchair with his leg up on a barstool; a single crutch was propped beside him. He was lying back with his hand on a glass that rested on the raised thigh, and a pipe between his teeth. The girl, blonde and pretty, in her early twenties Nick thought, seemed to be looking after the old man like a nurse. Except she had a glass in her hand too.

'Come on in with ye, my friend!' Other faces, shading from mahogany-brown to brick-red and most of them unshaven, grinned at him ogrishly from out of the clouds of smoke, and the girl, right there in the centre of it all, made him think, *Beauty and the Beasts* . . . Well, she wasn't exactly a beauty, not as one would use the term elsewhere, and they weren't beasts, just sailor-men. Barrie announced, in a voice like a shower of rusty scrap-iron, 'This is the feller pulled me out of the drink and had me use his cabin. Let me borrow his clothes, an' all!' Nick was shaking strong, horny hands left, right and centre; they were hands that had spent years grappling with wet nets in ice-cold seas. Barrie told him, 'Now here – meet Annabel. Annabel, she's – why she's my own little girl, my little darlin' . . .' She was smiling up at Nick, putting a hand to Skipper Barrie's mouth to check his flow of words; Nick hadn't found it easy to hear exactly what he'd said, in all this bedlam of talk and laughter – noise came not just from this bar but the other one as well, and men were singing in there now. Nick asked the skipper, 'Your daughter?' He had her hand in his: an incredibly small, soft hand, after the succession of vast fishermen's paws he'd been grasping; it was like holding something warm and living like a mouse or a bird: you didn't want to hold too tight and hurt any more than you wanted to release it and have it fly away. Laughter and guffaws shook the whole room: Barrie was shouting. 'Aye, my little daughter Annabel . . . Listen now, my precious: this is Lieutenant Everard, as won fame and glory at the Jutland battle. Hear me? Brung his destroyer home single-handed, half wrecked and full o' dead an' dyin' men: destroyer by the name o' *Lanyard*, ye'd 've read it in the newspapers . . .'

Nick would have liked to have shut him up, but the skipper was gathering an audience round him, shouting more loudly to gather others too. The girl hadn't said a word: her hand was still in Nick's, oddly enough, and she was smiling into his eyes as he stooped over her. Barrie roared, in the direction of the bar, 'Bring my friend a drink. What'll it be – rum?'

'No – beer, please.'

'Pint o' the horse here, Jack!'

'Aye aye!'

'Holdin' hands wi' him, are ye, darlin'?'

Applause, back-slapping. The girl – he'd let her have her hand back now – turned a chair round with her foot, and patted it. She had very wide-set, pale-blue eyes and a generous, full-lipped mouth; her nose had a slightly rounded end to it, a sort of blob that finished it off, but somehow it suited the rest of her face, the friendly and outgoing nature which he read in it. He didn't see the tot of rum someone poured into the tankard of beer on its way over to him.

'Here's health, a quick recovery, Skipper.' Funny taste, that first mouthful had. He sat down beside the girl. 'You're from Tyne-mouth, then?'

'If you say so.' She laughed. Barrie leant across her and hit Nick on his shoulder with a fist like a brick. 'She's a looker, eh?'

'Indeed she is.'

'Well, drink up!'

'How's the leg now?'

'*Told* ye I'd be hoppin' round!'

'Yes, you did.' He drank some more beer. Barrie shouted, 'You're our guest here. Private club, this is. Drink up, an' have another.' The girl asked him, 'What's your first name?'

'Nick. I think Annabel's a *lovely*—'

'Here's to us, Nick.' She raised her glass, and drank, with her eyes on his. Strangely enough, he wasn't in the least embarrassed; he felt he knew her and he knew he liked her, there was an immediate, ready-made *rapport* between them. She was rather, he thought, the 'Brickie' type: only less giggly. Her hand touched his where it rested on the arm of the wooden chair, between them; she leant closer, until her mouth almost touched his ear: she asked him, 'Do you like me?'

It was an extraordinary question to be asked, he thought, right out of the blue like that. But there wasn't any problem answering it. He nodded. 'Yes. Enormously!' Her eyes smiled, and her hand squeezed his; she was still leaning towards him and he wondered if she knew that she was showing rather a lot of bosom. Bosoms, plural. In a place like this, with only men – and not exactly a drawing-room lot, at that – around her . . . He realised that he felt protectively inclined towards her. She asked him, 'D'you think I'm pretty?'

He nodded. 'Pretty's not the word. You're *lovely*!'

'You're not bad yourself.'

He was astonished. Not exactly embarrassed: no, not at all embarrassed, just surprised . . . She was so – unusual. How and where, he wondered, had Skipper Barrie brought her up, and where was her mother now? He'd emptied his tankard, and Barrie had gestured, pointing, and one of the others had taken it to the bar and brought it back full again. Barrie was telling the story, somewhat exaggerated, of *Lanyard* at Jutland. The girl had been handed a new drink too; Nick asked her what it was.

'Eh?'

Leaning close again, smiling with her lips apart. From behind her shoulder, Skipper Barrie winked at him. Nick repeated his question; she told him, 'Gin. Only to keep the cold out, mind. And that's my ration now, I never have no more than two.'

This beer wasn't bad, when you got used to it. But it was strong stuff; Nick felt quite light-headed. He told Barrie, shouting through the din and narrowing his eyes against the swirls of smoke, 'I can't stay long. Have to go back aboard, in a minute.' He told Annabel, 'Might take a walk first, to clear my head. This beer's got Lyddite or something in it.'

'What's Lyddite?' She'd glanced at some man behind him, then back at Nick. 'What's Lyddite, when it's at home?'

'Explosive. They make it down the coast there, at a place called Lydd.'

She leant forward, waited for him to lean halfway and meet her; she murmured, with her face so close it actually brushed his, 'I could walk with you, if you like.'

'That'd be splendid!'

'Truly? You'd like me to?'

'*Like?* Why, I'd—'

'I could show you where I live, if you'd like that too?' Skipper Barrie broke in: 'Now drink up there, Lieutenant, lad!'

'No more, thanks. Very kind of you, very kind indeed, but—'

Annabel told her father, 'He's taking me for a walk.'

Barrie stared at her, then at him. Stubble-faced, and eyes red-rimmed: one didn't have to guess how he was spending his convalescence. What of the girl, though, did she have to sit with him all the time? The skipper laughed suddenly, and slapped his thigh: 'So *that's* how it goes, when a man's laid up?' He pinched his daughter's ear-lobe; she squawked, slapping at his hand as she wrenched herself away. Nick assured him, 'Don't worry, I'll take great care of her.' That, for some reason, practically brought the house down; Nick

274

realised they were all pretty well half-seas over. There was a glass – a small one – in his hand, in place of the empty tankard; how this one had got there he had no idea, he'd just looked down and there it was. He sniffed at the dark liquid in it: neat rum. Just that one sniff was enough to make his eyes water. Skipper Barrie boomed, 'Don't *smell* it, lad, *drink* it!' Nick would rather have poured it on the floor. He was already muzzy, and it was an effort to keep things in focus. All this smoke didn't help . . . He shook his head.

'Kind of you, but—'

The girl interrupted his refusal. For a moment he'd thought she was going to kiss him, her mouth came so close to his; she urged him, 'Do drink it down. He'll be upset if you don't. Fresh air'll see you right, and when we get to my room I'll make you some nice strong tea.'

Funny sort of evening. Particularly when one had only come ashore for a breath of air in the first place. He waved the little glass at Skipper Barrie: 'Happy Christmas!' The girl was watching him, and smiling at him as if she was pleased with him. He remembered – next morning, as he fought against a combination of physical sickness and mental shock – exactly how she'd looked at that moment; and then he'd been leaving with her: he could recall the vociferous farewells of Skipper Barrie and his mates, and then, on the way out through the other bar, Leading Seaman McKechnie and *his* friends greeting them with cheers and jokes about the differences between 'he-friends' and 'she-friends'; it was all extremely friendly and Annabel was laughing, enjoying it, clinging to his arm, but the whole feel of it was vague, clouded with smoke and the taste of rum and the roar of voices in the low-ceilinged room. He remembered telling McKechnie that Miss Barrie was the daughter of the skipper they'd rescued, and McKechnie's look of surprise; at about that point, when they were halfway across the room with the crowd of sailors opening to let them through, the town's air-raid alarm started up. A familiar sound, by this time, for the shoreside people: four short blasts and one long one, over and over again, from the siren on the Electricity Works. McKechnie told Nick, swaying like a palm-tree in a tornado and with a pint glass clutched in his tattooed fist, 'Ye'll likely lose her, sir. She'll be doon the *women's* shelter!'

The biggest air-raid shelters in the town were here in Snargate Street; the caves at the back of the old Oil Mills had been equipped with benches to hold thousands of people in complete safety from the Gotha bombers, with hundreds of feet of solid chalk above their heads. But it was true: they'd segregated the sexes, there were caves for men and caves for women. A very *proper* place, was Dover, under the eagle eyes of Lady Bacon and Mrs Bickford, wife of the general up at the Castle.

Annabel told McKechnie, 'You're mistaken. We're off to the Girls' Patriotic Club.'

Bellows of amusement . . . Nobody was taking any notice still of that siren as its last scream died away. The Girls' Patriotic Club was run by a Miss Bradley, and its club-room was over Bernards the grocers; its purpose – heartily approved of by Lady Bacon and Mrs Bickford – was to keep young ladies off the streets. Off Snargate Street in particular. Nick had had enough of the crowd and the din, he felt a strong need of air; he cut into the chat with 'We're going to take a walk along the Marine Parade.' He nodded to McKechnie: 'Goodnight.'

'If she's going for any walk – it'll be with *me* she'll go.'

A large man: trawlerman, by the look of him. In a heavy blue serge suit and a seaman's roll-neck sweater. He stood in front of them, between them and the door, and stared at Annabel.

'With *me*, Annie. Eh?'

Nick stepped towards him. The man put one enormous hand out, like a policeman stopping traffic, but he didn't take his eyes off the girl.

'Well, then?'

McKechnie hit him. Annabel screamed. Everyone was shouting, closing in. The big man raised both his fists together and crashed them down like a sledge-hammer on McKechnie's head; at the same time another of the *Mackerels* smashed a bottle against the challenger's ear. McKechnie had staggered from that blow, recovered as he swayed forward, stumbling; the trawlerman had clamped a hand on his throat and with the other he was belting him in the stomach. There was fighting all over the room now, trawlermen or driftermen against sailors. A *Mackerel* stoker, O'Leary, had climbed up on the bar; now he jumped, landing on the big man's shoulders and bringing him crashing down; Nick saw a sailor's boot connect against the trawlerman's jaw, and he thought it was probably McKechnie's. All Nick was trying to do was protect Annabel from flying fists: McKechnie yelled in his ear, 'Ye'd best be awa', sir, while the goin's good!'

'Come on!' Annabel tugged at him. Nick agreed: there'd be

redcaps here at any minute. Behind the Leading Seaman he saw a bottle raised – a big one, full of liquor – he shouted, and sprang forward: McKechnie swung round, the other man side-stepped and brought the bottle down; Nick saw it coming and he tried to dodge . . .

'There, my pet!'

Something cool was swabbing his forehead. Sarah's voice was gentle, loving, soothing in his ear and brain . . . Sarah?

Sarah was up at Mullbergh. He, Nick, was in Dover, wasn't he? What was—

He opened his eyes. Annabel smiled at him, her full lips only inches above his face, a damp flannel in her hand. They were on a bed: there was a cracked ceiling overhead, brown-and-grey patterned wallpaper. Grey morning light filtered through a dirty dormer window.

Morning light!

He felt his insides convulse with the shock of it. *Morning*. And he was still ashore. Then he remembered: Wyatt was still in London. He thought, *Thank God for small mercies*. He made a slight effort to sit up: Annabel gently pushed him back.

'Easy, easy now, my darling,' She rested on him. Bare, soft arms moved round his neck. Her breasts – full, heavy – pressed their nipples against his chest. He moved a hand down: she was naked, and so was he.

It had to be a dream. He shut his eyes. He'd been dreaming of – Sarah, his stepmother? Annabel asked him, 'Tell me something, as a favour?' He opened his eyes and found her pale-blue ones smiling into his; she asked him, 'Why d'you call me "Sarah" all night long? Who's this Sarah you're in love with?'

'Love?' It hurt, to move his head: he winced. 'No – no, I'm *not*, I . . .'

His own stepmother: his father's wife; how could one – even in a dream . . . It seemed the most dreadful thing of all. He tried to shake his head again, and felt the same sharp stab of pain. He told himself, *My skull's cracked, I'm deranged!*

'Liar. You *must* be.' She kissed him slowly, lingeringly. 'It doesn't matter. Whoever she is, she's a lucky girl.'

Impossible to *think* about, let alone discuss . . . 'How did I get here?'

'Two of your sailors brought you. They wanted to take you to

277

the ship, but I said no, not in *that* state, I'd look after you myself. So—'

'I must get back on board!'

'Now?'

'Yes – my God, I—'

'Pity.' She smiled, stroking him. 'I thought, when you woke up –' She shook her head. 'Never mind. Shall I see you again?'

He thought, *Sarah* . . . There were more immediate anxieties, but that was the deepest shock in his mind. Annabel was helping him to sit up. He told her, 'Of course. Yes, of *course* we'll –'

'Do you still like me?'

Standing beside the bed, looking down at him. She put her hands up, linking them behind her head. Then she bounced a little on her toes, and laughed at his eyes on her bouncing breasts. 'Well?'

'You're beautiful.'

'Really think so?'

He got off the bed. She touched him: 'Next time, you'll be well.'

Memory came in spasms. Underneath glimpses of last night, the constant thought of Sarah, his father's wife. Young enough to be his father's daughter, certainly, but still – to think of her – or *have thought* of her – like that . . . He told himself, *I don't: it was a dream. That bang on the head: and obviously they put something in the beer* . . . Sarah: distantly he heard her quiet, pleading tone between his father's angry, drunken shouting echoing through Mullbergh's cold stone corridors: waking, hearing that, feeling the racing of one's own heart, the misery for *her* sake, the loathing . . . Then the night she'd screamed: he'd rushed down, found her bedroom door with its top half smashed in and his father in a rage which faded to a sort of baffled shame when he saw Nick: and Sarah's tear-streaked face, her voice telling him, 'It's all right now, Nick. Truly. Go on back to bed.'

Cockcroft said, 'Lucky the captain's up in London. But there's bound to be the most frightful fuss, I'm afraid. The Military Police brought about a dozen of our chaps aboard, and they know the names of others who were in it, *and* that there was an officer involved!'

'God . . .' His head was spinning. 'Look here, I've got to sleep, I'm no good like this. If I can get a couple of hours with my head down before—'

'If you'd tell me what's to be done? Or perhaps it's Pym you ought to tell. But—'

278

'Mr Gladwish wants a signal made about changing one of his torpedoes. If the ready-use lockers are dry – you know we scraped and painted them out – the GM can see to refilling them. But the important thing is stores. I made a list – or started one . . . But see the cox'n, he'll know what—'

'All right.'

'Stores is the important thing. In case we finish the boiler-clean tonight—'

'They say they'll be done before that. They did a night shift – came crashing on board at midnight, and another lot took over about six—'

'*What!* I mean – *why?*'

'Heaven knows. What with one thing and another it's been a fairly hellish twelve hours, I can tell you. You realise I've had to put the defaulters in *your* report?' Cockcroft's long arms flapped hopelessly. 'Anyway, you sleep. I'll see the cox'n.'

'And fresh water. Ask the Chief Stoker—'

'Right. You turn in now. If anyone asks I'll say you've got a touch of 'flu. I'll give you a shake at noon – that do?'

It wasn't Cockcroft, though. It was Wyatt.

'Everard!'

There was a constant hammering and clattering overhead. Wyatt's small, furious eyes bored at him across the little cabin. 'Cockcroft informs me that you have influenza. Is that the case?'

Bulky, aggressive, filling the cabin doorway . . . Nick, even before he was fully out of sleep, out of a nightmare in which he was frantically trying to find Sarah while Mullbergh closed in on him, stone walls squeezing in on either hand and the ends of passages turning into dead-ends so that you turned and tried to run the other way with the narrowing passages trapping your feet, holding your ankles and cold terror everywhere – terror for Sarah more than for one's own predicament: the dream's content faded into confusion and in its place he had the certainty that Wyatt knew at least something of last night's riot.

'Well, is it?'

'All Cockcroft knows is I've been sick, sir. He may have assumed it was 'flu.'

'In fact it was – what?'

Nick slid off his bunk.

'I'll be all right now, sir.'

279

'Oh? Do you *really* think so? That you'll be *all right*?' Nick waited. He thought there was an element of satisfaction as well as anger in his captain's attitude. 'Listen to me, Everard. You remain in this ship and as my first lieutenant for the time being for one reason only – that I'm unable to replace you before we sail. I've tried to, and it's impossible; they've larger matters to attend to, in present circumstances . . .' A hand rose, pointing: 'You *were* in some bar-room last night, brawling over a tart's favours?'

'No, sir!'

'The Provost Marshal's made it up?'

'He's been misinformed, sir, by the sound of it. I went to meet Skipper Barrie – the man we picked up from the Carley float – at his invitation. He had his daughter with him. I was in her company when a man – a trawlerman, I think – accosted her. Then—'

'All right, Everard. That'll do.'

Nick stared at him. Wyatt said, 'I don't wish to hear about it.' He turned, hands clasped behind his back, stared out through the starboard-side scuttle. 'It's possible you were too drunk to know what was—' He shrugged, without finishing the sentence. Nick saw light reflected from the harbour's surface flashing in his narrowed eyes. '*Possible*. The matter will be dealt with – ashore – on our return. I should say a court-martial is the likely outcome. In my view it is an extremely squalid business, and I want no part in it . . . What I have to say to you is simply this: that we are coming to immediate notice for sea, and we are in the process –' he glanced upwards, at the upper deck where the noise was coming from – 'of converting for a minelaying operation. We shall fuel, embark our mines and sail as soon as that work is finished. Clear?'

'Yes, sir.'

Wyatt turned from the scuttle.

'Very well. Get shaved and properly dressed, and resume your duties as first lieutenant.'

'Aye aye, sir.' Nick slid off his bunk. Wyatt paused in the doorway, filling its whole width, looking back at him.

'How could you have been such a *damned* fool, Everard?'

He looked as if he was really trying to understand: or as if he wished there could be some hope of understanding. Then he'd shaken his head, dismissing the effort as futile, and turned away, and the curtain had fallen back across the doorway.

CHAPTER 4

Mackerel drove slowly eastward, a mile and a half offshore, approaching Dunkirk Roads. Six forty-five pm: seven o'clock was the ordered time for her rendezvous with the rest of the minelaying flotilla. Able Seaman Dwyer hailed again from the foc'sl break, below the bridge to starboard: 'By the mark, five!'

Pym said to Wyatt, 'As it should be, sir.'

Pitch-dark, bitter cold. Last night there'd been a sliver of moon, enough for the Gothas to see Dover and the coastline by; there was none tonight. Very little wind or sea. Christmas Eve: but it didn't feel like it, except for the biting cold, and even that wasn't the snowy-Christmas sort of cold. It was damp and penetrating, utterly un-jolly, Nick thought. They were all muffled up against it: great-coats or duffels or oilskins, sweaters over more sweaters over flannel shirts; scarves, gloves, Balaclavas – and either Gieves inflatable waistcoats or the issue swimming-collars. Thin men looked fat, fat ones like dirigibles. It didn't feel like Christmas or like anything else that anyone ashore could know about: only like the Dover straits and a black night and twenty tons of mines to plant in the enemy's front garden. The mines were aft there on their rails, with Mr Gladwish nursing them like a tomtit sitting on forty great cuckoo's eggs. Highly sensitive and destructive eggs: their presence and deadweight aft gave one the unpleasant feeling that one was piloting a floating bomb.

Dwyer had hove his lead again. It was far more of an expert job than anyone who'd never tried would have imagined, but he was an expert leadsman. He called now. 'And a quarter, five!' This was a narrow passage of comparatively deep water inside the shoals and minefields and with shallows and the land itself to starboard; one had used it so often in the past eighteen months that one could have told from the soundings as he sang them out if the ship had strayed so much as thirty yards to one side of the channel or the other. There was plenty of water here, for a destroyer drawing no more than sixteen feet – or a bit more than that now, with the extra weight of the mine-load on her – but depth enough, so long as she held her course well inside the channel, which narrowed, as it approached Dunkirk itself, to something like a cable's width. The leadsman hailed again: 'Less a quarter seven, sir!' Wyatt muttered. 'Very good' – as if the man could possibly have heard him . . . Since Nick had reported to him back in Dover that the ship was ready for sea with all hands on board, and Wyatt had curtly acknowledged his salute and told Mr Watson 'Stand by main engines', he and Nick hadn't exchanged a word. The night and the minelaying operation lay ahead of them, and that was all there was to think about now; soon after dawn they'd be back in Dover, and *Mackerel* would go alongside the oiler to top up her tanks, and he, Nick Everard, would presumably hand over to some new first lieutenant.

Where would he be sent – to a battleship, as a junior watch-keeping officer?

Much better *not* to think about it.

He'd been stupid. He could see that now. He'd played into Wyatt's hands. If you had a captain who'd speak up for you and fight to hang on to you, you could weather a scrape or two. When you hadn't – and your record hung on one single incident where you'd come out well instead of badly . . .

'And a half eight, sir!'

This was the deepest patch that they were passing over now. The sea hissed like a great cauldron of soda-water along *Mackerel*'s black sides as she slid up the channel at six or seven knots. About as dark as ever it could be. Dwyer wouldn't be seeing the marks on his line where it cut the water's surface; he'd be allowing for the two and a quarter fathoms between his hand and the waterline – the 'drift' was the technical term for it – and as the ship passed the lead's position on the bottom and the line came vertical he'd subtract that distance from the amount of line he had out.

'And a half, seven!'

Pym said, 'One thousand yards to go, sir.'

Converting for mines had taken five and a half hours. It wasn't a difficult evolution. *Mackerel* was one of a handful of destroyers fitted for it, with bolts and brackets all there in the right places, and her ship's company had done it often enough before. First the stern

282

gun and the after tubes mounting had to be unbolted, lifted on a crane and slung ashore. Then the crane picked up the mine rails and put them aboard, and they were bolted down like tram-lines to both sides of the quarterdeck and iron deck, with an extended chute from each set of rails over the stern, so that the mines would drop well clear of the propellers. A winch was fitted at the stern and another for'ard, respectively for hauling the mines aft and forward; the release gear at the chutes was operated by a single hand-lever.

It had taken another hour to load the forty mines, each weighing half a ton, and secure them properly. Each mine rested on its sinker, which was like a low trolley with wheels to run on the rails. These were the latest magnetically fired mines, called M-Sinkers; they'd replaced the useless Elias.

Dwyer called out, 'By the mark, five!'

Wyatt said, 'Starboard ten.'

'Starboard ten, sir.' *Mackerel* heeled slightly to the turn. Such breeze as there was crept up from astern, grew for'ard, blew in over the port side as she swung seawards under starboard helm, port rudder.

The old moon – in fact its last quarter had hardly been glimpsed by human eye – was dead, and the new one as yet unborn. A perfect night, therefore, for laying mines. Or, for that matter, for another German destroyer raid; and the purpose of this new minefield would be to catch any raiders on their return to base. The rest of the Patrol's destroyers – about two dozen, if you excluded the thirty-knotters and the ten or twelve M-class and Tribals on stand-off or under repair – would be at sea and hoping to catch them *before* they made for home. Dover harbour had been emptying fast by the time *Mackerel* had sailed.

The mines were to be planted between Zeebrugge and Ostend. The field's eastern end would be five thousand yards off Blanken-berg, and the western end seven thousand – three and a half miles – off de Haan. The approach was to be made from the north after a wide detour up around the outside of Bacon's summer netting area, his Belgian coast barrage from behind which he launched the monitor bombardments. The detour would take the flotilla clear of known minefields and shoals, avoid too close a proximity to the German coastal batteries, and take them clear, too, of Weary Willie, the trawler guardship off Middelkerke.

Wyatt said, 'Midships.'

'Midships, sir.'

Slow speed, and a black, quiet sea. A sharp awareness of the need to *keep* it quiet. Burglars embarking on a night's thievery might feel like this.

'Meet her, and steer north.'

'Steer north, sir . . .' The coxswain's small silhouette bobbed as he flung the wheel around. Wyatt must dislike this situation, Nick thought. His yearning to come to grips with Heinecke, who might well be at sea tonight with his 'Argentinians', would make the need to avoid any kind of action highly frustrating. Destroyers carrying mines were forbidden to engage an enemy unless that enemy fired first: then they'd be permitted to defend themselves. But one bullet, let alone a shell, would be enough to explode that cargo aft.

You had to shut your mind to everything except the simple object of the operation: sneak in, lay the mines, sneak away again.

'Course north, sir.'

'Should come up with 'em soon, pilot, shouldn't we?'

'We should, sir.'

Everyone was looking out, using binoculars, as *Mackerel* approached Hill's Pocket, the anchorage between the shoals where she'd been ordered to rendezvous with *Moloch, Musician* and two French destroyers, all of them carrying mines.

The leadsman's hail came up through the darkness: 'By the mark, ten!'

At ten fathoms the mark was a piece of leather with a hole in it. Dwyer must have had two fathoms in hand; so he'd have the mark for thirteen – a strip of blue bunting – in the slack of his line.

'Ship eighty on the starboard bow, sir!'

Charlie Pym sounded pleased with himself. Wyatt said, 'Slow together.'

'Flashing, sir!'

Porter was on to it. It was the challenge for the night, and he was already sending the reply on his hand-lamp. Wyatt told the coxswain, 'Port ten.'

'Port ten . . . Ten o' port wheel on, sir!'

The ship that had challenged was flashing something else now: Nick read, and Porter called out for Wyatt's information, *Take station astern of* Musician. *She is now four cables on your port bow. Course will be east-north-east speed ten. Subsequent alterations of course and speed without signal according to operation orders.*

'Midships – meet her!'

'Meet her, sir.'

'Steady!'

Pym said, 'I can see *Musician*, sir. More like three cables than four.'

'Good.' Wyatt told Leading Signalman Porter, 'Make to *Moloch, Ready to proceed.*' Porter's lamp began to spurt its dots and dashes; Wyatt ordered, 'Starboard five, half ahead together, two-five-oh revolutions.' Bellamy repeated the helm order, the telegraph bell clanged, and Pym was passing the speed order to the engine-room; out of the darkness to starboard came an acknowledging 'K' from *Moloch*. Wyatt told the coxswain, 'Midships, and steady on north-east.' *Moloch* was moving off; you could see the froth of white under her counter as she put on speed to give the Frenchmen room to drop into station astern of her. After them would come *Musician*, and *Mackerel* would bring up the rear; which meant that when they reached the laying position in three hours' time, *Mackerel* would be the first to get rid of her mines.

Nick wondered whether they'd allow him to volunteer for the RNAS. Learning to fly couldn't be all that difficult. Vereker and his friends were a splendid bunch, but they weren't particularly brainy. And flying would be a lot better than being sent back to big-ship life – with Wyatts lurking round every corner.

'*Musician*'s signalling, sir.'

Pym getting in first again. Charlie Pym the blue-eyed boy. Now *there* was someone who'd be right for a battleship appointment – with half a dozen snotties to do his work for him, and plenty of senior officers to suck up to . . . Pym knew, of course, what had happened ashore last night and what Nick's position was now; everyone in the ship must know it, by this time. It was more than likely that Charlie Pym would be nursing hopes of stepping into the first lieutenant's job.

If Wyatt allowed that, he'd be showing rotten judgement. Pym was lazy, and he had no understanding of, or level of contact with, the lower deck. The impression you got of Pym was that what mattered to him was his own position instead of what he could make of that position as a contribution to the ship's efficiency and happiness. The senior ratings – Chief Petty Officers Bellamy and Swan, for instance – disliked him; naturally they wouldn't say so or consciously show signs of it, but when you knew them and lived among them, worked with them, you could sense it; and it was virtually certain, Nick considered, that if Pym became first lieutenant *Mackerel* would go to pot.

285

Perhaps Wyatt knew it? He might. Wyatt was no fool, behind that bullish stare and aggressive manner. *Professionally* he wasn't, anyway. Might he be, in terms of personal judgement? Nick knew he didn't understand his captain. And could half the trouble be that they were simply different kinds of animal? The Navy's answer to that would be clear and blunt enough – and reasonably so – but perhaps for oneself it was something to give some thought to. Faced with authority in a form that seemed hostile or critical, did one tend towards a hedgehog attitude?

Nick had dim, approaching destroyer-shapes in the overlapping circles of his binoculars. The French destroyers. No need to report them: Wyatt had picked them up himself, and muttered something to Pym about them. Nick thought of himself as a boy at home at Mullbergh, and his father's dislike of him, the long years of mutual hostility, with David the heir as favourite and himself as the unwanted lout: that was how he'd felt. And curled up, inside the defensive spines?

Musician had signalled, *Let's go. Follow father*. Wyatt told Porter gruffly, 'No reply.' *Moloch*'s wake was a pale smudge in a black haze; the lean grey shapes of the French destroyers, closing in from eastward, shortened as they swung round to follow her. *Musician* was coming in from the opposite direction to take her place in the flotilla, but *Mackerel* was already where she had to be: *Musician* was therefore sliding into a gap in a formed line, as opposed to *Mackerel* tagging on astern of her. So much for 'follow father': that signal had been unnecessary in the first place, and Wyatt, without saying a word, had let *Musician*'s captain know it.

Able Seaman Dwyer's singsong tones cut upwards through the dark: 'And a quarter, ten!' *Mackerel* must be passing over the deepish patch inside the Breedt bank. Nick asked Wyatt, 'May we secure the lead, sir?'

'Yes please.'

He leant over the rail: 'Dwyer! Secure the lead!'

'Aye aye, sir!'

Wyatt said tersely as Nick turned inboard, 'We'll remain at action stations, Number One.'

In the chartroom, Midshipman Grant was preparing to keep a running check on *Mackerel*'s position, course and speed in relation to the operation orders, partly so as to be ready to give a dead-reckoning position quickly if Pym or the captain wanted one and also so as to be able to pass a warning up the voicepipe to the bridge when alterations of course or speed were to be expected.

The orders, in a heavily sealed buff envelope, had arrived after they'd converted and oiled and embarked the mines – great red-painted eggs as high as a man's shoulder as they sat on their wheeled, rectangular sinkers. Forty of them, twenty a side, brought in over the stern and hauled forward by winch, and each one then chocked on the rails before the next was run up against it. It was rather scary, to imagine them as they would be in a few hours' time, under water, tethered down in the cold and secret sea by the wire cables now coiled inside the sinkers: one could think of those great harmless-looking red things as monsters, evil, trying now to appear bland and stupid but ready at short notice to change into lurking, death-dealing horrors – which they would do within – what was it, half an hour? – when the soluble plugs on their firing-mechanisms melted in the water. Very different from the earlier British mines, the sort invented by the Italian Commander Elia. The Elias had had a mechanical firing device, a hinged lever that had to be tripped. As often as not, it stuck, and failed to do its job. The Board of Admiralty had distrusted such new-fangled ideas as electric detonation, so they'd opted for the mechanical system; whereas the Germans had had mines that worked, right from the beginning of the war, and it had given them a considerable advantage.

Those days were fading into history now. Jellicoe had pressed hard for hugely increased supplies of the M-sinker type, a year ago, and they'd recently been coming through in thousands. (It was the same sort of thing in the Air Service; a year ago, naval pilots had taken their rations of bombs to bed with them, to prevent brother-pilots pinching them while they slept.) Supplies of all these things had been greatly helped by America's joining in the war, this last April. But in any case this was a new Navy now, re-born out of war experience, and William Grant was extremely proud to have a place in it.

He put his face to the voicepipe.

'Bridge?'

'Bridge.' Pym's voice. Grant told him, 'We should alter to north twenty-one degrees east in two minutes, sir, and increase to twenty knots.'

'Very good.'

Grant lit a cigarette, taking it from a silver case that had his family's crest on it. It had at one time been a cravat-pin case, the property of his great-grandfather, who'd served at sea under Nelson. Grant's grandfather had been an admiral, following in the same tradition; but his father had been in the Army in India, and had died of typhus when his son had been only three. One of the greatest puzzles in William's mind, and one which he knew he'd never be able to solve, was what could possibly have induced his father to become a soldier – in India or anywhere else.

Perhaps he'd blotted his copybook, or the Navy for some reason hadn't wanted him.

He heard, through the voicepipe from the bridge, Wyatt ordering the change of course and increase in revolutions. One could visualise the dark, slim shapes of the destroyers ahead already filing round to port, lengthening as they turned, the white churn of foam piling as they put on power . . . Expelling smoke, he looked down at the chart again, where the track stipulated in the orders had been laid-off in pencil, with distances and compass courses pencilled in beside it. He called the bridge again, and told Charlie Pym, 'Forty-five minutes on this leg, sir.'

'All right, Mid.'

There'd been a period, when Grant had been fourteen and fifteen years old, when he'd been terrified that the war might end before he could get to sea. In 1914, Dartmouth had been emptied of its cadets, boys of thirteen upwards all sent straight to ships; but subsequent terms, new arrivals from the prep schools, had been held back, tied to school desks and the parade-ground, while the sands of war had seemed to be running out. All those 'big pushes' that had been so certain to end the war: how they'd been dreaded, at Dartmouth! But they'd fizzled out, one after another, and now one wondered whether it would *ever* end. Certainly the Americans were in now which should help; but to counter-balance their weight had come the Russian collapse and the transfer of thousands of seasoned German troops from east to west. Some newspaper articles had suggested that it could go on for years yet.

Anyway, he'd made it. If he hadn't, he'd have felt all through his life that he'd missed the greatest opportunity a man could ever have. And when one thought that some of one's friends, contemporaries, were actually still at school . . .

'Midshipman Grant, sir!'

The Leading Telegraphist, Wolstenholme, was peering at him

through the hatch from the wireless office. A normally placid, quiet man, a Yorkshireman, Wolstenholme looked agitated.

'Signal, sir – urgent!'

Grant leant over, and took the sheet of signal-pad on which the message had been scrawled in blue indelible.

It was from Flag Officer Dover to all ships and shore-stations in his command, and repeated for information to various other authorities; it said *Enemy wireless activity suggests attack on straits by surface forces is to be expected.*

Grant moved back quickly to the voicepipe. Wolstenholme was still craning through the hatch. He was a well-fed man, with small brown eyes set in a pale, roundish face. He said, nodding towards the signal, 'An' us wi' *mines* aboard!' Grant yelled into the voicepipe, 'Bridge!'

Able Seaman Dwyer stowed his leadline and canvas apron in the appropriate locker on the upper deck, just abaft the foremost funnel, and then began to pick his way aft. You had to go carefully in the darkness, and an old hand like Dwyer went *very* carefully; all there was to see by was the faint glow of phosphorescence from the broken water from the destroyer's black steel sides, and it wasn't much.

Cockcroft, at the midships four-inch – which was between the second and third funnels – was in the process of detailing two men to take round cutlasses, rifles and revolvers. He looked up, and saw Dwyer's grey head going by.

'Who's that? Dwyer?'

Dwyer admitted it. He explained. 'Been in the chains, sir – now I'm goin' aft to me action station.'

'Good.' Cockcroft handed him a .45 revolver on a webbing belt; a pouch on the belt held ammunition. 'Give this to Chief Petty Officer Swan, would you, and wish him a happy Christmas?'

'Aye aye, sir. An' all the best for 1918 to you, sir.' Dwyer went on aft. His station was in the emergency steering position, with Swan.

From the twenty-inch searchlight platform, where he was sitting with his boots dangling over his only remaining pair of torpedo tubes, Mr Gladwish watched him pass.

'Oh, Dwyer!'

Easily recognisable, that grey head. Most of the *Mackerels* were youngsters; most destroyer men were young, these days. There were still some old sailors about, of course, but since the outbreak of war one destroyer had been lost every twenty-three days, on average, while hundreds had been built; it thinned out the old hands, rather. Dwyer had stopped, and he was staring up at the gunner (T) on the searchlight platform.

'Sir?'

'Issuing small-arms, are we now?'

'I've a pistol 'ere for the Chief Buffer, sir, that's all.'

'Well, aft with it, and smartish, d'ye hear?'

'Aye aye, sir.' He shrugged to himself as he went on aft past the space where the other lot of tubes should have been. He knew what was agitating the gunner: Mr Gladwish didn't like firearms near his mines. Couldn't blame him, really; you only need to have one pistol dropped, and going off by accident. And you'd only to see Mr Gladwish and CPO Hobson, his torpedo gunner's mate, when they'd been priming the things, just before the ship sailed from Dover. The gingerly way they'd handled the cylindrical primers, carrying them like babies then lowering them as gently as if they were objects of the finest crystal glass into the primer-cavities in the mines. The signal from shore *Prime mines* was always the last to come, when everything else had been seen to and the ship was ready to sail. Then Gladwish and the TI, trusting none of the other torpedomen to handle so delicate a job, would each unscrew twenty cover-plates, fit twenty primers, tighten forty retaining screws . . . Dwyer sympathised. It was bad enough having the mines aboard, let alone messing about with them. The sooner the last one clanked down the rails and out of the stern trap into the sea, the sooner Dwyer – and about ninety other men – would feel safe again.

Squatting on the deck of the stern superstructure were the crew of the after four-inch, the gun which had been landed. They were the mine-handling party now, they and the torpedomen who would normally man the after tubes. Dwyer stopped, and stirred the gunlayer with his foot.

'Treat them 'orrors gently now, Archie lad!'

Archie Trew, who was also an AB but young enough to be Dwyer's son, pulled his legs back out of the way.

'Give each of 'em a good kick before we lets it go, don't we, boys?' Trotter, his sightsetter, commented, ' 'ighly disintegratin', that might be.' Dwyer went in through the screen door and down the ladder to the wardroom flat. Ammunition-supply ratings greeted him with a demand for news, information as to what was going on; he told them, 'Windin' up them mines, that's what . . . Course, if you *over*-winds 'em – well . . .' He gestured, rolling his eyes.

'*Bloody* things!'

The young stoker who'd muttered that sounded as if he'd meant it. He looked it, too: over-wrought, or ill . . . Dwyer told him, 'Keep your wool on, Sunny Jim. Steady does it . . .' He went aft again at this lower level, past the wardroom pantry and store and through two more stores to the steering-compartment, right by the rudder-head.

CPO Swan, extraordinarily, was shaving. He'd used scissors first to remove the bulk of his 'set', and now he was scraping his lathered chin with a bone-handled cut-throat razor. A bucket of water steamed gently between his spread feet. In this aftermost compartment of the ship there was quite a lot of motion on her, but it seemed not to occur to Swan – any more than it did to Dwyer, who'd been at sea at least as long as the Chief Buffer had – that using a cut-throat while standing on a deck that rose and fell six feet or more five times a minute might involve some hazard. In fact his hand's sureness seemed totally unaffected by the pitching.

Dwyer asked him, 'Shavin' off, then?'

An eyebrow rose. Swan said, without moving his lips, 'Sick of 'aving me soup strained.'

Dwyer smiled. 'You mean *she's* sick of it?'

The eyebrow flickered again. Swan took soap off the blade with his forefinger, and started on the other cheek. You could see already how different he was going to look. Dwyer sat down on the casing of the steering motor, and delved in his oilskin pocket.

'Brung me 'omework. They reckon we'll be three or four hours closed up, on this lark.' His homework was the final binding of a new tobacco prick. Leaf tobacco, Admiralty-issue and of course duty-free: you spread the leaves, sprinkled them with rum every day for a couple of weeks or so – a few drops from the daily tot wasn't much to spare – and then you rolled the leaves tightly into a hard-packed, rum-flavoured cylinder, which had then to be bound in a wrapping of tarry spunyarn. When it was finished and in its owner's expert view fit for smoking, he'd shave his daily requirement from the end of it, slicing the cross-section of the prick with his seaman's knife. He didn't call it a seaman's knife, though; he called it a pusser's dirk.

Swan drew the razor rasping down his throat, and flicked lather

291

off the blade again. Dwyer asked him, without looking up from his work, 'True about Jimmy, is it?'

By 'Jimmy' he meant 'the first lieutenant'. Swan murmured, 'McKechnie's the Scotch idiot as caused it, cox'n reckons. Wasn't no need at all.'

'Ah.' Dwyer wrenched the yarn tighter, and snatched another turn. 'Lose 'im, though, will we? Lose Jimmy, I mean?' Swan didn't answer. Dwyer went on, after a minute's silence, 'Always did seem daft, to me. If you got a good 'and aboard at sea, real *good* 'and, like – well, why bother 'im when 'e's ashore?' He gritted his teeth as he put more strain on the yarn. 'I never *did* see the sense in that.'

Swan put his razor on a ledge, and squatted down to sluice his face. He told Dwyer, with water streaming off it, 'That's why you never made more 'n Able Seaman, Dwye ol' lad.'

Pym answered a new call from the voicepipe. *Mackerel* was lifting slightly to the sea now, a short rocking-horse type motion that barely wet the foc'sl deck. Down there, the bow gun's crew were none the less crowded into the shelter of the gunshield; you didn't need to be wet to be freezing cold, in the Channel in December.

It wasn't Christmas Day yet. Not *quite* yet, Nick thought. *What do we do at eight bells, though – sing Old Lang Syne?*

No. That was for Hogmanay. And where might he be, by that time? In Scapa Flow? New Year horseplay in a battleship? Pym said, into the voicepipe, 'Bridge.'

'In about three minutes we should alter to east-north-east and stay on that for fifteen miles, sir. No change of speed.'

'Very good.'

Wyatt said, 'All right. I heard.' He had his glasses on *Musician*'s stern, that heap of white that you could see even when you couldn't see the ship herself.

A quarter of an hour ago they'd had the signal about Hun wireless activity. Wyatt had thought it out in silence; then he'd commented, 'Precautionary, one might suppose. Huns may be sending Christmas messages, for all we know.'

The thing was, Nick realised, that there was nothing they could do about it, except carry on with the operation and hope that if the enemy was at sea they didn't meet him. Not in this vulnerable, explosive state.

Pym failed to understand. He laughed, as if Wyatt's remark had been just a pleasantry. Wyatt cut into the false sound of it.

'Have small-arms been distributed, Number One?'

'Yes, sir.' Cockcroft had reported five minutes ago that he'd seen to it. Cockcroft's action station was aft, in charge of the midships and stern guns; but he had only one, tonight, to look after. The for'ard four-inch had Clover, the gunner's mate, as its officer of the quarters, and besides this Nick could easily control it himself over the forefront of the bridge.

He wondered about the whisper of some 'special operation', the rumour he'd heard them talking about the other night in *Arrogant*. It had been connected, or seemed to have been, with the gossip about a new admiral taking over. Nothing more than that, really, had been said, and it seemed to grow from a belief that if Bacon was being relieved it would basically be for not having pursued a sufficiently aggressive policy against the U-boats. So it could be just wishful thinking: or a harking-back to Bacon's own dreamchild, his plan for a 'Great Landing' which had now been abandoned. Its object would have been to land a force that would have linked up with the Army's advance – the one that had stopped at Passchendaele – and captured the Belgian ports. There'd been a mass of yarns about the plan: how it had involved using 600-foot floating pontoons, a kind of pre-constructed harbour jetty which monitors would push into position against the sea-wall at Middelkerke, four or five miles behind the German line. The pontoons had been designed by an engineer called Mr Lillicrap – which may have been partly why they'd been talked about so much. But that scheme had been abandoned, and this rumour might well be just wishful thinking: by the CMB men, for instance, who felt starved of action. Harry Underhill had said that several of the CMB officers had gone off on some mysterious course: and Elkington – Rogerson's guest, from the thirty-knotter *Bravo* – had a story that a friend of his just down from Scapa had told him privately that Admiral Keyes, who headed the Admiralty committee that had been putting pressure of one kind or another – this was gossip again, of course – on Bacon, and who was also director of the Plans Division at the Admiralty, had been up at Scapa having private talks with Beatty. That certainly did sound as if something was in the wind; and if it involved the whole Fleet, not just this Patrol, it would have to be something fairly big.

Keyes had been the commodore commanding submarines, at the beginning of the war. Rogerson had said he was a live wire, *he'd* give them something to do. And he'd been in the Dardanelles, as Chief-of-Staff to Admiral de Robeck. A man of action . . .

That was how rumours started, of course, and were built up. Adding to the structure, item by item, and probably none of them in any way connected with each other. It could be nothing – simply the expression of a *desire* for action. But – could one, all the same, volunteer?

Pym blurted suddenly, 'Sir, they're altering—'

'Damn it, pilot, I've got eyes!'

Wyatt had snapped Charlie's head off . . . Now he told CPO Bellamy, 'Port ten, cox'n.'

'Port ten, sir.' Following *Musician* round. This was the start of the second fifteen-mile leg of the roundabout route. It would bring them to No. 8 buoy, a fixed marker in 51° 30′ north, 2° 50′ east. From there they'd edge down south-eastward towards the Belgian coast. In fact, almost directly towards Zeebrugge; towards – conceivably – a head-on encounter with any German destroyers that might be coming out of Zeebrugge. But it would be no less surprising or unlikely to meet them here, now, or in half a minute's time: *there*, in that sea that looked empty, like an enormity of black ice crackling down the ships' sides as they pushed steadily, watchfully north-eastward. Air like ice too: and outside a radius of a few hundred yards it looked as solid as the water under it, as impenetrable and as good a cover to an enemy as it was to these minelayers. If you met raiding Germans the meeting would be at close quarters: sudden, savage, shattering.

There'd be no time to think. Not a spare second.

Nick got Cockcroft on the navyphone to the midships four-inch.

'Sub, make sure the guns' crews are on their toes, wide awake all the time. Go and tell the GM the same. There may be Huns about, and if we run into them we'll be alongside 'em before we know it. Understand me?'

'Absolutely!'

'But we do *not* fire unless we're fired at. Drive that home to Clover too. All right?'

'I'll have a chin-wag with him right away – I mean—'

Nick put the 'phone quickly on its hook. Cockcroft's manner and habits of speech would have been understandable if he'd been RNVR instead of RN. Somehow he'd survived the Dartmouth conditioning without letting any of it get inside his skin or skull. One might have thought that to achieve such a feat a man would have to be either incredibly strong-minded or thoroughly obtuse; but Cockcroft combined an easy-going lightheartedness with a brain that was in full working order. It was phenomenal.

Nick had his glasses at his eyes, adding his contribution to the general effort of looking out. *Mackerel* and the ships ahead of her were thrusting into the night at twenty knots, and if one reckoned on an enemy flotilla approaching at the same speed the gap between them would be reduced at a rate of almost one land-mile per minute. With a range of visibility of something like five hundred yards, there'd be no room for late sightings or slow reactions. He wondered, as he tried to distinguish where sea ended and sky began – but you couldn't, they were as black as each other – about that rumoured special operation. And about his own motives for wanting to volunteer for it. As an escape? But it wouldn't be: there'd be an inquiry into that pub row in any case, and nothing would save him from having to face it . . . But – well, if the worst came to the worst, to be allowed to volunteer for something of that sort would be quite a different matter from being simply kicked out of one's ship. Was that it: a question of how his leaving *Mackerel* would look to other people?

And by other people – Sarah?

There was no one else to consider. Uncle Hugh would know precisely what had happened.

The dream he'd had: calling her name, talking to her in his sleep, dreaming that he and she were – that Sarah, and not Annabel, had been in his arms . . . One had to face it, and – displace it. Otherwise it nagged on in one's thoughts. But the mind had a life of its own; this had nothing, surely, to do with will, intention, desire, any waking thought of her. To think of the dream wasn't to think as one had thought *in* the dream.

He'd thought he'd glimpsed something: something more solid than the empty night. In that split second he'd jerked the glasses back, holding his breath for steadiness and to keep the lenses from fogging-up.

Nothing. So easy to imagine . . .

Sarah – as close as Annabel had been?

CHAPTER 5

The inshore marker had been laid last night, probably by a CMB from Dunkirk. It was a small moored buoy with a black flag on it, ten miles east-south-east of No. 8 buoy, where at 8.45 the mine-laying flotilla had altered course and reduced speed to twelve knots.

Wyatt watched the destroyers ahead swing away to starboard. He knew they'd be turning round the buoy, but it wasn't yet visible from *Mackerel* here at the tail-end of the procession. *Musician* had put her helm over: you could see the swirl of white, like a pool of spilt milk spreading as the rudder dragged her stern round. Wyatt, with his glasses up, muttered to himself, 'There it is.' He meant the marker buoy. It was very small and so was the flag on it, and nobody who wasn't looking for it in this spot would have seen it except by purest chance.

'Port fifteen.'

'Port fifteen, sir!' Bellamy spun his wheel, putting on starboard rudder. Wyatt bent to the voicepipe and told the engine-room, 'Three hundred revolutions.' Acknowledgement floated hoarsely from the tube, and the coxswain reported, 'Fifteen o' port wheel on, sir.' Everyone spoke rather more quietly than usual, as they turned down towards the enemy-held coast. But it wasn't the nearness of Germans doing that, it was the load they carried aft. *Mackerel* swung round across a half-acre patch of ploughed-up sea, and as she went round it the marked buoy was bobbing like a float with some great fish nibbling at the hook below it. They swept round it, heeling, and Pym called down to the midshipman in the chartroom, 'Six miles from *now*!'

'Aye aye, sir!'

It was nine-eighteen. Not that timing was strictly necessary at this point; the next turn, like the others, would be a matter of following when *Moloch* turned. After that it would be stopwatch timing while the mines were laid. Meanwhile six miles at twelve knots meant another half-hour before they could begin to shed the explosive load.

'Midships.'

'Midships, sir.'

The brass caps on the wheel's spokes flickered dully in the binnacle's faint radiance as they circled. 'Wheel's amidships, sir.'

'Meet her—'

'Meet her, sir!'

'—and follow *Musician*, cox'n.' Wyatt left Pym at the binnacle, and moved into the starboard fore corner of the bridge. Nick transferred himself to the port side and further aft. Wyatt called to Pym, 'Come down to two-nine-oh revs, pilot.'

Wind and sea – about enough to make the snotty and the ship's cat seasick – were on the starboard bow now, on this course just west of south, and the ship was rolling as well as pitching. She'd get livelier when she'd lost the weight of the mines; and if the breeze had risen this much in the last half-hour there was no telling how it might be by midnight. Poor little Grant, he thought. There weren't many things worse than chronic seasickness. He had his glasses up and he was sweeping the darkness on the port side, starting at the bow and sweeping back across the black frozen emptiness towards the stern. The glasses were trained out at about seventy on the bow when the German destroyer-shapes swam into them.

Just suddenly – like that – there they were.

And only himself seeing them. For half a second perhaps they were his private, as well as hardly believable, enemy. Staring at them; and conscious of the mines . . .

'Enemy destroyers seventy on the port bow, moving right to left – three – no, *four*—'

'Very good.'

Very *good*?

It wasn't real enough to be a nightmare. One had thought of it, envisaged it: here it was, and it was as if it *wasn't*. Wyatt said, 'Yes, I'm on 'em! Pilot, keep *your* eyes on the next ahead.' Nick was telling Hatcher, 'Bearing red ninety degrees, range oh-one-oh.' Hatcher was setting it on his transmitter dial. Nick snatched up the navyphone. 'One and two guns, follow pointers, load and stand by!' He said into the torpedo-sight navyphone, 'Mr Gladwish – train your tubes port beam. Enemy destroyers passing on opposite

297

course, fifteen knots, range one thousand. Do *not* engage, just stand by.' His voice had been little more than a whisper, he realised. But *Mackerel* sounded like a brass band, felt like a cruise ship – floodlit, impossible not to see from miles away, let alone that bare five cables . . . He had his glasses on them again now; he heard Wyatt mutter, 'They're big destroyers. Almost certainly it's . . .' His voice faded out. For a small ship moving at only twelve knots, *Mackerel* seemed to be throwing an enormous wake. Were the Huns blind? Or still so near their base – Zeebrugge – that they weren't bothering to keep a proper lookout yet?

No. It would start, at any second. There'd be the blinding flashes of their guns: Nick had his eyes narrowed, actually ready for it. At this range, they wouldn't miss.

Bellamy's voice broke the silence.

'It's the schnapps they put away. Rots the eyeball, I been told.'

Nick was holding his breath. He thought, *Why don't we slow down and cut that bloody wash?* He answered his own question: if they did, they'd lose contact with *Musician*. And this was the run-in to the minelaying area, it would have botched the whole operation.

Might the Germans think these British and French ships, so close to Zeebrugge and steaming towards it, were Huns like themselves? If that was the case it would mean there were even more of them about, and at sea, in this area . . . But all four had passed the beam, which was the closest point. From now on the range would be opening, and the chance of some Hun opening his eyes or considering the possible rewards of turning his square head to the left were being steadily reduced.

Did Germans have square *eyes*, too?

He didn't think those were Heinecke's ships. They'd looked big at first, but—

Using the past tense, he realised. It was incredible: they'd passed, a whole flotilla of Germans had passed at no more than five cables' lengths and just – gone on . . .

Wyatt roared suddenly, 'Herr Heinecke! Damn sure of it! Of all the filthy luck!'

He was wrong. Nick was certain those hadn't been the 'Argentinians'. Ship recognition was something he was good at, and he'd have sworn they were either *Schichaus* or Krupp 'G' class. He also felt that there was luck *and* luck, and that *Mackerel* had just had her share of it. Touch wood . . . The enemy ships were still in sight: not separate shapes now, only a smear on the quarter drawing aft

298

and growing fainter, merging into the surrounding dark. He heard Wyatt ask Pym, 'How long before we're there?'

No relief in his tone: only a touch of impatience. One could guess the intention in his mind: to get rid of the mines and then go after those destroyers. But it would be necessary to contact *Moloch* by lamp first, and to use a lamp when they were as close inshore as they would be when the laying started – it simply wasn't possible. Any more than one could have sent an enemy report by wireless, giving German shore-stations a chance to take cross-bearings on the transmissions.

Pym had told Wyatt, 'Twelve minutes, sir.' And the Huns had disappeared north-westward. An enemy report would have been of enormous value to Admiral Bacon in his Dover headquarters, and to the other divisions of the Sixth Flotilla. But at least they'd been warned, with that signal about German wireless activity – which looked now as if it might have been well founded. Intelligence was pretty hot these days, under Admiral Hall. Nick heard Wyatt say to Pym, 'All right, I've got her.' He meant he'd taken over the conning of the ship again. Nick told Hatcher, 'All guns train fore and aft.' He went to the navyphone at the torpedo sight and spoke to Mr Gladwish.

'We were lucky, that time. Train fore and aft, please.'

Gladwish said, 'I lost a stone, that's all . . . Aye aye.'

Everyone knew how Gladwish felt about mines. He hated them. It happened that mines came into the scope of the torpedo department. Wyatt asked Pym, 'How long now?'

Pym got the answer from Grant, up the voicepipe, 'Seven minutes, sir.' Wyatt raised his voice above the ship-noise, wind-and-sea racket. 'Number One! Have 'em stand by aft!'

'Aye aye, sir.' He got Gladwish again. 'Stand by to lay mines. I'll use the voicepipe now. First one at my order when we finish the turn in about five minutes, then intervals of seven seconds.'

The explosive eggs had to be laid one hundred and fifty feet apart. At twelve knots the intervals between dropping them should therefore be seven and a half seconds, but to make sure of getting rid of them inside the distance it was better to ignore that half second and call it seven. The first twenty would be laid in one half-mile line, and then the ship would be turned four points, forty-five degrees, to starboard, to drop the second twenty in a line at that angle to the first lot. As the last mine, number 40, splashed into the wake, a flash on a shaded blue lamp would tell *Musician* to start laying hers. She'd spread her first twenty along the original straight course and then turn four points to port, not starboard as *Mackerel* had done, for the others. Ahead of her, as she finished laying, the rearmost Frenchman would put down the same right-handed dog-leg pattern as *Mackerel* had done; and so on, alternately one way and the other, so that the end result would be two hundred mines planted in a sort of fishbone pattern, much harder to locate and sweep than they would have been in straight lines.

Grant called up, 'One minute to the turn, sir!' Nick used the voicepipe to what was normally the stern four-inch gun. 'Stand by, Mr Gladwish. Less than one minute.'

The gunner would have a stopwatch in his hand. His right-hand man, CPO Hobson, would be operating the release-gear of the trap while CPO Swan supervised the business of winching the mines aft, one from each side alternately so the ship wouldn't take on a list. It was always tricky work, in total darkness on a slippery, pitching deck dotted about with gear and fittings to trip a man and send him skidding overboard. And it had to be kept moving smoothly: no jamming-up, no trolleys coming off the rails.

Wyatt said suddenly, 'There he goes.' He meant *Moloch*, turning hard a-starboard. Grant squawked in the copper tube, 'Should turn now, sir!'

The leading French destroyer was under helm. And now the second one . . . Just after 9.50: a few minutes ahead of schedule. Wyatt ordered, 'Port fifteen. Stand by to lay mines.'

'Port fifteen, sir!'

'Stand by aft!'

'Stand by!' Gladwish in one shout acknowledged the order and passed it to his minions. Even more faintly up the voicepipe came CPO Hobson's 'Ready, sir!' to Gladwish.

'Midships.'

Musician had steadied on the laying course, due west. The flotilla was now less than three miles off a coast bristling with Germans and heavy guns.

'Meet her!'

'Meet her, sir!' Wheel flying round . . . Wyatt shouted, 'Steady! Start laying!'

'*Go!*'

A bellow from Gladwish: a clanking sound echoing in the voicepipe: then Gladwish counted the first one as it went off the chute: 'One!'

Craning out over the bridge rail, looking aft, Nick saw the splash expanding in a white circle from the wake, and then the mine itself bobbing astern like some great toy before the sinker took charge of it, dragged it down to its set depth, which would allow for the rise and fall of tide. It was just about low water now: it had been half-tide when they'd groped their way past Dunkirk. Each time a mine dropped off the chutes Mr Gladwish called its number: 'Five . . . six . . . seven . . .'

Bellamy said, 'Steady, sir, course west.'

Gladwish's voice up the tube: 'Eleven . . . twelve . . . thirteen . . .' Lucky number: time for one of the rollers to jam in the rails, or the winch to break down, a wire to snap . . . 'eighteen . . . nineteen . . . *twenty*, sir!'

'Port fifteen!'

Bellamy's growl acknowledged it as he flung the wheel around. Gladwish's team continued sending mines over as the destroyer began her turn to starboard. 'Twenty-one . . .'

'Midships!'

'Midships, sir.' And from that after voicepipe, 'Twenty-two . . . twenty-three . . . twenty-four . . .'

'Meet her, cox'n, and steer north-west.'

'Steer north-west, sir!'

'Twenty-eight . . .'

'Course nor'-west, sir.'

'Very good.' Wyatt was staring aft through his glasses, seeing the mines bob and sway away and vanish into the grim cover of the sea. Leading Signalman Porter, with the signal lamp resting in the crook of his left arm, was using binoculars one-handed to keep track of *Musician*, so he could aim his lamp accurately when the moment came. Wyatt asked gruffly, 'Ready, Porter?'

'Ready, sir.' Gladwish shouted, 'Thirty-two!' Eight to go. Less than a minute's work. *Then* what? Nick asked himself what he'd do, in Wyatt's shoes. Chase that enemy flotilla? Or obey the orders, go to No. 8 buoy and wait for the other four to rendezvous there when they'd finished turning this strip of sea into a new death trap . . . He knew what he'd have done, all right. Now Gladwish's final yell was triumphant: 'Forty!' Porter's lamp clicked, emitting its bright-blue wink: *Musician* would have seen it and by this time her first mine would be trundling off its chute. Wyatt roared into the engine-room voicepipe, 'Seven-five-oh revolutions! I want all we've got now, Chief, full power!'

Full power . . .
Going hunting!

Racing north-westward, wind and sea on her port bow, *Mackerel*
plunged and rolled and shook, the high whine of her turbines and the
throaty roar of ventilators competing with the sounds of weather.
On the bridge you had to scream if you wanted to be heard, pitching
the voice high to cut across the cacophony of steel and sea and
engines and the howl of wind, wind mostly of the ship's own making
as she tore into it through the dark. Seas burst crashing against her
bow, flinging spray that lashed like hail across the forefront of the
bridge, ringing on the thin steel plating and drumming on the canvas
splinter-mattresses; the spray streamed overhead, slashed at icy,
numbed hands and faces, more like chips of ice than wind-driven
water. Wyatt yelled into the funnel-shaped opening of the engine-
room voicepipe, 'Seven hundred revolutions!' Reckoning that if they
were going to cut off those Germans at all they'd be within a few
miles of them by now, and that glowing funnel-tops wouldn't help
Mackerel to get in close: even Germans as blind as that lot must have
eyes for flames coming at them out of the night. Wyatt had shouted, a
minute ago, 'They can't see, so perhaps they can't *fight*, either!'

Guns' and tubes' crews were standing by: there was a chance, no
more than that, and if it came they weren't going to miss it. Not a
bad chance, more than the usual needle in a haystack; the enemy
ships had been steering a northerly course and it was virtually
certain they'd turn westward at some point, that by now they *would
have* turned; and they'd been doing roughly fifteen knots. *Mackerel*
was thundering north-westward at twice that speed, cutting the
corner; if it had been daylight she could have expected to run into
them, she'd have had a lookout up on the searchlight platform to
expand her range of vision and she'd have quite likely had them in
sight by now: by *now*, Nick thought, knowing they could at this
moment be a mile away, no more than a couple of thousand yards
and still invisible. There wasn't time to think about the odds of four
to one, or of having only two guns and one pair of tubes. If it did
cross one's mind one could also think of the four other ships, two
British and two French, just a few miles to the south'ard there; if
Mackerel managed to bring the enemy to action, gunflashes would
very soon bring up reinforcements. But that was something to
consider later, if at all: one thing mattered, one thing was to be
prayed for, and that was to find those four—

302

They found *Mackerel* . . .

An explosion of light: a searchlight: its beam burst in their faces. A great bayonet of light, bomb-like in its suddenness, blinding, mind-stabbing. Guns firing ahead, scarlet spurts in an arc across the bow, funnelling-in on the blinded ship as she rushed towards them.

'*Hit that bloody light!*'

Wyatt's bellow: men blinded, shielding their eyes. Nick was already telling Clover over the navyphone, 'Target that searchlight, rapid independent, *commence!*' It must have been three, four seconds since the light had first stabbed at them and transfixed them. Wyatt roared, 'Open *fire*, Number One!' The foc's'l gun fired before he'd finished the sentence, and *Mackerel* was already being hit repeatedly by the broadsides of the four Germans as they raced westward across her bow. All she could do for the moment was take punishment and use her one gun that could bear. Shellbursts flamed: the reek of cordite swept over and away in the wind: there was a shoot of livid flame on the port side for'ard and a clang as another hit skipped off the foc's'l and ricocheted away without exploding. You could hear shrapnel tearing into the splinter mattresses, battering the superstructure: another crash for'ard, and Nick saw the great spray of the explosion, orange and yellow with expanding points like shooting stars – that one had burst near the capstan, on the centreline. Wyatt was shouting above the din of gunfire and bursting shells and the roar of wind and sea, 'Tubes stand by starboard – I'm turning to port, Number One!'

'Aye aye, sir!' He got on the line to the torpedo gunner. 'We're altering to port. Train tubes starboard and stand by!'

Shells scrunched overhead: *Mackerel* bow-on was a small target, and more were missing than hitting. Then a section of one funnel flared orange, burnt crackling for a moment until the paint had scorched off it, died to a glow of red-hot, wind-fanned metal. Nick had Cockcroft on the gun-control navyphone; he told him, 'We'll be turning to port now and your gun will bear. Rapid independent and pick your own targets, right?' He heard the foc's'l four-inch bang off about its eighth or ninth shot, and at the same moment a tearing crash just below the bridge to port told of another hit. Stink of burning: the back of the bridge seemed to be all flames. Racket tremendous, deafening, shots and explosions and other noise merging into one continuous roar of sound; on the port bow, flames sprang up, danced long enough to silhouette black figures of

German sailors rushing aft along a destroyer's deck. Clover's gun was scoring, then. Nick yelled even louder into the navyphone, 'Sub, are you there, d'you understand?' Cockcroft said yes, he was and he did; he didn't sound as if he was shouting, just chatting rather more loudly than usual; Nick heard cheering, and that torturing light went out, as abruptly as if someone had pulled a fuse. The for'ard gun had hit the searchlight: he found himself waiting for another to take its place. Cockcroft added, 'Couple of chaps 've been hit by splinters, here.' Nick heard Wyatt shout to Bellamy, 'Hard a-starboard, cox'n!' He told Cockcroft, 'Helm's going over *now*.' He banged the 'phone down on its hook and half slid across an already tilting deck to the starboard torpedo sight. The searchlight beam and most of the gunfire had been coming from clear out on the port bow in the last – oh, minutes, seconds, you couldn't reckon time once all this started – so it would probably be the tail-end ships they'd fire their fish at. He lined his binoculars up with the pointers of the sight as *Mackerel* tightened her turn to port; the night was all flying, whistling, scrunching shells and blossoms of flame, thuds and crashes as shells burst and the sharper snapping crashes of *Mackerel*'s own guns firing: Cockcroft's was in it now, and getting hits.

Nick had the torpedo sight set – giving the enemy twenty knots and a course of west. It was a matter of waiting for the turn, for the ship to get round through ninety degrees and the aiming pointers to come on their target, and the hope was that the torpedo would streak out and find a meeting-point with the enemy destroyer. The third in the line of four, he was going for. All she'd have to do, to meet the torpedo which he'd be sending out ahead of her, was continue at her present course and speed. And now most conveniently one of *Mackerel*'s guns scored a hit on that German's stern and started a blaze going . . . But they were pumping shells over this way fast as *Mackerel* swung and exposed her length to them; there'd been a number of hits aft and there was at least one fire burning. Nick shut his mind to it: all that mattered was to get the torpedo on its way. You had to ignore distractions, concentrate on the fighting and cope later with the damage. There'd be plenty, he knew. An explosion just behind and above him threw him forward against the sight, and he thought he'd cut his face open: no time for anything but *Mackerel* swinging and not far to go now, no need for binoculars with the target lit up by her fires: the first one had taken hold and spread. He watched her along the pointers of the torpedo sight while *Mackerel* leaned hard over under helm and the sea crashed against her bow: both guns firing rapidly, using the enemy's blazing stern as an aiming point. *Mackerel* herself still being punished. Men would be dying back there where the German's shells were bursting, and more would be killed and maimed before they got that fish away and turned back out of this storm of high explosive. He was pleading through clenched teeth, *Come on, come on!* He heard Wyatt's shout to the cox'n, 'Midships!' and crouched intently behind the sight, narrowing his eyes against the gun- and shell-flashes; he knew that the after end of the bridge was wrecked and that there'd be frightful damage as well as loss of life and more surgical work than McAllister would be competent to handle; but both guns still fired and the sight came up passing the rearmost enemy: range what, three cables? – and touching now the stern of the target ship, moving on up – flames almost covering her, now – where *Mackerel*'s shells were driving in and bursting. He called Gladwish with the navyphone in his left hand, 'Stand by!'

Then the sight touched the German's for'ard funnel, which was part of the black mass of his bridge; in the second after he'd yelled 'Fire!' he realised that she was slowing and that the fourth ship was closing up on her quite fast. So the torpedo would miss: he'd had the sight set for an enemy speed of twenty, and she wasn't doing twelve now. A shell burst in the side of the bridge just below him: a white sheet of flame shot up vertically, with a thrust and roar of heat that pushed him back and scorched the skin of his face, momentarily blinding him. There was a smell like shoeing horses, and it was his own hair or eyebrows singeing off, but he was at the sight again hearing Wyatt ordering 'Port fifteen!' Somewhere in very recent memory Gladwish had reported 'Torpedo fired . . .' *Mackerel* was swinging back northwards again; it had all been for nothing, for one torpedo that would run out its range and then sink. Another hit close by sent the same whitish-yellow flashing upwards, scorching heat and blast. Slightly aft, to his right; he glanced that way half expecting to see Wyatt dead, the steering gone; but Wyatt was there, rock-like, silhouetted against the fires in the ship's waist and afterpart, and Bellamy sang out in his calm but strident, noise-beating tone, 'Fifteen o' port wheel on, sir . . .'

Turning for what, Nick wondered – to reduce their size as a target for the Hun gunners, or to pass under the last German's stern? There'd been two hits for'ard and now three enemy ships were on the port bow as *Mackerel* swung her stem past them; they were continuing westward while their guns still fired on the after bearing, over their port quarters. The other, the fourth of the line – no, the third, those two had changed places – the destroyer that was on fire was almost right ahead, just fine on the starboard bow; Wyatt yelled at Bellamy, 'Midships, and meet her!' Nick saw it suddenly: *he was going to ram* . . . The foc's'l four-inch was still banging away fast at the already hard-hit enemy, while Cockcroft's gun admidships was lobbing shells after the other three; Nick, wondering if they were getting any hits, had just raised his glasses for a look when the nearest of them – the ship that had originally been number four – blew up in a great gush of flame.

Mackerel's torpedo had missed one, hit another. Wyatt shouted, 'Every shot a coconut! Well done, Number One!' Guns' crews were cheering. Orange flame edged and patterned with black, oily smoke lit the night: the German had been struck abaft the bridge and almost certainly in a fuel tank. She was a torch – no, two torches, two burning halves drifting apart. A roaring sound ripped across the sea: then the sound died with the flames as both halves sank and the water snuffed out everything except oil floating on its surface. Wyatt bawled, 'Stand by to ram!'

The for'ard gun was still banging away and hitting the burning enemy ahead, but it wasn't deterring him from shooting back. But *Mackerel* had some advantage: she was a narrow, bow-on shape, and the German was broadside-on and already much worse hit. One cable's length away now, or even less. Nick leant over the front of the bridge and shouted to the gun's crew, 'Stand by to ram! Lie flat and hold on!' A shellburst drove him back, and at that moment he thought he'd seen Clover, the GM, fall. *Mackerel* was lurching, plunging forward, Bellamy handling the wheel with strength as well as skill, holding her against the thrust of wind and sea, grinning slit-eyed into the wind, his weight to the left to keep weather helm on her and Wyatt shouting in his ear, 'Make sure of it, now, cox'n!' Nick called Cockcroft – the after gun had ceased fire, lacking any target it could bear on – and told him, 'Stand by to ram – pass the word to hold on!' It was the last thing Cockcroft would ever hear from him. The German destroyer lay right ahead, lit by her own fires and with men running for'ard along her upper deck and two guns still firing. She was trying to turn away to starboard but she'd begun the attempt too late: *Mackerel* was rushing at her – a black, battered, flaming missile tearing across broken sea. Just before she struck she seemed to launch herself upward – as if the ship knew what she was doing and wanted to do the job as effectively as possible; then her stem with its underwater ram smashed like an axe-head into the German's side.

As if the world had been jolted off its bearings and stopped dead, and the sky had fallen in, blackness smothering, crushing, and light then springing through the wreckage, yellow leaping light of flames from the burning German with the British ship embedded in her. Some time had passed: moments, or a minute? Moments, probably. He heard, as he scrambled up, Wyatt shouting down to them to stop both engines. Shouts, screaming, and shots – small-arms – and suddenly the crash of the foc'sl four-inch: it had fired at maximum depression but its shell had passed over the German without touching him: he was ridden-down, still going over, under *Mackerel*'s forefoot. Rifle or revolver shots, and something whirred past very close. Looking for its source, Nick saw the flash of another shot, from the German's bridge: then Wyatt had lurched up against him at the front rail, and he was shouting to the gun's crew below them, 'Cutlasses! Cutlasses and bayonets, you men down there! Repel boarders, damn you, don't stand and *watch* 'em!' He'd swung round: 'Bosun's Mate!' The German destroyer was right over, practically on her beam ends and nearly cut in two; men were trying to scramble from her port side to *Mackerel*'s foc'sl. Boarders? Nick looked back over his shoulder for the bosun's mate, Biddulph; but there was no back to the bridge, only a tangle of twisted steel, torn plating, the mainmast's paint smouldering and the foremost funnel riddled, shot through like a colander, hardly enough of it left to hold up; in the remains of the bridge's afterpart Nick saw a foot in a boot with some shinbone sticking out of it, and what might have been the same man's (or another's) shoulder, and a pulpy mess in a Balaclava helmet dangling from something impaled on ribbons of black metal. Biddulph wouldn't be piping 'Hands to repel boarders', or anything else. And Porter, the leading signalman: he'd been at the rear of the bridge, and so must Hatcher have been: they too must be part of that horror-fantasy. Wyatt, leaning over the front of the bridge, was shouting '*Stop* them! *Stop* them!' He was sighting down the barrel of a pistol. Nick saw the coxswain, Bellamy, with his right hand on the wheel still but his left round Pym's shoulders; his face was all blood and you could see the bone of his skull. Pym looked dazed. Wyatt roared. '*At* them! Shoot 'em! Drive 'em back where they belong!' Nick looked down there, saw a group of Germans and some of *Mackerel*'s men rushing at them, and another German sailor coming over the side, climbing over laboriously with his mouth wide open, either screaming something continuously or his face distorted like that by fear: he was right up now, beside the clump cathead, with his hands up; Wyatt took aim, and shot him. Nick saw the man collapse and fall backwards into his own ship's flames. Wyatt was chuckling as he pointed the revolver at some other German, and bellowing encouragement to the men down there to clear the ship of boarders. Nick heard him shout, 'That's the way, young Grant! At 'em, seek 'em out, go *at* 'em!' Grant, that kid? Wyatt had fired again; he shouted, 'You *would*, would you, you damned Hun!' He turned to Nick, grinning happily: 'Here, Number One, want a shot?' Offering him the revolver. Nick didn't want it: Wyatt insisted, 'Here, take it, I've had *my* fun!' Nick, looking down at the mêlée on the foc's'l, saw that the bow seemed to have been forced upwards, out of line: there'd be plates strained and buckled and quite likely underwater damage. He opened his hand, let the revolver drop, turned to see Pym easing Bellamy down on to the deck with his back against the binnacle; Wyatt shouted, 'Pilot, get the Leading Tel up here, and a position from young Grant.' Then he remembered that Grant wasn't in the chartroom, and corrected, 'No – go down and work out a position, and have Wolstenholme send this: *To Moloch, repeated FO Dover and Captain (D) Six, from Mackerel: Have sunk one German destroyer by torpedo and rammed another. My position so-and-so. Two regrettably surviving Huns last seen proceeding westward twenty knots.* Got that?'

'Aye aye, sir!'

'Where are you going, Number One?'

'Below, sir, to inspect the damage for'ard.'

'Damage? What damage?' He'd been preoccupied with his 'fun'. Now he was gazing down at the bow itself, ignoring the few surviving Germans on it. They were being permitted to surrender, apparently. Nick didn't wait. The starboard side of the bridge was smoking, smouldering hot, and the ladder had been shot away; he crossed to the other side and went down the port ladder. There was a jagged-edged rip in the starboard side of the chartroom; inside, everything was smashed. He was looking in through smaller perforations in this near side. It was a miracle that Grant had survived. The wireless office seemed to be intact. Pym grasped Nick's arm: he was staring at what had been a chart-table, charts, instruments: 'How – how *can* I work out a position?'

'Tell them "vicinity No. 8 buoy". That's near enough. *Moloch* will have seen the shooting anyway.'

Pym nodded, as relieved-looking as if Nick had saved his life. Nick thought, *Bloody fool!* He turned aft, found that the ladder down to the iron deck was distorted but useable. The whaler's planks were still burning in the davits: on the other side the 20-foot motorboat was matchwood piled round a charred engine. He was wrenching at the buckled screen door, wanting to get in past the galley and down to the for'ard messdecks; a sailor stopped to help.

McKechnie. Last night they'd been in a different kind of fight together. It might have been a year ago . . . McKechnie added his weight to Nick's and they forced the door back; he asked Nick, 'Did ye know the sub-lieutenant's killed, sir?'

It sank in.

Cockcroft, dead. McKechnie added, 'There's a dozen or more, sir, and a lot wounded too. Back aft it's terrible.' Nick told him, 'Find the doctor, tell him the cox'n's on the bridge with a bad head-wound. Then go up there yourself and tell the captain I've sent you as relief helmsman.'

'Aye aye, sir.'

Memory was to come in fragments: like snapshots, impressions printed on the brain that would probably never leave it. Images, bursts of recorded sound that you heard again afterwards and thought about, glimpses of detail in a broad area of confusion. Important things and utterly unimportant ones – like Chief Petty Officer Swan, when Nick stared at him for a moment hardly knowing who he was, telling him 'I shaved off, sir.'

'I think we've some flooding for'ard. Come on down.' Then a hideous grinding sound, and the nightmarish impression that it was the bow breaking away from the rest of her; but it was the German destroyer rolling over, turning turtle, scraping against *Mackerel's* stem as she slid away and sank, the sea hissing, smacking its lips as it engulfed her and drowned her fires. Nick and Swan and the men on the bridge and foc'sl saw her go, a boil of foam and steam grey through the darkness, and light from that distant oil-slick flickering across the water. Then – suddenly – *Mackerel* lurched: as if she'd been relying on her beaten enemy's support . . . As Nick flung himself up the twisted ladder to the foc'sl he heard Wyatt bellow over the bridge rail, 'Collision mat, there! Get a mat over, *jump* to it now!'

The bow had changed shape: the foc's'l deck from just for'ard of the gun had folded downwards, so that it wasn't a deck anyone could have walked on now, only a sag of steel that groaned and creaked as the ship moved to the sea. Nick told Swan, 'Take charge here. I'm going below.' He saw Grant, and called to him, 'Mid, you come with me.' The snotty said, 'Two of the gun's crew are dead, and the GM's wounded in the stomach.' Nick thought, *Cockcroft's dead, too* . . . Someone had told him so – an hour ago? Cockcroft, with his small eccentricities and his amusing, pleasant manner . . . Grant asked him, pointing, 'What about *them*?' The German survivors: they stood in a close group, some of them frightened-looking and some hostile; two sailors with fixed bayonets faced them. Nick told one, a leading stoker, 'Take 'em below, and keep a guard on them.' He thought as he hurried down the ladder that with any luck the bulkheads down there might hold for a while, so long as Wyatt didn't try to use the engines. He thought, *They've got to, that's all! We've a lot of wounded, and no boats.*

CHAPTER 6

The collision bulkhead was bulging with the pressure of water on the other side of it. This seamen's messdeck with its ranks of scrubbed tables was at the best of times a cramped, gloomy cavern; now, sparsely lit by emergency lamps and with the deck-head crushed downwards and water seeping, it was a trap, coffin-like, echoing to the noise the sea made hurling itself against the thin steel plating, and the frightening racket from the damaged bow. You could imagine the compartment being crushed: the bulkhead splitting, a rush of sea . . . He said, 'Paint locker's flooded. Presumably all for'ard of this point is.' Watson, the commissioned engineer, nodded. 'Dunno about down below. Cable locker, an'—'

'We'll have a look, in a minute. Meanwhile –' Nick looked back at the cluster of tense faces behind him and the engineer – 'we'll get this shored. Allbright?'

'Sir?'

Leading Seaman Allbright squeezed forward, between two seamen. He was thin, young-looking for his leading hand's rate; now he could demonstrate his right to it. Nick told him, 'Get the bulkhead shored. Tables, mess-stools. Send to the Chief Buffer if you want spars or planks. He's on the foc'sl. Right?'

Allbright nodded, running his eye over the job and the men at his disposal. The ship's motion seemed more pronounced down here, and the noise – particularly the clatter and scrape of the ripped stem – added to the sense of danger. Imagination was half the trouble: better if one were bone-headed, solid. White-enamelled bulkheads glistened, ran with condensation; there were leaks from the perimeters of scuttles, dribbles from loose rivets. In bad weather, the for'ard messdecks were never dry. Dirty water, vomit, swept rubbish and gear to and fro across the corticene-covered deck: a shoe, a battered cap, empty cigarette packets, a half-written letter.

311

Stench: and men *lived* in this hole! Watson, his round face almost as white and as shiny as the bulkheads, pushed his cap back with a black-nailed thumb and ran the other oily palm across a dome of forehead. 'See what's what below, then?'

'Yes.' Nick, pushing aft through the crowd of men and with the engineer behind him, heard Allbright starting briskly, cheerfully: 'Right then – clear all this muck aft! Then let's 'ave them two tables flat ag'in the bulk'ead: mess-stools to 'old 'em . . . Jarvie, fetch us 'alf a dozen 'ammicks out o' the nettin' . . . Slap it abaht now, lads!'

Eyes wandering to that for'ard bulkhead. Shoring might strengthen it enough to make it hold. But if it didn't—

If it didn't, the compartment would have to be surrendered to the sea; the next bulkhead that could be shored, after that, would be this one through which they were passing now, leaving the big messdeck and going aft into the leading hands' space. From here a hatchway and steel ladder led down to the stokers' and ERAs' messes.

'Mid.' Nick stopped on the ladder. 'Tell the captain there's flooding for'ard, I'm still checking and I'll report soon as I can. Tell him I'm shoring the collision bulkhead and for the time being will he for God's sake not use the engines. Then come back.'

'Aye aye, sir.' Grant shot away. Nick, followed by the hard-breathing engineer, went on down. At the bottom, he turned for'ard, through the bulkhead door.

This stokers' messdeck was smaller than the seamen's mess above it; at its for'ard end, ten feet short of the collision bulkhead which now one could hear them working at overhead, was an engineer's store. Watson opened its steel door. Dark, wet-smelling, echoing like the inside of a drum; Prior, the stoker PO, peered in over Watson's shoulder. Nick passed him a lamp; they all went inside, and Watson held it up against the suspect bulkhead. He whistled, shook his head, glanced at Nick.

'We're in trouble, all right. An' all the way down, I'd say, would you?'

It was worse here than on the higher deck. The bulge was so pronounced that it looked as if the steel had actually stretched. It wouldn't do that, though; when the strain reached a certain limit, it would split.

Watson banged his heel on the rectangular hatch that led down to a lower store. 'Try it, shall us?'

Nick hesitated. He suggested, 'Leave one clip on, and just crack it.'

'Aye aye.' The engineer knelt down. *Mackerel* was rolling harder than she had been, and erratically; Nick realised she must be beam-on to the south-wester, which in any case was obviously blowing up still. He hoped Wyatt wouldn't be tempted to use the engines to keep her head into it. Watson had freed one of the two butterfly clips; now, squatting, he was using his heel to start the other one.

'God almighty!'

Fighting to screw it down again, with water spurting in a thin, hard sheet . . . 'Purchase-bar!' Watson looked round for help. 'Prior—' A savage lurch of the ship flung him back; Stoker O'Leary pushed in past Prior, jammed a section of steel tubing on one arm of the butterfly clip, wrenched it round; Prior stood on the hatch, and Watson, cursing fluently, joined him. Eventually they had it tight again and the spray of icy, dirty water stopped. Watson was dripping wet; he told Prior, 'Shore this bulkhead and the deck too while you're at it. *Some* bloody 'ow . . . But solid, make it rock 'ard top to bottom, can do?'

'Do me best, sir.' O'Leary, whom Nick remembered seeing in that pub brawl last night, muttered as he got off his knees, 'An' a very *very* happy Christmas to us all.' He got a laugh, for that. Nick went back into the messdeck and asked Grant, 'Did you tell the captain?'

'Yes, sir. He said will you be as quick as you can, please.'

No – I'm trying to give her time to sink . . . 'Chief –' he pointed downwards, as Watson came through and joined him – 'No. 1 oil-fuel's down there, right?' The engineer nodded. 'Well, if there's any leakage to it from the store that's flooded—'

'Wouldn't say it's likely.'

'If there is, there'll be an upward pressure here, this deck we're standing on. Isn't that so?'

'Could be, but—'

'We'll shore it, then.' He staggered, half fell across a mess table as *Mackerel* flung over. Watson, as if he was talking to a horse, 'Whoa-*up*!' He was holding himself upright on the open door. 'Fine time to blow up a force eight, ain't it though . . . 'Ere. Spo –' Prior, he was talking to – 'when you got that done, shore this deck down, right?' He looked around: 'Only joking, lads, it's no force eight.' Nick said, 'Let's check the magazine now.'

Aft through the bulkhead door, and down through the four-inch ammunition hatch to the lobby with shell-room to port and cordite-room to starboard. All dry: and there was no indication of any straining of the bulkhead. On the way up again he said, 'We'll get her back all right, Chief . . . Now what's *this*?'

They were bringing the Germans down. Lister, one of the crew of the foc's'l four-inch, asked him, 'Where'll we keep 'em, sir?' Nick looked at Watson, who suggested, 'Fore peak?' Men laughed: the fore peak was flooded. Nick said, 'ERAs' mess.' Watching them troop aft, Watson answered Nick's remark about getting back: 'Aye. Be all right if he keeps her slow an' steady, and the weather 'olds.'

'It *is* blowing up a bit.'

'Oh aye?' Rubbing his bald head. He'd got it well blackened; all it needed was a polish. 'How far 're we from 'ome, then?'

'About – sixty miles.'

'*That* much?'

Watson looked unhappy. 'Three, four knots is all that bulkhead's goin' to stand. Shored or not shored.' He pushed his cap on again. 'Fifteen, twenty hours – an' blowin' up, you say?'

Wyatt, feet wide apart for stability and an arm crooked round the binnacle, was using binoculars one-handed, whenever the ship was on a more or less even keel, to sweep the black seascape that surrounded them. Beside him McKechnie, feet similarly straddled, clutched the wheel although she was only drifting without steerage way. It was her beam-on angle to wind and sea that was making her this lively; so far it was only quite a moderate blow.

Enough to make that smashed-in stem sound like a busy smithy's shop, though.

'How long?'

'Perhaps another ten minutes, sir.'

He'd left Grant down there, with instructions to keep him and the captain informed, in particular to report when Allbright and Prior were satisfied with their areas of shoring, so that *Mackerel* could go ahead – or try to. Coming up from below a few minutes ago Nick had been disappointed not to find other destroyers standing by; he'd expected that *Moloch* and *Musician* would have found them by this time.

Dark all round: only white foam and wave-crests, close-to, broke up the blackness. The oil-patch must have burnt itself out.

'No signals, sir?'

'Wolstenholme's uncertain of the receiver. Transmitter's all right – so he *says*.'

314

Not so marvellous, Nick realised. He'd been quite confident they'd have had help close by. What if the transmitter was *not* working – if that signal hadn't in fact gone out, and nobody knew anything of what had happened?

'Do you know if he's checked the aerial, sir?'

'Yes.' Wyatt muttered furiously, under his breath, 'Come on, come *on* . . .' He twisted round: 'Reeves?'

'Sir!'

Reeves was the next senior signals rating after Porter. Porter was dead. So were a dozen other men, according to McAllister's preliminary count, and there were more than twenty wounded. Wyatt asked Reeves, 'Have you got a lamp there, and do you know the challenge and reply?'

'Yes, sir, I do.'

'H'm . . .' Studying the compass-card, glancing up to check the wind's direction and the ship's head. 'Coming up stiffer, Number One.'

'I'm afraid so.'

He'd left out the 'sir'. He didn't give a damn for Wyatt, he realised, or for Wyatt's opinion of him. The only thing that mattered was to get this ship back to Dover; for the sake of the men in her, particularly the wounded, and because it was a natural instinct to fight to keep one's ship afloat. Not to please Wyatt, though; *nothing* to please Wyatt.

'Can't they get a damn *move* on, down there?'

'They *are* trying to.' He added, 'Sir.' Wyatt was staring at him across the black, swaying, rackety bridge. 'You said the paint store's flooded?'

'Yes, sir.'

'Then the cable locker—'

'The bulge seems worse at that lower level.'

The collision mat was in place, over the outside of the crumpled bow. Swan had secured it there with steel-wire rope, and it would help, so long as it stayed in place; but with the motion of the sea increasing steadily, and when *Mackerel* went ahead—

The wireless office voicepipe: Nick answered it. Pym reported, 'Signal received from *Moloch*, saying *Use your searchlight to guide me to you*. Leading tel says it was a very faint transmission.'

Nick told Wyatt. It was a relief to know they could receive at all; and that the other signal had gone out. He added, 'Have to be the after searchlight.' This one over the back end of the bridge was part

315

of a tangle of junk which must still have parts of men in it. Daylight would be welcome, if *Mackerel* was still afloat to see it; but it would have its horrors to offer too.

'Have the light switched on, Number One. Point it upwards.'

'Aye aye, sir.' Nick got Gladwish on the voicepipe, and told him what was wanted; the gunner (T) answered flatly, 'Not a chance. Cables are shot away, and we can't rig jury connections until we've some light to work by.'

Nick wondered if he was trying to be funny. The situation seemed to be singularly unamusing. Except for the fact that *Moloch* and others knew *Mackerel* was in trouble and were looking for her . . . Wyatt was calling down to Pym, who seemed to have established himself in the wireless office, 'Pilot, take this down and send it off to *Moloch* repeated Captain (D) and FO Dover: *Have no searchlight working. Am hove-to while shoring collision bulkhead. Intend proceeding south-westward at slow speed shortly.* Got that?'

'Yes, sir . . . Captain, sir?'

'Well?'

'Barometer's falling fast, sir.'

Wyatt snorted angrily as he straightened up. As if it had annoyed him to be given information of that kind. His manner, Nick thought, suggested that he regarded the shoring of the bulkhead as a mere formality, a ritual drill he had to allow before he shrugged it off and shaped a course for Dover. As if he didn't realise that without the support of shores – and well-placed, evenly distributed ones at that – the bulkhead could rip open like a sheet of cardboard: might do so even when it *was* shored . . . But Wyatt perhaps felt superior to this kind of detail: his prayers had been answered, he'd met the raiders and sunk two of them – on his own, with no senior officer present to claim a share of the glory. He'd be expecting a DSO and a brass hat; he'd have liked now to be steaming proudly into Dover – not drifting, crippled, in a rising sea.

'Everard.'

'Sir?'

'Go down and see what's happening. Tell 'em I'm giving 'em five more minutes and not a second longer!'

Nick hesitated.

'Do you mean that, sir?'

A bull-roar: '*What?*'

316

'If the shoring's not done, would you risk carrying-away the bulkhead?'

Wyatt was a black mass hunched, head forward over massive shoulders, eyes gleaming in the binnacle's small light. McKechnie's head was turned towards him too. The questioning of orders was not an everyday occurrence. Nick added, 'We've only the Carley floats, and two dozen wounded men. If the bulkhead goes—'

'Everard!'

'Sir.'

'Do what I told you. Go down and tell 'em to get a damn wriggle on!'

'Aye aye, sir.'

Climb-down. Nick thought, *He won't love me for it*. But what difference, for God's sake, did that make . . . 'Everard.'

'Yes, sir?' He stopped at the top of the ladder, clung to the rail as *Mackerel* rolled and shipped green water that swamped across her gun'l and exploded against the bridge's battered side, swirled, came pouring out of the holed chartroom and over the side again as she hung for a moment and then flung herself the other way. You didn't need a barometer to tell you what was happening with the weather. Wyatt said, 'By daylight we may have a full gale on our hands. In the state we're in, we couldn't stand it. So we have no option but to make port at our best speed and as soon as possible. Understand?'

Best speed?

How much warning would one get of the bulkhead bursting? Time enough to evacuate the messdeck and the lower – stokers' – deck? He didn't think so. If it went there'd be a split and a sudden rush of sea . . . Might the answer be to finish this shoring operation and then clear everyone out from between the two bulkheads, shore up the second one as well?

He thought about it on his way below, weighing pros and cons. Grant met him in the leading hands' mess. 'Just about done, sir, except for the deck down there.' The midshipman was pale, ill-looking. Nick thought, *Poor little bastard* . . . He put a hand on his shoulder: 'Let's take a look.'

Wyatt staggered, caught off-balance as he moved to answer the wireless office voicepipe; he fetched-up in the corner of the bridge like a drunk colliding with a fence. 'Bridge!'

Pym reported, 'There's been a signal from the West Barrage

317

patrol, sir. They met two enemy destroyers and damaged one by gunfire, both last seen retiring north-eastward at high speed.'

'What ships are on West Barrage?'

'*Swift* and *Marksman*, sir – but *Attentive, Murray, Nugent* and *Crusader* are close by in the Downs.'

It was surprising that the Germans had pressed through that far, after losing half their force up here. The Hun raids were aimed at quick and easy killings with no losses to themselves, the 'fox in the hen-run' technique. This time, the foxes had got bloody noses.

Nick hauled himself off the ladder into the bridge. His seaboots were heavy, full of water; he'd timed his sortie from the screen door up on to the foc's'l badly, and a sea had caught him in the open, on that lower ladder.

He saw Wyatt at the voicepipe. Pym's voice was a faint gabble in the tube; Wyatt yelled, 'What's that?' The navigator told him, 'Signal just coming through from *Moloch*, sir, addressed to us.' Wyatt, holding himself at the voicepipe with an arm hooked round its top, the other hand grasping the bridge rail, shuffled his bulk around and stared towards Nick: 'Number One?'

'Yes, sir. The shoring's complete, as good as we can make it. Mr Watson's view is the bulkhead should stand up to a speed of three or even four knots, sir.'

He'd thought that to quote the engineer would be the best way to make the point about low speed. Wyatt wouldn't want *his* opinion.

'That's his *view*, is it . . . Yes, pilot?'

'From *Moloch*, sir: *I will continue to search for you. Are you under way yet?* That's the signal, sir.'

'Make to him: *Proceeding now course west-sou'-west*.' Wyatt straightened. 'How's her head, McKechnie?'

'North sixty west, sir!'

'Starboard ten, then.'

'Starboard ten, sir.' How she'd steer, with her bow askew as it was, remained to be seen. Wyatt, back at the binnacle now, called down to the engine-room, 'Mr Watson?'

'Sir?'

'I'm about to go ahead, Chief. I'll start at one hundred revolutions and work up to two-fifty.'

Ten knots?

'Sir –' hearing the engineer's instant reaction, Nick could imagine the alarm on his pallid, oil-smeared face – 'sir, that collision bulkhead—'

318

'Chief, I'm sick to *death* of being told about that bloody bulkhead! Slow ahead, one hundred revolutions!'

'One hundred revs, sir, aye aye!'

Wyatt might reconsider that intention, Nick thought, when he saw the sea's force on the damaged area for'ard. The man wasn't mad, he couldn't *want* to sink her . . . The turbine's low drone was a welcome sound, a stirring of life and purpose; the last hour's helpless wallowing had been far from pleasant.

'One hundred and twenty revs!'

'One-two-oh revolutions, sir!' Watson's acknowledgement came as a wail, a cry of despair from the ship's steel guts. Nick told himself *Imagination* . . . He raised his glasses, watched the movement of her stem against the background of white breaking sea; she seemed to be answering her helm quite normally, swinging steadily round to port. But the turning motion involved pushing that damaged bow against the resistance of the sea, adding the ship's own movement to the weather's force. He watched closely; he could *feel* the impact, the thudding jars crashing against split plating – and worse, forcing *in*, into the already flooded 'watertight' spaces and the cable-locker and paint store: already the pressure on the shored bulkhead would have increased considerably.

Wyatt too was angling his binoculars downward, watching the ship's stem. Nick heard him ask McKechnie, 'How's her head?'

'Just passing west, sir.'

'Ease to five.'

'Ease to five, sir . . . Five of starboard wheel on, sir.'

'Still swinging?'

McKechnie checked the lubber's line's movement round the card. 'Aye, a little, sir.'

'Bring the wheel amidships when you've ten degrees to go. And steady on south-sou'-west.'

'Aye aye, sir.'

The point being that she was turning so readily to port, and she might need compensating helm for the distortion for'ard, starboard rudder to keep her on a straight course. She was rolling less and pitching more as she came round closer to wind and sea. It wasn't good at all, that pitching. Wind, Nick estimated, about force four, rising five. *Rising* . . . If you had a huge net – say a single section of mine-net as the drifters handled it, which would be a hundred yards long and thirty feet deep – and filled it with scrap-

319

iron and then swung it from a crane against a solid wall time and time again, that would be something like the noise the sea was making against *Mackerel*'s bow. So what would it be *doing* to the bow, he wondered, and what must it be sounding like to the men who were watching the shores down there?

'Captain, sir.'

'Well?' Wyatt kept his glasses at his eyes. Nick said, 'I'd like to go down and see how the shoring's holding up.'

'Go on, then.' Wyatt bent to the voicepipe. 'One hundred and fifty revolutions!'

They'd brought some of the tables aft, out of the for'ard messdeck, to use them as bases for the shores on this second line of defence. They were working on it now, here in the leading seamen's mess and, at the foot of the steel ladder one deck down, the leading stokers'. CPO Swan had taken charge; the faces of the bulkheads were lined with upended mess tables, and hammocks placed to cushion the butt-ends of benches and spars which, with their other ends jammed against angle-bars and centre-line stanchions, held the tables firmly against the flat steel surface. Not too hard, because there was no pressure yet – hopefully never would be – on the other side of it . . . Planks had been criss-crossed where space didn't allow for tables. Swan shouted, over the fantastic volume of sound, 'That's all me timber, sir. The lot.' In the confined, below-deck spaces, the Chief Buffer looked bigger than ever; and without his beard, quite a different character.

Nick went into the stokers' messdeck. It looked something like a shaft of a coal-mine, only with more pit-props than any mine would have; Prior had hammered wedges in at deckhead level to jam spars down on to upturned tables that covered practically every square foot of deck. Now he was squatting on the sill of the door to the engineer's store at the compartment's for'ard end. He stood up, as Nick joined him.

'How are things here?'

He meant the shoring inside the store. Prior ushered him in to see for himself.

'Needs watchin' all the time, sir. You'd think nothing 'd shift it, wouldn't you, but – well, it's this pitchin' does it, the ends of the shores seem to keep slidin', sort o' – look, see there?' He used his mallet to knock it back. 'Wouldn't 've thought it, would you, sir? See it slide, did you?'

'Could you brace the feet from below?'

'If we 'ad more spars, I could.' Prior shook his close-cropped greying head. He had a reddish face, black-stubbled now, and very calm, steady eyes. The noise here in the store was appalling, to most people it would have been almost unendurable, but it didn't seem to bother him. He shouted, 'Chief Buffer's brought out all 'e's got, 'e *says*.' One eye winked. 'Not my part o' ship, sir, I can't tell.' He turned away, watching the shores again, mallet ready, as *Mackerel* plunged and shook. 'Be all right, sir, long as I'm 'ere wi' this.' He meant the mallet. And he was alone here, with the shored-up messdeck a dark and uninhabited cavern behind him; if the bulkhead gave way, the odds were he'd never reach the one aft, the one they were shoring now.

Nick said, pitching his voice up high, 'I'll ask for someone to relieve you presently. Every half-hour, say, watch and watch?'

Prior smiled. 'I'm quite 'appy, sir. We done a right good job on 'er, sir, don't you worry.'

Nick doubted whether it was a job to make anyone 'happy', hammering in shores as the ship's jolting shifted them, watching that bulkhead that had a whole sea's force only needing a bit of elbow-room on the other side of it – and the noise, the deafening metallic crashing, crashing . . . He was on his way aft and up to the other messdeck, and he found it much the same except that it was only the for'ard bulkhead, not the deck, that was shored; in spite of being stove-in at its for'ard end where the deckhead caved downward it seemed less gloomy, less of the trap-feeling about it. Grant had come into the messdeck behind him; he shouted, thin-voiced, 'Seems to be holding up, sir.'

Grant seemed to be holding up, too. Perhaps he'd just been sick; one always felt better, for a while. He was up close to the bulkhead now and he could see where a spar or two had shifted; by this time Prior would have knocked them back into position, but Allbright didn't seem to have noticed the change. Nick asked him, shouting above the din, 'Those need tightening, don't they?'

'What's that, sir?'

Allbright looked dead tired. Dark rings under hollow, dull eyes, and face thinner, paler than ever. Nick shouted in his ear, 'Time you had a rest, Allbright.'

'*Rest*, sir?'

The killick smiled. He seemed drugged, stunned – by the noise, perhaps – and puzzled at the suggestion that he might take a breather from this job of keeping sentry-go against the sea. Grant made an offer: 'I'll take over, for a spell.'

He took the mallet out of the leading seaman's hands, and began to knock the shores back into their original positions. Nick yelled, 'I'll send someone along, in a minute.' Allbright objected, 'Look, sir, *I* can—' Grant shouted, with his eyes fixed on the shore he was about to belt, 'Leave me to it, I'm perfectly all right.'

Nick took Allbright aft. He told Swan, 'Midshipman Grant wants a turn at the bulkhead. Give him half an hour, then have someone relieve him.'

'Aye aye, sir.' Swan peered for'ard through the shadowed messdeck. He glanced at Nick. 'Not the most salubrious of spots, sir.'

'You looked better with your beard, Buffer.' *Mackerel* was rising, rising: it was time she stopped and came down the other side. Here in the half-light, enclosed, ears ringing with the noise and mind full of what could happen at any moment and what could or could not be done to counter it, surrounded by men whose eyes were either alarmed or carefully controlled into showing *no* alarm as they watched the bulkheads and the props they'd placed – props which, in comparison with the weight and power of the sea out there, were really matchsticks – you could visualise the ship suspended on a wave-crest, hanging, tilting ready for the great rushing plunge: and then the feel of her moving, the downward slide, accelerating, falling almost as if through air not sea, and as suddenly brought-up hard, her bow deep in the next oncoming wave, sea rolling white and green, high, right over her, drowning the foc'sl gun and exploding in a mountain of foam against the foreside of the bridge superstructure: you heard it, felt it, knew that it had been the first big one of the night and that before long they'd be coming bigger.

Swan asked him, 'Don't really say so, do you, sir?'

Nick yelled back, 'I'd grow it again, if I were you.'

The flurry of sea ahead as *Mackerel* ploughed into it was all the wilder because of her misshapen bow; instead of a stem slicing knife-like into the waves it was a partly flattened, unwieldy mess of steel that smashed instead of cut, bludgeoned instead of lanced. From the bridge one looked down on a mass of white, a huge lathering that surrounded, smothered and moved with the ship, rose up around her as she wallowed into the troughs and fell away

322

again as she climbed the slopes. Through the froth solid seas, piles of black water, rolled like battering-rams, racing aft and bursting against the gun and superstructure, cannoning by and cascading aft on to the iron deck, boiling around the torpedo-tubes, ventilators and the bases of the funnels. Down below, one had been conscious mostly of the pitching, because that was the greatest danger to the shoring, with water hurling itself to and fro inside the flooded area; up here one realised that the weather was on the bow and she'd got into her familiar corkscrew action: bow up, roll port, bow down, roll starboard ... You could look down on that seesawing, foam-covered foc'sl and mentally see right into it, see the timber reinforcements to the bulkheads, the messdecks like narrow, ringing tunnels, and the men waiting, trying not to eye the bulging steel too often ... Wyatt moved, as if he'd suddenly become aware of his first lieutenant's presence.

'Satisfied with your shores, Number One?'

'Holding all right at the moment, sir.' He added, 'But the motion's tending to dislodge them, we're having to keep a close eye on it.'

'Naturally. But so long as it *is* holding—'

He was leaning towards the voicepipe, the tube to the engine-room. Nick, seeing the movement blurred by darkness, said quickly, 'With respect, sir, it might be premature to—'

'You're like an old woman, Number One!' Wyatt shouted, 'Engine-room!'

'Engine-room!'

'Two hundred revs, Chief!'

Wyatt straightened. He told Nick, 'That's revs for six or seven knots, Number One.' Pointing at the sea. 'We'll be making good – what, three?' He nodded. 'We'll do better, by and by. I'm going to berth this ship in Dover on Christmas Day – we'll have our evening meal alongside, d'you hear?'

What one heard was the rise in the turbines' note as they came up to the ordered speed. From one-fifty to two hundred revolutions per minute meant a third more thrust, a third more pressure on the bulkhead. Christmas Day? It *was* Christmas Day, it had been for the past hour. What did that have to do with seamanship and common sense? Wyatt shouted, 'Your fears, Number One – or Mr Watson's – are unjustified. I've been at sea in destroyers a great deal longer than you have. You might remember that, eh?'

'Yes, sir.' He wondered, as he watched the sea battering her

323

stem, whether it would be practicable and helpful to lighten her for'ard, so the bow would float higher and take less punishment. But there was really only the ammunition that one could shift. One might empty the for'ard shellroom and magazine, move the stuff aft or ditch it? The only other movable heavy weight was the cable, and that was inaccessible. Wyatt bellowed, 'Watch your steering, helmsman!'

'Aye aye, sir, but she's—'

'Pilot!'

He'd lurched over to the wireless-office voicepipe. Pym answered, and he told him, 'Make this signal to *Moloch: Happy Christmas. Am steering sou'-sou'-west at revs for seven knots. Owing to weather conditions regret may be late for turkey and plum pudding.* Got it?'

'Yes, sir!'

'Send it, then. Repeated Captain (D) and FO Dover.'

'Aye aye, sir. And a happy Christmas to you, sir!'

Wyatt groped back, chuckling, to the binnacle. Good humour faded abruptly as he checked the compass-card.

'McKechnie, d'you want to lose your rate? I said *watch your steering!'*

'Aye aye, sir. Sorry, sir. Only she's been gettin' a wee bit cranky. There's a change, sir, she's—'

'Rubbish, man! Just watch what you're doing!'

'Aye aye, sir!'

Then the bulkhead went.

CHAPTER 7

It went with a thump, heavy like a big gun firing, and a jolt that shuddered through the fabric of the ship. For about a second as he cannoned into Wyatt, Nick thought *Mackerel* had struck a sand-bank. Then he realised.

Wyatt had been flung against the binnacle. He'd recovered and he was yelling hoarsely into the voicepipe, 'Stop both engines!'

Nick had a vision of the bursting bulkhead as he threw himself down the port-side ladder and a sea broke on him, round him – it was thunderous, shoulder-deep. . . He had to stop, cling to the side rails of the ladder, wondering if they'd hold and if his arms would; he couldn't feel his hands, and the sea was over his head for a moment then dragging at him, like a live creature sucking at his body with its mouth, clawing tentacles of ice. Then the ship rolled hard to starboard, the sea let go of him and he was down, diving for the head of the next ladder, clambering down it, blind from cold and the sting of salt and the wind's black cutting edge, but the impulse to get down there making all of this trivial and inconsequential. He found the screen-door and blundered in, slipping on wet, slimy corticene, hurrying for'ard while *Mackerel* flung herself sideways and shot up, up . . . Tilting, now, bow-down; a crowd of men surged round him.

'We goin' to stay afloat, sir?'

'Of course. And by daylight there'll be other ships standing by us.' The words, the reassurance, came almost without thought as he pushed for'ard and the men let him through: he heard a cheer. Through the chiefs' and petty officers' messes, and the leading seamen's: the bulkhead door ahead of him was shut and in the process of being shored, all the other shores were in place and wedges were being driven in to brace them harder. Midshipman Grant said desperately, 'CPO Swan, sir – he's – he took over in there and—'

Mackerel plunged, digging her stricken forepart into the sea and at the same time sliding to port, a sideways slither with a rapid accompanying roll to starboard. Doing circus tricks, now; the men on the shores were having to stop work, cling to anything nearby and solid for support: one was vomiting. Grant had stopped whatever he'd been saying because he'd been hurled sideways and lost his footing: an OD, Jarvie, was hauling him up again.

'Chief Buffer was up the fore end, sir.' Trew, Able Seaman, layer of the stern four-inch, jerked a thumb towards the bulkhead. Little Grant's face was the colour of watered milk, it had that faintly blueish look; he gabbled, 'He'd just come along and said I'd – "done my spell", he said, *he'd* take a turn at it . . . I'd just got back here, literally *just—*'

'All right, Mid, all right.' Swan's death was a tragedy in ordinary human terms; in more practical ones the loss of a highly experienced and able seaman and NCO was as great a blow. Swan was – had been – a linchpin in the ship's strength and capability; to cope now, without him, would be just that much more difficult. Nick was studying the shoring. 'Looks solid enough here, Trew.'

'So did the other, sir.'

Nick scowled at him. *Mackerel* was climbing up another sea-mountain. He said, 'We're hove-to, now. There'll be much less pressure. Just keep your eyes on it; and if anything shifts or looks like shifting – well—'

Dropping: tilting over and rolling to starboard, like a barrel in a mill-race, and the thunder of big seas smashing down overhead. Trew nodded: 'Aye aye, sir.' He was a good hand, but unimaginative. Nick dropped down the ladder to the stokers' deck. It was the same scene here: door shut and being shored, the other shores being strengthened. Stoker Petty Officer Prior was in charge.

'You all right, Prior?'

'Not like up top, sir. It begun there, so we got warnin'. I was up for'ard, in the store there, I 'eard 'er goin' an' I run like 'ell.'

'Well done . . . Sure it is flooded, though, at this level?'

Prior rubbed his jaw. 'Care to go in an' see, sir?'

Men chuckled. Nick said, 'You mean it *is*.'

'It bloody *chased* me, sir!' More laughter; he added, 'She split right down.'

'Magazine?'

Prior glanced down at the hatch, right at their feet with its clamps screwed down tight. He shook his head. 'Don't like to open

326

up, sir, not really. But there's the oil for'ard; I reckon that might sort of cushion it, sir, I mean the bulkhead, 'old it firm d'you think?'

'Have you tried pumping?'

'On the – magazine . . .' Prior banged his forehead with a fist. 'I'm goin' *stupid* . . .' Glancing round: 'O'Leary! Where's that Irish—'

'Here, Spo . . .'

Nick left them to it, and went up again. To say he was glad he'd decided to shore this second bulkhead would have been to put it mildly. If he hadn't, *Mackerel* would be on the seabed now, and most of these men would be dead. Perhaps they all would; not only because she'd have gone instantaneously as the sea burst through her, but because in water close to freezing-point you couldn't hope to stay alive for longer than a quick Lord's Prayer.

He saw Grant, and considered sending him up to Wyatt with a report on the situation. But Wyatt might try to go ahead again, once he knew the flooding had been contained. Only a lunatic would try it; but Wyatt had, Nick thought, been showing signs of lunacy. He was obstinate, and basically – incredibly, for a comparatively young and well-thought-of destroyer captain – basically *stupid*. He'd want to prove his point: or something . . . And little Grant couldn't argue with him. Besides which he, Nick, couldn't stay down here, out of touch with what was going on; and it was as well that an officer of sorts should be here . . . He wondered what Gladwish was doing: he couldn't surely be on the tubes still, with the upper deck almost continuously under water.

Prior heaved himself up the ladder, hung on to the top of it through a savage roll . . .

'She's dry, sir. The magazine and shell-room – dry as a bone!'

'Thank God for small mercies . . . But now keep the hatch shut tight, eh?'

To have shifted the ammunition aft would make so little difference, now, in comparison with the hundreds of tons of water in the forepart of the ship, that it wouldn't be worth the work involved. Whereas keeping that space battened-down would maintain it as a pocket of air-pressure against any thrust from the oil-fuel tank for'ard of it. And it had the support, aft, of the second fuel tank, the after end of which was the for'ard bulkhead of No. 1 boiler-room. You couldn't shore that one, first because there was such a huge area of it and virtually no shoring materials left to work with, second because the for'ard pair of boilers were only about eighteen inches clear of it. There'd be no room either for shoring or for men to work there.

In other words, *this* bulkhead had to hold. If it didn't *Mackerel* would go to the bottom.

Trew said, 'Never knew a ship could roll so. Never . . .' He was flattened against the destroyer's port side, the curved steel of her hull, which for the moment had swapped places with the deck. Now she was whipping back the other way . . . Nick wondered whether it would be possible, by going slow astern on both screws, to hold her stern to the sea. It might be, he thought, if the rudder could hold her, if the force of the sea didn't constantly drive her off. But the waves would break right on her, they'd pile clear over her low stern and crash down on to the quarterdeck and iron deck, and they'd leave nothing there, everything would be swept away or flattened: but the hell with that, if it kept her afloat, at least until some other ship was standing by . . . He was thinking, he realised, as if he was *Mackerel*'s captain rather than her first lieutenant. The decisions weren't his to make. And it was high time now to be getting back up there and telling her real captain what had been happening down here.

'Grant – I'm going up to the bridge. I'll be back later, I expect.'

'Right, sir.'

He looked round. *Mackerel* was standing on her stern end, wallowing for a moment before the weight of the bow took charge and brought it crashing down like a great hammer . . . He told them, as that motion checked and she began to sway to port and rise again, 'We'll be all right now. We'll have our Christmas in a day or two. We'll have a devil of a good one to make up for all this, right?'

They cheered him, or the thought of Christmas. He was staring at the bulkhead. Swan was somewhere on the other side of it. Drowned. Washing to and fro.

Wyatt shouted, clutching the bridge rail with Nick beside him, 'When did you shore the second bulkhead?'

'Soon after the first, sir.'

After you'd said something about 'making our best speed' . . .

He waited, but Wyatt had no further questions or comments, apparently. He'd already concurred with the proposal to try her stern-on to the sea with engines slow astern, or as slow astern as might do the trick; they were waiting for Mr Gladwish and his torpedo gunner's mate to reach the bridge.

Wyatt leant sideways, to the wireless office voicepipe. Nick moved, to give him elbow room, but he made sure of not letting go. One slip, and a man could be over the rail and nobody'd even see him go: this bridge was something like a soaped saddle on a crazy horse. Wyatt shouted, 'Pilot!'

'Sir?'

'Take down a signal—'

He'd lifted his head from the tube as *Mackerel* wallowed over almost on her beam-end: she was hanging there as if she hadn't quite made up her mind whether to finish the whole thing off, go right over and be done with it. It was almost a surprise when she recovered and started to roll back. Wyatt dictated to Pym, 'To *Moloch*, repeated usual authorities: *I am hove-to and unable to proceed owing to extensive flooding forward. Request assistance at first light. Have twenty men wounded and both boats were destroyed earlier.* Send that off, right away.'

'Aye aye, sir!'

So now they'd know, Nick thought. It was as if Wyatt had only just begun to appreciate their predicament! Well, better late than never: and at the price of one life, Swan's . . . He saw Gladwish arriving in the bridge, with the lanky shape of CPO Hobson behind him. They'd been on the searchlight platform all this time; so far as Gladwish was concerned, the ship was at action stations, and nobody had told him until now to leave his.

Wyatt shouted, 'Hobson, you're acting cox'n.'

'Aye aye, sir.' A tall man, slow-moving and heavy-jawed, Hobson clawed his way in a bent position across the wet, gyrating bridge to take over the steering from McKechnie. At the moment, with the ship lying stopped, there was no steering to be done. Nick told McKechnie, 'And you're acting buffer. If anyone's kind enough to offer us a tow, at daylight, you'll have your work cut out.'

'Aye, sir.' The Glaswegian laughed as he fetched-up against the rail and clung to it. 'Be a lark, gettin' a line out in *this*!'

He was right, Nick thought, it would be. But you could only deal with one situation at a time; and in any case someone would have to find them first – find them still afloat . . . He heard Wyatt calling down to the engine-room, 'Is that you, Mr Watson?'

'Aye, sir!'

329

'I'm going to try her slow astern on both engines, Chief, and see if we can hold her stern to the weather.'

'Ready when you are, sir!'

'All right, then. Slow astern together!'

Leaning across Hobson, peering at the compass-card . . . 'Port fifteen, TI.'

'Port fifteen, sir.' The voicepipe squawked, 'Both engines going slow astern, sir!' Hobson said, 'Fifteen o' port wheel on, sir.'

It meant the rudder was angled fifteen degrees to starboard of the centre-line. As the ship had stern-way on, or would have at any moment, her bow should swing to port. Wyatt and Hobson both craned over the binnacle, watching the card and the lubber's line.

'She's not answering, sir.' The TI's voice was deep, gravelly, rather like Skipper Barrie's. Wyatt called down the pipe to the engine-room, '*Half* astern port!'

'Half astern port, sir!'

You could hear it now, the hum of the turbines through the louder but irregular buffeting of wind, the crash of seas . . . 'Port engine half astern, sir, starboard *slow* astern!'

McKechnie, staggering sideways as the ship rolled, crashed into Reeves, the signalman . . . 'Sorry, Bunts!'

'She's coming round, sir.' Relief in Hobson's tone. *Mackerel* wasn't only turning, though, she was climbing, pointing her broken snout at the sky. Nick asked Reeves, 'Still got your lamp?' He had. Wyatt shouted at the TI, 'I want her steadied on north-east, so her stern's into the south-wester. Understand?' Hobson checked the compass, and acknowledged, 'Aye aye, sir, steady on north-east, sir . . .' She was level-keeled for one long moment, balanced along a crest of white: then her bow was falling as she went into a long headlong rush ending in the fast, hard roll to starboard. She was halfway round now, with wind and sea driving at her starboard quarter; Wyatt told the engine-room, 'Slow astern both engines!'

'Slow astern both, sir!'

Hobson was still holding all the helm on, though . . . Nick proposed to Gladwish, 'Like to pay them a visit down below, at the shored bulkhead?' A sea came hurtling from astern, rose mountainous, black with white edging, white feathers streaming from it: it loomed higher as it caught the ship up, gathered size and weight, threatening anything that floated, anything in its way: then it crashed down, the size of a house, exploded where the stern gun would have been. *Mackerel* was floundering with her stern buried in black sea and leaping foam, and Nick was thinking of the men aft, the wounded in McAllister's care in the wardroom and his own cabin and the captain's; it wouldn't take many seas like that one to smash the after superstructure and sweep it overboard, and then there'd be only the hatchway with its lid of not-so-heavy steel covering the top of the wardroom ladderway.

And if *that* went . . .

Gladwish yelled, 'Won't long be dry aft!'

It wasn't dryness or wetness, mere discomfort, that Nick was thinking of. It was flooding, swamping. If *Mackerel* was going to get pooped like that every other minute – or several times a minute—

'Say you want me down for'ard?'

Nick nodded, put his mouth closer to the gunner's ear. 'And you might send young Grant up for a breather. Tell him I want to hear from him how it's going.'

'Aye aye—'

'Mind how you go!'

Gladwish growled as he moved to the ladder, scuttling crablike across the tilting bridge, 'Teach y' grannie . . .'

It would help that both screws were at slow astern now. If she could be held like this, with the lowest possible revs, just enough so she'd answer her helm and lie stern-on . . . Wyatt was of the same mind, Nick realised thankfully; he'd just called down, as Hobson was easing his helm, 'Stop starboard!' The less resistance the ship offered to the sea, the less thrust of her own, the easier she'd ride, the fewer missiles like that last one would smash down on her stern . . . He heard CPO Hobson report, 'Course north-east, sir!'

It would be surprising if just one screw would hold her. And thinking ahead – if they were taken in tow eventually, it would have to be stern-first: and *then* there'd be some seas pounding over that low counter.

He was thinking ahead too far, perhaps. The weather might have eased, by then . . . Nick delved through layers of wet protective clothing, found a handkerchief and used it to clean the lenses of his binoculars. Hobson was being hard-worked at the wheel, fighting hard with the rudder first one way and then the other to hold her as she lay; the fact that she was down by the bows meant that her stern rode higher, was more exposed to wind and waves trying to push her round. Wyatt was watching the compass, his wet face glistening bluish as he leant over in its pale light. Now he was moving to the voicepipe.

331

'Slow astern *both* engines!'

Nick began to study the bow through his binoculars. There was no visible change . . . Except that the water seemed calmer ahead. There was less of it breaking, less white showing than elsewhere; the calmer area seemed to be spreading out ahead of the ship, a broadening 'V' leading from her bow and fading outside the range of visibility.

The reason for it struck him suddenly. Oil – from the for'ard tank.

'Looks as if we're leaking oil, sir.' He pointed. Wyatt put his glasses on it. Now he'd gone back to the engine-room voicepipe.

'Chief – No. 1 fuel tank's leaking to the sea. You'd better shut it off.'

Nick heard Watson tell him it *was* shut off, that he'd done it as a precaution some time ago. His tone wasn't complacent, only reporting fact.

'Very good, Chief.'

But it wasn't good *at all* . . . It meant that, whether oil was leaking directly outboard or through the other flooded compartments in the bow, sea-pressure, wave-pressure, would be acting on the oil still inside the tank. So the bulkhead's lower section, to the magazine and shell-room which it had not seemed possible – or necessary – to shore, had the same force on it now from for'ard as the higher, shored part had. Nick felt a sudden tightening in his gut as this truth hit him and he realised there was a weak point in the defences he'd established, a back door left unguarded. The ammunition space had been dry when they'd put the pump to work, and he'd thought no more about it; now it might be flooded, or even if it wasn't it could become so at any moment – and it was *on the wrong side of the shored bulkhead*. The next break could be upwards into the stokers' accommodation space – where not one but twenty men would be trapped – or aft to No. 2 oil-fuel and the boiler-room . . .

'Number One, sir?'

Grant's pale face peered up at him.

'All right, Mid?'

'Yessir. Shores are all holding, and there don't seem to be any problems.'

'Has Petty Officer Prior been watching the magazine?'

'Not particularly that I *know* of—'

Grabbing for support, as she rolled . . . And now she was

digging her bow deep into the sea and wriggling, shaking like an up-ended duck. One thought of those flooded compartments, of the way the sea would surge through them, the pressures . . . Nick moved up the side-rail of the bridge until he was level with Wyatt at the binnacle.

'Captain, sir. Grant's here, if you need him. He says all's well below, but I'd like to go down and take a look.'

Wyatt had his glasses up. He didn't lower them; he yelled, 'Go on, then!'

'I thought I'd go aft, too, and see how McAllister's managing.'

'Very good . . . We must be losing the devil of a lot of oil there, Number One.'

He hurried, falling over himself to get down there quickly, rushing past Gladwish and down to the lower level. Prior seemed surprised by the urgency with which he put the question.

'Still dry, sir. I 'ad the pump runnin' not five minutes ago, and there's not a spoonful in there. I reckon she'll 'old up now, sir.'

The sense of relief was enormous; but it didn't last. There was a decision to be made now: to open up the magazine and try to shore it with such bits and pieces as were left to them, or keep the hatch shut tight and trust to providence.

Did one have any right to trust to anything except what one knew *should* be done? He asked Prior, 'If we got all the shells and cordite out and ditched it, could you make the timber of the racks into shores?'

'No, sir, I don't think so.' Prior shook his head. In the last couple of hours his stubble had developed into what was almost a beard; and while the first sprouting had seemed black, it had now turned out to be grey, to match his head. He said, 'All short sections, ain't it? An' too light, sir, any road. If you was askin' me, sir, I'd say leave well alone.'

The trouble was that with a fuel tank abaft it – No. 2 – if you didn't shore the magazine you couldn't shore at all. Nick felt the right way to go about this, the *thorough* way, would be to get down inside there and shore it up solid. Against that, however, was the fact they hadn't any materials; they'd lined and strutted two whole bulkheads and there was hardly a stick of timber or a mess-stool left.

'All right. We'll leave it.'

'I'll watch 'er, sir.'

Fat lot of good *watching* it would do.

333

'Don't run the pump more than you have to.' One wanted pressure in there, not a vacuum. He didn't feel at all easy about it, as he went up the ladder to the killicks' mess. Trew said cheerfully, 'Feels better, sir. Weather easing, is it?'

Nick shook his head. 'Just that we're riding stern-to, for the moment.' Men were sprawled about on the deck dozing, propped against bulkheads chatting, playing card-games. Unshaven, dirty-looking, a crowd of thugs . . . He felt his own jaw, heavily stubbled too, and he knew there was caked blood on his face from that collision he'd had, heaven knew how many hours ago, with the torpedo sight. He realised he must look as rough as any of them. Gladwish's eyes were red-rimmed, probably from his long ordeal on the searchlight platform; he had the look of a mad dog, Nick thought. He said, 'I sent three 'ands to the galley to knock up bully sandwiches an' tea. We'll let you 'ave some on the bridge, if you're p'lite to us.'

'How about aft, the wounded?'

'Well, they got the wardroom galley!'

'Not much in it for all that crowd.' Nick shrugged. 'Shouldn't think so. I'll let you know, anyway.'

He hoped they might be self-sufficient aft there, because it wouldn't be easy to get food and drink to them, carrying it over a deck that was behaving as *Mackerel*'s was now, rising and falling thirty feet at a time and pitching, rolling while seas broke on it and over it, and only lifelines to hold on to. If your hands were full of mess-traps, what did you hang on *with*? With nerve – and the balance of a trapeze artiste, a tightrope walker. It was something to face even now, this trip aft; it was time someone visited the wounded, and the only way to get to them was over the top, running the gauntlet of the seas right aft as far as the superstructure where iron deck met quarterdeck. There was no way through the ship, since the two boiler-rooms and the engine-room were three individually watertight compartments, divided by solid bulkheads without doors in them. For damage-control reasons, it had to be so; the compartments were so large, potential flooding area so great – from a torpedo hit, for instance, or ramming . . . From the screen-door by the galley Nick peered out into noisy, spray-lashed darkness. Holed, shot-battered funnels glistening to his left; the whaler's davits empty and the paint charred away. His eye marked the positions of the ventilators, charting a clear route aft: clear if you could call it clear, over that sliding, tilting, heaving deck that

334

was constantly being washed-down by breaking seas. But the sea helped, in one way: the phosphorescent effect of foam racing alongside and leaping and sliding along the whole cavorting length of her did to an extent outline the limits of the area through which one would have to pass. And by swirling round the obstructions it showed them up. The second funnel, he saw as he passed it, was almost untouched; the third, in steel tatters, made up for that, and a loose flap of it banging to and fro as the ship rolled rang like a great dinner-gong. He passed the tubes, which were trained fore-and-aft and seemed to be intact; a wave landed aft, crashing down around the mine-winch and the release gear, and water rushed for'ard knee-deep, but he was ready for it, in against the searchlight platform and holding tight to the rail that ran around it. The further aft one got, the greater was the pitch, the rise and fall, the dizzy roller-coaster swing of it. He stayed where he was until a new one poured down on her stern and spread in sheets and cataracts of foam: then he moved quickly, bent double against the wind and with the object of lowering his centre of gravity, crabbing his way across the space where the after tubes were normally, and heading for the lee of the quarterdeck superstructure. Just as he reached it, *Mackerel*'s stern was going down and on either side of her the sea was heaving, piling upwards: astern, too, it was hunching itself up menacingly as her bow angled skyward, and at any second now these piled tons of water would collapse across her afterpart, boil across her as much as six or ten feet deep. He finished a long, desperate slide down the wet slope of deck by crashing into the superstructure's vertical steel side; then he was around its corner and into the screen-door like a rabbit going to ground. He heard it happening out there: like big guns at close quarters, and the steel structure shuddering, booming from the water's impact: might *this* be the moment for the tin chicken-house to be flattened, flung overboard? A rush of invading sea burst through the screen-door just as he forced it shut. Knee-high: well, his boots had been full already, he'd have to empty them before he began the trip back for'ard. Full seaboots seemed to weigh half a ton. They'd shut the hatch-lid above the wardroom ladder, and secured it with one clip. The clips were operable from either side, of course; and he was glad they were having the sense to take precautions . . . He got down far enough on the ladder to reach up and pull it shut again above him. Then, at the bottom of the ladder, he found himself confronted by Warburton, the captain's steward.

Warburton grinned at him.

'Come for a spot o' breakfast, sir?'

McAllister had transformed the wardroom precincts into a sickbay and operating theatre. One that swung, rocked, slanted, soared and swooped, while the sea's crashing hammer-blows boomed and pounded at it. But the conscious wounded seemed in surprisingly good spirits, and McAllister seemed to be on top of things and to have their confidence. They had everything they needed. Nick had drunk a mug of cocoa while he chatted to them, and now he was back on the bridge, reporting to Wyatt.

'Nineteen seriously wounded, sir. Three have died since the action – Nye, Woolland, Keightley. The GM's a doubtful case, but McAllister's happy about all the others.'

Pym, back on the bridge now, asked how was Bellamy, the coxswain.

'He'll be all right.'

CPO Bellamy was in one of the wardroom bunks, turbanned like a Sikh. He'd asked Nick, 'Is it right you're leavin' us, sir? Leavin' *Mackerel*?' An odd time to ask, Nick thought; *everyone* might be leaving her, at any moment. No one was listening; he told him, 'I should think you can count on it.'

'Then I'll be puttin' in for a draft chit too, sir.'

Nick, looking down at the stubbly, weather-beaten face, shook his head. 'Better you stayed, cox'n. We can't all leave her at once. I'd hang on, if I were you.'

There would have, in any case, to be a ship to leave: she had to be kept afloat, and got home. It really did seem premature, trivial, to natter about draft chits. The magazine and shell-room was like a needle in his brain, a ticking bomb under all their feet, a bomb he could have defused and hadn't. He heard Wyatt call to Pym, 'I believe it's getting lighter, pilot!'

Wyatt was sweeping the sea ahead with his binoculars; and Nick thought he was right. In the east, on *Mackerel*'s starboard bow, there was a suggestion of greyness, a faint gleam like polish on the surface of the sea. The sea itself might be down a little, too . . . No. Studying it, he realised it was only that there was less broken water now. And working it out – from a year's experience as a navigator in the Patrol – well, about ten o'clock last night when they'd laid their mines it had been near enough low water; so for the last five or six hours there'd have been a south-running stream: and a southerly tide competing with a wind out of the south-west was a combination that invariably kicked up a breaking sea. Now, it would be roughly high water, so the tide would be north-running – for about four hours.

It made things *look* quieter, that was all. It didn't reduce the wind's strength or the size of the seas or *Mackerel*'s motion in them.

They'd had Mr Gladwish's tea and sandwiches up here. It had made everyone feel less exhausted, for the moment . . . Grant squawked suddenly, excitedly, 'Ship forty degrees on the starboard bow, sir!'

'Porter!'

Porter didn't answer. Only wind, sea, ship-noises . . . Porter couldn't have answered; not unless he was in those sounds. Porter had died, here on this bridge, last night. Nick prompted, 'Reeves—'

'*Signalman!*'

Wyatt had realised his blunder. But Reeves was already doing his job, and the signal-lamp was stuttering, piercing the gloom and illuminating the wrecked bridge with its staccato burst of flashes. It was the challenge he was sending, aiming his lamp out on the bearing Grant had named; Wyatt shouted, 'What should the reply be?'

'Baker Charlie, sir!'

That was what came back to them: by searchlight probing from the eastward.

'Ship's friendly, sir!'

Just as well, Nick thought. *Mackerel* was hardly in a state to cope with anything *un*friendly. Reeves was flashing her identity to the newcomer: and he'd got an answer from her . . . 'It's *Moloch*, sir!' The searchlight began to call again: he gave it the go-ahead with his lamp, and then called the message out word by word, although everyone on the bridge read it at the same time for themselves: *Good morning. Happy Christmas. Shall we wait for daylight before we pass the tow?*

337

CHAPTER 8

A final volley of rifle-fire crackled into the grey sky roofing Dover. Nick, standing to attention with half the ship's company behind him and the rest facing him behind Wyatt, was aware that the last of the coffins, draped in its Union flag, was being lowered into the chalky soil, and that Wyatt was staring at it – stern, granite-faced. Enjoying, Nick wondered, this parade? Would he feel gratified by the big turnout of townspeople who'd watched the slow march through the streets and then trailed along behind?

The *Last Post*'s bitter-sweet, lonely wailing had begun. Its notes soared, floated in cold December air, and Nick, looking up at the castle with its flag fluttering at half-mast, thought of Cockcroft, and of Swan; of Swan particularly, who'd been sacrificed to nothing but one man's obstinacy.

One should try, perhaps, not to entertain such thoughts? Shouldn't one simply grieve and glory over the passing of brave men? Accept the praise, honour, acclamation?

There'd been a lot of it. Cheers, to start with; then signals, telegrams and headlines. After the recent enemy successes in the straits it had come as a timely victory. Out of four German raiders, two had been sunk and one sent home badly damaged. This time, there'd been no German broadcast. And Wyatt, of course, was the nation's hero.

A crowd many yards deep encircled the naval funeral party. Children craned their necks for a better view. Women wept: men stood with bowed heads, with black arm-bands on their sleeves. Nick stared at his commanding officer across the damp strip of turf: he saw him looking down his pistol's sights, chuckling with delight; offering *him*, Nick, the pistol . . . Urging him to take it: 'I've had *my* fun!' Grant stuttered, 'CPO Swan, sir, he's—'

338

Swan was still inside the flooded bow, unless the sea had extricated him. *Mackerel* would be going in tow to the London dockyards for repairs. Tomorrow, probably: there was a need of calm weather for the tow, and the forecast was hopeful.

They'd buried twenty men. The twentieth, Clover the gunner's mate, had died of his stomach wound during the transfer from *Mackerel* to the hospital yacht.

Nick had an appointment ashore, this afternoon, and before that he had to see Wyatt. He dreaded it: routine contact with him was irksome enough, and the idea of a tête-à-tête was anathema. Formal correctness was one thing: to show personal politeness very much another: and knowing one had to hold one's tongue . . . He'd felt like an accessory, at first, and when the German prisoners had been marched ashore – a crowd of men on the jetty staring at them in frigid, hostile silence – he'd taken care to be out of the way, not to have to meet any of their eyes. Facing them, he'd have felt like Wyatt, as if *he* were a form of Wyatt: and he'd have seen it in their eyes, the dark figures struggling up against the flames of their own ship burning, spurts of small-arms fire and a rush of cutlass-swinging sailors, while Wyatt roared 'Shoot 'em! Drive 'em back where they belong!'

Into the sea, or the flames, he'd meant.

That German with his hands up: and the bark of Wyatt's gun . . . But *had* he had his hands up, in the sense of surrendering?

When you thought too hard about a thing, you confused the recollection of it. Then you found yourself faced with a question you couldn't answer positively, and suddenly what had been clear-cut wasn't so any longer. Last night in *Arrogant*, the old depot ship, drinking whisky round a table with Tim Rogerson, Harry Underhill and Wally Bell, he'd put it to them as a theoretical problem, a sort of 'what-would-you-do-if' exercise; but that hadn't fooled them. They'd glanced at each other quickly, understanding why he'd been quiet and thoughtful, gloomy, when he'd been supposed to be the guest of honour and chief celebrant. Bell, the former Law student, tried to change Nick's perspective of the incident.

'There's no accepted method of surrender for a ship other than by hauling down her ensign. And at night that's no use anyway, since no one sees it . . . But the Huns never actually did surrender their ship, did they?'

'Oh, she was done for!'

'*Did* they, though?'

'No.' And even 'done for', one or more Huns had still been shooting from their bridge or somewhere with a rifle.

Bell pontificated, 'Nobody's ever accepted the idea of individuals surrendering, at sea. If a ship sinks, or strikes her colours, you have survivors or prisoners – and that's clear, beyond argument. But suppose at Jutland when Jellicoe was lambasting some German dreadnought, if a couple of Huns on its signal-bridge had semaphored "Kamerad!"'? D'you think the Grand Fleet would 've ceased fire?'

Nick interrupted the other two's amusement. 'I'm talking about a man with his hands up and another with a pistol; not Jutland, or—'

'*Sure* he had his hands up?'

'Yes, of course I'm sure!'

'Like this?' Wally Bell had raised his hands in the 'Kamerad' position: 'or like *this*?' Hands forward: hauling himself aboard, or warding off attack, or reaching *at* someone . . . Wally added, 'You were looking down at an angle, so—'

'He was scared stiff. He had his mouth wide open, screaming or—'

'Or shouting "Charge!" . . . *Which* way were his hands out, did you say?' He only gave Nick a moment to find an answer; then he banged the table, making empty glasses jump. 'Can't be certain, can you? And that's hardly surprising – considering the distance from bridge-rail to stem-head, and the angle, and flames and smoke and the fact you weren't ever exactly an admirer of the man we're talking about – or –' he glanced round, lowering his voice – 'or *not* talking about . . . Tim, Harry, what d'you say?'

Rogerson shook his head. 'You *couldn't* tell. And you're right – in a mix-up like that, a few men shouting "I give in" doesn't stop the action.'

'Harry?'

Bell was asking Underhill for comment. The CMB man turned his deepset eyes on Nick. He growled, 'They shouldn't 've been there in the first place . . . Raiding – raiding the drifters on the minefield? A drifter's almost helpless – well, it *is*, it's a sitting duck to a destroyer, less use even than that clumsy thing Wally drives . . . Well – what'd those Huns 've done if they'd got through to the drifter patrols? Filled the lads' Christmas stockings? If a drifter skipper shouted "I surrender" and waved both hands at 'em – not that you could imagine any such thing – what d'you think, a Hun destroyer captain 'd cease fire?'

340

It was puzzling, and confusing. They were talking a certain kind of sense, and they were honest, decent men, his friends. Bell told him, while Tim Rogerson was calling to the steward for another round of drinks, 'We're on *your* side, Nick. Telling you not to be a mug!'

Admiral Bacon had issued a Press announcement about some action a year or so ago, and he'd included in it a statement that 'fortunately' many German sailors' lives had been saved. That word 'fortunately' had let him in for a barrage of newspaper criticism, and his mail for days afterwards had been full of vituperative letters from the public. The Germans were 'baby-killers' – because bombardments of East Coast towns, and Zeppelin bombs, had killed some children; and they'd sunk the *Lusitania*, torpedoed hospital ships. It was true, they had; hospital ships sailed unmarked now, for their own safety. And yet not long ago a German aeroplane had swooped low over the RNAS aerodrome at Dunkirk and dropped a parcel; it had contained the personal effects of a naval pilot whom they'd shot down, and a piece of ribbon from the German wreath on his grave, and a photograph of the guard of honour firing a salute over it at the military funeral they'd given him.

Nick asked the other three, 'Is it necessary to hate them, d'you think?'

Bell only raised his eyebrows and his glass. Underhill rubbed his cleft chin thoughtfully. Rogerson suggested, 'I suppose it does make the whole thing *simpler*?'

There was a dream-quality now about it all, a jumbling of recollections and detail. What had come first or last, what in between: fear of that unshored section of the bulkhead merged into a battle with the sea in which the weapons had been wires, lines, cables, men's strength and courage . . . Nick forced his mind away from it, back into the present: at least, he tried to: he saw Wyatt at attention, wooden-faced, staring straight at him, and behind Wyatt half the ship's company motionless, immaculate, parade-ground bluejackets: this was how the crowd saw them, the civilians packed tightly around this rectangle of ritual grief; but for one's own part one saw through to the dark foul-smelling crowded caverns of the messdecks and a threatened bulkhead, and tired, hungry, haggard men playing cards, joking, even singing . . . Cockcroft said suddenly, as clearly as if he'd been standing there at his elbow, '*Fine body of men, what?*' But nobody had spoken, and

Cockcroft had said it – what, four days ago? Only *four days*? Wyatt was still staring at him. Mr Gladwish was on Wyatt's right, while Grant and Watson were on either side of Nick. The bugle's last note blossomed, quavered, died. In the utter silence that followed it, he heard a man sob, somewhere close behind him. He nearly did the same himself: he could have, he could have let go completely, sunk to his knees and cried like a child. But it was over now, all over, and they were marching back through the town, through quiet, sympathetic crowds, grey streets and a bitter December noon.

'Sit down, Everard.' Wyatt pointed. 'Help yourself to a glass of that stuff.'

'No thank you, sir.' He sat down, though. Just a few days ago, this cabin had been an operating theatre: it seemed strange that it was now once again a place where one might be invited to sip pink gin. Wyatt looked surprised that he didn't want one: he stared at him for a moment, then he shrugged. He said, 'I wanted a word with you before you go to this – interview, or investigation, whatever it's going to be.'

It was to do with the trouble in the Fishermen's Arms, the brawl and the military police report on it. Nick had to report himself at an office in the secretariat at 2.30 pm; that was all he knew.

'Yes, sir.'

Wyatt stood up, and placed himself at the scuttle, staring out. Stooping slightly, and with his hands clasped behind his back. He cleared his throat.

'As you know, I washed my hands of the whole affair. I felt you'd not only behaved in – in an unseemly manner, but that you'd very badly let me down. Let this *ship* down. I –' he turned, glanced at Nick briefly and away again – 'I think in my position you'd have felt the same.'

Nick waited, through another interval of throat-clearing.

'But as I mentioned to you the other day –' Wyatt gestured towards the harbour entrance – 'when we were being brought in – as I said then, I've acquired a very high opinion of your professional abilities . . .'

Nick remembered, rather vaguely: but Wyatt had expressed it in terms of – *gratitude*? Emotionally disturbed, perhaps, by the reception which Dover was giving *Mackerel*. They'd been cheering her into harbour: ships and jetties lined with shouting, cap-waving sailors, and a bedlam of sirens shrieking from destroyers, trawlers, drifters . . . Dockyard maties, driftermen, trawlermen, and crowds of civilians all along the Marine Parade, cheering themselves hoarse. Christmas evening . . . Dusk had been seeping down over the inland hills, and the wind had dropped; it had been quite easy transferring the tow from *Moloch* to the two big tugs who'd brought her in and berthed her. Totally different to the struggle to get the tow connected in the first place – at dawn, working on a heaving, slippery deck with the sea breaking right over her and knocking men off their feet. *One hand for the ship and one for yourself* was the old sailors' phrase for it: but a man needed *five* hands, and preferably feet with suckers on them too. Nick had worked with his men, and the battle had gone on for hours: he still dreamt of it, of enormous seas mounting, hanging over the heads of sailors who couldn't see them coming, who were caught, trapped in loops of wire-rope, doomed: he'd be trying to shout, to warn them, and his jaw locked so he couldn't make a sound, only watch the sea break and boil . . . There'd been a light line to get over first – and heaving lines weren't easy to manage in a high wind from a tilting deck and when ships couldn't approach each other too closely for fear of being swept into collision – and then the grass, the coir rope that floated, had to be attached to the first line and hauled across; then, on the end of the grass rope came the 3½-inch steel-wire hawser. The mine-winch had proved useless, and the after capstan had been smashed in the action, so everything had to be done by manpower, muscle-power.

When the ships were linked and *Moloch* moved cautiously ahead, dragging at *Mackerel*'s stern to get her round on course for Dover, the wire had sprung bar-taut and snapped as easily as a banjo-string: two minutes, it had lasted, after two hours' back-breaking work – which had now to begin all over again. This time *Moloch* started by shifting two shackles of anchor-cable aft, and the wire was linked to it so that the chain-cable's weight acted as a spring and prevented further snappings under sudden strain. A pity they hadn't done it in the first place; it wasn't so unusual an evolution. It had worked, finally; but to get the wire inboard and secure it, with the cable's weight dragging at it and the ship flinging herself in all directions, had needed practically every fit seaman in the ship, like a tug-of-war team strung out along her upper deck – slipping, sliding, cursing. A dozen times he saw men slip or be knocked off their feet: seconds and inches more than once saved lives. In the end, hardly knowing how they'd done it, they had the two ships linked, and *Mackerel* was on her way to Dover.

They'd been entering the port, surrounded by the enthusiastic welcome, when Wyatt had called Nick to him at the front rail of the bridge. With the ship in the tugs' charge, there was nothing for anyone to do. Wyatt had said, 'If you hadn't shored that bulkhead, Number One, we wouldn't be here now. I'm very much aware of that. And your conduct generally has been of the highest order. I'm – grateful to you.'

'Thank you, sir.'

It hadn't meant anything to him. Nor had the cheering, hooting, waving. One knew what it was all about, and understood the meaning of Wyatt's words, but there'd been a numbness, a feeling of remoteness. And there were so many things that needed seeing to, to be getting on with as soon as the ship was berthed: even inside the harbour, until that bulkhead's lower part was shored one was aware of the weakness, one's own neglect . . . But now, forty-eight hours later, Wyatt was saying roughly the same thing again, and Nick's immediate reaction was a feeling of embarrassment, that he was sailing under false colours. What his captain was saying to him was *You're forgiven: you can stay with me, now* . . . And he didn't want to. It should have been possible to say so, and to say why: but he couldn't, they'd been right last night in *Arrogant*, it would have been the action of a mug – achieving nothing except damage to oneself.

All the same, this keeping quiet, letting Wyatt assume he'd want to stay with him, felt less like common sense or diplomacy than subterfuge.

Wyatt told him, 'I can't undo what's been said and done already, and I can't predict what sort of view they'll take. Un-officer-like behaviour ashore is not, even in wartime, something to be treated as of no account, or condoned.' He scowled, and cleared his throat. 'However, I've done my best to give you some support.'

He picked up a sheet of foolscap from the desk-top near him.

'I've sent a copy of this – an extract from my Report of Proceedings – with a covering letter expressing my wish to retain you as my first lieutenant, to Captain (D). He'll have passed it on to this chap Reaper, the man you'll be seeing. Whoever *he* may be.'

Wyatt sat down.

'There are – don't discuss this with anyone else, please – there are – new faces about the place. Sir Reginald Bacon is leaving Dover,

344

and Admiral Keyes is relieving him. With, I believe, more or less immediate effect. And naturally this will bring other changes at lower levels.'

It wasn't much of a surprise. There'd been talk of it for some while; and only last night Tim Rogerson had told Nick he'd heard it was imminent.

Poor old Bacon. He'd foundered, finally, on the floodlit minefield. And the Admiralty committee who'd forced that issue had been headed by Keyes, who'd now displaced him . . . Wyatt said, 'Here is what I said in my report, Everard.' He coughed, and read: *'I wish to draw their Lordships' attention to the high standard of leadership and initiative displayed by my second-in-command, Lieutenant Nicholas Everard, Royal Navy. First, as already stated, this officer aimed and fired the torpedo which sank one enemy destroyer. Subsequently throughout the hours following the action his personal energy, zeal and professional ability provided an example to the entire ship's company. Finally the passing of the tow, of which he took charge on deck under extremely adverse weather conditions, was a triumph of seamanship and good discipline.'*

Wyatt slid the document on to his desk, and asked Nick, 'Fair comment?'

'More than generous, sir.'

And neat. Commending Nick, it avoided – as no doubt it would in the main body of the report as well – any mention of it having been his decision, not Wyatt's, to shore the bulkhead – or that he'd felt it was necessary after Wyatt had talked of going at *Mackerel*'s 'best speed', against Nick's and the engineer's advice. Obviously, Wyatt wouldn't have filled in such details. *He* was no 'mug', either.

Nick looked down at his clasped hands, and thought: *But Swan's still in there* . . .

He glanced up, and met Wyatt's stare.

'I suppose you'll be putting in recommendations – with the report on the action – for honours and awards?'

Surprise: suspicion . . . Wyatt thought he might be about to propose some decoration for himself! He went on, 'Chief Petty Officer Swan, sir. Perhaps you'll have included him already. But in case not – well, he was at that bulkhead in full awareness of the danger of it bursting. Even *because* of that.'

'I'll – consider your suggestion.'

'Thank you, sir.'

*   *   *

345

Mr Gladwish, reclining in an armchair, looked up over his *Daily Mail* as Nick entered the wardroom.

'There's some mail for you, Number One.'

'Good.'

The gunner winked. 'How was –' He jerked his head, towards the skipper's cabin. Nick shrugged.

'Much as one might have expected.'

He was only just realising what Wyatt had done: that he'd offered him a trade. Nick should keep his mouth shut about bulkheads and speed and so on, and in return for that he'd have Wyatt's support and commendation.

The mail was on the table, and there were three letters for him. One was a bill, from Gieves. Needn't even open that one. On another he recognised his stepmother's writing, and the third was from his uncle. His spirits rose immediately; those were the two people he liked to hear from.

'Sherry please, Warburton.' He sat down at the table, and ripped open his uncle's letter first. 'How about you, Guns?'

'I don't mind.' Gladwish nodded. 'Very civil of you . . . Plymouth an' bitters, steward.'

'Aye aye, sir.'

Rear-Admiral Hugh Everard had written from his cruiser flagship in Scapa Flow, *I cannot tell you how pleased we have all been, and how delighted I am personally, by the news of your recent success in the Dover straits. Well done! Most refreshing, at a time when affairs seemed to be going less well down there. How splendid that it should have been your* Mackerel *that has – let us hope – turned the tide. I congratulate you most heartily and look forward to your account of the action.*

From this northern fastness I have no excitements to report. Our weather has been some of the worst in living memory, and very trying for all concerned, particularly of course for the small fry. But we keep the seas, and our powder dry, and live in hopes that the Hun may one day poke his snout out of his earth again.

I have been south only once since I saw you on leave at Mullbergh, and this time I did not visit the old place. Sarah has her hands full enough as it is, with her convalescents, and in any case I was obliged to spend some time in the vicinity of the Admiralty. I have had no word from, or news of, your father . . .

When he'd finished reading it, he folded it and stuffed it in his pocket. He had a great affection and respect for his uncle – whose

346

tales of the Navy, all through Nick's childhood, had fired him with the ambition to go to sea. Admittedly there'd been a period, of some years' duration, at Dartmouth as a cadet and later as a midshipman with the Grand Fleet when he'd been thoroughly disillusioned: his feeling had been that the Navy his uncle spoke of with such enthusiasm – Hugh Everard had never ceased to, in spite of the fact that it had once rejected him, virtually thrown him out – that this great Service he loved so deeply was the Navy of past years, changed now into something entirely different, while Hugh clung to his own image of it. Until Jutland, Nick had detested it. The Navy had seemed to be – well, all Wyatts, little ones and big ones; all pomp and humbug, dreary routine and self-importance, silly ritual. That described Dartmouth, all right, and it described a dreadnought's gunroom too if you added a generous measure of sadistic bullying. But the other side of the coin, which Nick had first glimpsed at Jutland, was there as well. If the Wyatts and other distractions could be cleared away, leaving the view of the purer concept, what might be thought of as an updated Nelsonian view . . . Perhaps it could happen. Meanwhile one needed to keep it in mind and see *past* the Wyatts . . . Returning to Hugh Everard's letter now: it was odd that he'd stayed away from Mullbergh. He and Sarah, Nick's young stepmother, got on so well, so obviously liked each other. Nick, adoring Sarah and admiring his uncle, had always been happy to see their friendship. Because Sarah needed support, and because he was ashamed of his father's treatment of her and glad Uncle Hugh existed as proof that not all Everards were brutes.

Sarah had once said to him, 'You're *so* like your uncle!' and he'd thought it was probably the nicest thing anyone had ever said to him.

He sipped his sherry, and read her letter eagerly.

My dearest Nick. Such wonderful, exciting news of you and your magnificent Mackerels! I must hear all about it – write now, at once, if you have been so churlish as not to have done so by the time this reaches you. Better still – take some leave. COME HERE and thrill me with the details! I have absolutely no doubt that you yourself will have been wildly brave and dashing again; please PLEASE send or bring me news as soon as you are able!

Life continues to be hectic here, now that we are a hospital-cum-convalescent home. I have an excuse, moreover – in fact dozens of them, some laid up and some hobbling about on crutches – to keep big

347

*fires blazing and warming this cold old place. It's so good to feel it's
serving a useful purpose instead of just rotting away. Meanwhile I
have heard from your father for the first time in two months; he tells
me that he is well, has a new address and is commanding some
training establishment which is also a remount depot. Alastair
Kinloch-Stuart, whom you may remember meeting here and who
is by chance in the district again – staying with the Ormsbys as it
happens – tells me that it must be a riding school. Apparently officers
are being commissioned now who do not know how to ride! One finds
it difficult to imagine your father in such company – and one would
certainly not wish to be one of his pupils!*

Nick skimmed through the rest of it: with the name and face of
Captain (or was it Major?) Kinloch-Stuart sticking in his mind like
grit. He'd arrived at Mullbergh for luncheon, one day when Nick
had last been there on leave; he'd been supposed to be staying with
friends nearby then too, and Sarah had introduced him as 'an old
friend from years ago' . . . A bit later, lunching with Uncle Hugh in
London and short of news or subjects for conversation, he'd
mentioned him, and Hugh Everard had bristled like a dog catching
a whiff of cat: and then denied having even heard the man's name
before.

Nick pushed Sarah's letter into his pocket. Her phrases 'by
chance' and 'as it happens' were mistakes, he thought. She'd
overdone it. And she needn't have mentioned the man at all:
she must have *wanted* to, wanted to put it before his, Nick's, eyes,
to *tell* him something . . .

He pulled the letter out, re-read that part of it. It was not, he told
himself, any of his business. Nor were his assumptions necessarily
correct. He was almost certainly doing Sarah a great injustice. Not
that anyone could have blamed her, if she *had*—

One knew nothing, so what was the point of brooding and
conjecturing? Kinloch-Stuart was a Cameron Highlander, so far as
he could remember. Might his hanging around Mullbergh explain
Uncle Hugh's staying away from the place? And what sort of
appointment might the man hold that seemed to keep him almost
permanently on leave, sponging on everyone in turn?

Forget it. It was fantasy and guesswork building on – on what?
On jealousy?

Annabel's voice like honey in his skull: *Why d'you call me 'Sarah'
all night long?*

Such nonsense, all of this. The mind played tricks – if one

348

allowed it to . . . He got up, walked to the scuttle, stared out over the harbour and the stone breakwater to the sea's grey-green swell. He made himself think about his father . . . Out of the fighting now, in a safe job. But still a command, of sorts; and to do with horses, so he'd consider it honourable enough . . . Might he have wangled it – or been shunted into it, out of the way? What it boiled down to was he'd survive, he'd return eventually to Mullbergh and to Sarah.

Gladwish raised his glass. 'Your 'ealth, Number One!'

He nodded. 'And yours, Mr Gladwish.'

'Good news from 'ome, I trust?'

'Oh – yes . . .'

He walked eastward along Marine Parade. It was cuttingly cold still, but there was hardly any wind. This morning the flag on the castle had fluttered strongly: now it drooped, hardly stirring, and the clouds were high and static. So *Mackerel* should be on her way soon, as intended; the thing was, would he go with her?

She'd have only a skeleton crew for the tow round. A third of the ship's company had gone off on home leave this morning; and more would be left in hospital beds . . . He saw motor-cars drawn up outside the Admiral's headquarters, and officers were hurrying in and out of the main door in the centre, where a sentry was constantly springing to attention and then standing at ease again. It was between the three adjoining buildings that the to-ing and fro-ing was taking place; the first house contained offices, the middle one – called Fleet House – was the Admiral's official residence, and the third held the secretariat. Including, apparently, this man Reaper, to whom Nick had been summoned. Room 14 . . . But he had time in hand; he walked on past, on the sea side of the road, looking the place over. Sandbags round the doors and windows stopped one seeing much. He wondered *which* great man would be in there at the moment – the usurper, or the evacuee?

He thought again, *Poor old Bacon* . . . 'Fred Karno' was his nickname amongst the destroyer men, on account of the ragbag collection of ships, establishments, aircraft and so on that comprised the Patrol. 'Fred Karno's Navy' . . . With, behind the scenes, such backroom wizards as the redoubtable Lillicrap; and Wing-Commander Brock, of the famous firework family, who was in charge of flares – the flares that lit the minefield at the Varne, for instance. Brock had a lot to do with Bacon's smoke-laying experiments, too; and a column of smoke rising now from the end of the naval pier showed that experiments were still going on. Testing the new burners that Bacon was so keen on, probably. The difficulty with the existing type, which were used in MLs, motor-launches – it was from Wally Bell that Nick had heard all this – was that at night the flames from the burning white phosphorus showed up through the smoke. They were trying out various kinds of baffle in metal funnels, trying to find a way of baffling flame without baffling smoke as well; and Bacon's inventiveness had devised a way of water-cooling the troughs in which the burners rested, thus thickening the smoke with steam. Cooling was desirable in any case; at a bombardment of the enemy coast during the summer the great man had had smoke-burners placed in rowing boats that were towed by the MLs, and two men in each rowing boat to ignite the burners and keep them burning properly, but the machines had become red-hot, and their attendants had had to swim for it as an alternative to roasting. Now there was a new plan, to hang burners from kites, to blind enemy spotter-aircraft . . . One wondered whether Admiral Keyes might yet appreciate the full scope of his inheritance!

But it was time to turn back, face his *own* problems.

He doubted whether Wyatt's new report on him would make much odds. At the time of the pub riot he'd stood aside and washed his hands like Pontius Pilate; and it was that incident, in its own context and circumstances, that was to be considered now. The fact that one had carried out one's duties at sea in a satisfactory way needn't come into this at all – any more than the fortuitous success at Jutland had lessened official rancour over that other, comparatively trifling misdemeanour. This one was not trifling. For an officer to become involved in a public brawl, and with members of his own ship's company – and at that, fighting (as *they'd* see it) over a woman who—

Who *what*?

In retrospect, he didn't know what to make of Annabel. There were certain possible conclusions from which he ran away when he thought about her. He liked to see her in his mind as she'd seemed to him in the early part of the evening, at first sight: and in any case she'd been kind, sweet to him. He *liked* her. Then there was another image of her in his memory: she leant over him, soothing his injured head, sponging it; she was naked and so was he, and her breasts swung, nipples brushing his chest. There was this enormously appealing warmth – and the concern, the anxiety in her eyes. It was a sexually stimulating memory but there was innocence in it too, a balancing degree of affection, of – using the word plainly, not in a hearts-and-roses sense – of love.

And he'd called her – dreamt of her as – *Sarah*?

He pulled his thoughts together. He was about to be hauled over the coals: and with good reason. He might, or might not if he was very lucky, face a court-martial after this, and be formally dismissed his ship.

Wyatt had been looking after his own interests, not Nick's. He'd tried to ensure that Nick wouldn't speak out of turn and upset his apple-cart, but at the same time his commendation of Nick over his usefulness at sea didn't in any way imply that he'd condoned or would want to condone *this* sort of behaviour.

A sentry shouldered arms, slapped the butt of his rifle. Nick returned the salute as he walked up the steps of what had been – and would one day be again – a seaside lodging-house.

In Room 14 a young paymaster with a rather supercilious expression stared at him from behind a desk. A coal-fire smouldered in a grate close to his chair, but here, ten feet away, the room was icy.

'May I help you?'

'Everard. *Mackerel*.'

'Everard?' He was checking in an appointment book. 'Oh, yes.' He didn't smile. 'I'll tell Commander Reaper you're here.'

'Hang on a moment.' Nick stepped closer. 'Tell me first – who is he, or *what* is he?'

The 'paybob' raised his eyebrows. It seemed he didn't much like the question. Or perhaps he didn't like any questions, from an officer who was on the carpet. He had a handkerchief tucked into his left sleeve, Nick noticed – a flag lieutenant's affectation. Was that how the fellow saw himself?

It looked as if he wasn't going to satisfy Nick's curiosity about the mysterious Commander Reaper. He was glancing downwards, now, at an elegant half-hunter that had materialised in his palm.

'I'll see if he's ready for you.'

He was getting to his feet, coming out from behind the desk. Nick moved, placing himself between the smooth young man and the door. 'I asked you a question. I'd like an answer, please.'

The paymaster's eyebrows practically vanished into the roots of his hair.

'Commander Reaper is seconded temporarily from the Plans Division at the Admiralty.' He frowned. 'Would you be good enough to step aside?'

'Of course.'

'Thank you.'

'Not at all.'

Reaper was a man of medium size; he had a narrow head, a beak of a nose, deepset eyes and a quiet, pleasant tone of voice.

Nick sat facing him across a littered trestle-table. On the far side of the room was a desk which presumably belonged to its more permanent occupant, and from that unoccupied swivel chair whoever it was would have a view down on to the harbour with the destroyer moorings in the foreground. He found that by turning his head and leaning back in his chair he had part of the same view. He could see several destroyers at their buoys; some were doubled-up, moored in pairs. The ship just entering now, with her whaler pulling like mad for the buoy to get there before the destroyer herself nosed up to it, was *Zubian*. She'd been put together from the bows of *Zulu* and the stern half of *Nubian*, after each of the two tribals had suffered appropriate damage. It had been Bacon's idea, to make one new ship out of the remains of two.

Reaper muttered, 'I shan't be long.' He was studying a file, frowning as he turned its pages. The invitation to sit down had surprised Nick; he'd expected to have to stand to attention, the accepted attitude for a junior officer being verbally flayed by a senior one. He waited; the whaler's bowman was on the buoy now, shackling *Zubian*'s cable to its ring.

'Well, then.' Reaper's eyes were on him. 'Everard . . .' He nodded. 'The name is not unfamiliar to me.'

He'd paused, and seemed to be inviting comment. Nick asked him, 'You know my uncle, sir?'

Reaper nodded. 'But it is *highly* unfamiliar in terms of any possible connection with fisticuffs in back-street bars.'

'Yes, sir. I'm very sorry it happened, sir.'

'Such behaviour, Everard, does not become an officer of the Royal Navy. It does not become a gentleman. It does not become *anyone* you, I imagine, would wish to be taken for.'

'No, sir.'

'And it is particularly, *totally* unbecoming –' Reaper pushed some papers about, then located and held up what looked like the

352

original of the report Wyatt had read out to him – '*totally* so to the officer whose abilities and qualities are referred to in this statement.'

'Yes, sir.'

Reaper leant back in his chair, but his eyes still rested hawkishly on Nick's.

'I have no disciplinary responsibilities here, Everard. And permit me to add that I *thank God* for that circumstance –' he leant forward, and his voice rose slightly as he tapped the file he'd been reading – 'since this kind of squalid time-wasting is utterly beyond my comprehension!'

'Yes, sir.'

'It is also beyond my capacity to tolerate!'

'Sir . . .'

For the last few seconds, he'd been feeling hopeful, but this last remark produced the reverse effect. There was a silence now; he raised his eyes, endured again that unrelenting scrutiny. He was at a loss to understand Reaper's position, attitude or purpose, and he suspected that this was precisely the effect the man was aiming at.

'Well. I presume, Everard, that there were circumstances which might throw a less harsh light on your conduct than the one which – er – shines from the report?'

'Only that I had no intention of getting into any sort of scrap, sir. I was there, and it sort of blew up all around me, and while I was –' he paused, searching for the word – 'while I was withdrawing, sir, I got knocked on the head.'

'Were you drunk?'

'I – well, not knowingly or intentionally, sir. But I think someone spiked my beer with rum.'

Reaper hit the table with the flat of his hand.

'Then you're a *colossal* fool, boy!' Nick frowned, watching him. Reaper blew out his cheeks. 'You enter the lowest drinking den in Dover, and don't keep your eye on your own glass of beer?'

'I hadn't imagined driftermen would be so keen to chuck their rum about, sir.'

'A chance to make a prize idiot out of a young pup with gold braid on his sleeve and the King's commission?'

'Oh.' He nodded, still frowning. Skipper Barrie, he wondered: would it have been *his* idea of a joke? 'Yes. I see, sir.'

Reaper took a deep breath, and let it out again. He asked him, 'You left the place with a girl. Is that correct? One of the town's—'

'Girl, sir?'

Reaper stared at him thoughtfully. Then he tapped the file again. 'According to the military police report—'

'My memory's none too clear on some points, sir. I suppose the rum in my beer . . .' He stopped talking. He could see that Reaper didn't believe him. But Reaper, extraordinarily, smiled.

'Quite.' He looked down, taking his eyes off Nick's face for the first time since he'd started the interview. 'Quite . . .' The smile faded as he glanced quickly through Wyatt's letter. Nodding slowly as he read. Now he looked up again.

'I have a certain function to perform here in Dover, Everard. So far as your own case is concerned, it so happened that this – this –' he poked at the file – 'degrading and time-wasting affair came up when your name was mentioned in another quarter – came up as something which had to be dealt with, decided somehow – and it fell to me to – er – kill several birds with one stone. *This* one is now – dead.'

He saw Nick's joy. He added quickly, 'Except to point out to you that your – your lack of wisdom, shall we say – has let down yourself, your uniform and a distinguished name. It has also wasted the time of quite a number of busy men. You'll see to it in the future, Everard, that you do not become associated with incidents of such a kind: and understand *this*, too: we are busy here, we are *extremely* busy and we have important, *very* important matters in our minds; we have an enormous amount to think about and to get on with. We *cannot*, cannot *possibly*, have our time wasted on such squalid trivialities. Were we *less* busy, and had the matter been referred to some different quarter for decision, you might very easily have found yourself facing a court-martial. Do you understand?'

'Yes, sir. Completely, sir.'

'You'd better not see that girl again.'

Nick stared at him. He hadn't admitted there'd been a girl, or anyway that he remembered one.

Besides . . .

'Very well, we can regard that unpleasant episode as concluded, I think.'

'I'm extremely grateful, sir.'

'What you mean, Everard, is you're extremely *relieved*.' Reaper nodded. 'Understandably. In your place, so'd I be . . . However – in all the circumstances, I hardly think we could leave you in *Mackerel* now.'

Nick waited.

'She'll be months in dockyard hands, in any case. You won't be missing anything worthwhile. D'you mind leaving her?'

'No, sir, I—'

'No . . .' He murmured as much to himself as to his visitor, 'And if you stayed in her, you might miss a great deal.'

'Sir?'

Reaper shook his head. 'It happens there's a job of work we want done. It's suggested you could be the man to do it.' The hawk's eyes were fixed on him. 'Know much about CMBs?'

'I've been out in one on engine trials, sir, and handled her a bit.' Harry Underhill's boat, that had been, on an occasion when *Mackerel* had been boiler-cleaning. He added, 'An RNR called Underhill has told me most of what I know about them.'

'That's the fellow you'll work with. Only –' Reaper pointed at him with a pencil – 'only for a short while, just this one – er – errand.' He got up, walked over to the window. Nick stood up too. Reaper said, staring out at the destroyers at their moorings, 'CMB officers are rather thin on the ground, at this moment. Experienced chaps, that is. Some are down at *Vernon* being told about the new mines we're getting, and the rest are up at Osea Island, the new base that's being built there. So there it is. I want you to take command of one of the forty-footers – I'm told CMB 11 is available and operational and suitable. Your second-in-command is an RNR midshipman by the name of –' he put his hand to his eyes, concentrating – 'Selby.' Turning from the window now. 'Have your gear sent over to *Arrogant*. I'll make a signal immediately, appointing you to her for special duties. It'll only be for a few days, though.'

'What after that, sir?'

'I don't command the Sixth Flotilla, Everard.'

'You mean it'll be decided by Captain (D), sir, after I do this – well, whatever this –'

'As it happens, a Captain Tomkinson will be arriving shortly to take over the destroyer command.' Reaper shook his head. 'Look, I've no time for chit-chat . . . I want you to spend as much time as you can in that CMB. Get the feel of her, and to know her crew, and Underhill can exercise his boat with you. There's still a swell running, but we're promised a period of calm. You've got two days to prepare yourself. Night after next should be right for our purposes, from the weather point of view; there'll be a moon,

355

and that might be the one thing that stops us; but with any luck we'll have cloud to cover it.' He'd spoken fast, disjointedly; now he went to his table, picked up some papers, dropped them, turned to Nick again. 'My reasons for offering you this, Everard, are that you've been in the straits for some while now, and as a navigator – so you know your way about. With the high speed of the CMBs, plus the fact you'll be carrying out the operation on a low-water spring tide, that's vital. Second, your ship's out of action, so you're available immediately. Third, you've shown you know how to keep your head in action. I need these qualities, and the CMB officers who have 'em aren't here, and it's not a thing that can wait. So – you'll command the operation.'

'Command it, sir?'

Reaper nodded.

'But Underhill's an experienced CMB officer, sir – and he can certainly navigate – and I'm coming in as an outsider—'

'He hasn't your experience of action.' Reaper was impatient suddenly. 'Look here, Everard – the nursery days are finished, you're *fledged* now, you can expect to be given quite considerable responsibility at any time . . . If you shirk your opportunities, you'll never amount to anything!'

He'd seemed more genuinely angry, in that outburst, than he'd been during the discussion of the Fishermen's Arms affair. Now he shrugged.

'I know it's – unorthodox. The job has to be done, that's all. And you're damn lucky to get the chance of it!'

'Sir.'

'You'll have an ML with you as well as the two CMBs. A launch will be allocated by Captain Edwards, and her CO will be told to report to you. Tonight, probably. I'll brief you and the other officers tomorrow evening aboard *Arrogant*, and that'll leave you part of the following day to decide how to set about it.'

How to set about *what*, for God's sake . . . He nodded.

'Aye aye, sir.'

Reaper said, 'Better get moving, then.'

CHAPTER 9

He eased down on the throttle. CMB 11's engine-noise dropped from its aeroplane-like roar to a quieter but deep-throated grumble, her bow dropped abruptly as the speed fell off and she levelled in the water, and her own wash came up from astern in a series of humps that lifted, rocked her, carried her bodily along. Then all that was over, and she was motoring quietly but powerfully across the swell.

Off to starboard, inshore, Nick saw Harry Underhill's boat curve hard to port, coming out this way to join him. He said to Selby, 'We'll go in, now.'

'Right!'

Selby laughed. He laughed at nothing: or rather, at everything. Nick found it irritating, and he wondered how Weatherhead could stand having him around on a permanent basis and at such close quarters. In a cockpit ten feet by six, which was roughly this one's dimensions, you couldn't get far from your companions. Midshipman Selby had yellow hair and a bright-red face pitted and scarred by acne; he was about nineteen. Nick had noticed how ERA Ross, the boat's mechanic and the third and last member of her crew, went deadpan at the sound of Selby's laugh: as if he'd have liked to have snatched up a spanner and hit him with it, and feared that one day he might.

Nick said, 'Flash *Let's go home* to him.'

'What?' Selby cackled. 'What—'

'Oh, Christ . . .' Nick pointed. 'Give me the lamp.'

Selby managed to hear that; he snatched it up and passed it over. Nick said, shouting in his ear, 'Now stand still!' He kept his left hand on the wheel and used the other one, balancing the lamp on Selby's shoulder, to call CMB 14, Underhill, and tell him it was time to pack up. Harry acknowledged it. Nick pushed the lamp into Selby's hands; he bent down, peered in at Ross through the small doorless hatchway in the centre of the cockpit's for'ard bulkhead.

'All right?'

Ross, squatting on his wooden seat on the engine's starboard side, grinned and raised a thumb. He was a long-boned man, and the seat was built against the inside curve of the boat's hull: it curved *him*, in conformity with her shape, and in that squatting position his knees stuck up like posts. Nick shouted to him, 'We're going in, now!' Then he straightened, opened the throttle to about one third, and pointed the boat's long, tapering bow at the eastern entrance.

They hadn't been over three-quarters speed this afternoon, on account of this swell that was still running. CMBs were fine-weather boats; in any sort of sea, at speed, they tended to leap from crest to crest, not only trying to knock their bottoms out but also tending to plunge *into* oncoming waves instead of over them. The larger boats – fifty-five-footers – managed a little better, but even they were too lightly built to stand up to the pounding a sea would give them at speed.

Underhill had swung his boat in astern of Nick's, and was following him towards the harbour. The light was going now, and it had been only a short outing, but Nick felt it had been worthwhile. He was happy with her; he could do anything with her, he thought, that anyone else could do. Leaving the jetty he'd been a bit clumsy – he'd forgotten how a boat's stern kicked off to starboard when a large single screw was put ahead and the deeper blade or blades of it, revolving in a greater density of water, had more effect than the upper ones – but he'd got it all under control now, he understood her and knew within reasonable limits what you could do and what you couldn't. At high speed, for instance, you couldn't safely slam on too much wheel; not unless you wanted to turn her right over. And she had no reversing gear: you couldn't go astern, so to come alongside you had to stop in time to get the way off her before she bumped.

The gap in the eastern breakwater wasn't far ahead, and he eased the throttle down. Keeping well to starboard, and being careful not to come in fast with an accompanying wash that would certainly infuriate and possibly damage ships alongside jetties or other ships, who'd be rocked and ground against each other . . . Inside he turned her to starboard, turning just short of three squat monitors at buoys. A Trinity House tender lay at anchor ahead; he turned the CMB close under her stern, then swung the other way to clear an anchored dredger. Now it would be a straight course and about five hundred yards to the camber, the inner basin. To starboard the sea heaved and boomed, lopping against the harbour wall; to port, the destroyer lines were almost empty. *Zubian* was still there, and beyond her lay a tribal, and near the centre of the harbour were two 'oily wads' and one of the big flotilla leaders; but all the rest were at sea – protecting the fishing-craft on the mine barrage, guarding Folkestone and the shipping in the Downs, watching the Dunkirk and Boulogne approaches, or patrolling in other set areas. Destroyers' daytime duties were more varied: escorting transports and leave ships between Folkestone and Boulogne, and hospital and store-ships between Dunkirk and Calais and Dover; escorting allied and neutral shipping through the swept channel that hugged the coast from Dungeness to North Foreland; protecting the sweepers who every single day swept all those routes clear of mines. Under Bacon, the Patrol had certainly earned its living.

But gossip had said that a change of admiral would be linked to a more aggressive policy: and gossip had connected Keyes, who was taking over now, with this rumoured attack or 'special operation'.

And Commander Reaper was from the Plans Division, which up till now Keyes had directed!

Nick thought, *Two and two makes nine, at that rate* . . .

He took the CMB in very gently, her engine barely mumbling to itself, and berthed her under the torpedo-loading derrick in the basin's north-west corner. There were three little jetties here, the spaces between them forming small docks about the same length as the CMB, and the shore-based gunner (T) with his working party was there standing by.

'Lieutenant Everard?'

'Yes.' The gunner looked at his pocket-watch as Nick joined him on the jetty. A small, grey-faced man. Nick said, 'Sorry if I've kept you waiting.' There was a torpedo ready on its trolley, and it had the distinctive orange-painted head that meant it was a practice one, a 'blowing head'. When it came to the end of its run, compressed air would be released to blow water out of it and make it buoyant, so it would bob upright on the surface with its orange nose easy to spot from the recovery-vessel. The gunner asked Nick, 'Want us to load 'er now? Morning won't do?'

He'd have a wife ashore, Nick guessed, a home to go to. Well, hard luck!

'Now, please. We'll be making an early start, tomorrow.'

CMB 11 had no torpedo on board at the moment. The trough that one would go in was a channel that extended, open-topped, from the after end of the cockpit to the boat's fantail-shaped stern. The torpedo – an eighteen-inch side-lug RGF – Royal Gun Factory, the Woolwich arsenal – would be lowered now and slid in from astern, under the steel arches that bridged the channel. It would be slid in nose-first, so that the head would lie pointing into the cockpit. Firing was by means of a hydraulic ram: its shaft passed centrally through the cockpit, and the white-painted, cup-shaped ram-head fitted over the curved nose of the fish. So it would lie there pointing the same way as the boat, and when it was fired the ram would discharge it tail-first over the boat's stern. The CMB would then be doing a few knots less than the torpedo's standard running speed of forty, so as the torpedo's own engine fired and its propellers drove it forward in the boat's wake and on exactly the same course, the driver would swing the wheel over and turn her aside, allowing the missile to travel on. Until the moment of firing he'd have been aiming the boat as if she herself were a torpedo – holding her on what would have become a collision-course with the enemy.

To anyone accustomed to more orthodox methods of firing torpedoes, it seemed an odd procedure. Nick thought it might take quite a bit of mastering. He told the gunner, 'I'll need you and your team standing-by tomorrow. We'll be practising all day, I expect. Can you muster three or four practice fish, so we don't have to wait long between runs?'

The motor-launch that was to join him for this mysterious expedition could make itself useful recovering the torpedoes and carting them in. And Underhill in CMB 14 could act as target ship.

Harry Underhill seemed a bit 'reserved' . . . He was a very direct, down-to-earth sort of man, and he disliked the present lack of information. He obviously thought Nick knew more than he was telling him; and under his skin he'd naturally resent an outsider bursting in and taking charge – all the more so, probably, when it happened to be a personal friend who was doing it. He wasn't unfriendly or uncooperative: just guarded, watching points.

It was still quite early, but already pitch dark, by the time he walked out over the floating brow and up *Arrogant*'s gangway.

He'd seen the torpedo loaded, and discussed the firing procedure and the ram's mechanism with the gunner from the shore base; then, by lamplight, he'd been over the boat's engine with Ross the artificer, and young Selby. It was necessary to know its quirks and foibles, what could go wrong with it, and so on, in case the mechanic got knocked out in action and one had to cope without him. Nick was surprised to find that the midshipman was about as ignorant as he was himself; it seemed logical to him that with only a three-man crew each of them must know the other's business. He mentioned to Selby a catch-phrase which had been familiar in training days: *Knowledge is the basis of initiative*. Selby only sniggered, as if he thought Nick was a bit of a card.

He went into *Arrogant*'s wardroom for a drink before he changed. He asked Underhill, 'Does *your* snotty know how your boat works?'

'Soon be over the side if he didn't.'

'Mine – Weatherhead's – doesn't know his arse from his elbow.'

Underhill nodded. 'Runt of the litter. Wethy's been trying to shed him, I think.'

'Is there one I could swap him for, temporarily?'

'Yes. Lad called Brown's kicking his heels, at the moment. If you've the wherewithal to swing it.'

He hadn't smiled at all. Beside him, Tim Rogerson looked just as serious. Nick thought, *He can't resent me, I'm not pinching his submarine* . . . 'What's up, Tim?'

'Johnny Vereker's dead.'

'Oh, no . . .'

'Shot down. Witnessed – 'plane exploded when it hit the ground. Two other pilots saw it. I've been talking to one of 'em on the blower – he was on his way through, on leave.'

Underhill sighed as he took two glasses from the steward's salver. He asked Nick, 'Gin?'

'Thank you. Of all the *rotten* things. Damn sorry, Tim.'

Rogerson nodded. He and Vereker had been in the same term at Dartmouth, and close friends all through. Nick sat down, and the steward brought him his drink. Tim Rogerson said, flaking his long frame into an armchair, 'I'll have to trundle his old motor over to his people's place in Hampshire, I suppose . . . Fine night to pick for a party, isn't it?'

'Are you having a party?'

'Oh, not really. Asked Bruce Elkington over, that's all. But you'll join us, won't you? Apart from the pleasure of your company, I'd like to hear what all this CMB business is about.'

'If *I could* tell you, I doubt if I'd be allowed to.'

'Nothing to do with the big thing, is it?'

Nick stared at him. 'What big thing?'

'For God's sake, *I* don't know.' His glance went past Nick's shoulder. 'Here's Wally. Now I'm afraid it *is* going to be a party.'

Wally Bell had a stranger with him, an RNVR lieutenant like himself. Half his height, though, and rotund. They came over.

'Thought you were at sea tonight, Wally. Shirking?'

'Donkey's giving trouble.' He meant his engine, his ML's. 'Look here, this is Sam Treglown. One of the élite.' By that he meant that Treglown was an ML man too. He pointed at Nick. 'Sam, that's the bird you're looking for.'

'Oh, are you Everard?'

Nick admitted it. Treglown smiled as he shook his hand. 'I've been told to report to you. Something special on?'

'Something. This time tomorrow we may find out what. Meanwhile you'd better have a drink.' He called the steward. Wally Bell was complaining. 'There's too much sea-time in this racket. Of *course* the damn thing breaks down occasionally!'

Treglown said, 'Yours is one of the Yank boats, isn't she? One of the Great Lakes products?'

'So what if she is?'

'Those engines are knocked together in some motorcycle factory!'

'No bearing on the subject whatsoever. In fact with *normal* usage she'd chug along for ever . . . But you know, what we ought to have is the Channel tunnel they've always talked about and never started. Think of the sea-time it'd save us all! No transports, no hospital ships, no escorts, no mine-sweeping – Lord, *think* of it!'

'And think also,' Rogerson added drily, 'of the Huns capturing the other end of it.'

Rogerson looked ill, Nick thought. Being red-headed he had a pale skin anyway, but tonight he looked like a tall, thin ghost.

'You'd have a damn great plug in it.' Wally stroked his beard. 'About halfway over. You'd have a cable attached to the plug and taken up to a buoy on permanent moorings. If the Huns got there, you'd just give the cable a jerk, and – *whoosh*!'

Treglown nodded. Frog-faced, podgy. He said, 'Glug glug.' Underhill commented, 'Be a hell of a job to pump the thing dry again.'

362

'Ah!' Bell shook his head, wagged a forefinger. 'The losing side – which means the Huns, naturally – would have the job of baling it out. In buckets. *Small* ones . . . Why, even Kaiser Willy'd think twice about going to war if he had *that* job in prospect!' He turned to Nick. 'What's this you're up to now? Left *Mackerel*, do I hear?'

'Over here, Elkington!'

Rogerson's guest had arrived. He waved, beckoning to him. He asked the new man, Treglown, 'You'll join us for dinner, won't you? We're celebrating the death of an old friend.'

He said later, after dinner, quietly to Nick, 'It's about the worst thing that ever happened, d'you know that? I still can't quite believe it. I tell you, Nick, I –' his hand fastened on Nick's arm – 'I could *cry*.'

'I know. I know *precisely*.'

Swan – Cockcroft – and so *many* of them . . . Like the ticking of a roomful of clocks, and every tick a life. One should weep, perhaps, not for individuals and friends so much as for England, for England's blood and strength that were draining out of her.

Elkington had left early; his ship was sailing at daybreak for patrol duty in the Downs. Nick had said to Rogerson, 'Pleasant fellow, that', and Rogerson had nodded. 'He's engaged to marry a girl I know.' He smiled now: it looked like a conscious effort to change his own mood. 'What's this I've heard whispered about some *fracas* at a local hostelry, involving a certain officer and a – er – young lady of the town?'

'I've no idea.'

It had surprised him that there'd been no gossip, so far as he'd known. But there'd had to be, of course, eventually. Rogerson said, still smiling, 'I might tell Eleanor, if you don't come clean.' He meant his sister, the pretty one who was a VAD. Nick said, 'You'd tell her if I *did* come clean.'

'Never!'

He sighed . . . 'Nick, would you say goodnight to the others for me? Being jolly's rather difficult, tonight.'

Nick told Treglown, 'We'll rendezvous with you three miles south-east of South Foreland at 9 am. All right?'

The ML captain nodded. 'Right. But I wish it'd only take *me* ten minutes to get there!'

He'd have to leave harbour a lot earlier than the CMBs

would. Nick explained that they'd have to be in from sea fairly early in the evening, in order to attend the briefing. So to get a full day's practice in, he needed an early start. He said goodnight to them.

'I'm off now. Going round to my old ship to make a few farewells.'

Mackerel was away at the other end of the port, in the tidal harbour where she'd boiler-cleaned, and the walk of about a mile and a half each way would do him good. He'd had no time for goodbyes this afternoon after the interview with Reaper. Wyatt had been waiting for him, though, and had accepted without much surprise or sorrow the information that Nick was being taken from him. Nick told him nothing except that he was being sent temporarily to *Arrogant*: which sounded, certainly, like an appointment for a man nobody had a job for. Wyatt had muttered, 'Well, I did try . . . I'm sorry, Everard', and on an afterthought he'd gone so far as to shake hands. Nick had arranged for his gear to be sent over, and left, intent on getting to grips with CMB 11 as soon as possible. Now he went down to his cabin on *Arrogant*'s main deck, to get his greatcoat. His stuff was all here, but he wasn't unpacking anything except immediate essentials. Might that be tempting Fate? After this one 'errand' – Reaper had used that term to describe the CMB operation – he'd no idea what they'd have for him to do next. It was distinctly possible that Reaper didn't know either. Reaper, for his purposes or the Plans Division's, wanted a job done, and they'd given him a man to do it. Someone they had no better use for. When Reaper had got whatever it was he wanted, he wouldn't give two farthings for Nicholas Everard's next appointment!

It wasn't a happy thought. He worried about it as he made his way out through the big old ship and down her gangway. Then he told himself not to think about it any more: he was tired, and depressed by the news about Johnny Vereker.

Get the CMB job done first. Then *start worrying*.

He'd turned the top corner and he was walking westward in the direction of the Marine Parade, with the submarine basin and the rest of the harbour shining like silver on his left, when it struck him suddenly that what was making it shine was the moon. The new one, just an infant moon, and only visible now because there was a great rift in the clouds: but it was there – and it might just as easily, therefore, be there again in two nights' time. Reaper had said something like *Moon may turn out to be a nuisance, but with luck there'll be cloud to cover it . . .*

With an absence of luck, there might not be?

CMBs needed dark nights to work in. Being so small and low in the water, hard to see except when they moved at speed, when they kicked up so much wash that they could be spotted as easily as battleships – they could lie stopped and be just about invisible. Being of shallow draught, they could sneak over shoals, too. Ideal for ambush, a quick torpedoing and escape. But a moon was as bad for them as daylight. They were no faster than the modern German destroyers, and they were made of wood and carried only one torpedo and the revolvers on their officers' belts, while the Hun destroyers were steel bristling with four-inch guns and quick-firing two-pounders.

Have your outing now, he thought, addressing the moon's sharp, fang-like shape. *And tomorrow night, if you like. But after that – please . . .*

Passing the naval headquarters buildings now, where this thing had been sprung on him this afternoon. A ray of light shone from one sandbagged doorway, glinted on a sentry's bayonet; otherwise it was all quiet, dark, either deserted or very well blacked out. He walked on, wondering if that bit of moon might bring the Gothas. They'd come without any moon at all, last time. But on recent visits they'd been getting a hot reception, and all because Lloyd George had been in the town on an official visit in September and bombs had been dropped in his vicinity – at least, close enough for him to have been aware of them. Anti-aircraft guns for which General Bickford had been pressing since last year had been delivered within days! Nick thought, with his eyes on *Zubian*'s black shape outlined against silvered water, *By this time tomorrow night I'll know where we're going, and what for* . . . He would not, he thought, swap Midshipman Selby for the other one. He'd make the best of Selby – who might, for all one knew, be worth his salt when it came to action. It was remembering Underhill's contemptuous expression 'runt of the litter' that had changed his mind. Hadn't *he* been that, in some people's eyes? If he dropped Selby he'd be doing him a thoroughly bad turn. If one knew for certain he wasn't up to scratch, it would be justified, but on such small knowledge of him he didn't believe it was.

The Prince of Wales pier was on his left, a long black finger poking south-eastward. He walked on, passing it, to where

365

Mackerel lay in the angle between the eastern wall of the tidal harbour and the small jetty that protected it. He hardly expected to find much life in her; but at least he'd have been aboard, tried to say goodbye to his former shipmates. By the time he finished the torpedo-firings tomorrow, she should have sailed.

The gangway sentry peered at him as he approached. Then, recognising him, saluted.

'Evening, Jarvie. All well?'

'Yessir, evenin' sir!'

'Anyone still about, d'you know?' He started up the gangway. Jarvie told him, 'They're all in the wardroom, sir. Bit of a do on, I believe, sir.'

Nick could hear it. *Mackerel*'s wardroom, evidently, were entertaining. Loud voices, laughter, party sounds . . . He stepped off the gangway and turned aft, went in through the blackout flap, painted canvas covering the doorway in the superstructure, and started down the ladderway. A voice from down there in the wardroom rose above the din: 'Speech! Speech!'

Nick stopped, wondering what was going on. He heard Charlie Pym's voice rise out of a sudden quiet.

'Gentlemen . . . Unaccustomed as I am—'

'Means 'e's a virgin!'

'Don' in'errupt y' first lieutenant!'

'—I should like to say how touched, how deeply moved I am by the enthusiasm with which you have welcomed my replacing one who – who—'

Laughter . . . Gladwish's voice cut through it: 'One who's come a cropper, that's—'

'One who's come to say goodbye to you.' Nick stepped through the doorway. He saw Gladwish, Grant, Watson; and Pym up on a chair, red-faced and with his mouth open. There were a couple of other men he didn't know, a warrant officer and a sub-lieutenant. They all looked quite shocked at seeing him. Grant was blushing scarlet as he jumped to his feet, and Gladwish stammered, 'Why, it's – why—'

'My word, you *have* surprised us.' Pym climbed off the chair. 'A little impromptu celebration of my elevation to first lieutenant. I'm sorry, it probably seems – well—'

'It seems –' Nick looked at him calmly – 'exactly what it *is*.' He saw Warburton, the leading steward, slip away. Pym offered, 'Well, good heavens, you must have a drink!'

'No thanks.' Watson, the engineer, was trying to claim his attention. He nodded to him. 'Hello, Chief.'

'Wanna say – it's a bloody rotten thing they done to you, it's more'n a bloody shame, it's—'

'What are you talking about, for God's sake?'

Gladwish nodded owlishly. 'He'sh right. They should 'a given y'a medal, not—'

'I wish I knew what any of you was talking about.' Nick looked at Pym. 'Can you tell me?'

'Well.' Pym shrugged. An exaggerated movement, but compared to Gladwish and Watson he seemed fairly sober. 'I've mixed feelings, naturally. I mean, I've got your job, I can't pretend I *mind* that . . . On the personal level though, of course, one's sorry—'

'I'm *extremely* sorry, sir.' Midshipman Grant, who evidently had not been allowed anything or much to drink, was still pink with embarrassment. Nick asked him, 'Sorry about what, Mid?'

'Well – you being pushed out—'

'Pushed out?'

He glanced round. They were all staring at him, doing their best to look sympathetic, on his side. He asked Pym, 'Do *you* think I've been *pushed out*?'

'Well.' Pym half smirked at Gladwish, then looked back at him. 'I'm afraid we *know* you have. That business ashore – the captain told me—'

'What, that I'd been dismissed the ship?'

'Nothing as definite as that, but—'

'I'll be damned.' He shook his head. It had been a long day, one way and another. 'Well, I won't try to convince you you're all jumping to wrong conclusions. You are, but it doesn't matter all that much . . . I only came along to say goodbye. I'll be at sea tomorrow before you sail, so—'

'At sea?' Grant had asked the question. What did they think, that he was confined to barracks? Nick looked back at Pym. 'I wish you luck. I hope you turn into a first-class number one.'

'Well, I'll certainly do my—'

'You won't, though. You're too soft with yourself and too damned idle . . . Goodbye.'

He went out and up the ladder, stepped out, pushing the canvas aside, on to the quarterdeck. Moving quickly, trying to master anger and disquiet, and wanting to be away from them. He turned for'ard, towards the gangway.

'Lieutenant Everard, sir?'

It was Leading Seaman McKechnie. There were quite a few other members of the ship's company behind him. 'Warby come an' tol' us you was aboard, sir.' Warburton, he meant, the captain's steward. 'Come to say goodbye, sir?'

'Yes, that's about it.'

'Sir – we want to say – well, the lads is sorry ye're awa', sir . . .' A murmur of agreement came from the others with him. 'Ship won't be the same, sir, not now.'

'Well – thank you.'

It was hard to know what to say. He certainly couldn't tell them the truth, that *they* were the people he should have come to say goodbye to, the only ones he regretted leaving.

'All I can say is I hope we may meet again.' It was a crowd, now, filling this port side of the iron deck. He raised his voice, and called out, 'Goodbye, and good luck to you all. You deserve it!' He put out his hand: 'We'll meet again, I hope, McKechnie.' Then he found that he was shaking *all* their hands, and they were singing all around him, *For He's a Jolly Good Fellow* . . . The Glasgow killick shouted in his ear, 'I seen the wee lass tonight, sir, she said tae gie ye her love!'

He got away. In the wardroom they'd have had an earful of that singing; and Wyatt, if he'd been asleep in his cabin, might well have been woken by it. It would annoy Wyatt – and mortify Charlie Pym!

She said tae gie ye her love . . .

McKechnie must have seen her in that pub. And the pubs were all shut now. But he remembered where she lived: at least, he was fairly sure he'd be able to retrace the hurried, rather painful steps he'd taken on that fateful, rum-flavoured morning.

Not only rum-flavoured though: there'd been the taste of Annabel. And her touch, and her gentle voice, the affection in her eyes . . .

Reaper's clipped tones echoed in his brain: *You'd better not see the girl again.*

Well, he'd given no such undertaking.

Left, here. Over the bridge at the end of Wellington dock. Now through there, the alley, and then right into Snargate Street. There was a side street forty yards farther down. He saw Pym's sneer, and stopped. Why give people like Pym what they wanted, why oblige the Charlie Pyms, for God's sake? And a thought on the heels of that one: wouldn't she have someone with her, by this time of night?

Reaper's voice again: *Nursery days are over, Everard. You're fledged, now!*

He turned about, went back across the bridge. Thinking of the man who might be with her now, this moment, making love to her, hearing that soft voice in his ear, seeing those wide eyes in the moonlight flooding in. But he was seeing a man with a ruddy-complexioned face and a black military moustache: not Annabel's client, but Sarah's lover.

The moon had slid behind a bank of cloud. Nursery days *might* have been over, and he *might* have been 'fledged'; but he felt cut off, rootless.

CHAPTER 10

He held CMB 11 on the course for Dunkirk. The weather forecast had proved accurate: only a light breeze ruffled the straits, and the swell was long, leisurely; the boat skimmed it, swooping in long shallow dives and climbs, a rhythmic, waltz-time motion accompanied by her engine's steady roar and the thudding of her bottom-boards against the sea's solidity. Harry Underhill in CMB 14 was in station one cable's length astern; there were thirty miles to go, two-thirds of the distance still to cover. Since these shallow-draught boats had seldom to bother about such nuisances as shoals, their route to enter Dunkirk Roads was 'as-the-crow-flies'.

Nick jerked his head to Selby.

'Here, you can have her. South seventy-three east.'

'Aye aye, sir.'

No snigger. Nick had asked him yesterday, during the torpedo firing practice, 'Why d'you giggle whenever anyone says any damn thing at all, Mid?'; and he hadn't done it since. It was surprising what a difference it made; when you separated Selby from his laugh, he became quite likeable. And yesterday afternoon Nick had made him take over for one of the torpedo shots, and he'd handled it perfectly.

Reaper had said to them in his quiet, matter-of-fact tone, 'I want you to go over to the Belgian coast and bring back Weary Willie. That armed trawler the Huns anchor every night off Middelkerke, you know?'

He'd looked round at them – at Nick, Underhill and Treglown, and they'd all nodded. He'd added, 'Intact.'

A cutting-out operation, in fact. Boarding-party in the ML, and the two CMBs to ward off interference. Very simple, really. Nick had been thinking about it ever since Reaper had given them the briefing, and he was still thinking about it now as he moved over to the cockpit's starboard side, leaving Selby to drive the boat. On the way across he stooped to look in at Ross. The ERA was on his little wooden seat, peering intently between tall, bony knees at dials that told him about such things as revs, oil-pressure, temperature. She was a good'un, CMB 11 was, he'd told Nick. Some of the others had to be nursed like babies and *still* gave trouble. He was nursing this one, Nick thought, very much like a baby.

The action torpedo rested where yesterday a succession of practice ones had lain. This one wore a warhead, though, three hundredweight of explosive. He stroked the ice-cold curve of silver steel, and wondered if there'd be a use for it tonight. He hoped not. What was wanted was speed and silence and no trouble, no Huns seeing or hearing or even suspecting anything. The cutting-out had to take place within spitting distance of the coast at Middelkerke and only about five miles from Ostend. Thirty years ago it would have been done with cutlasses and muffled oars.

CMB 14 was a dark blob bouncing in a welter of foam two hundred yards astern, in this boat's wake. They were travelling at twenty knots, a fairly economical speed that would get them to Dunkirk in plenty of time to refuel, have a snack and be on their way again. Treglown had set off in his ML much earlier in the day, and he'd have left Dunkirk before the CMBs got there. He had a PO, a stoker PO, three seamen, and one stoker as passengers; his own sub-lieutenant would be taking charge of them as a boarding party.

He moved to the for'ard starboard corner, leant with his arms folded on the coaming and his chin resting on his arms, watched the craft's long grey bow rising to the swells and carving a path across them. After each swoop up there was a fall and a thudding jar as her forepart smacked down again and her 340 horsepower flung her at the next one. Not difficult to imagine how uncomfortable she'd be in anything like rough weather.

Cloud-cover was thick, unbroken. It had to remain so. Provided the night stayed dark, and they had a modicum of luck: or at least an absence of *bad* luck . . . Such as meeting a destroyer or torpedo-boat coming out of Ostend. They had a habit of prowling round old Willie, snooping up between the Ostend Bank and Nieuwpoort Bank, then turning back into the port again or up-coast. The CMBs' function tonight would be to guard against any such interference, watch the approaches while the ML carried out her boarding and cutting-out, and then hang around to cover the joint retirement of the ML and her captive. If a torpedo-boat showed up, they'd try to lead it away and, if necessary, torpedo it. But only

371

if it *was* necessary. So close to Ostend – and to Zeebrugge, for that matter – the important thing was not to attract attention. A Hun destroyer flotilla could be whistled up within minutes. Ideally, the trawler's crew – although she was armed they weren't trained, fighting seamen, apparently – would wake up to find revolvers at their heads; and the Huns ashore would wake to find Willie gone.

'What the devil do they want us to pinch a trawler for?' Underhill had been puzzled, after last night's briefing. 'We've got – what, eighty here already?'

Nick had been thinking about it too, and he had a theory that explained it and pointed to a much bigger issue than this little jaunt. But he gave the CMB man the same vague reason that Reaper had offered: this was the beginning of a switch to the offensive, a policy of keeping the Hun hopping and spoiling his sleep.

'We want 'em on the *de*fensive,' Reaper had told them. 'We've still got to guard the straits, but we want to go out and hit 'em too. As you know, Vice-Admiral Keyes is in command now – and he's never been a man to sit back and let the enemy come to *him*.'

'Right we are, then.' Reaper had begun to roll up his chart. 'Any other questions?'

There weren't. He told Nick, 'Work out your own detailed orders and carry on from here. It's in your hands. Let's have a tidy and successful operation. You're not getting anything on paper – just go and do it . . . Perhaps you'll see me to the gangway, Everard.' He said to him privately, on the way down, 'I said I want this Hun intact. That will include, of course, her crew.'

Nick thought about it for a moment. Then he asked, 'Is that the priority, sir? Prisoners?'

Reaper frowned at him. 'Is there any reason we can't have the whole caboodle?'

'No, sir. Just a matter of priorities, if anything should go wrong.'

'I very much hope it won't . . . You're right to the extent that we haven't any great *need* of another trawler . . .' He'd said it vaguely, as if it didn't really matter either way. The fact was, it had been said.

Nick nodded. 'I understand, sir.' But Reaper had been at pains not to be too precise. 'The object is to take the trawler, crew and all.' He hesitated, near the gangway's head now. 'Look here – we wouldn't want the Hun to think we'd just gone after prisoners. The object is to let him know we're pushing him, that the straits belong to *us* . . . Makes sense, doesn't it?'

Nick saluted. 'Goodnight, sir.'

'Goodnight, Everard. And good luck.'

He'd thought, watching the gold-peaked cap disappear down the depot ship's gangway, that it was pretty obvious what was wanted, and what for, and why Reaper had been so mealy-mouthed about it. It was surprising Underhill hadn't caught on too. But he and Treglown might not have known where Weary Willie came from, where she and her crew spent their daylight hours.

They didn't ask, so he didn't need to tell them.

After supper he'd gone up to the chartroom, alone, to work out the orders he'd give them in the morning. To start with, for his own benefit, he jotted down the essentials of the situation they'd be facing. For instance, that the operation had been planned not only for a calm spell of weather but also for an exceptionally low low-water. The Huns might be thinking themselves safe behind the Belgian shoals; they were shoal-conscious, they'd left the channels un-dredged in order to keep the Royal Navy off their coast. They might not think of CMBs and MLs, which drew so little water they practically walked on it . . . Second, there were to be two Dover destroyers patrolling near the pillar buoy at the Hinder, twelve miles north-west of Willie; when the trawler had been taken, she and the ML were to head straight for their protection. While any destroyers – Germans – which the CMBs managed to entice away were to be led east-nor'-eastward, into the minefield which *Mackerel* and her friends had laid a few nights ago.

The emergency situations most likely to arise were (a) a breakdown, engine failure, of one of the three boats of the cutting-out flotilla, (b) encounter with enemy destroyer/s, (c) change of cloud/moon conditions. Nick's orders as he finally produced them dealt almost entirely with reaction to these contingencies.

Everyone knew exactly what to do, now.

He looked across at Selby. 'All right, Mid?'

The pink face turned to him; and this time, Selby laughed. He shouted, 'Bloody *marvellous*, sir!'

Treglown, they learnt, had arrived in Dunkirk and sailed again on schedule. The CMBs refuelled and were clear of the harbour by 9 pm. The route Nick had planned would take them about three miles offshore most of the way, after an initial zigzag to seaward to clear the silted east side of Dunkirk Roads and the Hills bank. They'd finish up only two miles off Middelkerke; they'd be just inshore of Weary Willie then, and over the top of a shallow patch which the Germans might well consider impassable and therefore an approach not worth watching very closely.

There was a danger that it *might* be impassable, places so shallow at this lowest of low tides that even CMBs and MLs couldn't scrape over them. The lack of dredging and the removal of navigational marks, all part of a deliberate enemy policy, created that uncertainty. There'd have been sifting into channels, and some of the shoals would have extended this way or that, even moved bodily to new positions.

The distance to cover was about twenty miles. The CMBs could have raced there in not much more than half an hour, but Nick had set a speed of twelve knots – which would leave virtually no wash or broken water to catch a German eye, and allowing for the tides would give a speed-made-good of ten and get them to the rendez-vous position by the zero-hour of 11 pm. Twelve knots was also about the slowest speed a CMB could manage; their engines couldn't put up with low revs for any length of time.

By eleven-ten the trawler should be captured and the flotilla – now of four instead of three – on its way seaward.

He looked to his right, at Selby. The midshipman had his glasses up and he was keeping a fairly constant watch on CMB 14, who was tucked-in close now, only fifty yards astern. Each snotty had the job of keeping track of the other boat; and since at this distance they were within hearing distance of each other's klaxons, a system of emergency sound signals had been established.

The monitor and its attendant destroyer off La Panne had been warned that they'd be passing. And it was a halfway point, a way of checking their position accurately for the last time before they found Weary Willie. The squat, black shape of the monitor loomed up ahead, and Nick moved the wheel gently, easing the CMB over to pass close to seaward of her. Ahead and to starboard a glow hung in the sky over Nieuwpoort, and the small sparks of distant starshell drifted downwards, flickered out to be replaced by others; Nick thought, *No starshell to seaward, please* . . . They'd be worse than searchlights, even; and the searchlight crews along this section of the coast had been warned of the boats' schedule. The rumble of gunfire from the Front was remote, impersonal. He saw the destroyer now: an 'M', lying at anchor beyond the monitor. Both ships were dark, dead-looking, silent; but there'd be more than a few pairs of eyes watching the CMBs slide out of the night and into it again. At Nieuwpoort they'd pass within two miles, four thousand yards, of the point where the trench-lines met the sea. Nick wondered if his father had even been that close

374

to the firing line, or whether his previous appointment had been of a similar kind to this riding-school job he had now. Something to do with horses, most likely. He'd never made any comprehensible statement about what he did. He'd implied, or allowed others to imagine, that he'd been actively involved in the various 'pushes', and talked about the fighting as though he'd been in it; but if it turned out eventually that he hadn't, nothing he'd said would prove him a liar.

He wished his elder brother David was still alive. They'd never got on; but David had been the heir to the baronetcy and Mullbergh, and now he was dead he, Nick, was in his place; he'd have preferred to have been detached, disinterested altogether in the inheritance, in whether his father lived or died.

Underhill was passing the destroyer. From this boat the monitor, well astern now, was just fading out of sight.

'What's the time, Mid?'

'Nine fifty-seven, sir.'

Three minutes inside schedule. A rocket soared, burst over Nieuwpoort, a greenish-yellow colour. He wondered what it meant. The land to starboard now was Belgium; France had ended just before La Panne – where, astern, a searchlight beam had just sprung out, lancing the darkness with its silver blade, sweeping the sea to the westward of the guardships. *Their* timing wasn't far out either, he thought; they'd been told to stay switched-off until ten.

'Selby – see if Ross is happy, will you?'

Selby ducked down for a quick chat with the ERA. He told Nick a minute later, 'It's all fine at the moment, sir. Except for the usual worry about oiling-up.'

It was a risk that had to be accepted. Gunfire was louder as they drew closer to the front line. You could see the flashes low down, sometimes, and bits of walls or broken buildings silhouetted for split seconds in their light; but no individual sounds, it was all one continuous background rumble. Inland searchlights wavered, fingering the clouds, searching for aeroplanes or Zeppelins; but those were too far east, he realised, to be anything but German. They'd be watching for the RNAS squadrons, Johnny Vereker's friends. A flare hung, the brilliant magnesium-white illuminating a black spread of land, the horror-ground of Europe.

Selby shouted, 'I think fourteen's in trouble, sir!'

Nieuwpoort was well astern. They'd been in what might be called enemy water for almost half an hour.

375

'*Think* – or *is* she?'

He heard the letter 'A' on Underhill's klaxon. In their code it meant 'am aground' . . .

With target almost in touching distance, and German batteries a bare two miles to starboard.

There was a quick remedy and a slow one; they'd practised both. This was a time for the faster, riskier method. He was turning the CMB to port, seaward, holding full rudder on her; at twelve knots no amount of helm would turn her over.

'Tell Ross I'll be opening right up in a minute!' He had her on the opposite course now, heading back the way they'd just come. He asked Selby, as the snotty came up from shouting in Ross's ear, 'Was she dead astern of us?'

'Bit out on the quarter.'

'You should've told me.'

Spilt milk . . . Underhill had let his boat swing off to starboard and he'd hit the mud and there he was . . . Nick swung the boat around to port again, taking her in two cables' lengths astern of the stranded CMB and holding on until he was inshore of her. Then hard a-port, right round quickly, aiming her at Underhill's boat, on a course of about east-by-north. When she was pointing the right way and he'd steadied her and centred the wheel, he pushed the throttle wide open. CMB 11's stern went down hard and she surged forward under full power. You could feel the thrust, the sea trying to hold her back and then its resistance lessening as she lifted in the water and began to skim it, bounce it, engine-noise a deafening roar now and sea flying past, wind ripping, whining, wash piling upwards and outwards, flinging high and white from her quarters as she drove forward. Underhill would be ready for the wash that – hopefully – would lift his boat off the sand and give him a chance to clear it. Nick moved the wheel a little, easing her to port and aiming to pass about ten yards clear of fourteen's stern. This boat was right up on the plane now, rocketing along, the sea crashing under her as she hurtled over it: and passing fourteen – *now* . . .

As soon as he'd passed, muttering thanks to God that he hadn't hit the ground himself – in fact with the boat up and skimming she was a foot or two further from that danger – he cut the power. There was an immediate sensation of drag: as if an anchor had been thrown out to pull them back: like brakes slammed on and as if she was stopping dead, and her own wash rushed past and under, lifting and then dropping her several times, making it difficult to hold glasses steady enough to see what had happened to Underhill.

'I think she's off, sir.' Selby was propped with an elbow over the torpedo warhead and glasses at his eyes. Nick was bringing the boat round to starboard, swinging her across the rolling ridges that still followed from that short, sharp rush. Rocking in towards the land again, dead slow. Now he had his glasses on the other boat: and he heard her hooter bleat the letter 'P', which meant 'ready to proceed'.

'See how Ross is, and tell him I want the revs for twelve knots again.' He'd control it by the throttle, but Ross down there could watch the revs minutely and keep them adjusted. That burst of speed should have cleared his worries over oiling-up; and fourteen had been got out of trouble without the delay of passing a line and trying to drag her off. The risks had been of grounding oneself, and of making such a display of wash. He'd been shown aerial photos of CMBs going fast in poor visibility, and the wash and wake was all you could see. Navigationally too it was a nuisance that it had happened; he'd been on the track he'd worked out and needed to be on, and now he couldn't be sure of it any more. If he went too far to starboard he'd do what Underhill had done, whereas if he came too far to port they might run straight into Weary Willie before linking up with Treglown. There was a strong element of chance in it, anyway, with so much uncertainty about what changes had or hadn't occurred in the shoals and channels. For that matter, Treglown could have run into trouble, could be stuck on some inshore bank; or been too cautious and stayed farther out, passed the luckless Willie and now be groping in the darkness, lost . . .

He decided to take Underhill's present position as being fifty yards too close inshore: and turn here, now, on to the old course.

'Tell me when he's back in station.' He waited, searching the sea ahead. It was all black, quiet, empty. The deep growl of the engine emphasised that surrounding emptiness. There was a special feeling, state of mind, when you were in enemy waters, close to his coasts and bases, a distinctly enjoyable sensation of loneliness and danger: a sharp consciousness of being there, armed and secret. You'd have to experience it, he thought, to know it, it wasn't something you could put into words. No sign of Treglown. Selby reported, 'Fourteen's in station astern, sir.'

'Good. Now look out ahead and both sides, help me find the ML.'

'Some way to go yet, sir, isn't there?'

The fireworks over the trenches were well abaft the beam. But perhaps Selby was right, perhaps they weren't yet far enough back. He checked: first that the boat's head was on the course – north 65° east – and then the relative bearing of the pyrotechnics. 130° on the bow: and he had the bearings in his head, memorised, as you had to when you couldn't use a chart: Nieuwpoort would have to be 150° on the bow when they were inshore of Weary Willie's regular anchorage. Selby was right: there was about a mile, or slightly more than that, to go. Say five minutes, then: and expect to meet Treglown in three?

'Time, Mid?'

'Ten-fifty, sir.'

Nicely up to schedule. His sense of timing had been thrown out by the emergency of Underhill's grounding. An excess of anxiety had given him the impression they were late and in danger of messing the thing up. In fact the incident with Underhill's boat had only so to speak taken up the slack.

Lesson to be learnt: to keep on the ball you don't have to *worry* . . . Command was a new experience, and one had to be careful not to allow it to distort one's judgement.

He told Selby, 'You're right. About a mile to go.'

Silence all around them, soaking up the engines' rumble. The sea's blank, dimpled surface hid its secrets. Shoal water: at times there was probably no more than a foot or even a few inches under the boats' keels. And any channels that were still deep enough for navigation might well have been mined. Two miles on the beam there, German gunners would be peering seaward. There was a sudden stench of petrol exhaust as a breeze swept up from astern. Wind rising? Wind didn't only make calm seas rough, it blew cloud-cover off the moon . . . He told himself, *It's moving according to plan, there's no point dreaming up problems that aren't here.* Selby was cleaning the lenses of his binoculars. The sea hissed as it swept along the CMB's wooden sides and the engine grumbled deep in its throat as it drove her steadily through the night. The midshipman had his glasses up again, now. Nick's own last spoken words, *a mile to go* hung in his brain as if he'd memorised them; he wasn't sure if it might be one minute or five since he'd spoken them. It was like a dream when something nonsensical or totally unimportant keeps running through your mind.

He checked the bearing again. Nieuwpoort was slightly more than 140° on the bow now. Almost there. The ML might appear at any—

378

'There she is, sir!'

Too good to be true . . .

But that odd, cuttlefish shape was too distinctive to confuse with anything else. He looked back, saw Underhill close astern, and put the wheel over, headed to close Treglown. Close up to him, he throttled right down and stopped, de-clutched. The CMB lay rocking on the swell, so close that if Treglown had come out of his little box of a wheelhouse and waved, he'd have seen him. Underhill had stopped too, after getting in much closer; the object was to let Treglown see them and identify them, without the need for exchanges of signals.

He *had* seen them. The ML was gathering way, on a northwards course. Half a mile in that direction, Weary Willie should be nuzzling sleepily at his anchor.

'Time now?'

'Eleven o'clock, sir.'

He checked the Nieuwpoort bearing. South 35° west.

Bang on. The main worry had been a variability of the tidal streams on this coast, but the allowances he'd made for them seemed to have been right . . . He told himself not to count his chickens, that things could still go wrong. He was edging CMB 11 out to a position one cable's length, two hundred yards, on Treglown's port quarter, and Underhill was opening out the other way to put himself on Nick's beam, the ML's other quarter. He could see both the other craft, he realised suddenly, with the naked eye . . . The clouds hadn't broken up, but they'd thinned, enough to let a suffused radiance filter through. Now, of all moments! White froth under the ML's counter suddenly: she'd speeded up.

'They must have the trawler in sight.'

'I have too, sir. Just to starboard of her.'

'Yes . . . Well done.' He pushed the throttle shut, and the engine-sound fell away to a harsh stuttering. Clutch out . . . He kept his glasses on Treglown's craft as it slid up towards the German trawler's tall black shape. It was Willie's funnel that gave him that high look. No light showing: no movement: only the ML sliding across the dark sea like a ghost-ship.

'What's fourteen doing?'

'Stopped, sir, level with us – abeam, I mean.'

Good . . . Except for the moon. Any moment now the ML would be spotted and there'd be shooting, or a rocket soaring . . . The two shapes merged into one as the ML crept up to the trawler.

One solid black smudge now, shapeless except for its height on the left edge: Willie's chimney. They could have been just in line from this angle, but they'd been united for so long that it was safe to assume they were alongside each other: Treglown's boarding-party would be aboard the German: if no alarm was raised *now*, why—

'Ship, sir! Starboard there, a—'

A searchlight beam sprang out, swept the sea in a short arc and settled on the ML and the trawler locked together. A German voice boomed gibberish over a loud-hailer. Selby had his glasses on her, and began shouting in a high, choked voice, 'Destroyer, sir, it's a dest—'

She'd opened fire. A gun on her foc's'l: a scarlet spurt of flame and now the sound of it, a sort of cracking thud: four-pounder probably. Moonlight brightening the whole scene now, but nothing like as bright as the searchlight still holding the ML in its hard steel clamp. That side was Underhill's. The ML had left the trawler's side, you could see a gap widening between them as she moved ahead and *towards* the German – whose shell hit her low down and for'ard, a shattering upwards disintegration of timber lit in its own shoot of orange flame. That was all it needed: she was built of half-inch planking, and ML 713 was finished, but the destroyer had fired again to make sure of her. Nick swung his glasses to CMB 14 and saw her gathering way, moving towards the enemy destroyer and rising in the water as she picked up speed, white sea boiling, piling from her stern, spreading as she slammed on power. The destroyer was stopped, or as near as dammit stopped. Harry had a sitting duck ahead of him. But the searchlight swung and picked him up, held him: the Huns would be staring down that beam at a welter of foam with a black dart cleaving through it, racing at them. Nick muttered under his breath 'Fire! Fire *now!*' If he didn't he'd lose his chance. The German was moving ahead, in the direction of the burning ML: no, he was turning, you could see his length shortening as he turned to put his bow towards his new enemy. Harry must have fired, because he was going over to starboard now, listing hard over as he swung away: the fish must be on its way, but the German would be bow-on to it, and unless there was a hit about . . . *now*? Nothing had happened: except that CMB 14's white wash was a brilliant fish-hook track across the sea to starboard, and the Hun was continuing his turn and putting on speed himself, still under helm: you could see his bow-wave lengthening, its white curve rising, extending now the full length of that rather high, level-topped foc'sl: a short, high foc'sl, probably turtle-backed, with a gun on its after edge and then a deckhouse in the well before the bridge: a 'V', he thought, built for thirty-five knots but getting a bit old now, probably do 30 at most flat out: a CMB should have the legs of him. Harry would *have* to have the legs of him, he'd nothing left to hit him with. The ML's flames were lower, almost extinguished as she settled in the water; she was only afloat now because she was made of wood. The Hun destroyer captain would be thinking he was on top of things: he was driving the CMB away and he'd smashed the ML, he'd think he'd saved Weary Willie from the English swine-hounds; he hadn't seen CMB 11, thanks to an extra couple of hundred yards and the fact that lying stopped like this there wasn't much to see.

Nick slipped the clutch in, and put the throttle to slow ahead. He told Selby, 'Watch the Hun and fourteen and tell me if anything develops.'

'They're chasing off, sir, that's all!'

'Keep an eye out that way.'

Harry would be heading for the new minefield. Nick steered CMB 11 for the ML. If the German had come from the west instead of the east matters would have been reversed, *he'd* have attacked it and CMB 14 would have lain doggo. He took her up towards the wrecked ML slowly: wouldn't help anyone if he flung up a lot of white water and attracted some Hun's attention. There could easily be another in the offing: or that first one might give up the chase and come back to see if there were any prisoners to be fished out. But most likely he'd be leaving that job to Willie.

There were two men standing on the ML's stern, and she was only just afloat, with her forepart buried in the sea. He shut the throttle and told Selby, 'Get up for'ard, help those two aboard.'

There were raised hand-hold strakes the whole length of the CMB's curved wooden topsides, and a bit lower another raised one was well placed for toe-holds. The top of the engine-space, immediately for'ard of the cockpit, was flat, but everywhere else you needed something to hang on to. Selby crawled for'ard past the round engine-access hatch at the for'ard end of the engine-space and halfway between the cockpit and the stem; Nick gave her another touch ahead, then shut down again: the CMB's stem-post nudged the ML's stern, and Selby was holding on to the bull-ring while he helped the two survivors climb up. Nick shouted to them to get down through the engine hatch, and saw them doing it as he

381

edged her away from the wreckage; it wouldn't be floating for much longer. Weary Willie was off on his port beam: black, quiet, and still at anchor. Then he saw men on her bow and heard a clank of cable-gear; those had to be British, because any Germans at liberty would have been blazing away with her four-pounder. Someone came out of this end of the engine-space and clambered up beside him.

'Glad you were around.'

Sam Treglown.

'Casualties?'

'None. There was only me and my leading hand – that's Eastman here – left on board. I'd decided the rest would be more use in Willie. She was ours without a shot before I shoved off, by the way.'

Too soon to express joy or even satisfaction. There was the question of what was happening to CMB 14. The leading seaman was in the cockpit now, and Selby was coming out of the engine-space behind him. Nick, with the CMB swinging to point her bow at the German trawler, was thinking about the likelihood of that destroyer coming back, and about the low speed of the trawler and the steadily increasing moonlight. That last factor was the clincher that was pushing him towards a variation of the plans made earlier. Treglown asked him, 'Will Underhill be all right?' He couldn't have put the question at a better – or worse – moment: gunfire crackled in the north-east, perhaps a couple of miles away: Nick was looking in that direction when he saw red sparks near the horizon, heard more shouting; then there was a whitish flash and the deep boom of an explosion. He answered Treglown: 'I wouldn't count on it.' He'd arrived at that decision. 'Selby – raise the firing-lever stop.'

'Raise it, sir?'

'Do it!'

'Aye aye, sir!'

If the stop was down, when the torpedo was fired it would knock back the firing-lever, starting the missile's engine so that as it dropped into the water its two concentric propellers would be whirring at full speed. If the stop was raised clear, there'd be nothing to hit the firing-lever, so the engine wouldn't fire and the torpedo wouldn't run. It would simply be pushed out astern and sink.

Selby came back into the cockpit. 'It's raised, sir.'

Nick moved the lever to withdraw the retaining-stops; they would have held the fish in its trough even against the ram's thrust. He put his hand on the firing-lever, and jerked it over, heard the thud of the cordite cartridge firing to create sudden pressure inside the hydraulic cylinder. The boat jerked with the force of it as the ram slammed back: the torpedo was a silver streak that sprang away over her low stern. They heard the splash that represented about twelve hundred pounds of taxpayers' money thrown away; then there was a long, sharp hiss of excess pressure leaking from the cylinder.

'Stand by to go alongside the trawler. Selby, Eastman – hold us alongside when we're there . . . Treglown – I want everyone out of her and into this boat. There's plenty of space where the fish was. I want the Germans – here, Selby – get one of these panels out. *That* one.' He kicked at the cockpit's after bulkhead, on the starboard side. 'We'll put the Huns in there, inside the stern.'

The panel could be removed, and there was room inside, between the heavy timbers that supported the torpedo channel, for several men to crouch or sit. They could be watched and guarded from the cockpit, and there was no equipment in there that they could do any harm to.

He told Treglown, 'Everyone into the boat, then have your stoker PO open Willie's seacocks.'

'Aye aye, sir!'

Selby had forced the plywood bulkhead panel out, and CMB 11 was sliding up to berth on the trawler's starboard side. As she loomed up closer, Willie looked surprisingly big. That tall funnel, and the high, square bridge with sandbags piled around it. Must make her top-heavy, he thought: and every little would help her down, presently. The moonlight was even brighter now. Treglown's sub-lieutenant, Marriot, appeared on deck and reported that everything was under control, they'd only to get the hook up: then they bumped alongside and Treglown sprang over and started passing out Nick's orders. There was a momentary hush of surprise, then a rush to obey. Nick was searching the sea to starboard, east and north-east: you could see quite a distance now and he knew he couldn't help Harry Underhill, to try to would be like throwing a chestnut into the fire in the hope of dislodging one already in it. And with this moon beginning to break right through now it was simply not possible to remain so close inshore . . . There was nothing to be seen, out there. Since those two spasms of gunfire and the explosion there'd been no sound, either. The explosion *could* have been the German hitting a mine. Otherwise . . .

'Get a move on!'

Four German prisoners were being hustled aboard. Nick told a seaman, 'Inside there. They'll have to crawl in.'

'Aye aye, sir . . . Giddahn, Fritz, giddahn there . . .'

Otherwise: well, a CMB wouldn't strike a mine, because they were moored too deep, those M-sinkers. But there'd been gunfire first: and the petrol tank was right under the cockpit floor. It was the only place they could have put it, he supposed. It would be well enclosed, reasonably protected; but still, a four-pounder shell . . .

If the destroyer came back, with this moonlight there'd be no escape from her. Not for a trawler that couldn't make more than about twelve knots. That was why there wasn't going to be a trawler for the destroyer to find if she *did* come back. Men were climbing over from her now. Treglown called, 'Stoker PO's below, sir, opening the seacocks. Only him and your midshipman and myself to come.'

'Very good.'

He waited. That calm 'very good' hung in his ears. Had it been *his* voice?

'She's filling, sir!'

'Come aboard, then.'

'Aye aye, sir!'

The stoker PO sounded like a Devonport man. Nick shouted, 'Treglown, Selby, come on!' They all three tumbled over. He called down to Ross, 'We're overloaded but we need some speed – all right?'

'She won't let you down, sir.'

The CMB was swinging round to point seaward. And Weary Willie was settling, lowering himself sedately but quite rapidly into the sea. When the Germans came back – or when any other German came – they'd think their Willie had been taken. Reaper had said, *We wouldn't want the Hun to think we'd just gone after prisoners.* There was no reason why the Hun should think anything of the sort.

Glancing round, a final look towards the east, Nick thought that if that explosion had been the destroyer going up on a mine, CMB 14 would have been back by now. But there was nothing in sight except the long, flat swells and the increasing moonlight. Reaper had said something about responsibility, and not shirking it. Here it was. Responsibility was here and now and this throttle his hand was resting on.

CHAPTER 11

Edward Wyatt, staring out of the carriage window at the familiar features of Dover's Marine Station, waited until the train had stopped before he stood up and beat at the skirts of his greatcoat to knock the dust off. The South East and Chatham Railway Company was a splendidly efficient organisation, and there had been times when its officials had worked miracles – at the time of the Somme offensive, for instance, they'd run twenty special hospital trains a day, on top of routine services – but it hadn't the staff to keep its trains as sparkling clean as they'd been before the war.

Wyatt wondered what the admiral was going to say to him. He'd hardly put *Mackerel* into the dockyard's hands, up in the Thames, before he'd had the telegram saying that Admiral Keyes wished to see him personally and as soon as possible.

To give him a new ship, perhaps. And just possibly, promotion! If they were giving him a brass hat, they might give him a flotilla-leader to go with it?

He stepped down on to the platform. It was about one mile to the headquarters houses, and the walk would be good for him. He hadn't seen Keyes since the Dardanelles, two years ago. Keyes had been a commodore then. Now he was an acting vice-admiral, promoted from rear-admiral in order to rank higher than Dampier, who was the admiral commanding the Dover dockyard, the engineering side of things. Last time Wyatt had met Keyes had been when Admiral de Robeck, Keyes's chief at that time, had sent for him to congratulate him on the taking of that Turkish battery, the landing party he'd led.

This time – what? Promotion, and a new ship, and a bar to his DSC? Even – possibly – a DSO?

Tim Rogerson had also just stepped out of a train, but at Portsmouth. He was here to have luncheon at Blockhouse, the submarine headquarters, with an old shipmate, 'Baldy' Sandford. He hadn't the least idea what for: or why one of Baldy's older brothers, who was a lieutenant-commander with a DSO and had apparently just arrived at Dover to join the new admiral's staff, should have sent for him and given him this cross between an order and an invitation.

On the part of the older Sandford it had seemed to be an order, but from the younger, Baldy, an invitation. One might hope to discover, over the meal perhaps, what the devil it was all about.

Rogerson walked out of the station precincts and down to the wooden harbour jetty. A twenty-foot motorboat lay alongside, and its coxswain was a leading seaman with an 'HM Submarines' cap-ribbon.

'Lieutenant Rogerson, sir?'

He returned the salute, and stepped into the boat's sternsheets.

Baldy Sandford was an archdeacon's son, he remembered. And one of a large brood: he was the *seventh* son, in fact. Which made one ponder on how archdeacons spent their leisure hours: and one could marvel, too, at such a churchly man having so unpious a son. Not a respecter of persons, old Baldy: a very humorous, jolly fellow, a terrific messmate. Determined as a character could be, in spite of that. The iron-jawed type. If Baldy wanted something done, it *was* done.

Even if he had to do it himself.

He greeted Rogerson on the Blockhouse jetty with a warm, bone-cracking handshake.

'How splendid you could manage it!'

'Oh, they don't exactly keep us on the hop, you know, in Dover.'

'They don't?'

'Not the submarines.'

'What *do* you get up to?'

'This and that. We've moored ourselves to anti-submarine bar-rage nets, pretending to be buoys and hoping Hun submarines might come and put themselves in front of our tubes. And we've done a lot of research on tidal ranges off the Hun ports – graphs of rise and fall, all that . . . I suppose it might come in useful, one day.'

Sandford nodded. 'Indeed it might.' His expression changed back to one of amusement. 'But you're bored stiff, eh?'

'Pretty well.'

'I can offer you something so unboring it might make your ginger thatch stand on end.'

He was a bit conscious of other men's 'thatch'. Rogerson nodded. 'I'll take it, sight unseen.'

'Third hand of an old "C"?'

'Now you're having me on.'

The C-class submarines were old, virtually useless, reserved for coastal-defence – and soon the breakers' yard. As they strolled up the jetty, he could see a couple of them anchored in the mud of Haslar Creek. Here, alongside, were two K-boats and an E. Sandford pointed at the two anchored boats.

'There they are . . . Listen to this, now. What about a C-class boat with a crew of six or seven picked men and her bow packed with five tons of Amatol?'

Rogerson rubbed his chin. He murmured, 'Sounds – explosive.'

'Oh, very.'

'What would we do with it?'

'I can't quite tell you that. What I mean is, I'm not allowed to. But you know that brother of mine who got in touch with you is now working for Roger Keyes?'

'One hears Keyes is collecting quite a large staff.' Rogerson nodded. 'Well?'

'This thing I'm on is part of some great stratagem of our former commodore's. Some kind of mad attack or other.'

'I'm in.'

Sandford glanced at him, surprised by the snap decision. Tim said, 'I'm *in*. Don't try to keep me out of it.'

'Well, there's a spot of preamble I'm bound to give you. It'll be more than ordinarily hazardous. The question of whether or not any of us will get away, or end up prisoners-of-war or blown to smithereens or – well, the point is, it's probably about as near to committing suicide as you could get without endangering your immortal soul. Are you sure you want to do it?'

'Never been more sure of anything.'

'Well, good for you!' Sandford held out his hand. 'I'm *so* glad.'

'Nothing to what I am.' Rogerson told him sincerely, 'I'm tickled pink. Damn nice of you to let me in on it.'

Wally Bell saw Captain Edwards, who was in overall command of the Patrol's MLs, striding towards him down the jetty. Wally stepped ashore to meet him.

'Morning, sir.' He saluted.

'Morning, Bell. Your boat likely to be fit for sea soon?'

'They're putting her together again now, sir. She'll be as good as new, the plumbers say.'

'Better be.' Graham Edwards stared with some disfavour at the litter of engine-room junk on the ML's deck. 'You've a lot of hard work ahead of you.'

Bell jerked his head towards his boat. He said, 'It wasn't just lying around doing nothing that cracked her up in the first place, sir.'

'Work of a particular kind, Bell.' Edwards told him, 'I'm taking you and a few others off routine patrol work, and giving you to Wing-Commander Brock for his programme of experiments. It'll be inshore smoke-laying, mostly.'

'Oh.'

Those bloody burners. Black mess everywhere . . .

'He's got a new system he wants to perfect. None of that messing about with burners. It involves using chlor-sulphonic acid in your boat's exhaust. Much more effective, apparently, as well as neater all round.'

'Chlor-sulphonic, sir?'

'Used in the manufacture of saxin. The sugar-substitute, you know? But that's to be stopped now. All the chlor-sulphonic they can make – or grow, whatever the hell they do – will be sent here, to Brock.'

'Sounds as if we're expecting to lay an awful lot of inshore smoke-screens!'

'Does rather, doesn't it?'

Reaper told Nick, 'You did well, Everard. Very well indeed.'

'Thank you, sir.'

'I'm sorry about Underhill.'

'Yes.' Nobody knew yet what had happened to CMB 14. The most likely theory was that the German destroyer had sunk her, or rather blown her up, and then hung around looking for survivors or trying to fish out wreckage for their intelligence people.

'In the circumstances, you took the best possible decision.'

'Are the prisoners proving useful, sir?'

Reaper's eyebrows rose.

'I beg your pardon?'

'I wondered if the prisoners I brought back were worth their salt, sir.'

'Why should you imagine there was any – any *usefulness* about them?'

388

'Well, sir, they're all I did bring back. And you've expressed satisfaction at the outcome of the operation. And before we set out I did rather understand you to say – well, to *indicate*—'

'You lost one CMB and her crew. Considering you'd had the bad luck to run up against a destroyer, and to find yourself having to cope with moonlight instead of total darkness, I can quite properly congratulate you on having made the best of a tricky situation. And since it was your first experience of command—'

'No, sir.'

He'd brought *Lanyard* back from Jutland.

Reaper raised one hand, and let it fall again. 'The first time you'd been *appointed* in command, then. In that consideration, your conduct of the affair was – impressive.'

'Thank you, sir.'

'Not only in *my* view, I may add.'

He glanced at his watch, frowned as he replaced it in his pocket. 'So *late* . . . What did you mean about those prisoners, Everard?'

'Weary Willie was based on Zeebrugge, sir. I believe – with respect, sir – I think prisoners are what we were really after. The Germans weren't to *think* so, so it was better if we didn't realise it . . .' Reaper was just sitting there and staring at him, listening. He went on, 'There've been rumours of an offensive. And – well, it would make sense from the anti-U-boat angle to attack Zeebrugge, blow it up or capture it or block the canal? Ostend as well, I suppose. But if—'

'It's a nice idea. And of course it's been mooted more than once, in the last two years.' A moment ago Reaper had looked sharply alert; now he'd relaxed. He smiled. 'You've a powerful imagination. But – don't broadcast your ideas, please.'

Nick felt fairly certain he'd hit the nail on the head. An operation against Zeebrugge and Ostend: block seaways out of Bruges and eliminate it as a base. Reaper murmured, 'Wide of the mark. But we don't want rumours flying.' He was looking at his watch again. Nick, worried that he might jump up and rush away, began: 'About what my next appointment's to be, sir . . .'

Reaper looked surprised: as if he thought it was an odd subject to bring up. Nick thought dismally that he'd guessed right in this area too: he'd done the Weary Willie job, and that was the end of this man's interest in him.

'Am I to remain in *Arrogant*?'

A shake of the narrow head . . . 'I've something else to tell you – and on which to convey to you Admiral Keyes's congratulations.'

As a result of *Mackerel*'s action on Christmas Eve, you'll be getting a DSC.'

He was astonished. Delighted, as it sank in, but as much surprised as pleased. He said, 'Very generous of – of the admiral.'

Might Keyes really have sent congratulations? Would he even have heard of Nicholas Everard?

'Lieutenant-Commander Wyatt gets a DSO.'

'Is there a full list available, sir?'

Thinking about Swan. About all of them, but particularly Swan. Reaper shook his head. 'Not yet.' Another glance at his watch. 'Have to cut this short, I'm afraid.' He closed his eyes, as if to concentrate his thoughts: then opened them again and reached for the telephone. 'Crosby. Telephone to *Arrogant*'s first lieutenant. Ask him with my compliments to have Lieutenant Everard's gear packed and sent immediately to *Bravo*.'

Nick stared at him. He couldn't surely have said *Bravo*? Reaper seemed deliberately to avoid his eyes.

'If you can't reach the first lieutenant, the officer of the day would do.' He put the 'phone down. Nick couldn't believe this. A 'thirty-knotter' – fit for nothing but defensive patrol work? and *Bravo* already had a first lieutenant – Elkington, Tim Rogerson's pal! Unless they'd moved Elkington elsewhere; that must be the answer . . . But – patrolling over the Varne minefield, or hanging around the Downs: no hope of any action or excitement. If you had enormous luck you *might* get a crack at a U-boat: but then, so might a drifter!

Reaper was on his feet. Nick stood up too. He felt sick with the let-down of it. They praised you, gave you a medal, then kicked you down the stairs!

'You'll be glad to be in a sea-going appointment, I'm sure. If you'd stayed in *Mackerel* you'd have been in a London dockyard for months on end.'

Sugaring the pill . . . Reaper added, 'But if in the future some offensive operation should be contemplated, I imagine you'd like a part in it?'

'Yes, sir. I should.'

What was he saying – that *Bravo* would be only a temporary billet? Until the attack on the Belgian ports? Or might she take part in it? Hardly . . . His mind was snapping at guesses like a fish at flies . . . And hard reality remained: *Minefield patrol. This is Wyatt's doing* . . . Reaper said, 'Look, I really must cut along.' Pausing, he looked quizzically at Nick. 'You're not a very *trusting* fellow, Everard.'

'I – don't think I understand—'

'Obviously not.' Reaper smiled. 'Never mind.' Offering his hand: 'Thank you again, for a job well done. And – happy New Year!'

New Year's Eve . . .

It didn't feel like it. It hadn't felt like Christmas, either. He shook Reaper's hand.

'Sit down, Wyatt.' The admiral drew his own chair closer to the desk. 'Last time you and I met was also an occasion for congratulation, as I recall.' He nodded at the ribbon on Wyatt's shoulder. 'That DSC, of course. But hadn't you been nicked by a Turk's bayonet?'

'A pinprick, sir.'

'H'm . . . Great days while they lasted, eh?'

'Damn shame we were obliged to withdraw, sir.'

'As you say.'

Nodding. Thoughts reaching back to the Dardanelles and to his own conviction that the Navy could have forced the Narrows, *should* have done. His commodore's rank then hadn't cut much ice.

'But it's the present and future we must think about, Wyatt. Not the games we've lost.' Fingers drummed briefly on the desk. 'Your ship's out of commission, you face a period of inactivity, and that's hardly to your taste. Am I right?'

Wyatt nodded. The admiral continued, 'Your talents in command afloat are undoubted. But you made a useful soldier of yourself, out there, too.' He wasn't just making conversation; he was watching his visitor closely, to assess reaction. 'How would you like to do something of the sort again?'

Wyatt started carefully, 'If you have some such employment for me, sir—'

'I'm planning a – a certain enterprise, Wyatt.' Keyes slid a drawer open, took out a folded sheet of paper, passed it across the desk. 'Read that, would you?'

It was a letter to him from Admiral Wemyss, who had now taken over from Sir John Jellicoe as First Sea Lord. Wyatt read,

In view of the possibility of the enemy breaking through the line on the North Coast of France, and attacking Calais and Dunkirk, a special battalion of Marines and a company of bluejackets will be placed at your disposal for reinforcements, and to act as demolition parties, etc., to destroy guns and stores. You are to make every preparation for blocking Calais and Dunkirk harbours at the last possible moment, with the ships whose names have been given to you verbally, so as to deny the use of these ports to the enemy if necessary.

Wyatt looked up. 'I see, sir.' He passed the letter back. Keyes contradicted him, with a smile. 'No, you don't. This is a great secret which we'll allow to leak out. It will explain to the overcurious why certain ships are having peculiar modifications made to them, and why we should be training a lot of sailors in various offensive and destructive arts which are more usually left to men in khaki. But I can trust you, I'm sure, to keep your own counsel. No need to burden you now with the details: suffice it to say that my operation will be not *de*fensive, but *off*ensive.'

'I'm pleased to hear it, sir.'

'But it will be an extremely hazardous undertaking. If you elected to join me, I'd be glad to place a section of the landing force under your command. You are, of course, exactly the sort of chap I need for it. But before you give me your answer, I must tell you that the chances of your returning alive from the assault would be – slender. One might say non-existent.'

Wyatt was looking as delighted as if he'd been offered the Crown jewels.

'Where shall I go, sir, and when, to study these esoteric arts?'

Crosby, the paymaster in the other office, was falling over himself in efforts to be helpful. Before, Nick had found him moderately insufferable. He took the long, buff envelope, containing his appointment to *Bravo*, from him; it bore the seal of Captain (D)'s office, and was addressed to Lieutenant Nicholas Everard, DSC, RN. The paybob said, 'Captain Tomkinson's only just in the process of taking over—'

'Tomkinson?'

'The new Captain (D).'

He remembered: Reaper had mentioned him. He was pushing the buff envelope into his pocket; Crosby asked him, 'Excuse me, but – shouldn't you read it?'

As if an appointment to an oily wad was something to drool over . . . Crosby said, 'I do think you *should*—'

'Yes. Later on.' He nodded at the fussy little man. Some of these office people lived for their bits of paper, records, memoranda . . .

As for Tomkinson, it seemed Dover was filling rapidly with four-stripe captains, as Keyes built up his staff. God help Dover, Nick thought; and God help Nicholas Everard, too. He told Crosby, 'I'll give it some undivided attention later. But now I think I'll go on down. You say there's a boat already waiting?'

'Should be.' Crosby nodded. He still looked worried. 'Or on its way in. By the time you get down there—'

'Right. Thank you.'

The boat *was* there, waiting for him – if that motorboat out at the naval pier steps was *Bravo*'s. He could see it as he crossed the Marine Parade. He could see *Bravo* herself too, in the centre of the destroyer moorings, rolling and tugging at her buoy. The wind was rising, high clouds scudding over; the usual south-wester was blowing up, and as usual there was ice in it. He pushed his hands deep into the pockets of his greatcoat and set off down the pier.

There was an RNR midshipman in charge of the boat. A skinny, dark-haired lad who looked as if he thought Nick might bite him.

He stepped into the sternsheets. 'Carry on, please.'

'Shove off for'ard! Shove off aft!'

Quite choppy in the harbour. The destroyer berths were in shallow water; tides ripped in from both entrances and met here in the middle, to the discomfort of destroyer men seeking a rare night's rest in port . . . He gazed at *Bravo* as the boat bounced out towards her. Strange-looking craft, the thirty-knotters. This one, a D-class boat of 1897 or '98, had two funnels instead of the more usual three. They were low, stunted-looking, and there was an absolute litter of ventilators all over her upper deck. A turtle-back foc's'l led to a bridge that was only about half the height of *Mackerel*'s and two-thirds of which was occupied by a twelve-pounder gun. There was a six-pounder aft, and two more on each side between bridge and after funnel. The pair of torpedo tubes just for'ard of the stern gun would be eighteen-inch. The general effect was of clutter, bits and pieces everywhere.

But she was clean, well kept. That would have been Elkington's responsibility, and it was obvious he'd been a very conscientious first lieutenant. The motor-boat curved in towards the port-side gangway. Nick wondered what sort of CO he'd be getting now; he couldn't remember Elkington having mentioned him.

The midshipman had cut the boat's engine. Almost at the gang-way's foot. Now he'd put her astern and he'd reversed the helm: and stopped again. It had been quite neatly done, and Nick told him so.

The boat's coxswain, a leading seaman, looked as pleased as the snotty did. Bowman and sternsheetman had their boathooks out and hooked to the boat-rope. Nick stepped on to the gangway.

Above his head, he heard the quiet order, 'Pipe!'

Pipe?

Only commanding officers – and foreign naval officers, and the King and members of his family, and certain other categories of visitor such as the officer of the guard and four-stripers and above – were entitled to be piped over the side of a Royal Navy ship. He didn't fit anywhere in that list. Someone, obviously, had blundered. He began to climb the gangway: the note of the pipe had risen, dropped, cut off. As he reached the top it began again. He saw Bruce Elkington standing stiffly at the salute, and a colossally broad CPO – it would be *Bravo*'s coxswain, probably – beside him, and two seamen, one of whom was the bosun's mate and doing the piping. Behind Elkington a sub-lieutenant and a warrant officer were also standing at attention. Finally, as he paused on the top platform of the gangway, he saw a long line of sailors fallen-in on the iron deck abreast the funnels, and a similar rank on the other side.

His hand snapped up to the salute, and he stepped aboard. The pipe's note fell, held for a few seconds, died. Elkington stepped forward.

'Welcome aboard, sir. On behalf of all hands may I say how delighted   '

His head spun. This was – it was happening, it was real, and yet—

His fingers touched the unopened envelope in his pocket. He could visualise one startling, glowing phrase in it: . . . *appointed in command* . . . Reaper's voice grated in his brain: *You're not a very trusting fellow, Everard* . . . Elkington said, 'Ship's company is ready for your inspection, sir. May I first present Sub-Lieutenant York – and Mr Raikes, torpedo gunner . . . This is Chief Petty Officer Garfield, our cox'n.'

Shaking hands . . . Still dizzy. *I'm dreaming this, I must be* . . . A destroyer command, at twenty-two? Oh – only an oily wad, but still a—

'Will you inspect the ship's company, sir?'

Walking slowly for'ard, past the tubes and then a dinghy in its davits. He glanced up at the masthead, saw the ensign fairly crackling in the rising breeze.

Not just *the* ensign. *His!*

PART TWO

St George's Day: Zeebrugge

CHAPTER 12

'Stop both.'

'Stop both, sir.'

Engine-noise, the thrum of vibrating steel, ceased. *Bravo*, in her station near the van of the assault force, rolled more heavily as she lost steerage-way and the northerly breeze slapped a choppy sea against her port side. More of a sea than there'd been when they'd sailed; but thank heaven the visibility had closed in at last. Cloud obscured the moon, and drizzle was an enclosing curtain.

Admiral Keyes's armada of seventy-six assorted craft lay stopped while MLs embarked surplus crews from the blockships. Stokers, mostly, who'd been needed for the cross-Channel passage but had to be removed before the actual assault. The fewer men on board the blockships when they were run into the canal mouth and sunk, the fewer there'd be to rescue.

To *attempt* to rescue. Nobody was in much doubt as to how the odds lay. And yet there was gossip – *Bravo*'s chief stoker had mentioned it to Elkington – that a lot of those engine-room ratings weren't intending to disembark at this point. Determined to be in on the attack itself, they were planning to lie low until the ships got under way again.

Nick moved out to the port wing of the twelve-pounder platform, which was a forward extension of the bridge, and trained his glasses aft. The CMB they'd been towing should slip now, and York, the sub-lieutenant, should be seeing to it. Elkington murmured at Nick's elbow, 'Slipping her now, sir. Starboard quarter.' As he spoke, the cough and spluttering roar of the CMB's engine proved he was right. And all through the mass of silent, rolling ships other CMBs would be casting off and getting away under their own power. They'd been brought this far under tow so as to conserve fuel. He could see a few of them now, in the lanes and gaps between bigger ships' dark outlines, slinking off like wolves to gather in their various packs.

They'd be the first craft in, laying smoke in the Hun defenders' faces to cover the attacking force's approach. Then MLs, plugging up more slowly – Bell's and Treglown's among them – would take over most of the smoke-laying work.

'Signal to proceed, sir!'

Leading Signalman Tremlett had been watching for it. Nick said, 'Half ahead together.'

'Half ahead together, sir!' Clark, bosun's mate, slammed the brass telegraphs over. There was a lot of brasswork in and on *Bravo*, and every bit of it gleamed like gold. Elkington and his chief buffer, PO Russell, made up for the ship's antiquity by keeping her so spick-and-span anyone might think she'd been prepared for an admiral's inspection, not for war. Every ventilator, for instance – and her upper deck was fairly dotted with them – had a brass rim which in sunlight was blinding to look at. *Bravo* was gathering way, responding to her helm again, and Chief Petty Officer Horace Garfield held her precisely in the centre of her next-ahead's wake. Garfield's cap was, as usual, slanted to the right, while his left eyebrow – also as usual – was cocked up. Whether he wore his cap at that angle to make room for the habitually raised eyebrow, or pushed the eyebrow up to fill some of the space left by the invariably askew cap, probably not even he himself knew.

Grebe, the thirty-knotter ahead of *Bravo*, was to be her partner in the inshore patrol. By way of contrast to these two relics, ahead of them steamed *North Star* and *Phoebe*, two new destroyers who were to patrol the area off the mole's end; and ahead of *Phoebe*, Roger Keyes's vast silk vice-admiral's flag flaunted its St George's Cross over the flotilla-leader *Warwick*.

Marker buoys had been laid with great accuracy to guide the attacking force and mark the stages of its approach. Where they'd just been stopped had been position 'D', and now they were steering for 'G', just a few miles farther east.

Astern of this group of ships – Unit 'L' in Keyes's operational orders – Unit 'M' consisted of two more destroyers towing the submarines C1 and C3. Seen bow-on – from here now, of course, they were quite invisible in the dark, and anyway hidden by the towing ships – seen end-on, they looked like nothing that anyone had even seen before. Spars had been mounted across the tops of their conning-towers, and motor-dinghies slung on each side from the spars. Rather like panniers slung on a donkey's back. The boats were for the submarines' crews to escape in, after they'd done their job of blowing the viaduct sky-high. But only an optimist could have believed they'd have much chance of launching those dinghies, let alone motoring away to safety in them.

Tim Rogerson was in C3.

The dark assembly of ships ploughed steadily, silently eastward. *Bravo* rattled, groaned, hummed and moaned to herself as she thrust across the waves; the wind sang in her rigging overhead. She was entitled, Nick thought, at her age, to talk and mutter to herself. He was used to her now, and loved her. As others had before him; and he wondered suddenly, the thought springing out of the darkness and the tension, the knowledge that before long the night would turn to flame and thunder, whether anyone else would after him.

Idle, dangerous speculation. He dismissed it. He had his glasses on *Greve*'s stern, and he thought *Bravo* was creeping up a bit, inside her station.

'Come down ten revolutions, Bailey.'

'Down ten, aye aye, sir!'

Astern of Unit 'M' steamed another pair of destroyers, one of them towing a picket-boat whose function would be to rescue the submariners after they'd transferred to their dinghies. Rogerson's captain in C3 was a lieutenant named Sandford, and it was this Sandford's elder brother, who was on Keyes's staff, who'd brought the picket-boat along.

The centre column, the line of heavyweights, was led by *Vindictive*. She was an old cruiser – the same class originally as *Arrogant* – but she'd been substantially modified now for her role of assault ship. She was carrying the main body of the landing force, sailors and marines who were going to storm the mole and neutralise the gun-batteries on it – particularly on its end part, what was referred to in the orders as the mole extension – so that the blockships could get past it and on across the harbour into the canal mouth. The rest of the bayonet-and-bomb brigade were in *Iris* and *Daffodil*, two old Mersey ferry-steamers. Not well suited to long journeys in the open sea, they were being towed now by *Vindictive*.

Behind that assault group came the Zeebrugge blockships, the old cruisers *Thetis, Intrepid* and *Iphigenia*. They'd been fitted out during the last few months at Chatham. All their control equipment had been duplicated, with alternative conning and steering positions protected by steel plating and splinter-mats. Concrete had been built in to protect their boilers and machinery and steering equipment, and charges fitted for blowing the ships' bottoms out, with firing keys in both conning positions. Their masts had been taken out of them, as had all their guns except those right for'ard, which they'd be able to use on their way through and in. Twenty rounds of ammunition for each gun were stowed in shot-ready racks. Every piece of unnecessary equipment had been removed, and so had all items of copper and brass, since the Hun was known to be short of both. Only just enough coal for the journey was carried in their bunkers; and finally all accessible and suitable below-decks spaces had been filled with cement blocks and cement in bags, and rubble and concrete.

All the blockship and submarine crews were volunteers – and there'd been hot competition for places in the ships. Command of *Iphigenia* had been given to a lieutenant of Nick's own age, twenty-two, a man named Billyard-Leake: Keyes had approved the appointment for the same reason he'd approved Nick's: Lieutenants Billyard-Leake and Everard had both acquired reputations for coolness, judgement and leadership in action. He'd said so. As a commanding officer, one actually met and talked with admirals!

Sarah had written, *Are you all puffed-up and important, with your medal and your ship, my famous stepson? If you are not, I shall be for you! I am! While your dear uncle – who so far forgot himself as to condescend to pay us a visit here last week – is so proud of his nephew that he can barely speak of him coherently!*

She'd had other cause than that for writing, though. The main content of her letter had been news of her own, and sadness and thoughtfulness, and a need to tell him about it. It had left him no less thoughtful, but perhaps – wrongly, he thought – less sad. *Much* less sad? No point trying to hide it from oneself: her letter had made him happy.

Not for a man's death, he tried to convince himself. By the fact she'd turned to him to confide in. And yet – one stranger, amongst the thousands dying . . .

Astern of the three Zeebrugge blockships steamed the pair that would be going to Ostend – *Brilliant* and *Sirius*.

'Coming up to position "G", sir!'

Bailey, *Bravo*'s RNR midshipman who'd seemed so timorous, was becoming a useful navigator. The previous captain – an RNVR lieutenant-commander, and he'd developed heart trouble

400

– had handled all the pilotage himself, but it had seemed a better idea to let the snotty earn his keep and gain experience.

'G' was the last checkpoint before they began the run-in to the target areas. It was also the point where the two forces would divide, the Ostend ships turning five points to starboard and heading almost due south to rendezvous with Commodore Lynes who'd be coming with small craft from Dunkirk. Lynes commanded the Dunkirk base, under Keyes, and the Ostend operation was being left to him.

Ahead, a shaded light flashed briefly. The Ostend blockships would be putting their helms over now, passing astern of this starboard column and disappearing into the night. Nick was watching *Grebe*, who seemed unable to maintain constant revs.

'Up ten revolutions, Mid.'

'Aye aye, sir.' He heard Bailey shout the order down the tube. Elkington reported, '*Brilliant* and *Sirius* passing astern, sir.'

'Mid, what's the time?'

'Ten-thirty, sir.'

Perfect. And the visibility was still closing in as the drizzle thickened. This was 'X'-hour, and in precisely ninety minutes, at midnight, *Vindictive* should be alongside the Zeebrugge mole with her assault force pouring ashore. She'd been fitted with special hinged gangways all down her length, which would be dropped to rest against the top edge of that massive stone barrier.

Elkington said, 'Wind seems to be holding, sir.'

'Yes. Touch wood.'

A change of wind from north to south had forced Keyes to cancel the operation and turn the force back to England when they sailed the first time, on April 11th. A northerly wind was an essential weather condition: the smoke-screens, vital to the whole business, had to be carried shoreward, not dissipated or blown back seaward. There'd been a second attempt on the 13th, but that had been abandoned too; wind and sea had risen to such an extent that a landing on the mole would have been impossible.

Third time, and third time lucky, Nick thought. This was the last chance they'd get, with high water falling in the right period of darkness; and if it had to be cancelled for a third time the Admiralty wouldn't let Keyes try again. There was the matter of security, for one thing; you couldn't go on for ever putting to sea and turning back again, and holding an assault force locked up in their ships in the Thames estuary, without some knowledge of it finally leaking to the enemy.

It could have happened already. Even now, the Germans could be waiting for them.

Nick asked Elkington, 'Is McAllister all set up, aft?'

'It's a daunting sight, sir. You wouldn't recognise your cabin.'

He'd got McAllister, who'd been *Mackerel*'s doctor, appointed to *Bravo*. She'd had no doctor, and Andy McAllister had proved his worth after that Christmas Eve action. He'd stayed in Dover when *Mackerel* had left for the London dockyard, and Nick on a visit to the hospital yacht to see *Mackerel*'s wounded had found him there still looking after them and hoping for a new destroyer job.

However well matters turned out in the next few hours, no hospital yacht would be much use. Whole wards of big hospitals in London and elsewhere were being held ready; special trains had been ordered, staffed by doctors. Even with total success, they'd all be needed.

The ruse of that letter from Admiral Wemyss to Keyes about a possible evacuation of Calais and Dunkirk, and perhaps having to block those two ports, had worked splendidly. Right up to the final briefings, everyone had believed it. And the German land offensive which Ludendorff had launched a month ago – with alarming success – had seemed to justify and support the fears of having to pull out. Now, with the German army still attacking and gaining ground, determined to make the most of their numerical superiority before enough American troops arrived to tilt the balance, this attack from the sea would be a timely diversion as well as a naval necessity.

Nick glanced round his bridge, at new steel plating that had been welded to its rails. There were splinter-mattresses outside that shielding steel. The guns – six-pounders – on the upper deck, and the torpedo tubes, had been given extra protection too. *Bravo* and *Grebe* were to be inside the mole, backing up the CMBs and MLs who'd be inshore to lay smoke and to rescue blockships' crews. Things were likely to be fairly brisk, inside that mole.

'There they go.'

Warwick – Keyes's flagship – with *Phoebe* and *North Star* astern of her, and with *Whirlwind* and *Myngs* on their port beam, were all putting on speed, drawing ahead to act as vanguard and deal with any enemy patrols that might be encountered between here and

Zeebrugge. Everything was happening exactly as planned and scheduled in the orders; and as each stage was reached there was a degree of relief in moving forward to the next.

Elkington said, his voice echoing Nick's unspoken thoughts, 'Be glad when we get to grips with it.'

What must it be like, Nick wondered, for the men in the landing parties, cooped up over there in *Vindictive, Iris* and *Daffodil*. For them, this raid would be something like Russian roulette – with five of the six chambers loaded.

He lowered his binoculars, and answered Elkington: 'Better than sitting over that damn minefield, isn't it?'

'Mind you roast 'em, eh?'

Edward Wyatt, in *Vindictive*, nodded to Brock, the RNAS Wing-Commander whose smoke, smoke-floats, flame-throwers and other pyrotechnical products were to be much in evidence during the coming battle. Brock was planning to land on the mole with the storming parties, too, to try to find some new sound-ranging apparatus which the Germans were believed to have installed there. He'd smiled at Wyatt's proposal: Wyatt added to it.

'Or boil 'em in oil, while you're at it?'

Brock was making adjustments to the after flame-thrower. Wyatt left him in the steel shelter they'd built for it, went down the ladder and over to the starboard side of the upper deck. There was plenty of time in hand, and he could still have been down in the old cruiser's wardroom, where coffee and sandwiches were available; but it was difficult, he'd found, to sit about, doing nothing. Tension, expectancy: it stretched the nerves, made you want to move, crack jokes, flex your muscles! Plenty of other men were doing the same thing: prowling to and fro, joking, laughing; or alone, silent and deep in thought. He walked for'ard along the starboard side; there was open deckspace here, room to move – unlike the port side, which was a mass of fittings and equipment for the mole boarding operation.

Destroyers' shapes were visible to starboard, and the white curls of their bow-waves. He stopped, leant with a shoulder against the cutter's after davit, and stared across a jumping, loppy sea at the attacking force's starboard column. Those two destroyers' silhouettes were unmistakable, dark or no dark: they were thirty-knotters. For inshore work, he guessed – expendable. Astern of them, just abaft *Vindictive*'s beam, were two much more modern boats – *Trident* and *Mansfield* – towing the submarines. Narrowing his eyes, he peered at them through the darkness. He could make out the destroyers well enough, but only one submarine. The leading one was there, in tow of *Trident*; but the other seemed to have disappeared.

The harder you looked, the less you saw. One needed binoculars to make sense of it. They must both be there. Otherwise surely both destroyers wouldn't be.

He pushed himself off the damp, grey-painted steel, and strolled on for'ard. Hardly any motion on the ship, but plenty of squeaks and rattles. Well, she'd seen a bit of service in her time, had *Vindictive*.

Nothing to what she'd see in the next hour or two!

Up on the level of the false deck, on his left, loomed one of the 7.5-inch howitzers that had been installed to bombard gun positions on the mole after the ship was secured alongside. She'd be below the level of the parapet, so howitzers were the obvious things, for their high trajectory. There was an 11-inch one on the quarterdeck, and another of these 7.5s on the foc'sl.

It was going to be hellish noisy, alongside that mole.

A false deck had been built on the skid-beams – the supports on which seaboats normally rested – all down the port side from foc'sl to quarterdeck. Wide ramps from this starboard side sloped up to it: three of them, providing ample and easy access to that higher level, which would be almost as high as the mole's parapet. Not quite, though; and there'd be a wide gap to be bridged as well, so there were eighteen gangways hinged to the false deck and triced up. Released, they'd crash down on to the parapet. The false deck provided cover, too; while they were waiting to be ordered up the ramps and over the gangways, the storming parties could take shelter under it.

Wyatt's palm stroked the butt of the revolver at his side. He'd like to be moving *now*: leading his company of fifty sailors with their grenades and rifles and machine-guns in a swift, wild charge on to the mole and over that shed's roof to the guns. Speed was the thing: speed and ruthlessness and the hell with what might be coming at you. *Attack*: and think of nothing else. Like a rugger dash, in a way; and as one who'd played rugger for the Navy, Edward Wyatt knew all about that.

Not quite as gentlemanly as rugger. Bullets and cold steel and high explosives and no handshakes either before or after. The training at Chatham had been rigorous and intensive: the men were hard as nails and they wouldn't be looking for prisoners.

He saw Harrington Edwards strolling aft with Peshall, the padre. They were coming this way, and he didn't feel like joining their conversation, so he turned away quickly and went up the nearest of the ramps to the false deck. Padre Peshall would be going ashore with the storming parties: he'd played rugger for England and he was unlikely to confine his activities to saving souls. Edwards, a bearded and one-eyed RNVR lieutenant-commander, had been all through the Gallipoli campaign and had since been wounded in France; it was odd, Wyatt thought, that a naval officer should be in a position to claim three years of trench fighting experience. But he was a good fellow. They all were: fighting-cocks, handpicked; it was just that he didn't feel in the mood, at the moment, for chatting.

At each end of this false deck a ladder led up to a flame-thrower hut. And all along it were the brows, gangways with hand-rails and transverse ladder-grips for footholds; they were upright on their hinges, angled slightly outboard and held there by topping-lifts which were secured to eyebolts in the midships superstructure. The mole would be something like six feet higher than this raised deck, and the brows would lead upwards to it across a gap of twenty or thirty feet. As well as the *flammenwerfers* and howitzers, there were three pom-poms, ten Lewis guns and sixteen Stokes mortars on this side of the ship; and in the foretop, which of course would be high above the parapet of the mole, were three more pom-poms and another six Lewis guns to fire downwards and sweep the mole's surface clear of Germans as the men rushed ashore.

Vindictive's port side had been lined with huge fenders to protect her as she bumped alongside; and the mainmast had been lifted out of her, and laid horizontally across the quarterdeck with its heel embedded in concrete and its end projecting over the port quarter. It would fend the stern off and keep the port propeller clear of the mole's underwater projection.

Wyatt heard someone coming up the ramp behind him. Glancing round, he saw that it was Cross, his second-in-command in E Company.

He frowned. 'Looking for me, Cross?'

'Not really, sir.' Jimmy Cross smiled. He was one of the contingent lent to the operation from the Grand Fleet in Scapa. Beatty had called on Flag Officers commanding the battlefleet's squadrons to provide selected volunteers from their ships; they were to be 'stout-hearted men, active and keen, who could be depended upon in emergency; and having regard to the hazardous nature of the enterprise, wherever possible, unmarried or without dependants'. Officers were to be those whose powers of initiative and leadership were known to be high. Flag Officers were to select officers, and Captains the petty officers and men. And one of those selected under this edict had been Cross, who was a gunnery officer and a fleet boxing champion. He stopped at Wyatt's side.

'Just it's getting a bit stuffy below, sir.' He stared up at the tracery of wires, jackstays and topping-lifts above their heads. Black parallels against a background of night clouds that were faintly lighter because they had a full moon behind them. He said, 'The Germans won't believe we'd be such idiots as to attack with a moon that could show through at any time it feels like it, d'you think?'

Wyatt didn't like that much. It sounded like a criticism of Keyes. He grunted, stared across a couple of hundred yards of sea at a whole pack of MLs keeping station on the beam. There was another horde of them, smoke-screen boats, further astern. Cross was looking aft, at the huge grappling-iron suspended from its derrick; there was another for'ard. He murmured, 'They've done a pretty thorough job of disfiguring this poor old hooker, sir.'

Wyatt growled, 'Dare say the Huns'll add their tanner's worth.'

'Anyway –' the younger man sighed – 'not long to wait for it, now . . . The men seem to be in good heart, sir.'

'Why shouldn't they be, for God almighty's sake!'

Explosive . . . You never knew, with Edward Wyatt. It was so easy to say the wrong thing, rub him up the wrong way. Crusty swine: worth his weight – which wasn't inconsiderable – of course, but – Cross shrugged it off. There was a touch of nervous tension in them all, just now. Wyatt added, as if he wanted to justify that outburst, 'They've all asked to be here, haven't they?'

Every man in the storming parties, whether marines or sailors, had expressed a personal wish to take part in what had been described only as a 'hazardous enterprise'. Then early this month Admiral Keyes had visited the ships at their anchorage in the Swin, the Thames estuary, described the operation in detail and told them that any of them who were married, or had other reasons to wish to withdraw, could do so without being thought the worse of. Not one man had expressed any such wish.

'I'm off for a word with Halahan.' Wyatt turned away. 'Join you down there presently.'

'Aye aye, sir.'

Not *much* later, Cross thought. It was past eleven o'clock. In less than an hour, they'd be leading their men up those gangways.

He turned his back on them, and went down to see if any of E Company might have last-minute queries. On the way down the ramp he glanced up at the clouds again. If they blew away, and the attack had to be carried out under a full moon, bright as day: *phew* ... There'd be the smoke-screens, of course, and they were necessary in any case because of starshell and searchlights; but with the whole area lit up by a moon, old Brocky's smoke would need to be five times as thick as smoke had ever been. *And* the wind must hold ... A story had gone round, leaked by one of Keyes's junior staff officers, that after the first two attempts to launch the operation had been abandoned the Admiralty had been about to call off the whole thing, pay off the ships and disband the marine battalion, send the Grand Fleet detachments back to Scapa. Keyes had pleaded with Sir Rosslyn Wemyss, the First Sea Lord, for his support in allowing a third sortie. Wemyss had said, 'But you wanted a moonless night, as well as a high tide at midnight!'

'No, sir.' Keyes had told him, 'I wanted a full moon. Couldn't wait for it, that was all.'

Wemyss had stared at him incredulously. Then he'd grinned.

'Roger, what a damned liar you are!'

Wyatt found Captain Halahan with Colonel Elliot of the Marines and Carpenter, who was commanding *Vindictive* but not her landing forces, in the cruiser's chartroom just abaft the bridge.

Halahan was in command of the naval landing force. Until he'd volunteered for this job he'd had the siege guns on the Belgian coast. He and Elliot had worked closely together and with Keyes, in the last three months, planning the mole attack; Elliot's Royal Marines had trained at Deal, and Halahan's bluejackets at Chatham. At Deal they'd built a mock-up of the mole, and stormed it day after day, putting the story out that it was a replica of some position in France which in due course they'd be attacking.

Carpenter, although he was now *Vindictive*'s captain, was primarily a navigator and staff officer who'd been with Keyes in the Plans Division in London and since then had been the prime mover and chief coordinator of all the planning.

There was concern now in his bony, sharp-featured face as he looked up, saw Wyatt, glanced back at Halahan. Wyatt asked Elliot, 'Something wrong?'

'Monitors haven't opened fire. They should have several minutes ago.'

Erebus and *Terror*, to the north-east of Zeebrugge, should have started their bombardment forty minutes after 'X'-hour. And when they did start, those big guns would be audible. Wyatt said, 'I saw three CMBs go tearing off, just as I came up here.'

'Units A and B.' Carpenter nodded. 'Laying smoke ahead of us as we approach. Three waves of it.' Halahan murmured, 'Oh, what a fount of knowledge.' He glanced at Wyatt. 'Problems?'

'None at all, sir.'

'Good. It's too late for problems.'

Carpenter had gone out on to the bridge. Lieutenant-Commander Rosoman, his first lieutenant, was at the binnacle, and Wyatt heard Rosoman's shout of laughter ring out at some remark his captain made. A happy, lively fellow, Rosoman. And keen as mustard, another of Keyes's personal selections. He'd had the responsibility of *Vindictive*'s fitting out, since Carpenter had been occupied with all the planning.

Osborne, the ship's gunnery commander, walked in.

'Shouldn't the monitors be doing something by this time?'

Halahan glanced up, nodded, returned to his quiet conference with Elliot. They were studying a plan of the mole, checking over the details of which company would do what, and when. Osborne looked at Wyatt, raised his eyebrows, and stalked out again. Wyatt looked over Elliot's shoulder at the mole plan.

The most vital objective was the capture or destruction of the guns on the end of it, where the blockships would have to pass. But there were other guns here and there, and a garrison with its living-quarters and other buildings on it; plus a seaplane base with four hangars, a railway station and two large goods sheds, and an overhanging submarine shelter. The mole itself was a massive stone construction just over one mile long, connected to the shore causeway by a 300-yard viaduct, a lattice-work construction of steel girders under which the tides raced and which carried a double railway line and a roadway to the mole. It was this viaduct that the submarines were intended to blow up, so that the Germans wouldn't be able to rush reinforcements over it.

The mole was eighty yards wide. On its outer side where the

assault ships would berth it had an outer wall twenty feet high; on top of this was a ten-foot roadway protected by a three-foot parapet. So the attackers would have to get over that little wall on to the roadway, then down the sixteen-foot drop to the broad surface that was concreted, dotted here and there with guns, buildings and so on.

Near the end of the mole a long building had been erected fairly recently, and its flat roof seemed to be more or less level with the raised roadway. This had been chosen as the place for the attack. The landing parties could rush over the flat roof and get close to the mole-end guns, thus avoiding the alternative of a painful advance up the mole itself against barbed wire and well-sited machine-guns. (There seemed to be trenches on the mole, too, with stone embankments protecting them.) The guns at the end, and on the extension – after the mole's full width came to its end, the ten-foot roadway alone was carried on for another 360 yards to a lighthouse on its tip – those guns were in an extremely exposed situation, and once over the long building's flat roof the landing force should be well placed to rush them.

The guns were thought to be 4.7-inch. Once they were taken, there was to be an advance westward down the mole, marines covering a demolition party of specially trained bluejackets whose orders were to do as much harm as possible to cranes, guns, the seaplane station and any ships or dredgers alongside. Sandford, Keyes's staff officer who'd planned the submarine attack and was now in the rescue picket-boat, had also planned the demolition work – in such detail that he'd borrowed wicker baskets on wheels, from the Post Office in London, for the explosive charges to be wheeled along in.

Thunder, suddenly, in the north-east . . .

Elliot and Halahan looked up, and smiled. Halahan murmured, 'Better late than never.'

Elliot ran a forefinger along his little clipped moustache: 'Thank God for it, anyway!'

The monitors had opened fire fifteen minutes late. Captain Carpenter pushed in through the doorway from the bridge. 'Hear that?'

'Late.' Halahan nodded. 'Rotten staff-work.' Carpenter opened his mouth to answer: but an aeroplane-like roar close by made speech impossible for the moment, drowned out the rumble of the cruiser's engines and the multiple rattlings of her fabric. As the noise lessened Colonel Elliot asked, 'What was that?'

'CMBs.' Carpenter had knitted this whole thing together, he knew each move, minute by minute. 'Units C, D and E, to be precise.' Halahan interrupted, teasing him again: 'You're showing off, Alfred.' Carpenter's deepset eyes smiled: he went on, 'C lays a smoke-float off Blankenberg and renews it with another every twenty minutes. D goes flat-out to the mole and lays smoke-floats in the western section, and patrols that line until he's relieved by Unit I—'

'Oh, for heaven's sake—'

'—which consists of eight MLs. And E does precisely the same thing in the eastern section.' He bowed to Halahan. 'Now if you'll excuse me—'

'Who wouldn't.' Halahan turned to the others. 'But –' he glanced at the clock on the bulkhead – 'we'd better go down. Fun starts in half an hour.'

Tim Rogerson stopped beside Petty Officer Harner. Harner was on the stool behind C3's wheel, in the dimly lit control room, although he wasn't doing anything about steering. Rogerson said, 'Permission for me to go up, please, cox'n.'

Harner leant sideways to the voicepipe.

'Lieutenant Rogerson on the bridge, sir, please?'

'Wait a minute!'

Baldy Sandford's voice. John Howell-Price, the submarine's first lieutenant, was doing the steering from the bridge; down here, Harner was only standing by a disconnected wheel. In the engine-room, ERA Roxburgh and Stoker Bindall had just started the boat's petrol engine; the rush of air through the control room, sucking down through the hatch and aft to the engine, was fierce.

Sandford called down, 'In engine-clutch, half ahead!'

Rogerson moved to the telegraph on the after bulkhead, passed the order through to the ERA. He heard Dick Sandford's voice in the tube again: 'Cox'n – what's the time now?'

'Eleven twenty-six, sir!'

'Very good.'

Rogerson wondered what was happening up top. They'd slipped the tow: that was obvious, from the fact that they were moving now under their own power. Altering to starboard, by the feel of her, the slight heel. They were supposed to wait, once they were clear of the main assault force, for C1 and the picket-boat to join them when they'd slipped *their* tows.

410

'Stop engine!'

Harner repeated the order as Tim whirled the handle of the telegraph. Stopping now to wait for the others, he thought. And then, *I make a first-rate telegraphman* . . . He was spare, really. If anything happened to Howell-Price he'd step into his place; or if Sandford was hit, and Howell-Price took over the command . . . But C1 had only two officers, and Rogerson wondered whether Sandford hadn't issued him with the invitation to this party before he'd known he had Howell-Price with him anyway.

She was stopped now, wallowing, rolling like a tub. An ancient craft. Built in 1906, the Cs were almost replicas of the earlier Bs. Single-screw, 200 horsepower out of a 16-cylinder petrol motor, 135 feet long and displacing 300 tons. Entirely fit, he thought, for this conversion to floating bomb.

One was acutely aware of that Amatol up for'ard. Of what might happen, for instance, if a shell hit it, on their way inshore. But it was easier when one turned one's mind elsewhere, and there were problems enough to come without considering the possibility of accidents, pure bad luck. Such misfortunes were insured against by having two submarines instead of only one; one would be enough to do the job, but the second was the back-up, making sure of it. Only one thing was sure, he thought: that within a very short time all this would be ripped apart, blown to shreds. He looked round the cramped, cave-like control-room. The two periscopes were down and housed; the single brass hydroplane-control wheel gleamed like dull gold. It was handy that in these old Cs and Bs there were no fore 'planes; it would have been necessary to have removed them, so as not to impede the boat's penetration of the viaduct.

The idea was that her forepart would drive in between the girders, and explode right in the middle of it.

'Time, cox'n?'

'Eleven-thirty and a half, sir!'

A moment's pause: a muttered exchange up there on the bridge. Then: 'Half ahead. And tell Lieutenant Rogerson he can come up.'

'Aye aye, sir!'

Leading Seaman Cleaver's seaboots came into sight at that moment, clumping down the ladder. Stepping off it, meeting the coxswain's enquiring stare, he announced, 'We're on our tod. No sight o' C1 and no bleedin' picket-boat neither. *I* dunno.' He shook sea off his oilskins. He'd been down on the fore casing, casting off

411

the tow. Rogerson went behind him and stepped on to the ladder, hauled himself up through the lower hatch and then the dark, salt-smelling tube of the conning-tower and up from there into the rocking bridge.

Sandford, leaning in the front curve of the bridge beside Howell-Price, turned and nodded to him.

'All well, below?'

'No problems, sir.'

'Well, we have one up here, old lad. The others 've gone the wrong way, or something. Silly cusses!'

A rumble of gunfire from astern somewhere. Turning, he saw flashes lighting a clouded horizon some miles off on the port quarter. Sandford murmured, '*Erebus* and *Terror* stirring the Hun up ready for us.' He laughed. 'But they're used to it, they won't think it's anything special. The idea's to make him keep his head down for a bit.'

Damp night air: drizzle and the stickiness of sea-salt. Swish of sea rushing aft over the saddle-tanks and washing through below this free-flood bridge. Racket of the engine, its exhaust drowned in the white-foaming wash. Rogerson thought, *So we're alone. All up to us.*

How long now?

It hit him suddenly, the reality of it. This wasn't something in the mind, a plan, something rather thrilling that one was thankful to have been let in on. It was *now*!

At least, in about twenty minutes . . .

In the circumstances, the need to make sure of it because the whole thing was in their hands alone, he didn't think Baldy would use the gyro-steering device. Both submarines had been fitted with it. When they were a hundred yards or so from the viaduct they could, if they wished, take to the dinghies and leave the submarine to steer herself on the pre-set course.

He didn't think Sandford would have used it anyway. Nobody had ever discussed doing so. And it would be frightful to get that close and then leave everything to a gadget that might let them down.

'Uncle Baldy' said, 'Lovely weather for a continental visit. Eh, you chaps?'

'Beautiful.' Howell-Price was still concentrating on the steering, and looking at the white wake astern you could see that the boat's track was ruler-straight. 'This sort of drizzle makes a man feel he's never left home.'

Sandford began to warble the Eton boating song. Rogerson wondered what the devil could have happened to the others. Might the picket-boat have been swamped? She'd very little freeboard. The people in C1 were pals, former shipmates and messmates. They'd be thoroughly fed up, to find themselves out of it. Engine-trouble, probably. It was sensible enough to use old scrap-iron ships for throw-away jobs, but there was that disadvantage, the element of unreliability.

He wondered how Nick Everard was getting on, in his old oily-wad. That was a throw-away job if there ever was one! And thinking of Nick, his mind turned to his own sister, Eleanor, who was – or *thought* she was – in love with him. Nick somehow held back: you could see he was attracted to Eleanor and that they got on well together, even got a bit spoony sometimes; but he was – oh, sort of detached, he acted like a man in love with someone else, or married, even . . . Strange fellow, in some ways. And mad keen – one might almost say a raving lunatic – these days about the Navy.

Howell-Price said suddenly, 'I can smell Brockish vapour.'

'Just as well.' Sandford had stopped singing, which was kind of him. He said, 'We're going to need that smoke of his. Unless they don't spot us at all, of course. And that *could* happen, don't you know?'

Howell-Price nodded, watching his course. He muttered, 'And pigs could fly.' Rogerson thought of something: 'Aren't the bird-men supposed to be plastering 'em with bombs, by this time?'

'So they are.' Sandford removed his cap, and scratched his head. Even in this darkness, you could see how he'd acquired his nickname. 'Weather, probably. Wets their feathers, or something. Shouldn't think it'd make much odds.' He stooped to the voice-pipe: 'Cox'n – time now?'

'Fourteen to the hour, sir!'

'Thanks.'

Smoke: they were running into the edges of it. Pungent, foul-smelling. It would be worse in a minute: you could see, ahead, a sort of bank of extra-thick darkness. A CMB had done that to it, pouring some chemical from its exhaust and depriving all the old ladies back home of their favourite sugar-substitute. *Vindictive* would be approaching the smoke-barrier too, Rogerson thought. The other side of it, they'd find the mole. Smoke – *thick* smoke – surrounded C3 now. Howell-Price called suddenly, 'Hey! I say . . . D'you *feel* that?'

'What?' Sandford stopped, leaning to put an ear to whatever his first lieutenant had to say. 'What's that, John?'

'Wind. Breeze. I'd swear it's – *off-shore!*'

'Oh, surely not . . .'

Rogerson felt it too. And realised what it meant. All the smoke the CMBs and MLs were laying to shroud the advance and the assault would be wafted out to sea: which meant total exposure to the German gunners on the shore and on the mole . . . But the shift in wind direction might not be permanent: it could be a fluke, a false alarm. Sandford called into the voicepipe, 'Cox'n – send Cleaver up, please.'

Harner's voice was thin in the copper tube: 'Leading Seaman Cleaver on the bridge!'

He was there almost instantaneously, a dark figure hoisting itself out of the hatch. 'Sir?' Rogerson edged sideways and aft, squeezing round the after periscope-standard, to make room for him. Sandford said, 'Go down on the fore casing, Cleaver, and turn on the smoke-canisters. Wait there and see how it drifts.'

'Aye aye, sir.' The killick cocked a leg over the side of the bridge, swung over, clambered down the rungs welded to the outside of it. Sandford began, addressing Howell-Price, 'If our own smoke could be persuaded to blow along *with* us—'

Westward, heavy guns crashed, flamed. Smoke made it confused, difficult to pinpoint them: but it was savage, continuous firing breaking suddenly out of silence, as if it had been held back, pent up and now suddenly released. Wreathing, eddying smoke watered the flashes still: but there were explosions of shells striking as well as the sharper spurts of gunfire: the roar of it spread, increased, thickened. A splitting crash, like close and vicious thunder, made them all look up; overhead, above the enshrouding smoke, a starshell burst into a source of brilliance that lit the clouds like daylight. The smoke was blowing past them faster than they were moving across the sea. Rogerson was sure of it. The wind *had* shifted: he thought of *Vindictive* suddenly exposed as she approached the mole at point-blank range. Sandford was shouting over the front of the bridge, 'Pack it in, Cleaver!' He raised his arms, fore-arms crossed, the visual signal meaning 'belay'. Cleaver waved acknowledgement, bent to the canister to turn it off; its smoke had been streaming seawards, useless. Sandford was at the voicepipe now: 'Cox'n?'

'Sir!'

Gunfire to port was tremendous. *Vindictive* must be getting hell. But whoever was being shot at, it wasn't C3. Not yet. Sandford shouted to the coxswain, 'Come up, all of you!'

'Aye aye, sir!'

Cleaver's head appeared over the rim of the bridge. Sandford ordered, 'After casing, old lad. Shelter behind the bridge. After we strike, take charge of the port dinghy's for'ard fall.'

'Port dinghy's gone, sir.'

'*Gone?*'

A great leaping flash to port: like a sheet of lightning. One could hear, between the thunder of big guns, the chattering of machine-guns and the steady thump-thump-thump of pom-poms. Sandford told Cleaver, 'Starboard dinghy, then.' Cleaver vanished, down on to the catwalk and aft round the conning-tower to the casing behind it. Stoker Bindall shot up out of the hatch, with Roxburgh the artificer behind him; Sandford told Rogerson, with glasses at his eyes and searching for the viaduct, 'Send them down to the after casing and then join 'em there yourself, there's a good chap.' Suddenly it was light. Starshell breaking overhead, hanging, flooding the whole area with their harsh magnesium brilliance, and the smoke drawing off them, pulling aft, shredding away and leaving them naked to German eyes: the sea leapt, shell-spouts springing up right ahead of the submarine as she clawed in landwards, floodlit, an easy target for gunners on the mole, on the viaduct itself when they chose to open fire. Gun-flashes in a ripple of bright spurts to the westward of where the mole must be: where the mole *was*, by God! You could see it, the great black bulk of it – and the viaduct too – as clearly as if this was midday, not mid*night*, and Howell-Price was altering course by about five degrees, aiming her to strike it in the centre and at right-angles. More shells fell – abeam, this time, to starboard – grey spouts jumping, hanging, collapsing back into black rings on the sea, and the rush of others ripping overhead. Now a searchlight beam sprang out – from the viaduct – swung to them and fastened. A second one joined it: C3 was speared on their points, held between them as if she was a piece of chicken and the beams two chopsticks. Sandford shouted in Howell-Price's ear, 'Hold hard now, John! Smack in the centre now, old lad!' Another shell plumped into the sea to starboard: and then the searchlights, to everyone's astonishment and relief, switched off. Gunfire to port was rising to a crescendo, a continuous and rising roar. Sandford grabbed Tim's arm: 'Damn it, I told you to go *down*!'

'Sorry!'

Not only had the searchlights switched off – which could have resulted from a power-failure, that was the most likely explanation – but that western gun battery had ceased fire. No easy explanation covered *that*. C3 had the viaduct right ahead of her; she was cutting a dead-straight white track across the sea towards it: and a flare burst suddenly to hang over the harbour on the other side of it, silhouetting its struts and girders and the high roadway it carried: a vast, looming, criss-cross structure – and men moving about on top of it: still no shots aimed this way. What did they think – that she was harmless, mistaking the viaduct for a gap she hoped to pass through, so she'd get stuck there and be easy meat? Rogerson, climbing over the side of the bridge, saw that towering lattice-work of steel etched black against the brilliance of the flare, growing, expanding across the sky as it towered towards them, and men running about on the roadway like upright ants, and he thought brutally *It'll be* German *meat* . . .

C3 plugged doggedly in towards it, her petrol engine hammering away: the Germans looked down, watched her come, did nothing at all to stop her. She had about a hundred yards to go.

Wyatt shouted back to Cross, 'Tell 'em to wait there till we send for 'em! There's no way up yet!' He was on the false deck: he'd been there all the time, and although it was littered with bodies and slippery with blood it was safer now, protected by the sheer wall of the mole. *Vindictive* still rang with the noise of her own guns and the crashes of German shells ripping into her and exploding, showering her decks with steel splinters which in turn drummed on steel, screeched away in ricochets, but for the same reason – the mole's protection – it was only in her upperworks now. The stone wall was a solid shield to her vitals – which, God knew, had suffered enough as she'd forged across the last few hundred yards of sea through a hail of shells. Now she was flinging herself about as if in agony, rising and falling and seesawing against the wall, rocking close to it and then away again, still nothing like close enough alongside. She'd come in at full speed and the surge had come in with her, her own following wash and the thrust of water from the bottom forcing up between herself and the mole: a maelstrom of her own making, and there was no escaping it. Half

416

the gangways had been smashed against the wall: three-quarters of the others had been shot to matchwood before she'd got that close, during that last murderous three hundred yards. When they'd burst out of the smoke they'd been too far east: Carpenter had swung the wheel over and increased to full speed, to save the ship and the men in her more punishment than they needed to suffer: in the process, conning her from the port flame-thrower hut, he'd overshot the mark – engines were going full astern now, Wyatt noticed, and they were adding to the turbulence and motion – overshot by nearly four hundred yards: she was that distance from where she should have been. It wasn't going to be at all easy to reach the guns at the mole's end: they were a quarter of a mile away, there'd be a quarter-mile of exposed, shot-torn concrete to cover . . . Well, they'd do it, somehow, E Company'd do it – for the simple reason that it had to be done, it was what they'd come here for. And the first thing was to *get ashore* . . . Another shell had just burst in the bridge: but the guns from the foretop were still blazing, and the howitzers were in it now. (Not the for'ard one. The *foc'sl* howitzer had had two complete crews wiped out, and then the gun itself.) Wyatt, staring upwards as the ship rocked away from the mole again, realised that the derricks carrying the grappling-hooks weren't tall enough: the hook on this for'ard one wouldn't – *couldn't* – be dropped to grab the parapet, which was what it was designed to do. If it could be got over, the ship could be secured – with the after one as well, of course: and the only way to effect it would be to *put* it there: to get up there and damn well *do* it!

He pushed past Cross, dodged round a hurrying stretcher-party – below, the doctors were already inundated with work – reached the derrick and began to climb it. The ship's superstructure was in ribbons, torn and shattered, sieve-like, and she was ringing like a gong – a *cracked* gong – from the ceaseless pounding she was getting. Bedlam: a screaming slaughterhouse. It would be all right, he told himself, deliberately steadying himself with the thought, once they could get ashore and sort things out a bit: this was just the awkward interval, the sort of thing you had to expect, should have expected, really. A sailor hurrying down the ladder-way from the *flammenwerfer* hut suddenly sprang off it, crashed down, bounced once, hit the deck below it and lay still in a spreading pool of blood. The higher you were, the more exposed, of course. He was getting to the derrick's curve, and this was the tricky part. He was no lightweight, no monkey, damn it. But it would be all right, everything would work out: a couple of the gangways were still intact and serviceable and several of the others could probably be repaired; when she was properly secured there'd be cover enough to do that, under the mole's wall. A cracking sound and a sting on the back of his neck was a splinter or a bullet passing. They'd been in against the wall and trying to get secured for – how long, two minutes? Three? It had been much worse before she'd got in close. The bridge had been hit for the first time within seconds of the Huns opening fire; Elliot of the Marines and his second-in-command, Cordner, had both been killed by that shell. Less than a minute later Captain Halahan had been cut down. Wyatt had been standing within feet of him at the time, on the false deck. Most of the senior men, company commanders and others, had been waiting there ready to lead their men ashore the minute there was a gangway to get over. Halahan had gone down, and Edwards had been shot through both legs; Harrison, who by that time had inherited command of the naval landing force, had been shot in the jaw. He was below now, unconscious.

Wyatt inched out along the derrick: it was an unpleasant thought that if he was hit he'd drop between the ship's side and the mole and be squashed. The foretop must have been hit a few times but the chaps up there were still blazing away with their pom-poms and Lewis guns and, please God, killing Germans. He was in semi-darkness here, shadowed as the lower part of the ship was by the mole, but a few feet above his head her upperworks were lit by the glare of German searchlights and shells were bursting on and in her several times a minute, machine-gun and small-arms fire continuous. The sharply etched dividing line between lower shadow and upper brilliance was the margin between life and death, and as he dragged himself out along the derrick and the ship rocked on the piling sea he was sometimes within inches of it. He had his legs behind him with their ankles crossed over the derrick's curve while his arms took most of the strain of hauling his own weight out towards the wires with the hook dangling on them; suddenly there was a crash that had nothing to do with gunfire, and an almighty lurch: the ship rocked, and he and the derrick rocked too, over towards the parapet: at the same time she was shooting upwards, lifting on the surge: he'd thought he was about to be flung off but in the next second he saw his chance and grabbed it, swung and swivelled, launching his body out to hang by his arms and swing with his feet and legs extended towards the grappling-hook: and he'd *got it* . . .

418

On deck they cast the wire loose as he forced the hook across: it dropped – over the parapet, and he was blinded, in the searchlight glare, hearing the slap-slap-slap of machine-gun bullets streaming past his ear: he didn't wait for the gunner to adjust his aim, but slid down the derrick head-first, ended in a thumping somersault on the deck. Cross began trying to haul him up, grabbing at his shoulders and stuttering congratulations or something of the sort; Wyatt shook the idiot off, snarled at him to go down and see what casualties they'd had. There'd been plenty, he knew, on the way in; if any company was up to half strength by this time, it was lucky. So many shells had penetrated and burst in crowded spaces. He could see what had happened to cause that sudden lurch: *Daffodil* had arrived, at last, put her great rounded, heavily fendered bow against *Vindictive*'s side and pushed her bodily against the mole. That hook was holding her, at this for'ard end. There was a tinny, rattling sound, what would have been a roar except for the bedlam of sound drowning it, as Carpenter let go his port anchor. And *Daffodil* was staying where she was, holding the cruiser hard against the wall. Plenty of movement still, though, on both ships. Where the hell was *Iris*? Those two brows crashed down: Wyatt heard a cheer, drowned in gunfire; he saw Bryan Adams – commander of A Company, and now after Halahan's death and Harrison's wounding Adams was in command of the whole blue-jacket landing force – leading his men up and on to the mole. Running, cheering: Wyatt whipped round to tell Cross to get the men up, but Cross had already gone: reappearing, now, with Wheeler and about twenty men behind him.

'All we have left, sir.' Two dozen at most, out of fifty. Royal Marines were pouring up the second of the two surviving brows. Wyatt roared, 'Forward!', drew his revolver, and flung himself up in the middle of them: it wasn't a time for 'after you's'. As he reached the top, Adams was leading one bunch of men straight down the roadway while others climbed down to the surface of the lower, broader mole; Brock was with the roadway lot. The guns in the ship's foretop were jabbering and thudding, firing fast to cover the rush of men on to the mole and down it; then a shell came from heaven knew where and burst right in the foretop, a gush of flame and objects whirring, trailing smoke, and now no covering fire. The flame-throwers would have been the thing: and Brock had even sworn that if *Vindictive* had been berthed in the right place – which everyone had assumed she would be – those *flammenwerfers* of his would even have wiped out the crews of the guns on the mole-end, without any other help from guns or landing-parties. In fact the oil-supply lines to both of them had been cut by German gunfire minutes before the ship had crunched against the wall. So there were no flame-throwers. The main body of the Marines was going westward: they had to ensure that no Huns could push up this way from the viaduct end and take control of the mole close to where *Vindictive* lay; if they did, the landing-parties would have been cut off. Adams had stopped to help Rosoman, the cruiser's first lieutenant, settle the after grappling-hook across the parapet; they weren't having much success. But the rush was slowing, bogging down, with mortars bursting here and there and machine-guns from the buildings farther up raking across the concrete. A, B, D and E companies were all earmarked to rush the mole-end guns, but 350 yards of open, flat concrete, enfiladed by machine-gun and mortar fire from half a dozen different places and directions – mostly at the moment from No. 3 shed, on the mole's inner side, and from actually *behind* the advancing bluejacket companies – *remnants* of companies – from where two Hun destroyers were berthed on the mole's inner curve almost opposite *Vindictive* – Wyatt admitted to himself, *It isn't going to be all plain sailing*. Noise indescribable. Adams going forward now, to a small blockhouse on the raised roadway: Wyatt decided to go for No. 3 shed, to try to knock out those machine-guns. The mortar-fire might be coming from somewhere close behind it, too. If E Company could deal with that lot, others – A Company of the Marines, for instance, who were moving up in support of Adams – could push on through, eastward.

There was one of the iron ladders just level with him now, leading down to the mole proper: stone chips were flying from the wall near it and from the parapet. He turned, looked back, saw Cross clasp both hands across his belly, sink down and double over in an attitude of prayer: Wyatt waved his revolver and screamed, 'E Company, *with* me!' and ducked down on to the ladder, half climbed down it and half fell, hit the concrete at its foot and started running, zigzagging towards No. 3 shed. It was about ninety yards long and he was aiming roughly for the centre of it. Behind him, Lieutenant Wheeler was limping as he ran, grasping the region of his hip with both hands and shouting to the men behind him. Shrapnel screamed from two successive mortar-bursts: Wyatt was halfway over, telling himself, *They can't hit everyone, the more of us*

420

there are the better the chance that some of us will get there. Poor old Cross: wasn't a bad fellow, bit slow-witted sometimes but – nearly there: and an open window or embrasure right ahead of him with the barrel of a machine-gun spitting fire towards a group of Marines with Adams's crowd; the Marines were setting up a mortar behind that little blockhouse on the higher level – well, they *had* been, the German gunner was scattering them now, he'd dropped two of them and the other three had dived for cover: Wyatt bent double as he ran and stopped zigzagging, aimed straight for the gun and pulled a grenade off its clip on his webbing: he tugged the pin out with his teeth, a sideways jerk of the head – and he was *there*, throwing himself flat then rising again to lob the grenade in the window. He'd dropped flat, heard it explode and a yell of pain or fear, sent another in after it to make sure. This was dead ground; he flattened himself against the wall while blue smoke eddied from the open window. Wheeler was still limping over, lumbering this way and that; there was a petty officer by the name of Shrewsbury with him, half a dozen E Company men and a mixed bag of others, including a Marine with a machine-gun. Wyatt grinned, waved his pistol, beckoning them to join him. *The more the merrier*, he thought. *We'll pull it off! By God we will!* On an impulse he hoisted himself up, right up with his head and shoulders in that window: it was a sort of bunkhouse, and he could see two dead men sprawled against the far wall: below him, a German groaned, called something in his own brand of Hun-talk: Wyatt leant right in, saw him, a boy of about sixteen, fair and pink-faced, scared stiff: he shot him in the head, and slid down again, turned to meet Wheeler who was only a dozen yards away: and it was at that moment that he saw it.

Westward – a mile or so away – the biggest sheet of flame he'd ever seen in his life before. The place was bright with starshell anyway, but that great tongue of fire dimmed everything with its own fierce brightness. Now as it dimmed, smoke poured upwards: black, pluming up and the plumes bending, carried northwards on the wind. But no sound came, and none had; there was so much noise close-to and everywhere else as well that nothing had been audible in any separate way – and yet it must have been a bang like the crack of doom. Wyatt roared with pleasure, exultation: there was only one thing it could have been, and that was the viaduct: the submarines had pulled it off, God bless them! He was bellowing, as Wheeler reached his side and sank down at the end of a trail of blood he'd left across the concrete, 'Well done, by God, well *done*!'

421

Shrewsbury said, 'Goin' to be tricky gettin' off this wall, sir.'
'What?'

The petty officer pointed. Two of Adams's party had just tried to rush across and join them there, carrying a mortar between them. They were both down: one lay still, sprawled on his face, and the other was trying to crawl in that way, dragging the mortar and using only his elbows for propulsion, his legs trailing and blood pouring from a black gash in his neck. Then as they watched the machine-gun found him again and the stream of its next burst of bullets bent him round in a sort of knot, eel-like: it stopped, moved on, leaving him to unwind slowly like a broken spring in a spreading, scarlet stain. Other men were joining Wyatt here against the wall, dodging as they ran, scrambling for the cover and diving, flopping into it. Over on the other side, the high-level roadway, a mortar-bomb landed and burst on the roof of the blockhouse behind which Adams's bluejackets were gathering. Wyatt saw them crouching, trying to make more of its cover than it was capable of giving them: and Adams was sending a runner back, either for reinforcements or for covering fire. If Osborn could use his stern howitzer, Wyatt thought, to drop a few shells on the mole just here to the east of them: that, or if they could bring up some of the Marines with mortars? He scowled, staring round: it wasn't in his nature to sit here and wait. They were wasting time: they hadn't been trained for months on end and then brought here just to *sit* . . . He stared at Wheeler.

'You fit? Eh?'

'Only a scratch, sir.'

Wheeler was bloody from the waist down. Wyatt nodded. 'Good man.' He looked round at the others. 'We'll make another move now. We've got to get to those damn trenches, that's the first thing. All we've got to do is move *fast*, surprise 'em, rout 'em out like winkles . . .'

Nick, on *Bravo*'s bridge, saw the leap of flame as the viaduct went up. He put his glasses on it: and that – what he was seeing now – had to be some sort of mirage . . . Men on bicycles, in mid-air. Then, as they whirled like leaves in a high wind and fell like stones into the rising gush of smoke, he realised what he'd seen: a German army bicycle platoon, hurrying to reinforce the mole defenders, had pedalled to a sudden, devastating doom. It was all smoke there

422

now, under the glare of starshells bursting intermittently. He looked at Garfield. 'Starboard twenty.'

'Starboard twenty, sir!'

Garfield was built like a GPO pillar-box. If you painted one navy blue and stuck a cap aslant on top of it, you'd have Horace Garfield, near enough. To knock him down you'd need to tie something like that charge of Amatol to his shortish, tree-trunk legs. Nick had wondered briefly about Rogerson: now his attention, only a part of which had in fact been diverted, was concentrated entirely on *Bravo*'s current manoeuvrings, on the smoke off the mole's tip, that gun battery on the extension which *Bravo* and *Grebe* had already engaged in passing – before they'd come across the moored barge with the gun on it, and sunk that . . . 'Midships!'

'Midships, sir.' Cap tilted left, eyebrow cocked, flinging the wheel over. *Bravo* slewing to port still, leaving the floating net obstruction on her starboard beam, turning her stern to it now as she swung on. At any moment *Thetis*, the first of the three blockships, should emerge from that smoke which Welman's and Annesley's CMBs had laid. The CMBs were everywhere, racing in and out of their own and the MLs' screens, replacing smoke-floats as they fizzled out or Hun gunners sank them; the screens had to be constantly renewed, since the wind had changed and was working in the enemy's favour.

Grebe was inshore, three or four cables' lengths to the south of *Bravo*, engaging and being shot at by the Goeben battery. Shell-spouts were round her almost constantly. Her own guns were toys compared to the battery's, but she was a small target for them – and she was under constant helm, circling and zigzagging, darting in and out, no doubt driving the Hun gunners berserk with fury. Foolhardy, Nick thought, much *too* close: Hatton-Jones was a poker player, and he was playing this like a game of chance too. But, at the same time, serving an undoubted purpose. The whole of this operation, everything, was aimed at one objective, namely getting the blockships into the canal mouth: and if guns that might interfere with that purpose could be kept busy, particularly now that the crucial phase was due to start at any second . . . Shell-spouts leapt close to *Bravo*'s stern: Nick told Garfield, 'Port fifteen'. He shouted to Elkington, 'Where did those come from?'

'End of the mole, I think!'

'Midships.'

'Midships, sir.'

Steering northwards, roughly. Mole-end fifty degrees on the port bow and about half a mile away. Smoke drifting clear of it: flaming onions – German flares – bursting brilliant above the smoke where it was thick offshore. Not brilliant enough to penetrate Brock's smoke, though. He saw the flashes of the guns, and then *Vindictive*'s howitzer shells exploding like black, red-edged mushrooms. It was *Vindictive*'s rocket-barrage – rockets designed by Brock and fired almost horizontally from her stern ports to light the end of the mole extension, where the blockship would have to turn – making *that* firework display. Really very clever: to show them where to turn, and at the same time provide them with thick smoke-cover within yards of the same spot. Nick told Garfield, 'Steady as you go . . . Number One – hold your fire!'

Thetis, plunging out of the smoke. He had his glasses on her. This was what really mattered, what the whole thing was *for*. A CMB raced in between *Thetis* and the mole extension, smoke belching from its stern. Brock-type smoke: what the hell would anyone be doing without Brock? He had no way of knowing, at this moment, that Brock was dead, killed on the mole. The mole-end guns were all flaming, and *Thetis* was shooting back at them. That CMB's captain – either Welman or Annesley, it must be – was a brave man. Welman, only two years Nick's senior, was commander of all the CMBs. *Thetis* had rounded the point: now she was swinging to port, either to avoid the barge boom or hit suddenly by the eastward-running tide. Nick wondered if her captain, Sneyd, knew there was a barrage of net obstructions just off his bow.

'Starboard fifteen.'

'Starboard fifteen, sir!'

Shell-splashes on the quarter, forty yards away. From the Goeben battery, probably. Elkington shouted, '*Grebe*'s been hit, sir!'

'Midships.'

'Midships, sir!'

'Steady on north twenty west.' He wanted to get closer to the end of the mole. Not *much* closer, but . . . He told Elkington, 'When *Thetis* has cleared the range, try a few shots at the mole guns.'

'Aye aye, sir.'

Elkington was trying to look impassive. It wasn't easy for him; he had the sort of pale-skinned, fine-boned face that tends to show its owner's state of mind. *Grebe*, inshore there, had a haze of smoke – or was it steam? – hanging over her amidships, and she'd slowed.

424

It could have been a hit in one of her two boiler-rooms. If that was steam, it *had* been. But she was moving again, picking up speed, and her guns were still busy.

'Tremlett!'

'Yes, sir?'

'Make to *Grebe. Are you all right?*'

'Aye aye, sir.'

Shells falling all round *Thetis* now. Some – too many – hitting her. And she was still swinging to port. At any moment she'd be in that net. The mole-end guns were firing at her about as fast as guns could be fired and reloaded. By this time the landing parties should have captured them. He focused his glasses on *Thetis*. She *was* in the net! Carrying it away with her. Fine for the two who'd be following her in – but if she got it round her screws . . . He saw that one of the two German destroyers alongside the mole was firing at her now, and he shouted to Elkington: 'Number One!' The first lieutenant turned, with a hand cupped to his ear: he'd been watching the mole-end and *Thetis*, waiting for a chance to get the four-pounder into action. *Thetis* herself was fairly well clear now but there was an ML there with her now, trailing her; her attendant rescue craft. Nick told Elkington, pointing at the Hun destroyer, 'Try a torpedo shot!'

'Aye aye, sir!'

Leading Signalman Tremlett reported, 'From *Grebe*, sir: *Thank you, but we Grebes are tough chickens.*'

'Right . . . Number One. Hold your fire till *Thetis* has gone by. I'll go in closer and we'll fire to starboard.' Elkington went to the torpedo-control voicepipe and began shouting orders down to Raikes, the gunner (T). Nick had intended to save *Bravo*'s two torpedoes in case of attack from outside, German ships coming from other bases, and also because the CMBs were supposed to be taking care of any destroyers inside the mole. But if those Huns were going to shoot at the blockships as they steamed in past them, it seemed a good use for torpedoes here and now. He told Garfield, 'Starboard twenty.' *Thetis* was passing now, about halfway from the mole-end to the canal mouth; she'd been hit hard, mostly by the guns on the mole extension; she'd developed a list to starboard and she seemed to be slowing. Garfield reported, 'Twenty o' starboard wheel on, sir!' Nick took a quick look at *Grebe*: he thought she'd been hit again, for'ard this time. Hatton-Jones might think of himself as a tough chicken, but he was a damn sight too close to that Goeben battery. On the other hand, if they were shooting at him they couldn't also be shooting at poor old *Thetis*.

'Midships! Stand by, Number One!'

Elkington was at the voicepipe, in touch with Raikes. They had a static target over there; it only needed a properly aimed torpedo that would run straight. You couldn't *shoot* at those destroyers, because you might hit British sailors and Marines on the mole behind them. *Thetis* was past, heading directly for the canal, listing harder and moving rather slowly and still being hit: Nick saw gunflashes in a new location, suddenly – a little way back from the foreshore but to the west of the Goeben battery and quite near the eastern arm of the canal entrance. It would obviously be more than just a good idea to knock *that* lot out.

'Steady!'

'Steady, sir – south ten west, sir—' Reversing the wheel . . . Nick heard Elkington yell, 'Fire!' Looking aft, he saw the splash of the torpedo's entry. He told Garfield, 'Steer that.'

Just off the mole extension, *Intrepid* burst out of the smoke.

Back at the binnacle, Nick beckoned to Elkington. He pointed out the position of that new battery: they were firing at *Thetis* now and the flashes were easy to see. *Thetis* was almost in the canal, just short of the two breakwater arms that made the approach to it funnel-shaped: he was thinking that it was a miracle she was still afloat when he saw that she was swinging off to starboard. He told Elkington, 'Hit those guns. See if you can't knock one or two of 'em—'

He'd seen a bloom of fire and a blossom of black smoke on *Grebe*. If she stayed where she was much longer, she'd be a *cooked* chicken. Elkington had rushed for'ard to the gun. It would have been nice, Nick thought, to have had *Mackerel*'s four-inch instead of these pea-shooters. *Intrepid* had cleared the barge boom – a string of barges linked by chains and probably with nets slung under them – and there was no net boom there now to impede her, since *Thetis* had towed it in. He looked back at *Thetis*: she'd stopped, aground, on the starboard side of the fairway, well short of the canal entrance. *One down, two to play!* That battery was raising spouts all round her. *Bravo*'s twelve-pounder fired: a surprisingly loud and penetrating *crack* for so small a calibre.

'Captain, sir!'

Tremlett was pointing out to starboard.

Against the mole: a great gout of smoke and spray, debris flying.

426

That German destroyer: *Bravo*'s torpedo had struck her right amidships, under her second funnel. Men were cheering – on the bridge and gundeck. Nick shouted, 'Well done, Number One!' The four-pounder fired again, recoiled: shell-splashes sprang up close to the ship's port side almost simultaneously. The battery was answering their attack: and that was to the good, it might even give *Intrepid* a clear run in.

'*Grebe*'s hit again, sir.'

Garfield said it; but his eyes were on the compass-card again now. They'd hit *Grebe* amidships again, as if they knew where it would hurt most and struck always at the same spot, like a cruel boxer inflicting a maximum of punishment.

'Tremlett – make to him, *Are you still all right?*'

'She's calling *us*, sir!' Tremlett jumped to the searchlight and gave them an answering flash. The four-pounder fired again. Garfield said, 'We're 'itting them guns, sir. Saw the muck fly, that last time.'

'From *Grebe*, sir: *Have been winged. A tow would help.*'

'Number One!' He yelled into the engine-room voicepipe, 'Full ahead together!' Elkington came aft quickly. Nick shouted in his ear as the gun fired again, 'Stand by to take *Grebe* in tow. Have to look slippy because we'll be damn close to the battery. See that the other guns engage it as soon as they bear. Starboard ten, cox'n.'

Intrepid was more than halfway to the canal mouth. Intact, going strong, hardly touched. *Thetis* had two cutters in the water, packed with men, and two MLs were closing-in on them, Elkington had gone down. Nick told Garfield, 'Steer for *Grebe*'s stern.'

'Aye aye, sir.'

Grebe shouldn't be there at all, he thought, let alone in an immobilised condition, which presumably was what Hatton-Jones meant by 'winged'. She was right opposite that battery, no more than half a mile from it, and only a little more than that from the Goeben guns. She was being hit repeatedly and the sea all around her was a mass of leaping shell-spouts. Hatton-Jones, who in civilian life was some kind of art expert and an international yachtsman, and was now an RNVR lieutenant-commander, could reasonably be granted a third description – that of bloody fool. It wasn't only *his* chicken's neck he'd put on the butcher's block.

'Aim in towards her quarter now, cox'n.'

'Aye aye, sir!'

427

'I'm afraid we may get knocked about a bit, in a minute.'
'I wouldn't bet against it, sir.'

C3 had hit the viaduct at nine and a half knots, right in the centre of a section between two rows of piers. Only her captain had been in the bridge by the time they'd struck it; he'd had all the others on the other casing, behind the bridge.

Striking, she'd ridden up out of water, on one of the submerged horizontal girders, smashed through the cross-braces and penetrated as far as the leading edge of the bridge. That had been the really solid point of impact, when the front of the bridge had slammed up against the lattice-work of steel and stopped her. So the Amatol charge had been thrust deep inside the structure of the viaduct, right in the centre of it and under the centre of the roadway overhead. When the bow had hit the underwater girder she'd jumped and jarred: on the casing they'd hung on, hearing the rush and scrape as steel struts snapped and ripped: then the final stop had knocked them off their feet, grabbing for fresh supports: above them in the darkness there'd been German shouts, yelled orders, then lights of torches, rifle-shots, bullets clanging and whirring off the casing. Tim Rogerson recalled a sense of confusion, of hardly knowing what had happened or was happening.

Sandford's voice cut through it.

'Get the dinghy in the water! Fast, now!'

Cleaver was at the for'ard fall. Rogerson cast off the after one, and the boat came down with a rush, its stern bouncing off the curve of No. 3 main ballast tank; the small, frail craft slid into the water almost on its beam-ends, then righted itself and floated.

'Get aboard, all hands!'

There was a lot of shooting now from directly above their heads. Now a searchlight blazed down, and the shots came faster. Scrambling into the little rocking dinghy: six aboard, and Roxburgh trying to start its engine. Sandford came down the side of the bridge like a trapeze artiste; he swung, landed on his feet on the tank-top where the sea washed over it: the submarine was stuck fast but the tide still moved her, grinding her against the girders that held her and supported her explosive bow. They were more than conscious of that five-ton charge now, because Sandford had lit the fuse before he'd left the bridge. He was climbing into the boat, shouting 'Come on, shove off!' The searchlight was blinding, petrifying, and a machine-gun opened up and fired one long burst that sent bullets screaming, rattling and ricocheting through the girders. The sea leapt all around the boat and splinters, large ones, flew from its port side. Rogerson heard himself say, 'She's holed. There's a great—'

The engine started. The machine-gun hadn't fired again but the riflemen were hard at it, bullets singing through the struts and beams, clanging off C3's tanks and sides and smashing into the boat's planks. The engine whirred, screamed unnaturally, jarring oddly on the transom. Roxburgh shut it off.

'Screw's damaged.' He shouted to Sandford, 'Bloody propeller, sir. It's no bloody good.' Rogerson, feeling water round his ankles, asked the ERA, 'Where are the bilge pumps, can we—' A whole section of the gunnel flew away. Sandford yelled over the noise of a fresh fusillade of shots, 'Get the oars out! Tim—' Rogerson's ears were singing from the rifle-fire. He was already groping for the oars, bent over and trying to get his boots out of the way, tugging at the loom of one of them. He pushed at someone else's legs that were in the light, got hold of the oar and dragged it up, and his own right forearm seemed to explode in front of his face. It felt as if it had been hit very hard with a hammer, but the skin and flesh had opened, tendons and bone flown out rather like the spines of a smashed umbrella: he was staring at it and thinking vaguely *dumdums, then*, almost impersonally as if it wasn't his own arm he was looking at. Cleaver had snatched the oar and shipped it in the port-side crutch, and Harner had the other one out to starboard; Harner was pushing at C3's black, wave-washed side with the blade of his, trying to shove off; there was a lot of water in the dinghy now, from the bullet-holes riddling her planks, but Roxburgh had just got the second of the two special bilge-pumps going and it didn't seem to be getting any deeper at the moment. The boat was slewing, coming clear, both oarsmen trying to get her moving out against the flood of tide: at any time it would have been hard work. Harner grunted, let go of his oar and rolled sideways: he was covered in blood and Rogerson suspected he was dead. He tried to take his place, seeing no reason he couldn't row with one good arm, but Bindall got it and slid into the coxswain's place on the thwart.

The boat began to move away from the viaduct, shots whistling round, ricochets whining, water leaping, more holes in the boat's sides. Bindall cursed, fell backwards, letting go his oar: Roxburgh grabbed its loom just before it vanished, sliding away out of the crutch – there were no spare oars, oddly enough, and there was a

429

five-ton pack of Amatol a few yards away with a fuse burning steadily towards it and only a few minutes left: Roxburgh and Cleaver knew it, and they pulled like fleet champions at a regatta. Howell-Price was dragging the wounded or dead men clear of the thwarts and Sandford was at the tiller. Rogerson felt two quick hammer-blows, one into the top of his left shoulder and the other lower, in his ribs on the same side: he remembered afterwards thinking at that moment, not actually feeling pain but knowing he'd been shot twice more and that it was against any sort of odds for any of them to live through this, *Well, that's it, we did know the chances weren't too bright . . .*

The boat was being forced out against the tide, half full of water, both oarsmen straining, grunting with the effort of moving her and her water-ballast and seven men's weight: another searchlight joined the first, and the machine-gun opened up again, and most of the stem and the starboard gunnel flew away like chips off a high-speed lathe: Howell-Price was taking over one of the oars, Sandford at the tiller had been hit, and a second machine-gun joined in. Sandford shouted, 'Keep it up just another half minute, boys, and the swine'll be blown to—' He'd been hit again. He was all blood and he couldn't finish his sentence but he was keeping the boat on course with his teeth gritted and his eyes shut: what made him open them was the Amatol exploding. It was as if the air, the whole night round them, were inflammable and someone had put a match to it: they were part of it, a deafening roar and an engulfing wall of flame. Rogerson, stupefied but vaguely aware that he was cheering, saw a lot of men on bicycles falling into space: some of them appeared to catch fire as they tumbled over. He thought he might be dead, or delirious, or mad. No searchlights now: the power cables to them had been blown apart, of course. Things were dropping everywhere, heavy things and small things, splashing down all round them: a wave came against the tide, lifted the dinghy and rolled it on its way. No shooting any more. Just one small foundering boat with dead or near-dead men in it. Sandford croaked, 'We've done it! *Look!*'

There was a hundred-foot gap in the viaduct. The mole was isolated from the shore. Howell-Price grinned sideways at ERA Roxburgh: 'Come on, *pull*!' Roxburgh complained, 'I'm no *sailor*, sir . . .' Howell-Price, Sandford, Rogerson, Roxburgh and Cleaver were all laughing, or making sounds that passed for it; Sandford told the rowers, 'Save your breath, you loonies. Pull.' There was starshell-light now, and flaming onions from this end of the mole, but nothing close or bright enough to show up details here in the boat. Just as well, Rogerson thought. We'd scare each other silly if we could see each other. We should all be dead. From the time they'd been dazzled in the beams of those filthy searchlights he had imprinted memories of what the others looked like. Sandford particularly, who'd been hit and hit again and still incredibly held the tiller and held it straight: Sandford, Uncle Baldy, should have a VC, he thought, and when he wore it he'd wear it for them all. His own numbness was wearing off and he was beginning to feel, to hurt: if it got much worse it might be difficult to keep quiet. But there was also a feeling of great tiredness, and in opposition to that a certainty that one should not give way to it, that it was imperative to stay awake. It was quite rough, out here, and he wondered where they were going; the little boat was sluggish with all the weight in her, and she must have sunk lower in the water because waves were lopping over the bow behind him.

'Boat *ahoy!*'

A light trained on them, its beam dancing on the water. He thought, *I'm delirious* . . . On the picket-boat the elder Sandford shouted to his stoker, 'Stop her! Slow astern!' He hurried for'ard, beside himself with excitement and relief, and tossed a line across the dinghy. Roxburgh caught it. Howell-Price shouted, 'We've several men quite badly hurt. Skipper needs attention urgently. So does—'

'He'll get it, don't you worry.' The skipper's elder brother knelt, grabbed the dinghy's gunnel; there were sailors behind him ready to get over and lift the wounded into the larger boat. Dick Sandford said in a surprisingly strong voice, 'See to the others first. Cox'n's worse than I am.'

'All right, old chap. Here – easy, now . . .'

'What happened to *you*?'

'Tow broke. Damn near capsized first. Miles back, right out at sea . . . Never mind, we're here now. We'll get you fellows to a destroyer with a doctor. My God, what a *splendid* job you've—'

'What about C1?'

'Broke her tow, too. She's all right, though. Fed up, I've no doubt, at missing it. Anyway, who cares, you did it! You *did* it, Dick!'

'Tow's fast, sir!'

Nick bent to the voicepipe as shells came whirring through

431

thinning smoke and their splashes sprang up to port. 'Slow ahead together.' The twelve-pounder let off another round: target the Goeben battery. *Vindictive*'s howitzers were blasting at that battery too; without their help things might have been a great deal worse.

'Slow ahead together, sir!'

'Keep the helm amidships, cox'n.'

'Aye aye, sir.'

Another salvo hurtled over: splashes all ahead, then one shell came late and short, burst on *Bravo*'s foc's'l: the capstan went up vertically, spinning like a huge top, splashed down a few feet clear of the bow as *Bravo* struggled to forge ahead with *Grebe*'s dead weight dragging at her stern. *Bravo* had lost her mainmast and the quarterdeck six-pounder; the superstructure that the after gun-deck was built on, which was also the wardroom access door, had been smashed in and set alight, but the fire was out now and Elkington had reported that there was no internal damage. Just as well – and lucky: McAllister had a lot of wounded below there in the wardroom. Looking aft over the stern as the wire came taut again, Nick saw *Intrepid*, lit by starshell, settling inside the canal entrance; two cutters and a smaller boat – skiff, probably – were pulling away from her, out into the harbour. There was a lot of machine-gun fire from the shore, and shell-splashes that must be coming either from the mole's inshore end or from that shore battery. An ML was laying smoke in there, and two others were heading to meet the blockship's boats. *Thetis* had been abandoned, but they'd left a green light burning as a guide to help the other two past. *Iphigenia* had rounded the end of the mole, and was halfway across towards *Thetis*: she seemed to be getting in unmolested.

The wire was taut and straining. Two shells dropped short of *Grebe*'s starboard bow, throwing a heavy rain of foul-smelling water across both ships. A starshell burst right overhead: with the smoke gone, they'd be punished again now; the Goeben gunners would want to make up for lost time and they wouldn't be pleased to see their prey escaping. The wire quivered, bar-taut, and *Grebe*'s bow hadn't moved yet.

'Starboard five.'

'Starboard five, sir!'

Turning to port – or trying to – so as to head out at an angle and drag *Grebe*'s bow round, get her pointing out the way they had to go. *Bravo*'s engines were only at slow ahead, but to put on more power at this stage would be to risk parting the tow. Then they'd have to start from scratch again.

'Damn . . .'

He'd whispered it, to himself, as a searchlight fastened on them. *Grebe*'s middle funnel exploded in a shower of steel. That damned light . . . But she was moving, just a little, and it was the start that counted. Once there was some way on her, the inertia overcome, you could put on more revs. It was a sudden strain on the wire that one had to guard against.

'Bosun's mate!'

Clark jumped forward. 'Sir?'

'Tell Maynard to shoot at that light until he hits it.'

'Aye aye, sir!'

Maynard, leading seaman, was the layer of the twelve-pounder. 'Midships.'

'Midships, sir.'

'One-five-oh revolutions.'

Flat out, for an oily wad, was about three-fifty. One-fifty would give her eight or ten knots on her own. Four or five perhaps with *Grebe* in tow. Straightening from the voicepipe he flinched as *Grebe* was hit again right aft. Smoke welled up from her quarterdeck. The twelve-pounder fired – going for the searchlight. Smoke was what they needed: not *that* sort, though. Stinking, blinding stuff, drifting seaward. *Iphigenia* was passing *Thetis*, and she was being hit: by the Goeben guns, probably, which would account for a slackening of the bombardment here. That was another hit on *Iphigenia*: the Huns had been getting too much practice, in the past hour, they were beginning to get the hang of it, God damn them! They'd cut a steam-pipe or something like that, in *Iphigenia*, you could see it pouring up, white in a searchlight's beam. *Grebe* was coming round nicely now.

'Starboard five, cox'n!'

'Starboard five . . . Five o' starboard wheel on, sir!'

Inching her round. Increasing the strain by degrees, getting her on the move, in the process turning her so she'd present a smaller target to the shore guns. The searchlight left them: swept across the harbour, lighting patches of drifting smoke – an abandoned ship's boat – sweeping on: fastening on an ML that was coming out stern-first from the canal entrance with tracer streaming at her from all directions and towing a cutter from her bow. Cutter and launch were both black with men. *Iphigenia* was inside the canal mouth:

433

from this angle she and *Intrepid* were one solid black mass against the light of flares.

'Midships.'

'Midships, sir.'

Elkington climbed into the bridge.

'So far so good, sir.'

'What?'

He shouted, 'Tow's holding, sir, so far!'

'You've done damn well.' It was no more than fact. Elkington had got the line over, then the grass and the heavy wire, in half the time it might have taken. Under heavy fire that wasn't as easy as the Manual of Seamanship Vol. I made it sound.

'What about casualties?'

'Rotten, sir. Nine dead and –' he hesitated – 'about sixteen wounded.'

Almost half the ship's company. And nowhere near out of this hole yet.

The guns in the waist were silent now. *Grebe* was in their way, and there were no targets they could bear on. The twelve-pounder sent one last shell crashing into the darkness: then that one was out of it too, blanked-off from its enemies by the smoking, smouldering ship astern.

'Steer north-east, cox'n.'

'Steer north-east, sir . . .'

That would take them wide of the mole's extremity, towards *Phoebe*'s and *North Star*'s patrol line to the east and north-east of it. Nick put his glasses up to see if either of them might be in sight, or even perhaps the flashes of their guns. He caught his breath: no more than four hundred yards off the lighthouse, one of them – impossible to see which – was stationary, and as he watched a sweeping searchlight gripped her, held her: shells burst all over her and all round her, for a moment she was hidden by their splashes and he thought, *She's done for* . . . How the hell she's got trapped in that position – she must have got lost in smoke perhaps, or – now he saw her partner, sister-ship, moving in at speed, laying a screen of smoke to hide her from that searchlight and the guns on the mole extension: he'd been stooping to the voicepipe while he watched it, all in the space of about four seconds: that smoke *might* save her, if she wasn't already finished . . . He called down to the engine-room, 'Two hundred revolutions.'

'Two 'undred revs, sir!'

434

'Number One, I think we'll—'

A flight of shells came screaming down and burst across *Bravo*'s stern. She seemed to convulse – to flinch and shudder, recoiling from the blows: flames leapt, died back, smoke expanded and came flying for'ard on the wind. Elkington shouted, 'The wire's gone, sir!'

Something like a brick had hit his right shoulder. It had knocked him back, throwing him against the binnacle, and Garfield had reached out one arm to steady him. He heard himself order, 'Starboard fifteen!' He'd been about to say it when the thing had hit him.

'Starboard fifteen, sir . . .' Garfield spun the wheel round. 'You all right, sir?'

'Yes . . . Stop port. Number One –' he couldn't feel his right arm, or move it – 'I'm going to lay smoke inshore of *Grebe* again, then go alongside, port side to his starboard side, and we'll lash him to us. Stand by on the upper deck, please.'

'Aye aye, sir!'

'And I want a report on how things are below . . . Half ahead port, two-five-oh revolutions both engines . . .' *Bloody* searchlight back again! He heard Garfield asking him, 'Are you *sure* you're all right, sir?'

'Midships . . . Cox'n, don't chatter at me.'

'Midships. Sorry, sir.'

The twelve-pounder was back in action. Shooting at the searchlight, Nick hoped. He actually hated it, that light, quite personally and viciously. He bent over the voicepipe: 'Engine-room – make smoke!'

'Make smoke, sir!'

Bravo was on fire aft. But she still wasn't as badly off as *Grebe*. Nick had to use his left hand to raise his binoculars. The right-hand side of his body was all wet: he could feel it running down. He told himself, pulling his thoughts together in order to clarify his intentions, his sense of direction and priorities, *The blockships are in, our job's done, in this state we can't be of any practical use to the MLs in there, so the thing is simply to get out of it – with Grebe* . . . The searchlight left them, swung to *Grebe*: there was a pom-pom firing at her from the beach. A starshell burst high over the middle of the mole: he saw a cutter pulling seaward, two MLs heading the same way, another stopped with a skiff alongside her and men being hauled up. He let his glasses drop on their strap and told Garfield,

435

'Starboard ten.' Black smoke had begun to flood out of both funnels. The top of the after one was shattered, and in the smoke you could see the glow from the furnace down below. For an old coal-burning oily wad there was nothing new in making smoke: only usually it wasn't deliberate, it made senior officers curse and send offensive signals. All *Bravo*'s surviving guns were firing as she swung inshore. He thought, *Better lay two lines of it, one parallel to the other* . . . That way, it might last.

'Midships.'

'Midships, sir.'

He felt ill, suddenly. A sickly weakness spreading from the gut. If one could have been sick it might have helped. The racket of the guns was bewildering, deadening to the senses: something in his head told him *Time to go round, lay smoke behind that lot* . . . 'Port fifteen.'

'Port fifteen, sir.'

Garfield was very steady, very calm. *Bravo* was lucky in her coxswain, Nick thought. Russell was a good hand too. Not as good a chief buffer as Swan had been, but—

There'd been no mention of Swan in the list of ship's company awards for *Mackerel*. Not that it would have made the slightest difference to Swan himself; but for his parents' sake, his people: they should have been allowed some sign, some acknowledgement of the man's quality. Too late now: and it all seemed so long ago. Shells screeched overhead; there were flames on *Grebe*'s iron deck. Her casualties must be terrible, much worse than *Bravo*'s. Now she'd vanished: the first line of smoke lay between them. It should be just as blinding to the Hun gunners. Nick thought he was falling: he held on with his left arm around the binnacle, bent his knees, slid down until the soft-iron correcting-sphere on this side was under his armpit. He let it take his weight, leaning towards it, resting for a moment with his eyes shut. It was amazing how the sick feeling drained away. Garfield boomed, 'Captain, sir!'

'Yes?'

Opening his eyes, and hoisting himself up.

'We've fifteen o' port wheel on still, sir!'

'Midships!' He checked the compass-card quickly. 'Meet her!'

'Meet her, sir . . .'

Gun-flashes ashore now. *Bravo* was inside her own smoke; it drifted seaward as it poured like black treacle from her funnels. And probably they'd made enough of it now: the next thing was to locate *Grebe* again.

'Port ten.'

'Port ten, sir.' Garfield seemed to be watching him all the time, and Nick found it irritating. He took the chance of another rest as he leant against the voicepipe. 'Slow together!'

'Slow together, sir . . .' The smell of the voicepipe increased the feeling of nausea. *Bravo* was turning to starboard into her own black, suffocating smoke. Elkington should have the wires and fenders ready down there by now. When they got through the smoke it should be easy enough to find *Grebe*, particularly if she was still on fire. He heard shells passing overhead, that cloth-ripping noise big ones made when they were passing mast-head-high or higher. They must have been firing blind.

'Midships.'

'Midships, sir.'

'Bosun's mate.' Clark moved towards him. 'Go down and tell the first lieutenant to stand by.'

'Aye aye, sir!'

'Wheel's amidships, sir.'

Able Seaman Clark had only got as far as the head of the ladder; he was coming back. Sub-lieutenant York was with him.

'First lieutenant says he's ready and standing by, sir.'

'Good.' He glanced round the bridge. 'Where's our snotty?'

'Aft, sir. Shell-splinter in his back.' York was goggling at Nick's arm and shoulder; Nick scowled at him, and turned away. It was a peculiar and very unpleasant sensation, to have feeling in only about half one's body and no control over one arm and hand. The limb just dangled. *Bravo* broke out suddenly into clear night air: starshells were drifting over the harbour and a flaming onion soared over the canal mouth. There were shells bursting on the mole extension and he thought those must be *Vindictive*'s howitzers still at it.

'Forty on the bow, sir!'

Garfield was pointing. *Grebe* looked like a wreck, burnt out. Nick shouted, 'Tremlett!' The coxswain said, 'He was hit just now, sir, he's been took down.' It was like a dream one had had before: hadn't Wyatt shouted at a dead yeoman? But he, Nick, hadn't known anything about Tremlett.

'Killed?'

'I don't think so, sir.'

That wasn't so bad, then. Signalman Jowitt asked him, 'Sir?'

'Make to *Grebe, Please stand by to take my wires on your starboard side*.'

437

'Aye aye, sir.'

'Sub, go down and assist the first lieutenant . . . Bosun's mate!'

'Yessir?'

'Go down to the chartroom and bring me up a stool,' He moved to the port side of the bridge, hooked his left elbow over the new protective plating – dented and scorched in places, it looked less new now: half the splinter-mattresses had been ripped or scorched away – and leant his weight on it. He called to Garfield, 'Port fifteen. Stop starboard.' Behind him he heard the clatter of the searchlight as his message was flashed to *Grebe*. He was glad he'd started it with the word 'please': Hatton-Jones was a touchy sort of man, he'd have objected to a signal from a junior that read like an order. Nick's head jerked towards the mole: that was a new sound altogether – the high shriek of a ship's siren.

The recall?

Vindictive's signal to the landing force. The order to start falling back to the ship. It meant the blocking had been completed, that the withdrawal would be starting now.

And consequently, that the howitzer plastering of the Goeben battery would be ceasing. *Damn!*

'Ease to five. Stop port.'

He watched carefully as the gap between the two ships closed. 'Midships.'

'Midships, sir!' Garfield unruffled, stoic.

Staring at *Grebe*'s battered, lacerated hulk, Nick thought *Have we pulled it off, then? Really?* But it was a detached, rather academic consideration. The smoke was already wafting out, surrounding them; *Grebe* was half hidden in it. All right, so there was another bank to drift up behind it, but that gave – what, five or ten minutes? To get two ships lashed together and under way, creep out of range?

Wyatt croaked, 'Hold on, damn you . . .' Crawling, sliding himself along with the Marine corporal on his back. This one seemed to have been shot in the lungs. His own wounds, Wyatt thought, were mostly superficial. His left leg was smashed from ankle to kneecap – *that* was bad enough . . . Whenever the pain of it reached his brain he had to stop, lie flat, press his face against the concrete and – he'd passed out, two or three times. It came in spasms, and when it ebbed – he said aloud, 'The *hell* with it!' His shoulder – no way of knowing whether that had been shrapnel or a bullet: and a

438

bayonet-stab in the neck. Flesh-wounds, those. Bled a lot, but –
nothing. He'd been stabbed when he'd led a rush of bluejackets
over some wire – they'd thrown planks on it and dashed over them
– and cleared out one end of the first lot of trenches. Huns back
there now, damn them! A long time ago, that felt like, but it
couldn't have been, they'd only been on the mole an hour. He told
the man on his back, 'Don't worry, you'll live to have another
crack at 'em! So'll I, by God!' Talking helped, now and then. One's
own voice reassured one. Almost as much as seeing Keyes's flag
had, just now: over the smoke out there, within a stone's throw of
the mole, he'd seen *Warwick*'s masthead go by with that great
banner of a vice-admiral's flag streaming from it – big because it
had been made to fly from a dreadnought battleship, Keyes's
squadron flagship up in Scapa – the St George's Cross and the
single red ball in its upper canton: it had passed by floating above
the smoke although the destroyer under it was hidden. Men had
cheered to see it, there'd been a shout of 'Here comes Roger!' A few
minutes before the recall signal, that had been; and now by
unspoken agreement, without any order being given, they were
bringing back the wounded and the dead. Wherever they could be
got at: some, you couldn't reach.

Wyatt had passed Padre Peshall half a dozen times: Peshall, not
even scratched so far – perhaps the Lord looked after his own
lieutenants? – had an odd way of running in a crouched, bear-like
shamble with a man across his shoulders. He kept delivering them
and going back for more. Wyatt was doing the same, a lot of chaps
were, but he couldn't move as fast as the padre, with this damn leg.
He'd saved three: this one would make four. It wouldn't be fitting,
to leave the dead for Huns to deal with; and the wounded, of course,
had to be brought out. In the last hour, Wyatt thought he'd seen
everything fine that there could be to see: he'd come to realise there
was no standard to which the British sailor or Marine could not
measure. Harrison, for instance, who'd been laid out half-dead by
that shot in the jaw: he'd come-to, and immediately rushed ashore
and taken over command from Adams. By that time Adams, who'd
led an assault on the wire and trenches beyond No. 3 shed, had been
hit several times himself and lost three-quarters of his men. He'd
reinforced them with some of B Company, whose officers had all
been killed, and led another rush along the parapet, but a machine-
gun had pinned them down and another one from a destroyer
moored on the inside of the mole had caught them in a cross-fire.

They'd had to retire again, leaving a lot of men dead out in front. Harrison, taking over, had sent Adams back to ask for Marine reinforcements, and Major Weller, the senior surviving leatherneck – the Marines by this time had cleared two hundred yards of mole to the westward of the ship and were holding out down there in the face of particularly fierce attacks – sent up a platoon. Meanwhile Harrison, who couldn't speak because of his smashed jaw, had led another dash along the roadway. He and every single man with him was either killed or wounded. Wyatt, who'd been flat at the time, temporarily knocked out by the shock of his leg-wound, had seen it, and helped some of them to crawl back. The half-dead leading the three-quarter dead. Able Seaman Eaves had tried to carry back Harrison's body, but Eaves was knocked out himself while he was doing it. Another sailor, McKenzie, a machine-gunner, had gone on working his gun long after he'd been badly wounded: he'd caught a group of Germans running from a blockhouse to the destroyer – which had shortly afterwards blown up, hit by a torpedo from God knew where – and he'd polished them all off, like a row of skittles, one behind the other. Wyatt asked the man on his back, 'Know your Captain Bamford, do you, eh?' The corporal didn't answer. Couldn't: couldn't hear, quite likely. Wyatt told him, not caring too much about being heard or not, 'Man's incredible. Never seen anything like it. Doesn't know bullets kill a man – or doesn't give a brass—'

'Hello there, Edward!' The padre crouched down beside him, staring at him anxiously. Probably thought he'd been talking to himself, gone off his head or something. He smiled. 'Give you a hand with this fellow?'

'No. You fetch your own.' Wyatt thought that was funny. He said it again, because Peshall hadn't laughed. The padre said, 'Ought to pack it in now, Edward. Let 'em take you aboard this time. The recall's sounded, did you hear it?'

Wyatt crabbed on towards the ship. A Royal Marine platoon was holding a small perimeter and providing covering fire, and there were scaling-ladders up to the higher roadway. Bluejackets were hauling the dead and wounded up as they were brought back from all directions, and carrying them across and lowering them down the brows. Four brows in commission now. Wyatt had one more chap he was determined to fetch: he had to, he'd actually told him he'd come back for him. He'd seen him sprawled in a half-sitting position in the doorway of a wrecked blockhouse or store near the Hun wire that started beyond No. 3 shed. There were some railway trucks lined up there, and they'd provide enough cover for a man on his own to crawl up under them and drag him away. The Germans were damn close by, since they'd reoccupied that trench: but if one was quiet, and as quick as this damned leg would allow ... Wyatt had been almost within touching distance of the wounded man already: he'd put the Marine corporal down, crept under the trucks and inspected him from not more than ten feet away. An able seaman with three good-conduct badges. Badly hit – his face all black on one side with crusting blood. Wyatt had called to him, 'Hold hard – I'll come back for you!' The recall wasn't an order to be obeyed promptly, it only gave notice of withdrawal. You couldn't just draw stumps and walk away. He lay flat while a machine-gun flamed and clattered from the left: there'd been too much light, one of their blasted flaming onions. *God*, he thought, *How I hate the bloody Huns!*

There was quite a bunch of men in the shelter of No. 3 shed now. A young Marine sergeant was controlling them, sending them across the open mole in small groups between bursts of enemy machine-gun fire. On one's own, keeping to the shadows and moving this slowly, as slowly as was necessitated by this damn-fool condition he was in, you had a certain advantage over men in groups legging it about. He grinned, muttered, *Marvellous chaps. Thank God I'm an Englishman!* Better cross over now. He'd been lucky with that parapet hook, he thought. That lift of the ship, just as *Daffodil* shoved her in, had done it. Wouldn't have, otherwise. Bargained for a tide three or four feet higher than tonight's. *Last* night's. One minute after midnight, *Vindictive* had bumped along-side. Young Claud Hawkins of D Company hadn't been so lucky, when they'd been struggling to get *Iris* tied-up alongside: Hawkins had used a scaling-ladder, got right up on the parapet to man-handle the hook over; he'd been on it when they opened up on him, and he'd started firing back at them with his revolver, and they'd killed him with the hook still not in place. Then George Bradford, Hawkins's company commander, had tried going up the derrick, and a machine-gun firing across the mole had cut him off the top of it: he'd fallen – his body had fallen – between the mole and the old ferry-boat, and one of his petty officers had gone down after it and that had been *his* end, too. The hook tore away in any case, as soon as the weight of the steamer came on it. But you felt so damn *proud*, to have had such friends . . .

441

Nearly there now. The shade under those trucks was deep: once he got under there, he'd be – Flattening, as a mortar thumped down somewhere behind him. Shrapnel lashed the trucks, splintering wood and striking sparks off metal, sang away into the flaming dark. Last trip, this. The ships wouldn't be alongside much longer. He was dragging himself forward again. Never mind about it hurting, you milksop, doctors'll fix all that up. What they're for. Had enough practice by this time to know how to set about it, too. That recall wasn't sounded on *Vindictive*'s siren, but on *Daffodil*'s. Reason: poor old *Vindictive*'s had her whistle shot off. She'd been shot to bits, above the level of the parapet she was a smashed-up scarecrow of a ship. God bless her! And Carpenter, Rosoman, Osborn, Bramble – what a crowd! Hilton Young with an arm half off: Walker waving without a hand: Keyes knows how to pick men, all right. Any man Roger Keyes picks for a job of work is fit to know. Under the second truck now . . . Putting his face right down on the cold concrete between the lines he could see light – radiance of distant starshell and closer flares, constantly changing but always there to some extent – and the black outline of the wrecked building where his three-badger would be waiting for him. *Told you I'd be back, my friend, eh?* Movement: scrape of a boot on concrete, and then a metallic click. Something bounced, skittered towards him under the truck. It touched his face. In the half-second that was left to him he realised it was a grenade.

Grebe was on fire again, and all her guns had been knocked out. He could see just one man moving on her after-part. The stern itself was shattered, funnels split and torn, her bridge was a charred heap of scrap-iron on which Hatton-Jones, recognisable by a bandage round his head, had a helmsman and a snotty with him. The fires aft provided enough illumination for the occasional starshell to be superfluous, from the shore gunners' point of view. *Grebe* was a dead weight to *Bravo*: it was probably only the fact that she was well down by the bow with her stern consequently raised high in the water that she hadn't flooded aft and foundered.

Bravo's twelve-pounder had been knocked to bits by a direct hit which had also killed all its crew; it was a miracle that shell hadn't killed everyone on the bridge as well. At least with the gun finished one wasn't obliged to go on bringing up more men to man it in the place of those already killed: stuck out there in front of the bridge, and with its protective screening shot away, it was about as exposed a position as one could imagine. Every shot that hit the foc's'l sent splinters screaming over it. More shells ripped overhead: Nick was tensed for new flame, blast, destruction, death: it hadn't come. Not this time. They'd *all* gone over. *The bastards have to miss sometimes . . . Bravo's* worst wound had been a hit in her for'ard boiler-room. Chief ERA Joseph had shut it off now: so long as the feed-water held out they could manage on the after boilers. She could make a few knots through the water; and while she could move, and float, and *Grebe* could float and move with her, there were lives in both ships that one could try to save.

'Port five, cox'n.'

'Port five, sir . . .'

To keep the for'ard wires taut. When they were slack, the sea's movement drove the two ships together – thumping, scraping . . . He saw flashes from the Goeben battery: he'd had his glasses on it, holding them in his left hand with his elbow on the top edge of the port side plating, looking aft over *Grebe's* smashed stern. With nothing shooting at those shore guns now – *Vindictive* and the others had left the mole some time ago – they were using the two old thirty-knotters for target-practice.

Wreaking some vengeance, perhaps, for the indignity their side had suffered, the rape of their stronghold.

Perhaps I'm being stupid? Perhaps there's no point in this now?

No alternative, though. Badly wounded men drowned, when a ship sank. *Bravo* and *Grebe* had more dead and wounded now than they had fit and living. Less than half *Bravo's* crew of sixty were on their feet.

Salvo scorching in now. He met Garfield's impassive stare. Behind the coxswain, young York. York had taken over from Elkington, who was dead. There wasn't anything one could do, except struggle on. At what – two knots? The only miracle that he could think of that anyone could have prayed for was the Goeben guns to run out of ammunition. It wasn't really likely. Nick said, 'One thing – they'll have to give us a new ship, after this.'

Garfield's raised eyebrow managed to climb another centimetre, then dropped back. He muttered, 'Don't make 'em like this no more, sir.'

'You think that's *bad*?'

Jowitt laughed. The shells came down in a hoarse rush ending in leaping fountains of black sea and a streak of flame across both ships, clap of thunder under your feet and inside your skull, stink of explosive and fried metal: on the starboard side abaft the bridge

443

yellow flames danced, crackling and spurting, leaping to throw the foremast into silhouette. The yard had gone and most of the rigging with it, the rest hanging in a tangle of steel-wire rope, halyards and aerial wires, but the mast still stood. Nick realised that the yellow burning was a cordite fire; bits of it were springing in the air, landing elsewhere and continuing to burn. Ready-use cartridges at the starboard for'ard six-pounder. He called to York, 'Sub – go round the guns and dump all the ready-use. Cartridges specially. Over the side.'

'Aye aye, sir!'

'*Bravo, ahoy!*'

Hatton-Jones was bawling through a megaphone as the shell-stink blew clear. Nick found his down by his feet. Moving was a strange business: you forced your limbs to travel in a desired direction, but when it started it felt like floating, lacking support or contact with the surroundings. He was up again, with the megaphone.

'Everard here. You all right?'

Hatton-Jones shouted, 'You'd better leave me. Cast off and get out of it.'

'What about your wounded?'

Shouting hurt him. He looked aft. 'Sub, wait here!' York came back from the ladder; there was a considerable gap in the bridge screening there at its head. He asked Hatton-Jones, 'Can you send them over to us?'

Garfield shouted, 'Captain, sir!'

Nick turned, looked at him. The coxswain was pointing out to port, across *Grebe*'s smoking, shattered waist. Nick saw, by star-shell light, a streak of white. Broken sea, some sort of—

'CMB, sir!'

He let the megaphone drop and put his glasses up. Left arm doing all the work. It *was* a CMB. One's mind was slow-moving, sluggish; one had to drive it, prod it. What could – well, take off some of the wounded, or—

Smoke!

Streaming from that racing, leaping boat's exhaust: lovely, heavy, Brock-type smoke! Jowitt cheered suddenly, a cowboyish whoop of joy. Garfield snarled, 'Quiet, you silly—'

'Sub.' Nick told York, 'Go down and empty all the shot-ready racks. Then see to the wires, see if anything needs adjusting or doubling-up. Look for fraying, and see the fenders are still in place. All right?'

Flashes of clarity. York was grinning as he turned away, looking at the CMB as she passed astern, rocketing by to spread her blessed smoke between these destroyers and the shore. Well inshore, plenty of room for it to drift out astern of them as they dragged themselves away like crippled animals. The CMB might even hang around, be at hand to lay another streak if that lot blew away.

It was all they'd needed. There'd been no hope of getting it, and the MLs had all been fully occupied getting the blockships' crews away. The launches had been packed to capacity, and it was obvious that a lot of the blockships' passage-crew stokers *had* defied orders and stayed on board . . . Shell-splashes sprang up way off on the quarter: the Hun gunners were trying to knock out the CMB now.

'*Grebe*, ahoy!'

'Yes, Everard?'

'Shall we proceed now, sir?'

Waiting for the answer, he leant against the plating and shut his eyes, whispered in his brain, *Thank you, God* . . .

More motion on them now, as the linked ships struggled seawards in a stiffening breeze. Crashing together, lurching, scraping . . . 'Like two junk-yards 'aving a go,' Garfield had rumbled. York had nearly split his sides. York said now, with binoculars at his eyes, 'Looks like *Warwick* coming back in, sir. The admiral.'

Nick was on the stool. They'd lashed it to the binnacle for him. He slid off it, moved to the side of the bridge and got his glasses up. He wasn't certain, but he felt as if he might have been asleep. Perhaps only for a second? Otherwise he'd surely have toppled off the stool.

It was *Warwick*, all right. Garfield said approvingly, 'Come to round us strays up, sir. Gath'ring 'is flock.'

Nick was remembering how a month or so ago, when he'd been getting to know his new coxswain and to like him, he'd asked him one day, 'What year did you join the Navy?' Garfield had told him, 'Nineteen-oh-three, sir.' Nick had thought, *When I was seven* . . . He'd asked another question: 'Why did you? What made you join?' The coxswain had glanced down at his boots, frowned, looked up again. He'd answered with one word: ' 'unger, sir.'

The Navy was made of men like Garfield.

Warwick passing close . . . Daylight coming rapidly: the Belgian

445

coast was a low black line with a haze of mauve-tinted dawn behind it. Nick had come back to the binnacle, but the stool seemed about twelve feet high. He let himself slide down, sat on the step and leant back against the binnacle's round solidity. He shut his eyes. Garfield said quietly, 'Sub-lieutenant, sir . . .'

Warwick had flashed, *I am ordering Moloch to stand by you. What is your situation?* Jowitt was using a hand-lamp; the twenty-inch had been blown overboard a long time ago. Raikes, the gunner (T), was crouching beside Nick. 'You all right, sir?' York looked down at him: 'Get McAllister and a stretcher, gunner, would you?' He turned to Jowitt, and told him, 'Make to *Warwick*: Bravo *towing* Grebe. *Believe can make Dover if weather holds. Very heavy casualties. Captain has just succumbed to wounds. Sub-lieutenant York assuming command.*'

Jowitt wanted to know how to spell 'succumbed'.

Sarah had said in her letter, *There is something I must tell you, because I must share it with someone and I believe that you, my dearest Nick, will at least try to understand. Please? You may remember that I introduced an old friend to you – Alastair Kinloch-Stuart, a major in one of the Highland regiments, here some months ago. Since then he has visited several times in this neighbourhood, and I cannot pretend otherwise than that his purpose has been to be close to me. I have not, I admit it and beg you to understand the circumstances, been as firm as I know I should have been in preventing this. He was such a very old friend, my family and his were on almost cousinly terms when he and I were only children. But – Nick, my dear, I should like to be speaking to you about this, not struggling to describe it so inadequately in a letter – he fell in love with me, and I have always had a high and warm regard for him; he was a good and honourable person and had no despicable intentions, indeed it was in some ways an agony for us both, and all the worse, that is to say more difficult for me at least to – oh, Nick, I am only saying what you know so well, that your father and I have not made the great thing of our marriage that I had hoped we should and intended. I must not ramble on, although I could scribble and scribble and still not tell you half of what I have in my heart and in my brain, of my feelings and deep sadness. But I did nothing wrong, Nick, ever. I promise you. And now poor Alastair has been killed in action. It was on March 22nd when the enemy broke through south of the Somme. Alastair had written a letter addressed to me, and it was brought to me here by his sister, to whom he had entrusted it. Now I have wept again. Nick, you are the one person on whose sympathy and love I place reliance: please come as soon as you can – please, Nick dear?*

McAllister was crouching beside him. Two sailors were opening the folding stretcher, placing it where they could lift him on to it.

Garfield asked without moving his eyes from the lubber's line, 'Will he be all right, sir?'

The surgeon-probationer looked up. He gestured to the stretcher-bearers. Rising to his feet, he answered slowly, emphatically, 'If he does *not* become "all right", cox'n, you may shoot me.'

The coxswain looked at him, and nodded.

'You said that, sir. There's some might 'old you to it.'

Nick murmured, 'Sarah. Oh, Sarah.'

McAllister and York exchanged glances. Nick spoke again; he'd been away somewhere, but for the moment he was back.

'Sub.'

'Yes, sir?'

'We're supposed to rendezvous at Thornton Roads. North-west for fifteen miles. Don't forget the tide. Transfer the tow when you get a chance.'

'Aye aye, sir.' They were lifting the stretcher, with Nick on it. York added, 'But now you – take it *easy*, sir, don't—'

Garfield laughed. Sudden, explosive. Then he was himself again – stolid, not even smiling. McAllister and York were staring at him, wondering what had caused that uncharacteristic bark of mirth. He wasn't bothering to explain.

PATROL TO
THE GOLDEN HORN

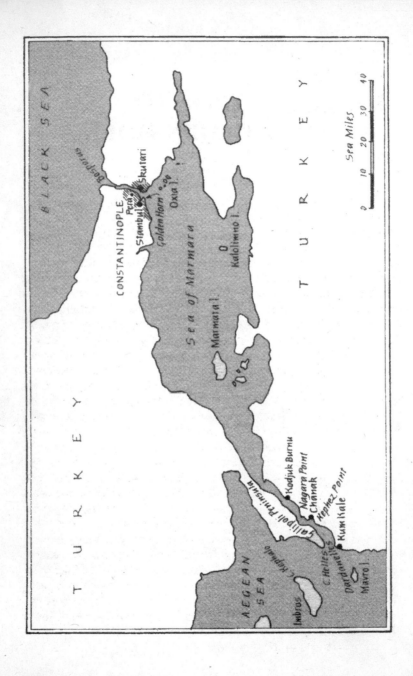

PROLOGUE

Mist curtained the exit from the straits, adding to the dawn a milky thickness that clung to the black water and allowed only sporadic glimpses of the land's outlines against a lightening sky, and the raiding ships came out through it like ghosts, grey-steel engines of destruction thrusting westward into the Aegean. The four destroyers which had escorted the big ships from Constantinople across the Marmara and through the winding, mine-sown Dardanelles were already invisible in the dark to starboard; Admiral von Rebeur-Paschwitz had detached them a few minutes ago, at five-thirty am, when by dead reckoning *Goeben*'s navigating officer had known that Cape Helles was abeam. The destroyers would sweep to the westward of Cape Helles now, and then if they drew a blank they'd turn and re-enter the straits while the more powerful ships pressed on in search of targets for their guns.

Goeben, battle cruiser, 23,000 tons and with a main armament of ten eleven-inch, led the four-funnelled cruiser *Breslau*. Both ships were closed-up at action stations, expecting at any moment to run into the British destroyer patrol which was known to haunt the approaches to the straits; and since any seaman knew that you could see over fog and under it but no distance through it, lookouts were stationed down on *Goeben*'s foc's'l and in the spotting positions on both mastheads. Seventy men manned each of the battle cruiser's five twin-gunned turrets, and the guns were ready loaded.

Goeben's wake curved as she swung to port, leading her consort round to a south-westerly course which was designed to take them clear around certain barriers of mines that the British had laid for the precise purpose of interrupting such a raid as this. Before the attack on Mudros which was the main target of the sortie, those British patrol ships had to be found and eliminated.

'Our course is south sixty west, sir.'

'Thank you, captain.' Von Rebeur-Paschwitz's intention was to sweep south-west for about ten miles and then, if the patrol hadn't been encountered either by himself or by his destroyers west of Cape Helles, he'd turn north and search for them off the coast of Imbros, where in any case there'd be other prey for his guns, perhaps inside Cape Kephalo and certainly in Kusu Bay. He walked out to the wing of the battle cruiser's bridge and gazed astern, watched *Breslau* tucking herself neatly into the bigger ship's wake after the swing to port. Light was increasing now but the mist still trailed over them like a blanket: it was a blessing, an unhoped-for bonus to their chances of success by prolonging the element of surprise, but he knew that at any moment it could begin to lift and dissipate. His force was at this moment seven miles west of Kum Kale and five miles due north of Mavro Island; there was a British lookout station on Mavro, and the longer this course was held the closer *Goeben* would be getting to those British eyes. But the temptation to turn away and cut the corner had to be resisted, because of the risk of finding himself in mined water. The admiral wished, almost desperately, that his intelligence reports of the British minefields could have been more precise.

Nine minutes past six: he'd gone into shelter from the wind, leaning over the covered chart-table in the forefront of the bridge, to light his first cigar of the day. He'd just emerged from under the canvas hood when he heard a shout from the young sailor who was manning the telephone from the foc'sl lookout: 'Mine, port bow!'

'Hard a-starboard—'

Goeben shuddered to the explosion. Black water leapt, cascaded across the bridge, a heavy stinking rain. Echoes of the crash still lingered ringingly; the captain was calling for reports from below. The bridge revolution indicators showed the admiral that his flagship hadn't slackened speed; nor had her course varied by as much as one degree. And reports were coming up from the compartments: damage was so slight that it could be ignored. The impact had been abreast the for'ard turret and thus against the eleven-inch-thick main armoured belt.

Von Rebeur-Paschwitz realised suddenly that he had a lit cigar between his fingers and that he'd been forgetting to smoke it. There was an inch-long cylinder of grey ash on the end of it. He drew pleasurably on the fragrance of the Havana leaf, enjoying simultaneously this proof of his flagship's contempt for British mines. Expelling smoke as her captain came to report to him on the

452

inconsequential extent of the damage below decks, he remarked to him that Messrs Blohm and Voss of Hamburg certainly knew how to build ships.

Ten minutes later course was altered to due west, and after another ten minutes – at six thirty-two am, by which time it was considered that they'd come right around the perimeter of the mined area – to north, towards Imbros. Mist still shrouded them. It was like – he heard the navigator remark to the torpedo lieutenant – steaming through potato soup. Luck, von Rebeur-Paschwitz appreciated, was certainly on his side, and he decided to make the most of it while it lasted. Aerial reconnaissance twenty-four hours earlier had shown that two British monitors were lying at anchor in Kusu Bay: he ordered *Breslau* to push on ahead at her best speed in order to block any possibility of their escape.

Breslau's best speed was about twenty-two knots; *Goeben*'s only twenty. Both ships had been capable of better than twenty-seven when they'd entered service in 1912, but four years holed up at Constantinople without dry-dock or dockyard facilities had taken a natural effect.

At seven am *Goeben* was five miles from the south coast of Imbros, roughly eight miles south-west of Cape Kephalo, and after a brief consultation over the chart the admiral ordered a four-point turn to starboard in order to skirt the island's south-east corner on a track that he reckoned would be well to the westward of the mine barriers. This north-east course was held until seven thirty-two, at which point the battle cruiser hauled round to port, to a northerly course that would take her exactly two miles off Cape Kephalo.

The mist was rising, at last. And the period of secrecy and silence was in any case about to be shattered by the thunder of the German guns. There was a wireless signal station on Kephalo, and it was to be *Goeben*'s first target for destruction: a warm-up, a chance for the gunners to get their eyes in. As the great ship steamed up towards the point her five turrets swung smoothly under electric power and under directions passed from two armoured control-towers amidships. In the spacious turrets – there were no divisions inside, between the individual guns – men grinned at each other, delighted at this prospect, finally, of action.

'Fire!'

One gun in each of the five turrets had fired, recoiled. Five other guns were ready for the second salvo. Reload projectiles and charges came up on the hoists between the pairs of guns and were presented to the breeches on rocking trays: the charges were in brass cylinders and in two halves, each half weighing 140 lb. Fumes wreathed acrid from the breeches: projectiles and charges rushed in, impelled by wooden rammers with spring-coil heads. Breeches slamming shut . . . 'Fire!' The second salvo was right for line, but short. Range had to be adjusted: and as Cape Kephalo was almost abeam now it would be opening, increasing, from now on. There was a rate instrument in each turret, and also a rangefinder, all of them connecting to one central transmitting station.

'Fire!'

Over . . .

'Fire!'

Flame, black smoke, flying masonry and rock and earth . . .

'Check, check, check!'

The gunnery lieutenant reported to the bridge by telephone, 'Target destroyed, sir.'

'Very well.'

It had been easy: much too easy for anyone to expect congratulations. Two miles, 4,000 yards, was really point-blank range. And having whetted her appetite *Goeben* now altered two points to port in order to run up past Kusu Bay.

Breslau, pushing on northwards to carry out the admiral's orders, had sighted a British destroyer. This was *Lizard*, and when the German sighted her she was about six miles to the nor'ard. *Breslau* gave chase, but *Lizard*'s better speed enabled her to stay clear of the more heavily gunned ship; she was waiting to be joined by the other patrolling destroyer, *Tigress*, who had been some miles to the west and was now hurrying back to join her.

The monitors in Kusu Bay, *Lord Raglan* and *M.28*, were shortening-in their cables and trying to raise steam; but their anchors never left the ground. *Goeben*, appearing out of still poor visibility around Grafton Point, began immediately to deluge them in a rain of highly accurate gunfire from which there was no possibility of escape. By eight am both monitors were sunk. It had been easy, unopposed, like target practice, and everything so far had gone exactly to plan. The only slight worry was that the explosion of that mine had upset *Goeben*'s compass; if the fault couldn't be rectified it might be necessary, von Rebeur-Paschwitz thought, to order *Breslau* to take the lead as guide. Meanwhile he ordered a reversal of course, in order to steam back and around the south of the island and thence westward for Mudros. At Mudros there'd be bigger prizes: bigger opposition too. Not that there'd been *any* here; and he had the satisfaction of knowing he'd left nothing afloat here that could bar his eventual line of retreat to the Dardanelles. By twenty minutes after eight *Goeben* was leading *Breslau* southward past the still smoking ruins of Cape Kephalo.

Then over that smoke-haze appeared a flight of British aircraft: bombers, from the Imbros airfield. *Goeben*'s 24-pounder AA guns swung their barrels skyward: and *Breslau*, to clear the flagship's range, swung out wide to port. Too wide: at eight thirty-one, by which time the first flight of bombers had dropped their loads into the sea and turned back for more, *Breslau* struck a mine.

She was under helm at the time, and the explosion was right aft: her steering was smashed, and so was the starboard turbine. With no operative rudder and with only one screw she was unmanoeuvrable. Von Rebeur-Paschwitz had no option but to order *Goeben*'s captain to take the damaged ship in tow. *Breslau* had in fact steamed into the western edge of the mine barriers: and *Goeben*, closing in to take up a towing position ahead of her, was now running into exactly the same hazard. While the cruiser's sailors worked frantically to range her cable on the foc'sl and prepare for the tow, and just as a second flight of bombers came racketing overhead – *Breslau*, lying stopped, took a direct hit in this attack – *Goeben* also hit a mine.

Suddenly the picture had changed entirely. There was a steady succession of attacks from aircraft: both ships were in clear Mediterranean water in which the dark shapes of mines could be seen all around them: and *Tigress* and *Lizard* were racing southward in the hope of a chance to use torpedoes. All the lighter guns in the German ships were blazing away at the persistent, mosquito-like bombers. *Goeben* was trying to pick her way between the mines: *Breslau*, unable to control her steering, hit another four in the five minutes after nine am. She was already listing to port: after the fourth eruption, the death-blow, she swung upright, lifted her bows high in the air and slipped swiftly stern-first to the bottom.

Admiral von Rebeur-Paschwitz abandoned all thoughts of an attack on Mudros. He had to accept now that he'd be doing well to get his ship back into the Dardanelles. He ordered a south-westerly course, then south, and finally north-east, in order to skirt around the mines; and *Goeben* was on that final north-east leg, very close to where she'd been when she'd hit the first one, when the third exploded against her quarter.

There was some extensive internal flooding, and she'd taken up a fifteen-degree list to port. Aircraft were still chasing and attacking, and the bombing continued even after she'd entered the Straits. Behind her the Aegean Sea was a furiously buzzing hornet's nest: and there was a lively awareness that the Germans wouldn't lose a minute in making good the damage to their battle cruiser and that what had been attempted once might very well be tried again. However safe *Goeben* might feel herself to be in her heavily defended Turkish hideout, she would now – somehow – have to be eliminated.

CHAPTER 1

'Steady as you go!'

'Steady, sir . . . South twenty-six east, sir!'

CPO Perry had flung the wheel back the other way; its brass-capped spokes flashed sunlight as they thudded through his palms and *Terrapin* steadied on her course across Kusu Bay, cleaving blue water under a cloudless sky. The bay mirrored a whitish crescent of beach framed in crumbly looking rock; higher up on the island, patchy green slopes broken by rock outcrops rose to support the canopy of Mediterranean sky. There were more strikingly beautiful islands in the Aegean than Imbros – Nick had had his first sight of some of them during the fast passage from Malta – but even this, to his home waters' eye, was fairly stunning.

Truman, the destroyer's captain, glanced again at his coxswain. 'Steer two degrees to starboard. Stop both engines.'

One island they'd passed within sight of had been Skyros; and on Skyros Sub-Lieutenant Rupert Brooke of Hood Battalion in the Royal Naval Division lay buried, his grave heaped with the island's pink-veined marble. Brooke's close friends had piled it over him – so Sarah had said, and Sarah knew everything about Rupert Brooke. Nick hoped that some opportunity might arise for him to visit Skyros.

Why? Because Sarah was so emotional on that subject? And he, Nick Everard, even more so over Sarah?

It was a shocking thing. Of *course* it was. Objectively, one knew that – and at the same time thrilled, thinking of her. You could lose yourself in a dreamworld filled with pictures, echoes of her voice. And worry, too – the puzzle – her actions since, and that she'd said *nothing* . . . As a passenger – he'd been sent out to assume command of *Leveret*, a five-year-old destroyer employed mainly as a despatch vessel between Mudros and Salonika – on passage, with nothing to do except sit and stand around, there'd been too much time for that kind of self-indulgence. He knew he'd surrendered to the temptation far too much, and he pulled himself back into the present and the sunlight now – to Cruickshank, the navigating lieutenant, at the binnacle and watching the transverse bearing as *Terrapin* slid up, with very little way on her now, towards her anchor berth; and to Truman, keenly aware – you could see it in his self-conscious manner – of the light cruiser two cables' lengths on his port beam, and the fact that *Terrapin* would be under close surveillance from that crowded quarterdeck. Truman was a stuffy, humourless lieutenant-commander. All the way from Plymouth he hadn't opened a single conversation, so far as Nick could recall, that hadn't borne directly on some Service matter.

A submarine lay alongside the cruiser, and a haze of smoke over her stern showed that she was charging her batteries. That would be E.57, presumably, the boat Jake Cameron was to join – in a hurry, which was the reason for *Terrapin* having been diverted here instead of going straight to Mudros, her original destination. Cameron was a passenger too, but he'd only joined in Malta. He was an immensely burly young RNR lieutenant – about Nick's age, but twice his weight. He was at the back of the bridge now, his wide frame squeezed into the corner between rail and flag-locker.

Cruickshank – bony, intent, crouched mantis-like at the binnacle – murmured, 'Five degrees to go, sir.'

'Stand by!' Truman had a rather plummy voice. Harriman, his first lieutenant, was at the bridge's front rail; he'd raised one stubby arm above his head, and Granger, down on the foc'sl with the cable party, waved acknowledgement. A languid wave: 'lounge-lizard Larry' was what the other officers called *Terrapin*'s dark-eyed sub-lieutenant. They were a good crowd; better, Nick thought, than Truman deserved. Cruickshank called, 'Bearing on *now*!'

'Let go!'

Harriman dropped that arm. On the foc'sl a hammer swung to knock the Blake slip off the starboard cable and send its anchor splashing, plunging into clear-blue sea. As the cable roared away and then slowed its initial rush until you could hear the separate *clank* as each link banged out through the hawse, Nick did some elementary mental arithmetic: eight fathoms of water, and three eights were twenty-four, so—

Truman had made the same calculation. He told Harriman, 'Veer to two shackles, and secure.'

Two shackles added up to twenty-five fathoms, and three times the depth of water was minimal for safe mooring. In this flat calm the minimum was as safe as houses.

Terrapin floated like a model ship in a bed of blue-tinted glass; the air was motionless, smelling faintly of the nearby island. Such picture-book stillness: it seemed incongruous to come to such a place for any warlike purpose. But Nick reminded himself, as he pulled the strap of borrowed binoculars over his head and slung them on the binnacle, that climate and scenery had nothing at all to do with it. Three years ago, when he – and the rest of Jellicoe's Grand Fleet – had been dying of boredom in the frozen wilderness of Scapa Flow, on sun-kissed beaches only ten miles east of this island a million men had died.

Near enough a million – counting Turks as well.

Cruickshank told Truman, 'Signalling from *Harwich*, sir.'

Harwich was the light cruiser, now on their quarter. Four-funnelled, *Bristol* class, with two six-inch and ten four-inch guns. Where would she have been, Nick wondered, a couple of months ago, when *Goeben* had come crashing out of the Dardanelles and caught everyone with their trousers down? He was looking over towards the cruiser and seeing that there were two submarines alongside, not just the one he'd seen before. *Harwich* was lying bow-on and you could see them both, one each side of her; the rumble of diesels from that battery-charging was a deep mutter across the quiet bay.

From a wing of the cruiser's bridge, a light was still winking its dots and dashes. Truman bent to the engine-room voicepipe.

'Finished with main engines. Remain at immediate notice.'

'Aye aye, sir . . . Shall we be fuelling, sir?'

That had been the voice of Mr Wilberforce, the commissioned engineer. And Truman evidently resented being asked a question he couldn't yet answer. It was a surprise that he'd been told to anchor; he'd brought Cameron to join his submarine, and the natural thing would have been to stop for long enough to drop him off and then push on to Mudros. He answered testily into the voicepipe, 'At present, Chief, I have not the slightest idea.' Now glancing round, he found Nick watching him, and raised his hooped, bushy eyebrows, his lips twisting in a smile inviting sympathy for the patience one had to exercise, tolerating unnecessary questions: one commanding officer to another . . . And Nick's facial muscles had gone wooden. He hadn't found himself exactly seeking Truman's company, during the passage out from

459

England; he thought the man was an idiot, and one of his own failings of which he'd always been aware was an inability to hide such feelings. Awkward, particularly when dealing with officers senior to oneself; and this personal Achilles' heel of his was likely to prove even more of a handicap, he thought, now that the war looked like ending pretty soon . . . *Terrapin*'s leading signalman saved him from the battle to contort his features into some sort of smirk; the signalman was presenting his pad to Truman.

'Signal from *Harwich*, sir.'

'Indeed.' Truman took the pad casually, glanced down frowning at the message. His frown deepened: 'Bless my soul!' He'd looked up, at Nick, with those thick brows raised again: now he was re-reading the signal. He told the killick, 'Acknowledge, and VMT . . . Everard, you and I are invited to luncheon over there. Eh?'

Nick shared the man's surprise. He didn't think he knew anyone in the cruiser; or that anyone aboard her knew of his, Nick Everard's, presence aboard *Terrapin*: of his existence, even. And the signalled invitation, to which the reply 'VMT', standing for 'very many thanks', was already being stuttered in rapid flashes from the back end of the bridge, would have come from *Harwich*'s captain. Truman had called to Jake Cameron, the submariner, 'They're sending a boat for you and us at twelve-thirty, Cameron.'

'Aye aye, sir. Thank you.' Cameron nodded – cheerful, enthusiastic. He'd been in a submarine that was refitting in the Malta dockyard, and they'd needed him here urgently to join another – E.57, which presumably was one of the pair alongside the cruiser.

Harriman reported to Truman, 'Cable's secured, sir, at two shackles. May I pipe hands to dinner?' Truman began to waffle – about not knowing yet what was happening, how long they'd be here . . . Nick checked the time, on his American wrist-watch. It was still a novelty; and it had been a present from his now famous uncle – Hugh Everard had become a rear-admiral after Jutland, but he was now a vice-admiral and *Sir* Hugh . . . Wrist-watches had been almost unobtainable earlier in the war; officers destined for the trenches and other forms of active service had advertised for them, as well as for revolvers and field-glasses, in the 'Personal' columns of *The Times*. Nick had been a midshipman then: it was just a few years ago, but it felt like a whole lifetime. To Sarah he must have been just a little boy in a sailor-suit.

How did she think of him *now*?

Back to carth again: or rather, to *Terrapin*'s bridge, where Truman had consented to his ship's company being piped to dinner and Harriman – thickset, monosyllabic – had passed the order to Trimble, the bosun's mate. Cruickshank, Nick saw, was taking a set of anchor bearings, noting the figures in his navigator's notebook; and Harriman was telling PO Hart, the chief buffer, to rig the port quarterdeck gangway. It still felt odd, to be a passenger, to see and hear the business of the ship being conducted all around one and just stand idly by: it wasn't at all a comfortable feeling.

The killick signalman reported to Truman, 'Your message passed to *Harwich*, sir.' A West Countryman, in voice and craggy features extraordinarily like another signalman, one named Garret with whom Nick had shared, at Jutland, certain rather hair-raising experiences; having survived them and returned, more by luck than good judgement, to the Tyne, he'd got himself and Garret into hot water by sending him off on a leave to which he had not been entitled. There'd been a stew over letting him have an advance of pay, too. The thing was – not that one had been able to explain it at the time – they'd found themselves home, and alive, when there'd been every reason for them to have stayed out there in the North Sea with six thousand others, dead . . . And Garret had been a newly married man, longing for the feel of his wife in his arms again: it had seemed *right* to send him off to her, and unlikely in the circumstances that anyone would give a damn.

One lived, and learnt!

From Nick's angle, it hadn't been a case of a swollen head, of his achievement in bringing the ship home in its shattered state having left him cocky. It had been a weird feeling, in those early days of June 1916: as if that sort of rubbish didn't count now, as if the experience of battle had taken one out clear of the morass of petty restrictions and red-tape that he'd often fallen foul of. And in the two years since then he'd observed what had seemed to be similar reactions in other men, after action. Survivors of sunk ships, for instance, hauled half-drowned over a destroyer's side, recovering into surprise at being alive and immediately emptying their pockets, throwing away money and papers and small possessions . . . He'd known how they'd felt.

After Jutland his uncle Hugh had suggested drily, 'Feeling your oats somewhat, Nick? That it?'

'No, sir, I—'

'Don't do anything so damn silly again, boy. You've a *chance* now. For heaven's sake make use of it!'

Before Jutland, Nick had not been reckoned to have any sort of chance. He'd been a failure, a sub-lieutenant 'under report' in a dreadnought's gunroom; and if there was such a place as hell, a Scapa Flow battleship's gunroom must surely come pretty close to it. Had done, anyway, in those days.

Uncle Hugh's star, of course, had risen even more dramatically than his nephew's. At Jutland as a post-captain he'd commanded the super-dreadnought *Nile* and earned promotion to flag rank; and now more recently his successful cruiser action resulting in the destruction of the *Göttingen* had won him the second promotion and a 'K'.

Nick joined the RNR submariner, Cameron, at the after end of the bridge. 'Which of those sinister-looking craft is yours?'

Jake Cameron pointed. 'Starboard side there. Other boat's French.' He rubbed his large hands together. 'Find out what all the flap's about presently, with luck!'

Obviously it was some kind of flap. *Terrapin* wouldn't have been diverted without good reason. En route from Devonport to Mudros she'd called at Malta for fuel and – hopefully – a day or two of shoregoing for her ship's company; but she'd only been alongside the oiler in Sliema Creek about ten minutes when a signal came informing Truman that he was required to sail again forthwith, taking one passenger to Mudros. One additional passenger, they'd meant. Later, when the ship had been well into the Aegean, another signal had changed the destination to Imbros. But alongside the oiler in Malta they'd been expecting some important personage to arrive on board – a general, or a politician – and what had turned up had been this outsize but otherwise very ordinary RNR lieutenant.

He and Nick had found they had a friend in common – Tim Rogerson, who'd helped to ram the old submarine C.3 and her cargo of high-explosive into the viaduct at Zeebrugge, to the considerable inconvenience of the Germans, at the same time as Nick in his 'oily-wad' destroyer *Bravo* had been playing Aunt Sally to Hun artillery inside the mole . . . It was like something one might have done, lived through, in an earlier age, not just six months ago. But the 'Zeeb' raid had taken place on St George's Day of this year, 1918, and it was only October now; and another odd impression was that one felt as if it had been experienced by some other person, not by oneself but by someone who up to that time had occupied one's skin.

Punctured skin. He'd been knocked about a bit, in *Bravo*, and

462

spent nine weeks afterwards in hospitals and another month convalescing at Mullbergh, his father's enormous, gloomy house in Yorkshire. Sarah, his father's young wife, ran Mullbergh as a recuperative centre for wounded officers, and it had seemed natural enough that he should go there. But given that decision to make again now – if he were back in Miss Keyser's private hospital in Grosvenor Gardens and Sarah in that funny little green hat had been asking 'Sister Agnes', 'Let me have him now? Let me fatten him up at Mullbergh, for a few weeks?' – given that situation again now, would one let it happen?

Well, it had seemed like an obvious move. And he didn't think – hard to turn the mind back, but he was fairly sure of this – he didn't think he'd ever regarded Sarah, up to that time, as anything more than a close, warm friend who happened also to be much nearer his own age than his father's, and yet his father's wife, and beautiful, and kind, and – well, nothing else. Not then.

He'd have given anything to know now, this minute, what she was thinking, feeling. When she'd written, she'd managed to say absolutely nothing; but almost immediately after he'd left Mullbergh she'd gone down to London to meet his father, who'd been sent home on an unexpected leave from France. Sarah had spent the ten days of it with him in some Mayfair house lent to them by friends. It had been an astonishing thing for her to have done: incredible, in the context of that miserable marriage. And in the letter when she'd told him, there'd been no explanation, no kind of comment. Nick had begun to think of her as suffering from remorse, as being *less* happy because of him, because of what they'd – well, become to each other; and thinking of her in that state it felt as if he, just like his father, had – oh, *fed on* her . . . It was an agony to think of it in that way: he shut his eyes, certain that if he could have been with her now to put his arms round her, reassure her . . . He asked himself, *Reassure her of what? Of my feelings for her? What use can they be to her?*

It was simply that he couldn't help them. And that despite the misgivings and a kind of loneliness he'd never experienced before, constantly thrusting through the worry and concern was a sense of excitement and happiness that was like being half-drunk.

Muffled piping from below decks broke into the jumble of his thoughts. The squeal of the pipe was followed by Trimble's roar of 'Ha-a-ands to dinner!'

Cameron levered his bulk off the bridge rail.

463

'I'm going down to see my gear's packed.' He jerked a thumb towards the cruiser. 'You're coming over too, did I hear?'

'Apparently.' Nick stared across bright water at *Harwich* and the submarine alongside her. He hadn't the least idea how or why he'd been honoured with this invitation.

The boat, with its three passengers in the sternsheets, sheered away from *Terrapin*'s gangway and headed for the cruiser. Truman had told Harriman, 'Get the ship cleaned up. If there's any news I'll give it to you by signal; otherwise assume we're here for the night. After tea you can pipe hands to bathe and non-swimmers to instruction.'

It was extraordinary how many non-swimmers there were in the Navy, and how many of them tried to shirk instruction.

Cameron, beside Nick in the boat's stern, was examining E.57 as they chugged down *Harwich*'s starboard side. She was just like any other submarine, Nick thought – a dirty, stinking tube, not in any sense a ship; he'd never understood submariners' fascination with their wretched craft. Now, as the boat curved round the big ship's stern, E.57 was out of sight and Cameron was studying the French one. Equally nasty . . . The boat's coxswain, nosing her up towards the gangway on the cruiser's port quarter, was slewing in too fast, and he'd put his engine astern too late: the boat thumped against the platform, bowman and sternsheetman struggling to fend off with their boathooks. From the quarterdeck up above their heads Nick heard the order, 'Pipe!' Truman glanced briefly at the somewhat chagrined coxswain.

'Devil's the matter with you, Markham?'

Then he was climbing the gangway into that squeal of piping. The custom stemmed from days of sail when captains, admirals and other dignitaries had been hoisted aboard in a boatswain's chair slung from a yardarm whip. Nick, hanging back to give Truman all the limelight, thought it must have been embarrassing for the gouty old men, to be dumped like sacks of spuds on their ships' decks . . . As the second wail of the pipes died away he went quickly up the scrubbed oak steps and over the cruiser's sides: saluting, finding himself on the edge of a group of officers, and having a quick first impression of a lot of gold-peaked caps; then, sorting wheat from chaff, he realised that actually there were only two of those: one was on the head of a small, pink-faced commander who was pumping Truman's hand, and the other—

Reaper!

Commander Reaper: who, as a staff officer on Roger Keyes's planning team at Dover before the Zeebrugge raid, had sent Nick on a crackpot cross-Channel raid in a coastal motor-boat . . . Narrow head: deepset eyes: his expression was one of mild amusement as he stared back at Nick's obvious surprise.

'Didn't I say we'd meet again, Everard?'

'You did indeed, sir.' Shaking his hand. Astonished, and pleased: but also puzzled . . . 'Did you know I was a passenger in *Terrapin*?'

Reaper nodded. 'From our exchange of signals with Mudros when we needed to divert you to this place.' He cocked an eyebrow. 'Last time we met, or thereabouts, I had the pleasant duty of telling you that you were getting a DSC. You've done better since, I hear.'

'Thanks to you, I think, sir.'

He'd won a DSO, at Zeebrugge – in a single hour when eleven other men had won VCs. But it could only have been on Reaper's recommendation that Nick had got his first command – *Bravo* – and taken her on that wild excursion . . . He saw a tall, rather benign-looking lieutenant-commander come hurrying on to the quarterdeck: he was looking from one face to another. 'Cameron?' Over Nick's head: 'Are you Jake Cameron?' Reaper, answering Nick's last remark, waved a hand dismissively: 'Nonsense. But I can tell you I'm extremely glad you've fallen into my hands again. You're exactly what the doctor ordered!'

'But I'm on my way to Mudros—'

'You *were* on your way to Mudros. I've arranged to borrow you, for this operation. In point of fact, Everard, you're the answer to my prayers.' The other commander, the little tubby one, was in the act of joining them, interrupting Reaper: but he broke off again, seeing the newcomer, the tall man who was latching on to Cameron: 'Ah, Wishart – wondered where the deuce you'd—'

'Frightfully sorry.' Wishart had quite a belly on him, for a man still under thirty. Reaper introduced Nick and the little commander: he was the executive officer of this cruiser, *Harwich*, and his name was Gillman. 'Heard a great deal about you, Everard. And you're Hugh Everard's nephew, I'm told. Delighted . . .' Rambling on, with a sort of boyish enthusiasm, as they shook hands: 'Never met your uncle, unfortunately . . . But what a corker, eh? I mean, dishing the *Göttingen*, eh?' Nick would have liked to listen only to Reaper, pump him, find out what he was being 'borrowed' for; but he was surrounded, getting bits and pieces of about three conversations at

465

once, and having to respond politely to Gillman's affability. He heard Wishart addressing Cameron just behind him . . . '*Just* in time, I may say. My navigator's John Treat – know him? Well, he went and exploded his appendix, and I had to leave him behind in Mudros. Furious, of course, to be missing this show . . .'

What show? And how could what was obviously a submarine operation concern him, Nick Everard?

Reaper tapped the tall man, Wishart, on his shoulder. 'Want you to meet Everard.'

'Why, of course!'

Wishart turned away from Jake Cameron, to shake Nick's hand. 'Very glad we'll have you with us. We'll try to see you're not *too* uncomfortable – but mind you, with two other passengers as well—'

'He doesn't know anything about it yet.' Reaper told Nick, 'Lieutenant-Commander Wishart is captain of E.57. You'll be sailing in her tomorrow.' He glanced over his shoulder: 'But come on down now. We're lunching with Captain Usherwood. We'll see you later, Wishart.'

Gillman and Truman had gone ahead.

'I'm taking passage somewhere in E.57?'

He could think of nothing he'd like less. The very thought of going inside a submarine sickened him. Reaper said, 'A bit more than just taking passage. You'll be going through the Dardanelles and into the Marmara, in order to sink or at any rate immobilise *Goeben*.' He glanced sideways at Nick, just very briefly, as he led the way in through the port-side screen door. 'All right?'

One could hardly have given a quick affirmative to *that* question . . .

Going through the Dardanelles would mean running the gauntlet of just about every submarine hazard that existed. And submarine hazards, one might reasonably feel, were things best reserved for the enjoyment of submariners. He certainly couldn't see how or why Reaper wanted to involve *him* in it.

Reaper had stopped at the top of a steel ladder that led down to the cruiser's main deck. Truman and Commander Gillman were still on it, going down. Reaper seemed to guess Nick's thoughts; he told him, 'This is not at all a straightforward submarine operation, you see. *Goeben* is at Constantinople – inside the Golden Horn, well protected from torpedoes. So she has either to be winkled out induced to put to sea so that our friend Wishart, or the French

466

boat which will also be in the Marmara, can sink her – or alternatively, blown up where she's lying.'

'Oh . . .' A chink of daylight. 'A landing party?'

The narrow head and its gold-peaked cap nodded. 'You'll have an explosives chap with you. But he's incredibly green. I need someone with him who's got a bit of savvy and can keep his head in an emergency. As you did once when you stole a trawler for me, eh?'

'A trawler's crew, sir.'

'Quite. You did the job we wanted done.'

A pause: Reaper peering down the ladder . . . It was difficult to believe in this business yet. It had been sprung too suddenly and unexpectedly. Nick sought escape in levity.

'So, for "trawler" read "battle cruiser", sir?'

Reaper didn't smile. He said gruffly as he started down the ladder, 'You won't have to steal her, Everard. Just destroy her.'

The brow down to E.57's casing was a ribbed plank with the unusual embellishment of a rope handrail. Wishart flipped it contemptuously as he preceded Jake Cameron down the steep incline. 'Guest-night stuff. They don't realise we develop sticky feet.' He stopped on the casing and a sailor in paint-stained overalls, emerging from the submarine's fore hatch, edged past him with a bucket in each hand.

'What's that lot and where's it going, Finn?'

'Spud peelings, sir. Goin' inboard, gash-bin.' The torpedoman grinned. 'Less the Frogs'd like it, d'ye reckon, sir?' He went up the brow chuckling to himself: stocky, fresh-faced, in his early twenties. Wishart told Jake, 'We've got a damn good bunch, you'll find . . . Come on down.'

Into the fore hatch, grabbing its upper rim and slinging themselves in feet-first on to a ladder that slanted down into the torpedo stowage compartment. Further for'ard, in the narrowing bow, were the two bow torpedo tubes; reloads for them were in here, one each side of the compartment. Behind the fish to starboard was the for'ard heads; opposite it, the officers' cooking stove. Lockers filled other ship's-side spaces, and any other gap not taken up with machinery and working gear had been crammed with crates, boxes, sacks of stores.

In the centre of the for'ard bulkhead was the big, brass hand-wheel that controlled the shutter-gear, hull doors protecting the firing ends of the tubes; about twenty pairs of socks hung on its gleaming rim and spokes. Wishart frowned at it, and a leading seaman – a large man with a smooth face and thick brown hair – told him apologetically, 'Won't let us 'ang no dhobey topsides, sir, not in workin' hours. Sailin' tomorrer, makes it awkward.'

'Who says you can't?'

The killick shrugged. 'Inboard, sir.'

'I'll have a word with someone.' Wishart told Jake, 'Leading Seaman Morton is second cox'n . . . Lieutenant Cameron's joined as navigator, Morton.' He asked him, 'Cox'n on board, is he?'

'Gone to dinner inboard, sir. Shall I fetch 'im?'

'Heavens, no.' He moved towards the bulkhead doorway. 'Let's have a chat, pilot, while there's some quiet. Then lunch in the wardroom inboard. Two o'clock there's a briefing session in Captain Usherwood's day cabin – you'd better join us.' He went through into the control room. Jake had come from one of the older E-class boats, and this was a much more recent version, but the variations in her internal layout were small and it was all familiar. The smells and sounds were familiar too: like the creaking underwater noises as she rubbed herself against the cruiser's side, and the oily smell that was part of a homey sort of warmth.

'Ah-hah!'

A small man – a lieutenant RN – looking up from paperwork spread around on the pull-out wardroom table and one of the bunks. Wishart nodded to him.

'As you say, Number One – ah-hah. Here's the johnny we've been waiting for.'

E.57's first lieutenant was small, sharp-faced; he had crinkly yellow hair, freckles and a belligerent expression. He stared at Jake like a hangman weighing up a customer for the noose.

'H'm. Have to take ten or twelve gallons out of the buoyancy tank.'

To compensate for Jake's extra weight, he meant. Wishart introduced them: 'Cameron – Hobday.' They shook hands. Hobday was like some kind of dog – a bull-terrier, Jake thought, shaking a hand that felt like the knuckle-end of a wheel-spanner. Wishart suggested, 'Let's have a welcome-aboard glass of gin – d'you think?'

'One excuse is as good as another.' Hobday's sentences came in short, clipped bursts, like sudden rattles of small-arms fire. He'd crossed the compartment to open one of the lockers above the chart table: Jake saw gin, bitters, glasses. He took the enamel jug from Hobday: 'I'll get that.'

'Good man.' Hobday began dripping Angostura carefully into three glasses, and Jake went for'ard into the TSC to fill the jug from a tap in the heads. A man his size could just squeeze into the tiny cabinet, when he needed to; now, he just reached in to the tap. Wishart asked him when he came back into the control room, 'Know what sort of a lark we're engaged on, do you?'

'No. I'm hoping you're about to tell me. Say when?'

'When. Sit down, old lad. You're at home now.'

Home from home . . . He sat facing them across the pull-out table. This corner of the control room had a curtain that could be drawn around it, and it constituted the wardroom. Two bunks were fixed against the curve of the pressure-hull, with drawers and this table under the after one; below the other was a third bunk, which was itself a sort of drawer that could be pulled out when it was wanted or shoved in out of sight. This one was the third hand's – Jake's. Its disadvantage was that when it was out it blocked the gangway, and you had to get used to being walked over.

He added water to his own gin. Plenty of it, knowing that later on today he'd have to check over all the charts they'd be likely to need, and the confidential books, signal equipment, compasses – everything in the navigator's department . . . Wishart raised his glass: 'Welcome aboard, old lad.' He put the glass down again. 'The point of all this, in a nutshell, is we've got to nobble the battle cruiser *Goeben*, alias *Yavuz*.'

Jake let that sink in. He nodded. 'So we're going through the Dardanelles.'

'That will certainly be the first step.'

Hobday murmured, 'No small step either.'

Wishart swirled the faintly pink liquid around his glass. A stoker came from aft, glanced curiously at Jake, passed on for'ard. Hobday called after him, 'There'll be no dinner left for you, Peel, if you don't run for it!' He told Jake, 'Stoker Peel. Twister, they call him.' Wishart admitted, 'We can't expect the welcome mat to be out for us, certainly. What we know is that the Turks've put in new nets and minefields, and more guns on the beach than they had before, plus – so we're told – hydrophone listening gear and fixed shore torpedo tubes. Also, their patrols have depth-charges now, which of course one didn't have to contend with in '15.' He sipped gin. 'We'll simply – well, deal with interruptions as they arise, that's all.'

For two years, Jake reflected, no submarine had attempted the passage of the Dardanelles. With the abandoning of the landing operations, there'd been no need for it. Then after *Goeben*'s recent sortie they'd sent E.14 up after her. Saxton White's boat. She'd been Boyle's, in the earlier campaign, and Boyle had won himself a VC in her. From this last excursion, White and that veteran submarine had not returned.

Jake said thoughtfully, 'It must be considered fairly important that we should have another go at it?'

'Yes.' Wishart nodded. 'You'll hear all the background this afternoon. From that chap Reaper. He's running the show – he seems to be some sort of specialist in planning unorthodox operations – and he'll be going along in *Terrapin* to act as a command and communications base, in the Gulf of Xeros so as to shorten the wireless range.'

'But surely we shan't be – well, advertising our presence in the Marmara?'

'Quite right.' Wishart looked approvingly at his navigator. 'We shall not. Not a peep – unless *Goeben* provides us with a target or – God forbid – gets past us, westbound . . . No, it's more for the benefit of the French. *Louve* – that's the Frog submarine on the other side, and it means "She-wolf", not some picture gallery as my uneducated first lieutenant chose to imagine – *Louve* is taking two evil-looking civilians to land somewhere or other and do heaven knows what. Political. This whole business is tied up with persuading the Turks to chuck their hands in, by the way. Reaper'll be explaining all that.' He shook his head. 'These chaps they're putting ashore look more like carpet-salesmen than politicians.'

Hobday agreed. 'Either of 'em 'd sell you his sister for the price of a pipe of opium, if you asked him.' He snorted. 'Personally I wouldn't.'

'Wouldn't what?'

'Touch either of their sisters with a barge-pole.'

Jake asked Wishart, 'Does anyone know where *Goeben* is exactly?'

'At the Horn. *In* it.'

'Above the bridge, where we can't get at her?'

'Two answers to that. One, she may not remain in cover. From the purely naval point of view, that's a worry: she may try to break out again. Our chaps have reason to think it's on the cards, in fact. And from our point of view   this boat's, I mean – let's hope she

470

does, so long as we're in position to have a crack at her.' He added, 'But they're nervy about it, up at Mudros. When she last popped out, they were caught very badly on the hop.'

'We heard there'd been a stink.'

'Did you hear the admiral commanding the Aegean had been sent home?' Jake shook his head. Wishart told him, 'You probably know we've two old battleships based at Mudros. *Lord Nelson* and *Agamemnon*. Well, the admiral wanted to visit Salonika, and his own yacht was temporarily out of action, so the old idiot took *Lord Nelson* away with him. As good as sending the Hun an invitation to come out and make hay . . . Mind you, *I'd* have sent him home just so as not to have to see him dribble. Perfectly awful – chin running with slobber . . . But as I was saying—'

'What about Saxton White?'

'What about him?'

'He went into the straits after *Goeben*, didn't he, almost on her heels?'

'Yes.' Wishart was silent for a moment. 'But – oh, I don't think it can help us much to talk about White, you know.'

Hobday backed Jake up. 'If we had some notion of what happened to him, surely—'

'You know, as I do, Number One, that E.14 was lost and that Saxton White is almost certainly dead.'

'Yes,' Hobday persisted, 'but until he went up, nobody had gone in there since – well, 1915, when we were doing it all the time. And as you've said, sir, the nets and minefields, and the shore batteries and so on will all have been changed, and—'

Wishart peered into his glass, frowning slightly. 'There's a new minefield between Kum Kale and Cape Helles. We know that because we saw them laying it.'

'If we could work out what White—'

'He got through the Narrows and close to Nagara. That's where *Goeben* had run aground. She hit a mine, you know, she had some minor flooding . . . She was stuck there, and bombs our 'planes dropped on her every day for about a week just bounced off her. During that week they were getting a boat fit to go up and torpedo her, and the only one available and within reach was Saxton White's. But by the time he went into the straits they'd refloated her and she'd gone. We *think* he then turned about and started back. But we don't know anything for certain, except they sank him. And just speculating, as everyone's been doing *ad nauseam* ever since, doesn't do anyone a shred of good. Saxton had bad luck at some point, that's all.'

Hobday waited to be sure that that was all his captain had to say. Then he argued, 'If they turned back from halfway up the straits, perhaps that was the worst thing about it. I mean, if the Turks had detected them on their way up, and then they turned sixteen points and gave the swine another shot at 'em—'

'Number One.' Wishart's easy manner was wearing thin. 'Either I've been failing to express myself clearly, or you're being particularly obtuse. The point I have been trying to make is that in my view it would be more helpful *not* to dwell on what might or might not have happened to E.14. All right?'

Hobday blinked at him. He looked puzzled.

'I beg your pardon, sir. I—'

'Where'd we got to . . . About *Goeben* being out of reach unless they shift her – and the French taking those odd characters with them . . .' He told Jake, 'We've our own landing party. Actually, we'll be transferring them to the French boat, and the Frogs'll do that part of it. But we're taking a chap called Robins – an RNVR two-and-a-half. I gather he works for the Foreign Office in some way. He talks French and Turkish and thinks rather well of himself – perhaps not the ideal passenger . . . I may be wrong, of course . . . The second man's a young Red Marine – Burtenshaw. Supposed to be an explosives expert and I believe he talks German. And finally this lad Everard, who seems to be Commander Reaper's afterthought.' Wishart asked Jake, 'What's he like?'

'Very decent.' Cameron nodded. 'Despite numerous medals – and having that uncle who's the admiral—'

'And a baronet for a father?'

Jake showed his surprise. 'I didn't know that.'

'Baronet, MFH, currently a brigadier in France. And this chap here is heir to the title and some huge estate in Yorkshire. If you spent several days in his company and didn't know it—'

'Not a hint.'

'Well . . .' Wishart glanced round the cramped compartment. 'Be a bit stretched, to make room for three extra bodies. Still, it won't be for long.' He pushed his chair back. 'We'd better go up while there's still some food left.'

Commander Reaper glanced round the table. Nick Everard was on his left, and the French submarine captain between Nick and the

472

RNVR lieutenant-commander, Robins. Burtenshaw, the Marine – he looked like a rugger player, and probably not long out of his public school, and very much under Robins's thumb – was at the bottom of the table, while Jake Cameron, Aubrey Wishart and *Terrapin*'s captain, Truman, occupied its other side.

Hobday had asked to be excused. He had a lot to do, and Wishart could brief him on any points that were new.

Reaper murmured, 'Smoke if you care to.'

'*Quoi?*'

He had to repeat it in French, to *Louve*'s captain. It was an embarrassing thing to have to do, because he'd just noticed, with a flicker of those deepset eyes in his bony, very English face, that Lemarie was already sucking a black cheroot. Odd, Nick thought, that he hadn't noticed its stink before. The Frenchman was short, muscled, swarthy, in his early thirties, and he wore the three narrow stripes of a *lieutenant de vaisseau* on his epaulettes. Hard brown eyes . . . A tough customer, Nick thought; might be a Corsican. Getting the translation from Reaper he raised his thick eyebrows, shot a glance at the cheroot in his fingers, and stuck it in his mouth with a kind of snort as he looked back at Reaper . . . Reaper leant forward, and clasped his hands on the table in front of him.

'My object in calling this meeting is to make sure we all have a grasp of the strategic background to the operation, the reasons for embarking on it and the absolute necessity of completing it successfully. Most of you already know your own sides of it; this is a matter of understanding the background from a common standpoint and, so to speak, in the round.' He glanced down the table. 'It's also, of course, for the information of those officers who have only just joined us.'

Robins muttered a rapid French translation into Lemarie's hairy left ear. Reaper paused now and then to give him time to catch up; and sometimes Robins paused, ignoring bits he didn't think worth translating.

'I'll begin with a reminder as to how *Goeben* came to be where she is.'

He embarked on a résumé of the scandal in 1914 when *Goeben*, one of Germany's newer battle cruisers, had been allowed to escape into the Dardanelles, to then neutral and undecided Turkey, instead of being brought to action and sunk. Rear-Admiral Troubridge, the cruiser admiral, had been court martialled for it; but there was a body of opinion in the Service which reckoned that

473

Troubridge's superior officer, 'Arky-Barky' Milne, should have been held responsible. Nick's uncle, Hugh Everard, had no doubt of it; and Jackie Fisher had said that *he*'d have had Milne shot. Though in fact – quoting Hugh Everard – there might not be many senior officers whom Fisher would *not* have had shot, at one time or another . . . But the messy business of *Goeben*'s escape was old-hat now – except to Troubridge, who'd been acquitted of all charges but still hadn't been given another job afloat. Not a happy situation, for a descendant of the Troubridge who'd fought at Nelson's side.

Reaper, luckily, didn't take the story back as far as Nelson.

'There's little doubt now that *Goeben*'s arrival at Constantinople was a major factor in Turkey's decision to enter the war against us.'

Robins snapped, without looking at anyone in particular, 'I'm sure we've all accepted *that* premise.'

Everyone except Burtenshaw glanced at him in surprise. Robins had very little chin, and the mouth above it was small, turned down at the corners. Dark hair, oiled, was swept back from a high swell of forehead. Probably very brainy, Nick thought, but also waspish, self-opinionated. He wondered why Reaper didn't pull him up. But the commander only continued in his even, quiet tone. 'The point I wish to make is that *Goeben* lying at the Horn now is still a factor in Turkey's *continuance* in the war. There are positive indications that the Turks would like to arrange an armistice. As you know, Damascus fell several weeks ago to Colonel Lawrence's Arabs; and now the Fifth Cavalry Division under General Allenby is advancing rapidly on Aleppo. More than halfway there, in fact . . . At the same time, we and our allies have changed the shape of things in France. So there's an end in sight, at last; and if we can push the Turks into surrendering, it should come more quickly.'

In July there had been the second Marne battle. Ludendorf's great offensive, aimed at snatching victory before the American armies could be trained and brought in to tip the scales, had been stopped, the initiative seized from him. Then in August an offensive by British, Canadian and Australian troops had been launched east of Amiens, in such secrecy that not even the War Cabinet had known it was being planned. Secrecy had paid off in the shape of 16,000 prisoners on the first day. And in September the Americans had been blooded when Pershing's 1st Army had struck at Mihiel and scored a knock-out; the momentum of victory was increasing now with American weight behind it.

Robins had just interrupted again.

'There are other *very* good reasons, of far-reaching political consequence, which suggest we should reach the Bosphorus with as little delay as possible.'

This time Reaper looked at him. His tone was mild enough, to start with.

'I've always found it easier to make one point at a time. Would you bear with me, meanwhile?'

The small mouth had compressed itself like that of an offended governess. He began thinly, 'As a representative of HM Foreign Office I should rather think it was *my*—'

'Foreign Office be damned!'

The lieutenant-commander looked shocked: as if he hadn't expected Reaper to be capable of anger. Reaper told him, speaking quietly again now, 'The only Whitehall authority identifiable to us here as your employer, Robins, is the Board of Admiralty. The Board's authority is vested in the Commander-in-Chief, who has seen fit to place you under my orders. I must ask you not to interrupt again.'

Lieutenant Burtenshaw, RMLI, was plainly embarrassed. He'd turned sideways, pink-faced, fiddling with a pencil, blinking into sunshine that streamed in through a scuttle.

Reaper cleared his throat.

'There are *several* reasons why it is necessary to eliminate *Goeben* as a fighting unit. The most obvious one to us here is the possibility of her breaking out of the straits again, as she did recently. The Hun might well try it. He's losing the war, he knows he is, and he might well prefer offensive action to simply waiting for the end . . . Last time *Goeben* came out, remember, was just after the Turks had lost Jerusalem, and it's considered that Admiral von Rebeur-Paschwitz was trying something dramatic to bolster the Turk morale. So far as we know, Paschwitz is still flying his flag in her – and Turk morale's right down the drain! Megiddo . . . Damascus . . . and very soon Aleppo . . .' He nodded. 'She may well come out again. If she did, what might be her objectives? We see three probables. One: break through into the Adriatic and link up with the Austrians. Two: inflict as much damage as she can on our supply routes and then dodge back into the Dardanelles or to Smyrna. Three: attack our bases at Mudros and Salonika – through which of course we're supplying the push against Bulgaria – or even Port Said and Alexandria.'

475

He was silent for a moment. Then he looked up again. 'I ought to mention that they've had time to get her back into fighting trim. You probably know she hit some mines during her last outing. Air reconnaissance suggests she's repaired and fit for sea.'

Truman asked, in his fruity voice, 'Is she definitely inside the Golden Horn, sir?'

'Yes. As recently as yesterday she was moored above the Galata bridge.'

Lieutenant de vaisseau Lemarie had a silver pocket-watch in his palm; he was staring down at it and making tut-tutting noises. He muttered in French now to Robins. Robins told Reaper, in a tone that suggested he'd rather have nothing at all to do with him, 'The *lieutenant* has to leave us now. He has matters to attend to before he sails.'

'Of course.' Reaper stood up, and the others followed suit. 'I wish you – we all do – a very successful voyage and a safe return . . . Naturally, we'll be on deck to see you off.'

Jake Cameron wondered how the Frenchman might be feeling about this jaunt. Everyone in the cabin knew roughly what sort of odds were to be expected – and they certainly weren't good ones. But a French submariner should be even more acutely aware of them. Since Dardanelles operations had begun, back in '14, there'd been dozens of successful British patrols in the Marmara, at a price of four E-class boats lost; but in the same period five French submarines had entered the straits and not one of them had come out again. Jake had been discussing it during luncheon, with Hobday and Wishart, and the names of the French boats ran through his mind now as he saw his new CO go round the end of the table to shake Lemarie's hand. *Saphir* . . . *Mariette* . . . *Joule* . . . *Turquoise* . . .

The fifth: he was stumped for it. And suddenly it seemed like the blackest omen that he couldn't name her . . . As if by not doing so he was putting *Louve* in that fifth place?

When the door closed behind the Frenchman, Reaper waved them back to their chairs.

'I've referred already to the fact that we know Turkey wants peace-talks. Now I'll tell you – in confidence – what puts it quite beyond doubt.' He glanced round at their faces. 'In the Mesopotamian campaign that came to grief at Kut – after one of the bravest defences, I may say, in the history of British arms – General Townsend and a Colonel Newcombe were among the thousands taken prisoner. Two-thirds of the other-rank prisoners have died since in Turkish hands – but that's digressing . . . What I'm telling you is that the Turks have let General Townsend and Newcombe out – shipped them out so they can help with armistice negotiations outside Turkey.'

Robins raised his head, stared contemptuously at Burtenshaw. Reaper went on, 'Fact is, Turkey's still at war with us *only* because of the German presence – General Liman von Sanders's troops, and *Goeben*. The troops are in poor shape and bad heart; ninety per cent of the Hun strength lies in *Goeben*'s guns. They call her *Yavuz* – in full *Yavus Sultan Selim*, meaning "Sultan Selim the Terrible". And her crew wear fezes, and she flies the Turkish ensign. So far as *we're* concerned they can wear top-hats and fly last week's washing – she's still *Goeben*, and she's manned by Huns . . . And she's more than just a symbol of German power – the Turks know perfectly well her guns could knock Constantinople flat, so she's *effective* power too. And you're beginning to understand, I hope, why we rather badly need to sink her . . .' He shook his head. 'That's not all, though. You're aware, of course, that the Russian Black Sea Fleet mutinied in February. Also that the Germans and the Bolsheviks signed what they call the Treaty of Brest-Litovsk in March – since when the Bolshies have started calling themselves 'communists' and murdered their royal family, and we've occupied Archangel to keep the Germans from getting there through Finland, and so forth . . . As far as the Black Sea's concerned, though, it's thought in London that there's some danger of the Huns taking over those Russian ships and using them against us. Quite a powerful fleet, it might be – and led, no doubt, by our friend von Paschwitz in *Goeben* . . . And we can eliminate this threat in two stages. First by action against *Goeben* as we now intend; and in the longer term by establishing ourselves at the Horn and controlling the – well, for the time being let's just say the Bosphorus. This we cannot do until we have a Turkish surrender, so that we can move the Fleet through the Dardanelles – and before we can do that, we have to deal with *Goeben*.'

He sat back, and his eyes flickered from face to face.

'I've explained all this in order that you should understand and accept one simple conclusion. That to destroy *Goeben* is worth any effort, hazard or cost. Quite literally – *any*.'

CHAPTER 2

On the cruiser's upper deck her ship's company were being fallen out from evening Quarters and mustered along her starboard side, ready to cheer E.57 off to patrol. This time yesterday they'd given a similar send-off to *Louve*.

Hobday shook Commander Gillman's hand. He'd only come up from the submarine to say goodbye to him: just as Aubrey Wishart would at this moment be saying goodbye to Captain Usherwood, down in the cuddy.

'Most grateful for your hospitality and help, sir.'

'Not a bit of it.' The small, rotund commander beamed. 'Just knock that damned Hun for six, now!'

From E.57's fore casing, Jake Cameron watched Hobday come down the sloping plank He'd given Jake until sailing-time – *now* – to know the name of every man on board. Twenty-four hours he'd had, to memorise nearly thirty names, as well as attending to all the small preparations, checking of chart-corrections, and so on. He'd been up most of the night, sorting out the charts and CBs.

The coxswain, Chief Petty Officer Crabb, was waiting for Hobday by the open fore hatch. Crabb was a grizzled, veteran submariner. Roman nose, cleft chin, voice like a dog's growl.

'Hydroplanes, diving rudders and steering gear tested in 'and and in electric, sir. Diving gauges open. All 'ands on board, all gear below secured for sea, sir.'

'Thank you, cox'n.' That had been the first of a long litany of reports which the first lieutenant had now to receive. 'Stations for leaving harbour, please.'

'Aye aye, sir.' Crabb yelled the order down into the hatch as Morton, the big, soft-faced second coxswain, came ambling aft with a meaty hand resting on the jumping-wire.

'Casing secured for sea, sir.'

478

The second coxswain, under Jake as casing officer, was responsible for ropes and wires and for the casing itself, this steel deck that was full of holes so that when the boat dived all spaces outside the pressure-hull filled with water. It was just staging, something to walk on. The bridge superstructure was the same; in the centre of it the conning-tower was a vertical tube with a ladder through it connecting from the control-room hatch to an upper hatch in the bridge deck, but the surrounding framework supporting that deck was free-flood, like a colander . . . Hobday told the leading seaman, 'Single up, and stand by the brow.' He looked past Morton at Jake. 'I want you to come through the boat with me, Cameron.'

He slid down the ladder into the torpedo stowage compartment; Jake and CPO Crabb rattled down behind him.

'Shut fore 'atch!'

'Anderson!'

CPO Rinkpole, the torpedo gunner's mate, had snapped the name over his shoulder, and Anderson, a dark-haired, very tall torpedoman, came aft from the tube space. Rinkpole jerked his bald head towards the hatch; Anderson reported to Hobday as he moved towards it, 'WRT's full, bow shutters open, sir.' From a few rungs up the ladder he reached up and dragged the hatch shut over his head. It wasn't only a matter of shutting and clipping it; there was a strongback to be bolted on inside it. Rinkpole told Hobday, 'Torpedo circuits tested, spare torpedoes lashed, sir.'

Forty-ish: not *entirely* bald . . . Rinkpole had been at sea for a quarter of a century and in submarines since the Navy had first recognised their existence. His torpedoes, Hobday had said, were his babies; if they hadn't been seventeen feet long he might have taken them to bed with him. Cole, the second LTO – electrical rating – was waiting to make his report: 'Bells, 'ooters an' Aldis tested an' workin', sir.' Cole's nickname was 'Blackie'; but it was uncertain whether it derived from his surname or from the thick mass of beard out of which his eyes seemed to glint like some animal's from a bush.

'Thank you, Cole.' It was already twice as cluttered in here as it had been yesterday. While they'd been alongside the cruiser the offwatch crewmen had been accommodated in her messdecks, but now hammocks and kitbags as well as extra stores, sacks of fresh vegetables, and so on, had been embarked. By the time the torpedomen's hammocks were slung in this compartment the only way to reach the tube space would be on all-fours.

Following Hobday aft, Jake saw Burtenshaw, the German-speaking explosives expert, perched on a chair in the control room; he had an open book on his knees and he was stooped over it, oblivious of the activity around him. No sign of his lord and master, Robins. But Everard was standing in the middle of the control room, staring up through the hatch at the bright circle of sky. As if, Jake thought, he was storing up a memory of it against the time when he wouldn't be seeing it much. Everard asked Hobday, 'Shall I be in anyone's way if I go up into the bridge?'

'Skipper'd like you to, I'm sure.' Hobday saw the gunlayer waiting to report. He cocked an eyebrow at Jake, who murmured, 'Roost'. A short, strong-looking man, with a broad face and wide-spaced eyes; according to Hobday, Roost had been a blacksmith's apprentice until 1914.

'Gun greased over, bore clear, gun secured, sir. Grenades, rifles, pistols and Lewis gun ready, sir.'

'Thank you, Layer.'

'Stowed 'is gear in the magazine too, sir.' Roost had nodded towards Burtenshaw. The Marine's gear was a large rucksack packed with demolition charges. Hobday nodded, moving aft through the control room. The signalman – Jake named him, *sotto voce* – reported, 'Challenges ready, sir.' Hobday nodded. 'Thank you, Ellery.' But they wouldn't be needing recognition signals. The destroyer patrol between this island and the straits would have been warned that they'd be passing; just as they'd have been warned yesterday to expect the Frenchman. And *Louve* should have got through by now, she'd be in the Marmara. If she wasn't, Jake thought, she'd – well, she *had* to be . . . He focused on the leading telegraphist, 'Professor' Weatherspoon, who behind his thick glasses and diffident manner looked fed up.

'Wireless and hydrophones correct, sir. But . . .' He shook his close-cropped, narrow head; the size of his ears and the high dome of skull made it look even narrower than it was. 'Well, I dunno, sir – I mean, there's me gear to be got at, maintenance an'—'

Hobday had caught on to the reason for his gloom.

'Only be for a day or two. And if we find it doesn't work, we'll change it. Meanwhile, when you have to get in there, he'll have to make way for you.'

'He' was the other passenger – Robins. They'd given him the little 'silent cabinet', the wireless office, to doss down in. It wouldn't give him room to stretch his legs out fully, but it would keep him out of the way and at the same time pander to his ego by making him think he'd been given a sort of minuscule cabin.

Jake, after a couple of gins and five minutes of Robins's conversation in the cruiser's wardroom last night, had said privately to Wishart, 'I'd put bloody bars on it if I were you.' On the silent cabinet, he'd meant . . . Hobday asked Weatherspoon, 'Is Lieutenant-Commander Robins on board?'

'No, sir. But 'is gear's all over the—'

'He's with your captain.' Burtenshaw took his nose out of his book. 'At least, he *was*.' He'd resumed his reading; Jake, peering over his shoulder, saw that the book was a rather battered copy of Tolstoy's *The Kingdom of God and Other Essays*. Strange reading, he thought, for an explosives expert. He followed Hobday aft. Finn, the man who'd joked about feeding spud-peelings to Frenchmen, was waiting near the control room's after bulkhead.

'Beam WRTs are full, sir.'

'Thank you, Finn.'

WRT stood for water-round-torpedoes. Each tube had to be filled with water around the fish inside it before it could be fired, and water was blown up by air pressure from the tube's own tank.

Chief Engineroom Artificer Grumman came lumbering for'ard to meet Hobday in the beam torpedo compartment. This was exactly amidships, halfway along the submarine's 180-foot length. Grumman was built like a prize-fighter; but he was an easygoing, kindly man.

'Engines ready, sir. No bothers.'

'Good. We'll be on our way pretty soon now, Chief.' Hobday squeezed past Grumman and went on aft, over the platform that bridged the pair of tubes. It was less easy for Jake and Grumman to pass each other. At the doorway ERA McVeigh, the 'outside' artificer – his responsibility was all the primary machinery outside the engine-room – glanced at Jake cautiously, as at a stranger whom he, McVeigh, would view with distrust until he had reason to change his attitude. McVeigh had a wild, uncouth appearance: his ginger beard was ragged, as if rats fed on it.

'Telegraphs tested, sir. Steering gear and Janney lubricated. Air on the whistle, sir.'

'Very good.'

Moving into the engine-room, they were met by the stoker PO. He had a wad of oily cotton-waste in his hand, and he was wiping his chin with it. A Yorkshireman, short-legged and thickset, with a

481

way of talking without any noticeable movement of the lips. Jake tried to adopt a similar technique as he murmured, 'PO Leech.'

'Comp tanks as per your orders, sir. Engine-room gear secured. External kingstons open.'

The amount of water in each compensation tank was decided after elaborate calculations concerning the boat's trim. Stores, fuel, fresh water, lubricating oil, extra personnel or gear – each change affecting the boat's weight in the water and balance fore-and-aft had to be taken into account. If you got the sums wrong and left her too heavy, when Wishart dived her she'd go down like a stone; if she was too light, she wouldn't get under at all. It would be just as bad too heavy or light at one end. Trim was one of Hobday's responsibilities.

In the motor-room Leading Seaman Dixon, the senior electrical rating, made his report. Dixon was short and fat: he was reputed – Hobday's story – to have been seen with seventeen boiled potatoes on one plate of mutton stew. He reported now, with the copper switchgear of the main switchboard shining like dull gold behind his overalled, egg-like shape, 'Main motors ready, sir. Motor bilges dry. Ventilator caps on, sluices 'alf closed.'

Hobday nodded. 'And the box is nicely up, eh.'

By 'box' he meant the battery – in fact four of them, each of fifty-five cells, each cell half the height of a man. The battery tanks were under the deck of the control room, and the cells stood in them on wooden gratings. They'd be getting a top-up charge this evening before the submarine dived for her run-in towards the straits and the Turkish minefield.

The *first* Turk minefield. Pretty well the whole way through there'd be mines.

Lindsay, one of the boat's two leading stokers, reported that the bilges were pumped out and dry and that the capstan had been tested. They went on aft, passing the humped casings over the actual motors and moving between banks of auxiliary machinery into the next compartment. Compressors, circulating pumps, pump motors. On each side, large handwheels to the kingstons of main ballast tanks – number 7 to starboard here, number 8 on the other side. Kingstons were large valves for opening or shutting flood-holes in the bottoms of the tanks; they were open now, as PO Leech had just reported, but the water stayed out because air pressure in the tanks kept it out. When the vents in the tops of the tanks were opened, though, the air would be released and the sea would rush up to fill the tanks and dive the submarine.

A mass of pipes continued on both sides and overhead: trim line, LP air-line, brass handwheels on the connections from the air-line to the tanks . . . Stores and gear filled any empty spaces. Some of the crew messed in here; the long mess table was slung up on chains under the deckhead, and could be let down when it was needed. Hobday stopped at the last bulkhead before the stern compartment, the after ends, and peered through. At the far end on the centre-line was the rear door of the stern tube. Emergency hand-steering gear was in the starboard after corner; and hand-operating gear for the after hydroplanes. Most of the off-watch crewmen slept in the after ends. A stoker sorting spanners glanced round from his crouched position beside a tool locker; Jake murmured, 'Stoker Peel'. He knew that 'Twister' Peel's diving-stations job was to watch the packing of the shaft bearings and help with the stern tube. Another man – a torpedoman – was squatting, writing in a notebook – diary, perhaps – writing slowly and laboriously, licking the pencil-lead between words. His name was – *oh, damn it all* . . .

He'd stood up. He was the after endsman and he had a report to make. He had a name too, but—

'After WRT full, sir.'

'Good.' Hobday cocked an eyebrow at Jake: and the name was on the tip of his tongue, but . . . Then the torpedoman reached out, hooking his hands over bunches of piping, exercising his muscles by swinging to and fro like a monkey in a cage: there were tattoos all over his arms. Tattoos triggered memory.

'Smith.'

'Cap'n comin' aboard, sir!'

Agnew, the Boy Telegraphist. Crabb must have sent him with the message. Sharp-faced like a weasel: pale: sixteen years old.

'Thank you, Agnew.' Hobday started for'ard, squeezing past individuals and through groups of men, to the control room, and up the ladder into the conning-tower with its thick glass ports, up again into the bridge and the brilliant sunshine. Jake, arriving close behind him, saw CPO Crabb at the wheel with the portable magnetic compass in its bracket in front of him. The signalman, Ellery, was at the after end of the bridge with his Aldis lamp ready, its cable trailing down through the hatch. Everard was back there too. Jake climbed over and down to the catwalk and for'ard along the casing; Wishart was halfway down the brow and Robins, strutting in front of him, looking irritatingly self-important. Jake checked that Morton had singled up the hemp breasts so that casting off would be quick and simple, and that the cruiser's first lieutenant had had a topping-lift rigged, with steadying lines to the end of the gangway, ready to haul it clear. He heard Hobday call down the bridge voicepipe, 'Stand by telegraphs and main motors. Group down.' Only the electric motors could be used for harbour manoeuvring, because the gas engines couldn't be put astern. Robins arrived on the casing, and Jake allowed him a perfunctory salute. Wishart got a proper one.

'All set, pilot?'

'Top line, sir.'

Hobday saluted the captain as he arrived in the bridge.

'Ready for sea, sir.'

'Splendid.' His easy manner made it seem like a personal favour he was acknowledging. 'Let go everything, then – as the bishop proposed to the actress.' He saw Nick Everard, and nodded to him. 'All right there? Looking forward to it?'

'Well . . .'

'Let go for'ard! Let go aft!'

The brow swung off the casing, and the ropes fell away from the submarine's bow and stern; they went snaking, wriggling up into the cruiser's waist. Jake took his stance up for'ard, where the casing narrowed and the hydroplanes stood out like fins, and Morton and the other hands of the casing party fell in on his left. He heard Wishart's voice back there on the bridge: 'Starboard ten, cox'n', and then, muffled by the voicepipe as he put his face down to it, 'Slow ahead starboard.' A touch of motor and a little port rudder, to swing her stern out . . . 'Stop starboard. Midships. Slow astern together.' Above them, on the cruiser's quarterdeck, Commander Gillman bawled, 'Three cheers for HM Submarine E.57! Hip, hip . . .'

Reaper, on *Terrapin*'s bridge and with binoculars at his eyes, heard the waves of cheering and saw a layer of white rising and falling above the heads of the men on *Harwich*'s decks as they waved their caps. Shifting the aim of his glasses he saw that the submarine had stopped her motors; you could tell, although she still had stern way on, by the fact that the white surge which her screws had flung up as she went astern had begun to melt, the blue surface to mend itself around her. She was swinging slowly, bringing her bow round towards Grafton Point.

She was moving ahead again now. There was a smoke-haze

above her after casing, and a powerful churning of the sea astern; the racket of her diesel engines reached his ears. And *Terrapin* could push on too. Reaper had wanted to see both the submarines on their way before he left Imbros himself, but now Truman could take his ship down south-westward to the main fleet base, Mudros, to refuel, and come back this way tomorrow and on into the Gulf of Xeros. At the eastern end of it, off the north shore of the Gallipoli peninsula, they'd be within a few miles of the Marmara, across the peninsula's thin neck.

He looked round at Truman.

'Whenever you're ready, then.'

The cable was already shortened in; all that was necessary was to pull the hook out of the sand and wind it up. Truman climbed ponderously on to the step that surrounded the binnacle; he told Harriman, 'Weigh.'

'Weigh anchor!'

Granger's 'Aye aye' floated up to them; the cable began to clank home as the capstan dragged it dripping from the sea. Two men with a hose angled down over the ship's side were cleaning the chain off as it rose. Truman looked round for his signalman.

'Mayne – make to E.57, *Au revoir. Best of luck.*'

He glanced at Reaper for approval, but the commander was busy with his binoculars. Harriman, observing Granger's signals from the foc'sl, reported, 'Cable's up and down, sir.'

'Very good.' The lamp was clacking away, and from the submarine's bridge a light winked acknowledgement of each word. At the same time, E.57 was piping *Harwich*; she'd backed away clear of her during the cheering interlude, and now as she went ahead she was saluting the senior ship. Presently she'd pass *Terrapin* at a distance of about half a cable, a hundred yards or so. The signalman, pushing his Aldis lamp back into its bracket on the side of the bridge, reported, 'Message passed, sir.' But now a light was flashing again from the submarine: flashing 'A's, the calling-up sign. Mayne snatched up the lamp again. Reaper, joining Truman on the binnacle step, took off his cap and began to wave it: Wishart and his first lieutenant – one tall and bulky, the other slight and short – were easily identifiable as they waved back. Further aft, another less distinguishable figure waved: Reaper put his glasses up again, and saw that it was Nick Everard. He waved again: and had to stop, lower his arm and stand to attention when he heard the pipe and saw Wishart at the salute. He hadn't known that Wishart

485

was junior to Truman in seniority as a lieutenant-commander. Now *Terrapin* was returning the compliment . . . Just as it all ended, Granger hailed from the foc'sl, 'Clear anchor!'

He hadn't reported it aweigh. Presumably the clarity of the water made it visible from the surface at the same time as it broke out of the seabed.

'Half ahead together. Starboard fifteen.'

'Starboard fifteen, sir.' The telegraphs clanged as the bridge messenger slammed their handles over. 'Both telegraphs at half ahead, sir.'

'Fifteen o' starboard wheel on, sir!'

'One-four-oh revolutions.'

Leading Signalman Mayne reported, 'From E.57, sir: *Why not meet us at the Horn?*'

Reaper smiled. He heard Truman ordering, 'Midships. Steer north ten west.'

Round the top of the island, then south. About sixty miles to go; then a hundred miles back and into the gulf. Flat calm, bags of speed and time in hand . . . Truman suggested quietly, 'Rather early in the day for cheers, was it not?'

Reaper knew what he meant. You cheered ships into harbour sometimes after successful operations, but not usually when they set out. It had been Gillman's suggestion, though, and Captain Usherwood had agreed to it. Reaper said, 'It's the devil of a job they're taking on, you know.'

'The straits?'

'Yes.' He settled the glasses at his eyes again. 'And what's in 'em.' He shrugged. 'We've nothing to go on, that's the snag of it. It's blind man's buff.' He nodded towards the submarine. 'As all of them know full well.'

E.57 was some way off now, with her diesels pushing her along at about six knots and the sea washing streaky-white over the bulges of her saddle-tanks, spreading in a broad, lacy track astern. She had a solitary, vulnerable look about her; he thought perhaps submarines always did have, at times such as this and to outsiders watching them, but it was disturbing to realise that tonight, when this ship would be safe and comfortable alongside an oiler in Mudros harbour, that one there would be groping blind through minefields, scraping under nets . . . He murmured, still with his eyes on her, '*Louve* must have got through to the Marmara all right.'

Truman asked him in a tone that could almost have held reproof, 'Do you have positive information on that score, sir?'

Truman wasn't his sort of man, and Reaper wasn't looking forward to the social side of life in *Terrapin*. The fellow had too keen a sense of his own importance. Reaper told him, 'No. But when the Turks sink a submarine they always make a song and dance about it. They'd have told the world, by now.'

CHAPTER 3

There was a scattering of white on the surface, a light breeze on the bow as the submarine ploughed south-eastward now, one diesel charging and the other driving her towards the spot where she'd dive for the run-in to the straits. Off to port, that distant haze of land was Cape Helles with the heights of Karethia and Achi Baba further back, vague as mist against the sky; where the land faded was the gap they'd soon be steering for and entering, and to the right of that were the ridges of hills on the nearer, Asiatic coast, ridges that slid down to the Plain of Troy.

Much closer – 3,000 yards on the starboard bow – was Mavro Island. They'd come in a wide circle around the British minefields.

Hobday lowered his glasses as Wishart heaved himself out of the hatch and joined him. E.57 was just about in the position to dive. A few minutes ago Jake Cameron had been up here taking bearings; then the signalman, Ellery, had come up to unship the portable compass. Steering was from the control room now, with the bridge wheel disconnected. Wishart said, 'No loafing, this time. You can do it. Wait one minute, then pull the plug and we'll see how long it takes.'

He'd spoken quietly so the lookout wouldn't hear him and be ready for it. After a spell of inaction even the best ship's company needed to be sharpened up a bit. Wishart went below again; when Hobday dived her, he'd be watching points down there.

The bridge was nothing but a platform now. Before they'd checked the trim with a slow-time, carefully controlled dive off Kephalo, the canvas screens had been unlashed from the bridge rails, the wires unrove and the stanchions unshipped, all of it carried below and stowed for'ard in the tube space. The wireless mast and its aerial and the ensign staff had been removed too. Then the engines had been stopped, and she'd wallowed, losing way, and Wishart had flooded her down by filling one pair of main ballast tanks at a time, so that she'd eased her way into the sea as gingerly as a flapper dithering off a beach. But this time, with only numbers 3 and 4 main ballast not already full of water, she'd make her plunge in seconds; and she wouldn't be coming to the surface again – please God – until she was through the straits and in the Marmara.

That one minute had passed. Hobday glanced round at the lookout – Rowbottom, a torpedoman. Placid, heavy-boned, slow-moving. He'd better not move slowly *now* . . . He was gazing out over the beam, eastwards towards the loom of land, blinking patiently into his binoculars. Hobday stooped, putting his mouth close above the voicepipe, and shouted, 'Dive, dive, dive!'

Turning his head, he glimpsed Rowbottom more or less in mid-air as the man seemed to take off, flash across several feet of bridge, and fall into the open hatch. In the same space of time Hobday had shut the voicepipe cock and leapt into the hatch on top of him. His thumb stabbed at the button of the hooter: the engine noise had died and he heard the vents in the tops of the main ballast crash open and a roar of escaping air as the sea rushed up into numbers 3 and 4. A rain of spray was falling as he dragged the lid down over his head; then he was forcing the clips on, engaging the links and pushing the levers over, using both hands to do it. He climbed down through the lower hatch into the control room, and Ellery shut and clipped that lower one as soon as he was off the ladder.

No sign of Wishart. He heard Cameron tell the coxswain, 'Forty feet', and Crabb, on the after 'planes, repeated the order. Cameron told his first lieutenant, 'Captain said I was to catch a trim at forty. He's gone aft.'

Giving them all a bit of practice, and having a bit of a snoop around meanwhile. Jake Cameron, glancing round as the hands settled into their places, met Nick Everard's eyes: just a pair of eyes and part of a face glimpsed through a lot of general movement. He was back watching the trim now. Crabb reported, 'Forty feet, sir. Touch 'eavy aft, sir.'

'Yes.' He did nothing to compensate for it, though. Being at forty feet instead of twenty made the boat heavier; when they came back to periscope depth again she'd be in trim. Also, her fore-and-aft balance would have been thrown out by Wishart having gone aft. One man's weight could make a surprising amount of difference when it moved more than a few feet. Hobday muttered in Jake's ear, 'Main vents'. Jake glanced at the panel: he snapped,

489

'Shut main vents!' and McVeigh's hands moved fast up the row of steel levers, slamming them back into line; the thuds of closing tank-tops ran like drumbeats down the boat's length. It was a crime to leave main vents open once the boat was dived, and many first lieutenants would have made a fuss about it. Jake nodded to him. 'Thanks.'

Wishart was back, though. 'Hundred and fifty feet. You carry on, pilot.'

'Hundred and fifty, cox'n.'

CPO Crabb and Leading Seaman Morton angled their 'planes to take her down. Jake said over his shoulder, 'Pump on the buoyancy tank.' ERA Knight opened the tank's suction and vent, and McVeigh started the pump motor. The buoyancy tank was a small one amidships, useful for minor adjustments to the boat's weight because it had no fore-and-aft movement. The trim had to be adjusted now because as she went deeper her hull would be compressed by the pressure of the sea; she'd thus displace a smaller volume of water and, in accordance with the principle of Archimedes, become heavier.

'Hundred and fifty feet, sir.'

'Very good.' Trim seemed about right; he had the tank shut off. He saw Burtenshaw leaning in the doorway of the silent cabinet; the dreaded Robins was presumably inside it. Nick Everard was on a chair pushed hard back against the wardroom bunks; he looked like a prisoner, Jake thought – trapped, and alert for a chance to make a break for it.

Hum of the motors. Warm, oily atmosphere. It would get a damn sight warmer before they reached the Marmara. Wishart cocked an eyebrow at his first lieutenant: 'Check for leaks while we're deep, Number One?' He told the helmsman, 'Port ten.'

'Port ten, sir.' Roost, the gunlayer, was helmsman at diving stations. He spun the wheel, and Wishart added, 'Steer oh-five-oh.'

That was the course to enter the Dardanelles – which about a million years ago had been a river and was no wider than a decent-sized one now.

Steering by gyro. The gyro wheel itself was inside a steel-mesh casing right against the steering pedestal. If Roost stuck his elbows out as he pushed the helm around he'd crack one on the conning-tower ladder and the other on the corner of the auxiliary switch-board. If you had a cat in an E-class submarine you wouldn't swing it round.

Having rudder on affected the boat's trim, and Morton had put some dive on the fore 'planes to counteract the bow's tendency to rise. Now Roost was easing the wheel off.

'Course oh-five-oh, sir.'

Wishart said, 'When the first lieutenant's finished his inspection we'll go to watch diving. What's our distance to the Kum Kale mines, pilot?'

'Six point one miles, sir.' He'd laid the tracks off on the chart and he had the courses and distances in his head.

'Three hours, then.'

A slow approach would conserve the battery's power – which was essential, with forty-five miles of straits ahead of them. It wasn't only a question of the distance to be covered under water; there'd almost certainly be some tricky bits on the way through – nets to break through, for instance – and to get out of difficult situations you needed, usually, at least spasms of full power on the motors. You had to save up, as it were, for the times when there'd be no option but to use the batteries to their limit.

Hobday had been right for'ard; now he passed through again on his way aft. He told Wishart, as he squeezed between Knight and Ellery, 'Dry as a bone so far.'

Morton murmured out of the corner of his mouth to Crabb, 'More 'n *I* am.' Sweat was running down his big, smooth face. 'Lover-boy Mort', they called him; something to do with a girl in Gibraltar, Hobday had said. Might she not have minded his tendency to stream with sweat? Only the 4th ERA, Bradshaw, was his equal at it, and *his* name to his friends was 'Polecat'. A wiry, very hairy man. He was at the port after end of the control room; his responsibilities at diving stations were number 3 external vent, the port ballast pump and the port main-line flooding valve.

E.57 had a complement of twenty-nine officers and men, and at diving stations fifteen of them had jobs here in the control room.

Hobday had been through to the after ends. He'd finished his tour now and he was coming back, coming from motor-room to engine-room. In the space between those two compartments, Stoker PO Leech was squatting between the engine clutches, paring his nails with a pusser's dirk. He edged sideways to let the first lieutenant pass.

'Shaft gland on the port side's seeping a bit, Spo.'

The Yorkshireman's left eyebrow twitched. 'Sweatin', more 'n seepin', sir.'

491

'I hope you're right.'

'Old chum o' mine, that port gland, sir.'

'Mind you look after it, then. And be sure Peel checks the bilges every watch.'

'Aye, sir.' Hobday went through to Wishart. 'No leaks, sir.'

'Heaven be praised.' Wishart told Jake, 'Bring her up to twenty feet.'

'Twenty feet, sir.'

The 'planesmen swung their brass handwheels round – big as bicycle wheels, brightly polished brass – and watched the dials that showed the angles of their hydroplanes and the boat's depth, and the tube of the spirit-level that showed her angle in the water. Now, as she rose towards the surface, Jake had to put back into the buoyancy tank as much water as he'd pumped out on her way down. And Wishart wasn't intending to make it easy for him; as she was slowing and levelling to periscope depth, he told Hobday, 'Fall out diving stations, Number One.'

'Which watch, cox'n?'

Crabb growled, 'First part o' port, sir.'

'First part of port watch, watch diving!'

Now instead of fifteen men in the control room, there'd be only four – plus the officers in the for'ard part of it, where they messed. Two 'planesmen, one helmsman, and one duty ERA would be all the watchkeepers on duty; of the others, some would be going for'ard and rather more than that going aft. The trim would be completely thrown out.

Jake told McVeigh, 'Stand by the trim-line.'

The for'ard trim tank held a ton-and-a-half of water, the stern one a ton. They were connected by a water-pipe called the trim-line and also by an air-pipe with a vent-and-blow cock on it, here in the control room. By putting the cock this way or that, you could blow water from one end of the boat to the other, to compensate for crew movements. It was a quick and simple system, and by the time the change-round was completed Jake had her back in trim.

Hobday nodded. 'Not bad.'

Jake looked down at him. 'I'm a clever bloke.'

'Just as well to be told. Nobody'd ever guess it.' Hobday joined Wishart and the passengers. Robins had emerged from the cabinet. Lewis, the gun trainer who acted as wardroom messman, was drawing the blue curtain which converted that corner of the compartment into what passed for a wardroom; he asked Wishart, 'Tea, sir?'

'*What* a good idea.'

Robins said, 'I was under the impression we'd *had* tea.'

Lewis told him, 'That were stand-easy tea, sir. Sardines with *this* lot.'

'Lord, but we're pampered . . .' Wishart winked at Burtenshaw. He'd brought the chart over, and he was spreading it on the pull-out table. 'Show you fellows our route and whatnot, so you'll understand what's going on . . . Here – this is where we've just dived. This line's the track we're following to approach the straits. We had to start some way out, you see, or they'd spot us from the shore and be expecting us – and that we *don't* want . . . The distance to run in is just about six miles. That's to the shaded area here, right across the entrance – the one enemy minefield we know about for certain. So at this spot here, in about three hours, we'll go deep and slip under it.'

Burtenshaw asked hesitantly, 'How do we know when we reach that point?'

'We'll be taking fixes – periscope bearings of the headlands – during the approach. We also have a check on the distance run, from log readings.' He jerked a thumb. 'The log's what makes that ticking all the time.'

It was quite loud, when you stopped to listen to it. Behind it was the low hum of the motors driving the submarine north-eastward at slow speed, and a thinner, whining whisper that came from the flywheel of the gyro compass.

Wishart explained to Robins, 'By the time we're under the mines and inside the straits it'll be coming up for sunset. The straits aren't what you'd call wide – in fact they're darned narrow in some places – so we won't use the periscopes more than we have to, when we're in there. Not even in the dark. But we can when it's really necessary, and land-shapes should be visible against the stars. That's why we decided to make this passage at night and on a night without a moon.' He paused, rubbing his jaw; then he went on, 'As far as possible, though, we'll stay deep. Several reasons. There'll be obstructions – nets, obviously – and they all start on the surface – buoyed, mostly. Lower down, depending on the kind of net and how they've laid it, we can either pass under its foot or break right through it. Same with mines – they tend to be nearer the surface than the seabed. That's a *bit* of an oversimplification, because the practice nowadays is to moor the beastly things in

493

lines at varying depths.' He shook his head. 'Very unsporting chap, the Turk. Not that it'll do him any good so far as *we're* concerned.'

Robins glanced up at him.

'Why not?'

Wishart turned a chair around, and sat down. 'Because – not that I'd want to boast, you understand – because I know my job, and I've an able and experienced crew, and this is a lucky ship.'

'What an experience to have.' There was a glowing smile on Burtenshaw's youthful, games-player's face. 'It's magnificent. Absolutely.'

Nick was looking at him as if he thought he had a screw loose. But Wishart patted him on the back. 'Extra rations for that kind of talk. But I'm afraid you may be disappointed if you're expecting thrills. Best way to pass the next eight hours 'd be to get your head down and sleep through it.'

'Eight hours?'

'Something of that sort.' Wishart looked at Nick. 'I was going to explain – reasons for staying deep rather than going through at periscope depth – the main one is the peculiar tidal picture in the straits. Nasmith was the chap who first rumbled it – you know, Nasmith VC? Well, he buzzed up and down the Dardanelles as if he owned them, once he got the hang of it. What he discovered was that near the surface you've got a tide from the Marmara into the Mediterranean – against us, in fact – of about one-and-a-half, two knots. If you have to knock those two knots off our dived speed you'd be adding forty per cent to the time it'd take us to get right through – and then the battery wouldn't last out. That's one of the problems they faced in those days – before Nasmith found that lower down, at say seventy or a hundred feet, there's a tide running at about three knots *into* the Marmara. *With* us.'

He paused, listening, as Jake ordered quietly, 'Raise the for'ard periscope.' They heard the slight *thump* as the ERA of the watch pushed the control lever to 'up', and the hiss of the hydraulic ram as oil-pressure sent the long brass tube sliding upward. Another soft thud as the ERA stopped it, and then a click as Jake jerked its handles down. Wishart went on, 'Surface water going one way, bottom water going in the opposite direction. That'd be odd enough. But it's more complicated than even that, in some places . . . One theory is that about halfway down, somewhere around the bottleneck there, the whole body of water in the straits does a sudden corkscrew twist – water from the bottom rises on one side, and surface-water slides

494

down on the other. Bit awkward if you get caught in it – as one or two boats have, in the past. But – well, knowing it can happen, and being ready for it – that's half the battle. If you find we're suddenly blowing and flooding tanks and generally pumping around in what may seem a rather disorganised manner, don't let it worry you – it won't be anything we can't cope with. Eh?'

Robins murmured, 'One might well *hope*—'

'Or for that matter if we bump into a net. It's not unusual. If we get snarled up, we unsnarl ourselves. Been done before, lots of times.'

Able Seaman Lewis pushed in through the curtain, using his elbows to part it. He was carrying a tin tray with mugs of tea on it. Jake, at the periscope, addressed the helmsman: 'Anderson – stand by to take down some bearings.' Hobday called out, 'Hang on there.' He grabbed the chart in one hand and a mug in the other, and went over to the chart table. Jake said, from the periscope, 'I'll have some tea here, Lewis, while you're at it.'

'Aye aye, sir.' The messman was putting the other mugs on the table, and Robins was staring disdainfully at his dirty hands and black fingernails. He was still staring at them when Lewis pushed his fist into an old toffee-tin and brought out a handful of sugar lumps. He began to thumb them one at a time into the lieutenant-commander's mug: 'Say when, sir . . .'

'One hundred feet.'

Wishart snapped up the handles of the periscope – the for'ard one, the big one with the sixfold magnification in its lenses – and McVeigh depressed the lever that sent it hissing down into its well. Wishart had just taken a new set of bearings – edges of land, and hilltops – to get a last fix on the chart before E.57 went in under the mines. At the chart table, Jake had marked the position on the chart and taken a reading of the log.

'Hundred feet, sir.' CPO Crabb spun the wheel of the after 'planes, and Morton put some dive on his. Key men had taken over the controls, although the rest of the hands hadn't been closed up at diving stations. No need for it, yet.

Robins was in the wireless cabinet. He'd said he was going to take Wishart's advice and sleep right through. Nick Everard and Burtenshaw were lying on Wishart's and Hobday's bunks, Nick with his eyes shut and Burtenshaw reading Tolstoy. Hobday watched the needles in the depth-gauges slowing down as the boat approached her ordered depth and the 'planesmen levelled her off.

495

'Stop the pump.'

McVeigh pushed the switch with the toe of his plimsoll. It was warm in the control room: quiet, comfortable, well-lit. Easy to drop off to sleep if you'd no special reason to stay awake. The quietest tone of voice was enough for orders and reports; if you spoke loudly you'd be heard at the far ends of the submarine.

'Hundred feet, sir.'

'Very good.' Wishart had to turn sideways to edge round the ladder; looking over Roost's shoulder he checked the ship's head by gyro. The course was 084 degrees, to run in between Cape Helles and Kum Kale.

'I'll sing out if I need you, pilot.'

'Sir.' Jake crossed from the chart table to the wardroom corner. The curtains were drawn back now, open. He sat down in the armchair, and Burtenshaw asked him if he wanted to stretch out.

Jake shook his head. 'I've my own bunk, anyway. This drawer thing here. Pulls out when it's wanted.'

'Oh yes, of course . . .' The Marine nodded. 'Er – mind if I ask you something?'

'I'll tell you when you've asked it.'

'Oh . . . Well, how did you come to be RNR, as opposed to RN or RNVR?'

'Merchant Navy. I was a cadet when the war started. Went to sea as a snotty – in a trawler based at Immingham. Then I sort of wheedled my way into submarines.'

'Will you go back to the Merchant Navy?'

'Lord knows.' Jake shrugged his heavy shoulders. The future and his place in it worried him; he didn't want to talk about it. Bad enough spending so many hours *thinking* about it – at night, even nights when you really needed sleep but you woke and it came into your mind and wouldn't go away. He asked Burtenshaw, not really giving a damn for the answer, 'What about you?'

The Marine laughed. 'Honestly haven't a notion, old chap.'

'You're not on a regular commission then.'

'Me?' He was tracing patterns in a glisten of condensation that was already forming on the white-enamelled deckhead above his bunk. 'Well, I was at Harrow, you see, and – how shall I put it – I unilaterally terminated my scholastic career.'

'French leave?'

'Almost. And the Royal Marines seemed as good a choice as

any, so I trotted down to Deal – the depot there, you know? – and joined up, in the ranks.'

'Did you, by George!'

'Spur of the moment, really. Just sort of happened.'

'Did your people mind?'

'Ah. Well, my father took it quite well, really. And now since I've been commissioned even my mother—'

'What does your father do?'

'Surgeon. Cuts up people who can afford his stupendous fees.' Burtenshaw's chuckle faded. 'He's in France now – disguised as a colonel, cutting up people who can't . . . Anyway, my life in the ranks didn't last long. When they found I had the rudiments of an education they told me it was my duty to accept responsibility, all that rot.'

'What about the explosives part of it?'

'Chemistry was about the only thing I was any use at, at school. And at Deal before the Zeebrugge raid there was a chap called Brock – son of the man who started the firework factory, d'you know? – and he's a *real* expert. I mean he *was*. He was killed on the mole . . . Anyway, I got tied up with some of his experimental stuff, bombs and things. I applied to go on the raid in his crowd, actually, but—'

'Wouldn't take you?'

Nick, who'd known Brock at Dover, had his eyes open, listening. He heard Burtenshaw answer, '*Everyone* wanted to go on the raid, you know. For every man that went, there were fifty wanted to.'

That was true enough. And the blockships' passage crews, mostly stokers, had been so determined to get into the action that they'd stowed away, hiding until the assault was launched. He heard Cameron ask the Marine, 'D'you really think you'll be able to blow up *Goeben*?'

'I've – well, not much of an idea about it, really. I mean, what I'm supposed to do. I've got this stuff with me, of course, but how or when or where – well, don't ask me, because I don't know *anything*.'

Silence . . . Nick turned his head, saw Jake Cameron looking puzzled. Then Burtenshaw's hand showed, pointing towards the wireless cabinet. 'Do what I'm told, that's all. *When* I'm told.' He leant right over the edge of the bunk and spoke in a whisper, but impersonating Robins: 'Fewer people know anything about it, the better for us all, Burtenshaw . . .' He'd pulled back into the bunk. 'Truly, I'm simply to do what I'm told when the time comes.'

497

'But if—' Jake waved in Robins's direction – 'if he went adrift, and you're left in the dark – surely—'

'Three of us now, thank heaven. I mean we've got this—'

A *clang* from the bow: from somewhere outside the hull.

'Stop both motors!'

Now a scraping noise. Jake Cameron had half risen in his chair, then sat back again and let his breath out. Burtenshaw was up on an elbow, pink-faced, goggling. Nick was on his back with his eyes open and staring at the deckhead. He hadn't otherwise moved although he could feel cold sweat all over his skin and his gut was tight. ERA Knight had jumped to the telegraphs to pass Wishart's order to the motor-room, and now the sound of the motors died away. But the scraping was continuous, from somewhere on the port side for'ard. Abrasive on the mind, *inside* it. Nick told himself, *Take it easy: they know their business, and this is only the first minute, we've a whole night to get through.*

He hadn't expected it to start this soon. He was getting his imagination and his nerves in hand now, hoping nobody had seen any outward sign of the sudden shock he'd felt.

'Starboard fifteen.'

'Starboard fifteen, sir.' Roost pushed the wheel around. He didn't look as if he thought anything out of the ordinary was happening. The wheel's polished brass glinted as it revolved; he'd checked it now. Morton, the second coxswain, reported an obstruction on the fore 'planes.

'Can't 'ardly shift 'em, sir.'

'It's an ill wind . . .' Wishart added, 'Midships. Slow astern together.'

'Slow astern together, sir.'

Calm, quiet . . . Voices so relaxed there was something almost artificial about them. Hobday asked Wishart over his shoulder, 'What ill wind, sir?'

'Tells us where it is, old lad . . . Stop port. Starboard ten.'

'Starboard ten, sir.'

ERA Knight, still acting as telegraphman, reported the port motor stopped. Burtenshaw whispered to Jake, 'What's going on?'

'For'ard hydroplanes have been fouled by something. Wire. So we're sort of backing off it.'

'Mine-wire?'

'Likely as not.'

A reverberating *twang*: still echoing: weird . . . Morton whispered, 'Bye-bye, dearie.'

'Stop starboard. Midships.'

Stopping the boat and then putting her astern – and with helm on, at that – had thrown out the depth-keeping. The jammed fore 'planes hadn't been able to help, either. The gauges showed a hundred and eight feet, and the submarine was still sinking slowly deeper. Hobday, trying to cope with the trim, not only spoke in the suddenly fashionable calm, quiet manner, but his movements were slower too. Normally he was an unusually brisk, jerky sort of man.

'Both motors stopped, sir.'

'Helm's amidships.'

'Port five. Slow ahead together. Knight, find someone else to work the telegraphs – you'll be cooking the breakfast, next.'

'Sir.' The ERA went to the bulkhead doorway. 'Pass the word for Davie Agnew!'

'Both motors slow ahead, sir.'

'Five o' port wheel—'

'Midships. Ship's head?'

Hobday said in a murmur to the 'planesmen, 'Get her up again now.' With the motors driving her ahead again, they'd be able to. The motors' hum was audible again: that, and men's small movements, quiet voices, and the steady ticking of the log. ERA Knight's voice in a whisper to someone near him, 'I'm right 'andy with a fryin'-pan, you'd be surprised, mate.' Nick lay still with his eyes on the sweating, painted steel above him, and tried to visualise what was outside it, the dark enclosing water and taut wires growing in it like graceful stems with the flower-heads of destruction, death, swaying to the tide. He heard Wishart tell the helmsman to steer 090 degrees.

Hobday asked him, 'Shut watertight doors, sir?'

He'd put the question casually, and for a moment Nick didn't think anything about it. Then he caught its import: Hobday was suggesting shutting the compartments off from each other so that mine damage wouldn't necessarily flood the whole submarine at once.

'Course oh-nine-oh, sir.'

'Very good . . . No, not yet, Number One.'

There must be pros and cons, Nick realised, and Wishart would have turned them over in his mind before he gave that answer. Perhaps communications and morale considerations versus that damage-control advantage. If one could work up a positive interest in the technical aspects of what was happening it might help, he thought. Jake Cameron had been over at the chart table; he came back now and told Nick and Burtenshaw, 'Chances of actually hitting one are pretty small, you know.' Nick wondered if Cameron believed it, or if he himself might be whistling in the dark. Agnew, the Boy Telegraphist, had obviously been fast asleep; he'd just come into the compartment blinking, stifling yawns, pale as a ghost. ERA Knight jerked his head towards the telegraphs and Agnew moved quickly to that port after corner. Jake told Burtenshaw, speaking very quietly, 'That ERA – Knight, his name is – he's from Newcastle, but his father's bought up some big London garage, and when the war ends Knight there takes over as the boss.'

He and the ERA had chatted last evening, while he'd been busy on chart corrections and Knight had been doing some job in the control room. Jake told the Marine, 'I warned him I'd be along for free gas.'

'Motor of your own, have you?'

'*I* wasn't at Harrow, my lad!' He didn't say it as if it mattered to him. He glanced up at Nick, and winked.

Clang . . .

'Stop together.'

The order had come quick as lightning, but not with any sense of alarm detectable in its tone. Now, on the port side, there was a noise like sawing. Not as far for'ard as the first lot had been. It was probably because it was closer, Nick told himself, that it sounded so much louder.

'Starboard twenty.'

Aiming, of course, to swing her to port around the wire, throwing her afterpart clear to prevent the mine-wire fouling the after hydroplane. Agnew reported, looking more surprised than sleepy now, 'Both motors stopped, sir.' Nick warned himself that this was only the first field of them, and that in the forty-five miles between this end of the straits and the Marmara there were bound to be plenty more. One might as well settle the mind to it, come to terms with it as an unpleasant interlude that had somehow to be lived through. But how might that be done? Surface actions and, in particular, destroyer actions were fast, brief, noisy and exciting enough to be – by and large – quite enjoyable. Utterly different. The scraping was still moving aft: a harsh, very unpleasant noise. Very close, too. He craned out of his bunk, to get a sight of the nearer of the two depth-gauges: a hundred and twelve feet: a hundred and thirteen . . . The submarine was not only scraping her side along the cable, she was also sliding down it. He realised that with her screws stopped, without any forward motion through the water, the hydroplanes could have no effect on depth-keeping. But perhaps that didn't matter much: since the mine would be at the top end of the wire, to slide down in the opposite direction wasn't such a bad idea. The thought made him smile: he was hardly aware of it, but he'd happened to meet Jake Cameron's glance and Cameron grinned back at him. Because the scraping noise had stopped? It *had* . . . But it might start again at any moment, he told himself, wanting to be ready for it if it did.

He wondered where the wire was now. And where others might be. One had no idea at all how thickly the Turks might have sown this minefield. Heaven knew, one had planted enough of them oneself: in the Channel, in the Dover days, those quick mine-laying sorties to the Belgian coast, always so damn glad when the last mine had slid off the destroyer's stern so that she was no longer a vulnerable floating bomb . . . Wishart blew his nose. Then he said calmly, pushing the handkerchief back into a pocket of his shabby grey-flannel trousers, 'Midships. Port ten. Slow ahead starboard.' He was using the screw that was on the side away from where the wire had been, and starboard rudder to counter the turning effect of using only one motor. Just to get past the infernal – Nick screwed up his eyes for about a second – *bloody* thing . . .

'Slow ahead both. Ship's head now, Roost?'

'Oh-five-seven, sir.' He left the port wheel on, to bring her round to starboard, which was the way they had to go. Agnew had reached up to swing the telegraph handles round. They were well above his head, on that after bulkhead, and it was difficult for him because he was so short. Hobday ordered quietly, 'Hundred feet, second.'

'Aye, sir.' Morton increased the up-angle on his 'planes. He was soaking wet by this time and he had his eyes slitted to keep the sweat from running into them. CPO Crabb glanced sideways at him, and sniffed; he muttered, 'Gawd . . .'

'Steer oh-nine-oh.'

Playing safe, Nick guessed, visualising the picture on the chart and trying to occupy his own mind by reading Wishart's. Going farther out to starboard as one passed through the entrance into the widening bay wouldn't make much odds, but getting too far the other way, towards Cape Helles, could spell trouble. Once this kind of zigzagging around started, so that one's position was uncertain, and on top of that not knowing much about what the tidal stream

501

might be doing at any particular depth, it would be reasonable enough to allow some extra margin of sea-room. Roost reported, 'Course oh-nine-oh, sir.' Morton whispered sideways at the coxswain, 'What d'*you* let out – rose-water?' It occurred to Nick that if this was a sample of what might be expected all through the straits, except that there'd be much narrower places and other forms of defences, one could almost say there wasn't a hope in ten thousand of getting through: he was trying to find a way of arguing against that, when they caught the wire.

The submarine jolted hard: an arresting jerk that sent men staggering, stopped her and listed her sharply to starboard. Men were grabbing at things near them for support: Nick, with one hand hooked over piping on the deckhead and the other clutching the edge of his bunk, heard Wishart order, 'Stop together!' Then, as Agnew reached to the brass handles of the telegraphs, the mine-wire sprang off the starboard hydroplane: you could feel the jump of it, the sudden powerful wrench, the quivery spasm of release. Wishart, glancing towards Agnew again and opening his mouth, hadn't had time to speak when the wire snapped back just as violently against the submarine's starboard side – here, amidships. Faces, eyes turned that way: it would be the saddle-tank, outside the pressure hull, that the wire had clanged against and where it was now scraping and creaking. She'd angled over to port, and now she swung back to starboard, a list towards the wire as it bent itself around her and exerted some kind of twisting force. Then the mine on the end of the cable crashed into the side of the bridge above their heads.

Echoes dinned through the boat: through men's eardrums, skulls . . .

Extraordinarily, there'd been no explosion.

Jake Cameron, finding Everard and Burtenshaw both staring at him, realised he'd been holding his breath. He let it out – slowly, not wanting it to be obvious. The vice which had clamped on his guts a few seconds ago was easing its grip. He crossed to the chart table, picked up a pencil that could do with sharpening and read the code letters on it: HB . . . Thinking about those two goofing at him like that, the thought of having let them see how badly he'd had the wind up in the last minute or two was about as disturbing as anything that was happening around them.

E.57 rocked back, settled on an even keel. The wire scraped jerkily along the starboard tanks.

'Port twenty. Slow ahead port.'

Wishart had his handkerchief in his hand, holding it ready as if he was about to sneeze. The urge to do so must have left him; he was pushing it back into his pocket.

'Twenty o' port wheel on, sir.' Roost was calm, expressionless. Agnew reported in a slightly breathless tone, 'Port – port motor goin' slow ahead, sir.'

'You're doing well, young Agnew.'

The boy grinned self-consciously. Aware of several other friendly glances, he turned slightly pink. No scraping noise, suddenly. They waited, thinking – or carefully *not* thinking – about the wire and the thing it held moored to the seabed and the protuberance of the starboard after hydroplane, whether the boat would be swinging fast enough to clear it.

Wishart gave it time. Finally he murmured – as if it didn't matter terribly – 'Lost it, I do believe.' Crabb grated, without taking his eyes off the dial in front of him, 'The 'un mines go bang when you 'it 'em. That must've been one of ours.'

Everybody laughed. Wishart said, 'When we get back, cox'n, I'll buy you a drink.' He looked at Hobday. 'Let's get down a bit before we hit a live one. Hundred and fifty feet.'

Hobday had the watch, and Burtenshaw still occupied his bunk. Reading the Tolstoy essays now. Wishart had turned in too; he was flat out and his eyes were shut, but Nick didn't think he was asleep. Probably only discouraging conversation. Nick was in the armchair, playing a game of patience with a pack of cards that Cameron had offered him. Cameron was on the other side of the table, facing him, writing letters or *a* letter: he wrote with his head bent low over the pad, so that all Nick saw was the top of his broad, dark head.

He'd found he had no urge to sleep, and that lying horizontal, wide awake, while other men were up and working within sight and earshot, imposed the irritating feeling of being an invalid of some sort. Which of course he had been, not so long ago – and might the difficulty he'd had in accepting that status be the cause of *this* restlessness?

There could be other, contributory causes. Sarah: not knowing why she'd rushed down to London like that, to spend time with his father – whom, God knew, she had reason enough to loathe. Could it have been anything else *but* remorse? And might she, through remorse, hate *him* now?

503

He was holding a seven of hearts, staring at it as if it had some great significance. He put it down, and brought the game back into focus . . . But being a passenger was irksome anyway: it had been in *Terrapin* and it was the same here in the submarine. He told himself, as he put a red queen on a black king, that giving way to the irritation was a weakness: that he should make himself relax and accept the unpalatable truth that ships and operations could be run quite well without his help!

Leveret – this new appointment – was another irritation. All right, so he'd be at sea – when the old tub wasn't laid up with boiler trouble or other ailments – and it *was* a command. But in that Mudros flotilla an old *Laforey*-class destroyer would be the runt of the litter, the ship that got all the dullest jobs . . . The game hadn't come out. He began to collect the cards, to start again. He could hear the sporadic scratching noise that Cameron's pen made as he wrote his love-letter – or whatever it was. Love-letters on the brain, he thought . . . Through wanting one so badly, and getting only those two matter-of-fact, stepmotherly notes from her. He'd been at Queenstown in Ireland when they'd reached him, working on Admiral Sir Lewis Bayly's staff at the liaison- and training-base for the new American convoy-escort flotillas. Sarah's letters had been brief, *polite* acknowledgements of his own long, impassioned ones. He'd been puzzled; but also he'd been hard-worked up there, and busy in any spare time composing letters and pulling strings in efforts to get back to sea; there'd been little time for worrying or working things out. And now, holding the pack of cards in his clenched left hand, he stared at Jake Cameron's bowed head and saw Sarah in his mind's eye: ghostlike, vague and enigmatic, because in the weeks since he'd left home waters and heard nothing more from her she'd become the centre of almost constant speculation and anxiety – as well as—

One baulked at the word. But *all right* . . . He fanned the whole pack in his two hands. All right: love.

She's my stepmother, for God almighty's sake!

Cameron had raised his head: they were staring at each other across the table.

'All right?'

'What?' Coming to earth . . . 'Oh yes, fine, thanks.' He shrugged. 'Not very good at just sitting about, though.'

'You won't have to, for long, will you?' Jake blotted a page of his letter and turned it over. 'Only a few days, then you'll be

504

having a run ashore in Turkey. All harems and 'Araq, so they say.'

Quiet, and warm. Since her brush with the mines, E.57 had been paddling along in perfect peace for about an hour-and-a-half. Against the background hum of her motors and the noise the log made – all of which disappeared if you didn't think about it or listen for it – one heard only the small movements of the helmsman and the two 'planesmen, a quiet order occasionally from Hobday, or some sound as the duty ERA shifted his position. Routine – homely . . . Jake went on with the letter to his mother.

Having had no excitements I really have nothing very interesting to say. The climate of course is wonderful although we have had some colder days and the nights are beginning to feel quite chilly. Mind you, by English standards you'd still think it was quite summery!

All she wanted was a few pages with her son's handwriting all over them. And the security – no, she didn't only *want* that, she *needed* it – to know he was alive and likely to remain so.

You needn't worry for two seconds about me, you know. The War is nearly over and in no time at all I shall be walking up the path and knocking on the door. In fact I have been thinking quite a bit about what I shall do when the time comes to leave the Navy. Apply to the old Line, I suppose; but then there may be rather a lot of chaps like me and not nearly enough berths for us all.

Now why had he written that? To test her reaction?

If he did apply, the Line would surely – he hoped – welcome him back. He'd become one of their cadets at the beginning of 1914; and his father Ewan Cameron had put in a lifetime's service with them. A tragically foreshortened lifetime; it had ended in the Atlantic two years ago, when the ship of which he'd been Master had been blown almost in half by a U-boat's torpedo and gone down in seconds. Jake had been allowed a fortnight's compassionate leave – two weeks in which to comfort an elderly, broken-hearted woman who even at the end of that leave, when Jake had had to return to his submarine flotilla at Blyth, hadn't learnt to believe in what had happened. The finality had been too much for her to accept as real; her emotional struggles had seemed to Jake rather like those of someone trying to condition their mind to accept the limitlessness of space, and finding the concept too elusive to be held on to. And at the same time, through the bewilderment, reality would strike in intermittently, bringing with it such an infinity of pain that it could only be described as torment. In trying to comfort her in that degree of agony, he'd been able to subdue his own quite powerful sense of loss; and after the fortnight's leave a submarine patrol in the German Bight had felt like a rest-cure. He'd felt guilty, for enjoying the relief of it.

Even now, although most of the time she *seemed* to have her feet back on the ground – as much as she ever had, anyway – wasn't she still half believing the old man would come home one day? Jake was fairly certain of it. The doubt, for him, was whether he should continue in a sea career; whether he shouldn't find himself some kind of job ashore so as to stay close to her.

I hope you are looking after yourself properly and seeing plenty of your friends. I am quite sure it won't be long before I am home with you, but until then you must try to . . .

'Captain, sir.' Hobday. Wishart opened his eyes and turned his head on the pillow. 'According to DR, sir, we should be in the middle.'

'Right.' Aubrey Wishart swung himself off the bunk, and slid down. Old flannels with frayed turn-ups, and a cricket shirt that must once have been white but was now yellowish with age. Tennis shoes. On patrol, nobody cared about uniform. Hobday, wearing his reefer jacket, was the only one who would have been recognisable to an outsider as a commissioned officer; and the rest of his turn-out was a pair of tweed trousers and a white shirt with no collar. Jake had an open shirt over a string vest; his trousers were blue serge from his cadet days.

He'd put the writing-pad away and crossed over to the chart table. Wishart joined him there.

By dead reckoning – DR, meaning an unchecked position estimated only from the courses steered and distances on each course by log – the submarine would now be five miles inside the straits and just about in the middle of Aren Kioi bay. It was the broadest stretch of water in the whole length of the Dardanelles: pearshaped, it narrowed up towards the bottleneck. If they were where they thought they should be, there'd be two miles of water on each beam.

Wishart glanced round the control room. Chief ERA Grumman had propped his bulk against the panel of vents and blows, Finn was on the fore 'planes and Anderson on the after ones. Ellery, the signalman, was helmsman.

'How long since the others got their heads down?'

Hobday looked at the clock. 'Hour-and-a-half, sir.'

'Damn it, they'll be getting bed-sores . . . Let's have the cox'n and second cox'n on the 'planes . . . You happy there, Chief?'

Grumman nodded, with that slow smile of his. 'Right as rain, sir, thank you.'

Hobday told Finn, 'Fore 'planes amidships. Go and shake the cox'n and second cox'n. Then go aft, and if there's a stoker awake I want him for the telegraphs. If there isn't, shake one.'

'Aye aye, sir.' When Finn moved away, Jake slid into his seat. Wishart nodded. 'Splendid. Bring her up, Number One. One hundred feet, to start with.'

'Hundred feet, sir . . .'

When she paused there, and while he made adjustments to the trim, the 'planesmen changed round.

'Fifty feet.'

The needle resumed its steady circling. CPO Crabb's eyes were like knife-holes in his leathery skin as he recovered gradually from a short, deep sleep. Morton was yawning, slumped damply on his stool.

'Stop flooding. Ease that rise, second.'

'Flood-valve shut, sir.'

Morton reduced the angle of rise on his 'planes. The boat was levelling at fifty feet. No scrapes so far. Higher up, there might easily be nets.

'Close up the hydrophones.'

Might be a patrol boat as well, of course, Nick realised. Just as well to listen for them before you pushed a periscope up under their noses. Hobday said over his shoulder, 'Burrage – shake the leading tel. Cameron – shake Lieutenant-Commander Robins, ask him to move out of the cabinet.'

The hydrophone listening gear was in the wireless cabinet. Wishart murmured as Jake went to its half-sized doorway, 'Forty feet, Number One.'

'Forty feet, sir.'

Sounds of Robins questioning the need to move; and Cameron's low-toned explanation. Leading Telegraphist Weatherspoon appeared, blinking owlishly through his thick-lensed glasses. Wishart told him, 'Listen all round for propeller noises, leading tel.'

He'd nodded; now he was in the cabinet, muttering to himself at the disorder in there. Robins was asking Jake what was happening and how far they'd come; Jake explained that they were coming up to get a fix, and led him to the chart. Robins was wearing uniform trousers and a shirt without a collar. Burrage was back at the telegraphs. Hobday, behind the 'planesmen, stood with his feet apart and hands on his hips: bouncy, alert, the look of a bantam cock . . . 'Forty feet, sir.'

'Very good.'

Waiting for Weatherspoon's report on the presence or absence of surface craft. And he appeared now in the doorway of the silent cabinet, headphones flattening his big ears against his high-domed head. 'Nothing moving up top, sir.'

'Good. But stay there now. Twenty feet, Number One.'

'Twenty feet, sir.'

The 'planesmen worked as a team, with Crabb putting the angle on her and Morton concentrating on the actual depth. The submarine rose slowly in a carefully controlled ascent. If she came up too fast and overshot, broke surface, she'd be certain to be spotted from the shore. If that happened, by the time she reached the Narrows they'd not only be floodlit but also swarming with patrol boats.

They might be, anyway. Twenty-seven feet. Twenty-six.

'Stop port. Full field starboard motor.'

Clink of the telegraphs: then Stoker Burrage's report, 'Port motor stopped, full—'

'Raise the after periscope.'

Nick, watching the processes of coming up to periscope depth, ignored Robins as he came over and eased himself into the chair that Jake Cameron had been using. Robins was rubbing his face and breathing hard, as if being turned out of the cabinet had imposed discomfort which he was stoically enduring. The periscope hissed upward. One could imagine the dark surface, glassy and reflecting starlight, and the periscope-top suddenly pushing up through it, a single eye peering into enemy territory. Wishart had cut the boat's speed to the bare minimum that would permit control of depth-keeping, one screw just idling; he'd done it so as to reduce the size of the feather, broken water where the periscope sliced the surface. Twenty-two feet: twenty-one. The top lens would be out of water now.

'Twenty feet, sir.'

The after periscope was the little one – unifocal, with only one-and-a-half times magnification. It was the attack periscope, for use at close quarters, its small-diameter top less easy to spot than the full-size one.

Wishart had swept round quickly. Now he stepped back, pushed the handles up, folding them so that the bottom end of the periscope would fit into the well, the deep tubular cavity in the control-room deck, that housed it when it was lowered.

'Down. Up for'ard periscope.'

Grumman pushed one steel lever back and pulled the other forward. Arctic oil under pressure hit one end of one ram and the other end of the second. The periscope wires, attached to the rams, ran hissing through their sheaves. Wishart had moved to the periscope: 'Depth?'

'Twenty, sir.'

He'd done a complete circle in low power. Now his right hand twisted the handle round, switching in the sixfold magnification. He circled again more slowly, his left arm draped over that spread handle. 'Stand by for some bearings, pilot.'

'Ready, sir.'

He got bearings of the land-edges of the entrance they'd come through, a summit to the north which could only be Achi Baba, and a cleft in the land-mass north-eastward. This last one, Jake pointed out, must be the line of the straits, their future course to clear Kephez Point. Wishart had sent the big periscope down and joined him at the chart table as he put the bearings on.

'This one as our course, sir – oh-three-eight?'

'Looks good enough to me.' Wishart gave that to Hobday as the course to steer. The boat was just levelling out at forty feet. Jake checked the run ahead of them: 'Good for the next eight miles.'

'Perhaps.' He might have been thinking that a great deal could happen before they'd got that far. You didn't want to be pessimistic about it, but it could be a mistake to count chickens, too. As far as Kephez the chart showed no sounding of less than thirty-five fathoms, but after the point it got shallower; and in that area two years ago there'd been a minefield and a net barrage as well. It was reasonable to guess there'd be something of that sort there now.

He moved back into the centre of the control room.

'Slow ahead together. Hundred and fifty feet.'

'Hundred and fifty, sir.'

The telegraphs clanked over. Burrage intoned, 'Both motors slow ahead, sir.'

Nosing down . . .

CHAPTER 4

Something had fastened on to Hobday's shoulder and was rocking it to and fro. He opened his eyes, focused muzzily on Jake Cameron's ill-shaven face. Jake told him, 'Coming up to Kephez. Wakey wakey.'

He'd just shaken Wishart. And he'd sent a hand for'ard for Crabb and the second coxswain. As E.57 moved into the narrow end of the pear and the land closed in on her track, it was time for key men to stand-to again.

Jake had explained the situation to Nick Everard and the Marine, Burtenshaw, who'd been up and about while Wishart and Hobday slept. Nick left the chart now, moved back to the wardroom corner as Wishart, humming some unidentifiable dirge, sloped across and let the chart table take his weight.

'How far have we come since the last fix, pilot?'

'Depending on tide, the five miles you reckoned on, sir.' Jake added, 'I've marked the DR.' He moved back into the centre, to watch the trim until Hobday had pulled himself together. With men shifting around, even just a few of them, there were adjustments to be made.

Wishart was studying the chart. E.57 was in something like thirty to thirty-five fathoms of water. Say, two hundred feet of it. Depth-gauges showed a hundred and fifty, at the moment. All right on the face of it: but if she was as much as five hundred yards to starboard of the track she was supposed to be on, the seabed ahead might shelve quite steeply upwards.

Hobday took over the trim. McVeigh, the ginger-bearded Glaswegian artificer, had relieved ERA Bradshaw. Young Agnew, leaning against the bulkhead under the telegraphs, might recently have crept out from under a wet stone. CPO Crabb slid in behind the after 'planes, displacing Able Seaman Smith, the tattoo'd torpedoman, without even looking at him. Leading Seaman Morton came shuffling zombie-like to the fore 'planes and tapped Louis Lewis, the wardroom messman and gun trainer, sharply on the crown of his scruffy head. He muttered, '*Got* it.'

Lewis scowled at him. 'Why'nt yer get a bloody 'ammer, make a job of it?'

Morton grunted as he took his place, 'Will do, next time.'

'Hundred feet, Number One.'

'Hundred feet, sir.' Hobday had got the fore-and-aft trim right; now he'd have to adjust her overall weight as she changed depth. Wishart went back to look at the chart again, and Jake moved over to give him room.

'*Like* to get a new fix . . . But if we can get by the point without showing any periscope—' Wishart tapped Kephez with the points of the dividers – 'and well into Sari Siglar here . . .' He'd paused. Jake knew he was thinking aloud and didn't want anyone else's comments. But he glanced sideways at him now. 'Might as well get your head down, pilot. With any luck this'll be plain sailing.'

Robins was back in the wireless hutch. Burtenshaw had flaked out in the pull-out lower bunk that was supposed to be the navigator's.

'One hundred feet, sir.'

'Very good.' Wishart sat down in the armchair, and opened Burtenshaw's volume of essays. Jake smoothed out the surface of Hobday's bunk, and climbed up on it. He lay back and shut his eyes, thinking of the bulge of Kephez Point out there – *up* there, half a mile to starboard. He could as good as see it: and the black, still water, and Turk eyes watching the surface for movement, perhaps Turk ears listening through headphones . . . The risks were there: so were the chances, the random rations of good luck and bad . . . Anyway, if the dead reckoning was more or less reliable they'd have a run of about three miles now past Kephez Point and into Sari Siglar bay, where Wishart intended to poke the stick up for another fix. From that new departure, they'd set a course through the Narrows.

He heard a kind of snort. Wishart muttered, 'Actually *read* this stuff?'

Jake turned his head, and Wishart realised – or thought – he'd woken him.

'Sorry, pilot – didn't mean to—'

'He does indeed. Fairly revels in it.'

'Extraordinary. Seems such a *normal* sort of chap.'

Jake craned over the edge of the bunk and looked down at Burtenshaw. Wishart evidently thought *he* was asleep too; but he'd opened his eyes, and seeing Jake looking down at him – and Everard too, who'd twisted round in his chair – he winked. Wishart was frowning as he leafed on through Tolstoy. Lying back again, Jake thought of the half-written letter in his drawer, and of that line *You needn't worry for two seconds about me, you know* . . . Not strictly honest, perhaps. An outsider might well have had doubts about the survival prospects of anyone in these circumstances. But when it was oneself in the middle of it, one didn't feel it to be so . . . He wondered, drifting out of actual thinking into a vague area between consciousness and sleep, whether when she read that line of assurance she'd believe it, or whether she lived in fear of losing him as well . . . He ought to write to her more often. Someone else had just told him that: he accepted it, murmuring assent, becoming aware only gradually of the emerging noise, voices sharpening, and the movement – rocking, shaking . . . But there were hours yet, at least two hours on this course before—

'Stop together! Diving stations!'

He was out of his bunk and passing that order for'ard, calling the hands, helping Burtenshaw to get the lower bunk shoved in out of the way, and now he was back in his own place at the chart table and Wishart had just ordered, 'Slow astern together!' Reality was displacing sleep and reactions that so far had been automatic, unthinking, and there were noises from the bow – external noises, scraping and a sort of steady grinding like metal being screwed up tight.

He heard Wishart say, 'We're in some kind of net.'

'Stern's sinking, sir. 'Planes aren't—'

'Wire round 'em, sir.' Morton was putting his whole weight on the wheel. Hobday said, 'Leave it, for the moment.'

'Stop starboard. *Half* astern port. Port twenty.'

The rush of men to their stations was finished now. Jake saw some were in the condition he'd been in half a minute ago: newly wakened, barely understanding what was happening. Nobody was stupid enough to ask. Roost said, 'Twenty o' port wheel on, sir,' and Agnew reported, 'Port motor half astern, sir, starboard motor—'

'*Full* astern port.'

'She ain't answering, sir.' Crabb had the after 'planes tilted to their full extent, but they were having no effcct. Held by her snout in the net, the boat had no way on, and her angle in the water was increasing steadily as her stern sank lower all the time. The racing screw wasn't shifting anything.

'Stop port.' Wishart shook his head. 'Damn thing.' He sounded disappointed but in no way anxious. 'Have to try t'other way. Starboard twenty.' He glanced at the bubble and told Hobday, 'Get some out aft.'

'I'm pumping on "Z", sir.' Hobday's tone was mild too. He'd just about emptied the after trim tank, and now he had the pump sucking on the after internal main ballast, 'Z'.

'Twenty o' starboard wheel on, sir.'

'Half astern starboard.'

He was trying to prise his way out of the mesh by twisting the submarine away from it. He'd tried backing straight out, but the net had clung to her. Jake, watching from his position by the chart table, could feel no movement other than the vibration of the screw. The net still held her, and one motor at a time with the batteries grouped down wasn't enough to tear her free. Meanwhile, the net's surface buoys would be dancing about like fishermen's floats, and if any Turks were even half awake in their lookout posts on Kephez Point they'd be whistling up the patrols by now.

Some nets were mined, and the mines' detonators controlled electrically from the shore.

'Stop starboard. Midships the wheel. Group up.'

The two pairs of batteries could be connected either in parallel or in series. Grouping down gave 110 volts, grouping up 220. On the main switchboards now – one on each side of the motor-room – Dixon and Rowbottom would be snatching out the rows of huge copper switches, each switch throwing a blue crackle of electric spark as it broke, then banging over the grouper switch and slamming the others shut again.

'Both motors stopped, sir, grouper up!'

'Wheel's amidships, sir.'

Hobday's yellow hair was standing on end: he had a habit of rubbing his head with both hands in moments of anxiety. He said, 'Stop the pump, shut "Z" suction and inboard vent.' He'd about checked the stern's tendency to sink. He glanced round, with a grimace that looked like a smile, as Wishart ordered, 'Full astern together!'

'Full astern together, sir . . .' Agnew, up on his toes for a bit of extra height, flung the brass handles round; the hum of the motors

513

rose to a scream as the hands on the switchgear wound out the fields and the screws spun fast in their own churned water. The submarine trembled, quivered, dragging at the net; if she broke free suddenly Hobday would have to flood that stern tank quickly through its kingston to stop her shooting up stern-first.

But she was *not* coming free.

'Stop both.'

A few more minutes of full power might have drained the battery flat. Without power, the only thing a submarine could do would be to surface. Then she'd be blown to pieces by the shore guns. Jake swivelled round, leant with his forearms on the chart and began to study the coastline of the straits and the names of mountains and rivers. *Mustchiof Tepe. Aski Fanar Burnu. Codja Flamur Tepe.* Remarkable, to think that Robins could speak it. He wondered what size of wire the net was made of and how wide its mesh might be. Big enough for E.57's bow to have thrust right in and for the folds of net then to have wrapped themselves round the hydroplanes. *Yapildak Chai.*

Wishart said, 'Have to enlarge the hole. How much in "A", "B" and "Z", Number One?'

'Less in "Z" now, sir, but otherwise all about half full.'

Jake saw that Burtenshaw was looking keenly interested but not alarmed. That was good, suggesting that the Marine saw no alarm in any of the submariners' faces. Nick Everard had resumed occupation of Hobday's bunk: he was on his back, eyes open and staring at the deckhead. Those three tanks – the ones Wishart had asked about – were all internal main ballast, and each of them held about five tons of water when it was full. Jake had often thought about being caught in submerged nets but this was the first time he'd actually experienced it. He'd guessed it wouldn't be a very comfortable sensation, and he knew now that he'd guessed correctly. *Chai* seemed to mean 'river'. Wishart had told his passengers, *If we get snarled up, we unsnarl ourselves* . . . Burtenshaw must have believed him; he was bolt upright in the armchair with his eyes darting this way and that, watching the unsnarling process demonstrated. He'd just jerked sideways as a drop of condensation falling from the deckhead made a direct hit on his ear. Wishart ordered, 'Stand by "A", "B" and "Z" kingstons.'

The order was being passed for'ard to the torpedo stowage compartment for 'A', back to the after ends for 'Z'. 'B' kingston's

514

operating wheel was here in the control room, and Burtenshaw was having to move to let Lewis get at it.

'Full ahead together!'

The boat surged against the net. Grinding and scraping as the note of the motors rose. You felt the tremble in her steel, through all her hull and fittings. She was a live thing, straining muscle, a trapped animal struggling for life.

'Stop both. Stand by those three kingstons. Full astern both!'

Power coming on again. Hobday wearing that odd grin, gritting his teeth in anguish at the draining away of his battery's strength. Wishart snapped, 'Open "A", "B" and "Z" kingstons!'

Adding, as the sea rushed in to fill the tanks, about eight tons to her weight. Flinging herself astern, she was dragging at the net and at the same time – now, suddenly, dropping like a dead weight, plummeting stern-first, falling . . .

It was a question of how strong a net could be. Whether it could stand the extra weight and still hold her, even now.

Jake's fists were side by side on the chart and he was holding his breath as he stared at their white knuckles. Then he was listening to something like machine-gun fire, from outside the hull, as wire strands parted. Bursting, snapping steel-wire rope: he let his breath out, and it was difficult not to cheer.

She'd torn free but she was still going down.

'Stop together!'

'Blow "A", "B" and "Z" main ballast!'

McVeigh pushed those three vent-and-blow cocks to 'blow' and wrenched open the master valve. '"A", "B" an' "Z" blowin', sir!'

'Group down. Slow ahead together.'

The gauges showed that she was still sinking, passing a hundred and fifty; she was slowing her descent but still going down and it was a bow-down angle now. Crabb said, 'Gone 'eavy for'ard, sir.' He'd glanced at Morton; the second coxswain reported, 'Fore 'planes ain't movin' proper, sir. Reckon there's wire still round 'em.'

Wishart was behind him. 'Do they move at all?'

'Yessir. But – not the full travel, sir. And – *stiff* . . . Seems there could be – like weight there, sort of.'

'Stop blowing "B" and "Z".'

McVeigh shut them off. He said, '"A"'s out too, sir.'

'Stop blowing "A" . . .' The boat was hanging in a bow-down position at a hundred and seventy feet. Hobday asked Wishart, 'May I put a puff in No. 1 main ballast, sir?'

515

'What's the state of the for'ard comp?'

'Only half full, sir. Three-fifty gallons.'

'Pump that out first.'

'Aye aye, sir.' Morton still couldn't move the fore 'planes except in a very limited arc and with great effort. Hobday got a pump sucking on No. 1 compensating tank. Wishart observed conversationally, 'Most likely there's a section of net hanging on the bow.'

'Unless it's the 'planes themselves, sir – if we've wrenched 'em out of kimber, bent the—'

'There's weight for'ard too, though.' Wishart hesitated for another second; then he turned away, moving decisively as if he'd got it all worked out now. 'Starboard fifteen. Stop port.'

Jake thought, *Turning back?*

He saw Nick Everard looking equally surprised. Nick had swung over on to his side and up on one elbow: like Burtenshaw, he seemed to be trying to follow and understand the various manoeuvres.

Roost and Agnew had repeated the helm and motor orders. Wishart explained, 'We can't carry on up-straits with the fore 'planes stuck and a load of wire up for'ard. Out of the question.'

He was right, of course, Jake thought. But to turn back—

'And we can't get rid of it without surfacing.' Wishart was addressing Hobday. 'Have to cut it off with hacksaws. Nothing much else we *can* do, is there . . . Pilot, what's the reciprocal of our former course?'

Thirty-eight plus one-eighty: Jake told him, 'Two-one-eight, sir.'

'Steer two-one-eight, Roost.'

'Two-one-eight, sir.'

CPO Crabb reported, 'Bubble's shiftin' for'ard, sir.' What he was telling them was that the angle was coming off her, that she was responding to the suction on the for'ard comp tank. Hobday told Morton, 'Leave your fore 'planes alone now with that rise on . . . All right, cox'n?'

'Aye aye, sir.'

Using the 'planes might damage them – the axle or the glands – or tighten the wire around them. The after hydroplanes could manage on their own, in Crabb's experienced hands. Older classes of submarine, the C-class and ones before that, had no for'ard 'planes at all.

'Course two-one-eight, sir.'

'Very good. Slow ahead together . . . Number One – we'll go

back a couple of miles, get into the wider part so we'll have some chance of not being spotted. Then we'll surface – trimmed right down – and get rid of that rubbish that's slung on us.'

Hobday said quickly, 'That'll be *my* job, sir!'

Leading Seaman Morton glanced round. Sweat was running in small streams down into his open collar. 'Beg pardon, sir. Casing work oughter be second cox'n's lot.'

'And the casing officer's.' Jake wasn't letting Hobday push him out of this. Work on the upper deck was the third hand's responsibility – and, as Morton had pointed out, the second coxswain's. He asked Wishart, 'May I take charge of it, sir?'

Wishart nodded. 'Need you on the trim anyway, Number One. *And* you'll have your work cut out. I want the top hatch and the bow out of water and damn little else.' He pointed at Jake: 'You'll have just one minute on the surface. *One*. That means ten seconds to get from the hatch to the fore 'planes, forty to do the job, ten more to get back. Hatch open – sixty seconds – hatch shut – *dive*.'

He added, 'Unless of course you find you can do it more quickly.'

Leading Seaman Morton looked thoughtful. Jake had an uncomfortable feeling that Wishart would stick precisely to his timetable. He looked across at Hobday. 'If you'd really *like* the job—'

Everybody chuckled. CPO Crabb suggested to Morton, 'Take a cake o' soap up while you're at it?'

'Stand by to surface!'

The reports came in: vents shut, LP air-line open to the main ballast tanks. High-pressure air was used to blow with, but it had to pass through reducers and the low-pressure line to reach the tanks.

Hobday had worked out a way to surface with not only the bridge-hatch out of water but also the for'ard end of the casing – the actual bow and the fore 'planes – which were well below the casing level. He reckoned he needed a bow-up angle of twelve degrees, so he was going to blow the for'ard pair of tanks until he'd got her to that angle, then puff water out of the next pair to them – three and four – to give her the buoyancy to stay up there.

They'd been up to twenty feet a few minutes ago, for a look round through the big periscope. Wishart had muttered, 'Searchlights, damn it . . .' Watching him as he swung around, Jake had seen a sudden brilliance that had made his eyes glow like a cat's as a searchlight beam swept past, flooding its harsh glare down the tube and through the lenses: then it had swung on by, leaving Wishart with his head back, blinking, momentarily blinded. He muttered, 'Have to chance 'em, that's all.' He snapped the handles up. 'Fifty feet, Number One. Pilot – you and Morton ready?'

Jake said yes, they were. He found the passengers – not Robins, who'd retired to the cabinet again – watching him. Burtenshaw, as it happened, had offered to go up with them and lend a hand. The offer had been refused, of course. For half a dozen reasons it had been a silly suggestion to have made; either he'd made it recognising that, or he was more stupid than he looked.

Wishart was giving them their final instructions. 'I'll open the hatch and get out first. You, then Morton, jump out, go straight over the front of the bridge and pull yourselves along the jumping-wire to the bow. The gun will be awash and there'll be four or five feet of water over the casing at this end, but the foremost thirty feet or so'll be sticking out and the 'planes should be well clear. Once you're there you'll have just over half a minute. Understood?'

The control room was a hot, stuffy, yellowish-lit cavern full of men with tense, sweat-damp faces. The depth-gauges showed fifty feet. Jake and the second coxswain had hacksaws, wire-cutters, cold chisels and hammers slung from their webbing belts. Apart from the webbing, they wore only shorts, swimming collars and engineers' gloves.

Hobday reported, 'Ready to surface.' Wishart gestured towards the lower hatch and Ellery unclipped it, pushed it up, the clang of its opening echoing in the hollow steel tube of the conning-tower. Wishart told Jake and Morton, 'If I blow this whistle, you two drop whatever you're doing and run like riggers for the bridge. Straight into the hatch. Understand?' They nodded. He added, 'Take no notice of the searchlights. We're a long way out and our silhouette won't be any bigger than a couple of floating barrels.'

'Aye aye, sir.' He heard Burtenshaw say rather shyly, 'Good luck.' Jake winked at him. *You needn't worry for two seconds about me, you know* . . . He hadn't reckoned on searchlights. Then he thought, *We're the lucky ones. We don't have to sit and wait. Months – years . . . Compared to what she has to go through, my life's roses.*

'Let's have that twelve-degree angle, Number One.'

'Blow one and two main ballast!'

Wild-eyed – scrappy ginger beard bristling – oil-stained – lips drawn back over narrow, yellowish teeth: a first-rate man, was

McVeigh, but if he'd walked into a Glasgow pub looking as he looked now the bar would have been evacuated in seconds . . . Air roaring: she'd already begun to tilt. Men were holding on, using anything solid to hang on to as the deck angled. Four degrees on the bubble: five . . .

Take no notice of the searchlights . . . The thing was, would the searchlights take notice of *them*?

Eight degrees. Nine . . . Wishart had one foot on the bottom rung of the ladder. Ten degrees. Depth-gauge needle circling faster now; one motor was driving her slowly ahead, and the angle of the boat was planing her upwards.

'Stop port.'

'Stop port, sir!'

Hobday glanced round at his captain. 'Eleven degrees, sir.'

'Surface!'

'Blow three and four!'

McVeigh wrenched the blows open, and the increased rush of air was deafening. Wishart climbed quite slowly up the ladder into the tower. Jake started up behind him, keeping his head well back so as not to get heeled in the eye, and using the sides of the ladder, not the rungs, as handholds. He'd had his knuckles crushed more than once, on submarines' ladders. He heard Hobday shout through the noise from down where Morton was crowding up behind him, 'Stop blowing three and four!' The conning-tower smelt of wet metal and old boots. Wishart was taking the first clip off the top hatch; he called down, 'Open the centre deadlight, pilot!'

The ports in the conning-tower had lids – deadlights – that screwed down over them. Jake set to work on the one in the middle, which faced exactly for'ard. He loosened the brass butterfly nut and banged the clip off with the heel of his hand, and the cover dropped clear on its hinge. From below, Hobday shouted, 'Twenty feet . . . eighteen . . .'

'Sing out when your port's clear, Cameron.'

'Aye aye, sir.' When this glass broke surface the top hatch would be well out. Surfacing as slowly as this and with so little positive buoyancy, it would be crazy to cut it too fine, in case something went wrong and she slipped back. If you went under with a hatch open and a man in the hatch – well . . . Hobday's voice came thinly, 'Twelve – eleven—'

The glass port in front of his face became suddenly alive with heaving frothing sea.

'Port's awash, sir!'

He heard Wishart push off the last clip and throw the hatch crashing back: air whooshed up through the tower like gas out of a bottle of beer. He was climbing, flinging himself up and out into the sloshing, seething bridge, the sea only a matter of a few feet away from him and boiling from the submarine's emergence, sluicing round and breaking, splashing over, surging powerfully around the bridge: he jumped for the wire that ran from the periscope standards to the bow, launching himself over the front of the bridge into black water frothed with swirling white. Sea heaved around the gun: he stood on its breech for a moment, shifting his grip on the wire, then swung himself for'ard, hand over hand; a few yards more and then he had his feet on the sloping, submerged casing. The wire's abrasive exterior – designed for cutting nets – ripped at his soaked wash-leather gloves as he dragged himself along it. Light – searchlight – a flash of it as it passed: well, it *had* passed. Morton close behind him, gasping and grunting. There were sharp edges to the gratings and he wished he'd worn plimsolls. The surface was quieter now, settling as the submarine settled too. The jumping-wire sloped right down to her sharp nose. Jake lay flat, clinging to flood-holes, peering down at the port hydroplane – horizontal, a dark ear-shaped thing with the gleam of starlight on its wet steel surface. No sign of any net or wire. He was straining his eyes to make sure there was nothing round it where its axle passed into the hull-gland; he heard Morton bellow, 'Over 'ere, sir!'

He scrambled over. Glimpsing, without looking straight at them, half a dozen wavering searchlights on the southern, Asiatic coast. Small-looking though, far off, farther than he knew they were. Morton slid over the side, right down on to the 'plane itself, and Jake hung over the casing's edge above him. Light swept over them: its brilliance hardened, lit everything: then it had passed, arcing across the sea, and Morton shouted, 'Like a lot o' bloody knittin'!' Jake could see only his hunched back: there wasn't room for two down there, and they were both big men. He heard Morton's hacksaw rasping at wire-rope, and called down unnecessarily, 'Room for me to help down there?'

'No, sir, not—' His voice rose: 'She's *away*, sir!'

He heard a clang. Then Morton's face, a pale blob in the dark, turning up towards him: 'Lost me bloody saw!'

'Here!' Hanging down half over the side, he caught a groping hand and pushed his own saw into it. The light's beam washed over them again. It crossed the bow, swept on thirty yards, paused. It was sweeping back again. Jake thought, *Oh God, now we're in for it!* Morton was sawing again – shouting – *singing*? The light picked them up briefly, and swung on. Glancing back, Jake saw it hover on the bridge, move on, stop again: he guessed they'd been spotted. Morton was standing, clinging to the side with one hand and heaving up a bight of wire in the other: 'Work 'er for'ard as I clear 'er, sir?' Dragging the bight with him, Jake crawled to the submarine's sharp bow. Straddling the bull-ring, he got the wire over his shoulder and began lunging and jerking at it, shifting it for'ard inch by inch. Morton would be working the mesh outward, he imagined, over the hydroplane's outboard curve. And – incredibly – Morton *was* singing! Gustily, panting the words out, a sea-song about a sailor and a tart: '*Saying take this my darlin' for the damage I have done, If it be a daughter or if it be a son . . .*' Gaining wire still, but too slowly, too damn slow by half. Light behind him, all around him: he wondered why Wishart hadn't blown his whistle. Morton shouted, 'Keep your weight on 'er, sir, she's partin', she's near . . .' Near *something*.

The light had left them again. It came from the northern shore and he knew he mustn't look that way, that he'd be blinded if it turned on him . . . Nothing coming in now, the wire felt solid: Morton's saw scraping and gasping spasms of that raucous song: '*If it – be a son – send the bastard – off to sea!*' Light fixed on them, holding them: a hoarse ripping sound like canvas tearing and from the north a crack of gunfire. Another shell scrunched over and the light still held them: Jake thought they were in the intersection of two beams. He was throwing his whole weight against the wire's resistance: a cross-piece, part of its mesh still intact, gave him a handhold. He was cursing, screaming at it. The sea leapt in a tall spout twenty yards off the bow, and another shell hurtled overhead. They were shooting faster now. Morton yelled, 'Stand from under, let 'er *go!*' Jake dropped his shoulder and twisted round, let the wire slide away, got his right leg up and out of it so the wire wouldn't be tempted to take his foot with it. It was an enormous weight of net. The light's dazzle was beaming from right ahead now; Wishart must have turned the submarine bow-on to it, so as to present a smaller target to the Turkish gunners. Morton's voice screeched suddenly, 'I'll *murder* you, you bloody 'orror!' Jake was where he'd been before, leaning out above him, trying to see what was happening. He heard clattering as Morton's dark bulk shifted and he strained at the wire: then a long, metallic slither and Morton's voice in its normal, deeper tone, 'Well, well, fancy *that* . . .' They'd been in darkness for several seconds, with no shooting, but as the second coxswain stood up on the hydroplane the light came back, blinding, savage. Jake yelled downwards, 'Is it clear?'

'All gone, sir!'

Two or three shells whirred over and one burst short, exploding as it struck the water. Stinking vapour-reek: metal racketed off the bridge and whistled off into the dark. One puncture in the hull and they'd be done for. A lot of gunfire, yellow-red flashes on the shoreline. Morton was clambering up: he assisted him, shouted, 'Back now – quick!' The light helped: you could see the jumping-wire and the gun. Another burst, with bits of shell screaming over and something clanging against the casing – aft, he thought. Morton had reached the bridge. Another yard – Jake swung off from a foothold on the gun – and he'd be there himself. Gunfire noisier now: Wishart bawled, 'Down below – *down*!' Brilliant light: Wishart's idea of helping someone into the bridge was to tear an arm or two out of its socket. Jake didn't pause to thank him. A shell came scrunching over; he landed in the hatch on top of Morton and then Wishart came down on top of him like five tons of pig-iron, only harder. The klaxon roared, shattering his ear-drums; cursing, he let go of the ladder and fell about ten rungs before Morton's bulk cushioned his fall and allowed him to catch hold again, cracking one elbow and a kneecap; the hatch had slammed shut up there, and Wishart called down, 'Fifty feet!' Jake told Hobday as he landed in the control room, 'Fifty feet. The 'planes are clear. Morton did it all.' McVeigh had opened the vents of those four main ballast tanks, and Hobday was flooding the for'ard compensating tank which he'd emptied because of the weight of the net on their bow. Jake saw the depth-gauge needle passing fifteen – sixteen – eighteen feet: safe from the Turk gunners now. He noticed McVeigh staring at him interestedly; looking down at what seemed to be the target of the scrutiny he found a mess of blood running from lacerations on that shoulder. He hadn't felt the net doing that to it. Morton was crouching in a pool of water with his head between his knees. Wishart came slowly down the ladder. He said, 'Lucky they're such rotten shots.'

* * *

Lewis had produced more tea. Hobday had the watch, and was sipping his with an eye on the depth-gauge and the trim. Wishart and Jake had theirs up on the bunks, while Robins, Everard and Burtenshaw sat at the pull-out table. Leading Telegraphist Weatherspoon was in the silent cabinet, keeping a listening watch on the hydrophones. Two patrol boats – small, high-speed launches of some kind, Weatherspoon had guessed – had gone down-straits half an hour ago; they'd passed close and then the sound of their screws had faded south-westward. A hopeful sign, possibly. If they'd come down as a result of E.57's fracas on the surface, the fact they'd continued in that direction suggested that the Turks thought they'd been shooting at a submarine on her way *out* of the straits . . . It was wishful thinking, perhaps; but the way those boats were going was the way they would have gone if that had been the enemy's belief. They'd have gone to sit over the minefield off Kum Kale – to wait for the bang and for bodies to float up.

Robins said, 'Midnight . . . And if my memory is accurate, we started under the minefield at seven-thirty. Four-and-a-half hours ago?'

Jake blinked at the gleaming paintwork on the pipes overhead.

'Right.' And they'd dived three hours before that.

'It was supposed to be an eight-hour passage from one end of the straits to the other, and we've used up four and a half. Are we anything like halfway through yet?'

'No.' Wishart had his eyes shut, but he was only resting. '*Nothing* like.'

'So it will take considerably longer than eight hours?'

'Reasonable conjecture.' He turned his head, and asked Robins mildly, 'Want to get out and walk?'

Hobday reported from the chart table, where he'd just checked the log reading, 'That's three-quarters of a mile, sir.'

'Good. Come round to oh-four-oh, please.'

Robins sipped his tea, made a face, put the mug down. He went on with his nagging.

'And we have now to start all over again, make a new attempt at getting through that net?'

Wishart shrugged. 'At getting past it, yes.'

'Might it not have been simpler, having torn a hole in it, to carry on through the hole?'

'Not with the torn-off section of it dangling from our 'planes, no.'

Nick, looking across the table at Robins's ratty little face, was surprised at Wishart's patience with him. But Robins wasn't letting go quite yet.

'Have we any reason to imagine it will be any easier this time than it was before?'

'Some.' Wishart nodded at the deckhead. 'Mind you, it's all a toss-up. One backs one's hunches, that's about the size of it.'

The helmsman reported quietly, 'Course oh-four-oh, sir.' Hobday came over and put his cup down on the table. 'Stay at this depth, sir?'

'Yes. I think we said one-and-a-half miles, pilot – that right?'

Jake Cameron, with his face buried in a pillow, mumbled yes, it was . . . They'd headed north, to get over towards the European shore. Wishart had reckoned that since the greater concentration of searchlights seemed to be on that coast, it was likely that any clear channel would be on that side too. So he'd decided to move over to that side and to take her down to a hundred and fifty feet when they came opposite Kephez. When they'd hit the net they'd been in the middle of the straits and at a hundred feet; if the thing extended right across and went down as deep as a hundred and fifty it would have to be fairly gargantuan. Perhaps it was. But the northern shore was steep-to, with thirty fathoms or more right up close to the beach, and that was an advantage for the submarine.

They needed an unimpeded passage from here on. The battery had already taken a beating, in the efforts to break out of the net; and as Robins had just been so kind as to point out, they weren't even halfway through yet.

Nick saw Robins returning from a visit to the chart table; his lips were pursed.

'It seems extraordinary that as the crow flies Imbros is no more than fifteen miles from our present unenviable position.'

He sat down. Burtenshaw looked embarrassed. In Robins's presence he usually did. Nick thought Wishart was going to ignore the comment; but Robins was beginning, perhaps, to get under even *his* skin. Apart from the irritation-value of the carping, it happened that Wishart's eyes had been shut, and for all Robins knew he might have been asleep; if he had been, the crime of waking him with another of his silly criticisms would have been fairly unforgivable. But the eyes opened, and the head turned slowly.

'One: we are not crows. At least, *I'm* not . . . Two: our

524

"unenviable" position is in the waterway through which we are bound to pass before we can deposit *you*, Robins, in the Marmara – and this I am as impatient to accomplish as you are yourself.'

Nick laughed. Robins shot him a glance of contempt. Then he muttered waspishly, 'The French seem to have found it easy enough.'

'Have we any way of knowing that?'

Robins shrugged. Wishart added, 'I hope you're right. Up till now the French haven't had much luck in these waters.' Nick could tell from his tone of voice that he was trying to keep things on an even keel. Because you couldn't afford quarrels in a submarine, because there wasn't room for them? On that basis, he realised he shouldn't have laughed just now. He was going to have to work with Robins, when the time came for the landing. Wishart said, 'Talking of *Louve*, though – the two civilians in her are politicals, aren't they? Wouldn't it have been simpler for the three of you to have formed one party?'

'Had the French proposed it – yes.' Robins shook his head. 'In fact it's on account of *their* ambitions that I have to – to go about things in my own way. Counteract – no, to *balance*—'

'Aren't we and the French on the same side any more?'

'A somewhat naive question, Wishart. The Eastern Mediterranean is – politically – a French sphere of influence. But we can hardly neglect our own—'

'Hydrophone effect, sir!'

'Diving Stations!' Robins had to move fast or Wishart would have flattened him. Jake, in a sort of flying-trapeze act, brought up hard against the chart table as Hobday repeated the order and the short, sharp rush swept through the compartments. Wishart was asking Weatherspoon about that HE – propeller noise.

'Astern an' like before, sir.'

'Two of 'em again?'

'Could be. Bit confused, sir.'

Ears like soup-plates, clamped against his skull by the head-set. His eyes were open but not focusing or seeing anything; his operative sensors were those great ears of his. 'Seems about steady, sir. Go over the top of us, I reckon.'

Wishart glanced round. The hands were closed up now, at their stations.

'Hundred and fifty feet.'

'Hundred and fifty, sir.' Brass wheels spun, reflecting yellow

525

light. Wishart gestured upwards and told Hobday, 'When he's gone over I'll have a shot at following him. We'll stay deep to get the tide's help, but it'll take both motors half ahead.'

Hobday met his captain's stare. It was a kind of challenge, inviting him to comment on the state of the battery. But if you could trail an enemy through his own defences it might save a lot more amps, in the long run, than it consumed.

CPO Crabb grated, 'Hundred an' fifty feet, sir.'

'Very good.' Hobday busied himself with adjustments to the trim. Wishart crossed over to the cabinet; Weatherspoon pointed a finger upwards, nodded. He was saying, *Here it comes* . . . And suddenly everyone could hear the rhythmic churning of the Turk's propellers: faint at first, rapidly growing louder . . . Weatherspoon said, ''nother astern of 'im, sir. Same pair as before.'

The pair that had gone *down*-straits earlier. Drawn blank, coming back up here to hunt? Wishart didn't question the leading telegraphist's judgement; different ships' propellers made their own individual sound-patterns, and an experienced operator could usually recognise screws he'd heard before.

'Half ahead together.'

Agnew repeated the order as he reached up to the telegraphs. In the motor-room Dixon and Rowbottom would be winding down on the rheostats, taking resistance out of the armature fields to allow the motors to speed up. Weatherspoon scowled, shook his head. 'Lost 'em, sir.'

'Stop together.'

If you made much row yourself, you couldn't hear the enemy's noise. Hobday told McVeigh, 'Stop the pump.' Weatherspoon's eyes blinked at Wishart as the hum of machinery died away. 'Close to the bow, starboard. P'haps green five, sir.' He jerked his chin upwards towards the deckhead. 'Other lad's comin' over now.'

'Steer oh-four-five. Slow ahead together.' Wishart went to the chart table. They could all hear the second Turk boat now. Jake pointed at the latest DR position. If it was accurate they were already in the narrow section created by a bulge of coastline that had Kephez Point as its northern tip. Wishart muttered, more to himself than to Jake, 'Even if we stick close to him we could still run into deep ones.'

Mines, he meant. It would be safe enough to follow an enemy on or near the surface, but at this depth it was anybody's guess. But they needed the depth so as to get the benefit of the deep tidal stream. The flatter the battery got, the more important that current was.

There could easily be a deep minefield on this side. It would make sense – Turk-type sense – to have one here. A net – the one E.57 had hit – on the other side where the inshore stretch was shallower, and deep layers of mines over here. So if the patrol boats were worth following at all, it would be better to do so at periscope depth.

It was a gamble, though. You had to stake thirty lives on it. Possibly much, much more than thirty, when you thought of the operation and the likely results of its success or failure. And the difference between that success or failure you could reckon, in a situation such as this, in inches.

'Come up to fifty feet, Number One.'

'Fifty feet, sir.'

'After that, twenty. But easy does it.'

Up by stages, so as not to risk the loss of control that could send her floundering to the surface. It was in this section that the straits had been known to go mad, turn upside down. Another point worth bearing in mind was that on each side here the shore guns would be less than a mile away.

At fifty feet, Hobday had the trim adjusted, and Wishart stopped the motors. Weatherspoon could still hear the second of the two patrol boats, and it was still right ahead.

'Slow ahead together. Twenty feet.'

Half a mile to starboard was where they'd tangled in the net. And three miles ahead was Chanak, the Narrows, the *real* bottle-neck.

'Down periscope.'

The small after periscope hissed down, and McVeigh eased the lever over gently to avoid the thud that always came with a more sudden check. Wishart had taken a few quick bearings; now he joined his navigator at the chart table to see what sense could be made of them.

If any. It was pitch dark up there, and with the coast inside spitting-distance he'd had to work quickly for risk of the feather being spotted.

Jake suggested, 'If the left-hand edge was *this*: and the tower could be this fort or whatever it is at Kilid Bahr?' Wishart agreed. 'Well, the last one would've been Kephez Point, and that fits well enough. Puts us *here*.'

Right in the Narrows. Between the points of Chanak and Kilid Bahr.

'Did it look like that, sir?'

Wishart shrugged. 'Looked like the inside of a pig's bladder, old lad.' Jake suggested, 'If we take this as our position, we ought to come round to about—' he moved his parallel-ruler across to the compass rose – 'three-five-oh?'

Wishart glanced round at Hobday. 'Alter course to three-five-oh, Number One.' He added, 'Gently. Five degrees of wheel.'

The less helm you used, the less effect it would have on the trim. There was land with Turkish gun batteries on it less than a thousand yards on one side and as little as five hundred on the other. It wasn't a place for mucking about in. Wishart glanced round to see what his passengers were doing. Robins seemed to be asleep, in Hobday's bunk, and Burtenshaw was on Wishart's, reading that book of his. Everard was sitting on a chair pushed back against the bunks. Wishart asked him, 'Like to see where we are?'

'Thank you.' Nick got up. He'd been wishing he could have had a look at the chart, but he hadn't liked to move, for fear of getting in the submariners' way.

'Cameron'll show you.'

Weatherspoon called sharply, 'Surface vessel closin' on us from astern, sir!'

Nick hesitated: then he sat down again. Jake Cameron smiled, spread his hands in a that's-the-way-it-goes gesture. Wishart was at the doorway of the cabinet and Weatherspoon told him, 'Comin' fast, sir, *very*—'

'Sixty feet!'

Now you could hear the screws: high revs, much faster than the others had been. Like being on a railway line with an express train rushing at you. Morton reported from the fore 'planes, 'She don't answer, sir!'

'Open "A" kingston, half ahead together!'

Lewis dived like a goalkeeper for the bulkhead doorway, to get at the kingston's handwheel in the next compartment, but Anderson was there ahead of him. The submarine's bow dipped sharply, and the speeding motors bit, drove her down. The propeller-noise rose to a crescendo, right on top of them.

'Shut "A" kingston!'

She was diving fast now, accelerating away from those screws

528

that must have passed perilously close to her up-angled stern. The Turk had gone over now. Jake thought, keeping his face expressionless, *Near squeak* . . . Wishart had slowed the motors and Hobday was getting a pump to work on 'A'. There'd be pressure in that tank now, so the pump should have an easy job of it. Needles still belting round the gauges. Sixty – sixty-five feet: he'd looked away from the gauges for a moment, and glancing back again he saw she was approaching eighty.

'Stop together – half astern together!'

She hit the seabed with a jolting crash that sent everybody flying. The lights went out. Nick, sprawled on the deck, heard men and objects falling everywhere. The gyro alarm-bell was an ear-splitting shriek, almost drowning Wishart's shouted order for the motors to be stopped. Jake Cameron was struggling across the compartment, aiming for the auxiliary switchboard, to shut that hideous noise off by breaking the main gyro switch. Bodies all over the place – men trying to sort themselves out, find out where they were. Wishart yelled, pitching his voice up to beat that bell, 'Emergency lights!' Jake reached the board and found the gyro switch and pulled it out. The racket stopped. Then by chance his hand touched another switch that was hanging loose and must have been thrown out by the impact. He wasn't certain he was doing the right thing – electrics weren't his strongest suit – but he took a chance and made the switch, and the lights immediately glowed up everywhere – not the emergency circuits but the main ones. A hand that had been groping close to his own turned out to be Hobday's. As first lieutenant he did know all about the boat's electrical systems, and he'd been trying to locate the switch that Jake had come across by chance.

Wishart said, 'Well done. Now give me a magnetic course, pilot.' For the time being, the gyro would be out of action. Wishart was as calm as a vicar at a garden party. Calmer – than some vicars. Dixon, the leading electrician, had come for'ard from the motor-room. 'Both motors stopped, sir.' Small round eyes in his moon-face were checking items on the auxiliary board. McVeigh reported, 'Still pumpin' on "A" tank, sir.' Everyone seemed to be back in their normal places. Hobday told Agnew, 'Ask PO Leech to check the bilges. All compartments check for leaks and report.' He looked at Dixon. 'Better have a sight of the battery tanks.'

If any cells had been cracked there'd be an acid spillage. Then any sea-water that might be in the tank already or that got into it later would create chlorine gas.

Reports were arriving to the effect that no leaks had been detected. The coxswain murmured, 'She's light enough, sir.' He'd seen a faint stirring of the needle on his gauge. There was a depth-gauge in front of each of the two 'planesmen. Hobday told McVeigh, 'Stop the pump.'

'Check the bow shutters, Number One.' Wishart, moving over to consult with his navigator at the chart table, asked Nick Everard, 'Are you all right?'

Nick was on his chair again. He indicated the bunk above him, where Burtenshaw was nursing bruises to various parts of his anatomy. 'Soldier took a bit of a high-dive.' Burtenshaw had been catapulted out of his bunk, and it was sheer luck he hadn't landed on top of Nick. Robins had managed to hold on, somehow. Burtenshaw told Wishart, 'I'm all right, sir, thank you.'

'Good.' Wishart leant on the table beside Jake. 'Well?'

'Our former course is north fourteen-and-a-half west, by magnetic, sir. But that last fix—'

'We must be here.' Wishart's finger tapped the chart. 'Somewhere near that nine-fathom sounding. So we're through the narrowest part already. The last bearing of that bunch must have been the high ground behind Kephez, not the point itself.'

Jake nodded. 'So now we need to steer – well, north thirty-five west, or—'

'That'll do.' Wishart turned away. 'Your gear in order, Weatherspoon?'

'Still 'earing 'im, sir. North-west – very faint now, an'—'

Dixon told Hobday, 'Dampish in the tank, but—'

'Any smell?'

The fat man wrinkled his nose. 'Always a bit of a niff, sir. Can't say it's no worse 'n what—'

'Tell Cole to wash through with soda. You'd better get back on the motors, yourself.'

'Aye aye, sir . . . I – do think it's all right, sir, in—'

Wishart cut in: 'Dixon – *I* thought we were in forty fathoms . . .' He asked Roost, 'Ship's head now?'

Cole was with Rowbottom on the main switchboard, freeing Dixon to work on the gyro. Jake had been tinkering at it with him; he came back now to join the others at the wardroom table. Passing Hobday, who was leaning against the ladder and humming to

530

himself as he watched the trim, he offered, 'Like me to take over for a spell?'

Hobday's otherwise sharp nose had a round end to it, like a knob. Gleaming with sweat on it, it was more noticeable. He shook his head. 'I'll tell you when I do.'

Wishart was saying, 'Mistake to take too much for granted, but it looks as if they must have reckoned we were on our way out of the straits when we popped up. Otherwise there'd be hunting craft now like fleas on a dog's back.'

Jake said, sitting down, 'You mean a Turkish dog.'

'You have a point.'

Robins had one too: 'What made us shoot down and hit the bottom as we did?'

'We had to get deeper quickly, to avoid that Turk. At twenty feet the bridge and periscope standards aren't far under the surface, you see. But we must've been in or on a high-density layer of water – to break through it we had to take in ballast and speed up. It did the trick rather too well. And we were in shallower water than we'd thought.'

Robins rolled over on to his back. Question-time was over, apparently. Jake asked Burtenshaw, 'Don't you want any explanations of anything?'

'Since you mention it.' The Marine pointed to a brass flap in the deck amidships. 'That bearded chap sloshed two bucketfuls of what looked like dirty water down through the hole there. Is that a reasonable thing to do?'

'The battery tanks are down there. Two of them. The cells stand on wooden gratings, and if you get a crack in one of them you get acid spilling. To neutralise it we dump in a solution of common soda that washes through under the grating and gets pumped out at the other end. If you didn't, the acid would burn a hole, eventually – and there are ballast tanks further down, under the batteries. Also, if salt water mixed with the acid you'd get chlorine gas, which – well, you're hot on science, aren't you?'

'Oh, *red*-hot.' Burtenshaw quoted from some textbook, ' "Yellowish-green gas of pungent and irritating odour and peculiar taste. Acts violently on the lungs and causes—" '

From outside the hull – for'ard somewhere – a harsh, rasping noise . . .

'Stop together – slow astern together!' Instantaneously, Wishart

531

had taken over. Nick thought, trying to keep out of everybody's way, *Here we go again* . . .

Jake Cameron headed for his chart table. Moving away, he'd knocked Burtenshaw's book off the corner of the table. He turned back, and picked it up.

'Sorry.'

Burtenshaw nodded, and finished that quote: '"– causes death by choking".'

'What?'

'Chlorine gas. Causes—'

'Oh, yes.' He went to the chart table. The scraping noise was drawing for'ard as the boat gathered sternway to clear the mine wire. Jake saw that Wishart had recently put a new DR on the chart and that at about this time they should have been altering course to starboard, eastward, to round Nagara Point.

'Stop port. Starboard ten. How much water here, pilot?'

'On the DR there's thirty-one fathoms, sir.'

'Magnetic course to clear Nagara?' Wishart saw Dixon still working on the gyro. 'Leave that. I want you on main motors, Dixon.'

The scraping noise stopped. In the thick silence Jake told his captain, 'Course of north sixty-six east should take us down the middle.' Wishart nodded, giving the thing time. Crabb's and Morton's eyes were fixed on their gauges; Morton, as ever, streamed with sweat. McVeigh's mouth was slightly open, showing his yellow teeth. The other two ERAs, Knight and Bradshaw, stood motionless, staring at fixed points on the deckheads, their expressions perhaps deliberately preoccupied. Signalman Ellery squatted near Agnew, close to the after bulkhead; his brown eyes in the monkeyish face never seemed to look anywhere except at Wishart. Agnew looked tired. He was a growing lad and he needed regular sleep. Burtenshaw, in the chair opposite Nick's, was leafing without much apparent enthusiasm through the pages of his Tolstoy, while behind his shoulder Able Seaman Louis Lewis leant against the curved edge of the latched-back bulkhead door and picked his nose with a thumb and forefinger. Lewis was not, Nick thought, the ideal choice for a wardroom messman.

'Stop starboard. Midships. North sixty east did you say, pilot?'

'Sixty-six, sir.'

Wishart cut into the helm and telegraph acknowledgements. 'Port fifteen. Slow ahead together. One hundred·and fifty feet.'

Roost's broad, countryman's face was placid, amiable as he spun the wheel. Port wheel, starboard rudder. 'Fifteen o' port wheel on, sir.' The motors' forward thrust allowed screws and 'planes to bite, and the 'planesmen had her edging downwards. Jake, staring at the chart, wondered whether the middle of the channel, the track he'd just pencilled on it, was really the best bet. One might alternatively have hugged the shoreline around the point or gone over to the northern side. But for that matter one might also have spun a coin. The mines might be anywhere. This might be the best track, or the worst. He saw again in his mind that line in his own erratic scrawl, *You needn't worry for two seconds about me, you know*. But thinking of her, of what might become of her if she were left alone, *that* brought worry. Real, and sharp. He told himself not to think about it: to remember that thing about the coward dying a thousand deaths. Of course, one could argue about whether it could really be considered 'brave' to be unimaginative; but that wasn't the point, it was a matter of control, of simply not allowing the imagination that much rope. Mental discipline, he told himself. He was leaning with his forearms on the chart, looking down at the shape of the Dardanelles and this zigzag bottleneck in the middle of them. He decided that even if it was not cowardly it was damn silly to allow oneself to think about the one and only aspect of one's situation that made this kind of ordeal difficult or frightening. (Begging a question slightly there: but never mind, the basic reasoning was sound enough.) The reason you did think about it, of course, was that it was there, real, and it was bad, so your mind dug away at it in order to flush it out, beat it somehow. But you couldn't: and you knew by now that you couldn't, so surely to God—

A *clang* – sharp, and then reverberating. On the other side, starboard side, amidships.

Several pairs of eyes – heads – had jerked in the direction of the sound. Jake had caught his breath; he let it seep away through clenched teeth. That clang had been the slap of a mine-wire against the submarine's side, and now it had begun its grinding passage aft along the saddle-tanks.

'Stop starboard. Port ten.'

Jake looked over at the passengers. Burtenshaw was facing the other way; he couldn't see if he was reading or just holding the book and listening. Robins, up on the bunk, had his eyes shut and he'd jerked his hands up to press their palms against his ears. Well, when you'd nothing to do except lie there and listen . . . Only

Everard was watching what was happening in the control room. Jake wondered if he was scared, or as unruffled as he looked. That lack of expression could well be a mask: as one knew only too well oneself . . . He turned back to the chart. He heard CPO Crabb's report, 'Hundred an' fifty, sir', and the other two – young Agnew's and the helmsman's. He realised, studying the chart, that in fact there wasn't really any alternative to this track that Wishart had put them on. The straits ahead at Nagara were less than one mile wide from shore to shore; there was very little room on the northern side, and closer to the point itself there were several shallow spots. Also, there was a note on the chart in his own recent Indian-ink lettering about a reported inshore current on that side. It had put *Goeben* on the beach here – obviously she'd tried to cut it too fine, but a submarine certainly couldn't afford to monkey with it. If she got swept up on those shallows the Turks would get some easy target practice, they'd take their time about blowing her to pieces. What it came down to was brutally simple: that to get through this narrow stretch you had to take your chances with whatever mines or nets they'd planted in it.

CHAPTER 5

'Down periscope.' Wishart told Hobday, 'Still too murky for a fix. But we're more or less in the middle, and that's what matters.'

The clock on the for'ard bulkhead showed two thirty-five. By dead reckoning E.57 should have been more than two miles past Nagara Point. After another two-and-a-half miles they'd be out of this widening funnel of land and in a position where an eighteen-mile run on one course would take them through to the Marmara. Two-and-a-half miles, with the submerged tide added to the boat's slow grouped-down speed, would take half an hour; and barring accidents or interference the final run could be expected to take another three or four.

Wishart moved over to the chart table and leant on it beside Jake Cameron. A favourite attitude for them both, Nick thought, glancing that way. Characteristic. Seen from the rear like this, their posteriors, side by side, looked elephantine. Burtenshaw pointed: 'You could move that column over to this one.'

'Ah.' Nick rather wished the Marine would allow him to play this game of patience on his own. He nodded. 'So I can.' Burtenshaw was on the other side of the table, seeing the cards upside-down and trying to spot each opportunity before Nick did. He moved the file of cards. 'Thanks.' Patience, indeed; and a card out of Wishart's hand, the example of his dealings with Robins. Wishart's voice reached them quietly from the other side of the compartment: 'I think we can trust the DR all right. We'll turn here—' he poked with dividers at the next and last turning-point, an alteration of about thirty degrees to port into that long home stretch – 'say at five past three.'

Jake nodded. 'Puts us about halfway.'

'It's not the mere distance that counts, pilot, is it? In terms of the bally awkward bits we're the devil of a lot better off than halfway!'

The Narrows were behind them. A few hours ago the thought of being through and on this side of them had been a kind of mirage thought, a distant dream to long for. In fact the process of getting this far hadn't been nearly as tricky as it might have been.

'Plenty of water.' Wishart was checking the soundings on the chart, along the pencilled track. The nearest sounding to the DR position indicated a depth of fifty fathoms – three hundred feet. He muttered, thinking aloud, 'Might try it at a hundred. Get us the tide and—' following the soundings all along that track – 'yes, safe enough all the way. H'm?' He nodded, and pushed himself off the table. 'Hundred feet, Number One.'

The farther out she got now, into the wider north-eastern reach, the less likely it was that there'd be mines or nets. The narrow sections were the obvious ones to block. A feeling of relief had begun to make itself felt as much as half an hour ago, when Nagara Point had been reckoned to be just abaft the beam. The preceding period had been unpleasant and getting more so, and it was about then that they'd begun to realise that intervals between mine-wire encounters had been lengthening. *Up to* that point, they'd been shortening. From there on until Wishart had ordered periscope depth for this last check on their position, the boat had been motoring quietly along without incident.

Now she was gliding down again. Hobday murmured, 'Easy with the angle, cox'n.' He was wary of the tricky densities, anxious to avoid another nose-dive or more bouncings on the seabed. If she tried one of those stunts here she'd hit nothing until she was three hundred feet down, and that was well below her tested depth.

After a period of tension, its lessening produced a sense of ease, even of exhilaration – at having come through, survived the hazards. You knew it could start again, but it never felt as if it would; it felt as if the strains were over, the testing process left behind for ever. There was a tendency to joke, and for the jokes to seem funnier than they were. Everyone was relaxing without anyone admitting to having been in a state of tension: and when you thought about it, even *that* seemed funny . . . A number of men requested permission to go aft to the heads; they'd been allowed to, one at a time. Not to the heads themselves, except for two men in the last few minutes, because at depths below thirty feet you couldn't use them. Sea-pressure prevented them being blown, discharged, when the boat was deep. For use below thirty feet there were buckets behind the engines.

Twenty-six feet: twenty-seven . . . The 'planesmen were easing her down very gently.

Robins, in Hobday's bunk, propped himself up on one elbow as the needles crept down past the thirty-feet mark.

'Are we past the Narrows yet?'

Wishart had just propped his weight against the control-room ladder. He glanced round, towards that corner, and nodded.

'Yes. We're—'

A jarring thump: and then heavy slithering noises overhead.

'Stop both. Half astern both.'

'Both motors half astern, sir!'

It sounded like something weighty being dragged along the casing. It had started up forward near the bow, but – well, whatever it was it must be sliding up the jumping-wire and the wire would be pushing it upwards, right over the tops of the two periscope standards if the boat maintained her forward motion. But she wasn't; she was going astern now. She jerked: it was a sort of lurch, quite a powerful one. A fish would be like this when it had taken a hook and the line suddenly tightened so that the fish felt it for the first time and tried to wrench away.

'Stop together. Group up.'

Robins had flopped down, and shut his eyes. Burtenshaw rested his forehead on his clasped hands on the table top. Everard was rather slowly shuffling the cards.

Grouping up was going to shake the guts out of the battery. Jake Cameron read the log, noting the figure and the time in his navigator's notebook, then marked a new and corresponding DR position. Doing that, he broke the lead of his pencil. He had plenty of spares in the rack, already sharpened.

Unlikely to be a mine-wire. Net? But when it had got hold of her she'd been at about thirty feet, and now she seemed to be right *under* it. A net with a bottom edge at thirty feet would hardly seem worth laying, in fifty fathoms.

The submarine's motors were stopped, and yet she was rock-steady, still. Wishart looked from the gauges to Hobday.

'Trim can't be all *that* perfect.'

The needles were so static that the gauges might have been shut off. The for'ard one read thirty-six feet and the coxswain's a foot more than that. The bubble in the tube reflected the same bow-up angle.

Nick was shuffling the cards still. If it was a surface net, there might be mines below it. It was a combination that had been used for some while in the Dover Patrol's defences in the Channel. You forced the U-boats to dive in order to pass under the net, and they dived into a curtain of mines. It had seemed a good idea, as a device for catching *German* submarines, but from where he was sitting now his view of it was somewhat different.

Wishart said, 'My guess is we're not *in* a net, but just hanging on the bottom of it somehow.'

He looked quite calm, thoughtful, trying to work it out. Hobday suggested, 'Might be the gun hooked in it.' Wishart nodded. 'I thought of that, but what about the jumping-wire?' Other faces reflected his own puzzlement. He shrugged. 'Anyway, let's see if we can spare the battery and break loose by flooding alone. As last time, only static.' He told Hobday, 'Stand by the internal main ballasts.'

He didn't mean all of them: just the ones that had kingstons. Hobday ordered, 'Stand by "A", "B" and "Z" kingstons.' Hobday had switched over to his 'calm' tone. Lewis scuttled over to crouch in the wardroom corner with his hands on the wheel of 'B'. That internal was under the for'ard battery tank, and the shaft from the wheel ran down inside the chain-locker, which was immediately for'ard of it. About six feet further for'ard, in the torpedo stowage compartment, Able Seaman 'Close-'aul' Anderson folded his long body down so he could get a grip on the operating wheel of 'A'; and in the after ends Stoker Peel would be ready by this time to open the stern tank, 'Z'.

Wishart called for'ard, 'Open "A" kingston!'

There was a small lurch, as the sea rushed into the tank. The bow might have dropped about an inch. The needle in the for'ard gauge had quivered; now it was still again.

'Open "B" kingston!'

Lewis wrenched the wheel round. You could hear the movement of the gearing in the shaft and the slam of sudden pressure entering the tank below. From above, outside the boat, there was a creak, a sound of straining; then nothing more.

Crabb muttered, 'Somethin' gave, up top, sir. By the gun, I reckon.'

'Third time lucky, cox'n.' Wishart ordered, 'Open "Z" kingston!' Ellery, at the bulkhead doorway, passed it aft, and a second later the boat trembled very slightly. Not enough to make any

538

difference on the gauges, but the bubble had shifted for'ard by about a quarter of one degree. And everything was silent now: warm, close air, nobody moving, smell of oil and sweat and the yellowish light glinting on brass and on the running condensation on the paintwork and on the shine of pale, sweat-damp, stubbly faces.

Wishart looked disappointed. Annoyed, perhaps – but not, Nick thought, particularly worried. It might be an act, he realised, or it might be that to the submariners this was less hair-raising than it seemed to an outsider.

'Pity. Have to use some juice after all.' Wishart rubbed his jaw. 'Never mind. Once we're past this lot we'll be home and dry. We're – what, grouped up?'

Agnew confirmed it.

Jake was thinking that dawn would be breaking soon, up there. Daylight would flush the surface of the straits and light the hills. This submarine was only ten yards below the surface, and she was suspended probably from large, brightly coloured buoys which presently she'd start tugging to and fro. Ten minutes ago they'd been preparing to congratulate themselves, thinking they'd come through the worst of it. He told himself soberly, *That was the silly thing. This is the reality. We knew it was going to be difficult and here we are, it is, and we've some way to go yet, that's all.*

Robins lay like a dead man, flat on his back with his eyes shut. What did a man like Robins think about, Jake wondered, when he wanted to turn his mind elsewhere? Bob Burtenshaw had climbed up on to Wishart's bunk, after first offering it to Nick Everard. Everard was sitting with his shoulder against the drawers underneath the bunks, and still fiddling with those cards. Not looking at them: just fiddling with them, shuffling, cutting, shuffling again.

'Half ahead together.'

The boat trembled as her motors, with 220 volts on them, sent her surging forward. The depth-gauge needles swung sharply – but not far: one to thirty-four feet and the other to just under thirty-five. She'd only made that lunge, and been brought up hard, stopped dead.

'Stop together.'

'Stop together, sir.' Agnew's voice was higher, thinner than it had been.

'Half astern together!'

For a second or two it felt as if she was going to pull clear. Then the rush astern stopped just as the other had. As if rubber bands of vast dimensions had been stretched to their limit and finally held instead of breaking.

'*Full* astern together!'

The note of the motors rose to a high, pulsating whine. From overhead they heard that same creaking noise. Straining metal. Wishart called, 'Stop both!'

If he'd let the motors go on racing he'd have burnt them out, as well as draining the batteries. Now all sounds died away again, gave place to new ones – the odd ticking of relaxing steel, easing of strain from rivets. Jake was thinking about rivets because of that creaking, which had sounded like metal bending, and because Wishart, moving as if for no special purpose, had just come to this end of the control room and stopped, quite casually, to examine the deckhead. He said to Hobday, still staring up at the lines of rivets, 'Better pump out those internals.'

'Shut "A", "B" and "Z" kingstons!'

Wishart was on his way back to his usual position by the for'ard periscope, midway between the steering pedestal and the 'planesmen. Jake asked himself, *Now what?* Around the stuffy, hot compartment he could see much the same question in other faces. Facial expressions, movements of the facial muscles, could very largely be controlled; but eyes, after a certain period of strain, tended to give the game away.

As navigator, of course, he was lucky in that respect. He could turn his back on the others while he studied the chart, and he could fiddle with the instruments while he rested his powers of resilience, recovered his mental breath. But there was only one answer he could find to the question he'd just asked himself, that *now what*? Simply that if you couldn't get out of a net when you were dived, you'd have to surface and cut it free as they'd done earlier in the night. But then two other questions came up at once. One: would it be possible for the boat to surface, with the enormous weight of the net on her? Two: if the answer to that question was 'yes' – which he rather doubted – could the job be done soon enough and quickly enough to take advantage of whatever period of darkness or semi-darkness was still left? Depending on how thoroughly enmeshed they might be, how long might they have to lie up there exposed to coastal batteries at point-blank range and illuminated by what would almost certainly, in these exotic parts, be a sensationally beautiful sunrise?

540

'Stop the port ballast pump. Shut "A" suction.' Hobday had already pumped out 'B' and shut it off, but the other pump was still sucking on 'Z'. He looked better now: during the burst of full-ahead grouped up his face had been stiff with agony – because his battery had been having its guts torn out and they might as well have been his own for the way he'd felt it. He told McVeigh now, 'Stop the starboard pump. Shut "Z" suction.' Shutting the inboard vents as well as the suctions would be automatic. Ellery was passing that last part of the order aft; Wishart looked across at Jake.

'Ready for another bathe, pilot?'

Oh, Christ . . . He nodded. 'Sir.'

'Second cox'n, you fit?'

'Aye, sir.'

'Get ready then.' Hobday told Morton, 'Ask the TI to come and look after the fore 'planes for you.'

'Signalman.' Wishart nodded towards the lower hatch. 'Open up.' He told Hobday, 'Might get a preview through the ports. See how we're snagged.'

Round the gun, Jake thought, that's where . . . He also guessed that the gun was being just about dragged off its mounting. During that surging to and fro it had felt as if the point of suspension was just about overhead, slightly for'ard of the conning-tower – which was where the gun was, the twelve-pounder, on its gundeck a few feet higher than the casing. Wishart had climbed up into the tower and Ellery was at the bottom of the ladder, peering up through the open lower hatch. Jake tied the tapes of his swimming collar, and Burtenshaw, up on Wishart's bunk, lifted a couple of fingers and muttered, 'Once again, best of luck.'

'Thanks.' He liked Burtenshaw. It was pretty sporting of a Harrow boy, he thought, to join up in the ranks. But none of these people, once the war was over, would want to know anyone like Jake bloody Cameron. As for Everard – still clutching those cards, for God's sake – Everard, a baronet's son who'd eventually become a baronet himself, might as well have been a creature from some other world. He *was*, in fact. Jake thought, *It doesn't matter: when the war ends I'll be too busy earning a living to worry about keeping up with baronets.* But did he care, really? He didn't know: and this was no time for considering one's place in the class system. The *war* wasn't a time for it: that was the whole point, surely, the way the question arose in the first place! The torpedo gunner's

541

mate – known as the TI, short for torpedo instructor – had come from his domain for'ard and was sliding on to the fore 'planesman's seat. CPO Rinkpole's bald head gleamed in its half-circle of greyish hair. Hobday murmured, 'Morning, TI.'

'Like old times, sir.' Rinkpole grinned sideways at the coxswain. 'All right there, Reggie?' Morton came for'ard in his net-cutting outfit, carrying tools for both of them. Jake relieved him of one set and told Hobday, 'We're ready.'

'Stand by to surface!' The routine reports began to come in, and Wishart climbed back down the ladder; he looked cheerful.

'We've got net – wire-rope mesh – all over the forepart of the boat, at right-angles to the fore-and-aft line. It's draped over the jumping-wire and the starboard side of the hanging edge has meshed itself over the twelve-pounder. All we've got to do – you and Morton, pilot – is get that clear and over the side. You may not even have to cut it, once it's slack all round – and I'm going to *try* to slip out of it as we surface.' He turned to Hobday. 'We need another trimmed-down surfacing, but it'll be stern-first and we'll have the weight of the net for'ard. We should be far enough up when there's ten feet on the gauges – so stop blowing at, say, twelve.'

Hobday nodded. He looked a bit doubtful, though. The big question was whether with the weight of the net on her she'd come up at all. It was quite possible, Jake thought, that even with all her tanks blown the thing would still hold her down. It was more than possible, it was *likely*, he thought. And in that case—

In that case she'd be stuck, in this outsize fish-trap.

'Now you two—' Wishart was addressing him and Morton – 'It's not as dark as it might be, now. We won't show more of ourselves than we have to, but we're certain to be spotted at once, this time, and obviously we'll be shot at. Consequently—' he smiled suddenly – 'don't loaf about, what?'

Morton had taken the point. 'Faster 'n that, sir.'

'Ready to surface, sir.'

Hobday meant, to *attempt* to surface.

'Number One – we'll go astern, slow grouped down, enough power just to pull us back from—' he jerked a thumb upwards and for'ard – '*that* damn thing, and get out from under at least some of its weight.' Hobday nodded. Wishart told him, 'Blow five, six, seven and eight to start with, then three and four if she isn't coming up. If you can get her up like that, leave one and two main ballast full. If the bow's awash it'll be easier to shove the net off or slide out from under it. Right?'

'Aye aye, sir.' Hobday looked happy enough with the programme. Wishart put one foot on the bottom rung of the ladder.

'Group down. Slow astern together.'

Jake and Morton, clanking with tools, moved up behind him. Agnew reported, 'Grouper down, sir, both motors slow—'

'Surface vessels closing from astern, sir!'

Weatherspoon: from the cabinet. Changing everything . . . *Ending* everything?

'Stop both.' Wishart, wooden-faced, stepped off the ladder. Weatherspoon reported, 'HE is confused, sir. There's more than one. Might be the same pair comin' back, sir.'

With his eyes on the gleaming, dripping deckhead, Weatherspoon frowned – as if, Jake thought, watching him – as if something most unpleasant had just been whispered to him through the earphones. He'd closed his eyes now, concentrating. Opening them, blinking, he eased the headset backwards, freeing his ears; he told Wishart, 'Two littl'uns coming from right ahead, sir, and this new 'un, bigger 'n slower, closing astern.'

Wishart nodded slowly, digesting that, putting the scene together in his mind. For just a moment as he turned away, Jake glimpsed a flash of anger – despair? – in his captain's eyes. Then there was nothing but the habitual calm appraising of a new situation. That would have been anger, Jake told himself, not despair: he'd be sick by now of being messed about. Who wasn't, for God's sake? Wishart announced quietly, 'Unlikely we'll be surfacing. But you two hang on—' he'd glanced at Jake and the second coxswain – 'in case they're just passing.'

You didn't need earphones now to hear the Turks' propellors. Like the first sound of a distant oncoming train: once you heard it, it got louder quickly. Weatherspoon, in the doorway of his cabinet where he could see and be seen, said, 'This pair's launches, sir. Other's more like a gunboat, trawler, somethin'.'

Wishart folded his arms on a rung of the ladder and rested his chin on his forearms.

'One of 'em's stoppin', sir.' The leading tel added, 'One o' the launches. Big one still closin'.'

That one was stopping was enough to confirm what it was about. The Turks knew they had a submarine in this net.

'Shut watertight doors, sir?'

'Not yet, Number One . . . But you two—' he meant Jake and Morton – 'get dressed. No outing this time. Number One – pass the word for all hands to keep quiet and not move about.'

Hobday sent Ellery aft and Lewis for'ard with that order. The propeller noise rose to a peak as it passed overhead; it drew away, lessening, on the other side. The net, evidently, could be crossed by surface craft. Weatherspoon reported, 'Slowin', sir. Stoppin', shouldn't wonder.'

You could hear the decreasing revolutions – slowing and fading. But through that disappearing sound a deeper, stronger rhythm was developing: the newcomer from the south. This would be the gunboat. Out of Chanak, probably. Burtenshaw whispered from his bunk, 'What's happening now?'

He wasn't deaf: he must have known. Jake guessed he wanted to be told it wasn't as bad as he thought it was.

'Patrol boats. They may start dropping charges, presently.' Everard had said it. Jake nodded. 'It's possible.' He went to the chart table before the Marine could ask a question that he'd have to try to answer and might find difficult. Something like *How can we possibly get out of this?* He pulled his serge trousers up and began tucking shirt-tails into them while he listened to the rising note of the approaching screw. Much heavier-sounding and slower than the first pair. A trawler of some sort, and it would carry depth-charges as well as at least one gun, and with E.57 immobilised in this trap they wouldn't have to *waste* any charges either. In the days of the first Dardanelles patrols, one had heard, when they caught submarines in this kind of situation they lowered small charges on wires from boats and detonated them electrically. In those days there'd been no such things as depth-charges. Just little ones on wires. They wouldn't be little ones today. The drumbeat of the trawler's screw was slowing.

Stopping.

Robins had his eyes open. He was lying on his back still and he didn't appear to have moved a centimetre, but his eyes were open and staring at the deckhead, the rivulets of condensation – or trying to see *through* it . . . Jake told him in his mind, *You won't see them floating down, chummy. You'll hear them, when they arrive.* Burtenshaw was looking at him: Jake winked. Everard was leaning forward in his chair and watching Wishart, who'd just told Hobday that he was going up into the tower to take another gander out through the ports.

Jake thought suddenly, *Surface, man the gun, chance our luck?*

If the trawler was really close to E.57, the coastal batteries would have their fire masked. Perhaps the submarine could pop up suddenly – if the net allowed her to – and loose off a few rounds from the twelve-pounder at point-blank range while he and Morton cut the net free: and the Lewis gun would come in handy too, spraying the Turks' decks to keep them away from *their* gun . . . A few seconds ago the idea had seemed crazy, a daydream – but wasn't it something more than that, when you thought about it? At least, a chance? Better than lying here like a salmon in a net, waiting to be gaffed? This way there was *no* chance, none at all. That was what he'd been anxious not to have to admit to Burtenshaw. He looked round now, a first move in what would be a hesitant, diffident approach to the skipper. Third hands weren't expected to advise their captains or propose tactics . . . One might also argue that if one had been anything other than a third hand one might not have allowed oneself to start thinking on such suicidal lines. And then again, which was suicide: trying that, or waiting to be blasted to the surface?

Wishart, returning from the tower, stopped halfway down the ladder.

'We might wangle ourselves out of it, if we're clever. Come up here, Number One. Pilot, take over the trim.'

Jake moved into Hobday's place behind the 'planesmen. 'All right, cox'n?'

'Never better, sir.' Jake thought, *Hell of a lad, old Crabb!* He added in that nut-cracking voice of his, 'Skipper'll soon 'ave us out o' this little lot, sir.'

'Of course he will!'

As if he'd never doubted it . . . And he could see more hopeful expressions all around the compartment. A swift and total change of mood. Ten minutes ago there hadn't seemed to be much anyone could do except wait for the bangs to start; now Wishart had his tail up again, and if whatever he was planning didn't work, Jake thought, he'd put forward his own scheme for a shooting-match.

Hobday came down the ladder. 'Cameron – you're wanted up there.'

He went up. No sound from the enemy over their heads. What might the Turks be so busy with – fitting detonators to the charges?

'Here, pilot. Take a look.'

He climbed a few rungs and joined Wishart in the tower. One

would hear the trawler's screws again, of course, before any charges came, there'd be that much notice. 'Here.' Wishart moved aside, giving him access to the little conning-tower port with its thick glass window. Between Jake and Wishart, there wasn't much room to spare.

Greenish-black water: but the shape of the submarine's forepart was clear to see. He saw the net too, a web overhanging everything. Only the half-light of very early morning made it hazy; the water itself was totally transparent. Wishart said, 'Look at the gun and the way it's caught up.'

Wiping the glass made it much clearer; condensation gathered quickly. The gun was a dozen feet for'ard and below the level of this observation port; its barrel pointed upwards at twenty degrees to the horizontal and was trained fore-and-aft, so that looking down from this angle you saw its whole length, breech-block to muzzle. The net was a pattern of loops and distorted rectangles shimmering in what looked like greenish jelly. He wiped the glass again, concentrated on the entanglement round the gun. Wishart said, 'The bights under the barrel can't be difficult to get rid of, once we dislodge the other bunch. We're double-hooked – that's why we couldn't clear it either ahead or astern. But I think if we lighten her and move ahead, with the angle right, that lot under the breech will swing clear – once the weight's off it, d'you see? Then I'll angle her the other way and come out stern-first. But the timing's got to be just right. What I can't have is any degree of time-lag between my orders and the motors doing what I tell 'em – and that's what *you're* for – there, in the hatch. Go on.'

He slid down the ladder and took up a position with his head in the rim of the hatch. He heard Weatherspoon report to Hobday, 'One launch on the move, sir – one o' the first lot.' Wishart called down, 'Blow three and four main ballast!'

No need to repeat it: those valves were already open on the tank inlets, and McVeigh had heard the order and wrenched open the high-pressure valve; there was a roar of expanding air as it ripped into the LP line and through it into the pair of midships saddle-tanks. Jake looked up, saw Wishart's face close to the glass port; he waited for the next order. With the noise of blowing, that roar of air, he'd be needed this next time.

'Stop blowing three and four!'

He yelled it almost instantaneously, and the noise cut off abruptly as McVeigh shut the blow.

'Slow ahead both!'

'Slow ahead—'

Ellery shouted the order aft. Quicker than using telegraphs.

'Stop together!'

Jake saved his breath: the signalman's shout had overlapped Wishart's order. But now a new sound was building up: fast screws closing, coming over. They were too fast-revving to be the gunboat's . . . Wishart shouted, 'Blow five and six!'

The rip of air again . . . And propellers passing over now: fast, loud, reaching a peak of sound and then – fading, into the blowing sound . . . 'Stop blowing! Slow ahead together!'

Jake yelled the orders down, and the noise cut off; he heard Ellery pass the slow-ahead order, and almost immediately after that the first charge exploded. A ringing crash: as if the submarine was a gong and they'd belted her with a hammer. The crash of the explosion reverberated away in jerky throbs as the boat flung over to starboard: lights flickered, went out, came on again. The launch, obviously, had dropped that charge, and Jake guessed that the larger ship had brought charges up, that the peaceful interval had been the time she'd taken to issue them to the launches.

'Stop together!'

Jake and Ellery in chorus . . .

'Open five and six main vents!'

McVeigh grabbed the levers and jerked them back, and Jake heard the thuds of the vents dropping open in the tank-tops.

'Blow one and two main ballast!'

Getting a bow-up angle now, so as to slide the gun's barrel out of its enclosing wires . . . The second launch – or the first one making a second run – passed overhead. Jake realised that Wishart must have got the breech-end of the gun clear in that first bit of joggling around; otherwise he wouldn't be angling her the other way now, he'd still be trying to shed the first lot. He had the shadowed, greenish picture of it in his mind, the net draped down over the jumping-wire, its starboard-side folds caught in and around the gun. She must have struck not quite at right-angles, for it to have swung in under the wire like that.

'Stop blowing!'

'Stop—'

The second charge was closer than the first. The boat rattled like an old tin can as the echoes of it boomed around her, through her. The lights went out: Wishart's voice called down into pitch

547

darkness, 'Slow astern together!' Jake heard Ellery pass that aft. Looking upwards he saw greenish light glowing through the little oblong window and illuminating the top half of his captain's face. That was daylight filtered through thirty feet of Dardanelles. He felt movement: she was responding, coming astern, pulling herself out of the net's grasp. He told himself, *Easy – don't count your chickens* . . . Lights came on: the emergency ones, fewer and less bright than the main ones. He moved down one rung on the ladder; he'd gone up one at some point without being aware of doing so.

'Stop together!'

But there'd been a flat, angry tone in that order. And if she'd been clear of the net, he wouldn't have stopped her, he'd have gone on, got her right out away from it; the net, after all, had to be the Turks' point of aim with their depth-charges. So what *now*? Jake stared up at his captain's dark bulk half-filling the tower; and distantly, but rapidly getting louder, he heard one of the launches starting another attacking run. A moment ago he'd thought they were free, on the move . . . Wishart told him, 'There's still some net caught round the trainer's handwheel, the base of it.' The enemy's screws were pounding closer, louder. If the launch passed close over the submarine's forepart, Jake realised, Wishart might actually see it, see the dark hull rush past and the whirring silver of its screws. He shouted upwards. 'Mightn't it part with some weight on it, sir?' Then he understood, while Wishart still peered out through the port and didn't answer, what his objection would be. They'd heard the strain coming on the gundeck earlier, and much more of it might wrench rivets loose in the pressure-hull. The gun was bolted to its deck, but the gundeck in turn was riveted to the hull; if the bolts held, the strain would come on the actual plates. The enemy launch was about to pass right overhead: the peak of its propeller noise was coming – *now* . . .

'Half astern together!'

Ellery had shouted it aft: Jake felt, through the rungs of the ladder, the vibration from the boat's motors. He looked up towards Wishart in the tower, and at that moment the charge exploded. He saw Wishart blinded by its flash and thrown backwards against the far side of the tower. Signal flares cascaded from a locker, rained down on him: everything was coming down, including Wishart, and he grabbed the ladder tightly, braced himself just in time to receive his captain's not by any means puny weight. The boat meanwhile seemed to have shot astern with a steep and increasing stern-down angle and a sharpish list to port: she was righting herself from the list now. Wishart roared beside Jake's ear, 'Open one, two, three, four main vents! Fifty feet!' Main vents thudding open: Wishart had hauled himself off Jake: he was up there shutting the deadlight on the observation port. He shouted, 'Go on down, pilot!' Jake dropped through the hatch. The submarine was on an even keel athwartships but still had stern-down angle. He glimpsed the needles in the gauges passing forty-two, forty-four feet, then he was at the chart table and Wishart, tumbling through the hatch, panted, 'Stop together. Half ahead together. Signalman, shut the hatch. Pilot, what was our last course?'

'North sixty-east six east, sir.' It felt like a hundred years since they'd run into the net. Wishart told Roost, 'Steer that.' Gathering way forward, the boat was levelling and the 'planesmen weren't having to work so hard. Fifty-four feet on the gauges. Hobday saw Wishart looking at them critically and said, 'Rather not change the trim until I have to, sir. I think she's settling down.'

'Sixty feet.'

'Sixty feet, sir . . .' Now he *would* have to pump some out. Jake was thinking that sixty feet was fine so far as passing under the net was concerned, but there was still the possibility of mines at lower levels. Wishart might have been considering the same point: he told Hobday, 'Three minutes, to make sure we're under, then we'll come up to forty.' These next few *seconds*, Jake thought, were surely the ones that counted. But you couldn't have it both ways: you either risked catching the bottom of the net in the periscope standards or you made sure of passing below it. They could have ripped it, too, and there might be pieces trailing.

'Slow ahead together.' Wishart had glanced at Agnew: Hobday told him, 'Telegraphs.' With the motors running, the surface craft could hear them anyway. If they stopped rushing about and listened; and not even Turks would be so daft as to have headphones on while they were dropping charges.

'Both motors slow ahead, sir.'

'Any damage, Number One?'

'Slight leaks under the gun-mounting, sir.'

Wishart went quickly to the for'ard end of the control room, and Jake turned from the chart table and stared up at the deckhead. At first he couldn't see anything at all; the softness of the emergency lighting didn't help. Then he spotted it: the smallest trickle, from one in a line of rivet-heads.

He reached up, touching it. 'Here, sir.'

'Couple here, too.' Wishart said as he walked away, 'We'll see to it in the Marmara. At least, our gallant engineers will.' McVeigh grinned at him wolfishly. Wishart asked, 'Dixon doing something about the lights?'

'Yessir.' Hobday turned and looked at him; he'd got the trim right, at last. He said, 'By the way, sir – congratulations.'

'Eh?'

CPO Crabb growled, with his eyes on the gauge in front of him, 'Lads 'd say the same, sir, I reckon.'

'Oh.' Wishart shook his head. 'That last charge did it. There was a double loop round the trainer's handwheel, and the charge snapped it like a bit of string . . . God knows what shape your gun'll be in, Roost.'

'We'll find out by an' by, sir.'

The lights came on. Seconds later, the emergency ones went out. A long way astern, a charge exploded. Laughter exploded too. It seemed hilariously funny, in that moment, that the Turks might be thinking they still had a submarine in their net.

'Forty feet.'

'Forty feet, sir!'

'How long on this course, pilot?'

'Two miles, sir – then north forty-one east.'

'We'll alter by log reading.' It would be full daylight up there now, and silly to shove up a periscope if you didn't have to. If they wanted to imagine they still had her trapped – well, that was fine! Wishart added, 'We'll go to a hundred feet when we alter, and catch the current. Meanwhile, Number One, let's spare the box. When you're happy with the trim, stop one motor.'

'Aye aye, sir.'

The battery would be just about at its last gasp, by this time. There was no point in taking readings, though; however flat it was, it would be flatter before they reached the Marmara.

The leaking deckhead, Jake thought, might not be quite so small a trickle when they went deeper. In about half an hour they'd find out.

'Forty feet, sir.' Hobday told Agnew, 'Stop starboard.'

'Stop starboard, sir.'

Wishart moved for'ard, in the direction of the chart table. 'All right, Stone?'

Leading Stoker Stone nodded. 'Thank you, sir.' He was a

railwayman from Newhaven. His job at diving stations was looking after the starboard ballast pump – the pump itself, not the starter and motor, which McVeigh had charge of. A thin, worried-looking man. He'd told Jake – the night before they'd sailed, when Jake had been nosing around, trying to get to know the ship's company in a hurry – how he'd come to 'volunteer' for submarines. He'd had a cushy number in HMS *Vernon*, the Portsmouth torpedo and mine school, and the drafting PO had remarked to him one day, 'Time you made killick, Stone. Make a right good killick, you would.' 'Killick' meant, in this context, leading hand; a killick was the fouled-anchor badge that a leading seaman wore on his left arm. Stone, flattered, had listened; the PO had flannelled him along and told him, 'They're cryin' out for killick stokers, down the road.' He'd let his name go forward – and a few days later found himself in Fort Blockhouse, learning about submarines.

'*Dahn the road*, 'e says! If 'e meant *acrorss the bloody 'arbour* whyn't the bugger say so?'

Wishart asked him, pulling in his belly in order to squeeze by, 'Heard from that young lady of yours lately?'

'Writes reg'lar, sir.' He looked pleased about that. Wishart propped himself in the doorway of the wireless cabinet. 'Anything happening up there?'

'Confused HE astern, sir. Reckon they're chasin' their tails, sir.' Wishart nodded. He backed out of the cabinet and told Hobday, 'Fall out diving stations, Number One. Let's have a cup of tea.'

CHAPTER 6

'When you were briefing Cameron the other day, remember you mentioned the Flag Officer Aegean being sent home after *Goeben*'s breakout?'

Hobday was in the armchair, addressing Wishart, who was on his bunk. Robins was on the other bunk, Cameron was on watch, and Nick and Burtenshaw were across the table from Hobday. Wishart asked, 'What of it?'

'Were you joking when you said he dribbles?'

'By no means.' Wishart shuddered. 'It's no joking matter. He smokes a pipe continuously, and slobbers down his chin. Politeness demands that one should look at him when he's mumbling at you, and looking at him makes one feel sick. Anyway he's back in London now. Dribbling over the Board of Admiralty, no doubt.' He nodded. 'Some justice in that, too.'

'C-in-C sent him home?'

'Yes. First-class man, Calthorpe.' He was referring to the Honourable Sir Somerset A. Gough-Calthorpe, Vice-Admiral. He shut his eyes. 'Look here, I think I'll try for a bit of shut-eye now.'

'Right. Sorry.'

Robins spoke from the other bunk. 'Want to use this one, Hobday?'

Hobday glanced up, startled. Nick and Burtenshaw looked just as surprised. He chuckled. 'Most kind. But I'll wait until we're in the Marmara, thanks all the same. Not much good at cat-naps.'

'I'd 've thought you'd have to be.' Burtenshaw asked him, 'D'you expect we'll be undisturbed, in the Marmara?'

'You lot won't be. That's when you start earning your pay, isn't it?'

Robins chipped in again. 'At what time *will* we get there?'

552

'Cameron?' Hobday twisted round in his armchair. 'What's ETA Marmara?'

Jake came over. Like a bear, Nick thought. It was that shambling walk of his. He told them, 'Can't be certain of the tide – but allowing three knots for it, plus the one or one-and-a-half we're getting from slow speed on one screw – well, eighteen miles from where we altered and went deep at four-twenty . . . Say eight-thirty, well clear?'

Robins observed that thirteen hours was a great deal longer than the passage had been expected to take. Nobody answered him. The assertion was undeniable, and his voicing it might have been intended as a criticism or might not. Nobody cared much, either way. Nick was conscious of a peculiar sensation of timelessness, of being shut off, of having left the world behind and no longer belonging to it. Even Sarah: he frowned, at the suggestion of disloyalty, desertion which came in with that thought. But in Sarah's case it wasn't only the cut-off feeling that the submarine and its situation gave him, it was also the lack of contact with her earlier, the sparsity and sterility of her letters.

'What?'

Jake Cameron had said something about having supper in the Marmara. He repeated it now. Nick thought, *If it's all plain sailing from here on.* He was beginning to get the shape of things – which included a certain unwisdom in taking anything for granted.

Supper in the Marmara . . . And then, as Hobday had just said, the business of the landing. It was an extremely vague briefing that Reaper had given him. What it amounted to was that Robins would introduce him and Burtenshaw to certain contacts ashore, and they – Turks, or at any rate local residents – would provide the information and guidance for an attack on *Goeben*. Nick was to take Burtenshaw and Burtenshaw's explosives under his command and see the thing through to the best possible conclusion, adjusting his plans according to the situation and developments ashore. Robins would be going his own devious, foreign-office way, politicking either with or in competition with the French. Reaper knew very little about that side of the business; his only instructions so far as Robins was concerned were that he was to be put ashore in company with the Frenchmen. But the outcome of the landing, of the political string-pulling or arm-twisting, and hopefully of the destruction of the *Goeben* – which was the *pièce de résistance* – all this superimposed on the wider strategic developments, was expected to take the form of a Turkish surrender, and Reaper wanted to have Nick ashore in Constantinople when and if this came about. He'd be in communication with Reaper, and through Reaper with the C-in-C, by clandestine wireless links now operated by the people to whom Robins would be introducing him. These included an English woman to whom Reaper had referred as the Grey Lady. Nick would be expected to report on what was happening ashore, and might be required later to make arrangements of one sort or another for the arrival and safe reception of the Fleet.

Tall orders, Reaper had admitted. Tall, and vague. They could hardly, in the shifting circumstances, be more definite. And the situation might well be complicated by Robins, who had his own instructions from London and would almost certainly want to throw his weight about. But Robins wasn't truly a naval man – Reaper seemed to expect to have his cake and eat it too, on this point – he wasn't a professional, and Reaper didn't trust him. Nick was basically to confine himself to the naval aspects of the situation; it was in areas where naval considerations overlapped political ones that he might find problems. He'd find problems anyway, and he was to act as he thought best in whatever circumstances arose.

'Whatever you do,' Reaper had told him, 'you'll have my support.' Nick had nodded, liking that assurance. The commander had added, 'But if you make a mess of it, we'll both be for the high-jump.'

Jake Cameron had gone back to the centre of the control room. He had Rowbottom at the wheel, Finn on the fore 'planes and Anderson on the after 'planes. Rowbottom stolid, slow of speech: Finn, stocky and curly haired, a complete contrast, one of the boat's humorists. Anderson, the tall torpedoman, was a close friend and shore-going partner of Finn's; he was nicknamed 'Close-'aul' Anderson, which had something to do with the belief that he sailed close to the wind in his dealings with the fair sex. He was alleged, certainly, to have one fiancée in Liverpool and another, a Greek girl, in Corfu town. E.57 had left Corfu only three weeks ago; until this *Goeben* flap had started she'd been part of the flotilla employed in blockading the Adriatic, keeping the Austrian fleet bottled up.

Dull work; but the general view was that having Corfu as their base compensated for it. And they hadn't been out from England long enough to get bored by the uneventful patrols.

ERA Percy Bradshaw leant against the panel of vent-and-blow controls. 'Polecat' Bradshaw had worked for Cammell Laird at Birkenhead until early in the war. He could still have been there, if he'd wanted to be, earning big money in a 'reserved occupation'. Bradshaw's beard, Jake noticed, had grown during the night to a remarkable extent. He ran a hand over his own jaw; he was in a similar condition. Anderson was looking fairly rough too; but on Finn and Rowbottom, who were fair-haired, the stubble didn't show so much.

'Bit light for'ard, are we, Anderson?'

'TI went aft, sir, did'n 'e?'

'Close-'aul' glanced over his shoulder as he said it. Most of his length was legs; he had trouble finding room for them when he was on the 'planesman's stool.

Jake had forgotten about Rinkpole having gone aft. At this slow speed through the water – hopefully the boat was moving faster in relation to the land – the trim was easily upset. He glanced at the clock; ten minutes to five. About three-and-a-half more hours in the straits, that meant. He felt hungry. It would be marvellous to be out in open water, to sit down to a meal, relax, have a smoke . . . He crossed over to the chart table and leant on it, studying the Marmara, the entrance to it where the Gallipoli Strait widened out from this miserable crack between two land-masses. Quite a sizeable piece of water, the Marmara. About 120 miles long and 50 wide, with these straits at its western end and Constantinople and the Bosphorus at the other, and various islands in the middle. Fascinating to look at it and think how, in 1915, British submarines had forced their way in through these straits and virtually ruled the area, sunk everything warlike that had moved on the Marmara's surface, closed it as a waterway to the nation who owned the land all around it. In the process, lost some ships and lives and made some reputations. When you considered the achievements of those early submarines, what was being asked of this one didn't seem so much. It also made it imperative that she should score her own success.

'Permission to go for'ard, sir?'

'Carry on, TI.'

He leant against the polished steel ladder. Peace and quiet, except for the murmur of Burtenshaw's and Hobday's occasional spasms of conversation. A heavy, drugging peace. Half of it was the stuffiness, warmth generated by the motors, batteries, breath. The leaking rivets were no worse than they had been. At a hundred feet sea-pressure might have made them *much* worse. Perhaps the trickles ran a little faster; but even that could have been imagined. It was what you expected to see, so you saw it. And as Chief *ERA* Grumman had observed half an hour ago, greater outside pressure might actually reduce the leaks by forcing the loosened rivets home.

Jake didn't believe it. He didn't think Grumman had either . . . He heard Burtenshaw ask Everard, 'You were at Zeebrugge, weren't you?' Everard must have nodded. Burtenshaw said, 'I tried to go on that stunt. I did some work at Deal with Brock – well, what I mean is he was in charge of all that side – Brock, d'you know who I mean, the chap who organised all the flares and smoke, rockets and—'

'I knew him quite well. At Dover. We all did.' He'd heard Burtenshaw mention Brock before, in a conversation with Jake Cameron. Hobday asked him, 'Did you know any of the submariners, the chaps who blew up the viaduct?'

'Yes. Tim Rogerson.'

Hobday smiled. 'Same term, Tim and I. Well, well!'

'He's about a year, year and a half senior to me.' It was Everard who'd said that. Adding now, 'Quite a pal, actually. D'you know his sister Eleanor, by any chance?'

'Can't say I do.'

Burtenshaw put in, 'Wasn't C3's captain one of the VCs?'

'Sandford. Yes.' Hobday added, 'Known in the trade as Uncle Baldy. Marvellous chap.'

'Have to be, I suppose, to be picked for a job like that one.' The Marine sighed. 'Not *my* luck, I assure you.'

Hobday chuckled. 'Not exactly long in the tooth yet, are you?'

'Perhaps not. But the war's likely to conk out soon, and all I've done has been loaf around such places as Deal!'

'Not loafing about Deal *now*, are you?'

'Thank heavens, no. But—' Burtenshaw hesitated: Jake murmured, 'Watch that depth, Finn.'

'Sorry, sir.' Jake thought, *Daydreaming about some Pompey tart* . . . Burtenshaw was saying, over in the corner, 'Compared to a chap like you, Everard – and if you'll forgive my mentioning it you're not such an awful lot older than I am—'

556

'Old enough to have been at sea before the war began, though.' Nick said, 'Over that period of time one could hardly *not* see a certain amount of action.'

'You've done damn well, by all accounts.' Hobday spoke without any sign of envy. 'And one needs no powers of second-sight to see you following in your uncle's tracks. Admiral Sir *Nicholas*—'

He'd pronounced it Nickle-arse.

'I don't think so.'

Jake turned, and looked across the compartment at Everard. He saw him shake his head.

'I'm not sure the peacetime Navy is quite my mark. I – er—' He was hesitant, looking at Hobday across the table. 'I don't know. I disliked Dartmouth, and Dartmouth wasn't frightfully keen on me. I've a feeling peacetime service might be rather like that: polishing the brightwork, minding one's p's and q's, being careful whom one knows and what one says to them, and – oh, I don't know . . .'

He'd heard himself saying it. He hadn't previously voiced such thoughts, except to really close friends like Rogerson, and quite privately. It was this shut-off feeling, he thought: as if this was another world – isolated from the real one.

Well, it *was*.

Hobday said, 'It'd be an awful lot to throw away. Being your uncle's nephew is a terrific card in your hand. And your record's fairly sensational. Those medals—'

'Chaps with a lot of ribbons were looked down on, before the war.' Nick's uncle had told him this. 'They used to call them glory-hunters. It wasn't at all a thing to—'

'Never mind about what happened *before* the war.' Hobday wagged a finger. 'If you wanted to make absolutely *certain* of reaching flag-rank yourself now, what you should do is marry an admiral's daughter.'

'Would you do that?'

'If I found one I could stand. Why not? You've got to fit in with things as they are, you know.'

'Well, that's not *my* meat.'

Jake Cameron, who'd spent several days in *Terrapin* as a fellow passenger with Nick Everard, saw it more clearly suddenly. It wouldn't have been *his* meat, either. Not that he, Jake, could have had any such opportunity; Lieutenant Nicholas Everard DSO DSC Royal Navy was a baronet's son and an admiral's nephew, and Hobday was right, the cards were ready to his hand if he chose to pick them up and play them. Jake's own options were the merchant navy or the alternative of some humdrum bread-and-butter work ashore. The two of them were miles apart. In spite of that, he felt instinctively that he and Nick Everard, if you cut through to the bone of it, were similar animals and might have more in common than – well, than Everard had with Hobday, say. Or Cameron with Hobday.

Not that he in any way disliked the little man. There was just that sudden picture of a peacetime Navy, all yes-sirs and no-sirs and admirals' daughters, and plenty of Hobdays willing to 'fit in' with it.

Might that make the Camerons and the Everards long-term losers?

He thought, *Thank God for the mercantile marine!*

Or for the tedious shoreside job? How would one react to a straight choice between that and Hobday's ceremonial sailoring?

'Sir.' Leading Telegraphist Weatherspoon saved him from having to resolve that less simple question. Weatherspoon had poked his head out of the silent cabinet; he had his headset pushed back off his ears. 'Reckon we're bein' follered, sir. That trawler.'

Hobday had gone over to him.

'Joined on astern, sir. Come up gradual – I was thinkin' I'd got some HE, then it'd stop, sort of before I was sure, an' I'd think *no, I'm wrong* – then—'

'Keep listening.' Hobday went back to the other side and shook Wishart's arm. 'Captain, sir . . .'

'Stop port.'

'Stop port!' Agnew passed the order verbally. In an effort to keep as quiet as possible they weren't using the telegraphs. This submarine was the mouse and there was a cat up there watching her every move.

'Port motor stopped, sir.'

That meant both motors were silent now. Wishart looked round at Weatherspoon, on his stool just inside the doorway of the silent cabinet. The leading tel nodded. 'Still closin', sir.' Then his eyebrows lifted. 'Enemy stoppin', sir!'

Which finally proved the point – that the trawler, or gunboat, was trailing them. Each time E.57 had stopped her motors, the enemy had stopped too. When the submarine's screws had stirred into life again, a few seconds would crawl by before the slower, more powerful screw would resume its leisurely beat. They'd checked it out several times now – hoping for a different explanation. It might, for instance, have been some patrol vessel making its way slowly up-straits and stopping now and then to listen through its hydrophones. Like a fly-fisherman working a stretch of river. But it wasn't so. Whatever E.57 did, the shadower kept his distance. His revs per minute increased when the submarine's did, lessened when she slowed. On the whole he was stopped more often than they were; he was obviously taking care to keep astern and at his chosen distance.

It was uncanny. Dislike for the Turk was mounting. You could see the anger in men's faces when they looked upwards.

McVeigh asked Wishart, 'Mak' a suggestion, sir?'

Wishart glanced at the wild-looking Glaswegian, and nodded.

'If we wen' up tae periscope depth, might we no gi'e the swine a bash oot the stern tube?'

'It's a nice idea.' Wishart shook his head. 'But we want all our fish for *Goeben*. Anyway he's a small target and he's watching us already – he wouldn't sit and wait for it.'

The ERA wiped the back of his wrist across his nostrils. He nodded angrily. 'Aye.' Wishart said soothingly, 'We'll shake him off, by and by. Once we get into the Marmara we'll lose him.'

'Losing trim, sir.'

'Slow ahead port.'

'Slow ahead port!' Finn passed it on aft from Agnew. Wishart joined Jake at the chart table. 'Where do we think we are?'

'Coming up to this point, sir.'

It was about an hour since they'd gone deep and turned on to the present course. If it was a three-knot tide as estimated they'd be roughly level with a place called Kodjuk Burnu. It was on the southern, Asiatic shore, and at this point the coastline bulged into the straits, narrowing them to about three thousand yards.

'Hadn't realised.' Wishart scowled at the chart. 'Narrowest since we cleared Nagara.'

'Yes.' Jake pointed with his dividers. 'And twenty-five fathoms is the shallowest mid-channel sounding we've come across.'

The same thought was in both their minds. A narrowing of the waterway with a rising seabed was a natural place to block with nets. Jake suggested quietly, 'That one may be following to see us get snagged up again.'

559

'Let us hope *not*.' The battery wouldn't stand for much more of the net games. Wishart stooped, peered more closely at the chart. 'Not a great deal we can do about it, old lad. Only way to locate a net, unfortunately, is bump into it . . . You know, I don't believe this Kodjuk is a place, as such. I reckon it means "headland" or "point". The *burnu* bit, I mean.'

There were quite a few other *burnus*, here and there, and they did all seem to be headlands. Jake remembered afterwards that he'd been looking for others along the coastlines, hoping to find one that might disprove that theory of Wishart's, and that Weatherspoon had just reported that the enemy had stopped his engine again – that word 'engine' was the last word, last moment – last *conscious* moment, before—

It must have been *in* that moment that the mine blew up.

As if all the sea they floated in had exploded. You had only one barely glimpsed flash of thought: *finished, over!* Your *mind* detonated . . . It was – total, so overwhelming that there was nothing else, nothing left or existing: the noise and impact and then the echoes and reactions all part of it, booming through hollow, shattered minds blanked-off from memory, will-power, consciousness. You were *in* it, part of it, you couldn't fight it or resist or – reason, comprehend . . . It was dark, absolutely black, and the universe was rolling over: the sound of shouting from all directions was far away, remote, although it might have had your own voice in it. A rush of water broke through then, roaring like thunder for a time before it stopped dead with an enormous jolt: and now trickling, splashing sounds growing fainter, fading into silence in the darkness, stillness. A swaying motion, and water-sounds soft and whispery through steel plating. In the rush of water – that hard, loud rush – he'd thought yes, this was how death came, how in his heart of hearts he'd always known it would; it was surprising now that he was dry and still drawing breaths and letting them gush out again. More voices suddenly, rising all together as if they'd been there all the time and now the volume was being turned up to normal: it was possible, he thought, that something had happened to his ear-drums. Now that had been a *lucid* thought: he clutched it and got more, an argument in favour of his ears being undamaged because otherwise he wouldn't have heard the water-sounds, the small ones. Someone was shouting about lights, and immediately there was a second crash of high-explosive: but that one had been farther away, enormous enough by normal standards and with a rocking effect that followed it, but compared to the first one – *nothing.*

'Dixon? Is Leading Seaman Dixon seeing about some lights?'

Wishart's voice. Insistent, but unexcited, rather as if this was another exercise, a practice evolution, one of his *out lights, main vents in hand* games. Jake struggled to his feet and began groping his way towards the auxiliary switchboard. Stumbling over someone who was crawling: cursing hard. A lot of cursing. Lights blazed suddenly: the main ones, not the emergencies. He found that he was facing the for'ard periscope, grasping its wires, his two hands slimy with its thick, grey grease. He thought he'd been unconscious, or semiconscious. The compartment seemed to be dry: and yet there'd been water forcing in – hadn't there?

'Check bulkhead voicepipes. Reports from all compartments, please. Are both motors stopped?'

You could see men trying to control their breathing, accept the surprise of being alive. Jake went to the chart table and found all his bits and pieces strewn around. Water was dripping much faster from the deckhead than it had been before. ERA Knight had come to this end of the compartment to have a look at it; he was muttering, 'Could be worse. Could be better but it could be worse, much worse.' Nodding, as if he liked the sound of that. He'd patted Stone's shoulder as he moved away: 'All right, Andy lad?'

Lewis had been lending his ear to a babble from the voicepipe in the for'ard bulkhead. He reported, 'Dry for'ard except a leak on the starboard torpedo tube, sir. TI says 'e 'as it in 'and, sir.'

'That's good, Lewis.'

Reality and normality returning as the elements of the machine recovered separately and began to mesh together. Hobday asked Wishart, 'Shall we keep watertight doors shut, sir?'

'For the moment, yes. Who shut them?'

Lewis admitted, 'I did this 'un, sir.'

'Well done you!'

'Polecat' Bradshaw kicked the after door. 'I got chucked ag'in it. Brought it to me mind, you might say.'

'Good man, Bradshaw.'

Burtenshaw put in diffidently, 'I think Lieutenant-Commander Robins is concussed, sir.'

Nick Everard said quickly, 'I'll see to it.' He looked fairly dazed himself. Wishart asked, 'Reports from aft?'

'Nowt from after ends yet, sir.' Stoker Adams was on that

561

voicepipe. 'No leaks nor nothin' in engine-room an' motor-room. Some fuses an' that gone, LTO says. Waitin' for after end's report, sir.' Adams was from Rochdale. Tall, stooped, yellow-headed. Wishart asked Morton, 'That gauge shut off, is it?'

'Aye, sir, but it's bust, too.' Crabb put in, 'This one'll do for 'im an' all, sir.' His gauge, the after one, showed a hundred and forty-three feet, and that matched the charted soundings off Kodjuk Burnu all right.

'Pilot, go for'ard, see how the TI's getting on and what the trouble is, and pass the word around that we seem to be intact and not much damaged. Tell 'em we'll open bulkhead doors soon as we know a bit more about the state we're in.'

'Aye aye, sir.' Jake told Lewis, 'Warn 'em I'm coming through.' The door had to be unclipped before you could open it. At the other end of the control room Lofty Adams reported, 'After ends dry 'cept for leaking shaft gland port side an' a spot of floodin' back through the 'eads. They're lookin' after it, sir.'

Wishart looked at McVeigh. 'And the outside ERA will see to it more thoroughly in a few minutes, the lucky dog . . . Number One, don't use the port screw unless we're forced to.'

'Aye aye, sir.' Hobday called to Adams, 'Tell the Stoker PO to see what Peel's doing about the shaft gland, and to have all bilges checked and auxiliary tanks dipped . . . Lewis, I want Cole to come and check the battery tank.' He added quietly to Wishart, 'Seems we've been lucky, sir.'

'Let's hope so.' Wishart was peering at the bubble and the depth-gauge, and now at the other spirit-level, the curved one on the deckhead that showed any list to port or starboard. 'Since so far as we know nothing's been flooded, there's no reason we should be bottomed, is there?'

'We aren't necessarily all that heavy, sir. A bit of pumping should bring her up. If the explosion pushed us downwards . . .'

'I'd have sworn I heard a lot of . . .' Wishart shook his head. 'We've this list to port.' He looked puzzled. 'Anyway, pump some out aft, let's have her tail up and the screws clear. Pump on "Z". If she looks ready to move, put a drop in "A" to hold her down. Can't move before we know what's happening up there . . .' Glancing round for Weatherspoon, he found the leading tel waiting to report to him.

'Can't 'ear nothin', sir. I don't *think* the gear's scuppered, but—'

'Your own ears, perhaps?'

562

'Not likely, sir. Didn't 'ave the 'eadset on when it went off. But there was that bloke up top there, and now I can't 'ear 'im, can't 'ear nothin', sir.'

'Let me have a listen.' Wishart took the headset from him, moving into the cabinet. Jake came back from the torpedo stowage compartment and tube space. Hobday had got the pump sucking on 'Z' internal main ballast now, and he beckoned him. 'Captain's using the hydrophone. Is it all right for'ard?'

Cole had come through behind Jake; he was clipping the door shut. Jake said, 'Sluice door on the starboard tube must have been jolted open and then banged shut again – enough to fill the tube under pressure and lift the relief-valve so hard it jammed open. Rinkpole belted it with a mallet and it's all right now. Anderson fell between the tubes and I think his wrist's broken . . . The fish in that tube – TI'll pull it back and do a routine on it as soon as there's a chance.' He nodded. 'That's all. Shall I take a look aft as well?' Hobday nodded, and Stoker Adams began to wrench the clips off the other door.

Wishart handed the headset back to Weatherspoon and backed out of the cabinet.

'I can hear water noises all round. Doubt if there's anything wrong with the gear. You'd better give yourself a break.' He looked round: 'Agnew – take over for a while. All right, leading tel?'

'Aye aye, sir.' Weatherspoon pressed his palms against his outsize ears, looking worried. But it was a relief to know the gear was working; without it they'd be deaf as well as blind. Wishart said, 'Our friend up there's waiting to see what floats up. Probably reckons we're a dead duck. Thanks to Messrs Vickers, we aren't, we're a *tough* one.' Men smiled, their faces glistening under films of sweat, eyes fighting not to show uncertainty. He told them, 'While he stays there, all we can do is sit tight . . . Adams – Lewis – pass the word to all compartments: no hammering, no spanners, no row at all.'

Adams had just clipped the door shut again behind Jake; now he passed that order through the voicepipe. Cole was shining a torch down one of the battery-tank sighting holes. Hobday had the port ballast pump working on 'Z' internal; he asked Bradshaw, 'Getting anything out?'

'Not much, sir.' He was crouched over the pump, which had pressure gauges on it. 'Relief-valve's gagged an' all.'

You had to gag the relief, which was set to lift at fifty pounds to the square inch. Hobday told McVeigh, 'Stand by to put some air in "Z".'

It was sea-pressure on the outlet valve that made the pump's work difficult. Increasing the pressure in the tank would balance it. McVeigh had his hands on the HP air-valve and his eyes on Hobday; Hobday said, 'Open . . . *Shut!*' The ERA had sent a burst of air thumping down the line. Bradshaw looked up from the pump. 'Lovely!'

Jake came back, and reported to Wishart. 'Leech doesn't think the shaft-gland'll get any worse, sir, and it's nothing much. The heads were in a foul state – still are – but there's no flooding now. The screw-down valve was shut, but not *tight* shut.'

The heads were McVeigh's bugbear. He growled, ginger beard wagging angrily, 'They dinna blow 'em richt, so it's solid muck they screw the valve doon on. Then ye get a *whumpf* like yon, an' it a' blows back an'—' He waved his hands, indicating that high-pressured shower of foulness. Jake nodded. 'I'm afraid it did.' McVeigh muttered to Bradshaw, his mate, 'Safer wi' a stack o' bedpans. It's the puir bluidy outside ERA has tae go an'—'

'Price you pay, McVeigh, for being a mechanical genius.' Wishart was looking at the depth-gauge. 'That tank must be about out by now.'

Emptying a tank that held five-and-a-half tons of water when it was full, and must have had at least half that much in it before they'd started pumping, seemed to have made no difference. And that made no sense. It was like two and two making three. Hobday said, 'I'll take some out amidships, sir . . . Although the bubble has shifted slightly, hasn't it, cox'n?'

'Less'n half a degree, sir.'

'Darn it.' Mysteries were irritating, as well as threatening future embarrassment. 'Stop the pump. Shut "Z" suction. Open "X" suction and inboard vent.'

Wishart was at the door of the silent cabinet. 'Hear anything, Agnew?'

The boy tel pushed the headset off his ears. 'Bit of a noise a minute ago, sir. Like – I dunno, sir, but I been thinkin' might it 'a been a ship lettin' 'er anchor go?'

'Why didn't you report it, for heaven's sake!'

'Did'n know what to call it, sir – I mean, I—'

'Report everything you hear. Even a lobster gargling – I don't care *what* you call it!'

'Aye aye, sir. Sorry, sir.'

Wishart leant with his back against the chart table. Hobday had just put some pressure into the midships tank, as he'd done for the other. Wishart began, thinking aloud, 'I'll accept it was the Turk anchoring. He'd have been following astern of us, with a good idea of where we were, and knowing – I'm guessing this – knowing they'd got a net ahead of us with controlled mines in it. Or not a net – just a line of mines wired to the shore. He'd have been signalling to his friends ashore – giving 'em lots of warning to be ready for us . . . Now he's dropped a hook and he'll sit up there until either he's sure we're done for or he hears us move.'

Jake had been checking soundings on the chart. He told Wishart, 'Shelves to eleven fathoms near the southern shore here, sir, and on the other side it varies between six and ten. He could be at anchor on either side and still be within a thousand yards of us.'

CPO Crabb reported, 'She's shiftin', sir!'

'Stop the pump. Shut "X" suction . . . Anchor her for'ard, sir?' Wishart nodded, and Hobday told Lewis, 'Open "A" inboard vent.' There was residual pressure still in 'A'; when the vent was opened, air hissed into the boat, and you had to swallow to clear your ears. But you couldn't flood water into a tank against pressure, and you couldn't vent it outboard without sending up a bubble to the surface.

A few seconds later Crabb reported that the spirit-level bubble was moving aft. Hobday stopped flooding the for'ard tank, and shut it off. Now the submarine's bow was weighted down heavily enough to hold her anchored to the seabed while her afterpart and screws floated clear of it.

Cole said – a mumble through his thick, black beard – 'No acid in the battery tanks, sir.'

'Good.' But there was still a sense of unreality. The uncertainty about what had happened – where all the extra weight had suddenly appeared from – added to the strangeness. It was like an aftermath of dying, of *having died* . . . As if they weren't intended to be alive, should not have been. But alive they were, and you couldn't lose track of several tons of ballast and just ignore it, pretend it didn't matter. You had to find out what had happened – before you found out the hard way, in an emergency, when it might be too late. It was like knowing there was a time-bomb somewhere, and searching and still not finding it. Wishart, of course, would be battling not only with that problem but with others too, the whole situation: the Turk sitting over them, and shore-controlled mines most likely covering the entire area – those were the *external* threats, and one had to consider them in conjunction with internal factors such as a battery that couldn't have much life left in it and air that was becoming thin and foul. He had to decide on *some* move. Eyes in tired, sweaty faces followed him, waiting for the decision. Robins was stretched out on Wishart's bunk, and Nick saw Wishart looking that way; he told him, 'He's all right now. Only had a bump.' Wishart turned as the stoker PO arrived from aft and asked Hobday out of that ventriloquist's mouth of his, 'You want *every* tank dipped, sir, that right?'

'Hang on, Leech.' Wishart ordered, 'Open watertight doors. Number One – we'll stay here. One officer and one hand on control-room watch. Everyone else turn in. Only one light's to be used in each compartment. No moving around at all.' He looked at Leech. 'Yes. Dip all the auxiliaries and check dry-stores, every space there is. And don't drop a pin while you're doing it, or I'll shoot you, d'you hear?'

'Can't kill a Yorkshireman wi' a bullet, sir.' Leech looked quite serious about it. Wishart said, 'All right, then, I'll hang you.' The stoker PO wagged his head, concurring. 'Ah. That's different.'

Robins, who'd admitted grudgingly that he'd sustained no lasting injury, asked Wishart what they'd do if the Turk sat tight – stayed up there, on top of them.

'Then we sit tight too. If necessary until it's dark again.'

Robins was in the bottom, pull-out bunk. Wishart and Hobday were in their own, and Burtenshaw was stretched out on a blanket on the deck. Nick had accepted a blanket for the same purpose but for the time being he was comfortable enough in the armchair; he'd be able to doze, he thought, by leaning forward across the table with the folded blanket as a pillow on it. Plenty of deck-space anyway, since there'd be no one moving around.

Wishart had explained to Robins that they couldn't move without making a periscope check of their position first. Which way or how far the boat had travelled between the explosion and bottoming was anybody's guess.

'You mean we'd lie here – what, *twelve hours*?'

'Nearer sixteen, if we have to wait for darkness . . . All the more reason to pipe down now and go to sleep.'

Jake Cameron had moved the telegraphists' stool to a spot just outside the cabinet. The headset's lead reached that far and the cabinet doorway served well as a back-rest. He'd be on watch for two hours now, and every half-hour he and his fellow watchkeeper, Stoker Burrage, would take turns on the listening gear. There'd be nothing else to do except keep quiet, stay awake, ensure that no noise was made from elsewhere in the boat. There'd been a period of noise-making, certainly, since the explosion, and the Turk would probably have heard some of it, but with any luck he might convince himself that he'd been listening to the submarine's death throes.

Making everyone lie down and do nothing was also the best way to conserve oxygen. It was stuffy in the compartments now, with a thick, oily, heads-reeking, submarine humidity. It wasn't pleasant to breathe, and yet you needed to take deeper breaths than usual. By nightfall it might be fairly horrible, Jake thought. Six or seven hours ago they'd had that short spell on the surface, but unless the diesels were started up – which unfortunately they had not been – you didn't get much fresh air into the boat just by opening a hatch. Hobday hadn't run the fans, during that minute on the surface, either. Hindsight told one that he should have, but like everyone else he'd had his mind on the net that had fouled them and on the shore batteries and searchlights.

All through the boat men slept, now. Asleep, you used less air, and minimal lighting saved power. Both commodities would be crucial to survival.

Sixteen hours, Wishart had estimated. Add that to the fourteen since they'd dived. And then there were still fifteen more miles of the straits to get through, and nobody would be so rash as to count on it being a straightforward, uninterrupted fifteen-mile run either. Count, Jake thought, on *nothing* . . . A couple of times in recent hours there had been a premature, illusory feeling that the worst was over . . . He glanced round the gloomy, deep-shadowed compartment. If one could have foreseen being in *this* situation . . . As well, perhaps, that the future hid itself, that one could only take things as they came. In any case – he told himself – they *were* winning: they'd got this far, and the rest of it couldn't be much rougher than some of the stages they'd already survived. Wishart was right to be cautious, to play for long-term safety rather than for a quicker breakthrough. The object was not to get into the Marmara in a hurry, it was to arrive there intact and fighting-fit.

Warmth, and silence. The Turk up there wasn't kicking any tin cans about either. Only soft water-sounds from outside the hull. Through the headphones the same sounds were greatly magnified. In many seas there'd be dead submarines lying much as this one was now, with dead men lying about, very much as E.57's crew were lying now and similar sea-sounds whispering on and on . . . If it hadn't been for the headphones one could easily have drifted into sleep. He could see that Burrage, blinking at the depth-gauges opposite him, was finding it hard to stay awake. Burrage was short, broad-shouldered, curly haired. If he'd been of lighter build you could have taken him for a jockey. He was sitting with his back against the HP compressor and he had his eyes open but switched off, as in a dream. Jake remembered ERA Geordie Knight telling him that Burrage's major enthusiasm was for motor-racing, his hero the great S.F. Edge. You could guess that at this moment Burrage wasn't here, trapped in silence at the bottom of the Dardanelles, but racketing along in a bedlam of roaring exhausts at Brooklands, risking his neck at speeds of up to sixty miles an hour.

Burrage hung around Knight a lot and talked to him about that sort of thing because he wanted a job in the motor business, after the war, and he knew Knight's father owned a garage.

The bulkhead clock showed six-twenty. By the original reckoning they'd have been in the Marmara hours ago. Eight hours from the Kum Kale minefield, the estimate had been. He wondered how long the passage might have taken *Louve*; even whether the French boat had got through at all. She might have been lucky and slipped through without much trouble. The Frenchmen were efficient enough, according to Wishart and Hobday; E.57 and *Louve* had exercised together on the way from Mudros to Imbros, and *Louve* had seemed to be well up to scratch.

When darkness came, the Turk might still be lying up there, like a cat over a mouse-hole. They'd have to be very canny, creep away from him. Not easy. Even less so if Wishart was right in his guess that the area might be sown with shore-controlled mines. If that was the case there'd be hydrophones ashore to pick up the sound of the boat's motors when she moved. Screws approaching their mine-barrage would be what they'd react to. You could imagine the Turks ashore there in headphones with their fingers on the firing keys . . .

Better not to.

He told himself, *It's all guesswork. Pointless. Wait and see what happens, no good trying to anticipate it.* He wished he could hit on some possible solution to the mystery of the trim. Leech had dipped all the auxiliaries – internal main ballasts, trim tanks, comps, buoyancy, WRTs, even the fresh water, oil-fuel, lub-oil and dirty-oil tanks. Bilges too, of course. Every other space – stores, magazine, every cubic foot of her – had been inspected. There was still no answer to that weight they'd had to shed. He remembered the flooding, rushing-water noise he'd heard. Or only imagined? He'd thought of himself as dead, or about to die, and one's mind might play odd tricks. He shifted his position cautiously. His damaged shoulder – the one the net had lacerated – still ached and smarted. The coxswain had painted the abrasions with iodine for him. He wanted to breathe deeply and at the same time not breathe at all. He looked at the clock again. The bulkhead behind it, an oval of white enamel lit by the glow of the single lamp, ran with condensation. Six-thirty. In Mudros, Imbros, and aboard *Terrapin* in the Gulf of Xeros, everyone would be counting on their being in the Marmara by this time.

Nick was thinking about Reaper, who'd be in the gulf now, in *Terrapin*. Reaper wouldn't hit it off with Truman, *Terrapin*'s captain, he thought. Truman had a pompous manner, a way of making his pronouncements sound weighty even when they were quite trivial. It wasn't just his awful voice, it was his style in general. Reaper, on the other hand, was an unassuming, straight-thinking man with no time for blather and no sense whatever of his own importance. Those exchanges he'd had with Robins at the meeting aboard *Harwich* – Nick had thought about it, and he realised that Reaper hadn't been quick to slap the man down for the sole reason that he wouldn't have wanted to waste that much time and effort; he'd wanted only to get on with the briefing. In the same way, when Nick had let Reaper see, at Dover at the turn of this year, that he thought Reaper was letting him down, that he'd had the job done for him – the trawler sunk and its crew brought back as prisoners – and no longer cared what happened next to the man who'd done it for him, Reaper hadn't said a word, he'd let Nick go off in that surly, let-down frame of mind, and left it to him to discover what had been done for him. His first command – of *Bravo*.

(With air as foul as this already, Nick wondered, what would it be like by nightfall? But lacking submarine experience, he couldn't tell *how* bad it was, or how much worse it could get and still be breathable. He shifted on the chair, pulled the rolled blanket closer and rested the other side of his head on it.)

No sufferer of fools, was Reaper. He wouldn't enjoy being cooped up with Truman, any more than Nick had; and being a destroyer CO himself he'd been treated as the captain's guest, not the wardroom's. For Reaper it would be worse, though, because loitering in the Gulf of Xeros and listening out for wireless messages wouldn't involve Truman in much work; he'd have time to play host, entertain his guest. Reaper would be bored stiff, Nick thought.

He had a French wireless expert with him, for communications with *Louve*, and a leading telegraphist from the Mudros staff, as well as *Terrapin*'s own operators. He wouldn't be expecting to hear anything from either of the submarines, but he'd have set a round-the-clock listening watch for shore transmissions – from the people the landing party were to tie-up with later – and after the landing he'd be expecting reports from Robins, and from Nick as well, through that same clandestine channel. Neither of the submarines was to break W/T silence except in a situation of drastic emergency; the hope was that the enemy in Constantinople wouldn't suspect the presence of submarines in the Marmara. But they'd be able to receive messages, and Reaper had drawn up a time-table of broadcast periods, alternating in English and in French, during which they were supposed to listen out. *Terrapin*'s wireless would transmit orders or information, particularly if anything reached him from the shore contacts if it affected the submarine's or the landing party's plans.

Reaper would be under strain, Nick thought. To sit there in *Terrapin* with no word from E.57 or from *Louve*, and knowing the hazards of this passage of the straits, and with the whole enterprise depending on their getting through. Then he'd be waiting for news from shore – from this Grey Lady and her friends – on some unreliable home-made wireless set . . .

He had said *something* about the 'Grey Lady', before he'd gone on to some other subject. He'd asked Nick, half jokingly it had seemed, 'Would you believe in an English maiden lady of middle age and impeccable social background having charge of our espionage and insurrectionary operations in Constantinople?'

Thinking back on it, it was like a dream that came and went. Breathing *through* the blanket, face-downward, as if it might filter the foetid air. Might Sarah be lying awake now, thinking about him, thinking of him with his head in the fresh air – in sunshine even, because he'd told her he was heading for a warmer climate?

Might Sarah have told the old man about what had happened at Mullbergh?

He'd been dropping off to sleep. The question burst like a fire-cracker in his brain, woke him with a start. He'd moved sharply, dislodged the blanket and practically dislocated his neck.

'Why not lie down?'

A murmur from Jake Cameron – who'd swapped places with the young stoker, Nick saw. He must have dozed for longer than he'd thought. He rubbed his neck: he'd pulled a muscle in it. Nodding to Cameron, and feeling sick now from the oppressive atmosphere. He moved as quietly as he could, hearing a gentle snoring which he thought came from Hobday, and spreading the blanket with two folds in it so that it was long and narrow, bunk-shaped. Cameron was back in his own thoughts, gazing tiredly at the shadowed, moisture-running deckhead. The dripping from it was as frequent now as if one was on the fringe of a thundery rainstorm, and the corticene covering of the deck had big wet areas from it. Nick still had that question in his mind as he lay down on his blanket: *Out of guilt, remorse?*

No. She was a very moral, self-disciplined person, and she'd been shocked at her own behaviour; but however badly she'd come to feel about it she was also a sensible, very level-headed creature. As well as beautiful and sweet and – *good*. And it had happened: it was still incredible, marvellous as well as frightening—

Why on earth had she gone down to London, of her own volition, to join a husband whom she loathed?

Whatever the answer was, it was *not* that she could have told him. She knew only too well what sort of man she'd married. Sir John Everard would have shown no mercy: he'd have destroyed her. He'd have destroyed Nick too, if he could have found a way to do it. And Sarah would have realised that; for his sake alone she wouldn't have dreamt of – of trying to ease her conscience by confessing. And yet she had gone down to London and spent ten days with her husband in the house in Curzon Street. She must have heard that he was back from France about a week after Nick had left Mullbergh to take up his job on Bayly's staff at Queens-town; and rushed straight down as if she and her husband were lovebirds who couldn't wait to be reunited!

In the middle of July, that had been. She'd told him about it quite matter-of-factly in the letter that she wrote soon after her return to Mullbergh. It had included the news that his father was likely to be sent home soon, for good. Brigadier Sir John Everard had been commanding an equestrian establishment – remount depot and riding-school for newly commissioned officers; it wasn't needed now, apparently, and the War Office had no other job for him. Well, the war was ending, anyway, and presumably they'd decided they had enough horses and enough officers to ride them. She'd written in that letter, *Whatever the reason, he should be home well before the end of the year, on what is called 'indefinite leave'. It was for discussions at the War Office that he had come back at such short notice. Have you written to him, in recent months? I think you should. There are matters that must now be forgotten, however we may feel about them . . .* Then there was a passage to the effect that the ending of the war would be a time for families to reunite, and how much happiness was in store; the suggestion seemed to be that she, Sarah, looked forward to some new kind of happiness with his father. Reading it through again he'd decided that she'd phrased it badly, that she'd really been talking about the country in general and not about herself at all. It was the only interpretation he could put on it, because if she'd intended it to be read exactly as she'd written it then it was a sham, a gross pretence. He couldn't believe that she'd be capable of such dishonesty.

She'd always been open and straightforward with him. And he'd doubted her only once. It hadn't been an honest or justifiable doubt, only his own jealousy sharpened by the knowledge that he'd be leaving Mullbergh next morning. His appointment to Admiral Bayly's staff had arrived in that day's post: he was to report in London forthwith for his routing instructions. He and Sarah were in the small morning-room at Mullbergh; it had a french window opening to a south-facing terrace and she'd turned it into a sort of office. She'd mentioned Alastair Kinloch-Stuart, an old, close friend of hers and of her family's, who'd been killed in France in April. For a while Nick had suspected the relationship between Stuart and Sarah; he'd thought he had some reason to, although he knew now there'd been nothing in it. He was ashamed that he'd thought such a thing of her, now. When the news of his death had reached her she'd written to Nick – wanting his sympathy, and telling him everything there was to tell: and he'd accepted without question that she'd done nothing to encourage the man's feelings for her. She'd been fond of him, and lonely, and that was all. There'd been no need, even, for her to tell him that much. He'd wished that he'd never doubted her, and thanked God that she was quite unaware he ever had. But now, suddenly, because she'd mentioned the man's name and he, Nick, was having to leave her and hating it, he'd uttered some sneering, offensive comment almost before he'd known he was going to say it. Something about 'replacing' him quickly enough.

Well, there was an RFC captain in the recuperative wing with whom he'd thought Sarah had been spending too much time.

She'd spun round from the window, bright and hard with quick surprise and anger.

'*What* did you say?'

Stupidly, he'd felt he had to stand by what he'd blurted out. She'd left him to dine alone, and he had plenty of time to realise what a mess he'd made. He'd gone up to bed about midnight, feeling absolutely miserable. Sarah meant everything to him; she had done ever since he'd been a child. Of all the people he could have hurt, she'd be the last he'd dream of hurting: and he'd done it on his last night. He couldn't sleep. He kept thinking of his departure in the morning, and Sarah taking care to be busy with her patients, shut away from him. He'd leave without seeing her, without a word . . . In the small hours, desperate now, he went to her room and knocked. After several minutes and more knockings, she called, 'What is it?' He told her, 'Me – Nick. Sarah, *please*—'

'Wait a minute.'

Her tone had been impatient, snappy. Well, he didn't expect much else. But at least he'd see her and apologise. Better than to leave Mullbergh without even saying goodbye.

Her key turned in the lock, and he saw the door pull back. She was wearing a silk dressing-gown and her brown hair was a wild, loose mass; it made her look even younger and more beautiful than she did when it was tied up in its bun. She stared at him calmly, appraisingly: for a second he was remembering another occasion on which he'd come to her room in the night. He'd been woken by her scream: there'd been a door smashed in, and his father in a violent, drunken rage. *Years* ago . . .

'Well, Nick?'

'I want to say I'm sorry. Terribly, *frightfully* sorry, I—'

Smiling at him now. That gentle, vulnerable mouth . . . 'You *were* a bit silly, I think. But—'

573

'You'll forgive me?'

'*What* a silly question!'

'Oh, thank *God*—'

He'd put his arms round her and kissed her cheek, and he felt *her* arms slide up round his neck. Relief was overwhelming: he was happy enough, suddenly, to weep for joy. And without knowing it was going to happen, he'd started doing exactly that. She felt the wetness on her face.

'Nick, my darling, but you're crying! Oh, my precious—'

He couldn't remember which of them pushed the door shut.

CHAPTER 7

Jake clenched his teeth as the chain-sweep clanked, crashed its way across E.57's stern. This was the second time the thing had found her: last time – ten minutes ago, but it felt like an hour – it had dragged over just like this, and gone on, leaving the silence to grow as the beat of screws faded across the straits. The trawler – a new one, not the one still anchored up there – had made another pass without the sweep locating her; now it was here again, and on the end of the chain there'd be grapnel hooks designed to claw and hang on to what it found.

The air was poisonous. Bulkheads running wet. The chain, moving in a succession of crashes linked by the steady, rasping slither, was an instrument of torture in itself. All you could do was wait – and stifle the imagination, not let your mind see what was happening outside. He began to use a soft eraser to tidy the chart, rubbing off old position lines. He thought the Turks might be under the impression they'd made a kill. If they believed otherwise they'd—

A jolt, and a heavy thud from aft: the grapnel had caught and held and now the strain was coming on the chain, taking the bight out of it while its weight acted as a spring. The submarine jerked and began to slew, pivot on her anchored forepart. Sweat-sheened faces stared upwards: then, as men took hold of their own reactions, glanced at each other and away again. Some frowns: a shrugging grin, a man's eyebrows raised disdainfully; Jake saw Louis Lewis's lips move, and it occurred to him that behind those stubbled, pallid faces there'd be a variety of prayers forming. Even if you weren't exactly devout in normal times it was almost physically impossible in a moment like this not to surrender to the urge to ask for help. He began his own: *Please God, let—*

'Time we moved, I think.' Wishart spoke easily but he looked

575

like something out of a grave. 'Don't know about the rest of you, but I'm—'

The noise – scraping, straining – was suddenly much louder. It had a penetrating quality like metal being gouged: and it gouged the mind, it—

Stopped!

Silence – except for that throbbing, high above them. The boat hung motionless, free again, while the slow beat of screws moved on like a churning pulse. Wishart finished the sentence that had been interrupted: 'I'm hungry.'

At noon, he'd had 'up spirits' piped – in a whisper – and as well as the issue of rum for all hands they'd had corned beef and pusser's biscuits. The extra rum would be written off in the books as spillage. For the brief period of the meal men had crept about barefooted and spoken only in whispers, and after it they'd all turned in again. Now it was just on ten o'clock. They'd been dived for nearly thirty hours.

CPO Crabb muttered, ''Ear, 'ear, sir.' His beginnings of a beard were jet-black, with none of the grey that patched his head. Wishart patted Hobday on his shoulder: 'Let's have her off the putty, Number One.'

'Open "A" suction and inboard vent. Pump from for'ard.'

Andy Stone had the suction valve open on the pump, and McVeigh pushed the starter-switch on its motor. Lewis had opened the main-line connection to the tank.

'Pumpin', sir.' Stone had gagged down the relief valve. Wishart murmured, 'Watch her like a hawk now.' He wiped his eyes; like everyone else's they were having fits of watering. It was the battery, the acid reek rising from near-spent cells into oxygen-starved air. Hobday nodded, acknowledging Wishart's caution. Nothing had turned up yet to account for the sudden heaviness, all the pumping they'd had to do after the mine had nearly finished them. These were hardly circumstances in which one would want to lose control and shoot up to the surface.

It all seemed to be happening in slow motion. And for the Turk with his sweep, third time might be lucky. *Don't worry for two seconds about me . . .*

'Bubble's shiftin', sir.' Crabb's voice was a rasp. Jake saw Burtenshaw watching from Wishart's bunk. When the chain-sweep thing had started half an hour ago and the hands had been sent quietly to their diving stations, he'd got up there out of the way.

Nick Everard was in Hobday's, and Robins for once was bunk-less, chair-borne, and peevish-looking perhaps because of that. Or just being his usual self. Jake felt his own weight leaning more heavily than usual against the chart table, and he realised that as the boat had lifted herself clear of the seabed her list to port had increased. Just as he noticed it he heard Hobday say, 'Stop pumping. She's off, sir.'

Anyone could have told him that. For nearly half a minute the feel of her had been quite different. Jake thought, *Come on, come on now . . .*

'Slow ahead starboard, full field. What's causing this list?'

'Slow ahead starboard full field, sir.'

'One hundred feet.'

'Hundred feet, sir.' Hobday's gingery stubble shone like pale gold around his sharp-edged jaw. The 'planes were tilting upward. Weatherspoon reported, 'Enemy surface vessel is turning, sir.' As she rose, the list was still increasing. Even two or three degrees could feel a lot, but this must be six or seven. Wishart said, 'Give me a course up-straits, pilot.'

'North forty-one east, sir, but—'

'Port five. Steer north forty-one east.'

'Port five, sir . . .'

Jake tried again: 'Sir, that course depends on—'

'I know, pilot, I know.' What he knew was that they didn't really know anything about their position, except so far as one might guess it.

'There's one shallow patch beyond the bulge – Kodjuk – and to starboard, sir. But if we clear the headland we should go wide of the shallows too.'

The gauge showed one-oh-seven feet. Hobday was adjusting her trim virtually by half-pints as she rose. Jake was trying to remember in fuller detail the confused minutes following the explosion of the mine, and in particular that noise – unless he'd dreamt it or imagined it when he was groggy-minded – of an inrush of water. Of *rushing* water. The recollection came to him because he was thinking about this list and whatever might have caused it: explosion, list, heaviness, all simultaneous and all therefore connected. There was a slant of about ten degrees on her now; you had to haul yourself up the incline or hold on to something so as not to slide down it. Wishart murmured to Hobday, 'Can't think why they didn't give us transverse trimming tanks.'

Some of the E-class had them, and some didn't. There wasn't normally much use for them; and even if they'd had them and been able to trim the list off her it wouldn't have answered the vital question – *why* was she listing?

'Course north forty-one east, sir.'

'Depth one hundred feet, sir.'

'Very good.'

'Stop the pump.' Apart from the list, he'd got her trimmed finely. Bubble a degree aft, 'planes amidships, needle static at the ordered depth and only one motor slow ahead. The lopsidedness spoilt the effect considerably. Hobday asked Wishart, 'Spare hands to the high side, sir?' He meant, use crew-weight to balance her. Wishart, instead of answering, pointed upwards. Jake heard it at once: it was the trawler coming back, the one towing its grapnel sweep.

He wondered if the Turks would have any way of knowing they'd hooked her once and that she'd spat out the hook.

'Slow ahead port, full field.'

'Slow ahead port, full field, sir . . . Both motors slow ahead, sir.'

'Seventy feet.'

The 'planes swung over again. Enemy propeller noise was louder and closer, but it was likely to pass astern, Jake thought. And Wishart was taking advantage of the Turk's own noise to speed up a little, hoping it would drown the sounds the submarine made and deafen the shore hydrophones. Jake thought, *Perhaps now we'll fool him, slip away* . . . But he checked that quick spark of hope, reminded himself that there could very likely be more nets ahead, or mines, or both, and that at this end of the straits, coming up towards the town and harbour of Gallipoli, there would as likely as not be a shoaling of patrol craft. One had also to bear in mind that there were still a dozen miles to cover before they reached the Marmara, and that plenty could happen in twelve miles of Dardanelles.

Condensation dripped like slow rain. Everywhere it glistened, trickled over sweating steel. The leaky rivets added their quota of wetness: the broad streak of it had a different shine from the wet enamelling over which it ran en route downwards to the bilge. He wondered about the shaft gland: that port screw was being used now. And using both motors meant using twice as much battery juice as running on only one had done. Theoretically the box should be flat already . . . Twelve miles: with the deep tide, say four knots. Not less than three hours – *un*interrupted. He wiped his eyes:

it would be wrong to rub them, rub the acid into them. McVeigh, who should have known better – he looked like some sort of hobgoblin over there, or a beast at bay crouching in its cave – had been rubbing his, and they were bright red, streaming. Breathing open-mouthed – one tended to, when the air was as poor as this, it made you feel as if you were jogging uphill all the time – McVeigh was displaying his narrow, ratty-looking teeth. He'd have looked at home gnawing the bark off trees, Jake thought; the image that came into his mind amused him and he must have smiled, because Wishart, glancing his way just then, looked surprised and asked him, 'Happy in your work, pilot?'

'It's a grand life, sir.'

'Ah. You'll *all* think so presently, when we're having our breakfast in the Marmara.'

CPO Crabb growled, ''Ell of a big breakfas' it'll need to be.'

Wishart looked just about played out. It must have come on suddenly; this afternoon, when Jake had been on watch and the skipper had sat chatting with him and the other watchkeeper for an hour or more, he hadn't looked tired at all. He asked Crabb now, 'Did they give us plenty of fresh eggs, cox'n, this trip?'

'Not so dusty, sir . . . But there's bacon an' beef sausage and fried bread – bread's 'ard, but *fried* it won't—'

'What'll we eat the rest of the patrol, for heaven's sake?'

'We're victualled for a month, sir. An' there's chickens in them Turk dhows, an'—'

Hobday reported, 'Seventy feet, sir.' He repeated his earlier suggestion: 'Try sending spare hands to the high side, sir?'

'If you like.'

'Or a puff of air in number four?'

'Not that.'

Weatherspoon said, 'Enemy passin' astern left to right, sir.'

Wishart nodded. 'We've slipped our chain, I think.'

'Not the one was sweepin', sir – the one what anchored. She's turnin' towards, sir.' Jake thought, *Damn them* . . . The leading tel said, 'Revs decreasin' – slowin', sir.'

'Stop port.'

'Stop port, sir . . . Port motor stopped.'

Wishart ordered, 'Everyone who's free to move, get over to the starboard side. Pass that for'ard and aft.'

Lewis sent the message into the torpedo stowage compartment. Ellery, sweat gleaming through the fuzz of brown beard around his mouth and running down the deep channels in the skin of his neck, passed it aft. Wishart stood watching the bubble in the small curved spirit-level on the deckhead.

'It's moving already, damn it!'

'Enemy's stopped, sir.'

Wishart nodded, still watching the bubble. Only a few men had had time to move, and the angle was already coming off her. Jake could feel her swinging over. Now a dozen or twenty men would have moved an average of, say, five feet; surely it oughtn't to make *this* much difference. She was on an even keel, already. Wishart's attention still on the bubble, which was the size and shape of a small broad-bean in the green-tinted tube. *She was going on over, listing the other way . . .*

'Back to your stations!'

But she was still swinging over – as if having once started she couldn't be stopped. Wishart muttered, 'She's gone cranky. Doesn't make sense, damn it. She's—' He pulled out a handkerchief to mop his streaming eyes with. Everard looked as if he more or less understood what was puzzling everyone; the Marine just as plainly did not. 'She's – stopped again . . .' Wishart, frowning at the bubble. 'Just gone over and – *hanging* . . .' He sounded relieved, Jake thought, that she hadn't gone right over – or at any rate far enough over to slop acid out of the battery cells. Weatherspoon reported, 'Enemy still layin' stopped, sir.'

Enemy listening to them, in fact. Just as he had before when he'd followed them along, starting and stopping and holding his distance astern of them. It struck Jake that if the Turk was out to drive them mad he was going about it in a very shrewd way. Also that the last time he'd trailed behind them like this there'd been a mine barrage ahead and he'd more or less herded them into it.

Wishart suddenly slapped his forehead.

'I'll be *damned*!'

Hobday glanced round at him. Wishart told the outside ERA, 'Get a wheelspanner on the conning-tower drain, McVeigh. Stand by to just crack it and then bang it shut again double-quick.'

'Aye, sir . . .'

Hobday muttered, staring at the hatch, 'Of course . . . I must be cuckoo!' Wishart told him, 'Get a pump working on the bilge. Account for everything, eh? The weight – and after the bang I heard a flooding sound – and now the list, and everywhere else normal. Top-hamper pulling her over . . . Be ready to run both pumps together if we have to.'

He watched McVeigh clamp a wheelspanner on the valve-wheel of the conning-tower drain. The pipe led from the bottom of the tower to the bilge; if there was water up there – if the boat had dived with her top hatch open, for instance – and you opened that valve, sea-water from the tower would flood down into the bilge at full sea-pressure.

Wishart must have been thinking about that, too, and decided to check his theory where the pressure wasn't quite so great.

'Belay all that. Wait, McVeigh.' He told Hobday, 'Come up to forty feet.'

Hanging over to starboard like this she felt like a duck with one leg shorter than the other. Clumsy: and in any emergency she'd be clumsy to handle too. But she was lumbering upwards now as the 'planesmen coaxed her towards the surface – a surface that would be dark now. It felt better – Jake thought – to be going up. Admittedly they could be rising into nets or mines; but by this time they'd be getting past that Kodjuk bulge of land, the rounded headland pressing in like a corset and giving the straits the inward curve of a belly-dancer's waist, and once the boat got out to where they widened again – *let's not*, he thought, *follow that simile too far* – her chances of running into lethal obstructions should become less with every yard she covered. His hands were resting palms-down on the chart, and he watched forefingers and middle fingers crossing. He didn't want to be caught off-guard again; too often, as one had begun to relax, something damnable had happened . . . Hobday was making adjustments to the trim as the boat came up; Wishart ordered, 'Thirty feet.'

'Thirty, sir.' Weatherspoon called out, 'Enemy movin', sir!'

'Which way?'

'Can't say yet, sir.'

Thirty-six feet. Thirty-five. Hobday glanced round at Wishart, obviously wondering whether he should still take her right up, with an enemy up there on the prowl. Thirty-four feet – thirty-three . . .

'Comin' towards, sir. Follerin' astern, like before.'

'Closing?'

'Very slow revs, sir.'

Following, then. *Exactly* as he'd done before.

Waiting for them to suffocate, or for the battery to die?

There was only one place where the straits narrowed again

significantly, and that was off Gallipoli, roughly eight miles further on. But in any case this stretch was only two miles wide. There could be minefields, or mined nets anywhere.

'Thirty feet, sir.'

Wishart looked at Weatherspoon. The leading tel nodded. 'Still comin', sir.'

'Closing?'

A shake of the head: 'Not *loud*, sir.'

'Right.' Wishart told Hobday, 'Pump on the bilge.' He looked at McVeigh: 'Ready?' The spanner was hanging from the brass wheel; McVeigh reached for it. 'Aye, sir.' Hobday reported, 'Pump's running on the bilge.' You could hear it, from down there out of sight, making a noise like some monster child sucking on an already empty mug. Wishart told the ERA, 'Crack it, and shut it again immediately.'

The Glaswegian took a grip with both hands on the shaft of the spanner, and swung his whole weight on to it. The noise of water jetting through the pipe had the suddenness of a gunshot: its roar stopped dead as McVeigh jammed the valve shut again. There was a slopping sound from the bilge; but the pump would be returning that gushing intake to the sea now.

'There's our answer, then.' Wishart reached up and banged his fist against the hatch. 'Tower's full. The one space we didn't think of checking. That's where the extra weight's come from and that's what's heeling us over.'

'Enemy closin', sir!'

'Seventy feet.'

Crabb and Morton flung their wheels around, and the 'planes slanted to drag her down. Morton hissed, 'Give us some angle, 'swain?' Crabb told Hobday, 'She's awkward, sir. Slow answerin'.'

'Bound to be.' Wishart didn't seem to have been made unhappy by his discovery. It would present certain immediate problems – surfacing would be a slow and rather dangerous procedure – but at least the mystery had been cleared up, and depending on precisely what the damage was it could probably be repaired, later on. He told Crabb, 'Have to manage as best we can, cox'n. Engine-room department'll have their hands full, though, once we get into the Marmara.'

He'd glanced round at the ERAs as he said it: at McVeigh, Knight, Bradshaw. Bradshaw looked as if he'd just climbed out of a bath, except that there was nothing clean about him; he'd tied a rag around his head to keep the sweat out of his eyes. Knight looked as if he'd been crying. Come to think of it, everyone looked pretty frightful. Eyes particularly. Holes in skulls with water running out of them. Little Agnew, propped against the after bulkhead under the telegraphs' brassy gleam, could have been the ghost of some lost child. Roost, square and upright at the wheel, blinked continuously and regularly, as if a motor moved his eyelids while he watched the lubber's line against the image of the compass-card. It was just as well that the master compass, above their heads in the flooded tower, lived in its own watertight binnacle. The long and stringy frame of Stoker Adams, in the starboard after corner, was drooped into a sort of S-bend: knees forward, head and shoulders slumped, the eyes red-rimmed and glaring murderously from under matted brows. None of us, Jake thought, can look much like the portraits in our parents' living-rooms. Even the passengers . . . Adams, though, looked particularly fiendish, possibly nastier even than McVeigh; he was yellow-skinned and the gloss of dirty sweat made him seem almost orange.

Wishart cocked an eyebrow at Weatherspoon. The leading tel told him, 'Close now, sir.'

The needle in the gauge was approaching the 55-foot mark, and Crabb, anticipating a sluggish response, was already easing the downward angle of the dive.

'Agnew – I shan't be using telegraphs. Go and sit in the doorway and pass orders by word of mouth.'

'Sir.' The boy looked grateful as he edged over past Ellery. Wishart said, 'Anyone who doesn't have to stand, sit down. Pass that through the boat.'

'Seventy feet, sir.'

'Very good . . . Here comes Willie.'

They could hear him suddenly – the thump-thump-thump of that churning screw. Trawler – gunboat, whatever Willie was . . . Almost over the top: but not quite, the volume of sound was still rising. Overhead just about – *now*. Jake wondered if the Turk might be dropping depth-charges.

If he was, they'd be on their way down now, floating down, turning end over end as they sank through still black water towards the submarine . . . The – *no* . . . He'd seen this point rather late, and he recognised an unusual slowness in his mental processes: if the trawler had been dropping charges she wouldn't have been moving at such slow speed. The Turk would blow his own stern off, that way. And one's brain was, undoubtedly, working at a similarly low speed. Oxygen starvation? He heard the enemy go over and the sound of him begin to fade, saw Wishart staring upwards at the deckhead as he listened too. Poor lookout if *his* brain had brakes on . . . Everyone was sitting, squatting on the deck, leaning against whatever came handy, and Jake let himself slide down too. Use less oxygen: skipper should've thought of it before. Hell of a good man, though. This afternoon – after the noon snack and tot of rum – Jake had taken over again in the control room, and Wishart had come and sat down too; they'd chatted for quite a while. At first Wishart had talked to Smith, the tattoo'd torpedoman who'd been sharing the watch with Jake; he'd talked about Smith's harmonica and how he'd learnt to play it, and from that to the Smith family in Hampshire. The torpedoman's father was a water-bailiff on some rich stretch of the Test, and Smith was full of stories about fish and fishing and poachers' ways. Wishart had had some fishing stories of his own to tell. When that conversation ran dry, he'd turned to Jake.

'Go back to the Mercantile Marine, will you, when their Lordships release you?'

He'd shaken his head. 'I don't know. It's a bit – difficult, in some ways.'

Eventually Wishart had got the whole thing out of him. About Jake's mother alone and panicky, and no one but him to care for her, take his father's place.

'Your father must have been away a lot, surely?'

'Then she had *me* with her.'

'My dear old lad—' Wishart had seemed genuinely concerned – 'parents do lose their children. Not *lose*, in any final sense, but—'

'Then most of them have each other to fall back on?'

'Listen.' Wishart waved a hand, wiping out Jake's arguments. 'Your mama isn't the only widow in the British Isles, not by a very long chalk. Thousands and thousands of 'em, *millions* of 'em, old lad. And some of 'em have lost sons as well as husbands, poor things.'

'Yes, yes, I know. But – well, some people take things harder than others do. And in this particular case . . .' It had been hard to explain. His mother wasn't at all worldly, she wasn't equipped for living on her own. She was childlike; at an early age he'd discovered that she needed him more than he needed her, and that she worried needlessly and constantly about any decision she had to make for herself. Like a child struggling to cope with an adult world. Jake's father would come home after a few months'absence, unravel her self-made problems and put everything straight for her, settle this and that and ask X and Y to keep an eye on her, and go off to sea again. Sighing, Jake suspected now, with relief? As *he* had done, after that terrible 'compassionate' leave?

'Enemy's stopped again, sir. Couldn't only just 'ear 'im – if 'e'd gone another minute I wouldn't 'a 'eard 'im stop.'

The pattern was not the same as it had been before. Before, the Turk had stayed back, kept his distance astern of them.

'Either he's changed his tactics, or he's lost us. Or he thinks we're sunk, left the other one trawling for us and he's gone on about his own business.' Wishart was talking to Hobday. Leaning on the ladder, mopping at his face with an already sodden handkerchief. He swivelled, leant on it frontwards, one foot on its bottom rung and his arms extended upwards, hands grasping a higher one. 'Number One.'

'Sir?'

Hobday's skin looked as white as paper; the lower half of his small face was gilded with ginger stubble. Wishart told him, 'I think we'll go up and have a look. Dark now – and we're doing no good as it is.' He pushed himself off the ladder. Jake thought he was working hard in the effort to think straight, act straight. 'Thirty feet.'

'Thirty feet, sir.' Hobday asked him, 'Use the port shaft, sir?'

'No.'

'Thirty, sir . . .' Crabb and Morton worked like machines, coping skilfully with the awkwardness of handling her with the list on. By 'going up', Jake realised, Wishart couldn't be talking about surfacing. It would be a dangerous thing to risk here even if she was in good shape and undamaged. With the tower flooded, they'd have to wallow up there while it drained down to the bilges and the pump shifted the water overboard; until the tower was empty you couldn't open the lower hatch, and until you were on the surface you couldn't start the draining process. So for several minutes the submarine would lie blind and helpless. But if only – he shut his eyes – if *only* it could be possible . . . To surface, get moving on the gas engines, with fresh air flooding through the boat!

Something to dream about . . .

585

He forced his eyes open, pulled himself together. They *would* be surfacing. Not yet, but a time would come – a little while yet, some way to go, just a matter of hanging on, and then there *would* be a moment when the engines would roar into life and you'd feel the sweet, cold air, drink it, wallow in it: the thought was enough to make you cry with longing for it . . .

You needn't worry for two seconds about me, you know.

Wishart had said to him this afternoon, 'Look here, old lad. You say you might take some job or other, anything to stay near her . . . Have you considered how that would be? Thousands and thousands of men have awful, humdrum jobs – jobs they loathe and just have to struggle on with, year in and year out – near killing 'emselves in the process. Would you contemplate that – when you don't have to, when you're a seaman, a first-class one, highly trained and experienced and a very, *very* useful man?'

There'd been a pause then: close to them, on his blanket on the deck, Everard had muttered something in his sleep. Wishart asked Jake, 'What advice d'you think your father would give, if he was here to give it?'

Jake had pointed out that if his father had been alive to give advice, the question wouldn't be arising in the first place. Wishart brushed that aside; and Jake had only been stalling, trying to stave off an argument that was entirely right and logical as Wishart saw it but which didn't take into account the deep, emotional feelings running counter to it.

'D'you think in the long run it'd do your mother most good for you to be in some frightful job, coming home each night done-up and dispirited – needing to get drunk to forget it, and turning green with envy when you run into some old shipmate who *hasn't* thrown up the life he was born for – that, or having a son who's happy, getting on, commanding his own ship soon enough – *that* fellow, coming home a few times each year, a son she'd be really proud of?'

'Well, it's more than—'

'Listen to me, old lad. *That* would be taking your father's place. *That's* what he'd like to hear about when she joins him!'

'Thirty feet, sir.'

Wishart checked the gauge and the bubble. He looked over towards Jake.

'May get a fix in a minute, pilot . . . Number One, bring her up slowly and carefully to twenty feet.'

586

'Twenty feet, sir. Handsomely now, cox'n.'

McVeigh hoisted his scraggy, scarecrow-like frame to its feet. He looked like something that had been run over by a horse-tram in Sauchiehall Street, but he was alert enough to realise he'd be needed now to operate the periscopes. Ellery got up too; Wishart was waiting near the after periscope, and on that small one it was necessary for relative bearings to be read off a bearing-ring on the deckhead.

'Twenty-two feet, sir.'

'Up periscope.'

'Twenty-one . . .' The brass tube was hissing upwards, drops of greasy moisture glinting on its bronze, grey grease clinging wetly to the wires. The bulky eyepiece end came up clear of the well; Wishart grabbed the handles at knee-height, and before the single lens jerked to a stop at eye-level he'd jerked them down and settled to the search.

'Twenty feet, sir.'

'Black as pitch . . .' Muttering to himself as he circled, right eye pressed against the lens, left eye shut. He stopped only halfway round, snapped the handles up. 'Down!' McVeigh depressed the lever, sending the periscope slithering back into its hole in the deck; Wishart murmured, squeezing for'ard between Roost's position and the ladder, 'Can't see a damn thing with that one.' Looking at McVeigh again he raised his hands and twitched the fingers, and McVeigh sent the big 'scope sliding up. A necklet of drops of water glistened like diamonds around the gland where the big tube passed through the deckhead.

'Depth?' He'd clicked the magnification in. Hobday answered, 'Twenty feet, sir.' Wishart circled slowly, his toes against the raised sill around the well . . . 'God almighty!'

He'd trained back the other way: his throat bulged as he swallowed.

'Port ten.'

'Port ten, sir.' Roost, rock-like, moved his wheel around.

'Ship's head?'

'North forty-five east, sir. Forty-six. Forty—'

'Midships. Steer north fifty east. Pilot – before I altered course there was a headland with a sort of beacon or sawn-off lighthouse on it about one hundred yards on our port beam.'

'*One hundred*—'

'Now – high bulk of land bearing . . . red 132 degrees.'

587

'Ship's head north forty-eight east, sir!'

Jake scribbled the figures down. On the big Grubb periscope a relative-bearing ring was etched on glass inside. Applying relative bearing to ship's head at the same moment gave you compass bearings.

'Hear anything, leading tel?'

'Nothin', sir.'

Circling . . . That was the *world*, up there, that he was staring into. Open, dark, clean, with a wind to ripple the surface and drive the clouds: up there, you could fill your lungs, let it all out, fill them again . . . Difficult to imagine! 'Pilot – other coast now – the highest bit of a longish line of ground, and the right-hand edge of it: bearing – green 93.'

'North fifty east, sir!'

And one more? No, he'd finished. Two position lines, plus what he'd said about being almost ashore on some headland. Compass variation of two degrees west. Lots of hills, mountains, edges on the chart: it was a matter of fitting those three items together so they'd make sense. He heard the periscope hissing down, and Wishart joined him.

'Point here, sir – *Karakova Burnu*. Then we'd have this height here called *Sarair Tepe* – for the first bearing . . .' He ran the parallel ruler across the chart from the compass rose. 'And then – this?' A longish ridge of high ground on the Asiatic coast, with an altitude of a thousand feet at its western end. It all fitted and there were no sensible alternatives; Jake ringed the point of intersection as a fix. They were close to the European shore and they'd come about two miles from where they'd lain bottomed all day. He laid off the present course of north fifty east.

'Three quarters of an hour, then back ten degrees to port?'

Wishart turned away.

'Have to get past that Turk, if he's still hanging about.'

Jake was suffering quite badly from the thin air and the stink in it; he was conscious of the shortness of his breath and a sort of fuddle growing in his brain. When you had something positive to do you could push the discomfort to the back of your mind, but as soon as you stopped it closed in on you again. Wishart had just ordered, some way off, 'Up periscope'. Jake told himself, *Stay awake* . . . Wishart asked Weatherspoon, 'Anything?' The leading telegraphist guessed what he was being asked, and shook his head. Drooping eyelids gave him a haughty look as he peered out from the cabinet. The periscope had thumped to a stop, Wishart had grabbed its handles and clicked it into low power, and he was making a rapid all-round search. In high power you had to sweep around more slowly, rather like using a telescope instead of binoculars; you saw further, in high power, with a narrower field of vision.

'Down.' He stepped back. 'Can't see much.' He'd shut his eyes, screwing his whole face up and shaking his head as if to clear his ears of something. He'd be having to work hard, too, to think straight. The mind had a tendency to go dim, drift away. Jake wondered, *We might surface, chance it? Better than playing safe and suffocating?*

'Seventy feet.'

'Seventy, sir.'

Wanting to get back into the lower tidal stream. Nick Everard, Jake saw, was lying on his back and reading Burtenshaw's Tolstoy book. Or just holding it up over his face as an umbrella against the dripping deckhead. Burtenshaw was at the table, making card-houses that never got to be more than two storeys high. He'd offered Robins the bunk he'd been on for a short while, not long ago, and Robins had accepted with a grunt that might have been taken as some form of thanks. He was asleep now. Burtenshaw had admitted during their snack lunch, his tongue perhaps loosened by that tot of rum, that he wasn't really getting much out of the Tolstoy. Jake had commented, 'Conan Doyle's *my* mark. Limit, just about.' They'd all agreed on the fascination of Sherlock Holmes. The ship's expert on the great detective, apparently, was Chief ERA Grumman; Hobday had said you couldn't trip Grumman up, he knew every detail of every case. Burtenshaw had opened Tolstoy, read a line of it, sighed, shut it again; he'd asked them, 'Anyone read the Guy Thorn book, *When It Was Dark*?' Hobday, who'd had the watch and had been keeping an eye on things at the same time as he munched his corned beef and biscuit, said he'd read some of it. He hadn't thought it worth his while to continue with it. 'I don't want some other fellow's quirky notions about religion. A man who tries to push those kind of views on other people – well, the *conceit* of it, the sheer—'

'Oh, I don't know.' Nick took up the argument on Burtenshaw's behalf, since the Marine was looking embarrassed by Hobday's vehemence. He seemed rather prone to this kind of awkwardness. Nick suggested to Hobday, 'You're objecting to it because you're seeing it from the standpoint he's proposing to reject. If your mind could allow the possibility that much of the stuff we've been taught to believe is up the pole—'

'I don't want it to, thanks!'

Jake grinning at them both. Like many large-built men he was easygoing, and it amused him to see others stung to argument. Burtenshaw licking corned-beef fat off his fingers. The rum had flushed his boyish cheeks; nobody guessed what a kick there was in navy-issue rum until they tried it.

'Seventy feet, sir.'

Jake looked up with a start: jerkily, as if he'd been woken out of a dream. He was sitting on the deck, leaning against the chart table. He couldn't recall the act of sitting down. Across on the other side Burtenshaw was dozing over the scattered cards. Nick Everard was still holding the book but it was resting pages-downwards on his chest, and his eyes were shut. His jaw was dark with stubble. Robins's embryo beard was blueish, and it gave him a Middle-Eastern look. Armenian, he could have been. Better be careful, Jake thought, when he landed; the Turks had nailed horseshoes to Armenians' feet, amongst other pleasantries. Everard had told him so, and Everard had had it from that chap Reaper. Robins, at the noon meal, had questioned Wishart about the rum issue. How officers could have been allowed it: and weren't the sailors supposed to have it diluted in water, in the form known as 'grog'?

Wishart had told him, poker-faced, 'Fresh water's one of our biggest problems, on patrol.'

'Hear anything, leading tel?'

Weatherspoon must have shaken his head. He was in the doorway of the cabinet, where he could see and be seen. Anyway, there'd been no answer, and Wishart seemed to have been satisfied. The ticking of the log was extraordinarily loud: like a heartbeat in the silent, airless, greenhouse heat and acid, lifeless air. If the submarine had a heart it was down below this deck, the battery. A miracle that it still beat at all. When it ceased to do so they'd have no option but to blow themselves to the surface and face the Turkish guns: and for a lungful of clean air might not the price be too exorbitant? He heard a rasping noise that pulled him out of the fringes of a daydream; the retch had come from his own throat, and he tried to turn it into a cough. Wishart said, 'Thirty feet.'

Jake *thought* he'd said it. Wishart was clinging to the ladder with his arms up and spread. He *must* have ordered that change in depth: leaning forward and rising slightly, one could see up-angle on the 'planes, and the needle in the depth-gauge beginning to circle slowly. Was he thinking of surfacing? Morton, at the fore 'planes, was rocking to and fro, his torso shifting rhythmically from side to side, about an inch in each direction. Keeping himself awake. Hobday, standing behind Morton and the coxswain, kept jolting up and down on his toes – heels – toes . . . He could have sat down and still done his job all right, *and* used less air, Jake thought.

Adjusting trim now as she rose, he'd stopped those irritating, jerky motions. Extraordinary to think of all that sea inside the tower. Observation ports blown in, probably. Perhaps Wishart hadn't clamped the deadlight shut over the middle one after the struggle in the net. But – it was getting harder all the time to concentrate one's thoughts – Jake *thought* he'd seen him doing it . . .

'Thirty feet, sir.'

Hobday had more or less whispered it.

'Leading tel?'

Weatherspoon's ears were blocked off by his headphones, but he didn't need to hear the question. He saw it, as Wishart glanced at him, and he shook his head. 'Nothin', sir.'

'Twenty feet.'

'Twenty feet, sir. Easy with her, now.'

'Aye, sir.' No change in Crabb's deep growling tone. Jake saw McVeigh drag himself upright, using the steel guard over the main vent levers as a handhold. Jake realised he might be wanted too, to take down some bearings. He had no idea, absolutely none, of how much time had passed since the last fix. When he was up on his feet he looked round to check the time by the bulkhead clock, but the clock was a whitish haze without hands or figures, more like a hazy full moon than – one lost track of one's own thinking. He was shaking his head, blinking, using his fingertips to clear his fogged-up eyes.

'Twenty-two feet, sir. Twenty—'

'Up.'

Hss – ss – ss . . . *Thump.*

Clack of the handles banging down. Hobday's report: 'Twenty feet, sir.'

'Well done, well done . . .' Calm, easy-mannered, friendly. Marvellous chap, Aubrey Wishart. 'Keep her up now though, don't for Pete's sake—'

Muttering as he swung around, his arms hooked gorilla-fashion over the handles, his weight hanging there so that his legs and feet hardly seemed to be supporting him at all, just sort of shoving around the circumference of the well as he trained the big periscope around. 'Better light now, I can—'

He'd gasped: and he was still for a moment, frozen . . .

'Down!'

The handles clashed up, McVeigh pushed the steel lever over and the gleaming brass barrel jerked, flowed downwards. All eyes were on the captain: mouths open, sweat running, breaths short like the panting of men running uphill under load.

'Seventy feet.'

'Seventy, sir . . .'

'Planes turning, digging into the sea to pull her nosing into its depths. Wishart told them, 'The Turk's about fifty yards – thirty, perhaps – on our port bow. I think he's anchored. It's a gunboat, like a big yacht with one tall funnel. He's showing a few lights through scuttles in his superstructure.'

He and Hobday exchanged glances. Now Hobday had turned back to the gauge, the 'planesmen. Wishart muttered, 'I could sink him, easily. One torpedo at close range – sitting duck.' Hobday whipped round eagerly; CPO Crabb growled, 'That's the ticket, sir!' Men were getting to their feet, wiping their eyes and blinking, happy. Jake quite suddenly felt better, really more or less back to normal. He slid open the chart-table drawer where he kept his navigational instruments, and took the attack stop-watch out of its box, so he'd be ready for the attack procedure when Wishart ordered it.

But why go deep, he wondered vaguely, if you were about to start an attack?

Wishart murmured, 'Can't do it, unfortunately, cox'n. Have to save all our fish for *Goeben*.'

Light of excitement fading. Like so many children robbed suddenly of a treat. Hobday said dully, 'Seventy feet, sir.' Wishart glanced round the disappointed faces. 'Not a squeak, now. Agnew, go aft very quietly, tell 'em I don't want to hear a sound. Lewis – tell 'em that for'ard.'

Object: sneak past Turk. Turk sitting up there in comfort, breathing fresh air. Jake had eased himself down to sit on the deck again. Condensation raining down everywhere. If you tasted it, it has a sweet, sickly rankness like human sweat. He found he had a stop-watch in his hand, for some reason. Must have picked it up without thinking. In the dream he reasoned carefully that not going for the Turk made sense, because if they could get past him and if he thought they'd been finished by that bloody mine, then they'd be creeping into the Marmara presently and the enemy wouldn't know they'd got through. He heard Wishart order, 'Twenty feet.'

'Twenty feet, sir.'

'*Certain* there's been no sound from him?'

Time had passed. He didn't know how much. Time was mixed up with the reek of the gassing battery and men's breath and sweat and the other stink wafting from the engine-room, from the row of covered sanitary buckets. The gas, of course, was hydrogen – described in the battery-maintenance manual as 'not actually poisonous, but will not support respiration'. Another way of saying 'It won't kill you, but it won't let you live.' But it was all one stench: indivisible, disgusting. Wishart's voice broke through: 'Up periscope.' It was part of the dream, it didn't concern reality. Then he heard the *thump* as McVeigh replaced the lever in its 'stop' position and the ram stopped sliding because oil at high pressure blocked its motion. When the ram extended, it increased the distance between sheaves around which the wires ran; that was what pulled them and hauled the periscope up or down. You could exercise your mind on visualising a thing like that, and it was better than thinking about fresh air or a cool night breeze dimpling the surface of the straits. He was in the process of getting to his feet: a big man, heavy, lurching upwards. Stop-watch: he pulled the drawer open, and put the watch carefully in its box. Shutting the drawer again, he glanced up and focused on the bulkhead clock. Twenty-five past twelve. Morning of day three, for God's sake! They'd been dived for – he made himself work it out – thirty-two hours . . . Submarine regulations still in force stipulated various impractical air-freshening routines after *fourteen* hours dived. They weren't out of the straits yet.

'We've passed him.' Wishart had his eyes at the lenses and he was facing aft. 'If it wasn't for his cabin-lights I wouldn't be able to see him. We're past and clear.' He began to swing himself slowly round, pausing now and then to study features of the shoreline. With only stars for illumination, you wouldn't see much else. Jake told himself, wanting to believe in it but still needing to be convinced, *We can go through now. Nothing left to stop us!* Except

– well, there could be more mine barrages, and nets. The fact they'd got past one Turkish gunboat didn't mean it would be all plain sailing from here on. Wishart turned up the periscope's handles and stepped back, and McVeigh sent it down.

'We're nicely out in the middle, pilot. What was that course you had us on?'

'North forty-one east, sir.'

'Ah, yes.' He turned, and rested a hand on the helmsman's shoulder. 'Starboard five, old Roost.'

'Starboard five, sir . . . Five o' starboard wheel on, sir.'

Roost was grinning, tickled by that prefix 'old'. There were glimmers of happiness in other faces too: in Stone's, Agnew's, Adams's, Knight's . . . Premature, perhaps; but Wishart's brighter tone and manner were infectious, and even a momentary lifting of spirits had its value. Wishart said, 'Steer north forty-one east, old Roost.'

'North forty-one east, sir.'

'Seventy feet, Number One.'

'Seventy feet, sir.'

Wishart joined Jake at the chart table. Leaning on it beside him, he lurched heavily against him. Jake glanced at him in surprise; Wishart said, 'Shove up, pilot. You're getting too damn fat, d'you know that?' He looked round over his shoulder: his face was bloodless, middle-aged. 'Lewis. You'd better reduce the navigating officer's rations.'

Crabb said, 'That's an extra breakfas' comes *my* way, Lewis.'

Jake told him, 'You'll need to be damn quick on your feet, cox'n!'

Laughter . . .

Wishart eased over, allowing him some room.

'Now then. Let's see where we think we are.'

Two-seventeen . . .

There'd been the orders, routine actions and reports of preparing to surface. It was a dream, of course. You went along with it because there was always the hope it might come true.

There had been other preparations too. Both ballast pumps were ready to start sucking on the control-room bilges, to pump out the water that would flood down from the tower. Wishart had said, 'Stop her at six feet', and Hobday had pointed out that she'd be unstable with the tower's weight out of water. Jake had thought, *Can't drain it any other way, you stupid clown*, but Wishart's answer had been more practical; he'd said, 'Blow port and starboard tanks separately if you need to. Just keep her upright till it's empty. Won't take many minutes.' Around them, men did their jobs mechanically, listened to the orders, made their reports, waited for whatever might come next. They didn't believe in it either, but he could see that like him they were ready to pretend they did. They were the faces of sick men who for some hours now had been breathing poison.

'Blow three, four, five and six main ballast!'

McVeigh snarling, panting like some wild beast as he sent air roaring to the saddle-tanks. Hydroplanes hard a-rise.

Going *up*!

Eighteen – fifteen – thirteen . . .

Watching the needle circle round the gauge: and the bubbles, particularly the transverse one, as the list increased and she began to sway over as she rose – ten feet . . .

'Stop blowing four and six!'

Those were the port-side tanks. The list was to starboard.

Eight feet. Seven. List coming off her now.

'Start the pumps!'

Deafening noise of expanding air: it filled the mind, allowed you to believe the dream was coming true while all the time you knew that at any second the whole procedure could be reversed by an order, 'Seventy feet: get her *down*!'

'Stop blowing one and three! Open the conning-tower drain!' The noise of blowing was shut off suddenly with the air, and Geordie Knight jerked the drain-valve open, starting it with the wheelspanner and then wrenching the thing around by hand. Water pounding in the pipe. 'Pumps are sucking, sir!'

There hadn't been anything sure about that, either. Battery readings taken just now by Blackie Cole had shown density readings that were horrifying, well below the safe-discharge limit of 1.180.

'Pilot – behind me on the ladder, on my legs.'

Jake shambled over. There was always pressure in the boat when she'd been down for a long time. You could see it on the aneroid. When it was really bad, a captain opening the hatch without extra weight to hold him down could be blown out and killed.

'Chief ERA in the control room!'

Lofty Adams called through for him. Grumman came in: vast, lumbering, nodding to the other ERAs, stopping with a hand like an oily leg of mutton on the edge of the bulkhead door.

'Sir?'

'The minute the top hatch is open, Chief, I want the gas engines started. Half ahead – three hundred revs starboard and a standing charge port. But no delay, not one second's.'

In case they met a patrol boat or other trouble, and had to dive again; at least the engines would have sucked the foul air out of her and drawn some of the fresh kind in.

Hobday had sent another blast of air into number three; and the list was no longer evident, as the tower emptied and she regained stability. Two hours, Wishart had said – so Jake remembered. If they were lucky enough to be left to themselves, they'd have two hours on the surface now, before dawn and daylight forced them down again.

Then what? For a full charge in normal circumstances the battery needed eight hours. Jake wasn't up to thinking that one out. His mind pleaded, *Let's just get up there – please?* Hobday told Wishart, 'The tower's empty, sir.'

Ellery jumped up on the ladder, pulled the pins out of the clips and then jerked the clips free. He grabbed the hinged bar and pushed upwards on it, climbing another rung on the ladder in order to force the hatch up and back, clanging heavily into the tower. A splashing of water, about a bucketful, rained down into the control room. The signalman jumped clear, and Wishart went quickly up the ladder. Jake followed him, into an odour of seawater and wet metal. Rush of air, a violent hissing, whistling: the port-side scuttle and deadlight had been stove in, leaving a jagged hole, and the boat's pressurised stink was gusting out of it. Higher up, he grabbed hold of Wishart's legs, wrapping his arms round him above the knees and holding tight. He heard him working at the clips on the top hatch, and suddenly the hiss of escaping pressure thickened to a roar as Wishart eased the last clip off and held the hatch's opening force on it. Foul air rushed up round them: a fog came with it, an evil-smelling mist pouring out of the boat's sewer-like compartments. Wishart flung the hatch open and yelled downward, 'Start the engines!' Jake bawled it down and climbed after him, heaving himself up out of the hatch's rim and into the wet bridge and the incredibly clean night air. In the pause before the diesels coughed and spluttered into life he heard, from not far away in the darkness on the beam, a dog's high, mournful howl.

A *Marmaran* dog!

CHAPTER 8

'Let us pray.'

Fifth day: Sunday morning . . . Wishart glanced around the control room at the bowed heads of his ship's company. CPO Crabb's grey-streaked one was immediately in front of him, and Rinkpole's dome gleamed beside it. Leech, the stoker PO, had cut himself shaving, and a twist of blood-soaked cotton-waste clung to the side of his thick neck. Wishart's eyes rested for a moment on the depth-gauges with their needles static at seventy-five feet; E.57 was bottomed, off the west coast of Kalolimno Island, and there wasn't a hint of movement on her. Satisfied, he opened his prayer-book at one of the strips of signal-pad he'd put in as markers, and began to read into the warm underwater quiet, *O most blessed and glorious Lord God: we thy poor creatures whom thou hast made and preserved, holding our souls in life and now rescuing us out of the jaws of death, humbly present ourselves again before thy Divine Majesty to offer a sacrifice of praise and thanksgiving, for that thou heardest us when we called in our trouble, and didst not cast out our prayer . . .*

There'd have been some prayers all right, Jake thought. Most likely every single member of the ship's company had asked the Almighty for assistance at least once during the passage of the straits. Wishart had whisked some pages over, switching adroitly from one prayer to another: that first one, if he'd gone on with it, would have let him in for asserting that at some point they 'gave all for lost, our ship, our goods, our lives', and this would have presented an unjustifiably defeatist attitude. He continued instead, *Thou hast showed us terrible things and wonders in the deep, that we might see how powerful and gracious a God thou art, how able and ready to help them that trust in thee . . .*

Jake had been looking at ERA McVeigh when Wishart had spoken of 'terrible things and wonders in the deep', and he'd

597

almost burst out laughing, thinking that Angus McVeigh might be about the most terrible and wondrous of the lot . . . It was astonishing to think that only five days ago he'd had his work cut out just to remember these men's names; he felt now as if he'd known them all for years.

It had been about two-thirty on the morning of the third day when they'd surfaced at the Marmara's western end. There'd been two hours of darkness left; they'd spent them travelling eastward at six knots with one engine pumping the beginnings of new life into the tortured battery. Before dawn Wishart had dived her and taken her in close to the northern shore, to lie bottomed all day in twelve fathoms near a headland called Injeh Burnu. A day's rest, proper meals, clean air to breathe . . . During the day, Rinkpole and his torpedomen had drawn back the torpedo from the starboard tube, the one that had been flooded when the mine went off, done a full maintenance routine on it and then reloaded it. And Leading Seaman Dixon, the LTO, had got the gyro compass back into commission. The bigger repairs – to the conning-tower and the leaky control-room deckhead – had had to wait.

That evening they'd got away from the coast and surfaced well out in the deep water. Heading north-east on the gas engines and charging all the time, they'd met no surface craft at all, and they'd taken this as evidence that the Turks had no idea they'd got through. Otherwise they'd have been hunting for them. Wishart, on the bridge with Jake that night, had murmured, 'Probably imagine they've made their straits impassable. Silly asses!'

'Wonder how *Louve*'s come through it.'

'Oh, those froggies'll be all right.'

There'd been hammering and filing noises from the tower under their feet, and for some time Grumman and Knight were down inside the casing, under the gundeck, using a shaded torch to examine the rivets that fixed it to the pressure hull. Those were the loosened ones – from the strain of pulling against that net – and Grumman's view was that the flooding of the tower had loosened them still further.

'Tower made 'er list; an' when she lists over you got the weight o' the gun pullin' sideways.' He'd moved one ham-like hand at an angle to the other. 'So there's all that movement actin' on the rivets, twistin' at 'em. I reckon we oughter take the gun an' the gun-mountin' right off 'er, sir.'

They'd done it yesterday, in daylight, right out in the middle with no land or ships in sight. ERA Knight had taken care of technical problems while Roost and his gun's crew did the donkey-work. Barrel and breech had been manhandled into the fore hatch – which had been opened for the bare minimum of time needed to get the loads struck down into the submarine – and were now stowed up for'ard in the tube space. The heavy circular mounting had then been unbolted from the gundeck, manoeuvred along the casing to the bow in order not to risk damage to the saddle-tanks, and there eased overboard to sink into four hundred fathoms of water. Leaving a slight trim adjustment for Hobday to attend to. And while that had been going on, Grumman with McVeigh and Bradshaw had bolted a steel patch on a rubber seating to the outside of the hole in the tower, and welded a back-up patch to the inside of it, with packing between the two to guarantee its water-tightness. Hobday meanwhile had had both engines pounding away to bring his battery up to scratch; it hadn't been quite up, although the repair jobs had been completed, when the lookout on the bridge had sighted a wisp of funnel-smoke and they'd had to dive. Mid-morning, that had been; Hobday had grumbled at having had to cut the battery charge.

'Another half-hour, she'd have been right up.'

'We can't risk being spotted, Number One. The most vital thing now is not to let 'em suspect we're here.'

During the day, paddling eastward at periscope depth, they saw two freighters, one gunboat and about a dozen sailing craft, most of them dhows. The gunboat hadn't been patrolling, and her behaviour had reinforced their belief that the enemy were quite unaware of a submarine having gate-crashed their private sea. She'd been making about eight knots on a straight course, heading towards Rodosto; she hadn't been zigzagging, there'd been men lounging on her upper deck, and both her guns had canvas covers on.

E.57 had surfaced at five in the evening; there'd been nothing at all in sight, and Wishart had ordered 'hands to bathe'. They came up in groups of four men at a time; the procedure was to dive in, climb out, work up an all-over lather with salt-water soap and then go in again to wash it off. Nick had jumped at the chance of a swim, and so had Burtenshaw, but Robins had passed his up. And last night when all nominally clean-shaven men had shaved, preparing themselves for the Sunday morning service, Robins had abstained and advised the other two to do likewise. Nick had seen the point;

it would be better to look scruffy and un-British when the time came to land. They were to be provided with some kind of local garb – whatever Turks or other denizens of Constantinople wore – and clean-shaven faces would have looked out of place. So now the three passengers were the only men in E.57's control room who weren't spruced up.

The rendezvous with *Louve* was scheduled to take place at dawn. Nick was more than ready for the move. Being a passenger had been bad enough in *Terrapin* but in this submarine it was worse still. One felt not only useless and idle but actually an encumbrance, an unnecessary body getting in the way of men with work to do. It would be a relief to move under one's own power, make one's own decisions. Not that he'd much idea *what* decisions, what sort of problems he'd be faced with. It was no good even trying to guess what opposition or what help there'd be. Robins was certainly *no* help: Nick had tried to get some background information out of him, about the situation ashore and so on, but the man was either as ignorant as he was himself or jealous of his special knowledge. It was just as well, Nick thought, that he wasn't going to have to rely on Robins later, that they'd be splitting up as soon as they'd got ashore and met Reaper's people – whoever, for God's sake, *they* might be . . . Robins had said once, answering a probe of Nick's, 'The Grey Lady's the king pin. You'll get everything from her, or she'll see you get it from some other quarter.' Then, realising he'd actually given a fairly straight answer to a question, he'd turned testy, asking, 'Did Commander Reaper not brief you fully?'

'Well, yes. As far as he could.'

'Ah.' Smirk. 'Quite!'

Robins, of course, loathed Reaper. Nick didn't bother to stand up for him, though. A sneer as nebulous as that wasn't easy to take issue with; and Reaper was capable of fighting his own battles.

What *had* Reaper told him? Anything else that he ought to have in mind and hadn't? He didn't think so. Only the times and positions for the two rendezvous appointments. Beyond that, one had a free hand to act as circumstances dictated. It had been Reaper's personal decision to bring Nick into it. As the operation had been conceived originally, he'd said, Burtenshaw had been no more than a ferret to flush *Goeben* out of her hole. He'd been a throwaway: no great difficulty in putting him ashore with Robins, and while he wasn't expected to achieve anything directly with his bag of explosives the hope was that his having been put ashore at all would alert and alarm the Germans to the possibility of sabotage attempts; so they'd move her out of the Horn, to where E.57 or *Louve* could get at her. Reaper's intention was that with Nick to steer him along, the Marine might make a real job of it. Implicit in the London plan – the one Reaper had been saddled with and which he'd now amended – was that Burtenshaw was likely to be caught, soon after he'd landed. It was the kind of Whitehall cynicism that Reaper said he'd met before and never put into action in any of the stunts he'd handled. Nick had wondered whether his own participation was likely to make all that much difference. Reaper, he was aware, had a high opinion of his abilities, but that opinion was based on a performance – the Flanders coast raid – which Nick felt owed a great deal to sheer luck. Mightn't Reaper be only throwing away two amateurs instead of one?

Remembering that talk with him, pacing *Harwich*'s quarterdeck as night closed down on Imbros . . . Reaper had gone on to discuss what was expected to happen after Turkey capitulated. He'd said it was virtually certain that a British naval force would be sent through the Bosphorus into the Black Sea to support the White Russians in the Caucasus and Crimea.

'Not that your poor old *Leveret* is likely to be part of that.'

'I suppose not.'

And damn *that*, too. To have had a prospect of action – surface, destroyer action – instead of just the fizzling-out of the war and the onset of peacetime formality, would have brightened things considerably. It might even have made this submarine trip tolerable. He'd have been able to look forward to getting back to a world he knew and understood and could handle, felt at home and happy in. As it was, he faced a dogsbody job with little prospect of excitement in it. But he didn't want to show Reaper how low his spirits were; he said, 'At least it *is* a command, sir.'

Reaper had laughed. 'You've learnt not to look gift-horses in the mouth then, Everard!'

Bravo, he'd been referring to. And what *that* appointment had led to.

Wishart had read out a prayer for the King's Majesty. Now he turned the pages to another of his markers, and started on the 'Prayer to be said before a fight at Sea'.

O most powerful and glorious Lord God, Lord of Hosts, that rulest and commandest all things: Thou sittest in the throne judging right, and therefore we make our address to thy Divine Majesty in this our necessity, that thou wouldst take the cause into thine own hand, and judge between us and our enemies. Stir up thy strength, O Lord, and come and help us, for thou givest not always the battle to the strong, but canst save by many or by few . . . And how often in past centuries, Nick mused, must Christian invaders of these territories have asked their God to 'judge between them and their enemies'. A nicely preconceived judgement they'd have been expecting too, seeing that the enemy in those days had been Islam. It wasn't now: despite what the Turks were up to at the moment, the real enemy was as Christian as they were themselves, and would probably be requesting much the same degree of assistance. Only Christian pressure from one side and Christian bungling on the other had brought Islam into *this* war: plus the fact that a small group of thugs in Constantinople had all the power in their hands . . . McVeigh was staring at the deckhead, and Lewis was counting something on his fingers. Eggs? Potatoes? Wishart had shut his prayer book; he glanced at the depth-gauge and then said, 'The Grace of the Lord Jesus Christ, and the love of God, and the fellowship of the Holy Ghost, be with us all evermore.' A general growling of 'Amen' finished it. Heads that had been bowed turned upwards as he cleared his throat, looking round at them.

'It wasn't any joy-ride, was it? But you came through it splendidly. I knew you would, and you proved me right. Thank you, and well done.'

He met Weatherspoon's eyes, small-looking behind those thick glasses. The telegraphist's head shook briefly, answering the unspoken question. Wishart told his ship's company, 'About dawn tomorrow we'll be meeting the French boat and transferring our passengers to her. After that we'll settle down to patrol across the exit from Constantinople. *Louve* is watching it at the moment. We'll be there all ready for *Goeben* if she obliges us by coming out and providing a home for Chief Petty Officer Rinkpole's torpedoes.'

The TI smiled faintly, ran a hand over his bald head. Wishart went on, 'It's vital that if *Goeben* does come out we should sink or cripple her. That's what we've come this far for. Don't imagine that getting through the straits was the tricky bit and now it's all routine. It won't be. We're in the enemy's back-yard and the game's only about to start. So – on your toes every minute, eh?'

He turned to Hobday. 'All right, Number One. Fall out, please. Get her off the putty when you're settled.'

'White watch, watch diving!'

As the compartment emptied, leaving only watchkeepers at the controls, Wishart invited Nick and Robins to join him at the chart table. He used dividers to measure the run to the dawn rendezvous.

'Eighteen miles. We'll potter up that way all day, surface when it's dark in order to charge the battery, and we'll be there on the spot in plenty of time. *Louve* at the moment is *here*: so she has hardly any distance to come to meet us.'

He'd pointed at a pencilled rectangle a mile wide and eight miles long straddling all the likely courses out of Constantinople. He told Robins, 'After we put you in *Louve*, we take that area ourselves, and after she's dumped you off she'll be going to a long-stop patrol line at the western end.'

In case *Goeben* got past E.57. She'd have to get by the Frenchmen as well before she reached the Dardanelles. Wishart asked Robins, 'Where's your landing spot, d'you know?'

Robins stared at him for a moment, then glanced at Nick. There'd been a policy of not letting the left hand know what the right hand was planning. E.57 might have been sunk, in the straits, and there had been no reason for the submariners to know the details of the shoreside operation. But now, there didn't seem much reason why they should *not* know. Nick told Wishart, 'Constantinople.'

'What?'

'We shan't be landing from *Louve* at all. Twenty-four hours after we join her, she has a rendezvous with a dhow.' Robins pulled a notebook from his pocket and flipped some pages over. 'Ten miles north-west of Ag.Etias Point.'

'I see . . .' Ag.Etias was the top-left corner of Kalolimno Island. Wishart ran the parallel ruler over and marked off the distance. 'There, then.' He looked at Nick. 'The dhow takes you right into Constantinople?'

'Where she's from. And we'll be got up to look like her crew – they're to have clothes for us on board. With the whole coast watched and guarded, it's really the safest way in, I suppose.'

'Oh Eternal Lord God, who alone spreadest out the heavens and rulest the raging of the sea . . .' Terrapin was as steady as dry land, slicing through a sea like marble, marble that veined white astern

and then gradually reverted to unbroken blue. Truman, her captain, had no need to look down at the book in his hand: this was the everyday naval prayer and by the time he'd reached his fifteenth birthday he could have recited it in his sleep. He was on the gundeck of his destroyer's stern four-inch, while below him on her quarterdeck and up both sides of the iron deck as far as her foremost funnel the ship's company had assembled for Divine Service, their heads bared to the Aegean sun. *Terrapin* steamed slowly but in erratic zigzags across the wide entrance of the Gulf of Xeros. Astern and at this moment on her quarter was the brownish mass of the Gallipoli peninsula, while ahead and much further off was the lower and less distinct outline of the European mainland. A single higher point of land on the port bow was Mount Chat; the rest was an uneven blur shimmering in warm, still air. Summer was lingering into autumn, autumn refusing to be squeezed out by winter; any day now it would change abruptly to grey skies, cold winds, heaving sea.

Nights had to be spent at the gulf's eastern end, the end nearest to the Marmara. Each day Truman brought his ship out twenty-five miles westward, and during that passage westward watched the sun rise, flooding the barren hills with colour. Reaper slept at those times. He had to be awake all night, or most of it, the hours set for wireless contact with the submarines and for messages from shore. It was because of the weakness of the shore transmitters that it was necessary for a communication link this far east; the submarines' sets had the range for Mudros easily. Or *should* have had. But any enemy observers ashore, or in the recce 'planes which from time to time came dithering like nervous moths along the coastline, were supposed to believe that *Terrapin* was just another patrolling destroyer. They weren't intended to know that she slipped back into the gulf at nightfall.

'. . . *that we may be a safeguard unto our most gracious Sovereign Lord, King George, and his Dominions, and a security for such as pass on the seas upon their lawful occasions* . . .'

Reaper was a difficult man to entertain, Truman had found. He was prone to long silences: he seemed to switch off, often in the middle of some interesting discussion, and then not to hear any more of what was being said to him. Of course, he had a great deal on his mind; but it was still exasperating. And it would be a great relief to have this business done with, join the flotilla at Mudros and resume normal destroyer duties. He shut the prayer book as he

604

finished, '—*and the love of God and the fellowship of the Holy Ghost be with us all evermore*—'

He let them have the last word. Then heads lifted; there was a general stirring, straightening. Even *Terrapin* moved, heeling as she altered course to a new leg of the zigzag. Funnel-smoke was acrid, drifting downward in the windless air; it swept across the raised gundeck where he stood, curled lazily and dirtily across the wake. Harriman, with his cap pushed under his left arm and his bald patch strikingly evident from this gull's-eye view, was looking up at him expectantly. Truman nodded. 'Carry on, please.' He went down to the quarterdeck to join Reaper, and told him in case Harriman hadn't, 'We're invited to luncheon in the wardroom, sir.'

'Yes. Very kind of them.' Reaper added, 'I'll take the opportunity to give them the latest news.'

'Eh?'

Truman blinking owlishly . . . A cold fish, Reaper thought. At this moment history was being made, the shape of the world was changing, and all he could talk about was nuts and bolts, problems of engineering, fuel consumptions, changes in the signal code . . . It would be a pleasant change not to lunch alone with him today. Reaper was aware that his own nerves were on edge. Trying to be patient while the days passed and others did the work and faced the danger . . . Not a word from either submarine – well, that was good – and not a peep from inside Turkey either. No sudden flurry of Turk wireless activity, for that matter. It was probably what one dreaded most, at this stage of the operation: so thank God for all the silence. But – he shook his head, staring out astern over the pile of white that rose under the destroyer's counter – as a staff man, a planner and organiser, he should have been used to the waiting, guessing. He wasn't, though, and he doubted if he ever would be.

He turned, strolled for'ard – making himself stroll and not walk briskly. There were a few minutes to pass before it would be time to go down to the wardroom, and a circuit or two of *Terrapin*'s upper deck might save him from being trapped again by Truman. Walking for'ard now, past the after set of torpedo tubes, hearing the pipe, 'Hands to dinner!' So the rum issue had been completed; time *did* pass, if you made yourself relax, forget it. Strolling on . . . There'd be no work done this afternoon by the two off-duty watches; it would be a traditional Sunday afternoon of letter-writing, sleeping, patching clothes, haircuts on the foc's'l during the dog watches while the killicks' mess gramophone churned out *Dixie* or *Alexander's Ragtime Band*.

Remarkable, how cheerful and enthusiastic the men kept, considering how little entertainment or shoregoing came their way. From the regulars you could understand it, because this was the life they'd chosen for themselves; but even the Hostilities Only ratings seemed content enough. One tended to look carefully, listen hard, these days, when there was so much talk about discontent in the Fleet. It was about pay, mostly. Their Lordships at the Admiralty were aware of the grouses, and in sympathy; Beatty had written from his Grand Fleet flagship urging an overhaul of all rates of pay, and the First Lord, Geddes, had been pressing the Treasury hard. The Treasury, used to pressure and to ignoring it, hadn't so far responded. It was not a case of discontent between the men and their officers – in that respect the situation was excellent, generally speaking, and officers' pay was as badly in need of reform as the lower deck's. Flag Officers, for instance, drew the same money they'd had in 1816 – 102 years without a rise. But sailors on leave in England had seen civilian earnings soaring while their own families couldn't make ends meet; they'd also seen how civilian rates had been pushed up by strikes. There'd been talk in Fleet canteens of a naval strike: but in naval terms 'strike' and 'mutiny' were synonymous; mutiny was mutiny, and there was only one face that any commissioned officer could show to it.

There was certainly no sign of unrest here in *Terrapin*. Truman seemed to take that for granted: when he and Reaper had discussed it, the suggestion that there could *ever* be such disturbances had shocked him. Not a very long-sighted man, Reaper thought. To put it more plainly, Truman was rather a damn fool. Because if the Navy was to be sent into the Black Sea after the Turks surrendered, and sailors came under the influence of Russian Bolsheviks, and if the war against Germany ended and the HO ratings, burning to get home to their families, were kept out here in some kind of policing job, while back in England men who hadn't fought at all were getting home to their wives every night and drawing four times the pay . . .

The Treasury would have to wake up, and quickly. And, please God, let any intervention in South Russia be a very temporary affair. There were British troops in Archangel, of course – but that was primarily to stop the Hun drive through Finland, since the Bolshies had declined to stand up for themselves. Reaper found himself walking, still deep in thought, into *Terrapin*'s wardroom. Harriman asked him, 'Gin, sir?'

'How very kind. I'm afraid I've warmed the bell somewhat—'

'You're precisely on time, sir.' Harriman had beckoned to Link, the steward, and Link was bringing a glass of gin and the bitters shaker on a silver salver from the sideboard. It was lower deck pay that had to be seen to most urgently, Reaper thought. Never mind the fact that he as a commander drew the same money as a Scottish dockyard matey whose only responsibilities were a hammer in one hand and a cold chisel in the other. Mr Shriver, the gunner (T), came over. Grey-haired, long-nosed, close-together eyes . . . 'A pleasure to 'ave your company, sir.' Granger, the tall young sub-lieutenant, asked him, 'Any good buzzes, sir?' Granger was sipping Tio Pepe. *Terrapin*'s wardroom had stocked up with it at Gibraltar, on the way through.

Reaper nodded. 'I've quite a bit of news for you, as it happens . . . Thank you, Link.' He accepted a cigarette from the wardroom's silver box. Gough-Calthorpe's staff in Mudros kept him informed of everything that mattered, in their daily ciphered signals. In an operation like this one, with so much politics involved and at least one nation's surrender imminent, it was vital to have a broad and up-to-date picture of the developing strategic situation. He added, expelling smoke, 'But we'll wait for—'

'Oh. You're here already.'

Truman's surprise at finding him down here was *almost* a criticism. Link had Truman's sherry ready-poured for him, and Granger was offering him a light for his cigarette. Harriman asked Reaper, 'May we hear your news, sir?'

'Quite a few bits and pieces.' He sat down on the padded fender. 'For a start, we sent some 'planes over Constantinople yesterday, calling on the Turkish people to kick the Huns out. In view of what I've to tell you in a minute, that *might* have been rather a waste of effort . . . Second point, though, is the Aegean squadron's being reinforced with two dreadnoughts from home waters – *Superb* and *Temeraire*.'

Truman had raised his eyebrows: 'Suggesting that a sortie by *Goeben* is considered likely, eh?'

Explaining the obvious to his officers. There'd been no need for him to comment; Reaper had given him all this news earlier on.

'There's certainly no other enemy unit in these waters worth two dreadnoughts. Four, counting the pair we have already.' He

607

thought it was possible that London was taking a longer view than just the *Goeben* threat; the Black Sea was very much in mind now, and the Russian ships there, the possibility of their falling into German hands. He nodded. 'But here's the more important news. The Turks are sending a delegation to talk about an armistice, and London has authorised Admiral Gough-Calthorpe to receive them on board *Agamemnon* – any day now, in Mudros. How's *that*?'

'Calls for another drink.' Harriman looked round for the steward. Truman said in his fruity voice, 'Armistice talks do not inevitably result in a cessation of hostilities. One may *hope* for—'

'Yes. Let's hope.' Reaper put his glass down on Link's salver and took another in its place. 'But one warning I must give you – mum's the word.' He glanced up. 'Hear that, steward?' Link nodded. Wardroom stewards were the eyes and ears of the ship's company. Harriman raised a forefinger at him warningly: Link grinned, moved with his tray to Truman's elbow. Reaper explained, 'As you know, we've this French wireless chap Rostaud on board. And for the time being we aren't letting the French in on our negotiations with the Turks. London's view is that *we* are the naval power here. We've taken the brunt of the action and it's become our show. So to that extent . . .' He shrugged. 'I don't *feel* perfidious. But you see, the fact that Turkey wants to make peace does make a raid by *Goeben* rather probable. If the Huns see the ground being, so to speak, cut from under their feet – eh?'

The rest of his news came from farther afield. The German lines in France were disintegrating. The enemy had evacuated Zeebrugge and Ostend. Scheer had recalled his U-boats from patrol; it was believed in London that his intention was to redeploy them in support of some offensive action by the High Seas Fleet. It made sense, Reaper explained. With defeat in sight, Scheer would be bound to come out. He'd attack the Channel ports, perhaps, and have submarines patrolling outside fleet-bases to catch Beatty's ships when they emerged to counter the assault. But not just to counter: this might be the battle for which, ever since Jutland, the whole of the Royal Navy had longed. One could imagine the excitement and high spirits prevailing now in Rosyth, Invergordon, Dover, Harwich, Immingham . . .

Reaper read the expressions on the faces round him, and understood them. Any one of these men would have swapped a year's seniority to be back in home waters now.

*   *   *

608

By nightfall, he could feel the tension in his nerves again. In a few hours the cogs he'd set in motion would be meshing. He stared into the darkness, towards the Marmara. 'Not long now . . .' It was a mutter, and more to himself than to Truman, but as he said it he realised he'd used exactly the same words not more than ten minutes ago. A give-away: as good as an announcement of the state of anxiety he was in. He could have kicked himself, for exposing that degree of weakness, particularly to a man like Truman. He was with him on the destroyer's bridge now as she nosed into the rounded cul-de-sac that had Cape Xeros to the south and Saros Adalari Island in the middle. The nearest piece of the Marmara was only eight miles away, across the narrow Gallipoli peninsula; and eighty miles east was the rendezvous position where at dawn the two submarines would surface, link briefly in that alien and secret world, then separate again to perform their respective tasks. If one of them failed to keep the appointment, the other was authorised to break wireless silence.

So the best news, from Reaper's point of view, would be none at all. But even that wouldn't be positive evidence that all was well. Conceivably, and knowing how hazardous the passage of the Dardanelles must be, *neither* submarine might keep the rendezvous.

He heard Cruickshank, *Terrapin*'s navigator, order quietly, 'Port fifteen.'

'Port fifteen, sir.' That was PO Hart, Chief Buffer, at the wheel in the centre of the bridge. *Terrapin* was moving at slow speed but with frequent applications of rudder. The odds were that she could have anchored and lain in peace all through the wireless broadcast hours, but there was just a chance that the enemy could have got wind of something and sent a U-boat prowling after her. Even at long odds you couldn't accept that risk.

'Midships.'

'Midships, sir.' Quiet voices broke the silence like stones falling into a still surface. The land was a dark hump in the south and a vaguer, more distant one to nor'ard; you saw the land's shape where it blotted out the lower stars. Eastward one could see nothing. Reaper said, 'I'm going down. Be in the W/T office or the chartroom.'

'Very well, sir.' Truman had a canvas bed up here on the bridge. The black shape that was Reaper melted towards the ladder. He'd only been on the bridge for half an hour, a breather from the stuffiness below. Now he'd be returning to the wireless room because it was about one o'clock and the change-over time from a French language broadcast hour to the second English language one. One of the two sets was used for listening all through the dark hours for any transmissions from shore, while on the other the two submarines had been allocated alternate hours.

Reaper went down the starboard ladder to the foc's'l deck, and in at a steel door abaft the ladder's foot. This was the W/T room, under the rear half of the bridge; a hatch in its for'ard bulkhead connected it to the chartroom.

The Frenchman, Rostaud, had just handed over the Type 15 to Telegraphist Michaelson. Leading Tel Stewart was on the Type 4. Reaper leant sideways to let the tall Frenchman edge past. The compartment was only eight feet square and half its depth was taken by the operators' bench, under the sets along the after bulkhead. Rostaud muttered, *'A deux heures, alors.'* His droopy moustache gave him a downcast, apologetic air. Reaper pulled the door shut behind him. The little space was fuggy with cigarette smoke and the peculiar hot-metal smell of electrical equipment.

'All quiet, I suppose.'

'Graveyards get jumpier, sir.' Stewart sniffed. This wasn't the most exciting job a man could have. He was young, studious-looking. Michaelson, on his right, looked older than the leading hand. Reaper said, 'This is our last English transmission period before they join up at the rendezvous.'

'Don't worry, sir.' They seemed to read his thoughts. 'Anything comes up, you'll get it.'

Michaelson had the easier job. Stewart on the Type 4, which was tuned to short-wave shore transmission, had to be sharp-eared and sharp in more general terms, too, to recognise what might concern them and what didn't. Reaper said, 'I'll be next door.' He went outside and into the chartroom, where he'd be near enough if anything developed and where he had a bunk-settee to relax on. He sat down on it, and swung his legs up.

Quarter past one. Lying back, he stared sightlessly at the deck-head with its heavy steel I-section beams. It was one thing to make plans, another to have to live with them. He allowed his eyes to close. When it was a plan on paper, ships and men were symbols; now the ships had names and the men were people he'd come to know. He thought he'd only just shut his eyes when the door banged open, waking him with a jolt.

610

Mayne, the leading signalman.

'Sorry, sir. Didn't know you was kippin'. Come to ask would you like a cup o' tea, sir?'

He'd never intended to let himself fall asleep.

'Thank you. Nothing I'd like better.' Except, he thought, powers of telepathy.

Half an hour later Mayne pushed into the wireless office and shut the door. You could hardly see the operators for the cloud of cigarette smoke. He jerked his thumb at the chartroom hatch and told the leading tel, 'Out like a light again.' Stewart nodded. Mayne said, 'Been like a scared cat all day.'

Stewart adjusted the position of the headphones on his ears and leant forward again across the bench, his weight resting on his forearms. There was an anchor tattoo'd on the left one and a heart with initials in it on the other. *Terrapin* heeled as she swung to a new course. Mayne was leaning against the for'ard bulkhead and he'd begun to roll himself a cigarette; he did it without looking down at his fingers, and the cigarette seemed to form itself as if by magic. He saw Stewart jerk upright, grab a pencil in his right hand while his left flew to a tuning knob on the Type 4. Mayne began slowly stowing the tobacco tin inside his jumper; the cigarette was in his mouth, unlit. Stewart had begun to scrawl on the pad in front of him. Plain language, not code.

Control from Kitten – French subma

'Bloody 'ell!'

Fiddling at the set's adjustment . . . Mayne pulled back the hatch to the chartroom. 'Signal comin' in, sir!'

Submarine captured intact and brought Constantinople where papers given commander German U-boat which now sailed intention ambush E57 at rendezvous – ends . . .

Reaper snatched up the pad. The door swung open behind him, banging to and fro. Mayne reached past him and shut it. Reaper drew a sharp, hard breath, as if something had kicked him in the stomach. Then, just as quickly, he'd recovered and reacted.

'Start calling E.57.'

Michaelson's hand began rattling the key like some kind of machine. Reaper leant between the two men and began to write on a fresh sheet of pad, *Control to Wishart. German U-boat waiting at rendezvous in place of Louve. Keep clear of R/V position. Louve intact in enemy hands. Will transmit new orders midnight tomorrow Monday.*

611

'Code that up.'

Mayne edged over to the pile of code-books at the end of the bench. Michaelson was still tapping out E.57's call-sign. Smoke wreathed away from the stub which Stewart had spat into a shellcase ashtray. The other two were setting the message up in five-letter code groups. Reaper asked Michaelson, 'Are you sure it's going out?' The telegraphist pointed with his spare hand at a quivering needle in a dial. 'Full power, sir.' Reaper looked at the clock again: he was almost as white as the enamel on the bulkhead it was fixed to. In two minutes the submarine would be closing down her listening watch, and in about ninety she'd be expecting to meet *Louve*.

CHAPTER 9

E.57's diesels rumbled steadily into the empty, pitch-black night. It wasn't going to be pitch-black for long, though: eastward, a glimmer of brightness pushing up from an invisible horizon showed where presently the first-quarter moon would come sliding up. Wishart had lowered his binoculars and he was staring in that direction, over the submarine's quarter as she forged slowly north-westward. Trimmed right down, she was showing very little of herself above the flat plane of the sea.

Stoker Burrage, on watch as lookout, had moved up to the for'ard side of the hatch to make way for the two telegraphists, Weatherspoon and Agnew, who'd been sent for to strike the W/T mast and aerial. They'd just about done it now; they were man-oeuvring the coiled aerial and its insulators, and the dismantled mast, to the hatch; Agnew had slipped down inside, on the ladder, and Weatherspoon was passing the gear down to him. Burrage went back down the other side to the after end of the bridge; Weatherspoon reported to Wishart, 'Mast and aerial's struck, sir. Goin' down now.'

'Very good.'

They were in position, near enough, and the battery was just about fully charged. There was no point in waiting for that moon to rise and floodlight them. Wishart said quietly, matching his tone to the surrounding silence, 'We'll sit on the seventy-foot layer while we wait.'

Submariners in 1915 had discovered a high-density barrier at seventy feet, in this and some other areas of the Marmara, on which a boat could lie as securely as she could on a seabed. As the seabed hereabouts was two or three thousand feet below her safe diving limit, it was a useful phenomenon.

'Stop together. Out both engine clutches. In port tail clutch. Shut off for diving.' Wishart straightened from the voicepipe and glanced towards a vague shape in the after, end of the bridge. 'Down you go, lookout.' Burrage vanished into the hatch like a genie returning to its bottle. The engines' grumble died; you heard the sea now, loud because it was so close, the hiss of it along the tanks and under this platform where it swept across the pressure-hull and washed around the tower's base.

'You can dive her, pilot.' The submarine wallowed sluggishly, losing way. Wishart called down, 'Group down, half ahead to-gether.' Straightening from the pipe again he told Jake, 'Give 'em a minute, then pull the plug.'

'Aye aye, sir.' This was doing it gently, diving in slow time, being kind to men off watch who could sleep on and only discover when they woke later that she'd submerged. They'd be shaken in an hour or so anyway, in preparation for the meeting with *Louve*. Wishart had gone down, and Jake was alone on the bridge, thinking what luxury it was going to be – to have no passengers and all that space. He bent to the voicepipe: 'Open main vents!' As he was shutting the voicepipe cock the vents crashed open, air roared up out of the tanks; then the sea slid over the tanks' tops and spray plumed up in the escaping air, salt water raining on him as he reached up to grab the hatch by its brass handle and drag it down over his head. When he stepped off the ladder into the control room the depth-gauge needles were swinging past the twenty-foot mark.

'Seventy feet.'

'Seventy, sir.' Hobday was at the trim. 'Slow together.'

'Slow ahead together, sir.' That was Burrage at the telegraphs. Smith's tattoo'd hands caressed the wheel. Morton and Rowbottom were on the 'planes. ERA Knight had just slammed in the main vent levers. Passing forty feet: forty-five now . . . Wishart sloped over to the wardroom corner, and tossed his old reefer-jacket on to his bunk. Jake ambled that way too as he peeled off a sweater. Burtenshaw was stooped over a letter he was writing, Robins was reading, and so was Nick Everard. Everard had borrowed a Sherlock Holmes story from Chief ERA Grumman and he was trying to finish it before the rendezvous with *Louve*. Jake rested his bulk against the edge of the chart table and waited for Hobday to be ready to hand back the watch to him. He'd be due to relieve him of it again at half-past: hardly worth changing over, really. Hobday said like a mind-reader, 'I'll hang on now, Cameron.'

'Thanks.' Decent of the little man, he thought. He was about to

614

retire to the wardroom corner, that living-area which in an hour and a half would seem so palatial, when Burtenshaw came over to him.

'Where are we now?'

Jake began to point out positions and future movements on the chart; then he realised the Marine wasn't really listening. He'd brought the letter with him – the one he'd been writing – and he pushed it towards Jake. It was addressed to Colonel J.H. Burtenshaw RAMC, with a War Office address. He asked quietly, 'D'you mind? Only – oh, you know, if one came to grief?'

Blushing with embarrassment . . . It wasn't easy to imagine this schoolboy character performing usefully in a place like Constantinople. One could see him as a hero on some cricket field, but that was about the limit of it. He had Everard to hold his hand, of course; but even Everard, for all his medals and his reputation, was a destroyer man, not a cloak-and-dagger merchant. Burtenshaw murmured, even pinker now, 'Only if things went smash, you know?'

Three-fifteen: the hands had closed up at diving stations. And only just in time, because Weatherspoon had picked up distant HE, propeller noise. He was listening to it now, and for a change all eyes were on him instead of on Wishart.

Roost had opened the twelve-pounder magazine and brought up Burtenshaw's rucksack of demolition charges. It was under the chair that he was now sitting on, and it was all that any of the passengers would be taking with them. They had some personal kit in *Louve* already, and in the dhow tomorrow there'd be the Turkish gear for them to change into.

'Starboard beam, sir. Faint, still.'

Wishart checked the ship's head by gyro. Starboard beam: it meant that *Louve* was approaching from the eastward, and that was as anyone would expect. He glanced at Hobday, '*Punctual* frogs.' Weatherspoon's eyes rested on Wishart for a moment; he shook his head slightly, as if something was puzzling him. Now he'd looked down again, concentrating on whatever he was hearing. He was on his stool, in the doorway of the cabinet. Wishart said quietly, 'Let's have her up, Number One.'

'Aye aye, sir.' Hobday set the pump to work on 'A', which an hour ago he'd weighted to hold her on the high-density layer. Weatherspoon blurted suddenly, 'It's a submarine, sir – not the Frog boat, though.'

615

Everyone looked at him. One or two men smiled. 'Professor' Weatherspoon was a bit of a joke, for'ard. Wishart moved towards him, squeezing behind Hobday. 'Think you may have forgotten what she sounds like?'

The two boats had spent a day exercising together between Lemnos and Imbros, and Weatherspoon should have had plenty of time to familiarise himself with the characteristics of *Louve*'s HE. But this was precisely the time for her to show up, and exactly the right place, and so far as anyone knew there were no other submarines in the Marmara. Jake looked across at the passengers: Robins was staring impatiently at Weatherspoon, and Everard looked puzzled. Wishart said, going back to his usual position, 'See how she sounds when we're closer. Know her then, I dare say.' Hobday ordered, 'Stop the pump. Shut "A" suction and inboard vent.' He asked Wishart, 'Twenty feet, sir?'

'Yes, please.'

'Slow ahead together. Twenty feet.'

Agnew pushed the telegraphs around: *Louve*'s hydrophone would hear that noise echoing through the sea between them, and now she'd be listening to E.57's screws as they stirred into motion. Jake thought of that little tough-nut skipper, Lemarie, the glint in his hard brown eyes as the French operator picked up the HE and reported it. One couldn't envy Lemarie *his* passengers; and now he'd be very crowded indeed, for the next twenty-four hours. Jake looked over at the wardroom corner again: he'd never appreciated before how generous the designers had been, with all that space for only three officers. A bunk *each*, for heaven's sake! Sixty feet on the gauges: fifty-eight . . . Hobday muttered, 'Easy does it, cox'n.' Crabb grunted; he'd already started to bring the bubble back a bit, and Hobday must have seen it, so all he'd been doing had been anticipating a similar instruction from Wishart. Fifty feet. Jake saw Weatherspoon staring fixedly at Wishart, and an urgent gleam behind the spectacles.

'Def'nitely not 'er, sir.'

Jake felt a first twinge of doubt. It came from Weatherspoon's tone of certainty. He wasn't a very self-confident or self-assertive man. Wishart seemed to have been pushed into a moment's doubt, too. He was looking at Weatherspoon and frowning, hesitating. Now he'd turned away. It couldn't, he knew, possibly be anyone but the Frenchman.

Jake wondered if *Louve* might have damaged a propeller – caught it against a net and chipped a blade, for instance. Anything like that would dramatically change her signature-tune.

'Captain, sir?'

Wishart's head jerked round towards the telegraphist. The gauges showed thirty-five feet: thirty-three. E.57 was approaching a surface that by now would be streaked with silver. Weatherspoon said doggedly, 'Boat I'm listenin' to ain't *Louve*, sir. Certain pos'tive it ain't. Nothin' *like* 'er, sir.'

Wishart stood silent, staring at him.

'What's she bear now?'

Weatherspoon was right: this was not the Frenchman. Jake *knew* it, suddenly. Other thoughts followed quickly: the Turks had no submarines, so that left only one thing it could be. But the sheer coincidence of time and place . . . Coincidence? *If she'd been sunk, and a survivor hadn't stood up to interrogation?*

Weatherspoon, jaw set hard, looked simultaneously determined and scared.

'Up periscope.'

The big for'ard one. Depth-gauge needles moving more slowly as the 'planesmen levelled her towards the ordered depth. Twenty-five feet. Twenty-four. The glistening tube rose, a bronze pillar with McVeigh watching it and his hand on the lever ready to bring it to a stop. Hobday reporting quietly, 'Twenty-two feet, sir . . . twenty-one . . .' Wishart snatched the handles down, rose with the periscope, training it round as he straightened up. His eyes were at the lenses and McVeigh had stopped it.

'Twenty feet, sir.'

Weatherspoon's voice cracked across the silence: 'Torpedo fired, starboard bow!'

'Hard a-port, down periscope, forty feet, group up, full ahead together!'

'Torpedo approaching starboard!'

Weatherspoon was rising from his stool – eyes dilated, finger pointing out towards the oncoming missile that only he could hear. Crouched, gesturing, gargoyle-ish as the boat swung over and angled downwards and the grouped-up full-ahead power began to drive her down. Then they all heard it: a rushing, churning noise with a steeply rising note, sound surging up, expanding: Nick sat frozen, brain-bound and muscle-bound: then it had passed, whooshing by overhead, and he found that the Conan Doyle novel in his hands was bent hard back along the spine, that he'd practically torn it in half.

'Midships. Starboard fifteen. Group down, half ahead together. Bearing of the submarine's HE now?'

'Right a'ead, sir.' Weatherspoon corrected, as the boat swung on, 'Five to port – broadenin'—'

'Ease to five. Twenty feet.'

'Dead a'ead, sir.'

'Twenty, sir.' All calm, laconic now. Roost, mild as a church-warden, reported he had five degrees of starboard helm on. That meant five degrees of port rudder. Weatherspoon had settled back on his stool again. His breathing was short and jerky and he was still chalk-white. Gauges showed twenty-six feet: twenty-four . . .

'Up.'

Periscope shimmering greasy, wet-running as it rose.

'Twenty-two, sir—'

'Midships. Bearing now?'

'Ten on the starboard bow, sir, movin' left.'

'Twenty feet, sir.'

Training the periscope slowly left . . . Then he stopped, and they heard him gasp. Weatherspoon didn't hear it: he was on his own, reporting, 'Very close, sir – revs increasing – *very*—'

'Shut watertight doors! Group up, full ahead together, starboard five!'

Lewis and Ellery dragged the doors shut at each end of the compartment and began slamming the clips over. Jake saw Weatherspoon pull the headphones off his ears. Wishart ordered, 'Midships . . . Steady!'

'Steady, sir – oh-eight-four—'

'Stand by to ram!'

Hunched at the periscope, not training it at all. Steady bearing meant collision course. Now he pulled his head back and snapped the handles up, grabbed elsewhere for support, clutching the ladder just as she hit the U-boat. It felt more like steaming full-tilt into a cliff-face. An enormous jolt, and from for'ard the noise of tearing metal. Some who hadn't caught hold of solid fittings had been sent flying. Wishart shouted, 'Stop both!' The impact had flung her bow upwards: she'd be on top of her victim but her own foreparts might easily have been holed. There could be *two* victims. Bow sinking now; and still that noise of metal being wrenched apart. She *felt* heavy for'ard. Morton reported, 'Fore 'planes won't budge, sir.'

If her for'ard half was flooded—

Jake Cameron heard himself whisper, *Christ, now here we go!* He was sweating suddenly: he begged himself, *Oh, steady now . . .* On the other side of the compartment Nick thought, *Well, here it is after all.* During the passage of the straits, even in the bad moments when they'd seemed trapped and done for, the calmness of the submariners had made him doubt whether matters could be as touch-and-go as they'd seemed. Then when the torpedo had been coming straight for them he'd felt numb with hopelessness: there'd been an unexpected thought of Sarah knowing nothing of all this, living her own life and guarding her own secrets, Sarah in a world he couldn't share with her now because he'd already left it. Now as the submarine began to plunge downward, angling steeply towards the seabed three thousand feet below, he understood suddenly that it was inevitable, that he might have known it was, if he'd let himself face it squarely. The landing business – all that – well, at least he wouldn't have to play *that* game now . . .

But he'd glimpsed the truth, similar awareness, in several other faces. Masks had slipped, just momentarily. Even Cameron's: and Cameron was in control of himself again now, glancing round in that mild, rather deadpan way of his . . . 'Report from for'ard!' Urgency in Wishart's tone: even Wishart had forgotten his customary drawl. Lewis jumped to the bulkhead voicepipe and began to unscrew the cock on it. With so much bow-down angle and such a rate of descent it seemed quite likely her forepart might be flooded. If the TSC was full there'd be a jet of water through that voice-tube. And there *wasn't*. But that still left the tube space, the bow compartment. Hobday asked Wishart, 'Blow one and two main ballast, sir?' Wishart shook his head: 'No.' But the needles were rushing round the gauges, the angle steepening. Jake Cameron thought – hoped – *The seventy-foot layer'll stop us.* He'd crossed his fingers. Burtenshaw was staring at him wildly with his mouth open: Jake winked at him. Everard saw that, looked round at the Marine, smiled and said something to him. Burtenshaw seemed to have snapped out of it. E.57's stem would be embedded in the enemy's side, and whether or not she herself had any flooding for'ard the other boat's weight would be dragging her down; the German would have at least one compartment torn open to the sea. Out there, just a few yards away, there'd be men dead, drowning, struggling to live. If they shouted, might Weatherspoon hear them through his earphones? Jake saw the needles passing sixty feet as

619

Lewis reported that the tube space and TSC were dry and had sustained no damage.

'Open bulkhead doors.' Less than forty-five seconds had passed since the ramming. Lewis and Ellery working at the doors' clips. And a different kind of noise from for'ard suddenly; Weatherspoon looked up and swallowed, agitating his adam's apple.

'Blowin' 'is tanks, sir.'

Wishart nodded as if he'd been expecting it. It was a loud, harsh noise, like sandpaper rubbing on a drum. Jake leant across the chart, resting on his elbows, hearing it and guessing what was happening in the other boat. Men trapped, frantically trying to break free by blowing themselves to the surface. Their submarine was speared on E.57's bow, held by her deadweight, like a swimmer being pulled down by a shark.

Seventy feet. Seventy-one . . .

The angle was lessening and she was settling very slowly. The racket for'ard suddenly shut off. Seventy-three feet on one gauge and seventy-four on the other. Bulkhead doors open now. Close-'aul Anderson, one arm in a dirty sling, had stuck his head through the doorway to mutter something of Louis Lewis. Blowing noises again: at this rate it wouldn't be long before the Germans ran out of bottled air. You built up reserves of it by running a compressor that filled the groups of air-bottles in various places in the boat. If you emptied all the groups you'd have nothing left to blow with; and you could only run the compressor on the surface with a hatch open. A lot of this Hun's air might be just bubbling up through holes in his ripped hull.

E.57 lurched, resettled with a bow-up angle.

'Open "A" and "B" kingstons!'

Lewis dived for the wheel that opened 'B'. Beyond the bulkhead Close-'aul would be working one-handed on 'A'. The enemy was trying to lighten himself and for that moment his efforts had looked as if they might be about to succeed, but now Wishart was adding ballast to E.57's for'ard section to counter that lightness and hold her down.

'Bubble's coming back, sir.'

Hobday had said it as detachedly as if this was some ordinary trimming problem they were dealing with. Jake remembered sparrows that he'd drowned: in a sparrow-trap, made of wire netting, which his father used to set in the vegetable patch. Often there'd be a dozen or twenty birds in it; his father had shown him how to take

620

the whole cage and hold it under the surface of the pond while they died. It was the kindest way, he'd explained, of doing it. Jake thought, leaning on the chart table, *We're being kind to Germans, now* . . . Well, if the Huns had been luckier with that shot, E.57 would be a tangle of metal on the seabed by this time. Two thousand feet down: and in a drawer here in the middle of the wreckage would be a letter which until it disintegrated would still read, *You needn't worry for two seconds about me* . . . He heard the blowing start again: it had stopped for about half a minute and now they'd opened up again: and vibration suddenly, a terrific shaking: he realised what it was just as Weatherspoon reported, 'Using 'is motors, sir. Full group up, sound like.'

'Shut "A" and "B" kingstons.'

Precaution. Might want to pump out or blow those tanks in a minute, and you couldn't when they were still open to the sea. Wishart had moved in beside Hobday where he could see what was happening to the bubble. He'd want to make sure the German didn't get any up-angle on her through his blowing; if he managed that he might be able to slip off.

'Group down, slow ahead together.'

'Slow ahead together, sir!' Agnew whirled the telegraphs. By putting the motors ahead Wishart was maintaining a pressure that would keep his stem dug into her.

The vibration stopped suddenly: Weatherspoon met Wishart's enquiring stare as he looked round over Hobday's head: Weatherspoon opened his mouth to say something, and the shaking began again. He told Wishart, 'Tryin' it astern now. Or it was astern before an'—'

'Yes.' Wishart looked at Agnew. '*Half* ahead together.' He turned to Hobday. 'Number One – if he's blowing bubbles under our bow, we could be getting some of his air into our for'ard tanks.'

He meant, through the open kingstons in the bottoms of them.

'Could be, sir.' Hobday sounded doubtful. Wishart glanced over at McVeigh. 'Open and shut one and two main vents.' McVeigh grabbed the levers and wrenched them back; the noise from for'ard muffled the sound of the vents opening, but the bow dropped suddenly in a downward lurch: eyes flew to the depth-gauges as McVeigh shut the vents again. Seventy-five feet: seventy-six . . .

'Through the barrier, sir.' There was alarm in Hobday's voice. And some reason for it: with the deadweight of the part-flooded submarine on her stem to drag her down, fore 'planes jammed and

621

four hundred fathoms under them . . . They'd passed eighty feet
and the needles were circling faster now – eighty-five – ninety—

'Stop together.'

'Stop together, sir!'

One hundred feet. Wishart muttered, to nobody in particular,
'It's worse for him than it is for us.' Jake guessed at what might be
in his mind: the U-boat would have leaks, strained plates and
rivets: as depth and sea-pressure increased she'd suffer more and
more. And in his state the German couldn't do much to help
himself: he was being dragged down, drowned, getting heavier all
the time. If as they went deeper the two submarines broke apart,
the damaged one would almost certainly go on down – and
down . . . Until the sea crushed him, burst him like a nutshell.
But there was still that rather colossal 'if' – *if* they broke apart: it
was possible, conceivable, that they might not. If when Wishart
tried to separate he found he couldn't, the German would still go
on down but he'd be taking E.57 with him.

One hundred and twenty feet. Wishart was watching the depth-
gauge intently. Hobday had just muttered something to him; he'd
frowned, shaken his head, glanced at his first lieutenant as if he was
surprised at him: and just at that moment, everything went quiet. It
was the enemy's motors that had stopped, and the vibration they'd
been causing. The difference – silence – was uncanny . . . The two
submarines were locked together, sinking towards the seabed quite
fast, gathering downward momentum . . . Hundred and forty feet.
Hundred and fifty. Roost said, 'Lost steerage way, sir. Turnin' all
the time an' I can't stop 'er, sir.'

Like something dead, spiralling down. Visualising it as it would
look from the outside, the sea out there, one couldn't help seeing it
as a wreck on its way to the bottom. Two locked into one. Jake
heard Hobday ask Wishart very quietly, almost whispering, 'Permission to blow "A" and "B", sir?'

Wishart shook his head, without taking his eyes off the depth-
gauge. There was a grim, shut look on his face: as if he had
pressures in himself too, and was holding them back, forcing
himself to see the thing through to its end, not to let go now as
perhaps he'd have rather done. Everyone's eyes were on him: he'd
be used to that by now, but this time they weren't just standing by
for orders or clues to his intentions, they seemed to be trying to
hypnotise him into some action they all passionately wanted. Such
as blowing main ballast before—

'Blowin' again, sir!'

Half a second later you didn't need hydrophones to hear it. It was the same sound as before, a rip of high-pressure air racketing out: then, within seconds of it starting, it was weakening, fizzling out.

Stopped.

Hobday said, 'His air's done.'

'Yes.' Wishart turned quickly, decisively. Jake guessed this was the climax he'd set himself to wait for. 'Blow "A" and "B" main ballast. Half astern together.'

'Open "A" and "B" kingstons! Stand by to blow—'

'Both motors half astern, sir!'

Blowing the extra ballast out, and pulling astern to clear the German. If there was anyone alive in that boat now, there wouldn't be much longer. The two internals' kingstons were open: McVeigh sent air booming into the tanks to force the sea out through them.

Passing two hundred feet: and no change to the bow-down angle.

'Stop together. Group up.'

Hobday pitched his voice up over the air noise: 'Stop blowing! Shut "A" and "B" kingstons!'

'Grouper up, sir!'

'Half astern together.'

Agnew flung the telegraph handles round. 'Both motors half astern, sir.' Hobday asked Wishart, 'Shall I put a puff in one and two main ballast, sir?' He wanted her bow up, the angle reversed. Wishart shook his head: *he* wanted to get her unlinked from the German first, not waste E.57's air on slowing the wreck's descent as well as his own.

Two hundred and twenty-five feet on the gauges now. Twenty-five feet below tested diving depth.

Two hundred and thirty . . .

'*Full* astern together!'

The motors' note rose as the screws speeded . . . Jake saw the needles circling on. Loss of ballast and all that power astern wasn't stopping her. He wondered if Wishart wasn't going to have to change his mind: whether they weren't close to a point of no return.

Wishart must have come to the same conclusion . . .

'Blow one, two, three, four, five six, seven and eight main ballast!'

The whole lot: too late for half-measures. McVeigh had flung himself like a mad dervish at the panel and he was wrenching the valves open. Even now there was no certainty – and if it failed: well, the German had been forced to use every ounce of air he'd had: now it could be a taste of one's own medicine that was coming. Blowing: and motors grouped up: nothing in reserve if this failed . . . Air at three thousand pounds to the square inch smashing through reducers into the LP line and through it to the tanks: depth two hundred and forty-five feet. Two-fifty . . .

'Stop blowing seven and eight!'

Keeping the bubble from going mad: and shouting to beat the din of air – which dropped slightly as McVeigh shut off the after pair of tanks. Two hundred and sixty feet: and suddenly alarming noise from for'ard: creaking, straining . . . Jake leant over the chart table, listening to it and at the same time not wanting to hear it. It sounded like the bow being torn off.

'Stop blowing one, two, five and six! *Half* astern both!'

Like a section of hull-plates being ripped away. Jake told himself, *Always sounds worse than it is* . . . Under water every sound was magnified, distorted. But *something* was being wrenched apart . . . 'Stop blowing three and four!'

The boat jerked, tilted as her bow hauled free and began to swing upwards – much too fast . . . 'Open one and two main vents! Stop together – group down!'

It was going to be a tussle now to get her back into control and trim: but she was already rising fast towards depths that she was tested for. The quiet, after all that noise, was startling. There was no sound at all from outside: nothing out there that anyone could have heard. Only wreckage sinking into a half-mile depth of sea. It would be a long way down by now and it would only stop when it hit the bottom. He felt sick and shaky, as if his own hands had been locked on someone's throat.

The sparrows, he remembered, had always fluttered, for a little while.

CHAPTER 10

'Not *cold*, is it?'

Nick had only this moment woken from a heavy sleep: and he was warm, in the bunk. Wishart's bunk. He'd opened his eyes to see Jake Cameron pulling on an extra sweater, on top of a sweater he had on already. Obviously he was going up to take over the watch from Hobday. He'd sat down now, to lace his canvas shoes, and he was looking up quite angrily at that question.

'No. It's like a greenhouse. If you're swathed in layers of bloody blankets.'

Nick grinned. The more he saw of Cameron the more he liked him. 'Sorry.' Turning out for night watches wasn't most people's idea of happiness. He looked across at the clock and saw that it was two twenty-five – in the morning of day seven, Tuesday. And – almost fully awake now – he realised that it *was* cold. The diesels were sucking a torrent of night air down through the conning-tower, and the boat had quite a bit of movement on her as she rumbled eastward with a southerly breeze and a choppy sea on the beam.

Eastward, because the rendezvous had been changed. Reaper had moved fast after he'd had E.57's wirelessed report last night. Within minutes he'd replied with confirmation that *Louve* had been captured intact and that the submarine they'd sunk had been German, and he'd told them to keep listening-watch for further orders. Then he must have been in contact with his friends ashore, and half an hour after midnight he'd come on the air again, switching the R/V position eastward, twenty miles nearer Constantinople, and telling Wishart it would be a caïque, not a dhow, he'd meet.

Robins had been quietly jubilant. He was in command now. And Reaper's orders had said he was to represent French as well as

625

British interests. But an hour ago he'd complained of 'slight indisposition' – he'd meant sea-sickness. He was on the bridge now with Wishart and Hobday. But Burtenshaw, Nick thought, was much the sicker of the two. Pale and sweating, corpse-like on Hobday's bunk. Kinder not to speak to him.

It had been a trying day. After they'd sunk the U-boat Robins had wanted Wishart to surface and send off a report immediately; even if *Terrapin* hadn't been listening at that time, Mudros would have got it. But Wishart, much to Robins's indignation, had preferred to lie low until nightfall – and Nick had agreed with him. If they'd broken wireless silence at once, the Germans and Turks at the Horn would have had notice of their survival and therefore of the U-boat's destruction; whereas if they kept quiet, the enemy might believe his U-boat was keeping silence in order not to alert the Aegean end of the British operation. If nobody went on the air until dark, the enemy would have only a few hours between hearing the transmissions and the time arranged for rendezvous with the dhow, and hopefully that might not give them time to interfere.

The German had known the time and position of the E.57/*Louve* link-up, so perhaps they'd know about the next appointment too. But if all *Louve*'s papers had been given to the U-boat commander and he hadn't shared his knowledge with the authorities ashore before he sailed, then only the fishes had it now. The considerations had been: one, Reaper had stressed how vital it was to push this business through to a successful conclusion; his phrase had been 'any effort, any risk', and if that meant anything at all it meant exactly what it said. Two, at this time – when they'd been discussing it – the rendezvous with the dhow had seemed the only way they could get the landing party ashore. So the appointment had to be kept. If the enemy did have that much information, it could be highly dangerous, even suicidal. On the other hand, a lack of sound alternatives put it into the 'any risk' category. The alternatives were first to make a landing elsewhere, using the submarine's Berthon collapsible boat; but this would be even more chancy, since no information was available about landing places, patrols, shore-guards or observation posts. Second – Nick's suggestion – was to capture some small sailing craft, keep its crew prisoners in the submarine, and let him sail into Constantinople. He'd proposed loading it with Burtenshaw's guncotton and a torpedo warhead as well, laying it alongside *Goeben* and detonating it. Robins had opposed this plan strongly, on the grounds that it wouldn't get him ashore. Nick had seen a snag or two in his idea, but he still thought it would have been the best way to carry out Reaper's orders – *his* part of them – and it would have been a straightforward, basically *naval* plan of assault, the sort of thing he'd have felt at home with. Wishart had been in sympathy, but had felt bound to accept Robins's veto. Robins was the man in charge, and Nick was a latecomer to the operation. Wishart's decision had been to reconnoitre the R/V area thoroughly in the hours before dawn, and then to make a very cautious approach to the dhow, making certain there were no other ships about and that the dhow wasn't armed, and so on. After he'd transferred the passengers to it he'd accompany it at periscope depth as far as he safely could, on its passage to Constantinople.

One other area of danger couldn't be insured against. This was the possibility of the dhow's identity being known ashore, so that they'd be met on arrival. This was their personal risk, not the submarine's, and Wishart left that decision to Robins, who said he'd make up his mind after he'd been aboard the dhow and questioned the Turks in it.

Then Reaper's latest signal had arrived and cleared away all the question-marks.

Nick heard Burtenshaw groan that sea-sickness was a pretty rotten thing. Jake Cameron looked up at the bunk. 'Not your first experience of it?' The Marine must have nodded, or something; Cameron told him, 'It'll be worse in a caïque, my lad. Much worse.' He added, when Burtenshaw didn't answer, 'Never mind. You'll have Robins to hold your hand. Or you can hold his. Take it in turns, perhaps.' He stood up, ready for the bridge; Burtenshaw stopped him.

'Won't forget that letter?'

'I'll hang on to it. Give it back to you later.'

'Thanks.' Nick guessed at what sort of letter it must be, and he wondered if he should have written one for Sarah. But saying what? And if his father should be at Mullbergh, released from the Army, and *he* opened it? A fine legacy to Sarah that would be . . . He slid down off the bunk; he'd slept enough and he was wide awake, and one of the others would be wanting to turn in presently. It truly *was* cold . . . Burtenshaw asked plaintively, 'Is there anything one can do, for sea-sickness?'

'Yes.' Cameron answered over his shoulder, 'Be sick.' He went over to the helmsman. Nick told Burtenshaw, 'Wear a tight belt, eat dry biscuit, don't drink anything at all.' Cameron had told the helmsman, Finn, 'Relief OOW.' He glanced back to the wardroom corner: 'It'll be much, *much* worse in the caïque.' He winked at Nick. Finn was yelling up the voicepipe, 'Permission to relieve officer of the watch sir, please?'

Wishart called down, 'Ask Lieutenant Cameron to wait until I get down.'

There was good reason not to let the bridge get overcrowded on patrol, when the boat might have to be dived quickly in emergency. Jake sloped over to his chart table, pausing halfway to let CPO Rinkpole get by. Rinkpole, heading aft, had a gloomy look about him.

'Still having bad dreams, TI?'

Earlier in the day he'd told Jake that he'd had a nightmare about the torpedo in the starboard bow tube, the one that had been flooded under pressure of the mine's explosion. He'd completed a maintenance routine on it since. In the dream it had done something-or-other that had greatly upset him.

He shook his head. 'Not sleepin', sir.' With his torpedoes he was like a hen with chickens. Jake picked up the dividers to measure the run to the caïque rendezvous; they'd be diving in an hour or less, so as to be out of sight before daylight came. The same routine as yesterday: except this time Wishart would believe anything Weatherspoon told him.

'All right, pilot.' Wishart came off the ladder. 'Room up top for you now.' He eyed Jake's solid frame meaningfully as he said it. Jake stared back at him: he didn't think there could be more than a few pounds between their weights.

'D'you mean you'll be staying below now, sir?'

Wishart jerked his head. 'Get up there.'

'Is Lieutenant-Commander Robins staying on the bridge?'

'He's under the weather. Has to be fit for when we meet our caïque.' Wishart shrugged. 'Not for long.'

The bridge seemed to be full of very little men. One of the pair abaft the hatch would be Robins, of course. Jake asked Hobday, 'Who's the lookout?'

'Stone.'

Andy Stone, Leading Stoker, Hostilities Only, railwayman from Newhaven. In the dark, he and Robins, lieutenant-commander from the Foreign Office, were identical black gnomes. Hobday said, 'That's ten minutes watchkeeping you owe me.'

'If you'll agree it's ten minutes hanging around the control room you owe *me*.'

'Damn sea lawyer . . .'

He wasn't a bad fellow. A bit pompous sometimes, but quite a decent sort. Jake's eyes were adjusting to the dark; it took a few minutes to tune them in, which was partly why OOWs and lookouts didn't change watches at the same time. Hobday told him, 'Course oh-seven-six, three-two-oh revolutions, running charge port side.'

'Any special orders?'

'None except we'll be diving on the watch before long, and I'd like a shake before we do.'

'Why?'

'What d'you mean, *why*?'

That was the area of pomposity. Thinking the boat couldn't be dived unless he was there to catch a trim. Jake shrugged in the dark. 'No skin off my nose . . . Anyway, I've got her.'

Alone – except for the two silent figures further aft – with the throaty grumble of the diesels and the wash of the sea, a little spray occasionally flashing over from the starboard side. There was more motion on her up here, of course, since the bridge's fifteen feet of height made for an upright pendulum effect, swaying to and fro while waves broke regularly against her sides, swept aft, frothed over the saddle-tanks and surged across the trimmed-down hull. If she hadn't been as trimmed down as she was, low and weighted in the sea by full or half-full tanks, there'd have been a lot more roll on her. He'd jammed himself against the for'ard periscope standard; there was a bracket at just the right height for his elbow to hook over. In worse weather than this, bridge watchkeepers would lash themselves to the standards with ropes' ends, and now it was just a matter of steadying oneself well enough to be able to concentrate on a careful looking-out with binoculars. The other two were propped against the after standard. Like twins, book-ends, one each side. Astern, beyond their silhouettes, white froth alternately heaped up or spread, disintegrating, as the submarine's afterpart swung up and down; at one moment you'd glimpse the shiny black whaleback of her, then it would be all churned sea humping, bursting upwards as the two sides met and merged. There was only a faint whiff of exhaust fumes; the wind was taking it away to port. Leading Stoker Stone, with glasses at his eyes, was like a small statue slowly turning, the binoculars' length foreshortening as he swung, pivoting on his heels. A serious, very reliable man, was Andy Stone. His 'young lady' in Newhaven – Lewis had said her name was Florence – would be getting a very steady, sound provider, when she took him on.

When the war ended . . . That phrase, that idea, was everywhere. Jake was sweeping down the port side. He didn't know what the answer was going to be to his own post-war problem. See what *she* thought about it, perhaps. Wishart had been right, but Wishart didn't know it all, didn't know *her*, for instance. In the sense that Stone was a railwayman and took it for granted he'd be a railwayman again, he – Cameron – was a seaman, and could see a similar sense in continuing to be one. If he found that she could take it in the same way – for granted, something she wouldn't question unless he questioned it himself? The problem had come close to solving itself more than once in the last few days. Once or twice in the straits, and yesterday's Hun . . . Spin of a coin. But a certain amount of skill and watchfulness came into it, it wasn't *only* luck. Lowering the glasses, resting his eyes for a moment as he turned back to start on the port bow and sweep across and down the starboard side, he saw Robins standing hunched, inactive, useless. If he was so determined to stay up here, couldn't he at least add a pair of eyes to the looking-out?

Beneath his dignity, perhaps. What a creature to send on a jaunt like this one! Only kind of chap they could get for it, perhaps. Others all fighting, and plenty of them dying, dead. When you thought of the horrors of the trench-lines . . . He'd paused, sweeping back now, over a place where he thought there'd been a flash of broken water. Nothing, though. Easy to imagine things. He thought, starting a search on the bow again, that he – all of them – were lucky, truly *very* lucky, with this job. Nothing could be as awful as that sort of fighting. *Nothing*. But the static war had ended now, by all accounts; armies were moving forward, sweeping across Europe. Swinging down past the beam now: he'd thought suddenly that the diesels' note had changed, risen and thickened: then the truth hit him in two stages, the first a suspicion of what it was and the second a jolting awareness of danger and the need to act. In the next fragment of the same split second he'd thought it might be more distant – *not* dangerous, only sound carried in the wind; then it was loud again, louder, beating down out of the night sky astern, everything at once and no time to think, he'd shouted, 'Down below!' and the other two were a blur in the dark as he yelled into the voicepipe, 'Dive, dive, dive!' Flashes – fire-stabs and cutting streaks and an explosive hammering, a black bat angling over – seaplane, he glimpsed its cigar-shaped floats and its gun-muzzle flaming, engine-noise deafening as it crashed over. Stone yelled then, 'This orfficer's 'it, 'e's—' *Something* . . . Pieces of metal flying from the after standard: but noise receding, black as pitch, main vents crashing open: he'd got hold of Robins and Stone screamed at him, 'Done for – no *use*, sir—'

'Get below!'

Dragging Robins, hearing the engines cut out and the dwindling racket of the seaplane, the pounding of the sea as the submarine wallowed down. His hands were wet, sticky: Robins had been hit and badly hit, but that didn't necessarily make him dead. Inside now on the ladder, trying to get Robins down inside too: it was incredibly difficult and the sea was loud all around him, gurgling and thumping, crashing against the plating as she dipped under, angling down. He had one hand on the grip under the hatch's rim, the other wrenching to free a leg that was still in the way. Sea would be flooding over at any moment. A hand from below grabbed his own leg, let go and struck at him, and Wishart bellowed, 'Get down and shut the hatch!' He'd accepted Stone's belief, obviously, that Robins was dead. But the hatch still had that leg in it – or something; water spouted, leapt over. There'd been spray and splashing but this was solid, lopping over, green sea beginning to pour in and no chance whatsoever of getting the hatch shut. So – *lower* hatch . . .

He let go of everything, and dropped. One foot hit the rim of the lower hatch, twisted, and pain shot through his ankle: then his shoulder had struck in about the same place and he'd cracked his face hard on some fitting in the tower; the sea was a flood now, drenching down. He heard a shout of 'Shut main vents!' and thought of the seaplane up there quite likely circling for another run: if Wishart took her up this soon they'd – Jake had fallen through the lower hatch and on his way through he'd grabbed its handle so as to drag it down and shut the sea out. Robins's body must have been carried through the top one by the rush of water, and now it came thumping down like something falling off a butcher's hook. The hatch was swinging down with Jake's weight on it and the sea on its other side to add to that: he saw Robins's face in sharp, clear close-up, a death-mask sheeted in blood and with one eye open and entirely white, and then the hatch had crunched down like a nutcracker crushing bone and brain and flesh. Nightmare: beyond it, the scene in the control room was a

631

reality in which he, part of the nightmare, was an intruder. Above him the hatch was ringed with pink and scarlet, a dripping stain . . .

'Cameron!'

He focused on someone who turned out to be Aubrey Wishart. 'Seaplane, Stone said?'

Jake nodded. 'By the time I heard it, its gun was—'

'All right.'

Wishart wasn't looking at him now, and Jake was aware, mostly from expressions on other faces, of the state he was in. He wasn't seeing only the horror of Robins's death, he was looking beyond it too, wondering whether the operation, the landing part of it, had been knocked out in that burst of machine-gun fire. And shock at the danger he'd put the boat and all her ship's company in, by messing about up there: although what else he could have done – not knowing whether he was dead or—

'Go and wash, pilot. Signalman – get a bucket and swab, clean this up.'

'Aye, sir.'

'Thirty feet, sir.'

'Bring her up to twenty. But don't rush it.' He glanced round, frowned at seeing Jake still standing there. 'For God's sake, man—'

'Sorry, sir, I—'

'Everard, you'll go ahead with Burtenshaw, the two of you, I take it?'

Hobday suggested, 'Doesn't the seaplane's attack on us suggest they're wide awake, know we're here and know we've sunk their U-boat?'

'They'll know we're somewhere about, I'm sure.' Wishart's tone was patient. This was a council of war. They'd surfaced, drained the tower, buried Robins's remains. Dawn had given him a colourful send-off, theatrical lighting effects in silver, bronze and crimson while Wishart had read the burial-at-sea prayer and they'd put the body over, weighted with twelve-pounder shells. McVeigh meanwhile had examined the periscope standards and found that apart from chipping and scoring by machine-gun bullets there'd been no damage done. Six minutes later they'd dived again. Jake had the watch now and the meeting with the caïque was to be at five am.

Wishart answered Hobday, 'They'll have heard our wireless transmissions, for one thing. But the seaplane attack was nearer

632

the old rendezvous position than the new one, and I'd say it was unlikely that Reaper's friends ashore would have set up a new plan that wasn't secure. Their necks are just as much at risk as ours, one might suppose. But we won't just charge up to the caïque without taking a damn good look around first – if that's what's worrying you.' He turned to Nick. 'You haven't said much, Everard.'

Nick glanced up. 'Isn't much to say, is there?'

'Well, you were expecting some sort of help from Robins—'

'Only that he was going to pass us on to someone or other when we got ashore. Now the caïque's crew'll have to do it. Or there may be a reception committee in the caïque, for all we know. Alternatively—' he looked at Burtenshaw – 'we have the name of a hotel or hotel bar in Pera – place called the Maritza – and the code-name of a – er – lady-friend of Commander Reaper's.'

'And you're happy with that?'

'Happy?'

Hobday chuckled at his surprise at such a question. But Wishart was waiting, apparently expecting some sort of answer. Burtenshaw did look quite happy, now he'd got over the shock of Robins's death. At least he was under the orders of someone who'd talk to him occasionally. Nick saw Jake Cameron hovering close by, listening to the discussion; he asked him, 'Are *you* happy?' Cameron shrugged. He looked tired and withdrawn. Nick offered, 'Come along with us, if your skipper'll spare you.'

'Not a chance.' Cameron's eyes met Wishart's for a moment. Wishart said, 'Best navigator I ever had. I'm hanging on to him.' Cameron felt himself colour slightly, and turned away. He'd been thinking, in the last grim hour or two, wondering if he hadn't been taught something, given a lesson in priorities and clear thinking. Robins hadn't been helped, and the boat might easily have been lost. Now if when he left the Service he took a shore job, would it do the old woman the slightest good, long-term?

The parallel was a loose one, but it was there all right. It told him that he needed to acquire a capacity for ruthlessness: not just for his own sake, but for everyone else's too. As he moved back towards the 'planesmen he heard Wishart explain to Everard, 'What I meant was, are you worried at going ahead with this now?'

There wasn't time to be worried. There wasn't time to *think* about being worried. Nick told Wishart, 'I'd be far more worried *not* to be going ahead with it.'

Burtenshaw, still pale although the boat was steady now, nodded

633

faint agreement. Wishart looked thoughtful. 'Not a bad answer, that.'

Not bad: but *mad*?

Nick was reacting to events as if they were real – as if he'd seen Robins dead, Robins's skull crushed in the hatch, Robins's blood and brains all over Cameron: and as if he, Nick Everard, was actually going to make this attempt to blow up one of the most powerful fighting ships afloat; but he didn't believe in it, any more than someone tossing about in a half-waking nightmare believes in what he's dreaming.

'Good God, look at this!'

He focused on Hobday, who'd come up from somewhere below the table. There *was* a dream-like element . . . But it was a canvas parcel – bag – that Hobday had thumped down on to the table.

'Gold sovereigns, by golly!'

Wishart murmured, as if he didn't believe it either, 'I'll be damned.'

Hobday had found it in a drawer that Robins had used. Burtenshaw said he knew about it. He'd forgotten: but Robins had mentioned that he'd be taking five hundred pounds in gold for someone ashore. Burtenshaw didn't know *who* for. They counted it: there were twenty rolls and twenty-five sovereigns in each roll.

'Better take it with you, Everard. Dare say someone'll pop up and ask for it.' Wishart glanced round at the hovering messman. 'What d'you want, Lewis?'

'Spot o' breakfast, sir?'

'Well – if you're quick with it . . .'

Pilchards, washed down with what Lewis thought of as coffee. Burtenshaw closed his eyes and turned away from it, although Nick warned him there was no telling when they'd next get a meal or what it might consist of. There were some jokes then, about Turk menus, which didn't make the Marine feel any better. Nick ate rapidly and hungrily, with a pistol already strapped to his side in a webbing holster, while E.57 closed in towards her appointment with the caïque.

CHAPTER 11

The caïque's crew certainly weren't feeding them. No food, no drink. No sign of anything like friendship either. They were sailing them into Constantinople all right, but whether they'd cut their throats before they got there or sell them to the authorities on arrival was anybody's guess.

At first Nick had hoped it was only a strangeness that would wear off, mutual suspicions that should dissipate as they all got to know each other. Now, the best part of a day later, he'd no wish at all to know them any better than he did already. There were four of them: wolf-like men with cunning, vicious faces, and all four were armed with knives. When Nick had asked for water to drink there'd been whines and finger-twisting gestures: *money* . . . Then unmistakable threats.

No money, no drink . . .

The money was in Burtenshaw's rucksack with the demolition stores. It would obviously be far too dangerous to let these people get a sniff of it.

A day of dirt, discomfort, hunger and – above all – thirst. But now Constantinople, which for hours had been a shimmer of white and green in a distant, bluish haze, was enclosing them as the caïque's sails drove her in on the southerly breeze. Three cities in one, glowing in the light of the dying sun. The mosques and minarets of Scutari to starboard and Stambul to port burnt like the embers of a fire; ahead lay the entrance to the Bosphorus, the gateway to the Black Sea – to Odessa, the Crimea, Batum; and on the caïque's port bow, beyond Serai Point and on the far side of another half-mile of blue water, Pera's white buildings gleamed among the dark slim cypresses. Blue water, white stone, green foliage, white sails everywhere, and the sun setting it all alight. Here to port Stambul's sea-walls showed double, reflected upside-down in the water at their feet. It was startlingly beautiful, making you believe in the most highly coloured travellers' tales; with more immediacy one was aware that beyond this point of land – Serai – where presently the caïque would swing round on to the port tack, Galata Bridge straddled the entrance to the Golden Horn, where *Goeben* lay. A kind of Holy Grail built of grey steel, armed with eleven-inch guns, scheduled for destruction.

By two men in a sailing-boat with pistols and a bag of bombs?

It could be a mistake, Nick realised, to let the mind dwell on the sheer unlikeliness of such a hare-brained scheme succeeding. Just press on, he told himself. Like bringing a ship into a tricky, windswept anchorage in the dark: no good dithering, taking her in too slowly, or you'd just drift into *worse* danger. You had to grit your teeth, get on with it.

Burtenshaw, happy to be leaving the responsibility to Nick, was suffering now from nothing except thirst. He waved a hand in the direction of Stambul.

'Santa Sophia.'

'What?'

'That big dome with the four minarets round it. Built by the Emperor Justinian in about five hundred AD as a symbol of Byzantine Christianity. Gone Mohammedan now, of course. Hence the added minarets.'

'Where d'you get all this from?'

'Well, it's famous.' He shrugged. 'And one learnt a certain amount about the ancient world – at school, you know?'

'I didn't. Except which way Rodney turned in some battle or another . . . Talking about learning, though, how do you happen to talk German?'

'Ah. Well, to start with, I had an Austrian governess. And my mother's half French, so I wasn't too bad at that, and when one had reached a certain standard – at school, I mean – there was the option of doing German instead. So—'

'Are you fluent?'

'Oh, not by a *very* long chalk!'

'No . . .' Nick stared at the slowly passing scenery. The whole thing was hopeless. If one could have put the clock back, been back in Wishart's submarine, would one still agree to go ahead, elect to be here now?

Lunacy . . . And yet, how could one have backed out – having got this far, having been brought through the straits, and with Reaper back there expecting miracles?

He sighed. The thing was, to shut one's mind: move from moment to moment, not think about what was happening in any general way . . . He unfolded his hand-drawn map – traced from the chart of the Bosphorus – and studied it. It was enough to show the rough layout of the three cities: this entrance, with Stambul on the left and the Horn like a wide river behind it, separating Stambul from Pera but with two bridges – the Galata and the Old Bridge – spanning it. Scutari was the city on the Asiatic side, over there to starboard and linked only by ferry-boats to the European shore. Simplified, the waterway could be thought of as having the shape of a capital Y. The lower part of it, the stem, was the entrance from the Marmara, the channel they were sailing up now. On the right was Scutari, and the right-hand branch of the 'Y' was the beginning of the Bosphorus. The left-hand branch was the Golden Horn, a cul-de-sac of protected anchorage dividing Stambul from Pera. That was about the sum of it.

Nick folded the map and pushed it into a pocket of the jacket they'd given him, a loose garment of stained and threadbare linen. Under it he had a sort of vest, and his trousers were sailcloth. He didn't know what he might pass for in this get-up: an Armenian horse-trader, an off-duty kitchen porter? The fez made him clearly a Mohammedan – Burtenshaw had one too, with *his* jumble-sale outfit. The caïque's captain had invited them to select garments of their choice from a heap on the cabin deck, and it had been a matter of picking out what came closest to fitting. They weren't the only living creatures in this gear, and they'd stood the greasy fezes upside down in the sun in the hope of baking out whatever forms of insect life resided in them. After the clothing issue and a parade in the open for the amusement of Aubrey Wishart at his periscope, the Turk captain had made his first demand for payment: Nick had refused it, and initial fawning had changed immediately to animosity.

He'd been thinking about the money. He told Burtenshaw, 'See if you can get a couple of the sovereigns out of the bag without our friends seeing what you're doing. And slip them to me. I'll pay them when we land.'

'Just two?'

'Someone ashore may well be expecting to get the whole five hundred, intact. And I doubt if these chaps see gold very often, anyway.'

Near Oxia Island, eight miles and several hours back, Wishart had raised and lowered his periscope three times, the prearranged signal that he was leaving them to go on alone. They'd been careful not to wave, since the crew were watching them and they hadn't wanted to advertise the fact that the escort was deserting them. Nick had pictured mentally the other end of that bronze tube, the now familiar control-room scene. It had felt like leaving home: and he'd never expected to have such feelings for a submarine! He'd heard in memory Wishart's final words: 'Best of luck, old lad. You'll make a job of it, I'm sure.'

He might have been sure!

Grey Lady: Maritza Hotel: it wasn't much to go on. Nick had counted on finding some reasonably helpful character aboard the caïque.

Coming up close to Serai Point now. On the other bow the entrance to the Bosphorus seemed to be widening as the caïque moved into the wide joint of the 'Y'. Sails flapping as the wind faltered and then returned: gear creaking. Slap of wavelets against the timber hull . . . Wishart had observed, not long before he'd surfaced this morning, that however hazardous the landing operation might seem, it was a fact that submariners in this Marmara had done things just as crazy, in the earlier Dardanelles campaign. Two submarines' first lieutenants, for instance, had swum ashore pushing explosives along with them on home-made rafts, and blown up railway lines under the noses of Turk soldiers. There'd been all sorts of improbable adventures. He'd added, 'Truly, you're in the best of company.'

Some of which, Nick recalled, was dead. Wishart hadn't mentioned this point, of course.

Burtenshaw pointed suddenly, and announced, 'Galata Bridge!' At the same time his other hand nudged at Nick's side. 'Here. The money.'

They'd rounded Serai Point. To their left a narrowing sheet of blue water was the approach to the Golden Horn; the Galata Bridge, straddling the 200-yard wide waterway, had its central span pulled aside. The bridge was of masonry resting on floating iron pontoons, and to open it they towed the middle ones outwards, like opening double doors. The caïque was swinging round now under rudder, and one of the crew had padded for'ard to tend its foresail as the craft turned close in around the point, almost in the shadows thrown by the walls of some kind of fort or castle. About four hundred yards to go, to that gap in the bridge: and then they'd be actually inside the Horn – with *Goeben* practically within spitting distance!

They'd have some sort of guard, surveillance of the traffic entering, surely. He turned to Burtenshaw as he pocketed the two sovereigns.

'If we get any problems like police boarding us, keep your mouth shut and give the crew a chance to talk us out of it. And do what I do.'

'What will that be?'

Of all the damn-fool questions . . . 'If we have to split up, rendezvous in the Maritza bar. Right?'

Burtenshaw licked his dry lips. 'Right.'

'Whatever happens, don't lose that rucksack. And don't let your pistol show.'

The Marine pulled his rubbish-heap jacket together, to hide the webbing belt. The sun was a blinding golden halo around a mosque near the south end of the bridge. Two other caïques had emerged from the opening in the bridge's centre: black silhouettes, dramatic on silver water, creeping up the northern shore towards the Bosphorus. Some steam-driven craft – tug or launch – was fussing about near the gap. The low sun was dazzling: but the tug, if that was what it was, seemed to have gone through, into the Horn . . . His nerves were a bit taut: they were close to the target now, the prize that had drawn them through so many obstacles, for which *Louve* had been lost, E.14 sunk – and a lot more, more distantly, an enormous lot more besides. She was *there*, somewhere beyond that bridge . . . He leant forward, shielding his eyes against the yellow searchlight of the sun: his throat felt as if it was lined with brick-dust. Burtenshaw, also peering towards the bridge, was humming a tune he must have picked up from Leading Seaman Morton, E.57's second coxswain. Morton was always humming it – an old sailors' ditty about a seafarer who spends a night with a girl, and, leaving her bed in the morning, gives her certain advice. The song was familiar enough to Nick, and he sang the words of the chorus now for the education of the ignorant leatherneck.

'Saying "Take this my darling for the damage I have done,
If it be a daughter, or if it be a son;
If it be a daughter dandle her upon your knee,
If it be a son send the bastard off to sea"'—

He'd caught his breath: and his thoughts had flown a couple of thousand miles: to Sarah's precipitate visit to his father and to the lack of any sort of reason or explanation . . . He, Nick, had been with her at Mullbergh: they'd spent that night together on some other planet and in the morning he'd left – because he'd had to – and within a very few days she'd—

If it be a daughter or if it be a son . . .

Sarah? As ruthless as that – as decisive and guileful? Just like that, seizing a chance so that if he, Nick, had fathered a child by his own stepmother, Sir John Everard would accept it as his own?

Burtenshaw said, 'I think they're about to shut the bridge. They would do, I suppose, at sundown. But we'll get through, all right – so long as the wind doesn't die on us, or—'

Babbling about wind . . . Nick told himself to think about something else: about *now*, for instance, and what the hell they were going to do when they got ashore. Maritza Hotel. Grey Lady. Find the first, ask for the second. It was all one *could* do. What had Reaper told him about the situation ashore, the general background? Reaper's calm tones drawling as they trod the oak planks in step, their hands behind their backs, turning at precisely the same moment at each end of the cruiser's quarterdeck: 'Remarkable place, Constantinople. Beautiful and sophisticated, and under the surface it's a snake-pit. Now more than ever. The Turks are – well, unpredictable. "Changeable" might be a better adjective. At the moment, luckily for Robins, they're in a flat spin.'

'Having to surrender – and the Germans there to stop them doing so, you mean?'

'They're split. Only the Young Turks are pro-German and pro-War. The Young Turks, I suppose you know, are the ruling faction. The new Sultan – old one's drunk himself to death, one hears – this young one, Vahid-ed-din Effendi – hates them like poison. Which is what they are, of course. The three top ones are Enver Pasha, Talaat Bey and Djemal Pasha. They'll do a bunk, I'm advised, once they find their German friends aren't there to protect them any longer. Enver's a small, vain man, with curly ends to his moustaches. Ruthless as a snake. Talaat's a vast brute, like a gorilla only more vicious. Djemal's the Minister of Marine – sports a heavy black beard. Enver got himself and Talaat into office by shooting their C-in-C, old Nazim, back in '13. *And* it's pretty clear he's the chap who murdered the Heir Apparent. The story they put around was that he'd killed himself – opened the arteries inside his arms – here and here, in the crooks of the elbows. But both arms at once really needs a contortionist – specially as he was lashed to a chair at the time. Those three'll have to disappear, I'd guess, or swing.'

'Will Robins – will we – find a welcome, d'you expect?'

'From the underground, yes. All the Christians, and what's left of the Armenians. The Turks have massacred most of the Armenians, or transported them. Not that there's much difference – they sent one caravan of eighteen thousand men, women and children away to Aleppo in '15, and exactly one hundred and fifty got there . . . But yes. I'd say we'll find plenty of co-operation when the balloon goes up.'

The caïque was inside: the bridge had been towering up, and in the last seconds it had swallowed them. Now the Turks could shut it for the night. But there were no big ships in here: certainly no *Goeben* . . . The crewman who'd let down the foresail sprang ashore with a rotten piece of frayed rope, passed it round a bollard and leapt back on board again: he was walking aft along the top of the gunwale, balancing effortlessly on wide, bare feet whose thick skin must have been splinter-proof. His eyes were on the Englishmen and one hand hovered near the hilt of his knife. Two other crewmen were between them and the jetty; and the skipper was coming for'ard too now. Nick murmured, 'Strap the rucksack on, Bob.'

'Shall we ask for directions to the Maritza?'

'What, tell these thugs where we're going?'

'Oh. No – I suppose not . . .'

Ashore, lights were being turned on. This was Galata, and they were berthed on a stone quay not far beyond the bridge. There were other small craft about, but very little movement anywhere; it was as if with their arrival everything had suddenly closed down for the night. But against a corner of a warehouse sixty yards away, two policemen lounged, smoking and spitting: it was the sound of expectoration that had drawn his attention to them, and the gleam of light on brass buttons that revealed police-type uniforms.

Goeben was not between the two bridges, so she could only be in the larger anchorage above the second one, the Old Bridge. The distance between the two was about half a mile. Nick thought it might be their good luck that she wasn't in a Galata berth, because if she had been there'd surely have been German sentries and boat patrols all over the place. As it was, with both bridges shutting off the waterway, they probably didn't think much more protection could be necessary.

641

Nearer to the higher bridge, just this side of it, he could see a yacht moored alongside. She was about a hundred and fifty yards away and the flag over her stern was the Stars and Stripes. Puzzling over this, he remembered that America was not at war with Turkey.

From shorewards came the familiar sounds of urban life. Voices, hooves and iron wheels on cobbles, snatches of music, tram bells clanging, a general background hubbub with individual sounds rising from it. The caïque's skipper shuffled closer and stuck his hand out.

It wasn't a request. His three crewmen were barring the way to the jetty. Nick looked over their heads, towards the corner where the policemen had been leaning. They'd gone.

He said, holding out one sovereign towards the malevolent-looking skipper, 'You ought to be paying *us*. Here, take it.' The last words had been hardly necessary: the man had snatched the coin, examined it, and now he was testing it with his teeth. The crewmen were crowding closer and there was a mutter of what appeared to be dissatisfaction; now one dirty hand was out again and the other was gesturing, pointing at the men behind. The swift, unintelligible gabble might have been to the effect that one coin was all right for him, but what about the staff?

Nick made a show of conferring with Burtenshaw. He said, 'He can have the other one, but he's got to believe it's all we've got. Argue with me – tell me I mustn't give it to him.'

'You mustn't give it to him.'

'Damn it, can't you put some *feeling* into it?'

The Marine bawled, 'You must not give it to him, I say!'

'Well, you can go to blazes!'

Staring at each other: Nick apparently angry, and Burtenshaw bewildered. Nick glanced back at the caïque's captain, and produced the other sovereign; he also turned the pocket of his jacket inside out, as proof that there wasn't any more.

'Here. And may you break a tooth on it.' The hand clawed out; Nick muttered, 'Come on, Bob, while the going's good.' He pushed past the rabble and vaulted over to the jetty. Cobbles. 'This way. Let's not look as if we're *running* away.' All very well to *talk* like that, but as he said it he was sharply aware of his own exposed back and the knives in the crewmen's sashes. Burtenshaw, at his side, marched as if he was on parade – Beating the Retreat, perhaps – with his jaw out-thrust and eyes glaring straight ahead, arms swinging stiffly from the shoulders. He was going to need quite a lot of jollying along, Nick suspected; he told him, 'There's no one on the saluting base today, Bob.'

'What's that?'

'Relax. We aren't on a parade ground.'

'Perhaps not. But I think they're following us.'

'Oh, rubbish!'

'Just listen, then . . .'

Three women – dark shapes, veiled and shawled – appeared out of one of the alleys that joined the quay, and watched them as they passed. An old man popped out of an arched doorway, stared at them, shot back inside and slammed the door. Nick heard a sudden twitter from those women, and an answering growl in a man's voice: he glanced over his shoulder and caught a glimpse of the three figures huddled close together and another skulking past them, yet another showing very briefly and nearer, ten yards further this way: then there was nothing, only the women walking back the other way along the cobbled quayside and a long area of darkness in the cover of the wall, pools of it blacker still in the angles of buildings shielding alley-ways. Burtenshaw said, 'Two of them at least. I heard one call the other, or swear at him. Actually I heard them when they were coming ashore from the caïque and I thought you must have too.'

'You've got damn good ears.'

'They're closer than they were.'

The Turks, he meant, not his ears. But what to do now, Nick wondered. Stop and face them? But they'd have knives, and it would hardly be wise to use revolvers on them. Those two police-men couldn't be far off, and shots would bring them running – plus any other guards there might be in the vicinity. The crewmen following must either suspect that there'd be more gold where that sample came from or be wanting to know, for their own ulterior purposes, where their former passengers were going. They might easily draw *baksheesh* from both sides, from the Turk authorities as well as from Commander Reaper's contacts.

Make a break for it – run, hope to lose them?

No. Daft. They'd know these alleys thoroughly, and to try anything of the sort would be playing right into their hands. As well as attracting the attention of any policemen or German sentries who might be about. It was a fairly weighty problem and there wasn't much time, he felt, for dithering; then, suddenly and not far ahead, he saw the Stars and Stripes.

It was floodlit, on the yacht's ensign-staff, and her name – *Scorpion* – was painted in gold letters across her transom. In all the circumstances, he decided instantly, to pass her by would be looking a gift-horse in the mouth.

'We'll go aboard that Yank.'

'Could be a trap. How *can* there be an American—'

'They aren't at war with Turkey. And anyway, it's our only hope.' He heard the footfalls behind them, very much closer than they had been, and he grabbed the Marine's arm: 'Now – run for it!'

As he rushed to the gangway where it slanted down abreast a tall, slim funnel, his eye recorded a clean sweep of deck and a high clipper bow and twin raked-back masts. A pretty ship: and if American hospitality was what it was cracked up to be she was in the right place at the right time. He swung himself on to the lit gangway between polished brass stanchions, and Burtenshaw came pounding up the planks close behind him. As they reached the top, a large individual in the uniform of a petty officer in the US Navy stepped forward into the light.

'Far enough, till I know who you might be!'

'Friends! Allies!'

Burtenshaw had yelled it. Nick amplified, 'There are some Turks with knives chasing us. I think they intend to rob us.' But now another man had materialised from a shaded deckhouse doorway. He was tall, slim, about Nick's age, with shiny swept-back hair and spectacles that flashed in the radiance of the gangway lamps. He was dressed in immaculate evening clothes. The other man, after a word from this newcomer, had gone down to the shore end of the gangway, and could be heard now talking to one of their pursuers. It was one of the caïque's crew, all right, and he'd stopped on the edge of the pool of light down there.

The well-dressed American turned to Nick.

'That is no Turk, sir. That is a Lazz – else I'm a Dutchman.'

'A Lazz?'

'Scum of the earth. Smugglers, thieves, murderers. They'll smuggle gold out and kidnapped virgins in. Whatever you may have a hankering for, a Lazz will quote you a price for it: or if someone else pays him more, he'll cut your throat.' He listened for a while, cupping a hand to one ear; then he turned back to them, satisfied that the other man was handling the shoreside situation well enough. 'If I were to make what you might think was a somewhat personal comment, gentlemen – I wouldn't say you were dressed quite like you sound?'

Nick admitted, 'By and large I suppose we're dressed Lazz-style.'

'Allies, you did say?'

'Well, most certainly—'

'Counsellor.' The petty officer stepped off the gangway. 'We have a coupla dog-collar men headin' this way.'

'Might have known there would be.' The tall man told Nick, speaking more quickly now, 'I'm Benjamin Mortimer. This yacht is the ambassador's *stationaire*. Ambassador Morgenthau is in the States at this time, the embassy's closed during his absence and I'm sort of looking after what still has to be done . . . Might I assume you two are British, perhaps escaped prisoners of war, something like that?'

Nick agreed. 'Something like that.'

'Well, as you are probably aware, the United States and Turkey are not at war, and it so happens we represent British interests here when we're called upon to do so. Regrettably, that does not permit me to – ah – harbour you, as it were . . . They still coming, Parker?'

'Sure are.' The petty officer stepped on to the gangway and headed down towards the jetty. Benjamin Mortimer murmured, 'He'll stall 'em, but I'm the one talks their lingo . . . We might say you were Bulgarian soldiers – fought in Turk formations and gotten wounded, now you're fresh out of hospital, and in the goodness of my heart I'm contemplating employing you as maintenance hands aboard this yacht?'

Nick smiled gratefully. 'Your heart's good, all right.'

'Blood's thicker 'n water, I guess. Now look, though – aren't that number of Bulgarians walking around talking your kind of English. Stay dumb, eh?'

He turned away towards the quayside. Parker was coming back up the gangway. At its foot, two swarthy, fattish men in dark uniforms like the pair they'd seen earlier but with brass crescents slung across their chests were blinking upwards at the lights. Mortimer went on down, and Turkish compliments flew to and fro. Parker said, getting off the gangway, 'Special police. They have this ship under surveillance most days an' nights. Anyone comes or goes, they show up.'

'Dog-collar men, you said?'

'Says *Quanum* on them brass tags. Means "Law". They're

worse'n the regular ones. Mr Mortimer pays 'em plenty not to bother us more'n they have to.'

The conversation down there still sounded polite enough. Nick commented, 'Very pretty ship, this. Do you take her to sea at all?'

'Not so often.' Parker stared at their clothes as if he'd only just noticed them. Now he noticed Nick noticing the inspection, and he politely glanced away. He nodded. 'Time o' the Spanish-American war, this little lady was a blockade-runner. Had steel armour fixed all down her sides.'

'She's used to troubled waters then.'

'You could say that.' He looked round as Mortimer, smoking a black cigar now, came back up the gangway. 'All serene, sir?'

'Well.' Mortimer waved the strong-smelling weed. 'Let's say they found it difficult not to accept the facts as I described them.'

Parker rubbed his heavy jaw. 'Ain't much they don't find it difficult not to accept.'

'They are indeed – receptive.' Mortimer smiled drily as he reached for his cigar-case. 'Care to smoke?'

They both declined. Nick said, 'What we *would* care for – if it's not overpresuming on your kindness – is something to drink.'

'Brandy? I've only a Greek variety, but—'

'Water – please?'

Hard to think about it . . . Burtenshaw ran a dry tongue over dry lips. 'Yes – if—' Mortimer had suddenly understood. 'Parker, whistle up that steward. Gentlemen – please, if you'd step inside . . .'

'Inside' turned out to be a warmly lit saloon, all mahogany, soft carpet, oil paintings and the gleam of crystal glass and silver: and within minutes, cool fresh water trickling down one's throat. Burtenshaw sighed, 'Oh, delicious!' and poured himself another glass. Nick said, 'Can't tell you how grateful we are to you for taking such a chance on us.'

'Coupla months back, don't know I would have.' Mortimer wagged his head. 'Now – well . . .' He'd a tumbler of brandy and water in his fist. 'There's a rumour around suggesting your British fleet won't be long coming.'

'Let's hope rumour's right for once.' Nick asked him, 'Any rumours about a French submarine called *Louve*?'

'Sure is.' The American put his glass down. 'Towed her in right past us here, coupla days back. She's higher up – beyond where they have *Yavuz* now.'

646

'*Yavuz* – that's—'

Nick cut across Burtenshaw's quick excitement. 'Crew still on board *Louve*, d'you know?'

'They have them in the Military Prison. That's in the Ministry of War compound in Stambul.' He'd jerked a thumb south-eastward. 'Seems she got beached under the guns of one of their Dardanelles forts. Don't know how. Some place near this Marmara end. Her captain wasn't able to blow her up on account he had certain civilians on board and when he passed the word "abandon ship" they wouldn't budge. Too scared, I guess. And she got taken in one piece.'

Nick glanced at Burtenshaw. They'd been an odd-looking bunch, that French cloak-and-dagger party. Mortimer added, 'The civilians did 'emselves no damn good, by all accounts. Bedri Bey had 'em tortured and the word is they're dead. Bedri's old Talaat's right-hand man – and he's one mean Turk.' He looked from one of them to the other. 'Care for some'n stronger, before you leave us?'

Nick declined, but he also took the hint. 'Before we do leave you – one more bit of information? You mentioned *Yavuz* – the battlecruiser we still call *Goeben*—'

'Well, I have to call her *Yavuz Sultan Selim*. She flies the crescent and star, and her crew wear fezes. Not my business what language they converse in. I can fly *my* country's flag here because we don't happen to be at war with Turkey. But if I had to say that ship was a goddam Fritz, well . . .'

Nick saw the point. 'But – is she anchored or moored out in the stream, or is she alongside?'

'The latter. They had her between buoys, but she berthed on the quayside yesterday. Last evening. Looks like she could be going someplace. Been loading stores all day, taking in fresh water, had a collier alongside too. Parker here reckons she's raising steam.'

Nick was up on his feet, trying to look as if he wasn't in a hurry. Burtenshaw, half up, was reaching for the rucksack which he'd kept beside him. Mortimer sank lower in his chair. Smoke drifted from his lips as he smiled gently, watching them.

'Boy, you're subtle. I'd *never* guess what brought you here. Never in a billion years.'

'One more favour.' Nick was thinking about the two dog-collar men. Somehow they'd have to get past them without being stopped and questioned. 'Tell us how we can find the Maritza Hotel?'

The American stared at him, as if he'd asked for something difficult this time. He shook his head slowly. 'I guess I better not.'

'Why—'

Mortimer took the cigar out of his mouth, and sighed.

'They raided the Maritza, last evening. Tell you the truth I wouldn't know what delayed 'em this long. *Bakhsheesh*, no doubt . . . Dog-collar men took off a whole load of the regular clientele, so I heard. If I were you, I'd stay clear.'

Nick stared at him while it sank in. He was thinking of *Goeben* raising steam, sailing at dawn, taking everyone by surprise again. The least he'd be expected to do was get a signal out. But without contacts, *how*?

Benjamin Mortimer had risen to his feet.

'Your intention had been to meet a friend or friends there, I might suppose.'

'Never know your luck.'

'Quite so.' The Counsellor nodded seriously. 'But it's not impossible I might be able to point you the right way – if you'd tell me the identity of the person you're hoping to locate.'

Nick wondered if he'd already said too much. You could take risks when it was just your own neck at risk – but other people's? The Grey Lady's?

Mortimer frowned.

'My credentials – if that might be what's causing you to hesitate – are flying over this ship's stern, sir.'

'I'm sorry.' He was embarrassed. 'I'm not for a moment questioning your—'

'Then permit me to make it simpler for you. Would your contact happen to be of the female sex and your own nationality?' Nick nodded. The American crossed the saloon and stooped to a bureau drawer: cigar in mouth, groping in the drawer . . . 'Street map here, some place . . .'

E.57's diesels growled steadily into the darkness, a white-flecked blackness that felt so thick with danger that you could imagine something there every time you put your glasses up; this close to Constantinople there'd *have* to be destroyer or gunboat patrols. Particularly with a flap on – the Germans knowing that at least one hostile submarine was patrolling in the Marmara – and even more so if there was any likelihood of *Goeben* breaking out to sea . . . The boat was trimmed down so low in the water that there was no more than her bridge to be seen; but standing on it, in these circumstances, it felt as big as a haystack and illuminated by the white foam flooding over the hull and tanks below it. One felt – in a word – conspicuous . . . Wishart, Jake and Ellery were on the bridge, and all three pairs of binoculars were busy all the time, lowered only for the few seconds it took occasionally to wipe lenses fogged by the sea-dew. They'd been on the surface for about half an hour now, straining their eyes to probe the night, breathing the faint reek of oil exhaust, and conscious of the closeness of the Turkish coast. The voicepipe squawked, and Jake answered it.

'Bridge.'

'Permission to rig W/T mast, sir?'

Wishart muttered an affirmative, and Jake passed it down.

But they wouldn't be transmitting. It wasn't only the breaking of wireless silence that would be bound to alert the enemy: there would also be the customary display of blue sparks from the aerial connections – a frightening piece of self-advertisement when one was as close inshore as this. Jake, sweeping with his glasses across the bow and trying to keep track of the dividing line between sea and sky, heard Weatherspoon and Agnew clattering about and muttering to themselves as they rigged the mast and aerial at the back of the bridge. Wishart called, 'Quick as you can, leading tel.'

Five men on the bridge were about three too many, in this situation.

'Aerial's rigged, sir!'

'Well done.'

Familiarity with the job made for speed. The telegraphists practised in harbour with blindfolds on and stop-watches timing them. They'd left the bridge, now.

'I'm going below, pilot.'

'Aye aye, sir.'

Now it was only himself and the signalman; both of them circling slowly, continuously. No good staring at any one point for more than a second: the eye was best at picking up a 'foreign body' as it passed over them. It wasn't the object that you saw, it was the difference between it and its dark surroundings. Over the bow, and down the starboard side; the voicepipe yelped, 'Bridge!'

'Bridge.'

'Time for the next leg to port, sir.'

'Starboard ten.' They were carrying out a programmed zigzag, and the helmsman down below watched the times for each

649

alteration. Jake called down, 'Ease to five and steady on one-two-oh.' He straightened, raised his binoculars again, leaving Anderson to get on with it; he'd covered about ten degrees of black horizon before something glimmered white. Back on it now: it looked like a small, dim light, but he knew it was a fast ship's bow-wave.

'Dive – dive – dive!'

Racket of the klaxon – vents thudding open . . . Ellery was down inside and Jake followed down on top of him, dragging the lid shut and jerking its clips over, shouting to Ellery to tell Wishart, 'Bow-wave – destroyer or patrol-boat – northerly bearing about five cables, coming towards!'

Bearing and range were rough, just guesswork . . . He heard Wishart order forty feet, felt the angle as she tilted downwards, nosing deep; then he was off the ladder and Ellery had climbed up to shut the lower hatch; Weatherspoon reported, 'HE – true bearing oh-one-four – fast, reciprocating, closing, sir!'

'Group down, stop starboard.' Agnew repeated the orders as he clanged the telegraphs around; Hobday was getting the trim adjusted for the forty-foot depth. Glances drifted upwards as the Turk patrol craft, whatever it was, thrashed overhead. Wishart asked Jake, 'Any chance he could have seen us?'

'Doubt it, sir.'

'Fadin', sir.' Weatherspoon added, 'Bearing just west of south now, sir.'

Holding a straight course, then. Which meant he had *not* seen them.

'Twenty feet.' Wishart looked over towards the silent cabinet. 'Still on to him?'

'Just about gone, sir.'

Hobday was having to work on the buoyancy tank now, as she came up again. Jake wondered how far Nick Everard and the Marine had got. He heard Hobday order, 'Stop flooding.'

Twenty-four feet: twenty-two . . .

'Stand by to surface.' Wishart told Weatherspoon, 'Be ready to come up when I pass the word. You'll have to bring the aerial down and dry out the contacts, then re-rig it, and I want it set up and working before we have to dive again.'

So he thought it was to be *that* sort of a night. And it would be, probably. You couldn't expect to be left undisturbed this close to an enemy port. Weatherspoon stared commandingly across the compartment at his assistant. Agnew, who'd be doing all the

650

donkey-work with the aerial, looked fed-up and sucked his teeth. ERA Bradshaw muttered reprovingly, 'It ain't *all* beer an' baggy trousers, lad.'

'Ready to surface, sir.'

Ellery pushed the hatch open and got down off the ladder; Wishart started up it.

'Surface!'

Hobday snapped, 'Blow three, four, five and six main ballast!' He'd only blow them half out. She'd lie like a hippo with her nostrils just clear of water, practically invisible and ready to slip under again in seconds. Nobody was going to get much sleep tonight.

Nick and Burtenshaw had been ready to leave the yacht, but Mortimer had stopped them.

'You want to meet Bedri Bey? The dog-collar men'll be on you before you're round that corner!'

Burtenshaw looked glumly at Nick. 'Not to mention the caïque's crew. Be out there somewhere, won't they?'

'We'll have to run for it, dodge 'em somehow.'

'Wait.' Mortimer had sent for Parker, the PO. Waiting for him, he'd explained, 'He can send some of the boys ashore on a punishment fatigue. With you two in among 'em. Once you're at the bridge in the traffic, your own mothers wouldn't find you.'

Parker had rounded up a dozen volunteers. *Scorpion* had a crew of seventy men, Mortimer had told them, and twisting Turks' tails had become their favourite sport. Within minutes they were all moving off at the double, Nick and Burtenshaw in the centre of the squad. Long before they reached the north end of Galata Bridge they could see the dense tangle of carts, cabs, motors honking impatiently, and moving like glue all around and through it, a mob of pedestrians. The sailor doubling on Nick's right told him as they jogged along, 'We'll wheel left and left again on the first block up from the bridge, sir. At the second turn you go straight on up the hill. You'll be like part of the crowd there got caught up with us.'

'Very much obliged.'

'Our pleasure, sir.'

Twenty minutes later they were entering the exclusive European district of Pera. The Galata Tower had been the first landmark; then the Tokatlian Hotel, where behind plate-glass windows facing the street fat Turkish officials and pompous-looking German officers were entertaining richly dressed, jewelled women at supper tables. Glimpses of champagne bottles in silver ice-buckets, obsequious waiters scurrying around. A bored-looking girl stared straight at Nick with an expression of disdain: he smiled at her, and saw her companion half turn in his chair and glower: he was a scrawny, beak-nosed German, something in the region of a colonel, and his anger was directed at this low-class street-lounger who'd insulted the girl with his grin . . . Hurrying on – and getting into smaller, confusing streets now, ten minutes later. Still quite a sprinkling of pedestrians: but all hurrying, not looking at each other, each minding his own business.

'Which?'

Burtenshaw pointed.

'How d'you know?'

'See trees through that other gap. And we had to pass between two areas of park?'

'Right.' He muttered as they started off again, 'You'd make a navigator.'

Young cypresses now, and old houses; little courtyards roofed with vines. A smell of dusty flowers: lights glimmering, passers-by fewer and flitting quickly through the quiet, near-deserted alleys.

'Left here . . . I think.' Burtenshaw whispered it as they paused; it wouldn't do to be heard talking English. 'The curved street, he mentioned – and the side-road across the hill behind it?'

'Right.' They were getting close now. 'Look for a courtyard entrance and trees at the back of it before the house.'

And the house would stand well back and have blue shutters and vines over a long veranda. The American had sounded as if he knew it well. The narrow curve of street was silent except for their own thudding footfalls. They stopped at an archway, tall and narrow with a curved top coming to a point. High, grey wall – and ten yards farther down, heavy wooden gates, shut. Nick slipped in through the archway with Burtenshaw close behind, looking back down the street to be sure no one had followed. Sweet-scented bushes: ahead, a cluster of feathery-looking trees stood out against the sky. The gleam of light from behind them must be coming from the house, and in the house – please God – they'd find the Grey Lady. The American had professed not to know any other name for her. He moved to the left; from the locked gates there was a carriageway to the house, and to walk along the side of it would be easier than groping through this perfumed jungle. Burtenshaw had stopped to change the rucksack from one shoulder to the other for about the sixth time; after the runs and the long uphill trek he was evidently feeling its weight. Well, *he* was the explosives expert. Approaching the trees and the house, Nick saw light pouring from an unshuttered window; he also saw what looked like an exceptionally large motor standing in front of the house. At closer quarters it turned out to be an open tourer – but a huge, swagger-looking contraption. This was the back end of it. Its long, silvery bonnet was bright and gleaming in the pool of light flooding from the window.

Burtenshaw had grabbed his arm, hissed something in his ear. Nick stopped. 'What?'

'Mercedes Benz. German!'

He thought, *Oh God, what next* . . . Then he rose over the quick reflex of despair: the mere presence of a Hun-made motor-car meant really nothing. Burtenshaw, he thought, tended to become alarmed too easily . . . There was an emblem of some kind on the motor's near-side door; Nick stooped to examine it. Beside him Burtenshaw whispered, 'That's the German eagle! Must be some official—'

'Oh, shut up!'

Think, now . . .

They'd raided the Maritza. And discovered there what might have led them here? In that case, the Grey Lady herself might be under arrest. But – not Germans, the raid had been made by the police, the dog-collar men, Mortimer had said. This was all guesswork: and Mortimer's account, for that matter, had been only hearsay. The thing was, Nick realised, to get a look inside the house and see who might be in occupation. If this was the Grey Lady's house and it was full of Germans, then he and Burtenshaw were on their own entirely. He began to creep quietly towards the window. His aim was to get to the side of it, keeping out of the light, and stand up slowly and look in. He was stooped like a baboon, passing between the motor and the house; he heard a sharp *click* and the headlamps sprang up like great floodlights. A man's voice shouted some sort of command.

The language matched the eagle crest. German.

Nick had frozen, with one hand covering his eyes against that blinding glare. He thought, *Finished* . . . Burtenshaw, right behind him, had yelped like a kicked dog and now stood facing the lights, blinking, with his hands up at shoulder-height. That shout had come from the driving-seat of the Mercedes Benz. Ten to one the Hun would have a pistol or rifle aimed at them from behind that dazzle of brilliance. He'd shouted again: and this time another German answered – from the house, behind them. But – ten to one? One chance in ten would be better than none at all, and he *might* not be armed.

'We'll have to make a dash for it.' Nick spoke out of the side of his mouth to the Marine. 'When I say *Go*, shoot at the lights and run. Out through the arch and turn left. Make for the nearer park. I'll go right and join you later.' You had to *move*, that was the thing. The Germans were exchanging shouts as if in disagreement over something; or they were shouting at the Englishmen and getting angry at the lack of response. Of course, Nick realised, neither he nor Burtenshaw could easily be taken for English. He asked the Marine, 'What are they saying?'

'Well – it's – it's a bit difficult to—'

A woman's voice: a stream of – Turkish?

From the house. *Grey Lady?* If so, free or captive?

'We're English! British officers!'

Clutching at straws: and giving the game away. Why had he done it? He didn't know. Except the urge to do *something* . . . The echoes of his shout rang through the darkness. Nobody answered: then the silence was broken by the snap of a rifle-bolt being jerked back. It convinced him that he'd blundered. He took a breath, *knowing* suddenly that this was as far as they were going to get. Then a new thought – that anything, even a bullet in the back, would be better than an interview with Bedri Bey. He murmured, 'Stand by again and be ready to run like blazes. If I don't meet you at the park try to get back to the Yanks.'

The woman's voice called again, but this time in very clear, educated English and from only a few yards away: 'English, indeed . . . You certainly don't *look* it.'

CHAPTER 12

The Grey Lady was tall, angular, authoritative. No beauty, but she had a certain charm that was entirely feminine. Forty, forty-five? About that, he thought. She wore a serge suit, and brogues; she could have been some country squire's unmarried sister, organising a village out of its mind.

She'd already had reports on the battle cruiser *Yavuz*'s preparations for sea, but the raid on the Maritza had disrupted her communications system and she hadn't been able to signal Reaper.

'Not that it matters now, since your submarine is waiting to torpedo her and you've arrived to play *your* part.'

She seemed unaffected by the knowledge that she was talking to two amateurs. Nick had told her about Robins being killed, and he'd been quite open about his own and Burtenshaw's lack of experience of this kind of clandestine operation. She'd shrugged it off: *nobody* had such experience, she said, until they found themselves involved in such work. And the business before them now, of sabotaging *Goeben* alias *Yavuz*, had nothing to do with the late Lieutenant Commander Robins. She was to have put Robins in touch with a certain individual in the Sublime Porte – Turkey's 'Whitehall' – but otherwise she'd have had no dealings with him. *Goeben* was what mattered here and now.

Nick gestured towards Burtenshaw. 'Really *his* pigeon.'

'Pigeon?'

'Burtenshaw here is the explosives wizard.'

'But you are in command of the operation?'

He had to admit it. But had anyone, he wondered, ever been less qualified or trained for such command? He hadn't the least idea what he was going to do. He didn't say so now: there was a brisk impatience in her manner, a touch of steel in the large, really rather captivating eyes. Her contempt for cold feet would, he felt, be blistering. In any case, she proceeded now to solve the problem for him – casually, as if this sort of thing was only part of an ordinary day's work.

'I've sent the other two Germans – on foot, of course – to fetch uniforms for you from their barracks. You—' she looked at Nick – 'would do well to shave. You'll find a razor in the bathroom upstairs. Shaving may be less important in your case, Mr Burtenshaw, since you are not so dark and it shows less. Besides, many of the German troops are quite shabbily turned out these days. *Quite* going to the dogs.' She smiled, pleased about it. 'But you must board *Yavuz* before sunrise, which I understand is the likely hour for her sailing. You'll have little time for sleep, I'm afraid.' Another smile. 'Never mind. We all have our small discomforts, do we not.'

It was rather like sitting in some country parson's study and being briefed on a plan to rob the Bank of England. You could listen and nod agreement from time to time, but if you really thought about it – about, for instance, the intention that they should actually walk on board a German battle cruiser within the next few hours . . . Better *not* to think. The only dividends from it were cold shivers and a sense of madness. Just listening to her was bad enough. The Mercedes Benz outside, for instance, belonged to the German C-in-C, General Liman von Sanders. She'd bought it from the general's driver. The driver and another German soldier – one who spoke some English and acted as interpreter – were the pair who'd now gone to steal uniforms. The third Hun, a partner of the driver's, was outside on guard, but the Grey Lady had the ignition-key on the table in front of her. She did not, she said, trust Germans.

She had arranged several days ago to buy the huge motor, not for the purposes of the present operation but because arms dumps had been established in various parts of the city, ready for an uprising by Christians and other anti-German elements, which would take place before the arrival of the British fleet. A large, fast vehicle had been needed to tour the dumps and collect the weapons quickly when the time came for action. She'd fixed it through a Greek henchman of hers named Themistoclé, and her plan now was that the motor should be used to take Nick and Burtenshaw, dressed as German soldiers and carrying baggage belonging to von Sanders, to *Goeben/Yavuz* just before she sailed.

It was a very simple plan, and there was virtually nothing that could go wrong with it, she said. Nick asked her soberly, 'Do you really believe that?'

'Why, most certainly!' She looked genuinely surprised. 'Don't *you*?'

'Well . . .'

'In more normal circumstances, I agree, it might seem – perhaps reckless. But this country is in a state of near-collapse, and the Germans are nearly as demoralised as the Turks. They know we have the upper hand in Europe now, and they also know their Turkish allies will round on them as soon as they can do so with impunity. As for the Young Turks – our lords and masters – well, they're said to be preparing to abandon the sinking—'

The lights went out. In here, and outside too. No gleam through the trees, no glow above the distant roofs. In pitch darkness, the Grey Lady laughed delightedly. Nick wondered if she might be off her dot.

'What a perfectly *splendid* coincidence!' She laughed again. 'I was on the point of mentioning that the Young Turks are rumoured to be getting ready to make a bolt for it – and in fact only this afternoon I was told that a plan had been laid for the fuses at the power-station to be drawn for an hour or two tonight, in order to facilitate the departure of those frightful rogues Enver, Talaat and Djemal. And – lo and behold!'

Nick murmured, 'Not beholding much, myself.' Burtenshaw asked, 'Doesn't this mean it's good as ended? The war – at least Turkey's—'

'Hardly *that*. I should say it marks the *beginning* of the end, and that it should greatly help the progress of the armistice negotiations . . . Did you know that discussions were in progress?'

They'd heard nothing of that sort, Nick told her. He explained to Burtenshaw, 'We still have to dish *Goeben*. Long as she's in fighting trim she could stop the Turks signing any armistice. She could keep us out, too – stop our minesweepers getting in, to start with.'

'Very true.' A match flared: they saw her face close to it, its harsh light darkening her deepset eyes, deepening the lines in face and neck. Then the gentler glow of candlelight spread through the room and she'd blown out the match, lost ten years of age and become softer, feminine again. Leaning towards the candle, peering at a little watch on a loop of chain: 'High time those wretches were back here . . . Lieutenant Everard, you did not by any chance bring with you a parcel of sovereigns?'

'Why yes, we did.' Burtenshaw stooped to grope in his rucksack.

Nick told her, 'We didn't know what it was for. But if it's intended for you . . .'

'Only too glad.' Burtenshaw put the canvas bag on the table. 'Weighs a ton.'

'Heavier the better!' She whisked it away, to a cupboard. Nick apologised, 'Two sovereigns short, I'm afraid. We had to pay the caïque's skipper something or they'd have cut our throats.' She frowned at that; then she explained, 'I was forced to pay three hundred for the motor. Exorbitant, of course; but they wanted *five* hundred to start with, and of course Themistoclé takes his commission. I could only scrape up a hundred, and I promised them the rest of it would be here within a day or so. So when you told me of Commander Robins's death . . .' She sighed, and smiled; you could see she'd been worrying about it. Nick was impressed by her not having mentioned the money until now. He told her, 'We'd have lost it very quickly if the caïque's crew had had a sight of it.'

She had already apologised for the Lazz fishermen. Faced with the sudden emergency when she'd had Reaper's distress call, she'd had to give Themistoclé his head, and that had been his easy answer to the problem. She said, 'They're all *so* mercenary. And once a German decides to sell out – well . . .' She sighed. 'There'll be a price on the uniforms, of course, too.' She'd glanced up at them, smiling suddenly: 'I have a bottle of Kirsch here, if you'd care for some. *Also* from the Germans, I might say. Shall we have a glass now, while supper's cooking?'

Supper was a mutton *pilaff*, followed by bread with a kind of raisin jam called *pekmes*. She apologised for so strange a meal; food-rationing and shortages were a curse, and a cause of unrest particularly in the poorer quarters of the town. She introduced Celeste, the young girl who'd cooked the *pilaff*, as one of about sixty convent girls, mainly of French parentage, whom she'd rescued from Bedri Bey's intention of turning them out into the streets. It would have meant the brothels. She'd found safe homes for all of them. Nick gathered, from as much as she told them, that by standing up to such moves as this openly and fearlessly she'd won the authorities' respect, or at least their tolerance, while her charitable work among the poor had not only made her well liked in the city but had also cloaked her more clandestine activities.

He'd dozed off. He came-to once, to hear argument or hard bargaining in progress between their hostess and the Germans.

Then – only minutes later, it seemed – she was waking him and the electric lights were burning.

So it *hadn't* been a dream?

'Time to put on these dreadful uniforms. They won't fit at all well, but we can't expect miracles.' Dressing, he'd still been muzzy with sleep and a kind of horrified disbelief, but returning to the living-room he'd found more of Celeste's thick, aromatic coffee ready, and it had brought him back to life – in no kind of comfort, but more or less clear-headed.

The Grey Lady showed them two heavy leather suitcases. Her manner was brisk but entirely calm, and the effect of it, Nick found, was steadying.

'These belong to von Sanders. Quite a *nice* man, really. No business at all being German. See – his name on them. One each to carry – otherwise they might wonder why there should be two of you. How fortunate that you should speak German, Mr Burtenshaw.'

Nick was wondering how much German the Marine *did* speak.

They were to go on board as the general's personal servants. Ostensibly coming from so high an authority, they'd almost surely be let by without question. Germans were like that, she said. As a matter of fact, we English were like that too. Herman, the driver, who was a familiar figure behind the wheel of the easily-recognised official motor-car, would declare at the gangway that he was delivering the Herr General's baggage as previously arranged. Nick and Burtenshaw would haul it up the gangway, and once inside the ship they – presumably – would know what to do. Herman would wait on the quay until nobody much was looking at him, and then drive away, and when anyone noticed that he'd gone they might assume the baggage porters had gone too.

Burtenshaw was speechless: numb – Nick thought – with fright.

As a target area for the explosive charge Nick had first thought of the midships torpedo flat. If a biggish amount of guncotton could be detonated close against a torpedo warhead, or better still in the warhead store, the results might be rewarding. But access would not be easy. It would be four or five decks down and through armoured hatches, well below the waterline. Modern German warships were honeycombs of small compartments all subdivided from each other: this was why they tended to remain afloat even after substantial damage . . . On reflection, he'd decided it might be best to go for the steering compartment, right aft and in the bottom of the ship. To set the charge off there probably wouldn't sink her, but with smashed steering gear she'd be immobilised, which would be enough for Reaper's purposes. It would also make her a sitting duck for Wishart.

He asked the Grey Lady how she could be sure Herman wouldn't blow the gaff once she'd paid him.

'He has at least as much to lose as you have, Lieutenant. He'd be shot out of hand.' She was looking them both over, as that triggered another thought; she murmured, 'Such a pity you haven't your own uniforms to wear under those dreadful suits.'

Nick caught the reference: the possibility of being shot. To be caught dressed as German soldiers would qualify him and Burtenshaw for 'out of hand' treatment, too . . . But they were starting now, actually walking out of the house. The guncotton, divided between the two cases, weighed very little. Climbing into the back of the car . . . If ever there'd been a truly madcap scheme, it was this one: and he, Nick Everard, was in command of it! Panic flared: but there was no *time* for panic . . . He told Burtenshaw as the Mercedes Benz backed out into the road with one of the Germans yelling advice to Herman, 'Once we're up the gangway, turn aft as if we're heading for the admiral's quarters where the luggage is supposed to go. Then duck inside and out of sight. We'll need to get right aft and down as many decks as she's got – that'll be the deuce of a long way down.'

They were out in the road and the other Hun was shutting the gates. Herman sent the big motor trundling along the narrow curve of street. Nick added more advice: 'And keep well closed up. If anyone questions us, say we're looking for the store for General Liman von Sanders's baggage. Naturally *you'll* do all the talking, if any has to be done.'

Burtenshaw, white-faced, turned and looked at him.

'You don't honestly think we can get away with this, do you?'

'Not get away with it?' Nick hoped his astonishment looked real. 'But why shouldn't we?'

The Marine shrugged. He looked away again, keeping his mouth shut tight as if he couldn't have trusted himself to speak again. At the end of the street they'd turned downhill across the intersection, and now the driver eased his wheel over to slant away north-westward, switching to the road that led down to the quayside on that higher reach of the Golden Horn. Motoring down to the Horn, for heaven's sake – to *Goeben* herself . . . No daydream either, the action had started and there was no way of stopping it. High above them, somewhere off to the right, a *muezzin* greeted the dawn, bearing witness in a raucous chant to Allah's greatness, calling the Faithful to their daybreak devotions. Visualising the robed figure aloft on some minaret that he couldn't see from the rumbling motor, Nick was reminded of a diving platform high above the Dart, a plank protruding from a hulk's side, and himself aged thirteen on the end of it. It was a very high board and until he'd got out on it he hadn't appreciated how far below the water would be. Looking down at it had brought a chill of fear: an instructor's bellow had floated up to him – 'What are ye waitin' for, the tide?' The only way off that platform had been over its edge, into the gulf: and it was just like that now. *Oh Sarah, my darling . . .* What had sent her image into his mind? What about her anyway – suddenly even his own feelings were uncertain, whether he regretted, would have put the clock back if that had been possible, undone what had been done . . . *Would* one? There'd been no moment of decision, no conscious act: it had happened, as something natural and inevitable: for both of them, he thought, it had been like that. And no, he did *not* regret it, because if it had not happened there'd have been an ingredient missing, something that was important now. Might she feel the same? And if the reason for her rushing to join his father in London was the one he'd guessed at, how would it seem to her – if it had all happened, and she'd buried the truth so well – as time passed, how would it be for her?

The possibility that she'd keep the secret even to the extent of never discussing it with *him* was a new and startling concept. It had sprung, of course, as an answer to the puzzle about those letters she'd written – the attitude of detachment, mild stepmotherly affection . . . If it turned out that he was guessing correctly now, receiving finally the message that she'd been trying to impart to him, would he be able to play that game, act as if nothing had ever happened between them? Could so large a lie be so firmly established that to all intents and purposes it would become the truth?

Burtenshaw's voice croaked beside him, 'It's – God, it's *hopeless*!'

'What is?'

He wouldn't have to tell any lies, or live one. He couldn't, he knew, possibly survive this – Burtenshaw was right, this *hopeless* operation. Gleam of water ahead: dawn's silver on the Golden

Horn. That dark mass rising against godown rooftops was smoke – a big ship's funnel-smoke. Burtenshaw answered him: 'This stunt, this attempt to blow up a—'

'God's sake, man, who'd have thought this time yesterday that we'd get *this* far?' He wished at once that he hadn't said that. One shouldn't admit to *any* doubt. He added, 'You'll feel better when the action starts.'

The motor's tyres thrummed as Herman turned without slackening speed around the corner of an ugly red-stone building. Port offices of some kind. Now the tyres sang on cobbles. Quayside: a wide area like a square in a small market town. The water was right ahead, its black sheen broken by the silhouette of a waiting tug. There was a graving dock between the waterfront and the building on their left. But they'd swung right, behind a long cargo shed with chains on its doors and a stink of wet hides in the air around it. Near the farther end of it, Herman turned his head and shouted, pointing a gloved hand towards the left; then he had both hands back on the wheel and he was leaning sideways in the effort of turning the Mercedes around the end of the warehouse and towards the quay.

At the same moment, almost like a fanfare greeting their appearance, Nick heard a bugle-call. The Prussian equivalent of a *muezzin*, he realised, a Hun sun-up ceremony. Shades of a dreary youth-time spent in Scapa Flow! On *Goeben*'s stern the black cross with the eagle in its centre would be mounting the ensign-staff. Guard and band to welcome them, now? By God, there was! A double rank of guard with rifles at the 'present', right aft on the great expanse of quarterdeck; and the band was striking up now, brass instruments cocked up under the looming barrels of the after eleven-inch turret. All the Germans were wearing fezes. The band had thumped out its short ditty and the bugles blared what must have been their form of 'carry on'; rifles were thudding to the 'slope', a rippling flash as the ranks of bayonets swayed over and the dawn light caught them, silvery-pink light glittering across the *Halic*, the Golden Horn. Looking upwards, he saw that at the main *Goeben* was flying a broad-pendant with a black cross on it, a commodore's flag.

No vice-admiral then, on this trip?

They were rumbling straight towards the after gangway, which led up to the quarterdeck near the stern turret. A point he'd overlooked in his thoughts of where to place the charge struck him as he

662

stared up at the ship's impressive twenty-three thousand tons of fighting power: since there'd be a bow torpedo room and a stern one in addition to the torpedo flat amidships, it might be possible to get close enough to the after one to blow the whole back-end off her. Drums were beating a tattoo now, boots crashing on oak planking as the quarterdeck was cleared, guard and band marched for'ard. All horribly familiar from one's own big-ship days: a slightly different, foreign flavour to it, but otherwise much the same. He leant forward and tapped Herman's shoulder, pointed at the other gangway, up near the first funnel.

'That one. Stop *there*.'

Herman was used to driving his general and other senior officers, who invariably would be received on quarterdecks. He was chauffeuring private soldiers now. Lights still burnt somewhat unnecessarily at the tops of both gangways. Officers on *Goeben*'s quarterdeck stared down at them; the quay was shadowed here by the ship's bulk. As they passed the bottom of the after gangway Nick saw a one-stripe officer in front of a single rank of men with bayonets on their rifles. He looked ahead, at the gangway they'd be stopping at: there was a similar guard at the foot of that one too. Mustering sentries, perhaps, men recalled from posts elsewhere on the quayside. He saw Burtenshaw staring at the bayonets as if he was mesmerised by them: he looked sick. The motor stopped, and Nick muttered, 'Come on.' He pushed the door open, grabbed one suitcase, and stepped out on to the running-board and down on to the cobbles, wet from the sea-dew of dawn. Glancing back, he saw the Marine standing, holding the other case and staring up nervously towards the ship. Turning, Nick saw a two-striper coming down the gangway with his eyes fixed on them and far from friendly.

'*Was ist das?*'

One didn't have to be a linguist to get the drift. He was pointing at the suitcases and he wanted to see inside them. Nick was thinking, *Caught. Already. Well, it was a pretty hopeless thing to have tried.* He grinned, as a dim-witted soldier might, and turned the case so that the German could see von Sanders's name on it; then Burtenshaw, joining him quite suddenly as if he'd that moment snapped out of a trance, stared rather haughtily at the *Kapitan-leutnant* and let rip with a string of German. Nick swung round, astonished; afterwards he realised that his open-mouthed surprise must have been goofy enough to have matched the earlier grin. The *leutnant* shrugged, and pushed past them on his way to muster the squad of sentries: and the gangway was unguarded, reaching up into the great grey ship above them.

It felt about as long as Piccadilly: and as exposed as a high-wire in a circus. Burtenshaw was leading: he'd taken the initiative on the quayside and it looked more natural for him to go up first. Halfway up Nick told him, 'At the top, slant right, go in the screen door and take the first ladder downward.' Burtenshaw nodded. The head of the gangway rested a few yards for'ard of the foremost of the battle cruiser's secondary armament of six-inch guns on this starboard side, and the screen door led into the ship at the lowest level of her bridge superstructure. Stumbling up the ribbed slope behind the Marine, Nick was trying to work out the probable location of the beam submerged torpedo flat. It had to stretch clear across the ship, in order to have one tube on either beam, so it had to be somewhere where there was no gun-turret, since the lower parts of each turret, ammunition hoists and so on, extended right down to the bottom of the ship. And with the layout of *Goeben*'s main armament that really left only the area below the bridge – roughly, therefore, this point of entry. Which would be excellent, because the sooner the charge was placed, the better; and the torpedo flat, with its own explosive content and its location below the waterline, would be a splendid place for guncotton.

Burtenshaw was off the gangway, crossing the ten feet of steel deck towards the open screen door. Now he'd paused, glancing back over his shoulder; Nick passed him and led the way inside.

There was a ladderway leading upward, another downward, and a transverse passageway over to the port side. Guessing there'd be the same up-and-down ladder system duplicated over there and that on the outboard side there might be less coming and going, Nick went straight ahead. And he'd guessed right: there was a matching down-ladder leading through an open rectangular hatch and with a taut chain for a handrail. He went down it quickly, with Burtenshaw's German boots close above him clumping on the steel treads. At the bottom they were in a fore-and-aft passageway with various doors leading off it and dim lights glowing on the painted bulkheads; and they were still well above the waterline. A group of sailors came by, hurrying, glancing at the soldiers curiously as they passed. One of them shouted something that made others laugh, and Burtenshaw waved his free hand, grunted in a friendly way. Five minutes ago he'd seemed to be a dead loss; now, he was worth

664

his weight in diamonds. Nick clapped him on the shoulder: 'Marvellous . . . We need to get down a couple more decks. Perhaps three.'

The head of the next ladderway was a dozen feet aft: they clattered down it, clutching their cases of explosive. Ladders and passages were narrower than in large British ships and deckheads were much lower: had one been a claustrophobiac, Nick thought, one might well feel uncomfortable, down here. More so, oddly, than in the submarine. Burtenshaw panted, close behind him, 'This is absolutely – *impossible*, it's—' and Nick cut him short: 'Don't think about it. Too late for thinking.' He thought it might be the key to Burtenshaw: keep him moving, doing. Well, it might be the key to anyone. Down another ladder, and he thought they'd be roughly at the water-level now. He was stepping off the ladder when a hand grasped his arm.

A petty officer: the insignia suggested some engine-room rate. He'd barked a question – loudly but in quite a friendly, semi-amused manner, something like *Where the hell d'you think you're going?* Nick let his lower jaw sag, assuming a baffled expression which was less a matter of acting than of having no other way to react, and Burtenshaw came up trumps again, saying they were searching for the officers' baggage store. He showed the PO the name on the cases: the man's eyebrows rose and fell, and he looked vaguely contemptuous – perhaps to make up for the fact that for the moment he'd been impressed – as he jerked a thumb, told them to get back up three levels and then right aft; and get a move on, or they'd find themselves at sea . . . He'd pushed them towards the ladder, one hand on each. By the time they were halfway up it, though, he'd moved away for'ard and swung a bulkhead door shut behind him, and they started down again. They were below the waterline now, and the lower they went in the ship the hotter, clammier it got. Inside the coarse uniform, Nick was already streaming wet. He muttered to Burtenshaw, 'Your German gets by, all right'; the Marine made a face, as if he wasn't all that sure of it.

Where this ladder ended – it took them into the centreline of the ship, port and starboard ladder-systems combining – was an entrance for'ard to a messdeck, and a transverse passage with humming machinery behind steel-mesh cages, and over on the port side another passage of some sort led aft; but at this point there was no way on down. The messdeck, however, was deserted, and a short way inside it was a closed hatch.

'See what's down here.'

Better than dithering about: and the sooner they got this stuff planted, the better.

Only two clips held the hatch shut. Nick loosened them by kicking the butterfly nuts round with his heel, and Burtenshaw knocked them off; then they pulled the hatch up, and Nick slid through on to the ladder. Dim lighting, and a peculiar smell that was in a way familiar and yet out of place, seemed not to belong. Thrum of machinery: not down here, but aft, trembling through the ship. Moving off the quay? There'd be help from tugs until she was out clear of the floating bridge. Here was a wet-smelling, *odd*-smelling, cramped steel flat, and on his left at the ladder's foot was a hammock-netting – a railed enclosure like a stall in a cattle-market – full of hammocks and kitbags. Near it a door, which he opened, and found himself looking into a bathroom flat, or wash-place. Steel basins, lavatories, lagged pipes, and a grating overhead with the whirr of fans sounding from it. Burtenshaw mutterered, 'No torpedoes. Just—'

'What's that say?'

Outside, and on the far side of the ladder, a small, elliptical door was set high in the after bulkhead, and there were German words stencilled in red beside it. Burtenshaw translated, 'Entry forbidden except to authorised personnel on duty'. There was a padlock on one of the retaining clips, and it was about two inches thick. Nick thought this might well be a way into the torpedo flat. Almost certainly there'd be something in there worth damaging, and the odds were that it would be explosive. It might, he thought, be the torpedo warhead store, connecting to the flat itself on the other side. In any case it was as good a bet as any. Then, looking round, he saw the concrete.

This was what he'd smelt. It was the bulkhead nearest to the ship's side, beyond the hammock netting. They'd painted it grey, which was why he hadn't noticed it at first, particularly in this rotten light. It was a concrete lining to the real bulkhead, and the only possible explanation was that this was how, with the extremely limited repair facilities here at the Golden Horn, they'd repaired the ship's action damage – quite possibly mine-damage sustained during her last sortie, when she'd sunk the monitors in Kusu Bay.

It was a perfect spot for the explosion. Smash through that concrete, and you'd be blasting into previous – existing – damage.

'Set your charge up.' He put his case down. 'I'll make a space for it.' He began to drag hammocks out of the netting, dumping them temporarily against the ladder. They'd be useful, to tamp down the charge as well as to hide it . . . Working fast, before someone might come down and catch them at it. 'Quick as you can, Bob.' Burtenshaw had the cases open and he was piling all the guncotton into one, lashing the whole lot together with tape, in the shape it had been in before they'd divided it. Nick pulled out one more hammock, leaving a hole deep enough to drop the charge right down into the angle between deck and bulkhead – the concrete one. He looked round again: Burtenshaw had taken a detonator out of a little tin that held half a dozen of them, and he was fixing one end of the white coil of fuse into it, squeezing it tight with pliers and then sliding the detonator into the middle of the charge, with a loop of tape around the fuse to hold it in place. He looked up.

'Ready.'

'Light it, then.'

'Right.' His hands were shaking as he set it going. For a moment nothing happened, then the end of the fuse glowed red and began to fizz. He shut the case: then hesitated, opened it again. 'Best not have it airtight. Might put it out.' Nick helped him lower the suitcase with its lid slightly open into the nest among the hammocks and other gear, and then they piled the rest back in on top of it.

Done. And if they could get well away from this part of the ship, it would be a thousand to one against the thing being found before it went off. Burtenshaw murmured, as if struck suddenly by the enormity of what they'd been doing, 'It's a *huge* charge.'

'Good.' Nick turned to the ladder, and picked up the other case. 'Back up now, up at least two decks, then aft. Far away from here as possible.'

'I'm – with you there.' He'd actually smiled. Nick told him, 'You lead. If we're stopped again, ask to be directed to the admiral's quarters.'

'Couldn't we get right up on the upper deck?'

'Not yet, anyway . . . Up you go.'

How would one explain an empty suitcase with two men to carry it? Not easily, he thought. But the general's name might pull a certain amount of wool over Teutonic eyes. They'd reached the top of the second ladder; he answered Burtenshaw's backward glance with a nod. 'Up one more, then turn right.' Climbing again: and the ship was definitely under way, the machinery noise a steady, throbbing hum. He wished they *could* have gone up top, into fresh air and where they could see what was happening; it occurred to him that while they'd been down in that empty messdeck they should have borrowed some sailors' gear instead of the field-grey they were wearing so conspicuously. *Damn* . . . Worth going back, he wondered? Dressed as sailors, in a ship with a complement of about a thousand men, you could hide for ever, with any decent ration of luck . . . But he decided against it: now, leaving harbour, all the hands not working would be fallen in, lined up on the upper deck and fully fezed, no doubt; but at any moment *Goeben* would be out clear of the Galata bridge and the hands would be dismissed and go pouring down the ladders. The possibility of being caught down there where they'd placed the charge wasn't one that could be taken. Tramping aft now, boots ringing on the steel deck. The ship had a sparse, stripped-down look: when you looked closely you saw that there was nothing inflammable anywhere, only bare steel, not a stick of wood in sight. A ship intended for fighting, not for living in. Bulkhead doors on either side at intervals, with high sills: machinery noise getting louder as they went towards the stern. Now and then a sailor glanced at them, muttered something as they squeezed past, or stared through an open doorway: all right so far, but luck had some limit to it: and God, Nick recalled suddenly, helped those who helped themselves. Helped themselves to sailors' uniforms – from some other messdeck? Now, quickly, while there was still a chance and before the hands were sent below?

'Hey, Bob.' Burtenshaw looked round. Nick beckoned him: 'Down here.'

Back into the great ship's guts. There'd be messdecks pretty well all through her, for'ard of the machinery spaces. So the route had to be downward and certainly no further aft. He explained, 'We must find another messdeck and swap this gear for sailor-suits.' One could see that the idea didn't much appeal to the Marine. And he himself was aware of two obvious dangers in it. One: being caught in the act of stealing the uniforms and shifting into them; the answer to it was to be very quick, get it done before the ship relaxed into watchkeeping routines. Two: there was a risk that the theft might be discovered and the soldiers' uniforms found, and an alarm raised. But it was still a better chance, he thought, than continuing to parade around in these clowns' outfits. He led the way down: into a wider passageway with a row of doors with

German labels on them. Officers' cabins? Not far enough aft for that, surely. Offices, perhaps. Not wanting to waste time in asking Burtenshaw to tell him, he'd turned for'ard, looking for another down-ladder: and a voice barked, '*Halt!*'

Burtenshaw, behind him, gasped.

It was the *Kapitan-leutnant* who'd come strutting down the gangway and looked like stopping them and then, at the sight of Liman von Sanders's name on the cases, thought better of it. There was a one-striper – *Oberleutnant?* – and also an older man, some kind of senior rating, with him.

'*Ziegen Sie hier! Aufmachen!*'

Burtenshaw was stuttering uselessly: his nerve had gone, and so apparently had his linguistic powers. It seemed to be the suitcase again that the German was interested in. Burtenshaw looked round despairing at Nick, then back at the trio advancing on them. Nick snapped, 'Here, quick . . .' He turned back towards the ladder they'd just come down; but the CPO, whatever he was, barred his way, while behind him the other two had grabbed Burtenshaw and the empty case.

CHAPTER 13

'Smoke, all right. Lots of it.'

Wishart, hunched at the for'ard periscope, muttered it to himself. Hobday, who'd been keeping the periscope watch ever since they'd dived before first light, and who'd spotted the smoke and shaken Wishart, was terrier-like with excitement.

Goeben?

'Port ten.'

'Port ten, sir . . . Ten o' port wheel on, sir.'

That was Louis Lewis at the wheel. Finn was on the fore 'planes and Morton, stripped to his bulging waist and as usual shiny with sweat, was on the after ones. Depth-gauges showing twenty feet. Wishart told Lewis, 'Steer oh-three-nine.'

'Oh-three-nine, sir.'

It was the bearing of the Horn, according to a fix Hobday had taken a few minutes ago. Jake, disturbed by the flurry of activity, had rolled out of his bunk and sloped over to the chart. Distance to the Horn nine point five miles. If *Goeben* was coming out she could be passing over this spot in half an hour.

Wishart was taking a careful all-round look. No good getting excited about a target and letting some patrol boat jump on you from the other direction. No good getting excited anyway – not even if it did turn out to be *Goeben*; and the odds were heavily against that dream coming true so fast. The smoke might be from a factory or a fire or from a freighter of some sort. Jake, slumped across the chart table, begged silently *Please God, let it be* Goeben.

Wishart was motionless again, with the periscope trained on that north-easterly bearing. All their eyes on him – on as much of his facial expression as was visible. Faces ready for disappointment, but with hope in them too. Wishart glanced sideways, at Hobday's sharp alertness.

'Close the hands up, Number One.'

'Diving stations!'

A swift, quiet rush of men . . . They'd gone to diving stations a thousand times, and quite often there'd been some degree of tension or expectancy. This was different: if you hadn't known it, Jake thought, watching them as they settled to their jobs, you'd have read it in their faces.

Goeben: the big one, the one they'd come for, through steel nets and minefields.

'I want a word with Rinkpole.'

'Pass the word for the TI!'

CPO Rinkpole came aft looking interested but calm. He was too old a hand to get excited all that quickly. Wishart stepped back from the periscope and McVeigh sent it hissing down.

'TI – presently we'll stand by all five tubes. That means your chaps'll have to slap it about a bit.'

Rinkpole ran a horny hand over the dome of his head. 'Aye aye, sir.'

'She's worth everything we've got. If we get the chance to use it. But we certainly shan't get *two* chances.'

'One'll do us, sir.'

'Yes.' Wishart nodded. 'All right, TI.' He looked towards McVeigh and moved his hands slightly, and the periscope came rushing up. Rinkpole went aft to lecture his beam- and stern-tubes' operators – Finn with stokers Lindsay and Burrage amidships, and Smith assisted by Peel in the after ends. Hobday was using the trim-line to get her back in balance after the move to diving stations. Trim would be vital now: if you lost control during an attack you could lose your target: and the effort of the entire operation felt cumulative now – minefields, nets, near-suffocation, *everything*, building towards this coming moment in which you'd hit or miss. To miss was in fact unthinkable, and Hobday wanted his trim right to the nearest half-point. From that point of view, Rinkpole's meanderings through the boat were a nuisance. Wishart was circling quickly; he paused to check the bearing of the smoke and then began another circle much more slowly in high power. Back on the smoke: a long, careful study of it, while the low eastern sun blazed down the tube and threw discs of fire into his eyes.

'Down periscope. Half ahead both.' He looked fleetingly at Jake and told him, 'The bearing's steady.' Jake had the stop-watch ready on his plotting diagram, instruments and sharpened pencils at hand. It was extraordinary how brittle pencil-leads became in times of stress. The fact of the target's bearing being steady could mean that E.57 was in the right place; alternatively, and if this *was* their target, that she hadn't cleared Seraglio Point yet. In which case she might alter course sharply as soon as she was clear, and then the submarine might be in very much the *wrong* place.

It would, anyway, be quite a while before they knew for certain what sort of a hand they were being dealt: and slightly longer than that, even, before they'd be in a position to attack.

Burtenshaw had finally regained the power of speech, and asked to be directed to the admiral's quarters. The request had seemed to annoy the *kapitan-leutnant*, who'd had them frogmarched to the lower bridge instead. There he and the ship's captain had questioned them. The captain was a tall, angular man with hooded, bird-like eyes; he wanted to know where was the other suitcase and what had been inside the empty one. He spoke reasonably good English, and Burtenshaw didn't have to translate as he'd been doing for the other man, the two-striper.

Two sailors with bayonets on their rifles guarded them from the rear while the questioning continued. Burtenshaw had said he didn't know *what* had happened to the other case; the captain swung round to fix his sharp stare on Nick.

'You, *you* will tell me. *Kapitan-leutnant* Heusinger has reported that you came with two cases from the shore. Now we see only one case. Where is the other one?'

Nick looked surprised. 'Other one?'

The expression turned colder.

'You know that I can order you to be shot, since you are not wearing your own uniform?'

'Well . . .' He was about to say something about the end of the war being imminent, and how pointless it would be – which seemed rather a weak argument unless he could frame it better – when he saw the commodore arriving. A medium-sized, intelligent-looking man in his middle or late forties; he had a face that could easily have been English. The captain saw Nick's glance shift, and looked round; then he drew aside, making way for the senior man.

'Which of them is Everard?'

The question had been put in German, but Nick heard his own name. He was taking a quick check on the surroundings as the land fell away astern; the ship was under helm, altering from a course of

672

south-south-west to about west-south-west. A course which would take her, he hoped, to where Aubrey Wishart should at this moment be waiting for her. And if the Germans could be stalled for that length of time, he thought, if they could be dissuaded from ordering up the firing squad until E.57 got her attack in, the execution might with any luck be postponed indefinitely. They'd be within their rights to do it, certainly, and he thought bird's-eyes quite likely would have; but this commodore had rather a gentlemanly, civilised look about him.

Goeben's captain had returned to his bridge. The commodore, flanked now by the *kapitan-leutnant* and a young commander – rather, *corvetten-kapitan* – was staring at him interestedly.

'Your father is Admiral Sir Hugh Everard, perhaps?'

'No, sir. That's my uncle.'

'Indeed.' The commodore nodded. 'You should be proud of such an uncle.'

'Yes.' Nick nodded. 'I am.'

'I should regret very much to be forced to deprive him of a nephew. Or to deprive you, of the possibility of following in his footsteps in your Royal Navy.'

His English was almost perfect, with only the slightest trace of accent. Coupled with his appearance and pleasantly affable manner, it felt as if one was having a friendly chat with a fellow countryman.

But the affability was fading.

'As I have heard Captain Steinhoff remind you, you *are* in a position to be shot, you know. And since we are not particularly stupid we must believe that your other portmanteau contained some kind of explosive charge. It would spare me the discomfort of ordering your execution if you were to tell me where it had been placed. The ship is being searched, of course, and it is probable that we will find it quite soon in any case; I am simply giving you this opportunity to save yourself . . .' Glancing at Burtenshaw: 'Your-*selves*, I should say. How do you decide?'

'There's nothing I can tell you, sir.'

The German looked at Burtenshaw.

'You, sir?'

Burtenshaw shook his head. The commodore sighed, and asked the *kapitan-leutnant*, 'I am told you have an idea of the approximate location?'

'That is correct, Herr Commodore. The point of entry was at the for'ard gangway with two cases, and taking that into consideration with the place where they were apprehended with only *one* case I believe the other must be somewhere amidships, roughly.'

'And below the waterline, of course.'

The *kapitan-leutnant* agreed. The commodore added, 'The explosion, moreover, might occur at any time.' He looked thoughful, not at all worried. In spite of what he'd just said – which was true, the charge *could* explode at any moment . . . Nick wondered how long that fuse was: it was a point which, in the tension and rush of getting aboard and placing the charge, he hadn't raised. Meanwhile, the commodore was a man in full control of himself as well as of his surroundings, he'd know the fuse would be burning and that getting excited wouldn't slow it. But there was anger in him too – and – as he turned his head and stared at Nick – menace, suddenly. Quiet menace, much more frightening – if one gave way to fright – than rage or threats would have been. He was a quiet man who worked logically: and cold logic wasn't noisy, any more than a snake was before it struck – well, *most* snakes . . . He'd nodded slightly as he reached a conclusion, and now he'd swung to face the man with three stripes.

'My compliments to Captain Steinhoff, and I suggest that all men not essential to the working of the ship below decks should be brought up. These two—' one hand gestured towards Nick and Burtenshaw – 'are to be confined below, amidships, in the bottom of the ship. You—' glancing sideways at the *kapitan-leutnant* – 'will go with them. Should they attempt to escape, you will shoot them dead. If on the other hand they should decide to disarm or remove their bomb from wherever it may be, you will permit them to do so and then bring them back here. Is that understood?'

Jake Cameron had fingers crossed on both hands. He heard the soft thump as McVeigh pushed the telemotor lever to 'raise' and the tube began its upward slither; then the sound of the handles clicking down as Wishart grabbed them. Glancing back over his shoulder he saw the skipper circling, checking the surroundings before he settled on the crucial bearing. Rinkpole passed through the control room on his way for'ard.

'Ah . . .'

The men whose jobs allowed them to watch Wishart brightened suddenly as they caught the sudden gleam of pleasure in his face. He said, 'I can see her foretop. It's *Goeben*. Stand by all tubes. Down periscope.'

McVeigh sent it down like a shiver of yellow light. Everyone taut with excitement now. Any one of them would have said that in all their lives they'd hardly expect anything to matter quite so much: that was how it felt – like a moment you'd lived for and would live *on* afterwards. Glancing round, Wishart saw them feeling it, and murmured, 'Easy does it, now. This'll be an attack like any other . . . Slow together. Up periscope.'

'HE right ahead, sir.' Weatherspoon added, 'About three hundred revolutions, sir.'

'*Goeben*'s maximum is about three-twenty.' Jake said it for Wishart's information. He'd done his homework. Wishart had finished a precautionary all-round search and he was rock-still again, watching his target.

'Stand by to start the attack.'

'Standing by, sir.' Jake's finger on the button of the stop-watch.

'Starboard ten.'

'Starboard ten, sir.' Roost spun his wheel. Even Roost, behind those flashing spokes, was under tension. Muscles at each side of his square jaw bulged in and out like pulses, and for Roost this was about the equivalent of a fit of hysterics. 'Ten o' starboard wheel on, sir.'

'Start the attack. She bears – *that*. Range—' Jake noted range and bearing and began to lay it off on the plotting sheet. 'Masts are in line bearing—' He checked it, and it hadn't changed. So enemy course was two-two-oh, Jake noted. Wishart said, 'I'm opening off-track on her starboard bow. Midships.'

'Midships, sir.'

'Down periscope. Steer oh-one-oh.'

'Steer oh-one-oh, sir.'

The time of starting the attack was zero minutes. Jake marked *Goeben*'s position on the diagram accordingly. When Wishart gave him a second fix on her he'd measure the distance between the two points and estimate her speed. Meanwhile he had to keep the submarine's own track, her courses and speed, up to date, extending the pencil record of it every few seconds, because the second enemy range-and-bearing wouldn't be taken from the same place as the first had been.

'Course oh-one-oh, sir.'

'Half ahead together.'

Agnew pushed the telegraphs around. Wishart would be visualising the oncoming battle cruiser – her course, speed, range, her bearing from the submarine, the boat's own movements and the two ships' shifting positions relative to each other. You needed a kind of insight and a sportsman's eye and a touch of gambler's instinct too. Hobday, intently watching the trim, was ready to correct the smallest imbalance if one showed up. The greatest hazard was the possibility of varying densities, hitting a freshwater patch or an area of increased salinity. Such a phenomenon could hit them at any second, and if he or his 'planesmen were too slow to react and counter the change, the result could be disaster. You stuck to your own job and at the same time there was a moving picture in your brain of the shape of the developing attack. Wishart was taking the submarine out clear of *Goeben*'s track so as to get into position to fire from her starboard bow. The torpedoes would be sent out ahead of her so that they'd strike her finally at an angle of ninety degrees, on her beam. If they were aimed right and she held her course, they and *Goeben* would converge and meet.

'Slow together. Up.' The periscope was already rising. McVeigh watched him all the time and acted on periscope orders before they could be uttered. McVeigh was like a fighter poised for the bell to start the fight: on his toes, crouched a bit, beard bristling. As if he had springs inside him. Wishart, with his eyes at the lenses, asked Jake, 'Masthead height's what, a hundred and sixty?'

'Hundred and eighty, sir.'

You needed that height, for periscope ranging. You took the angle subtended by waterline and masthead; the periscope's gra ticulated glass was marked off in one-degree spaces. (In high power you had to remember to divide the angle by four.) With that angle, and knowing the vertical height, you had a range that was the baseline of a right-angled triangle. Wishart gave Jake his second range-and-bearing, and pushed the handles up. 'Down. Half ahead together. Starboard ten.'

Circling round to port, increasing the off-track range slightly as he brought her right around to end up on a firing course. Joining Jake now at the chart table.

'Two-two-oh's dead right if she hasn't altered. And twenty knots won't be far out. Give you another set of figures in a minute.' He'd absorbed the plot's information and now he was going back to the periscope. 'Ease to five.'

'Ease to five, sir . . . Five o' starboard wheel on, sir.'

'Tell the TI I'll be firing both bow tubes, to start with. Midships.'

'Midships, sir. Wheel's—'

'Steer one-three-oh.'

'One-three-oh, sir!'

'Slow ahead together.'

Roost was easing the helm as she approached her firing course. Wishart was reducing speed each time he pushed the periscope up, because at lower speeds there'd be less feather where it cut through the calm surface. Calm-ish, anyway. But there was enough white flecking for reasonable security, thank God. The closer E.57 came to her target, the briefer would be her periscope's appearances.

'Twenty-two feet.'

'Twenty-two, sir.'

To show less periscope. The less that stuck out, the less there was to catch an enemy eye. The alternative to holding the boat a couple of feet deeper would be to lie or crouch low, not have the stick hoisted right up. The best answer was a bit of both. Wishart muttered, 'May they all be cross-eyed with schnapps. Up periscope.'

'Course one-three-oh, sir!'

'Twenty-two feet, sir.'

'Very good.' He jerked down the handles. 'Stand by for enemy range-and-bearing.'

Up for'ard in the tube space CPO Rinkpole, with Blackie Cole and Close-'aul Anderson, was going through the routine of bringing his bow tubes to the stand-by position. Firing reservoirs had been charged, shutter doors opened and the clutch reported clear. Now they were blowing water up from the WRT tanks to surround the fish inside the tubes and at the same time equalise the pressure inside with that beyond the sluice doors, the front caps of the tubes, so that those doors could be opened.

'Starboard tube full!'

Rinkpole shut off the air to the starboard WRT. Cole reported the port tube full as well. You knew when they were full because water shot out of the vents. So much machinery, pipes, pumps, wheels, air-bottles and so on in this cramped, cave-like space that the torpedomen had to worm about like reptiles.

'Open sluice doors!'

There was a wheel with geared shafts on each tube. The shutter doors, beyond the sluice doors, were opened or shut by one larger, central wheel, between the tubes. Stinking hot . . . Anderson was using both his hands now; his messmates had got tired of his famous broken wrist and he'd been shamed into declaring it fit for use again.

'Clutch up side-stops to firing bars!'

When the firing mechanism was activated, the side-stops that held the fish from sliding about inside the tubes were automatically withdrawn. Rinkpole saw those connections made. He ordered, 'Open screw-down outboard vents', and reported back via Lewis to the control room that bow tubes were standing by. Wishart had already received a similar report on the stern tube from AB Smith, and Finn had the beam tubes standing by as well. Wishart sent the big periscope down and moved to the smaller, after one, the attack periscope. He ordered, 'Bow tubes to the ready.'

'Open stand-by valves.' Rinkpole snapped it, and Cole and Anderson moved like lightning: 'Tube ready, tripper down, vent closed!'

Rinkpole eased the two safety-pins out of the firing gear. He called back to the control room, 'Bow tubes ready.' Wishart could fire electrically from the periscope now; alternatively, Rinkpole could do it in the tube-space by hand, triggering the shots from his wooden seat between the white-enamelled tubes. In his mind the TI was whispering to his torpedoes, his babies whom he'd nursed and cosseted for so long against just such a moment and purpose as this one; he was asking them, *Now don't you go and let me down, my dears* . . .

Deep in the ship's belly, as far below the waterline as E.57 would be at periscope depth and with half a dozen vertical ladders and solid hatches between this point and the nearest exit to fresh air, the messdeck was identical to the one they'd come to before. And there was a hatch in it and a ladder leading down, just as there had been from that other one. The *kapitan-leutnant* sent them down it; he had a revolver in his fist and, behind him, a sailor with a rifle and bayonet.

Nick went down – into a flat with a hammock-netting and a door through to a bathroom flat. And in this space at the foot of the ladder where the hammock stowage was, one bulkhead was faced with concrete . . .

It was like a dream with elements of reality distorted, lopsided, a nightmare in which you'd come to a place you'd been in before, and yet hadn't. The effect was muddling, disorientating, and when you set it into the background knowledge that somewhere quite close by there was a burning fuse and enough explosive to split the ship's side open . . . He got it, suddenly. The messdeck above them now had to be immediately aft of 'their' messdeck. This bathroom flat would share plumbing with that other one – adjoining it, and with only a thin sheet of steel dividing the two. The two access flats connected with the washplaces in an athwartships direction and must be similarly close. That concrete-strengthened ship's side bulkhead ran along the outside of both. It meant that the gun-cotton and the smouldering fuse could be no more than ten feet from where he stood now as Burtenshaw, white-faced, came down the ladder to join him.

The *kapitan-leutnant* sat in the hatchway above them, pistol held loosely in one hand with its barrel pointing downwards, towards them. He was looking up into the messdeck, passing some order to the attendant rifleman.

'What's that he's saying?'

'Telling him to report that we're in 4C messdeck's washplace. There's a telephone just up there, apparently.'

'How long a fuse did you set?'

They were both whispering, with their backs to the man on the ladder up above them.

'The whole lot. I don't know how much there was. I should have cut it to a set time but I didn't think of it. I don't *know* how long.'

'Half an hour? An hour?'

'I tell you I don't *know* . . .'

Or he wasn't capable of putting his mind to it. He looked terrible. Not only sheet-white, but sweaty, wet-faced. He'd muttered on the way down, 'We can't just stay there – to be blown up or drowned, like rats in a trap—' The *kapitan-leutnant* had shut him up, then, while Nick had thought about rats in traps, and that German U-boat they'd drowned here in the Marmara, and thoughts like *tit for tat* . . . Burtenshaw said it again now: 'We can't just – *stay* here, and—'

'We can't do anything else, Bob.'

It was what they'd come for. What a submarine and her whole crew had risked their necks for. And Reaper had said, 'Any effort – or cost.'

Wishart had accepted Jake's estimated enemy course and speed of two-one-eight, nineteen knots. He threw a glance at McVeigh, and the attack periscope slid up.

'Watch your depth!'

She'd slipped downwards by six inches. Coming back up now.

Wishart was crouched at the periscope with his knees bent and his arms draped gorilla-fashion over the spread handles. McVeigh's pink-rimmed eyes never left him. Young Agnew was twitching with excitement and trying not to show it. ERA Geordie Knight, usually calm and placid, was flushed, aggressive-looking. Stoker Adams was stooped like a mantis, breathing jerkily, eyes glaring under jutting brows. Ellery quick-eyed, hovering behind Wishart. Wishart had the periscope set at the firing-angle he'd worked out; he trained left now though, checking on how far his target had to come before her stem would cross the hairline in the glass. Resetting it before he sent it downward: and now he'd stopped it, brought it whizzing up again. Bit of a periscope artist, Aubrey Wishart. He was making one more quick check: and snapping the handle up. 'Down.' On his knees: counting seconds like a man praying. He moved his fingers, curling their tips upward about an inch, and McVeigh caught the signal, pulled the lever: the bronze tube was a pillar of greasy yellowish metal skimming up. He grabbed the handles and stopped it three feet off the deck.

'Stand by.'

'Stand by, sir!'

Seconds crawling past. Jake, leaning over the chart table, shut his eyes and thought *Please, God . . .*

'Fire one!'

Triggering the starboard tube, he'd also given the order verbally in case the electrical firing system might have failed. A thud, long hiss of venting air, rising pressure in the boat: Wishart shouted, *'Damn* the bloody thing!' His eyes stayed at the lenses. Hobday had whipped round, and Wishart snapped, 'Fire two!' Another thud and hiss; that was the tube venting after the discharge and then filling from the compensating tank. Wishart ordered, in a state of fury, 'Port fifteen, port beam tube to the ready!' He snapped at McVeigh, 'Dip!' He meant him to lower the periscope and raise it again immediately: a periscope kept up for longish periods of time was far more likely to be spotted. Wishart told Hobday, 'First one broke surface and ran wild.' Pointing suddenly over Hobday's shoulder – 'Keep her *down!'*

Nineteen feet – eighteen – and bow-up angle increasing. Sixteen . . .

'Open "A" kingston!'

For'ard, Rinkpole felt the upward lurch and heard the order to flood that for'ard tank. He guessed there'd been some hang-up in the timing of the inflow of water compensating for the loss of the torpedoes' weight, and that Hobday couldn't have seen the upset quickly enough to have dealt with it before she started tilting up. Now the bow dipped from the extra weight in 'A': she was bow-down, diving. He ordered, 'Shut sluice doors!' One of his fish – the one he'd done a routine on and then dreamt about – had run amok, and he was shamed, mortified. Climbing off his seat he rasped at Anderson, 'Goin' aft to the beam tubes.' But Wishart's warning echoed in his memory: *We certainly shan't get* two *chances* . . .

On *Goeben*'s bridge they'd seen the first torpedo leap almost right out of the water and then topple in a great splash and vanish. Steinhoff had barked a helm order and twenty-three thousand tons of German steel had heeled hard as she swung away to starboard, turning her bows towards any torpedo that might *not* have gone crazy. The battle cruiser had been about halfway through her turn when E.57's periscope standards, and then the top of her conning-tower, had come foaming up into sight; another sharp command had increased the angle of rudders, tightening the turn in some hope of catching the submarine, ramming her. But she'd dipped under long before there was any chance of it, and a few seconds later the second fish had streaked past, leaving its effervescent trail fifty feet clear to port.

Helm was now reversed, to bring her back on course. There was a lot of shouting into voicepipes and telephones, and turrets were training back to where they'd started from. The English submariners had certainly got their boat down again quickly: but in terms of an attack they'd really made a mess of it.

Below, they'd felt the lurch and heel of the big ship's full-rudder turn, and heard the whirr of machinery as the turrets near them trained around; then they heard the *kapitan-leutnant* ordering the rifle-toting sailor to find out what was going on. He'd gone to the telephone on the messdeck up there, and Burtenshaw told Nick what he was doing. The man was coming back now, and reporting to his officer.

Burtenshaw said, 'There's been a torpedo attack. Missed. The submarine's well astern now.'

He was panting, needing a breath between each two or three words. Nick stared at the sick-looking face; he thought, *That only leaves us, then* . . . He felt ill himself: until now, he realised, there'd been some hope that they might not have had to see it right through to its highly unpleasant end. He told Burtenshaw – as much as anything to keep his spirits from rock-bottom – 'If or when the charge goes off, go straight up that ladder. Well, I'll lead, if you like – but don't think about his revolver, because for one thing he'll probably miss and for another he'll more likely be running like a rigger for the upper deck.'

Burtenshaw shook his head. 'When it goes off – I told you, it's *big*, there'll be no hope of—'

'Bob, there's *always* hope!'

Cock-and-bull, he thought. *And never know now, about Sarah . . .* But in the same mental breath he realised that he *did* know: as clearly as if she was speaking to him inside his head he knew for certain that he'd guessed the truth. And nobody else now would ever know it. Only Sarah herself. Would she ever tell the child, he wondered? She might: honesty, her forthrightness, might make her do it. But on the other hand – Burtenshaw's eyes on him, all fear as they shifted to the bulkhead, visualising (Nick guessed) the explosion, the steel splitting and the concrete cracking open, the inrush of sea and the hatch up there slamming shut on them: Nick shut his mind to it, tried to shut it also to the sense of suffocation, claustrophobia much stronger than anything he'd felt in Wishart's submarine. He told himself that Sarah would *not* tell her – *his* – child the truth, because she'd realise that to do so would be to shift the guilt, lump a burden on the child which it had done nothing to deserve. Not its fault, and not Sarah's: only his, Nick Everard's, and he'd be gone, leaving her to carry it alone. Burtenshaw whispered hoarsely, his eyes frantic, 'Don't you feel *anything*?'

Difficult to know, for a moment, what he'd meant. Nick had closed his eyes: like a long, slow blink. Now he'd opened them and nodded. Burtenshaw was glistening: all sweat. Nick was too: thinking about it, he could feel it.

'Yes. As much as you do, probably.'

Or more. Like a suppressed scream in the mind, a scream you needed to let out and couldn't. Not *shouldn't*, but *could not*. Like the man up top who knew your uncle and coldly, politely, sentenced you to this. Expressionless, to all intents and purposes mute – as Sarah would have to be about the most important, vital thing in all her life. She'd have the urge to scream it, too. If one could have grovelled, sobbed or—

Please God, let us out of this?

* * *

682

Wishart had spun her fast to starboard, using one screw full ahead and the other full astern, risking the trim they'd only just recovered and weren't too sure of yet – risking *anything* for the unexpected second chance. A very long-shot chance – if it existed at all. Long range, and with the submarine badly placed; she was just about on the German's beam, which meant the fish would approach him from abaft it, actually having to chase after him to some extent instead of going in to meet him at something like right-angles to his course.

They'd been deep, struggling with a haywire trim. When Hobday had regained control and they'd got back up to periscope depth Wishart had expected to see nothing more than *Goeben*'s smoke as she steamed away towards the Dardanelles.

Rinkpole reported from the beam tube space, 'Starboard beam tube ready!'

'Up periscope.' He'd only briefly dipped it. 'Stand by. Ship's head?'

'Two-six-oh, sir.'

'Twenty-one feet, sir—'

'Fire!'

He'd slammed the handles up. 'Thirty feet. Full ahead port. Port fifteen. Port beam tube to the ready.'

Another shot – at even longer range and a still worse angle?

'Thirty feet, sir.' Hobday wasn't taking his eyes off the trim for a second, this time. He'd no idea what had gone wrong before. Agnew had swung the telegraphs around and Roost had spun his wheel; Rinkpole called, 'Port beam tube ready, sir!' Firing from this other beam would mean sending the fish off to chase *Goeben* from her quarter. The rate of closing, Jake realised, subtracting *Goeben*'s speed from the torpedo's, wouldn't be much more than twenty knots.

'Slow ahead both.' Wishart watched her head as she swung. If that last fish had been going to hit, Jake thought, they'd have heard the bang by this time. Range, torpedo speed and stop-watch time told him so quite clearly. Wishart said, 'Midships. Steer oh-six-five. Twenty-two feet.'

'Twenty-two, sir.'

The 'planes angled to bring her closer to the surface. Twenty-five feet. Twenty-four.

'Up periscope.'

The small, low-powered one again. Even at this range he wasn't taking chances of being spotted.

The *boom* of the torpedo exploding was a smaller sound than they'd have expected. The long range, of course – and the much louder bangs they'd been subjected to in the straits. It was such a small sound that Jake hadn't thought of it as a hit at all. But now shock-waves following the explosion came like a double echo to confirm success: unless, of course, the fish had only dived and exploded on the bottom . . . Wishart grabbed the periscope's handles, jerked them down and put his eye to the single lens. They heard him gasp, saw the flash of incredulity and then joy. He'd swallowed, found his voice.

'Right aft. God, what a *fluke!*'

He whooped, suddenly, flung his arms up, did a little dance. Men were cheering, slapping each other on the back. CPO Crabb muttered, glowering at his depth-gauge, 'Bloody mad'ouse . . .'

As the crash of the torpedo-hit boomed and shuddered through the ship, for a second Nick's taut nerves reacted as if it had been the much closer, louder bang which he'd been expecting, trying to be ready for. In that second he thought his heart had stopped: and beside him Burtenshaw had jerked rigid as if he'd had an electric shock . . . Then there was a stillness, a sensation of the surroundings dying: and *that*, Nick realised as reality and sense came back, was the machinery slowing, stopping. Lights began to flicker and weaken as power failed. Somewhere in the distance there was muffled shouting and an alarm-bell ringing: and immediately above their heads the *kapitan-leutnant* was sending his man to the telephone again, to find out what was happening. Burtenshaw croaked, 'Make a dash for it?'

The man on the ladder was watching them. In the half-light his face was indistinct but Nick had an impression that he was smiling, *hoping* they'd try to rush him. Imagination, perhaps: but he could see the pistol, light gleaming on its barrel. Also, they could hear the sailor bawling into the telephone: and now it sounded as if he'd got an answer, that he was in conversation with someone up there.

Nick muttered, 'Must have taken a second crack at it, out of his stern tube or a beam one.'

He *hoped* that was it. And that the hit had been in some vital spot, not something they'd be able to deal with and get the ship moving again. If she was stopped permanently she'd be a sitting duck, at Wishart's mercy.

Burtenshaw suggested in a hoarse, pleading whisper, 'If she's done for couldn't we give up now?'

'Wait.' Overhead, the sailor was back and reporting to the *leutnant*. 'What's he telling him?'

'I missed the start of it, but—'

The *kapitan-leutnant* was shouting down to them in German. Nick caught one word – a German version of 'torpedo'. He could have cheered – for Wishart, and with personal relief; but relief was premature, because the guncotton could blast them at any moment. Burtenshaw translated in a fast, excited gabble, 'It was a torpedo-hit aft and she's stopped because the steering's smashed and they think one shaft as well. He says they're finished anyway so why don't we—'

'Yes.' Nick cut him short. 'Tell him we'll disarm the charge.'

Or rather, he thought, as the Marine began shouting up towards the hatch, *You*'ll disarm it . . . But he'd go with him, to see he didn't bungle it. It was a matter of getting to that other messdeck and down to its bathroom flat, digging the case out from the hammocks and yanking the detonator out of the explosive. It would serve no purpose to have it go off; if *Goeben* was immobilised, the job – Reaper's job – was done.

CHAPTER 14

'What we knocked off was her main rudder. She had two, you know, one behind the other. Stern's so narrow they couldn't fit 'em side by side, and they needed a certain rudder area and that's how they achieved it. The little one on its own is quite useless. But we'd bent the port shaft too, and made quite a decent hole in her quarter, with surprisingly extensive flooding.'

Wishart was filling in some details of the story, in Truman's cabin aboard *Terrapin*, at anchor in the entrance to the Bosphorus. Truman wasn't present; he'd been summoned to an interview with the Chief of Staff, aboard the flagship. Wishart was telling the story mainly for the benefit of Johnny Treat, his navigator who'd been stricken with appendicitis back in Mudros. Treat had come through as a passenger in one of the other destroyers; he was still pale, convalescent-looking, and fed up at having missed this Dardanelles trip which looked sure to have been the last offensive submarine patrol of the war.

His CO went on, 'I had the other beam tube ready, and the stern tube as well. After that hit she'd stopped, so of course we were able to catch up with her quickly enough, and I was about to make a real job of it at close range when damn me if I didn't see her ensign being struck. By courtesy of Everard here. He'd had the gall to point out to the German commodore that they'd no hope of getting anywhere – except to the bottom when we put some more fish into her – and that it'd be Turkish colours, not German, that he'd be hauling down, and that even if by some miracle he managed to get her back into Constantinople it'd be about as humiliating for him as anything could be . . . Not bad, on the spur of the moment, and after spending half an hour or more sitting on a bomb. Eh?'

Reaper nodded. 'Not at all bad.'

'They weren't far off shooting us as spies.' Nick explained, 'The mind does tend to concentrate.'

'Whatever the circumstances—' Reaper stubbed out a cigarette – 'the fact remains, it worked. And the Commander-in-Chief is by no means displeased. As you'll be discovering for yourselves presently.' He looked from Nick to Wishart. 'Both of you. What's impressed him most, apart from the achievement of the desired result, is the way you pushed ahead with the operation in the face of numerous setbacks. *Louve* – Robins – the lack of a reception committee for the landing party . . .' He glanced up. 'Oh, one thing I'd best mention – the Admiral has had champagne put on ice for us.'

Wishart licked his lips. 'Crikey.'

'His flag lieutenant was kind enough to warn me. In case any of us had thought of taking a stiffener before we went.'

Great days were upon them suddenly . . .

The war wasn't *quite* dead. But the German fleet had mutinied. Admiral Scheer had been preparing a fleet sortie, offensive action that would have led to a showdown such as the Royal Navy had been praying for ever since the inconclusive results of Jutland. But the men of the High Seas Fleet had refused to take the Kaiser's ships to sea. They'd seen enough of British guns at Jutland: their propagandists might claim they'd won that battle, but it was significant that they weren't ready to come to the test again. Significant, and also bitterly disappointing for the Royal Navy.

The news had come yesterday by signal. So in the letter that Nick had just had from his uncle, in the first mail to be brought through to Constantinople, there'd been mention of the battle that was expected. By now, Vice-Admiral Sir Hugh Everard would be as disappointed as any other of Beatty's officers. As Beatty himself must be . . . But Hugh Everard had had no other news. He'd not seen or heard from Sarah. So the sense of vacuum persisted: and Nick realised, after he'd read quickly through the letter, that he'd been *expecting* news – of Sarah, and of the kind he'd guessed at. Because Sarah might have arranged for him to hear of it through his uncle. Because she couldn't send it to him herself, directly, and also because – well, if he'd been right with that other piece of guesswork, the idea that he and she were never to discuss it or even to admit that there could be anything *to* discuss . . . Family news, reaching him by a roundabout route of her own devising – implying nothing, compromising no one . . .

Well, it *could* have been like that.

Nick had never appreciated how deeply his uncle felt for Sarah until a few months ago when Hugh had come to visit him in hospital, after the Zeebrugge raid. He'd said quietly, privately, 'Look after her, Nick, if she should ever need it. *I* should, if I were ever in a position to be of service – but none of us can tell what's in store . . . I know you're fond of her, and that she is of you; and we both know she's drawn a wrong card, eh? She'll not complain of anything – she's too brave, by half – I mean she'd never *ask* for help. That's my point – without asking, she may need it. Be ready, Nick, and a weather eye open?'

If he had any sense of shame or guilt, it was from knowing how shocked Hugh Everard would be if *he* knew. Nick had a greater respect and affection for his uncle than he had for any other man on earth.

Coming out of his thoughts, he focused on Reaper, who'd just lit another cigarette and was regarding him steadily through its smoke.

'Well, Everard? Now this is over, what's *your* future?'

In the long run – unpredictable. In the more immediate sense it was cut-and-dried and dull as ditchwater. He told Reaper, 'Suppose I'll beg a passage to Mudros, to take up my appointment to *Leveret.*'

'Ah.' Reaper blinked. '*Leveret.* Quite.'

Something odd in his expression, though. Some private knowledge or speculation?

As if he was holding back a laugh . . . And Nick was back in memory in a room in a requisitioned boarding-house overlooking the destroyer anchorage in Dover harbour; he'd faced Reaper across a work-littered table and tried to mask his disappointment at the news that he was to join *Bravo* – a shaky old relic, outdated and outworn. Nobody had mentioned that he was being appointed *in command*.

Reaper was wearing that same secretive, tricky look that he'd worn then. He murmured, watching smoke drift towards the deck-head, 'Yes. Of course.' Johnny Treat, Wishart's navigator, asked, 'What happened to the Marine?'

Reaper turned to answer him. 'Burtenshaw is busy demolishing gun-emplacements and other fortifications in the Dardanelles. It's what he knows about, d'you see?'

There'd been some demolition and gun-spiking by landing-parties from destroyers moving up-straits behind the mine-sweepers, but only a preliminary clearance, enough to ensure the safe passage of the fleet. It had been a biggish fleet that had come through, a procession of warships sixteen miles long. Most of them had been British, but there'd been some French and Greek flags among the White Ensigns. The Greek battleships *Kilkis* and *Lemnos*, for instance, which, before they'd been presented to the Greeks, had been the USS *Idaho* and *Mississippi*.

Nothing German floated here now. *Goeben* lay in the shallows of the Gulf of Izmid, where if her bulkheads collapsed from the weight of water inside her she'd have a soft bottom to sit down on. She'd struggled into the gulf on one screw and well down by the stern, and lain for nearly a fortnight with E.57's reloaded bow tubes trained on her while her own men removed the breech-blocks from her guns and the warheads from her torpedoes. Nick, as prize master, had supervised this drawing of her teeth.

A fair part of the British force that was anchored here now would be going through the Bosphorus in a day or two, into the Black Sea. Reaper, who was abreast of all the Intelligence reports, had said they'd probably see action soon enough. If not against Bolshevik-manned warships, at least in support of shore operations. General Denikin's drive into the Caucasus, for instance: he had 30,000 White Russians in his force, and the Cabinet in London had decided that he should be supplied and supported through Novorossisk, which he'd captured from the Reds at the end of August. And there was another White army in the Crimea: and the new Republic of Georgia, which had declared its independence from the Bolsheviks, was most likely going to need help in defending its littoral and the oil port of Batum against invasion from the north.

Action soon, then: and *Terrapin*, this destroyer in which he was sitting so comfortably now, was to be part of the squadron that was going in. While he, Nick, would be back in the Aegean, his enemies: boredom, officialdom, envy of *these* people . . . Reaper was looking at his watch. The motor-boat had just been called away, and presently it would be lying at the gangway waiting to carry the three of them to the flagship. Reaper nodded: 'Five minutes. Are we all chamfered up?'

Spit and polish for the C-in-C. Admiral Sir Somerset A. Gough-Calthorpe had scored his own huge success: his armistice negotiations had been brilliantly conducted, entirely off his own bat, and the extent of his command and responsibilities was enormous now: he was High Commissioner of Turkey, Commander-in-Chief of the Mediterranean and of the Atlantic as far as Cape St Vincent: the Black Sea, Caspian, Red Sea and the Danube were all in his command. General Allenby was his subordinate: Gough-Calthorpe, in fact, was God, so far as the Middle East was concerned. Wishart suggested to Nick, 'If you want passage westward, wait two days and you can come back with us. That'll make *two* passengers – you and Jake Cameron.'

'Well, that's very kind, and—'

Reaper interrupted. 'He may *not* be requiring passage westward.'

'Sir?'

'Would you be terribly chagrined, Everard, if someone else took over *Leveret*?'

So he'd been right about that hooded, secretive look. He sat watching Reaper, waiting for whatever this new thing was. Not allowing himself to hope *too* strongly . . .

'Well?'

'No, sir. I'd presume there was some – some interesting alternative.'

Reaper laid his half-cigarette down in the silver ashtray.

'Following the mutiny in the High Seas Fleet, a German naval surrender has to be prepared for. Amongst other needs is that for officers in certain categories of seniority and command experience who speak good German. Chaps of that sort are wanted back home immediately. And—' he paused, just fractionally – 'Lieutenant Commander Truman is one of them. Consequently—'

'*Terrapin!*'

'Damn it, if you'd allow me—'

'I'm sorry, sir.'

'As you say – *Terrapin*. I've suggested to the Chief-of-Staff that you might be considered suitable to relieve Truman in command. Should he agree, and should the Admiral concur, a signal will have been exchanged by now, I imagine, with Captain (D) in Mudros. On the other hand—'

On the other hand . . .

At odds of ten to one on, it would have been agreed by now. If Truman was to be relieved, he'd have to be relieved at once, since *Terrapin* had been earmarked for the Black Sea expedition. What other destroyer captain would they find available here at Con-

690

stantinople? Reaper knew it too: if he hadn't been sure of it he wouldn't have raised the subject, not until he'd had an answer to his proposal. Nor, probably – come to think of it – would he have expanded as he had earlier on the subject of what awaited a Royal Navy squadron on the other side of the Bosphorus.

He wouldn't be grinning at him like that, either.

Wishart was smiling too. Benign, big-brotherly: fresh from the deep minefields and the nets.

Nick found himself on his feet. 'Sir – I really don't know what to say, I—'

'Let it wait, then.' Reaper stood up too. 'Over the champagne, I dare say you'll think of something.'

691

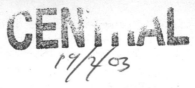

AUTHOR'S NOTE

The Englishwoman who appears here as the Grey Lady was in fact known – according to Francis Yeats-Brown in his book *Golden Horn* – as the White Lady of Pera. In using her as a fictional character it seemed best to change her shade. But she did (Yeats-Brown records) buy General Liman von Sanders's Mercedes Benz tourer, for the purposes stated and from his soldier driver, and for a while she had it guarded by a performing bear.

Enver, Talaat and Djemal escaped that night while the fuses were drawn, but all three came to sticky ends soon after. And *Goeben*, when Admiral Gough-Calthorpe reached Constantinople, was indeed in the Gulf of Izmid and, with extensive flooding aft, was moored in shallow water in case she foundered.

For readers to whom technicalities are of interest I would mention that details of E.57 were obtained from builders' plans in the National Maritime Museum at Greenwich, and from *General Orders for Submarines 1913, Notes for Officers under Instruction November 1918* and an E-class crew-list and watchbill, all in the RN Submarine Museum at Fort Blockhouse, Gosport.

The submarine-ambush episode is factually based. It happened in 1915. The French submarine captured intact by the Turks was the *Turquoise*, and operation orders found in her led to the German submarine UB 15 keeping a prearranged rendezvous with the British E.20. E.20, a sitting duck, was torpedoed and lost with all hands.

E.57 is of course a fictional creation; only 56 E.'s entered service. But Saxton White's attempt to reach *Goeben* in E.14, after the German sortie in which the monitors were sunk, did take place and did result in the loss of E.14 and the death and posthumous VC of her captain. White's was in fact E.14's second VC: the first had been awarded to Lt.-Cdr. E.C. Boyle, who commanded her in 1915.

A.F.